PENGUIN (P) CLASSICS

JOSEPH ANDREWS AND SHAMELA

HENRY FIELDING was born in Sharpham Park, Somerset, in 1707, the son of an army officer of aristocratic descent and profligate ways. In 1725 he was bound over to keep the peace after attempting to abduct an heiress. He was educated privately at first, then at Eton, and from 1728 to 1729 at Leyden University. He went to London in 1728 and published his first literary works, a satirical poem *The Masquerade*, and a comedy, *Love in Several Masques*. From 1729 he managed a theatre and wrote a prolific series of comedies and experimental and politically outspoken plays, such as *Pasquin* (1736), and *The Historical Register for the Year 1736* (1737), which lampooned Sir Robert Walpole and his government. It was partly because of this last play that Walpole introduced the Licensing Act in 1737, which effectively ended Fielding's career as a dramatist. After this Fielding embarked on a career in the law and was called to the Bar in 1740. He was commissioned as a Justice of the Peace for Westminster in 1748. With his half brother, John, he established the Bow Street Runners and did much through his writings and actions to address crime in London. He never made enough money in the law for his needs and was always engaged in schemes such as the Universal Register Office (an information and employment agency), as well as literary ventures, to try to improve his income. In 1734 he married Charlotte Cradock, the model for Sophia Western in *Tom Jones* (1749) and for the heroine of his last novel, *Amelia* (1751). He was distraught when she died in 1744, but in 1747 married her maid, Mary Daniel.

Fielding began his career as a novelist in 1741 with *Shamela*, written as a negative response to Samuel Richardson's *Pamela* (1740), the tale of a virtuous servant who marries her master. The following year, he published *Joseph Andrews*, a more positive demonstration of his skills and beliefs; by taking his characters on the road, he departs from the concerns and narrow plot of *Pamela*, and anticipates his masterpiece, *Tom Jones*. His last novel, *Amelia*, was much darker in tone, and less popular with critics and readers. He also produced political and satirical journals which unite the concerns of his literary and public life: *The Champion* (1739–40), *The True Patriot* (1745–6), *The Jacobite's Journal* (1747–8), and *The Covent-Garden*

Journal (1752). He published his *Miscellanies* in 1743; his final work *The Journal of a Voyage to Lisbon*, a poignant description of his last days, was published posthumously in 1755. He died in physical pain and mental distress in Lisbon in 1754.

JUDITH HAWLEY was educated at Christ's College, Cambridge, and Lincoln College, Oxford. She lectured in English Literature at Newcastle University from 1992 to 1995, and is currently a Lecturer in English at Royal Holloway, University of London. She has published articles on Laurence Sterne and on eighteenth-century women writers, as well as editing Jane Collier's *Art of Ingeniously Tormenting (1753)* (Routledge/Thoemmes, 1994) and Elizabeth Carter's *Selected Works* (Pickering & Chatto, 1999).

HENRY FIELDING

Joseph Andrews

and

Shamela

Edited with an Introduction and Notes by
JUDITH HAWLEY

PENGUIN BOOKS

PENGUIN BOOKS

Published by the Penguin Group
Penguin Books Ltd, 80 Strand, London WC2R 0RL, England
Penguin Putnam Inc., 375 Hudson Street, New York, New York 10014, USA
Penguin Books Australia Ltd, 250 Camberwell Road, Camberwell, Victoria 3124, Australia
Penguin Books Canada Ltd, 10 Alcorn Avenue, Toronto, Ontario, Canada M4V 3B2
Penguin Books India (P) Ltd, 11 Community Centre, Panchsheel Park, New Delhi – 110 017, India
Penguin Books (NZ) Ltd, Cnr Rosedale and Airborne Roads, Albany, Auckland, New Zealand
Penguin Books (South Africa) (Pty) Ltd, 24 Sturdee Avenue, Rosebank 2196, South Africa

Penguin Books Ltd, Registered Offices: 80 Strand, London WC2R 0RL, England

www.penguin.com

Shamela first published 1741
Joseph Andrews first published 1742
Published in Penguin Classics 1999

6

Introduction and Notes Copyright © Judith Hawley, 1999
All rights reserved

The moral right of the editor has been asserted

Set in 9.5/11.75pt Monotype Baskerville
Typeset by Rowland Phototypesetting Ltd, Bury St Edmunds, Suffolk
Printed in England by Clays Ltd, St Ives plc

CONTENTS

ACKNOWLEDGEMENTS

In the course of preparing this edition, I have been the recipient of much good-natured advice and generous aid from a number of people, and I have accumulated many debts of gratitude. I am grateful to the helpful staff of the following libraries: the British Library; the Cambridge University Library; the Founder's Library, Royal Holloway, University of London; the Houghton Library, Harvard University; the Robinson Library, Newcastle University; the University of London Library, Senate House. Many friends and colleagues have offered help on specific points, or have lent support in more general ways, and I would especially like to thank Linda Anderson, Linda Bree, Peter Caracciolo, Tom Keymer, Claire Lamont, David Nokes, Adam Roberts, Mike Rossington and Peter Swaab for their time and trouble. I would also like to thank John Lanchester, Tim Bates, Susan Piquemal and Anna South for their patience. I could not and would not have done it without the support of Philip Horne.

The text of *Joseph Andrews* is based on, but does not reproduce, a copy of the second edition held in the British Library and microfilmed by Research Publications International; I would like to thank Lorna Batten of Research Publications for making it available for my use.

If it is possible to dedicate an edition, I dedicate this to my grandfather, F. T. Hawley.

INTRODUCTION

When Henry Fielding turned his skilful hand to prose fiction in 1741, after his political satires had been so successful in the theatre that Walpole had driven him from the stage with the Licensing Act of 1737, his first effort, *Shamela*, was a burlesque of a novel too prominent to be ignored. *Pamela: or, Virtue Rewarded*, a vivid tale of a servant girl who resists her master's sexual advances and later becomes his wife, caused a sensation when it was first published on 6 November 1740 (dated 1741 on the title page). Fielding would not have known that the author was the printer Samuel Richardson because *Pamela* was first published anonymously and presented as the genuine letters of Pamela Andrews. Richardson was not named as author on the title page until the posthumous sixth edition (2nd issue), in 1772.

From the beginning, readers divided into pro and anti Pamelist camps, the latter endorsing Fielding's caricature of Richardson's heroine as a hypocritical prude who sets out to trick her master into marrying her. Fielding's Edwardian editor, W. E. Henley, stoutly declared:

Harry Fielding . . . for one thing, knew the worth of a wench's humour, and for another how the noble Mr. B. should have done by Pamela, and would assuredly have done by Pamela, had he not been the creation of a Vegetarian who knew nothing of life, and wrote of women only from their own report of themselves. (Henley, *Works* (1908), III, 51)

In *Shamela*, Fielding signals his refusal to believe Pamela's report of herself by inserting 'I pretended' in his shamming heroine's protestations of innocence. In *Pamela* we find a circumstantial account of Mr B's attempted rape of Pamela; he pretends to be Nan the Maid disguised in drink and, while the wicked Mrs Jewkes holds Pamela down, attempts to rape her: 'he put his Hand in my Bosom. With Struggling, Fright, Terror, I fainted away quite, and did not come to myself soon; so that they both, from the cold Sweats that I was in, thought me dying —' (*Pamela*, 2nd ed. (1741), I, 273). In *Shamela*, the affair is a plot framed by Shamela and Mrs Jervis (who appears as a virtuous character in *Pamela*) to entrap the foolish and faint-hearted Mr Booby and to profit by his bungling lust. Parodying Pamela's habit of 'writing to the moment', Fielding draws out the inflaming possibilities of the scene:

Well, he is in Bed between us, we both shamming a Sleep, he steals his Hand into my Bosom, which I, as if in my Sleep, press close to me with mine, and then pretend to awake.—I no sooner see him, but I scream out to Mrs *Jervis*, she feigns likewise but just to come to herself; we both begin, she to becall, and I to bescratch very liberally. . . . I counterfeit a Swoon. (*Shamela*, Letter VI)

Pamela's spontaneous physical responses become tricks in a whore's trade to trap a rich husband. However, while Shamela's behaviour is deplorable, there is something appealing about her sexual honesty and energy.

A recurring theme in appreciations of Fielding is praise for his 'healthiness'. Thus Coleridge, whose initial liking for *Clarissa* was overturned by his reading of the published correspondence of Richardson, exclaimed 'how charming, how wholesome, Fielding always is! To take him up after Richardson, is like emerging from a sick room heated by stoves, into an open lawn, on a breezy day in May' (Thomas M. Raysor, ed., *Coleridge's Miscellaneous Criticism* (1936), 437). Many critics have implicitly or explicitly associated Fielding's 'healthiness' with masculinity, and Richardson's 'sickliness' with femininity. For Charles Burney, 'His novels are *male* amusements, and very amusing they certainly are' (*Boswell's Life of Johnson* (1934), II, 495). On the other hand, while Fielding's reputation was enhanced by his being opposed to the supposedly neurotic Richardson, he was prone to being associated with lowlife because of his comparative openness about sexuality. Richardson's supporters might be expected to take this line; his friend, the prominent physician George Cheyne, spluttered that Fielding's 'wretched Performance . . . will entertain none but Porters or Watermen' – people who were a byword for obscenity (Letter to Richardson, 9 March 1742, quoted in Ronald Paulson and Thomas Lockwood, eds., *Henry Fielding: The Critical Heritage* (1969), 118).

In more recent years, the tide of critical opinion has turned in favour of Richardson; *Pamela* and *Clarissa* attract more critical attention than *Joseph Andrews* and *Tom Jones*. This change in taste restates the gendered characterization of Fielding and Richardson which was established in the eighteenth century. Thus, Katherine Rogers starkly declares: 'while Richardson was a radical feminist, Fielding accepted the male chauvinism of his culture' (*Novel* 9 (1976), 257). While in many ways Fielding and Richardson are antithetical to each other, this gender polarity is not accurate as a characterization of the cast of mind and imaginative capabilities of these writers. In *Clarissa* (1747–8), Richardson is frighteningly convincing in his portrayal of the accomplished rapist Lovelace, while Fielding sympathetically depicts the impressive feminine virtues of the heroine of his last novel, *Amelia* (1751).

Furthermore, critics who play up the healthy appetites of Fielding the man and artist misdirect our reading of his works. First-time readers of *Joseph Andrews* expecting to find a light-hearted novel unencumbered by serious intent, a bawdy romp through the English countryside peopled by hearty vicars, lusty lads and buxom wenches, may well be surprised by what confronts them in the opening pages: not a jolly jape, but a serious treatise invoking Homer and Aristotle in support of the author's theories about the relationships between comedy, tragedy and epic. That Fielding should open his 'novel' with a disquisition on the aesthetics of the 'comic Epic-Poem in Prose' is both surprising and fitting. It is entirely characteristic of Fielding's manner and his energies that he should cut both ways at once, combining classical learning and comic vitality.

Shamela was published anonymously and was probably considered by Fielding to be a minor piece, but he wanted *Joseph Andrews* to be taken seriously. To make it easier to appreciate Fielding's development as a writer, *Shamela* has been placed before *Joseph Andrews* in this edition, rather than being included as an appendix to his more mature work. Fielding had made his reputation with a succession of theatrical pastiches, burlesques and pantomimes, and in *Joseph Andrews* he wished to scale greater artistic heights and establish a higher moral purpose. It was important to him to give his new species of writing a distinguished genealogy, adopting Homer for his forefather rather than the writers of 'those voluminous Works commonly called *Romances* . . . which contain . . . very little Instruction or Entertainment' (Preface). While his writing was a new species, it was not a 'novel'. The term novel did not then have the status it does now, being rather associated with scandalous love stories of the sort written by Aphra Behn and Eliza Haywood. In his adherence to the values associated with classical learning, Fielding also differs from the boldly modern Richardson. In his Preface, Fielding marks himself off from the merely contemporary in a series of finely balanced distinctions between tragedy and comedy, epic and romance, painting and writing, demonstrating his knowledge of various arts and authorities and his skill in dissecting them.

At the same time, his rational evaluation has a certain lightness and freedom to it, a playfulness which suggests that while Fielding took himself seriously as a cultural critic and literary artist, an important part of his theory was that it should be comic in practice. 'Mirth and Laughter', the Preface states, 'are probably more wholesome Physic for the Mind, and conduce better to purge away Spleen, Melancholy and ill Affections, than is generally imagined'. Thus, the careful discriminations between comic history-painting and *caricatura* are as important for the fact that the potential discrepancy between subject and treatment is disguised by a finely turned syntactical balance as for any point of principle they may establish.

Fielding does not present a complete theory of his art of fiction in his Preface; he does not even fully account for what he achieved in *Joseph Andrews*. In *The Moral Basis of Fielding's Art* (1959), Martin C. Battestin reminds us that Fielding's theory of the Ridiculous is 'an account of *satiric* laughter only; as Arthur Murphy pointed out long ago, it does not explain the pure, warm-hearted *comedy* of Parson Adams' (103).* Even so, the Preface introduces an important distinction between the Comic and Burlesque which helpfully orientates the relations between *Pamela*, *Shamela* and *Joseph Andrews*:

no two Species of Writing can differ more widely than the Comic and the Burlesque: for as the latter is ever the Exhibition of what is monstrous and unnatural, and where our Delight, if we examine it, arises from the surprizing Absurdity, as in appropriating the Manners of the highest to the lowest, or *è converso*; so in the former, we should ever confine ourselves strictly to Nature, from the just Imitation of which, will flow all the Pleasure we can this way convey to a sensible Reader.

Burlesque exaggerates distortions and perversions of value; it claims that the figures it mocks have a false sense of importance by reversing and inverting the behaviour appropriate to social status (for example, in *The Grub-Street Opera*, Fielding makes His Majesty's government behave like a household of squabbling servants, which is probably why this play, written in 1731, was suppressed until 1755). The comic, on the other hand, claims to draw on and draw out natural characters, characters whose follies may be amusing, but do not provoke scorn or condemnation. It is important

* For Arthur Murphy, Fielding's friend and biographer, see *Gray's Inn Journal*, 17 August 1754. See also Fielding's discussion of technique in *Joseph Andrews*, III, i; his Preface to Sarah Fielding, *David Simple* (1744); his review of Charlotte Lennox's *Female Quixote* (1752), in *The Covent Garden Journal* (24 March 1752), and the many narratorial intrusions in *Tom Jones* which further his meditations.

to realize that the comic epic poem in prose is not a mock epic. The characters themselves are not burlesqued, although the diction may be locally mock-heroic, especially when people exert their sexual prowess. Mrs Slipslop, for example, becomes both grand and bestial when aroused: 'As when a hungry Tygress, who long had traversed the Woods in fruitless search, sees within the Reach of her Claws a Lamb, she prepares to leap on her Prey . . . so did Mrs *Slipslop* prepare to lay her violent amorous Hands on the poor *Joseph*' (I, vi). *Joseph Andrews* is intended as a comic romance along the lines of *Don Quixote*, as we are told on the title page. (Fielding used the 1725 Motteux-Ozell translation of Cervantes's great work, first published in Spanish in two parts in 1605 and 1615; more will be said of the Don later.) Roughly defined, a comic romance, or a comic epic poem in prose, is an invented story with aspects of the epic and romance, such as quests, adventures, love and conflict; the characters are treated comically in that they are drawn from everyday life and are seen in a humorous light, but they are not mocked or travestied as they would be in burlesque. His chief aim, Fielding claims, is the ridicule of affectation, not the satire of vice.

In Fielding's terms, *Shamela* is a burlesque. Monstrosity, absurdity, hypocrisy and the inversion of high and low are a challenging source of 'Delight' throughout. For example, Shamela's whorish mother, Henrietta Maria Honora Andrews, is dignified with the name of a queen (Henrietta Maria was the Catholic wife of Charles I), but also endowed with the skills of a prize fighter – she cuts short letter VIII to Mrs Jervis explaining that she has sprained her right hand 'with boxing three new made Officers. — Tho' to my Comfort, I beat them all.' The incongruity between her name and her behaviour, like the discrepancy between Shamela's words and deeds, is a sign of the debasement of standards, a corruption which Fielding symbolizes in linguistic abuse such as Shamela's 'vartue', or what her mother in the same letter calls the 'Poluteness, which you learned when you was in keeping with a Lord'. Burlesque deliberately distorts the picture in order to render a true image of vice.

It is difficult to get an undistorted image of *Pamela*, not least because the book provoked so many spin-offs, continuations and merchandise, including waxwork models of Pamela in high life. Something of a cult of its cult has grown up around it: critics repeat with awe the anecdotes about how villagers rang bells to celebrate Pamela's marriage to Mr B, how vicars recommended the book from their pulpits. Furthermore, this combination of morality and commercialism in the afterlife of *Pamela* the book owes something to the life of Pamela herself, and to the complexities of literary form and ethical values of Richardson's remarkable epistolary novel. The fact that Pamela eventually succumbs to the man who pursued, kidnapped and assaulted her has been taken by many as a sign that she was shamming resistance: according to the anti-Pamelists, she says 'no' to him at first in order to gain greater rewards when she says 'yes' later. Furthermore, the subtitle, 'Virtue Rewarded', could be taken to suggest that a woman's only 'virtue' is her virginity, and that this is indeed her chief asset. In this view, Richardson is advocating a utilitarian ethic, recommending a narrow version of moral rectitude on the basis that it will be repaid with cash benefits in this life. The dangerous implications of Pamela's teachings for both masters and maids are pointed out by Parson Oliver at the end of *Shamela*:

Young Gentlemen are here taught, that to marry their Mother's Chambermaids, and to indulge the Passion of Lust, at the Expence of Reason and Common Sense, is an Act of Religion, Virtue, and Honour; and, indeed the surest Road to Happiness.

. . . All Chambermaids are strictly enjoyned to look out after their Masters; they are taught to use little Arts to that purpose: And lastly, are countenanced in Impertinence to their Superiors, and in betraying the Secrets of their Families.

Fielding is caricaturing *Pamela*'s 'message', but his argument has some purchase on the text. While Richardson would not wish to recognize this account of his doctrine, he was sensitive enough to criticism of Pamela's outspokenness and of the social distance between his hero and heroine to smooth away in later editions some of the vulgarities and the 'Impertinence' in her speech which had imparted such energy and vividness to the first edition. However, to be fair, because the marriage does not take place at the end of the book (in the second edition, there are another 121 pages still to go), it is not the *end* Pamela has in view. Moreover, by resisting Mr B, Pamela reforms him: she transforms his lust into love and makes marriage strictly speaking honourable, even if not psychologically convincing.

Modern readers may be particularly alert to the gender and class politics of Richardson's tale, but the abuse of power by masters was an issue of public concern in the eighteenth century too, as the Charteris case demonstrated. A notorious gambler and rake, Colonel Francis Charteris maintained a supply of women for himself by hiring naive country girls as servants and then seducing them. In 1729 he was charged with the rape of one such servant, Ann Bond. Surprisingly, he was found guilty and condemned to death, but predictably this friend of Walpole's was able to use his influence to obtain a royal pardon in 1730. His abuse of power was not uncommon, but so extreme that at his funeral in 1732 an outraged mob raised a riot. They almost tore his body out of the coffin, and threw dead dogs into the grave along with it. Fielding had Charteris in mind in 1730 when writing his comedies *Rape upon Rape* and *The Lottery* (his allusions to Charteris suggest that he may have seen Hogarth's depiction of him in plate 2 of *The Harlot's Progress* before it was published in 1732). He was certainly angered both by Charteris's vice and by Walpole's ability to 'screen' his friends from prosecution.

The extraordinary hold *Pamela* has over its readers is derived not just from its potentially (but perhaps only potentially) radical criticism of sexual and class relations, but also from the obsessively detailed and subjective way in which it is narrated in Pamela's own interrupted and self-absorbed correspondence. While Pamela endures an intense power play of desire and resistance, the reader is forced to work through the seemingly interminable minutiae of Pamela's 'writing to the moment', a literary method which is both inept and super-subtle. Observing Pamela's inner drama of resistance and seduction, the reader gradually develops an insight into a young woman's psychological world unprecedented in English prose fiction; not even Defoe's *Moll Flanders* (1722) nor his *Roxana* (1724) convey such a detailed impression of the heroine's inner life.

Richardson's first person narrative places a strain on the credibility of Pamela's character: she has to present herself as modest yet at the same time busily records all the praise that comes her way. Fielding greatly objected to Pamela's apparent vanity and the even greater vanity of the then anonymous author who prefaced his novel with numerous testimonials and eulogies affirming the moral beauty of the work. Fielding almost certainly worked with the second edition of *Pamela*, which was swollen by 38 pages of puffery. (Unfortunately no modern edition reproduces *Pamela* as it would have appeared to early readers.) In effect, Richardson was running his own fan club and employing friends to defend himself against his critics. The prefatory letters, most of them written by Richardson's friend Aaron Hill, are so inflamed with zeal for Pamela that they break out into a vein of amorous imagery. With very little re-writing, Fielding was able to tease out innuendos for the prefatory letters to *Shamela*. Parson Tickletext's letter to Parson Oliver condenses several pages of one such letter, and the slightest omission produces fruity double-entendres. Richardson's correspondent had gushed:

The Comprehensiveness of his Imagination must be truly prodigious! – It has stretch'd out this diminutive mere *Grain of Mustard-seed*, (a poor Girl's little, innocent, Story) into a Resemblance of That *Heaven*, which the Best of Good Books has compar'd it to. (*Pamela*, 2nd ed., I, xvii; cf. Matthew 13.31–2)

Tickletext enthuses:

The comprehensiveness of his Imagination must be truly prodigious! It has stretched out this diminutive mere Grain of Mustard seed (a poor Girl's little, *&c.*) into a Resemblance of that Heaven, which the best of good Books has compared it to.

Like 'Fanny' and 'the dear *Monysyllable*' (Letter X) which Shamela professes not to understand, '*et cetera*' was a slang name for female genitalia. Fielding liked attractive women (all his heroines – Fanny, Sophia, Amelia – are beauties), and he did not seem to expect absolute standards of sexual rectitude from them (Betty is admired for her good nature rather than condemned for her looseness). Yet Richardson was for him a legitimate target for ridicule because this combination of eroticism and modesty appeared to be a hypocritical and affected purity.

The poet laureate, playwright and actor-manager Colley Cibber and the Reverend Conyers Middleton, Cambridge librarian and contentious scholar, are strange companions for Pamela Andrews, but Fielding runs them all together when he names the author of *Shamela* Mr Conny Keyber. To Fielding, they were all guilty of affectation. All three were in the public eye as Cibber's autobiography, *An Apology for the Life of Mr Colley Cibber . . . Written by Himself* was published in April 1740 (*Apology* here means 'defence'; Cibber was not saying 'sorry', or suggesting that his was a mere apology for a life); Middleton's *The History of the Life of Marcus Tullius Cicero*, with its fawning dedication to John, Lord Hervey (Fielding's Miss Fanny), was published in February 1741, the same month as the second edition of *Pamela*. A measure of his dislike for Cibber, Middleton and Hervey is the fact that Fielding also wove criticisms of them into *Joseph Andrews*, and repeatedly attacked Cibber in his journal *The Champion* (April–May 1740). Fielding sees them all as politicians, in the sense of schemers and self-promoters, and he objects to them on party political grounds. Cibber, like Richardson, was aesthetically and politically at odds with Fielding, who at that time was writing for the Opposition coalition. Soon to be promoted to the King of Dunces by Alexander Pope, the Tory Cibber rivalled and libelled Fielding in his theatrical career and toadied to the corrupt Prime Minister, Sir Robert Walpole. Middleton's *History* slighted *Observations on the Life of Cicero* (1731), a book by Fielding's friend and patron George Lyttelton, and sucked up to Hervey, whose own sucking up to Robert Walpole had earned him a powerful place in the King's Household. Here, ridiculous affectation merged into vice and gave Fielding's burlesque more force and a wider range of targets.

The combination of topical politics and timeless satire is common in all of Fielding's fictions. The variety of subject matter and stylistic devices he employs, including precise parody, slapstick humour, touching sentiment, legal dispute and journalistic essays, demonstrates that Fielding could engage with the nitty gritty of the day and keep his eye on enduring moral values. At the same time, it gives the novel a formal and ideological range which may be unnerving to those unfamiliar with the eighteenth century.

Joseph Andrews treats many of the same issues as *Shamela*, but, whereas the latter works by burlesque and satire, the former opens up into a broader comedy about the life and manners of a greater cast of characters. It has a positive spirit which takes it beyond the parody of a particular novel. *Pamela* supplies framing devices for Fielding's comedy of the road, but the movement of the middle section of the quest owes more to the comic romances of Cervantes and Scarron than to the moral tale of Richardson. Indeed, the tenor of the main body of the text can be taken as a corrective to Richardson's way of thinking. There are various verbal allusions to *Pamela* at the start of *Joseph Andrews*. The action is set in motion by the attempted seduction of a servant, and closure is achieved at the end of *Joseph Andrews* with further reminders of Richardson's novel as the characters return to Booby Hall for an *éclaircissement* of events and relations. The matter-of-factness of Gaffar and Gammer Andrews provides a contrast with Richardson's description of Pamela's tearful reunion with her parents: 'Gaffar *Andrews* testified no remarkable Emotion, he blessed and kissed her, but complained bitterly, that he wanted his Pipe, not having had a Whiff that Morning' (IV, xvi). Fielding's Pamela is not the minx that Shamela is, but what tells very badly against her is that, provoking the solemn wrath of Abraham Adams, she and Mr Booby laugh during the wedding of Joseph and Fanny (IV, xvi).

Indeed, the wedding is strikingly different from that in *Pamela*, not least because it is the climax of the book and represents the happy resolution of all the problems. It is as if Fielding were saying that the medial position of the wedding in *Pamela* is a sign of Richardson's failure of form and judgement. The blissful sexuality of the wedding night is also a rebuke to Richardson's neurotic withholding. Squeamish Pamela continues writing to her parents until eleven o'clock at night, and then casts a veil over the events of the bedchamber. Fielding's narrator, however, takes us into Fanny's bedchamber and helps her undress:

Undressing to her was properly discovering, not putting off Ornaments: For as all her Charms were the Gifts of Nature, she could divest herself of none. How, Reader, shall I give thee an adequate Idea of this lovely young Creature! the Bloom of Roses and Lillies might a little illustrate her Complexion, or their Smell her Sweetness: but to comprehend her entirely, conceive Youth, Health, Bloom, Beauty, Neatness, and Innocence in her Bridal-Bed; conceive all these in their utmost Perfection, and you may place the charming *Fanny*'s Picture before your Eyes.

Joseph no sooner heard she was in Bed, than he fled with the utmost Eagerness to her. A Minute carried him into her Arms, where we shall leave this happy Couple to enjoy the private rewards of their Constancy; Rewards so great and sweet, that I apprehend *Joseph* neither envied the noblest Duke, nor *Fanny* the finest Duchess that Night. (IV, xvi)

Fielding makes Fanny's beauty poetic (deliberately cutting against the bawdy associations of her name), but does not completely refine her into abstraction; rather, he elevates her into the essence of natural beauty, in herself a marriage of fine qualities which is both a description of the actual marriage taking place and an epitome of it. The reminder of social rank (Joseph and Fanny are as happy as nobility) also marks the distance between the potentially radical *Pamela* and the more conservative *Joseph Andrews*. Whereas Richardson elevates Pamela to the status of the gentry through her marriage to Mr B, Fielding, in a typical device of romance (the baby-swap and later recognition scene), reveals Joseph to be a true-born member of the minor gentry. His marriage to Fanny, now the daughter of Gaffar and Gammer Andrews, does not violate social class as much as that of her sister and, because they are as happy as dukes and duchesses, they do not need to change their rank.

As well as realigning social relations at the end of *Joseph Andrews*, Fielding inverts gender relations at the start. Instead of depicting a lusty squire pursuing a shy serving maid, he has a lascivious mistress make advances against a comically chaste but virile manservant. When Lady Booby recovers from her stultifying surprise on meeting resistance from Joseph and exclaims, 'Your Virtue! Intolerable Confidence!' (I, viii), she is presented as monstrous because she is violating decorums of feminine as well as class behaviour, as she herself acknowledges: 'Have you the Assurance to pretend, that when a Lady demeans herself to throw aside the Rules of Decency, in order to Honour you with the highest Favour in her Power, your Virtue should resist her Inclination?' (I, viii). Coupling her with the vulgar, pretentious, self-deluding and cow-like Mrs Slipslop reinforces the hideous image of the self-demeaning lady. Nevertheless, we should respond with sympathy to this odd coupling of desire and actuality.

At the same time, the joke is partly on Joseph, whose behaviour and language are unnaturally constrained. Fielding sets him up as the butt of a joke in these early chapters by concealing from us the information that Joseph is not a chaste prig, but a faithful lover of the charming Fanny Goodwill, and it is this affection, rather than any lack of natural passion on his part, which governs his restraint. For at least the first ten chapters, Joseph is little more than a rhetorical object of the narrator, a figure used to demonstrate his values. He rarely gets to speak directly, and is called Joey until the narrator wishes to draw a typological parallel between his hero and his biblical namesake (who was sexually harassed by Potiphar's wife in Genesis 39.7–20). Joseph's first employment is as a scarecrow or, as the narrator terms it, 'His Office was to perform the Part the Antients assigned to the God *Priapus*' (I, ii). We are more likely to recall another part of Priapus than his bird-scaring role, and the narrator here wishes to alert us to the virility of which Joseph is as yet innocent (see *Joseph Andrews*, I, ii, *n.* 6). Joseph's characterization differs in several vital respects from that of Shamela. Although we see him playing several roles in the opening chapters, he is not an actor like Shamela; he has a core of virtue and good nature which is untouched by the world he inhabits. Furthermore, we focus *on* him, not *through* him; the shift from the first person narrative of *Pamela* and *Shamela* to the third person narrative of Fielding's detached narrator in *Joseph Andrews* signals a major change in the triangular relationship between reader, characters and author, a difference which is loaded with aesthetic and ethical values.

The narrator, who was to become even more of a controlling presence in *Tom Jones*, intruding commentary and digressive chapters into the narrative, is one of Fielding's most important characters. He is with us throughout *Joseph Andrews*, yet he is an elusive and protean figure; not quite Henry Fielding the author, nor a full character with his own biography, he slips in and out of irony. The first description of Parson Adams, for example, seems to be entirely reliable, authoritative and without irony. The narrator simply states: 'Mr *Abraham Adams* was an excellent Scholar.' (I, iii). Yet by juxtaposing this stable characterization of his fictional creation with the shiftiness of the self-presentation of Colley Cibber in his *Apology*, he modulates into a skilful irony which preserves Adams' reputation intact while undermining that of the poet laureate:

He was besides a Man of good Sense, good Parts, and good Nature; but was at the same time as entirely ignorant of the Ways of this World, as an Infant just entered into it could possibly be. As he never had any Intention to deceive, so he never expected such a Design in others. He was generous, friendly and brave to an Excess; but Simplicity was his Characteristic: he did, no more than Mr *Colley Cibber*, apprehend any such Passions as Malice and Envy to exist in Mankind, which was indeed less remarkable in a Country Parson than in a Gentleman who hath passed his Life behind the Scenes, a Place which hath been seldom thought the School of Innocence . . . (I, iii; cf. *Apology*, 2nd ed. (1740), i, 7)

Fielding is able to praise Adams' simplicity – a vital clue to the rest of his behaviour – in a sophisticated manner without making him appear a fool. Cibber comes off as the fool for thinking he can get away with pretending that he is as innocent as an infant; we are later to learn that it is precisely Adams' childlike innocence which gets him in trouble.

Adams' other characteristics – his learning, generosity, friendliness and bravery – also ally the parson with the values of Fielding and his narrator. Fielding's sense of himself as a gentleman possessing exactly these qualities lies behind the witty aloofness of the narrator. He maintains a posture of urbanity and probity which at once lends support to the sense of the trustworthiness of his judgement and separates the narrator from the pains and pleasures of the people he describes and assesses. All of these features can be found in this example of the narrator's description of Adams in action:

Upon these Words, *Adams* fetched two Strides across the Room; and snapping his Fingers over his Head muttered aloud, He would excommunicate such a Wretch for a Farthing; for he believed the Devil had more Humanity. These Words occasioned a Dialogue between *Adams* and the Host, in which there were two or three sharp Replies, 'till *Joseph* bad the latter know how to behave himself to his Betters. At which the Host, (having first strictly surveyed *Adams*) scornfully repeating the word *Betters*, flew into a Rage, and telling *Joseph* he was able to walk out of his House as he had been able to walk into it, offered to lay violent Hands on him; which perceiving, *Adams* dealt him so sound a Compliment over his Face with his Fist, that the Blood immediately gushed out of his Nose in a Stream. The Host being unwilling to be out-done in Courtesy, especially by a Person of *Adams*'s Figure, returned the Favour with so much Gratitude, that the Parson's Nostrils likewise began to look a little redder than usual. Upon which he again assailed his Antagonist, and with another stroke laid him sprawling on the Floor. (II, v)

The forcefulness of Adams' first verbal outburst is set against the casualness of the violence ('with another stroke . . .'). The exchange of blows is described as if it were a polite dialogue, which it is far from being, even though it is all about social proprieties. The fight is provoked by the landlord's outrage at his wife's attentions to a footman and by the intervention of one who appears to be a tramp.

For the comedy of this violence to work as slapstick and for the sufferings of the assailants not to cause the reader pain, Fielding has to maintain his arch detachment. The controlled syntax and incongruous diction ('offered', 'Compliment', 'Courtesy', 'Gratitude') cast an air of artificiality over this lowlife brawl which anticipates the greater mock-heroics of the fight in the churchyard in *Tom Jones* (IV, viii). Sometimes the narrator's irony is in excess of the situation; it appears to be a fallback position for Fielding. (Even in his plays he managed to work in a version of irony by adopting the structure of the rehearsal play which featured a commentary on the action.) It probably stems from national and class – as well as personal – attitudes to the expression of feeling. Fielding could be forthrightly sentimental, especially in *Amelia*, his last and least popular novel, which pays tribute to Fielding's beloved first wife Charlotte. Sentimentalism is, though, itself an artificial way of displaying emotion, suggesting perhaps an embarrassment about sincerity. Leslie Feidler associates Fielding's apparent distrust of feelings with the kind of defensive masculinity with which we began:

The fear of not seeming manly enough haunts him everywhere, inhibiting reflection and delicacy and subtlety alike; and leading to the exaggerated heartiness, bluffness and downright crudity of manner required in a society where the male has continually to prove that he is one of the boys. (*Love and Death in the American Novel* (1967), 157)

While exaggerated, Fielding's arch irony is far from crude, though it does deliberately inhibit certain kinds of reflection, as William Empson points out when he relates Fielding's irony to his distrust of Richardson:

I think it was mixed with a class belief, that well-brought-up persons (with the natural ease of gentlemen) do not need to keep prying into their own motives as these hypocritical Nonconformist types do. As a novelist he never actually asserts this idea, which one can see is open to misuse. (*Kenyon Review*, 20 (1958), 224)

Without wishing to present Fielding as tied obsessively to refuting Richardson, I would suggest that many aspects of his work revolve around the religious and class attitudes crystallized in *Pamela* which Empson in his brilliant and cavalier manner identifies in this passage. The role played by the narrator in mediating the story, and his lack of involvement with the inner life of his characters, are related to a distrust of the habits of self-scrutiny developed by the Dissenting middle classes in the early modern period.

The tone of the narration and the comic treatment of the action have troubled readers of *Joseph Andrews* in different ways. Simon Varey argues that the moral message of his novels is undermined by his ironic manner:

Although he promoted the cause of virtue in *Tom Jones* and *Joseph Andrews*, his undercutting irony ultimately compromised his position in these novels by making concessions to his readers' scorn. (*Henry Fielding* (1986), 121)

Varey's criticism indirectly suggests one of the central concerns of Fielding's experiment in comic epic: how can moral heroism be treated in an age which found Pamela and Colley Cibber to be suitable paragons? The Augustan satirists belittled the actions of the moderns by submitting them to absolute standards; Pope had already mocked feminine virtue in his *Rape of the Lock* (1712, 1714), and masculine literary power in *The Dunciad* (1728–43). Fielding, something of a latecomer and holding more flexible attitudes to human weakness, experiments in *Joseph Andrews* with a method more humane than *Shamela*'s burlesque, but also more risky because more likely to be misunderstood. Joseph's mighty cudgel in III, vi is an example of Fielding's complex reworking of Augustan mock-heroic. The description burlesques Homer's epic descriptions of Agamemnon's sceptre and the shield of Achilles in the *Iliad* (2, 100–9; 18, 478–607), both of which had already been feminized in Pope's *Rape of the Lock* (1714) (II, 117–22; V, 87–

96). Yet Fielding whittles away the trinkets which embellish modern canes and bodkins, restoring an aspect of the heroic to Joseph's priapic cudgel. With it, he cracks the heads of eight hunting hounds which were attacking Parson Adams. Although the style of the passage is decidedly mock-heroic, Joseph genuinely represents 'at once the Idea of Friendship, Courage, Youth, Beauty, Strength, and Swiftness' (III, vi). As Fielding says in his preface, the diction may be burlesqued, but the characters are not.

In *Joseph Andrews* and later in *Tom Jones*, Fielding develops a theory and practice of comedy which shifts the response to the signs of the times away from the negative power of satiric scorn to the positive example of amiable humour. Parson Abraham Adams, whose vitality and complexity hijack the novel, leaving even Joseph in the shade, is the key figure for testing these problems to do with irony and virtue. Fielding's concern for and with Adams is felt in the fact that the Parson is the only character referred to explicitly in the preface, and that Fielding went to some trouble to touch up his character in the revisions in the second edition of *Joseph Andrews*. The revisions tend to add to the Parson's ridiculousness. In the preface Fielding anticipates that 'the low Adventures in which he is engaged' will upset clergymen, but insists that 'no other Office could have given him so many Opportunities of displaying his worthy Inclinations' (nor of displaying Fielding's own response to the chief religious controversies of the day). Adams has a motley heritage: he is part clergyman, part Quixote. On the one hand, many of his religious doctrines are derived, as Martin C. Battestin argued at length in *The Moral Basis of Fielding's Art*, from the Latitudinarian divines of the Anglican church, who, reacting to the violent differences of opinion which fuelled the civil war, and to the cynicism of Hobbes, argued that an active social benevolence was more important than the niceties of dogma. On the other hand, his chief literary model is a crazy knight of La Mancha, Cervantes's hero whose head was turned by reading chivalric romances. How could readers take seriously moral teaching which came from the mouth of a ragamuffin parson or a madman, as Don Quixote was usually taken to be at this point in the eighteenth century? In *Rape upon Rape* (1730), Fielding himself suggests that the modern world is so made that the practice of virtue always seems foolish. In a scene which anticipates elements of Adams's first rescue of Fanny (II, ix), the character Constant exclaims: 'Good nature is Quixotism, and every Princess Micomicona will lead her deliverer into a cage' (III, ii).* This is not quite the same as saying that virtue is mocked (as George Cheyne did in a letter to Richardson); the point is that Adams is a touchstone whose virtue shows up the corruption of the world he inhabits.

The notion of the wandering journey beset with perils, the attempt to protect one's ideals in a corrupt world, and the encounters at inns, all owe something to Cervantes's influence. There are specific parallels, such as the encounter with the 'roasting squire' in III, vii, which is modelled on *Don Quixote*, II, xxxi–ii. The Squire's plots to humiliate the Parson backfire and he and his cronies end up looking foolish. (Further parallels are cited in the notes.) Fielding's attitude to Don Quixote was sympathetic and idealizing; previously, people had tended to read Cervantes's anti-romance as a satire on the eccentric knight. The first to draw attention publicly to Fielding's new interpretation was his sister, Sarah. *The Cry* (1754), written by Sarah Fielding in collaboration with Jane Collier, complained that

that strong and beautiful representation of human nature, exhibited in *Don Quixote*'s madness in one point, and extraordinary good sense in every other, is indeed very much thrown away on such readers as consider him only as the object of their mirth. Nor less understood is the character of parson *Adams* in *Joseph Andrews* by those persons, who, fixing their thoughts on the hounds trailing the bacon in his pocket (with some oddnesses in his behaviour and peculiarities in his dress) think proper to overlook the noble simplicity of his mind, with other innumerable beauties in his character. (*The Cry*, 169)

Fielding was one of the leading figures in a new tendency in comedy to promote the lovable, laughable, amiable humorist. From this period, the combination of nobility and simplicity in the characters of Adams, Don Quixote, Falstaff and their kind was appreciated with humorous indulgence. Hazlitt later concluded of Adams that 'Our laughing at him does not once lessen our respect for him' (*Comic Writers*, in *Works* (1930), VI, 115).

Yet folly and virtue coexist in a precarious tension in Adams; the suspicion that Fielding ridicules virtue is hard to shake off entirely. Even though he insists on the dignity of his hero and the virtue of his words

---

* To trick Don Quixote into captivity, the curate and the barber persuade Dorothea to pretend to be the mythical Princess Micomicona who needs his aid (see *Don Quixote*, I, iv).

and deeds, he seems to delight in humiliating him. Nabokov described *Don Quixote* as 'a veritable encyclopedia of cruelty', 'one of the most bitter and barbarous books ever penned' (*Lectures on Don Quixote* (1983), 52). Adams too is treated with barbarism: his clothes, already disfigured by having been torn ten years ago, and not helped by the casual way with which he tops off his outfit with nightcaps, handkerchiefs, short coats and so on as if deliberately to disguise his cassock, bear much of the brunt of the attack: they are soaked, doused in blood, thrown into pigs' mire, torn by dogs, dunked in a barrel, splattered by the contents of a chamber pot, and left off altogether in the farcical bedroom scene. Surely people can be forgiven for laughing at him and failing to recognize his status when he presents such an appearance. Parson Adams's physical appearance is of less concern to him than the figure he cuts as a man of learning, but here too he is vulnerable and subjected to numerous attacks and humiliations: at least half a dozen times his learning is called into question by men more stupid and less well-read than he is. In terms of classical learning he always comes off better than his detractors, but his ignorance of the ways of the world is often brought to our attention.

Adams at least has the power physically to defend himself, whereas poor Fanny Goodwill is an example of the vulnerability of innocence. She is sexually harassed more often than is Pamela, and by half a dozen different men. Even Adams gets into bed with her, albeit by mistake. Like Hitchcock, Fielding likes to torture his heroine. His willingness to put his favourite characters in positions of stress seems perverse. Yet, just as the violence is always treated as slapstick, his victims are always rescued, disaster is always averted. While Fielding reveals a dark side to the landscape, peopling his countryside with thugs and villains of all sorts, he also fits this threat into a comic frame. The fact that these victims are always rescued attests to his belief in a divinely ordered universe, a benign providence. Yet the fact that his heroes always end up in trouble bears witness to his more pessimistic sense that good nature is not only not enough to get you by in this world, but that it is actually likely to lead you into difficulty.

Several of the essays and articles that Fielding wrote while he was working on *Joseph Andrews* provide an insight into his dual sense of the power and the vulnerability of goodness. In *An Essay on the Knowledge of the Characters of Men* (written around this time, though not published until 1743), Fielding describes the quality which Battestin argues is the moral basis of his art – good nature – but in terms which hint at its limitations:

Good-Nature is that benevolent and amiable Temper of Mind which disposes us to feel the Misfortunes, and enjoy the Happiness of others; and consequently pushes us on to promote the latter, and prevent the former; and that without any abstract Contemplation on the Beauty of Virtue, and without the Allurements or Terrors of Religion. Now Good-Humour is nothing more than the Triumph of the Mind, when reflecting on its own Happiness, and that perhaps from having compared it with the inferior Happiness of others. (*Miscellanies*, Wesleyan Edition (1972), I, 158)

Good nature, in this account, is a secular version of what Fielding believed was the highest duty and virtue of a Christian: charity. While good humour is self-centred, good nature is active and outgoing, as Fielding was to insist in *Tom Jones* (see especially XV, i). The danger is that good nature or charity can be something of an unreflecting habit: not only does it not entail the abstract contemplation of virtue or religion, it is, as Fielding explained in an article written in 1740, 'void of Suspicion, not apt to censure the Actions of Men, much less to represent them in an evil Light to others' (*The Champion*, 5 April 1740). The good-natured man is thus easily duped, as Adams is by the false-promiser (II, xvi). (The vulnerability of the good-natured is a constant preoccupation of Fielding's works, witness Heartfree, Tom Jones and Amelia.) Sympathetic identification with the plight of others is dangerous because it leads you to expect that other people think and feel as you do. Fielding, whose first literary works were explorations of masquerade, repeatedly warns his readers that most people go in disguise, 'under false visors and habits'. Good nature is vulnerable to abuse unless it is armed with judgement.

Tho' Virtue and Wisdom be in Reality the Opposites to Folly and Vice, they are not so in Appearance. Indeed, it requires a nicer Eye to Distinguish them, than is commonly believed. The two latter are continually industrious to disguise themselves, and wear Habits of the former. (*The Champion*, 4 March 1740)

Abraham Adams, who both recommends and represents good nature, is not intended as a role model; we are to admire his virtue, but not to imitate his behaviour in all respects because we will be constantly duped, dunked and bespattered. Fielding, suspicious of Pamela's role as an ideal standard, suspicious too of Richardson's subjective narrative technique which encourages the reader to identify with his example of injured innocence, deliberately sets the reader at a distance from his characters and the action by means of the ironic narration. He forces his readers to think about, not identify with the character. His irony sees with 'a nicer Eye', and is aware of other, more worldly ways of viewing the situation. On the one hand he perhaps makes concessions to the reader's scorn; on the other, as Empson argues, he employs a double irony in which he is seeming to please both the scornful and the sympathetic reader simultaneously.

It would be a mistake to see Adams as an embodiment of unthinking benevolence and spontaneous sympathy; he also counsels rational restraint and is firmly attached to the legalistic and ritualistic practices of the Church of England. The marriage of Joseph and Fanny, in fact the subject of marriage in general, including his own, is an occasion for the exercise of rational principles. He insists that Joseph and Fanny go through the full procedure of publishing banns rather than follow their impetuous desires and be married by licence straight away. Furthermore, when Fanny has been kidnapped by the 'roasting squire', Adams delivers an oration on the importance of restraining the passions (III, xi). The dichotomy between the perspectives of reason and passion is visually symbolized in this 'scene' in which Joseph and Adams are tied back to back, unable to see what the other person sees. We should note, firstly, that Adams is not all benevolence and, secondly, that he is frequently unable to produce the correct response to a situation. When Joseph is racked with torment at the thought of Fanny's ravishment, Adams's rational severity is no comfort to a friend in pain. The imperfection of Adams's view of the situation is even more starkly presented when one of his own loved ones is threatened. Setting him up for a fall, Fielding makes Adams preach against rushing passionately into marriage and illustrates his argument that we must 'not set our Affections so much on any thing here, as not to be able to quit it without Reluctance', with the example of his namesake's willingness to sacrifice his son Isaac:

'no Christian ought so to set his Heart on any Person or Thing in this World, but that whenever it shall be required or taken from him in any manner by Divine Providence, he may be able, peaceably, quietly, and contentedly to resign it.' At which Words one came hastily in and acquainted Mr *Adams* that his youngest Son was drowned. He stood silent a moment, and soon began to stamp about the Room and deplore his Loss with the bitterest Agony. (IV, viii)

Joseph reminds him of his own arguments about the need to conquer the passions, but Adams, we are told, 'was not at leisure now to harken to his Advice'. Adams is not able to learn from his experience because he lacks self-knowledge; he does not reflect on his behaviour, or on his inner self. *Joseph Andrews* functions like a parable in which the lessons enforced by the narrator are to be learnt by the reader, not by the characters. Reform of character is not possible for everyone; many characters, such as Miss Grave-airs, or those on the coach who are reluctant to aid the naked Joseph, are representatives of particular vices or weaknesses rather than psychologically plausible individuals capable of development. In this sense, Bunyan's *The Pilgrim's Progress* (1684), as well as *Don Quixote*, is a model for *Joseph Andrews*. It is debatable how far Fielding expects his own readers to mend their ways. Perhaps they are to be educated in the ways of the world, so that reform is then in their own hands.

Fielding's writing is frequently organized around a series of contrasts and conflicts. Flat characters such as Miss Grave-airs are contrasted with rounded ones like Parson Adams. Words are set against actions: Trulliber often has the word charity in his mouth, but never performs a charitable deed. Division is possible within an individual too, as we have seen with the juxtaposition of Adams's two ethical principles: rationalism and benevolence. Adams is unaware of this internal division, but he accepts other kinds of inconsistency in his character. Speaking of himself in the third person, he explains this dualism: 'he always asserted, that Mr *Adams* at Church with his Surplice on, and Mr *Adams* without that Ornament, in any other place were two very different Persons' (IV, xvi). What makes sense of Adams's two bodies is the fact that he is governed by a superior order: 'he was a Servant of the Highest'. Ultimately it may be possible to reconcile all the contradictions in the text by appealing to a third term and a higher principle. Modern readers, however, may be struck rather by the clash of contrary values and by a sense of ambivalence in the text.

Fielding was driven by conflicting impulses. As a lawyer and moralist he was concerned with maintaining order in society, but as a comic writer and as a man he was fascinated by the vitality of disorder. It is noteworthy that both Adams and Shamela manifest their spontaneity by snapping their fingers. For Fielding, antithesis is both a rhetorical device and a world view. He juxtaposes classical reference and topical issues. He praises good nature while cruelly tormenting his best characters. One possible analogue for the tension between Fielding's high moral purpose and his low comedy is the fact that as a lawyer he was exposed to some very mixed company and diverse experiences. On hearing of his death, his cousin, Lady Mary Wortley Montagu, remarked of his life and his career as a magistrate: 'no man enjoyed life more than he did, though he had few reasons to do so, the highest of his preferment being raking in the lowest sinks of vice and misery' (*Complete Letters* (1967), III, 140). In a similar vein, the preface to a French translation of *Joseph Andrews*, published in 1744, sheds light on the heterogenous nature of Fielding's work when it explains the routine of the circuit judges at the assizes: they hear trials during the day and in the evening attend balls: 'This mixture of joy and sorrow, of comedy and tragedy, of business and pleasure, lasts four or five days' (*Henry Fielding: The Critical Heritage*, 133; translation by the editors). Fielding's fiction is marked by a kind of festive comedy which is aware of vice and pain, but chooses to downplay vice by treating it as folly and to minimize pain by celebrating violence as a kind of moral slapstick.

He does not achieve a comic balance merely by offsetting bad characters with attractive vitality against boring good characters. His mixed mode countenances contradictory characteristics in the same person. Simon Varey points out that Fielding's good characters always have something wrong with them: in *Tom Jones*, X, i, he makes this a principle; in *Joseph Andrews*, Adams is vain, Fanny conceals her love, Joseph cannot muster perfect Christian forgiveness. 'The difference is that Adams, Joseph, Fanny, and those who help them are *natural*, but among those whom they encounter, the proud, vain, hypocritical, and evil are unnatural, or artificial' because their flaws have become their defining characteristics (*Henry Fielding*, 65). Many early readers praised the 'naturalness' of Fielding's novels: Elizabeth Carter wrote of *Tom Jones* that it 'is the most natural representation of what passes in the world, and of the bizarreries which arise from the mixture of good and bad which makes up the composition of most folks' (*A Series of Letters between Mrs Elizabeth Carter and Miss Catherine Talbot* (1808), I, 207).

Yet Fielding is not really a naturalistic writer, though literary realism is often associated with 'low' characters, such as Defoe's Moll Flanders and Dickens's Bill Sikes. Not only does Fielding protect himself from the lowness of his characters with his ironic detachment, he abstracts himself from reference to the merely topical with allusions to classical, biblical and traditional precedents. The classical allusions and the insistence on the timelessness of human nature give Fielding's account of contemporary England depth and perspective, and are a sign of the conscious artificiality which invests his style and plot structure. In the final chapters of *Joseph Andrews*, romance overtakes the realism of the adventures of the road and of Fielding's satire on the state of the nation. Good nature is not powerful enough on its own to counteract Fielding's satiric vision and to achieve a happy resolution of the plot. Chance, in the form of the kindly pedlar, intervenes to effect a *dénouement* in a story of romantic loss and recovery of identity. Yet, just before this fairy-tale ending, Fielding introduces another dark stroke as the shadow of incest falls over the lovers.

Fielding flirts repeatedly with the theme of incest in his plays, poems and novels. The danger is raised, but always averted by some providential intervention which reveals that the lovers are not really related. Martin C. Battestin argues that this preoccupation is highly unusual in the literature of the first half of the eighteenth century; it 'is matched in only one other author of the period . . . his sister Sarah' (*Henry Fielding: A Life* (1989), 27). Sarah Fielding's first novel *David Simple* (1744) recounts the suffering caused by the injustice of a stepmother who accuses a brother and sister of incest. Henry Fielding as a child was himself accused of incestuous relations with his four-year-old sister Beatrice in an ugly Chancery suit concerning the custody and the financial circumstances of the Fielding children after the second marriage of their father. Whatever the truth of these accusations, Henry maintained close and loving relations with his sisters. In his fascination with the subject of incest in his writings, it is as if he is flaunting his ability to raise and settle this demon.

Fielding enjoys teetering on the brink, but in the end imposes order on the flux. *Shamela* seems to be about to end with vice in the ascendancy, but the triumph of the minx over Mr Booby and the gullible reading public is reversed as her true letters are published and her husband catches her in bed with Parson Williams. The spirit which presides over the close of *Joseph Andrews* is a cross between a Justice of the Peace and Santa Claus, acting in accordance with the laws of poetic justice, if not an absolute moral code. Joseph and Fanny are united with all due ceremony, and no one goes home without something, as cash prizes are distributed to the deserving. Abraham Adams is rewarded with a profitable living even though his principles are against pluralism, and Fielding's satirical account of the usual political business of appointments makes such a gift unlikely. The only punishment meted out is to the fellow who attacked Fanny; he is committed to Salisbury gaol.

This happy contrivance, with Mr Booby emerging as a subaltern Providence, although not a paragon (and thereby anticipating the role of Allworthy in *Tom Jones*), is in accordance with literary convention; however, it suggests something about Fielding's view of things and the nature of his realism. It is significant that the good-natured characters, Joseph Andrews,

Abraham Adams and Fanny Goodwill, could not engineer this resolution themselves: Fielding is sceptical about the power of benevolence in the real world. However, as an artist and a moralist, he is very concerned with the conventional happy ending because it represents a conjunction of art and life. In *Amelia*, Fielding gives us the term 'the Art of Life' (I, i). By this I think he implies that life is an art, that one must learn how to live, but not by becoming an artful dodger; 'the Art of Life' is not just the art of survival. Also, it implies that life is a work of art, a work of conscious design created by a combination of Providential authorship and individual free will. Through his stylized plots, language and characters, he is working out the design which both makes life possible and renders it meaningful. Not all readers feel that Fielding's characters grow and learn ways of living, or agree with his view of the world, but they are at least encouraged to learn the art of flexible judgement, thereby finding out how to read other people and to enjoy the benevolent 'Triumph of the Mind'.

1707	22 April: Henry Fielding born to Edmund Feilding or Fielding (1680–1741), a raffish and prodigal army officer, and his wife, Sarah (1682–1718), at Sharpham Park, near Glastonbury, Somerset, home of his maternal grandfather, Sir Henry Gould. Distrusting the improvident Edmund, Sir Henry leaves an estate in trust to provide for Sarah and her children.
1709–19	Early years spent on a farm at East Stour, Dorset, provided by Sir Henry's bequest.
1718	14 April: death of Fielding's mother.
1719	Possibly in January, Edmund marries Anne Rapha, a widow and Roman Catholic with children of her own. HF is sent to Eton, and his surviving siblings, Catherine (1708–50), Ursula (1709–50), Sarah (1710–68), Beatrice (1714–51) and Edmund (1716–?), are taken care of by Lady Gould in Salisbury. Meanwhile, Edmund cuts into the profits of his children's estate.
1719–24	Educated at Eton; a contemporary of William Pitt and Henry Fox, and a friend of George Lyttelton, who later becomes an important patron. Although he seems to have studied his lessons at school, HF is reported to have run wild during his youth, probably in reaction to the family problems which arose after his mother's death.
1721–2	Lady Gould sues Edmund in Chancery for custody of the children and of what is left of the farm in East Stour. In the protracted and bitter court case, Lady Gould's supporters accuse the second Mrs Fielding of mistreating the children and of trying to convert them to Rome; and claim that HF had incestuous relations with his sister Beatrice, then aged four and a half. The court gives judgment against Edmund so the children and the farm come under the control of Lady Gould.
1725	24 May: witnesses execution in London of the notorious criminal Jonathan Wild.
	November: attempts unsuccessfully to carry away by force one

Sarah Andrew, a wealthy heiress, whose guardian had refused to allow her to marry HF.

1726   When Sarah Andrew marries someone else, HF vents his spleen by translating part of Juvenal's misogynistic Sixth Satire. He also presses his father for money and assaults one of his father's servants.

1727   July: stepmother, Anne, dies. Submits a comic play, *Love in Several Masques*, to his cousin, Lady Mary Wortley Montagu, for her revision and patronage.

        10 November: his first published works, now lost: *The Coronation. A Poem, and An Ode on the Birthday*, to celebrate the accession of George II.

1728   29 January: *The Masquerade*, a satiric poem, published under the pseudonym 'Lemuel Gulliver'.

        16 February: *Love in Several Masques*, his first play, produced; published 23 February.

1728–9 16 March 1728–30 April 1729: registered as a student of letters, University of Leyden; stays only three months at first, then, after having turned his hand to political journalism in England in summer 1728, returns to Leyden in February 1729. Little is known of his time here. HF drafts the play *Don Quixote in England*, and seems to have left in a hurry because sued by creditors.

1729   January: father marries Eleanor Hill, a wealthy widow from Salisbury.

        Autumn: moves to London and, with some difficulty, establishes a theatrical career.

1730–37 Has numerous plays – all of them comedies – performed at various London theatres, including *The Author's Farce* (1730), *Rape upon Rape* (1730), *Tom Thumb* (1730), *The Lottery* (1732), *The Modern Husband* (1732), *The Mock Doctor* (1732), *The Miser* (1733), *Don Quixote in England* (1734), *The Universal Gallant* (1735), *The Virgin Unmasked* (1735), *Pasquin* (1736) and *The Historical Register for 1736* (1737). In February 1736, as 'The Great Mogul', he takes over management of the Little Theatre in the Haymarket where he stages most of his experimental plays. His personal life continues to be restless and often troubled. In the early 1730s he spends his summers in Salisbury and winters with his free-thinking and free-living friends in London, running up debts and getting into scrapes.

1734   28 November: elopes with and marries Charlotte Cradock, after which he spends more time at East Stour and gradually reforms his friendships, behaviour and beliefs.

1737   June: the Theatrical Licensing Act, partly prompted by *The Historical Register for 1736*, effectively ends HF's theatrical career, though he tries to have plays performed in later years (e.g., 1742, 1743 and 1745).

1 November: enters the Middle Temple and begins studying law.

1737–8   Writes for the Opposition paper *The Craftsman*.

1738   February: the farm at East Stour sold to raise money; the Fieldings are no longer landed gentry.

1739   15 November: sets up *The Champion*, a periodical along the lines of *The Spectator*, and contributes leaders, literary criticism, and moral, topical and political essays, until early November 1740, after which his partner, James Ralph, takes over.

1740   20 June: called to the bar earlier than is customary; strings were presumably pulled for him.

July–September: begins pattern of spending the summer on the Western Circuit, and, from 1741, September in Bath.

10 October: still short of funds, HF publishes his translation of Gustave Adlerfeld, *Histoire militaire de Charles XII, Roi de Suede* (first published 1739).

November: his father is committed to the Fleet Prison for debt.

6 November: Samuel Richardson publishes *Pamela; or, Virtue Rewarded*.

1741   7 January: *Of True Greatness*, a poem, published in pamphlet form.

15 January–6 March: *The History of our own Times*, intended as a fortnightly magazine, runs for a few issues.

22 January: *The Vernoniad*, a mock-epic poem.

9 March: while still confined for debt, Edmund marries Elizabeth Sparrye, probably his servant.

March: HF held for a fortnight in a sponging house, a halfway station to debtors' prison, for a debt he did not finally clear until 26 May 1742.

4 April: *Shamela*.

18 June: Edmund Fielding dies without leaving anything to his children.

25 June: selections from *The Champion* reprinted in 2 vols.

December: *The Opposition: A Vision*, a pro-Walpole poem.

1742 22 February: *Joseph Andrews*.

6 May: *Miss Lucy in Town*, an unsuccessful attempt to resume writing for the stage.

31 May: Aristophanes's *Plutus, The God of Riches*, translated with Revd William Young, on whom Abraham Adams is modelled.

1743 12 April: *Miscellanies*, in 3 vols., including *Jonathan Wild* and *A Journey from this World to the Next*, published by subscription.

1744 4 May: Sarah Fielding, *David Simple*, with a preface by HF.

November: death of HF's beloved wife, Charlotte, in Bath.

14 November: she is buried in London, but HF does not attend her funeral.

23 November: *An Attempt towards a Natural History of the Hanoverian Rat*, a pro-Opposition satire.

1745 2 July: *The Charge to the Jury*, satirical pamphlet about the death of Walpole.

3 October: *A Serious Address to the People of Great Britain*, warning about the consequences of the current Jacobite rebellion.

7 October: *A History of the Present Rebellion in Scotland*.

5 November–17 June 1746: edits *The True Patriot*, an anti-Jacobite journal.

1746 12 November: *The Female Husband*, a pamphlet loosely based on the true case of the lesbian transvestite, Mary Hamilton.

1747 25 February: *Ovid's Art of Love Paraphrased, and Adapted to the Present Time*.

10 April: Sarah Fielding, *Familiar Letters between the Principal Characters in David Simple*, with a Preface and contribution by HF.

27 November: marries his cook-maid, Mary Daniel (d. 1802); their first child, Henry, born three months later and baptized 25 February 1748.

5 December–5 November 1748: edits *The Jacobite's Journal*, a pro-Government paper.

1748 28 March–2 June: with his wife serving refreshments under the name of 'Madame de la Nash', runs 'a Puppet Show after the Antient Manner' from his house in Panton Street, London.

30 July: entered in the Commission of the Peace for Westminster; his appointment as magistrate is confirmed by oath on 25 October.

9 December: takes up residence in Bow Street, London.

1749   12 January: is finally able to act as magistrate for the county of Middlesex, his name having been entered in the Commission of the Peace 20 June 1747 before he was fully eligible. HF pursues his office with great diligence; in January 1750 he institutes raids to break up gangs of street-robbers – the origin of the 'Bow Street Runners'; he drafts bills and publishes pamphlets on ways to combat crime; his strenuous campaign against violent crime in the autumn and winter of 1753 hastens his death.

3–10 February: *Tom Jones*; four editions published by December of this year.

18 November: *A True State of the Case of Bosalvern Penlez*, a pamphlet defending the unpopular decision to execute a rioter.

1750   19 February: with his blind half-brother and fellow lawyer John, HF opens the Universal Register Office, an advertising and employment agency.

1751   19 January: *Enquiry into the Causes of the Late Increase of Robbers*.
19 December: *Amelia*.

1752   4 January–25 November: edits *The Covent-Garden Journal*, an entertaining and moral journal which publicizes HF's activities in combatting crime.

13 April: *Examples of the Interposition of Providence in the Detection and Punishment of Murder*.

1753   29 January: *Proposal for making an effective Provision for the Poor*.
20 March: *A Clear State of the Case of Elizabeth Canning*, a pamphlet in defence of a supposed victim of abduction (who later turns out to be an imposter).

1754   January: John Fielding takes his brother's place as Magistrate for Westminster and Middlesex, but HF continues performing his duties until his health gives way completely.

19 March: revised edition of *Jonathan Wild*.

26 June–7 August: travels to Lisbon in the vain hope of restoring his health.

8 October: HF dies at Junqueira, near Lisbon, and is buried in the Protestant burial ground in Lisbon.

1755   25 February: *The Journal of a Voyage to Lisbon*, HF's lively and irrascible account of his last voyage, published simultaneously in two versions.

SUGGESTIONS FOR FURTHER READING

EDITIONS

The Wesleyan Edition of the Works of Henry Fielding is the most scholarly collection of texts, but is not yet complete. Martin C. Battestin's edition of *Joseph Andrews* in this series (Clarendon Press, Oxford, 1967) is splendid, but does not include *Shamela*. The most comprehensive collection was edited by W. E. Henley (Drury Lane Edition, 16 vols., Croscup & Sterling Co., New York, 1902). *Shamela* has been reliably edited by R. Brimley Johnson (Golden Cockerel Press, Waltham St Lawrence, 1926); Sheridan W. Baker (University of California Press, Berkeley and Los Angeles, 1953); and Ian Watt (Augustan Reprint Society Publication No. 57, Los Angeles, 1956). *Joseph Andrews* and *Shamela* appear together in paperback editions by Douglas Brooks-Davies (World's Classics, Oxford, 1980) and Homer Goldberg (W. W. Norton, New York, 1987), which has a very helpful appendix of critical and contextual material. *The Correspondence of Henry and Sarah Fielding* has been edited by Martin C. Battestin and Clive Probyn (Clarendon Press, Oxford, 1993).

BIOGRAPHY

Battestin, Martin C. and Ruthe, R., *Henry Fielding: A Life* (Routledge, London, 1989).

Cross, Wilbur L., *The History of Henry Fielding*, 3 vols. (Yale University Press, New Haven, 1918).

Rogers, Pat, *Henry Fielding: A Biography* (Scribner's, New York, 1979).

GENERAL WORKS ON FIELDING

Alter, Robert, *Fielding and the Nature of the Novel* (Harvard University Press, Cambridge, Massachusetts, 1968).

Battestin, Martin C., 'Henry Fielding, Sarah Fielding and "the dreadful Sin of Incest" ', *Novel* 13 (1979), 6–18.

Cleary, Thomas R., *Henry Fielding: Political Writer* (Wilfred Laurier University Press, Waterloo, Ontario, 1984).

Hatfield, Glenn, *Fielding and the Language of Irony* (University of Chicago Press, Chicago, 1968).

Hume, Robert D., *Henry Fielding and the London Theatre, 1728–1737* (Clarendon Press, Oxford, 1988).

Hunter, J. Paul, *Occasional Form: Henry Fielding and the Chains of Circumstance* (John Hopkins University Press, Baltimore, 1975).

Johnson, Maurice, *Fielding's Art of Fiction* (University of Pennsylvania Press, Philadelphia, 1961).

McCrea, Brian, *Henry Fielding and the Politics of Mid-Eighteenth-Century England* (University of Georgia Press, Athens, 1981).

McKillop, Alan Dugald, *The Early Masters of English Fiction* (University of Kansas Press, Lawrence, 1957).

Paulson, Ronald, *Satire and the Novel in Eighteenth-Century England* (Yale University Press, New Haven, 1967).

Paulson, Ronald and Thomas Lockwood, eds., *Henry Fielding: The Critical Heritage* (Routledge & Kegan Paul, London, 1969).

Rawson, Claude, ed., *Henry Fielding: A Critical Anthology* (Penguin, Harmondsworth, 1973).

Sacks, Sheldon, *Fiction and the Shape of Belief* (University of Chicago Press, Chicago, 1964).

Smallwood, Angela, *Fielding and the Woman Question: The Novels of Henry Fielding and Feminist Debate, 1700–1750* (Harvester Wheatsheaf, Hemel Hempstead, 1989).

Varey, Simon, *Henry Fielding*, British and Irish Authors: Introductory Studies (Cambridge University Press, Cambridge, 1986).

Watt, Ian, *The Rise of the Novel* (University of California Press, Berkeley and Los Angeles, 1957).

Wright, Andrew, *Henry Fielding: Mask and Feast* (University of California Press, Berkeley and Los Angeles, 1965).

STUDIES OF *JOSEPH ANDREWS* AND *SHAMELA*

Battestin, Martin C., 'Fielding's Changing Politics and *Joseph Andrews*', *Philological Quarterly* 58 (1979), 39–55.

Battestin, Martin C., 'Fielding's Revisions to *Joseph Andrews*', *Studies in Bibliography* 16 (1963), 81–117.

Battestin, Martin C., *The Moral Basis of Fielding's Art: A Study of Joseph Andrews* (Wesleyan University Press, Middletown, 1959).

Goldberg, Homer, *The Art of Joseph Andrews* (University of Chicago Press, Chicago, 1969).

Goldberg, Homer, 'Comic Prose Epic or Comic Romance: The Argument of the Preface to *Joseph Andrews*', *Philological Quarterly* 43 (1964), 193–215.

McCrea, Brian, 'Rewriting *Pamela*: Social Change and Religious Faith in *Joseph Andrews*', *Studies in the Novel* 16 (1984), 137–49.

Nokes, David, *Henry Fielding: 'Joseph Andrews'*, Penguin Critical Studies (Penguin, Harmondsworth, 1987).

Rothstein, Eric, 'The Framework of *Shamela*', *ELH: A Journal of English Literary History* 35 (1968), 381–402.

Schneider, Aaron, 'Hearts and Minds in *Joseph Andrews*: Parson Adams and a War of Ideas', *Philological Quarterly* 66 (1987), 367–89.

Spilka, Mark, 'Comic Resolution in Fielding's *Joseph Andrews*', *College English* 15 (1953), 11–19.

Staves, Susan, 'Fielding and the Comedy of Attempted Rape', in Beth Fowkes Tobin, ed., *History, Gender and Eighteenth-Century Literature* (University of Georgia Press, Athens, 1994), 86–112.

Woods, Charles, 'Fielding and the Authorship of *Shamela*', *Philological Quarterly* 25 (1946), 248–72.

NOTE ON THE TEXTS

The texts printed here are based on the second edition of each novel. *Shamela* was first published on 4 April 1741, price one shilling and sixpence. A second edition appeared on 3 November 1741 and there was a pirated Dublin edition in the same year. All of these editions were published anonymously, and Fielding never acknowledged the work as his own. However, there is enough internal and external evidence to suggest that he was the author and, since R. Brimley Johnson's Golden Cockerel edition of 1926, it has generally been agreed that *Shamela* is from the same pen as *Joseph Andrews*. The second edition was partly reset and partly reimpressed; spelling, punctuation and capitalization were slightly altered; some errors from the first edition were corrected, some were retained, and a few minor errors were introduced. There is evidence that some of the emendations can be attributed to the author; therefore, having collated the first and second editions, I have taken the second as my copy text.

Joseph Andrews appeared in five authorized lifetime editions, the first four of which Fielding saw through the press. Fielding put his name to the third and all subsequent editions, but his authorship was an open secret from the start. The first edition was published in two volumes costing six shillings on 22 February 1742; the second appeared on 10 June 1742; by March 1743, three editions had been called for, totalling 6,500 copies. (In addition, pirated editions appeared in Dublin in 1742 and 1747.) Fielding made alterations in each of the first four editions, but his revisions for the second were the most thorough-going, and give us pretty much the text that has come down to us in the twentieth century. For the second edition, Fielding corrected some but not all of the errors and inconsistencies, polished his style, pointed his irony with minor changes, and added several of his most humorous passages, significantly affecting the meaning of the work, especially with respect to the characterization of Abraham Adams. I have compared the first five editions and have selected the second as a copy text on the grounds that maintaining the integrity of a particular text is in this instance preferable to a conjectural reconstruction of the author's final intentions.

Obvious errors in both books have been silently corrected, and a few changes have been made to typographical features which could interrupt the pleasure of the modern reader: quotation marks and the long 's' have been modernized. No attempt has been made to impose artificial consistency on these idiosyncratic works; spellings have not been modernized, nor rendered consistent when they were not so in the original. To retain the flavour of the original and the subtlety of Fielding's address to the reader, certain typographical features such as capitalization and italics have been retained. In common with mid-eighteenth-century practice, most nouns are capitalized (though in the reimpressed sections of *Shamela*, there are fewer capitals, and this anticipates the practice of Fielding's later works). Italics are generally used for foreign words and phrases, but Fielding also uses typography for effect: for example, he italicizes Trulliber's dialect words and the foreign jargon of fops. My aim has been to reproduce a text which is as close as possible to that which the author wrote and his contemporaries would have read, but which does not alienate readers in the twenty-first century.

Rather than printing *Shamela* as an appendix to Fielding's more mature work, I have placed it as a curtain-raiser so that readers can see how *Joseph Andrews* grew out of it.

SHAMELA

AN
APOLOGY
FOR THE
LIFE
OF
Mrs. SHAMELA ANDREWS.

In which, the many notorious FALSHOODS and
MISREPRSENTATIONS of a Book called

PAMELA,

Are exposed and refuted; and all the matchless
ARTS of that young Politician, set in a true and
just Light.

Together with

A full Account of all that passed between her
and Parson *Arthur Williams*; whose Character is
represented in a manner something different from
that which he bears in *PAMELA*. The
whole being exact Copies of authentick Papers
delivered to the Editor.

Necessary to be had in all FAMILIES.

By Mr. *CONNY KEYBER.*

LONDON:
Printed for A. DODD, at the *Peacock*, without *Temple-bar*.
M. DCC. XLI.

DEDICATION

To Miss *Fanny*, *&c.*[1]

Madam,

It will be naturally expected, that when I write the Life of *Shamela*, I should dedicate it to some young Lady, whose Wit and Beauty might be the proper Subject of a Comparison with the Heroine of my Piece. This, those, who see I have done it in prefixing your Name to my Work, will much more confirmedly expect me to do; and, indeed, your Character would enable me to run some Length into a Parallel, tho' you, nor any one else, are at all like the matchless *Shamela*.

You see, Madam, I have some Value for your Good-nature, when in a Dedication, which is properly a Panegyrick, I speak against, not for you; but I remember it is a Life which I am presenting you, and why should I expose my Veracity to any Hazard in the Front of the Work, considering what I have done in the Body. Indeed, I wish it was possible to write a Dedication, and get any thing by it, without one Word of Flattery; but since it is not, come on, and I hope to shew my Delicacy at least in the Compliments I intend to pay you.

First, then, Madam, I must tell the World, that you have tickled up and brightned many Strokes in this Work by your Pencil.

Secondly, You have intimately conversed with me, one of the greatest Wits and Scholars of my Age.

Thirdly, You keep very good Hours, and frequently spend an useful Day before others begin to enjoy it. This I will take my Oath on; for I am admitted to your Presence in a Morning before other People's Servants are up; when I have constantly found you reading in good Books; and if ever I have drawn you upon me, I have always felt you very heavy.

Fourthly, You have a Virtue which enables you to rise early and study hard, and that is, forbearing to over-eat yourself, and this in spite of all the luscious Temptations of Puddings and Custards, exciting the Brute (as Dr *Woodward* calls it)[2] to rebel. This is a Virtue which I can greatly admire, though I much question whether I could imitate it.

Fifthly, A Circumstance greatly to your Honour, that by means of your extraordinary Merit and Beauty; you was carried into the Ball-Room at the *Bath*, by the discerning Mr *Nash*;[3] before the Age that other young Ladies generally arrived at that Honour, and while your Mamma herself existed in her perfect Bloom. Here you was observed in Dancing to balance your Body exactly, and to weigh every Motion with the exact and equal Measure of Time and Tune; and though you sometimes made a false Step, by leaning too much to one Side; yet every body said you would one time or other, dance perfectly well, and uprightly.

Sixthly, I cannot forbear mentioning those pretty little Sonnets, and sprightly Compositions,[4] which though they came from you with so much Ease, might be mentioned to the Praise of a great or grave Character.

And now, Madam, I have done with you; it only remains to pay my Acknowledgments to an Author, whose Stile I have exactly followed in this Life, it being the properest for Biography. The Reader, I believe, easily guesses, I mean *Euclid's Elements*; it was *Euclid* who taught me to write. It is you, Madam, who pay me for Writing. Therefore I am to both,

> *A most Obedient, and*
> *obliged humble Servant,*
> Conny Keyber.

LETTERS TO THE EDITOR

The EDITOR to *Himself.*[1]

Dear SIR,

However you came by the excellent *Shamela*, out with it, without Fear or Favour, Dedication and all; believe me, it will go through many Editions, be translated into all Languages, read in all Nations and Ages, and to say a bold Word, it will do more good than the *C*—*y* have done harm in the World.[2]

> *I am, Sir,*
>
> > *Sincerely your Well-wisher,*
> >
> > > Yourself.

JOHN PUFF, *Esq*; *to the* EDITOR.

SIR,

I have read your *Shamela* through and through, and a most inimitable Performance it is. Who is he, what is he that could write so excellent a Book?[3] he must be doubtless most agreeable to the Age, and to *his Honour* himself; for he is able to draw every thing to Perfection but Virtue.[4] Whoever the Author be, he hath one of the worst and most fashionable Hearts in the World, and I would recommend to him, in his next Perform- ance, to undertake the Life of *his Honour*.[5] For he who drew the Character of Parson *Williams*, is equal to the Task; nay he seems to have little more to do than to pull off the Parson's Gown, and *that* which makes him so agreeable to *Shamela*, and the Cap will fit.

> *I am, Sir,*
>
> > *Your humble Servant,*
> >
> > > JOHN PUFF.

Note, Reader, several other COMMENDATORY LETTERS and COPIES OF VERSES will be prepared against the NEXT EDITION.

AN APOLOGY FOR THE LIFE OF
MRS SHAMELA ANDREWS

Parson TICKLETEXT[1] *to Parson* OLIVER

Rev. SIR,

Herewith I transmit you a Copy of sweet, dear, pretty *Pamela*, a little Book which this Winter hath produced; of which, I make no doubt, you have already heard mention from some of your Neighbouring Clergy; for we have made it our common Business here, not only to cry it up, but to preach it up likewise: The Pulpit, as well as the Coffee-house, hath resounded with its Praise, and it is expected shortly, that his L—p will recommend it in a —— Letter to our whole Body.[2]

And this Example, I am confident, will be imitated by all our Cloth in the Country: For besides speaking well of a Brother, in the Character of the Reverend Mr. *Williams*, the useful and truly religious Doctrine of *Grace* is every where inculcated.[3]

This Book is the 'SOUL of *Religion*, Good-Breeding, Discretion, Good-Nature, Wit, Fancy, Fine Thought, and Morality. There is an Ease, a natural Air, a dignified Simplicity, and MEASURED FULLNESS in it, that RESEMBLING LIFE, OUT-GLOWS IT. The Author hath reconciled the *pleasing* to the *proper*; the Thought is every where exactly cloathed by the Expression; and becomes its Dress as *roundly* and as close as *Pamela* her Country Habit; or *as she doth her no Habit*, when modest Beauty seeks to hide itself, by casting off the Pride of Ornament, and displays itself without any Covering;'[4] which it frequently doth in this admirable Work, and presents Images to the Reader, which the coldest Zealot cannot read without Emotion.

For my own Part (and, I believe, I may say the same of all the Clergy of my Acquaintance) 'I have done nothing but read it to others, and hear others again read it to me, ever since it came into my Hands; and I find I am like to do nothing else, for I know not how long yet to come: because if I lay the Book down *it comes after me.* When it has dwelt all Day long upon the Ear, it takes Possession all Night of the Fancy. It hath Witchcraft in every Page of it.'[5] —— Oh! I feel an Emotion even while I am relating

9

this: Methinks I see *Pamela* at this Instant, with all the Pride of Ornament cast off.

'Little Book, charming *Pamela*, get thee gone; face the World, in which thou wilt find nothing like thyself.'[6] Happy would it be for Mankind, if all other Books were burnt, that we might do nothing but read thee all Day, and dream of thee all Night. Thou alone art sufficient to teach us as much Morality as we want. Dost thou not teach us to pray, to sing Psalms, and to honour the Clergy? Are not these the whole Duty of Man? Forgive me, O Author of *Pamela*, mentioning the Name of a Book so unequal to thine: But, now I think of it, who is the Author, where is he, what is he, that hath hitherto been able to hide such an encircling, all-mastering Spirit,[7] 'he possesses every Quality that Art could have charm'd by: yet hath lent it to and concealed it in Nature. The Comprehensiveness of his Imagination must be truly prodigious! It has stretched out this diminutive mere Grain of Mustard-seed (a poor Girl's little, *&c.*) into a Resemblance of that Heaven, which the best of good Books has compared it to.'[8]

To be short, this Book will live to the Age of the Patriarchs, and like them will carry on the good Work many hundreds of Years hence, among our Posterity, who will not HESITATE their Esteem with Restraint.[9] If the *Romans* granted Exemptions to Men who begat a *few* Children for the Republick, what Distinction (if Policy and we should ever be reconciled) should we find to reward this Father of Millions, which are to owe Formation to the future Effect of his Influence. — I feel another Emotion.

As soon as you have read this yourself five or six Times over (which may possibly happen within a Week) I desire you would give it to my little God-Daughter, as a Present from me. This being the only Education we intend henceforth to give our Daughters. And pray let your Servant-Maids read it over, or read it to them.[10] Both your self and the neighbouring Clergy, will supply yourselves for the Pulpit from the Book-sellers, as soon as the fourth Edition is published.[11] I am,

Sir,

Your most humble Servant,
THO. TICKLETEXT.

Parson OLIVER *to Parson* TICKLETEXT

Rev. SIR,

I received the Favour of yours with the inclosed Book, and really must own myself sorry, to see the Report I have heard of an epidemical Phrenzy now raging in Town, confirmed in the Person of my Friend.

If I had not known your Hand, I should, from the Sentiments and Stile of the Letter, have imagined it to have come from the Author of the famous Apology, which was sent me last Summer; and on my reading the remarkable Paragraph of *measured Fulness, that resembling Life out-glows it*, to a young Baronet, he cry'd out, *C——ly C——b—r* by *G——*.[1] But I have since observed, that this, as well as many other Expressions in your Letter, was borrowed from those remarkable Epistles, which the Author, or the Editor hath prefix'd to the second Edition which you send me of his Book.

Is it possible that you or any of your Function can be in earnest, or think the Cause of Religion, or Morality, can want such slender Support? God forbid they should. As for Honour to the Clergy, I am sorry to see them so solicitous about it; for if worldly Honour be meant, it is what their Predecessors in the pure and primitive Age, never had or sought. Indeed the secure Satisfaction of a good Conscience, the Approbation of the Wise and Good, (which never were or will be the Generality of Mankind) and the extatick Pleasure of contemplating, that their Ways are acceptable to the Great Creator of the Universe, will always attend those, who really deserve these Blessings: But for worldly Honours, they are often the Purchase of Force and Fraud, we sometimes see them in an eminent Degree possessed by Men, who are notorious for Luxury, Pride, Cruelty, Treachery, and the most abandoned Prostitution; Wretches who are ready to invent and maintain Schemes repugnant to the Interest, the Liberty, and the Happiness of Mankind, not to supply their Necessities, or even Conveniences, but to pamper their Avarice and Ambition. And if this be the Road to worldly Honours, God forbid the Clergy should be even suspected of walking in it.[2]

The History of *Pamela* I was acquainted with long before I received it from you, from my Neighbourhood to the Scene of Action. Indeed I was in hopes that young Woman would have contented herself with the Good-fortune she hath attained; and rather suffered her little Arts to have been forgotten than have revived their Remembrance, and endeavoured by perverting and misrepresenting Facts to be thought to deserve what she now enjoys: for though we do not imagine her the Author of the Narrative itself, yet we must suppose the Instructions were given by her, as well as the Reward, to the Composer. Who that is, though you so earnestly require of me, I shall leave you to guess from that *Ciceronian* Eloquence, with which the Work abounds; and that excellent Knack of making every Character amiable, which he lays his hands on.[3]

But before I send you some Papers relating to this Matter, which will set *Pamela* and some others in a very different Light, than that in which they appear in the printed Book, I must beg leave to make some few Remarks on the Book itself, and its Tendency, (admitting it to be a true Relation,) towards improving Morality, or doing any good, either to the present Age, or Posterity: which when I have done, I shall, I flatter myself, stand excused from delivering it, either into the hands of my Daughter, or my Servant-Maid.

The Instruction which it conveys to Servant-Maids, is, I think, very plainly this, To look out for their Masters as sharp as they can. The Consequences of which will be, besides Neglect of their Business, and the using all manner of Means to come at Ornaments of their Persons, that if the Master is not a Fool, they will be debauched by him; and if he is a Fool, they will marry him. Neither of which, I apprehend, my good Friend, we desire should be the Case of our Sons.[4]

And notwithstanding our Author's Professions of Modesty, which in my Youth I have heard at the Beginning of an Epilogue,[5] I cannot agree that my Daughter should entertain herself with some of his Pictures; which I do not expect to be contemplated without Emotion, unless by one of my Age and Temper, who can see the Girl lie on her Back, with one Arm round Mrs *Jewkes* and the other round the Squire, naked in Bed, with his Hand on her Breasts, *&c.* with as much Indifference as I read any other Page in the whole Novel. But surely this, and some other Descriptions, will not be put into the hands of his Daughter by any wise Man, though I believe it will be difficult for him to keep them from her; especially if the Clergy in Town have cried and preached it up as you say.

But, my Friend, the whole Narrative is such a Misrepresentation of Facts, such a Perversion of Truth, as you will, I am perswaded, agree, as soon as you have perused the Papers I now inclose to you, that I hope you or some other well-disposed Person, will communicate these Papers to the Publick, that this little Jade[6] may not impose on the World, as she hath on her Master.

The true name of this Wench was SHAMELA, and not *Pamela*, as she stiles herself. Her Father had in his Youth the Misfortune to appear in no good Light at the *Old-Bailey*; he afterwards served in the Capacity of a Drummer in one of the *Scotch* Regiments in the *Dutch* Service; where being drummed out, he came over to *England*, and turned Informer against several Persons on the late Gin-Act; and becoming acquainted with an Hostler at an Inn, where a *Scotch* Gentleman's Horses stood, he hath at last by his Interest obtain'd a pretty snug Place in the *Custom-house*.[7] Her Mother sold Oranges in the Play-House; and whether she was married to her Father or no, I never could learn.

After this short Introduction, the rest of her History will appear in the following Letters, which I assure you are authentick.

LETTER I

SHAMELA ANDREWS *to Mrs* HENRIETTA MARIA HONORA
ANDREWS *at her Lodgings at the* Fan *and* Pepper-Box *in*
Drury-Lane.[1]

Dear Mamma,

This comes to acquaint you, that I shall set out in the Waggon on *Monday*, desiring you to commodate me with a Ludgin, as near you as possible, in *Coulstin's-Court*, or *Wild-Street*, or somewhere thereabouts; pray let it be handsome, and not above two Stories high: For Parson *Williams* hath promised to visit me when he comes to Town, and I have got a good many fine Cloaths of the Old Put[2] my Mistress's, who died a wil ago; and I beleve Mrs *Jervis* will come along with me, for she says she would like to keep a House somewhere about *Short's-Gardens*, or towards *Queen-Street*; and if there was convenience for a *Bannio*,[3] she should like it the better; but that she will settle herself when she comes to Town. — *O! How I long to be in the Balconey at the Old House* [4] —— so no more at present from

Your affectionate Daughter,
SHAMELA.

LETTER II

SHAMELA ANDREWS *to* HENRIETTA MARIA HONORA
ANDREWS.

Dear Mamma,

O what News, since I writ my last! the young Squire hath been here, and as sure as a Gun he hath taken a Fancy to me; *Pamela*, says he, (for so I am called here) you was a great Favourite of your late Mistress's; yes, an't please your Honour, says I; and I believe you deserved it, says he; thank your Honour for your good Opinion, says I; and then he took me by the Hand, and I pretended to be shy: Laud, says I, Sir, I hope you don't intend to be rude; no, says he, my Dear, and then he kissed me, 'till he took away my Breath —— and I pretended to be Angry, and to get away, and then he kissed me again, and breathed very short, and looked very silly; and by Ill-Luck Mrs *Jervis* came in, and had like to have spoiled Sport. —— *How troublesome is such Interruption!* You shall hear now soon, for I shall not come away yet, so I rest,

> *Your affectionate Daughter,*
> SHAMELA.

LETTER III

HENRIETTA MARIA HONORA ANDREWS *to* SHAMELA ANDREWS.

Dear Sham,
Your last Letter hath put me into a great hurry of Spirits, for you have a very difficult Part to act. I hope you will remember your Slip with Parson *Williams*, and not be guilty of any more such Folly. Truly, a Girl who hath once known what is what, is in the highest Degree inexcusable if she respects her *Digressions*; but a Hint of this is sufficient. When Mrs *Jervis* thinks of coming to Town, I believe I can procure her a good House, and fit for the Business; so I am,

> *Your affectionate Mother,*
> HENRIETTA MARIA HONORA ANDREWS.

LETTER IV

SHAMELA ANDREWS *to* HENRIETTA MARIA HONORA ANDREWS.

Marry come up, good Madam, the Mother had never looked into the Oven for her Daughter, if she had not been there herself. I shall never have done if you upbraid me with having had a small One by *Arthur Williams*, when you yourself — but I say no more. *O! What fine Times when the Kettle calls the Pot.* Let me do what I will, I say my Prayers as often as another, and I read in good Books, as often as I have Leisure; and Parson *William* says, that will make amends. – So no more, but I rest

> *Your afflicted Daughter,*
> S———.

LETTER V

HENRIETTA MARIA HONORA ANDREWS *to* SHAMELA ANDREWS.

Dear Child,

Why will you give such way to your Passion? How could you imagine I should be such a Simpleton, as to upbraid thee with being thy Mother's own Daughter! When I advised you not to be guilty of Folly, I meant no more than that you should take care to be well paid before-hand, and not trust to Promises, which a Man seldom keeps, after he hath had his wicked Will. And seeing you have a rich Fool to deal with, your not making a good Market will be the more inexcusable; indeed, with such Gentlemen as Parson *Williams*, there is more to be said; for they have nothing to give, and are commonly otherwise the best Sort of Men. I am glad to hear you read good Books, pray continue so to do. I have inclosed you one of Mr *Whitefield*'s Sermons, and also the Dealings with him,[1] and am

Your affectionate Mother,
HENRIETTA MARIA, *&c.*

LETTER VI

SHAMELA ANDREWS *to* HENRIETTA MARIA HONORA ANDREWS.

O Madam, I have strange Things to tell you! As I was reading in that charming Book about the Dealings, in comes my Master — to be sure he is a precious One. *Pamela*, says he, what Book is that, I warrant you *Rochester*'s Poems.[1] — No, forsooth, says I, as pertly as I could; why how now Saucy Chops, Boldface,[2] says he — Mighty pretty Words, says I, pert again. — Yes (says he) you are a d—d, impudent, stinking, cursed, confounded Jade, and I have a great Mind to kick your A——. You, kiss — says I. A-gad, says he, and so I will; with that he caught me in his Arms, and kissed me till he made my Face all over Fire. Now this served purely you know, to put upon the Fool for Anger. O! What precious Fools Men are! And so I flung from him in a mighty Rage, and pretended as how I would go out at the Door; but when I came to the End of the Room, I stood still, and my Master cryed out, Hussy, Slut, Saucebox, Boldface, come hither —— Yes to be sure, says I; why don't you come, says he; what should I come for, says I; if you don't come to me, I'll come to you, says he; I shan't come to you I assure you, says I. Upon which he run up, caught me in his Arms, and flung me upon a Chair, and began to offer to touch my Under-Petticoat. Sir, says I, you had better not offer to be rude; well, says he, no more I won't then; and away he went out of the Room. I was so mad to be sure I could have cry'd.

Oh what a prodigious Vexation it is to a Woman to be made a Fool of.

Mrs *Jervis* who had been without, harkening, now came to me. She burst into a violent Laugh the Moment she came in. Well, says she, as soon as she could speak, I have Reason to bless myself that I am an Old Woman. Ah Child! if you had known the Jolly Blades of my Age, you would not have been left in the lurch in this manner. Dear Mrs *Jervis*, says I, don't laugh at one; and to be sure I was a little angry with her.

—— Come, says she, my dear Honeysuckle, I have one Game to play for you; he shall see you in Bed; he shall, my little Rosebud, he shall see those pretty, little, white, round, panting —— and offer'd to pull off my Handkerchief. — Fie, Mrs *Jervis*, says I, you make me blush, and upon my Fackins,[3] I believe she did: She went on thus. I know the Squire likes you, and notwithstanding the Aukwardness of his Proceeding, I am convinced hath some hot Blood in his Veins, which will not let him rest, 'till he hath communicated some of his Warmth to thee my little Angel; I heard him last Night at our Door, trying if it was open, now to-night I will take care it shall be so; I warrant that he makes the second Trial; which if he doth, he shall find us ready to receive him. I will at first counterfeit Sleep, and after a Swoon; so that he will have you naked in his Possession: and then if you are disappointed, a Plague of all young Squires, say I. —— And so, Mrs *Jervis*, says I, you would have me yield myself to him, would you; you would have me to be a second Time a Fool for nothing. Thank you for that, Mrs *Jervis*. For nothing! marry forbid, says she, you know he hath large Sums of Money, besides abundance of fine Things; and do you think, when you have inflamed him, by giving his Hand a Liberty with that charming Person; and that you know he may easily think he obtains against your Will, he will not give any thing to come at all ——. This will not do, Mrs *Jervis*, answered I. I have heard my Mamma say, (and so you know, Madam, I have) that in her Youth, Fellows have often taken away in the Morning, what they gave over Night.

No, Mrs *Jervis*, nothing under a regular taking into Keeping, a settled Settlement, for me, and all my Heirs, all my whole Life-time, shall do the Business —— or else cross-legged, is the Word, faith, with *Sham*; and then I snapt my Fingers.[4]

Thursday Night, Twelve o'Clock.

Mrs *Jervis* and I are just in Bed, and the Door unlocked; if my Master should come — Odsbobs![5] I hear him just coming in at the Door. You see I write in the present Tense, as Parson *Williams* says. Well, he is in Bed between us, we both shamming a Sleep, he steals his Hand into my Bosom, which I, as if in my Sleep, press close to me with mine, and then pretend to awake. — I no sooner see him, but I scream out to Mrs *Jervis*, she feigns likewise but just to come to herself; we both begin, she to becall, and I to bescratch very liberally. After having made a pretty free Use of my Fingers, without any great Regard to the Parts I attack'd, I counterfeit a Swoon. Mrs *Jervis* then cries out, O, Sir, what have you done, you have murthered poor *Pamela*: she is gone, she is gone. —

O what a Difficulty it is to keep one's Countenance, when a violent Laugh desires to burst forth.

The poor Booby frighted out of his Wits, jumped out of Bed, and, in his Shirt, sat down by my Bed-Side, pale and trembling, for the Moon shone, and I kept my Eyes wide open, and pretended to fix them in my Head. Mrs *Jervis* apply'd Lavender Water, and Hartshorn,[6] and this, for a full half Hour; when thinking I had carried it on long enough, and being likewise unable to continue the Sport any longer, I began by Degrees to come to my self.

The Squire who had sat all this while speechless, and was almost really in that Condition, which I feigned, the Moment he saw me give Symptoms of recovering my Senses, fell down on his Knees; and O *Pamela*, cryed he, can you forgive me, my injured Maid? by Heaven, I know not whether you are a Man or a Woman, unless by your swelling Breasts.[7] Will you promise to forgive me: I forgive you! D—n you (says I) and d—n you, says he, if you come to that. I wish I had never seen your bold Face, saucy Sow, and so went out of the Room.

O what a silly Fellow is a bashful young Lover!

He was no sooner out of hearing, as we thought, than we both burst into a violent Laugh. Well, says Mrs *Jervis*, I never saw any thing better acted than your Part: But I wish you may not have discouraged him from any future Attempt; especially since his Passions are so cool, that you could prevent his Hands going further than your Bosom. Hang him, answer'd I, he is not quite so cold as that I assure you; our Hands, on neither side, were idle in the Scuffle, nor have left us any Doubt of each other as to that matter.

Friday Morning.

My Master sent for Mrs *Jervis*, as soon as he was up, and bid her give an Account of the Plate and Linnen in her Care; and told her, he was resolved that both she and the little Gipsy (I'll assure him) should set out together. Mrs *Jervis* made him a saucy Answer; which any Servant of Spirit, you know, would, tho' it should be one's Ruin; and came immediately in Tears to me, crying, she had lost her Place on my Account, and that she should be forced to take to a House, as I mentioned before; and that she hoped I would, at least, make her all the amends in my power, for her Loss on my Account, and come to her House whenever I was sent for. Never fear, says I, I'll warrant we are not so near being turned away, as you imagine; and, i'cod,[8] now it comes into my Head, I have a Fetch for him, and you shall assist me in it. But it being now late, and my Letter pretty long, no more at present from

> *Your Dutiful Daughter,*
> SHAMELA.

LETTER VII

Mrs LUCRETIA JERVIS *to* HENRIETTA MARIA HONORA ANDREWS.

Madam,

Miss *Sham* being set out in a Hurry for my Master's house in *Lincolnshire*, desired me to acquaint you with the Success of her Stratagem, which was to dress herself in the plain Neatness of a Farmer's Daughter, for she before wore the Cloaths of my late Mistress, and to be introduced by me as a Stranger to her Master. To say the Truth, she became the Dress extremely, and if I was to keep a House a thousand Years, I would never desire a prettier Wench in it.

As soon as my Master saw her, he immediately threw his Arms round her Neck, and smothered her with Kisses (for indeed he hath but very little to say for himself to a Woman.) He swore that *Pamela* was an ugly Slut, (pardon, dear Madam, the Coarseness of the Expression) compared to such divine Excellence. He added, he would turn *Pamela* away immediately, and take this new Girl, whom he thought to be one of his Tenant's Daughters, in her Room.

Miss *Sham* smiled at these Words, and so did your humble Servant, which he perceiving, looked very earnestly at your fair Daughter, and discovered the Cheat.

How, *Pamela*, says he, is it you? I thought, Sir, said Miss, after what had happened, you would have known me in any Dress. No, Hussy, says he, but after what hath happened, I should know thee out of any Dress from all thy Sex. He then was what we Women call rude, when done in the Presence of others; but it seems it is not the first time, and Miss defended herself with great Strength and Spirit.

The Squire, who thinks her a pure Virgin, and who knows nothing of my Character, resolved to send her into *Lincolnshire*, on Pretence of conveying her home; where our old Friend *Nanny Jewkes* is Housekeeper, and where Miss had her small one by Parson *Williams* about a Year ago. This is a Piece of News communicated to us by *Robin* Coachman, who is intrusted by his Master to carry on this Affair privately for him: But we hang together, I believe, as well as any Family of Servants in the Nation.

You will, I believe, Madam, wonder that the Squire, who doth not want Generosity, should never have mentioned a Settlement all this while, I believe it slips his Memory: But it will not be long forgot, no doubt: For, as I am convinced the young Lady will do nothing unbecoming your Daughter, nor ever admit him to taste her Charms, without something sure and handsome before-hand; so, I am certain, the Squire will never rest till they have danced *Adam* and *Eve*'s kissing Dance together. Your Daughter set out Yesterday Morning, and told me, as soon as she arrived, you might depend on hearing from her.

Be pleased to make my Compliments acceptable to Mrs *Davis* and Mrs *Silvester*, and Mrs *Jolly*, and all Friends, and permit me the Honour, Madam, to be with the utmost Sincerity,

Your most Obedient,

Humble Servant,
Lucretia Jervis.

If the Squire should continue his Displeasure against me, so as to insist on the Warning he hath given me, you will see me soon, and I will lodge in the same House with you, if you have room, till I can provide for my self to my Liking.

LETTER VIII

HENRIETTA MARIA HONORA ANDREWS *to* LUCRETIA JERVIS.

Madam,

I received the Favour of your Letter, and I find you have not forgot your usual Poluteness, which you learned when you was in keeping with a Lord.

I am very much obliged to you for your Care of my Daughter, am glad to hear she hath taken such good Resolutions, and hope she will have sufficient Grace to maintain them.

All Friends are well, and remember to you. You will excuse the Shortness of this Scroll; for I have sprained my right Hand, with boxing three new made Officers. — Tho' to my Comfort, I beat them all. I rest,

Your Friend and Servant,

HENRIETTA, *&c.*

LETTER IX

SHAMELA ANDREWS *to* HENRIETTA MARIA HONORA ANDREWS.

Dear Mamma,

I suppose Mrs *Jervis* acquainted you with what past 'till I left *Bedfordshire*; whence I am after a very pleasant Journey arrived in *Lincolnshire*, with your old Acquaintance Mrs *Jewkes*, who formerly helped Parson *Williams* to me; and now designs I see, to sell me to my Master; thank her for that; she will find two Words go to that Bargain.

The Day after my Arrival here, I received a Letter from Mr *Williams*, and as you have often desired to see one from him, I have inclosed it to you; it is, I think, the finest I ever received from that charming Man, and full of a great deal of Learning.

O! What a brave Thing it is to be a Schollard, and to be able to talk Latin.

Parson WILLIAMS *to* PAMELA ANDREWS.

Mrs Pamela,

Having learnt by means of my Clerk, who Yesternight visited the Revd Mr *Peters* with my Commands, that you are returned into this County, I purposed to have saluted your fair Hands this Day towards Even: But am obliged to sojourn this Night at a neighbouring Clergyman's; where we are to pierce a Virgin Barrel of Ale, in a Cup of which I shall not be unmindful to celebrate your Health.

I hope you have remembered your Promise, to bring me a leaden Canister of Tobacco (the Saffron Cut) for in Troth, this Country at present affords nothing worthy the replenishing a Tube with.[1] —— Some I tasted the other Day at an Alehouse, gave me the Heart-Burn, tho' I filled no oftner than five times.

I was greatly concerned to learn, that your late Lady left you nothing, tho' I cannot say the Tidings much surprized me: For I am too intimately acquainted with the Family; (myself, Father, and Grandfather having been successive Incumbents on the same Cure, which you know is in their Gift)[2] I say, I am too well acquainted with them to expect much from their Generosity. They are in Verity, as worthless a Family as any other whatever. The young Gentleman I am informed, is a perfect Reprobate; that he hath an *Ingenium Versatile*[3] to every Species of Vice, which, indeed, no one can much wonder at, who animadverts on that want of Respect to the Clergy, which was observable in him when a Child. I remember when he was at the Age of Eleven only, he met my Father without either pulling off his Hat, or riding out of the way. Indeed, a Contempt of the Clergy is the fashionable Vice of the Times;[4] but let such Wretches know, they cannot hate, detest, and despise us, half so much as we do them.

However, I have prevailed on myself to write a civil Letter to your Master, as there is a Probability of his being shortly in a Capacity of rendring me a Piece of Service; my good Friend and Neighbour the Revd Mr *Squeeze-Tithe* being, as I am informed by one whom I have employed to attend for that Purpose, very near his Dissolution.

You see, sweet Mrs *Pamela*, the Confidence with which I dictate these Things to you; whom after those Endearments which have passed between us, I must in some Respects estimate as my Wife: For tho' the Omission of the Service was a Sin; yet, as I have told you, it was a venial One, of which I have truly repented, as I hope you have; and also that you have continued the wholsome Office of reading good Books, and are improved in your Psalmody, of which I shall have a speedy Trial: For I purpose to give you a Sermon next *Sunday*, and shall spend the Evening with you, in Pleasures, which tho' not strictly innocent, are however to be purged away by frequent and sincere Repentance. I am,

Sweet Mrs Pamela,
Your faithful Servant,
ARTHUR WILLIAMS.

You find, Mamma, what a charming way he hath of Writing, and yet I assure you, that is not the most charming thing belonging to him: For, tho' he doth not put any Dears, and Sweets, and Loves into his Letters, yet he says a thousand of them: For he can be as fond of a Woman, as any Man living.

Sure Women are great Fools, when they prefer a laced Coat to the Clergy, whom it is our Duty to honour and respect.

Well, on *Sunday* Parson *Williams* came, according to his Promise, and an excellent Sermon he preached; his Text was, *Be not Righteous over-much;*[5] and, indeed, he handled it in a very fine way; he shewed us that the Bible doth not require too much Goodness of us, and that People very often call things Goodness that are not so. That to go to Church, and to pray, and to sing Psalms, and to honour the Clergy, and to repent, is true Religion; and 'tis not doing good to one another, for that is one of the greatest Sins we can commit, when we don't do it for the sake of Religion. That those People who talk of Vartue and Morality, are the wickedest of all Persons. That 'tis not what we do, but what we believe, that must save us, and a great many other good Things; I wish I could remember them all.

As soon as Church was over, he came to the Squire's House, and drank Tea with Mrs *Jewkes* and me; after which Mrs *Jewkes* went out and left us together for an Hour and half — Oh! he is a charming Man.

After Supper he went Home, and then Mrs *Jewkes* began to catechize me, about my Familiarity with him. I see she wants him herself. Then she proceeded to tell me what an Honour my Master did me in liking me, and that it was both an inexcusable Folly and Pride in me, to pretend to refuse him any Favour. Pray, Madam, says I, consider I am a poor

Girl, and have nothing but my Modesty to trust to. If I part with that, what will become of me. Methinks, says she, you are not so mighty modest when you are with Parson *Williams*; I have observed you gloat at one another, in a Manner that hath made me blush. I assure you, I shall let the Squire know what sort of Man he is; you may do your Will, says I, as long as he hath a Vote for *Pallamant-Men*, the Squire dares do nothing to offend him; and you will only shew that you are jealous of him, and that's all. How now, Mynx, says she; Mynx! No more Mynx than yourself, says I; with that she hit me a Slap on the Shoulder; and I flew at her and scratched her Face, i'cod, 'till she went crying out of the Room; so no more at present, from

Your Dutiful Daughter,
SHAMELA.

LETTER X

SHAMELA ANDREWS *to* HENRIETTA MARIA HONORA ANDREWS.

O Mamma! Rare News! As soon as I was up this Morning, a Letter was brought me from the Squire, of which I send you a Copy.

Squire BOOBY *to* PAMELA.

Dear Creature,
I hope you are not angry with me for the Deceit put upon you, in conveying you to *Lincolnshire*, when you imagined yourself going to *London*. Indeed, my dear *Pamela*, I cannot live without you; and will very shortly come down and convince you, that my Designs are better than you imagine, and such as you may with Honour comply with. I am,

My Dear Creature,
Your doating Lover,
BOOBY.

Now, Mamma, what think you? — For my own Part, I am convinced he will marry me, and faith so he shall. O! Bless me! I shall be Mrs *Booby*, and be Mistress of a great Estate, and have a dozen Coaches and Six, and a fine House at *London*, and another at *Bath*, and Servants, and Jewels, and Plate, and go to Plays, and Opera's, and Court; and do what I will, and spend what I will. But, poor Parson *Williams!* Well; and can't I see Parson *Williams*, as well after Marriage as before: For I shall never care a Farthing for my Husband. No, I hate and despise him of all Things.

Well, as soon as I had read my Letter, in came Mrs *Jewkes*. You see, Madam, says she, I carry the Marks of your Passion about me; but I have received order from my Master to be civil to you, and I must obey him: For he is the best Man in the World, notwithstanding your Treatment of him. My Treatment of him, Madam, says I? Yes, says she, your Insensibility to the Honour he intends you, of making you his Mistress. I would have you to know, Madam, I would not be Mistress to the greatest King, no nor Lord in the Universe. I value my Vartue more than I do any thing my Master can give me; and so we talked a full Hour and a half, about my Vartue; and I was afraid at first, she had heard something about the Bantling, but I find she hath not; tho' she is as jealous, and suspicious, as old Scratch.[1]

In the Afternoon, I stole into the Garden to meet Mr *Williams*; I found him at the Place of his Appointment, and we staid in a kind of Arbour, till it was quite dark. He was very angry when I told him what Mrs *Jewkes* had threatned —— Let him refuse me the Living, says he, if he dares, I will vote for the other Party; and not only so, but will expose him all over the Country. I owe him 150 *l.* indeed, but I don't care for that; by that time the Election is past, I shall be able to plead the *Statue* of *Lamentations*.[2]

I could have stayed with the dear Man forever, but when it grew dark, he told me, he was to meet the neighbouring Clergy, to finish the Barrel of Ale they had tapped the other Day, and believed they should not part till three or four in the Morning —— So he left me, and I promised to be penitent, and go on with my reading in good Books.

As soon as he was gone, I bethought myself, what Excuse I should make to Mrs *Jewkes*, and it came into my Head to pretend as how I intended to drown myself; so I stript off one of my Petticoats, and threw it into the Canal; and then I went and hid myself in the Coal-hole, where I lay all Night; and comforted myself with repeating over some Psalms, and other good things, which I had got by heart.

In the Morning Mrs *Jewkes* and all the Servants were frighted out of their Wits, thinking I had run away; and not devising how they should answer it to their Master. They searched all the likeliest Places they could think of for me, and at last saw my Petticoat floating in the Pond. Then they got a Drag-Net, imagining I was drowned, and intending to drag me out; but at last *Moll* Cook coming for some Coals, discovered me lying all along in no very good Pickle. Bless me! Mrs *Pamela*, says she, what can be the Meaning of this? I don't know, says I, help me up, and I will go in to Breakfast, for indeed I am very hungry. Mrs *Jewkes* came in immediately, and was so rejoyced to find me alive, that she asked with great Good-Humour, where I had been? and how my Petticoat came into the Pond. I answered, I believed the Devil had put it into my Head to drown my self; but it was a Fib; for I never saw the Devil in my Life, nor I don't believe he hath any thing to do with me.

So much for this Matter. As soon as I had breakfasted, a Coach and Six came to the Door, and who should be in it but my Master.

I immediately run up into my Room, and stript, and washed, and drest my self as well as I could, and put on my prettiest round-ear'd Cap, and pulled down my Stays, to shew as much as I could of my Bosom, (for Parson *Williams* says, that is the most beautiful part of a Woman) and then I practised over all my Airs before the Glass, and then I sat down and read a Chapter in the Whole Duty of Man.

Then Mrs *Jewkes* came to me and told me, my Master wanted me below, and says she, Don't behave like a Fool; No, thinks I to my self, I believe I shall find Wit enough for my Master and you too.

So down goes I into the Parlour to him. *Pamela*, says he, the Moment I came in, you see I cannot stay long from you, which I think is a sufficient Proof of the Violence of my Passion. Yes, Sir, says I, I see your Honour intends to ruin me, that nothing but the Destruction of my Vartue will content you.

O what a charming Word that is, rest his Soul who first invented it.

How can you say I would ruin you, answered the Squire, when you shall not ask any thing which I will not grant you. If that be true, says I, good your Honour let me go home to my poor but honest Parents; that is all I have to ask, and do not ruin a poor Maiden, who is resolved to carry her Vartue to the Grave with her.

Hussy, says he, don't provoke me, don't provoke me, I say. You are absolutely in my power, and if you won't let me lie with you by fair Means, I will by Force. O la, Sir, says I, I don't understand your paw[3] Words.

—— Very pretty Treatment indeed, says he, to say I use paw Words; Hussy, Gipsie, Hypocrite, Saucebox, Boldface, get out of my Sight, or I will lend you such a Kick in the — I don't care to repeat the Word, but he meant my hinder part. I was offering to go away, for I was half afraid, when he called me back, and took me round the Neck and kissed me, and then bid me go about my Business.

I went directly into my Room, where Mrs *Jewkes* came to me soon afterwards. So Madam, says she, you have left my Master below in a fine Pet, he hath threshed two or three of his Men already: It is mighty pretty that all his Servants are to be punished for your Impertinence.

Harkee, Madam, says I, don't you affront me, for if you do, d—n me (I am sure I have repented for using such a Word) if I am not revenged.

How sweet is Revenge: Sure the Sermon Book is in the Right, in calling it the sweetest Morsel the Devil ever dropped into the Mouth of a Sinner.[4]

Mrs *Jewkes* remembered the Smart of my Nails too well to go farther, and so we sat down and talked about my Vartue till Dinner-time, and then I was sent for to wait on my Master. I took care to be often caught looking at him, and then I always turn'd away my Eyes, and pretended to be ashamed. As soon as the Cloth was removed, he put a Bumper of Champagne into my Hand, and bid me drink —— O la I can't name the Health. Parson *Williams* may well say he is a wicked Man.

Mrs *Jewkes* took a Glass and drank the dear *Monysyllable*; I don't understand that Word, but I believe it is baudy. I then drank towards his Honour's good Pleasure. Ay, Hussy, says he, you can give me Pleasure if you will; Sir, says I, I shall be always glad to do what is in my power, and so I pretended not to know what he meant. Then he took me into his Lap. — O Mamma, I could tell you something if I would — and he kissed me —— and I said I won't be slobber'd about so, so I won't; and he bid me get out of the Room for a saucy Baggage, and said he had a good mind to spit in my Face.

Sure no Man ever took such a Method to gain a Woman's Heart.

I had not been long in my Chamber before Mrs *Jewkes* came to me, and told me, my Master would not see me any more that Evening, that is, if he can help it; for, added she, I easily perceive the great Ascendant you have over him; and to confess the Truth, I don't doubt but you will shortly be my Mistress.

What, says I, dear Mrs *Jewkes*, what do you say? Don't flatter a poor Girl, it is impossible his Honour can have any honourable Design upon me. And so we talked of honourable Designs till Supper-time. And Mrs *Jewkes* and I supped together upon a hot buttered Apple-Pie; and about ten o'Clock we went to Bed.

We had not been a Bed half an Hour, when my Master came pit a pat into the Room in his Shirt as before, I pretended not to hear him, and

Mrs *Jewkes* laid hold of one Arm, and he pulled down the Bed-cloaths and came into Bed on the other Side, and took my other Arm and laid it under him, and fell a kissing one of my Breasts as if he would have devoured it; I was then forced to awake, and began to struggle with him, Mrs *Jewkes* crying why don't you do it? I have one Arm secure, if you can't deal with the rest I am sorry for you. He was as rude as possible to me; but I remembered, Mamma, the Instructions you gave me to avoid being ravished, and followed them, which soon brought him to Terms, and he promised me, on quitting my hold, that he would leave the Bed.

O Parson Williams, *how little are all the Men in the World compared to thee.*

My Master was as good as his Word; upon which Mrs *Jewkes* said, O Sir, I see you know very little of our *Sect*, by parting so easily from the Blessing when you was so near it. No, Mrs *Jewkes*, answered he, I am very glad no more hath happened, I would not have injured *Pamela* for the World. And to-morrow Morning perhaps she may hear of something to her Advantage. This she may be certain of, that I will never take her by Force, and then he left the Room.

What think you now, Mrs *Pamela*, says Mrs *Jewkes*, are you not yet persuaded my Master hath honourable Designs? I think he hath given no great Proof of them to-night, said I. Your Experience I find is not great, says she, but I am convinced you will shortly be my Mistress, and then what will become of poor me.

With such sort of Discourse we both fell asleep. Next Morning early my Master sent for me, and after kissing me, gave a Paper into my Hand which he bid me read; I did so, and found it to be a Proposal for settling 250 *l.* a Year on me, besides several other advantagious Offers, as Presents of Money and other things. Well, *Pamela*, said he, what Answer do you make me to this. Sir, said I, I value my Vartue more than all the World, and I had rather be the poorest Man's Wife, than the richest Man's Whore. You are a Simpleton, said he; That may be, and yet I may have as much Wit as some Folks, cry'd I; meaning me, I suppose, said he; every Man knows himself best, says I. Hussy, says he, get out of the Room, and let me see your saucy Face no more, for I find I am in more Danger than you are, and therefore it shall be my Business to avoid you as much as I can; and it shall be mine, thinks I, at every turn to throw my self in your way. So I went out, and as I parted, I heard him sigh and say he was bewitched.

Mrs *Jewkes* hath been with me since, and she assures me she is convinced I shall shortly be Mistress of the Family, and she really behaves to me, as if she already thought me so. I am resolved now to aim at it. I thought once of making a little Fortune by my Person. I now intend to make a great one by my Vartue. So asking Pardon for this long Scroll, I am,

Your dutiful Daughter,
SHAMELA.

LETTER XI

HENRIETTA MARIA HONORA ANDREWS *to* SHAMELA ANDREWS.

Dear Sham,

I received your last Letter with infinite Pleasure, and am convinced it will be your own Fault if you are not married to your Master, and I would advise you now to take no less Terms. But, my dear Child, I am afraid of one Rock only, That Parson *Williams*, I wish he was out of the Way. A Woman never commits Folly but with such Sort of Men, as by many Hints in the Letters I collect him to be: but, consider, my dear Child, you will hereafter have Opportunities sufficient to indulge yourself with Parson *Williams*, or any other you like. My Advice therefore to you is, that you would avoid seeing him any more till the Knot is tied. Remember the first Lesson I taught you, that a married Woman injures only her Husband, but a single Woman herself. I am in hopes of seeing you a great Lady,

Your affectionate Mother,
HENRIETTA MARIA, *&c.*

The following Letter seems to have been written before *Shamela* received the last from her Mother.

LETTER XII

SHAMELA ANDREWS *to* HENRIETTA MARIA HONORA
ANDREWS.

Dear Mamma,

I little feared when I sent away my last that all my Hopes would be so soon frustrated; but I am certain you will blame Fortune and not me. To proceed then. About two Hours after I had left the Squire, he sent for me into the Parlour. *Pamela*, said he, and takes me gently by the hand, will you walk with me in the Garden; yes, Sir, says I, and pretended to tremble; but I hope your Honour will not be rude. Indeed, says he, you have nothing to fear from me, and I have something to tell you, which if it doth not please you, cannot offend. We walked out together, and he began thus, *Pamela*, will you tell me Truth? Doth the Resistance you make to my Attempts proceed from Vartue only, or have I not some Rival in thy dear Bosom who might be more successful? Sir, says I, I do assure you I never had a thought of any Man in the World. How, says he, not of Parson *Williams!* Parson *Williams*, says I, is the last Man upon Earth; and if I was a Dutchess, and your Honour was to make your Addresses to me, you would have no reason to be jealous of any Rival, especially such a Fellow as Parson *Williams*. If ever I had a Liking, I am sure —— but I am not worthy of you one Way, and no Riches should ever bribe me the other. My Dear, says he, you are worthy of every Thing, and suppose I should lay aside all Considerations of Fortune, and disregard the Censure of the World, and marry you. O Sir, says I, I am sure you can have no such Thoughts, you cannot demean your self so low. Upon my Soul, I am in earnest, says he, —— O Pardon me; Sir, says I, you can't persuade me of this. How Mistress, says he, in a violent Rage, do you give me the Lie? Hussy, I have a great mind to box your saucy Ears, but I am resolved I will never put it in your power to affront me again, and therefore I desire you to prepare your self for your Journey this Instant. You deserve no better Vehicle than a Cart; however, for once you shall have a Chariot, and it shall be ready for you within this half Hour; and so he flung from me in a Fury.

What a foolish Thing it is for a Woman to dally too long with her Lover's Desires; how many have owed their being old Maids to their holding out too long.

Mrs *Jewkes* came me to presently, and told me, I must make ready with all the Expedition imaginable, for that my Master had ordered the Chariot, and that if I was not prepared to go in it, I should be turned out of Doors, and left to find my way Home on Foot. This startled me a little, yet I resolved, whether in the right or wrong, not to submit nor ask Pardon: For that you know, Mamma, you never could your self bring me to from my Childhood: Besides, I thought he would be no more able to master his Passion for me now, than he had been hitherto; and if he sent two Horses away with me, I concluded he would send four to fetch me back. So, truly, I resolved to brazen it out, and with all the Spirit I could muster up, I told Mrs *Jewkes* I was vastly pleased with the News she brought me; that no one ever went more readily than I should, from a Place where my Vartue had been in continual Danger. That as for my Master, he might easily get those who were fit for his Purpose; but, for my Part, I preferred my Vartue to all Rakes whatever —— And for his Promises, and his Offers to me, I don't value them of a Fig — Not of a Fig, Mrs *Jewkes*; and then I snapt my Fingers.

Mrs *Jewkes* went in with me, and helped me to pack up my little All, which was soon done; being no more than two Day-Caps, two Night-Caps, five Shifts, one Sham,[1] a Hoop, a Quilted-Petticoat, two Flannel-Petticoats, two pair of Stockings, one odd one, a pair of lac'd Shoes, a short flowered Apron, a lac'd Neck-Handkerchief, one Clog, and almost another, and some few Books: as, *A full Answer to a plain and true Account,* &c. *The Whole Duty of Man,* with only the Duty to one's Neighbour, torn out. The Third Volume of the *Atalantis. Venus in the Cloyster: Or, the Nun in her Smock. God's Dealings with Mr Whitefield. Orfus and Eurydice.*[2] Some Sermon-Books; and two or three Plays, with their Titles, and Part of the first Act torn off.

So as soon as we had put all this into a Bundle, the Chariot was ready, and I took leave of all the Servants, and particularly Mrs *Jewkes*, who pretended, I believe, to be more sorry to part with me than she was; and then crying out with an Air of Indifference, my Service to my Master, when he condescends to enquire after me, I flung my self into the Chariot, and bid *Robin* drive on.

We had not gone far, before a Man on Horseback, riding full Speed, overtook us, and coming up to the Side of the Chariot, threw a Letter into the Window, and then departed without uttering a single Syllable.

I immediately knew the Hand of my dear *Williams*, and was somewhat surprized, tho' I did not apprehend the Contents to be so terrible, as by the following exact Copy you will find them.

Parson WILLIAMS *to* PAMELA.

Dear Mrs PAMELA,

That Disrespect for the Clergy, which I have formerly noted to you in that Villain your Master, hath now broke forth in a manifest Fact. I was proceeding to my Neighbour *Spruce*'s Church, where I purposed to preach a Funeral Sermon, on the Death of Mr *John Gage*, the Exciseman; when I was met by two Persons who are, it seems, Sheriffs Officers, and arrested for the 150 *l.* which your Master had lent me; and unless I can find Bail within these few Days, of which I see no likelihood, I shall be carried to Goal. This accounts for my not having visited you these two Days; which you might assure yourself, I should not have fail'd, if the *Potestas* [3] had not been wanting. If you can by any means prevail on your Master to release me, I beseech you so to do, not scrupling any thing for Righteousness sake. I hear he is just arrived in this Country, I have herewith sent him a Letter, of which I transmit you a Copy. So with Prayers for your Success, I subscribe myself

Your affectionate Friend,
ARTHUR WILLIAMS.

Parson WILLIAMS *to Squire* BOOBY.

Honoured Sir,

I am justly surprized to feel so heavy a Weight of your Displeasure, without being conscious of the least Demerit towards so good and generous a Patron, as I have ever found you: For my own Part, I can truly say,

Nil conscire sibi nullæ pallescere culpæ. [4]

And therefore, as this Proceeding is so contrary to your usual Goodness, which I have often experienced, and more especially in the Loan of this Money for which I am now arrested; I cannot avoid thinking some malicious Persons have insinuated false Suggestions against me; intending thereby, to eradicate those Seeds of Affection which I have hardly travailed to sowe in your Heart, and which promised to produce such excellent

Fruit. If I have any ways offended you, Sir, be graciously pleased to let me know it, and likewise to point out to me, the Means whereby I may reinstate myself in your Favour: For next to him, whom the Great themselves must bow down before, I know none to whom I shall bend with more Lowliness than your Honour. Permit me to subscribe myself,

> Honoured Sir,
>> Your most obedient, and most obliged,
>> And most dutiful humble Servant,
>> ARTHUR WILLIAMS.

The Fate of poor Mr *Williams* shocked me more than my own: For, as the *Beggar's Opera* says, *Nothing moves one so much as a great Man in Distress.*[5] And to see a Man of his Learning forced to submit so low, to one whom I have often heard him say, he despises, is, I think, a most affecting Circumstance. I write all this to you, Dear Mamma, at the Inn where I lie this first Night, and as I shall send it immediately, by the Post, it will be in Town a little before me. — Don't let my coming away vex you: For, as my Master will be in Town in a few Days, I shall have an Opportunity of seeing him; and let the worst come to the worst, I shall be sure of my Settlement at last. Which is all, from

> Your dutiful Daughter,
>> SHAMELA.

P. S. Just as I was going to send this away a Letter is come from my Master, desiring me to return, with a large Number of Promises. — I have him now as sure as a Gun, as you will perceive by the Letter itself, which I have inclosed to you.

This Letter is unhappily lost, as well as the next which *Shamela* wrote, and which contained an Account of all the Proceedings previous to her Marriage. The only remaining one which I could preserve, seems to have been written about a Week after the Ceremony was perform'd, and is as follows:

Shamela Booby *to* Henrietta Maria Honora Andrews.

Madam,

In my last I left off at our sitting down to Supper on our Wedding Night,* where I behaved with as much Bashfulness as the purest Virgin in the World could have done. The most difficult Task for me was to blush; however, by holding my Breath, and squeezing my Cheeks with my Handkerchief, I did pretty well. My Husband was extreamly eager and impatient to have Supper removed, after which he gave me leave to retire into my Closet for a Quarter of an Hour, which was very agreeable to me; for I employed that time in writing to Mr *Williams*, who, as I informed you in my last, is released, and presented to the Living, upon the Death of the last Parson. Well, at last I went to Bed, and my Husband soon leap'd in after me; where I shall only assure you, I acted my Part in such a manner, that no Bridegroom was ever better satisfied with his Bride's Virginity. And to confess the Truth, I might have been well enough satisfied too, if I had never been acquainted with Parson *Williams.*

O what regard Men who marry Widows should have to the Qualifications of their former Husbands.

We did not rise the next Morning till eleven, and then we sat down to Breakfast; I eat two Slices of Bread and Butter, and drank three Dishes of Tea, with a good deal of Sugar, and we both look'd very silly. After Breakfast we drest our selves, he in a blue Camblet Coat, very richly lac'd, and Breeches of the same; with a Paduasoy Waistcoat,[6] laced with Silver; and I, in one of my Mistress's Gowns. I will have finer when I come to Town. We then took a Walk in the Garden, and he kissed me several times, and made me a Present of 100 Guineas, which I gave away before Night to the Servants, twenty to one, and ten to another, and so on.

We eat a very hearty Dinner, and about eight in the Evening went to Bed again. He is prodigiously fond of me; but I don't like him half so well as my dear *Williams.* The next Morning we rose earlier, and I asked him for another hundred Guineas, and he gave them me. I sent fifty to Parson *Williams*, and the rest I gave away, two Guineas to a Beggar, and three to a Man riding along the Road, and the rest to other People. I long to

* This was the Letter which is lost.

be in *London* that I may have an Opportunity of laying some out, as well as giving away. I believe I shall buy every thing I see. What signifies having Money if one doth not spend it.

The next Day, as soon as I was up, I asked him for another Hundred. Why, my Dear, says he, I don't grudge you any thing, but how was it possible for you to lay out the other two Hundred here. La! Sir, says I, I hope I am not obliged to give you an Account of every Shilling; Troth, that will be being your Servant still. I assure you, I married you with no such view, besides did not you tell me I should be Mistress of your Estate? And I will be too. For tho' I brought no Fortune, I am as much your Wife as if I had brought a Million — yes, but, my Dear, says he, if you had brought a Million, you would spend it all at this rate; besides, what will your Expences be in *London*, if they are so great here. Truly, says I, Sir, I shall live like other Ladies of my Fashion; and if you think, because I was a Servant, that I shall be contented to be governed as you please, I will shew you, you are mistaken. If you had not cared to marry me, you might have let it alone. I did not ask you, nor I did not court you. Madam, says he, I don't value a hundred Guineas to oblige you; but this is a Spirit which I did not expect in you, nor did I ever see any Symptoms of it before. O but Times are altered now, I am your Lady, Sir; yes to my Sorrow, says he, I am afraid — and I am afraid to my Sorrow too: For if you begin to use me in this manner already, I reckon you will beat me before a Month's at an end. I am sure if you did, it would injure me less than this barbarous Treatment; upon which I burst into Tears, and pretended to fall into a Fit. This frighted him out of his wits, and he called up the Servants. Mrs *Jewkes* immediately came in, and she and another of the Maids fell heartily to rubbing my Temples, and holding Smelling-Bottles to my Nose. Mrs *Jewkes* told him she fear'd I should never recover, upon which he began to beat his Breasts, and cried out, O my dearest Angel, curse on my passionate Temper, I have destroy'd her, I have destroy'd her! —— would she had spent my whole Estate rather than this had happened. Speak to me, my Love, I will melt myself into Gold for thy Pleasure. At last having pretty well tired my self with counterfeiting, and imagining I had continu'd long enough for my purpose in the sham Fit, I began to move my Eyes, to loosen my Teeth, and to open my Hands, which Mr *Booby* no sooner perceived than he embraced and kissed me with the eagerest Extacy, asked my Pardon on his Knees for what I had suffered through his Folly and Perverseness, and without more Questions fetched me the Money. I fancy I have effectually prevented any farther

Refusals or Inquiry into my Expences. It would be hard indeed, that a Woman who marries a Man only for his Money, should be debarred from spending it.

Well, after all things were quiet, we sat down to Breakfast, yet I resolved not to smile once, nor to say one good-natured, or good-humoured Word on any Account.

Nothing can be more prudent in a Wife, than a sullen Backwardness to Reconciliation; it makes a Husband fearful of offending by the Length of his Punishment.

When we were drest, the Coach was by my Desire ordered for an Airing, which we took in it. A long Silence prevailed on both Sides, tho' he constantly squeezed my Hand, and kissed me, and used other Familiarities, which I peevishly permitted. At last, I opened my Mouth first. — And so, says I, you are sorry you are married; — Pray, my Dear, says he, forget what I said in a Passion. Passion, says I, is apter to discover our Thoughts than to teach us to counterfeit. Well, says he, whether you will believe me or no, I solemnly vow, I would not change thee for the richest Woman in the Universe. No, I warrant you, says I; and yet you could refuse me a nasty hundred Pound. At these very Words, I saw Mr *Williams* riding as fast as he could across a Field; and I looked out, and saw a Lease[7] of Greyhounds coursing a Hare, which they presently killed, and I saw him alight, and take it from them.

My Husband ordered *Robin* to drive towards him, and looked horribly out of humour, which I presently imputed to Jealousy. So I began with him first; for that is the wisest way. La, Sir, says I; what makes you look so Angry and Grim? Doth the Sight of Mr *Williams* give you all this Uneasiness? I am sure, I would never have married a Woman of whom I had so bad an Opinion, that I must be uneasy at every Fellow she looks at. My Dear, answer'd he, you injure me extremely, you was not in my Thoughts, nor, indeed, could be, while they were covered by so morose a Countenance; I am justly angry with that Parson, whose Family hath been raised from the Dunghill by ours; and who hath received from me twenty Kindnesses, and yet is not contented to destroy the Game in all other Places, which I freely give him leave to do; but hath the Impudence to pursue a few Hares, which I am desirous to preserve, round about this little Coppice. Look, my Dear, pray look, says he; I believe he is going to turn Higler.[8] To confess the Truth, he had no less than three ty'd up behind his Horse, and a fourth he held in his Hand.

Pshaw, says I, I wish all the Hares in the Country were d————d (the Parson himself chid me afterwards for using the Word, tho' it was in his

Service.) Here's a Fuss, indeed, about a nasty little pitiful Creature, that is not half so useful as a Cat. You shall not persuade me, that a Man of your Understanding, would quarrel with a Clergyman for such a Trifle. No, no, I am the Hare, for whom poor Parson *Williams* is persecuted; and Jealousy is the Motive.[9] If you had married one of your Quality Ladies, she would have had Lovers by dozens, she would so; but because you have taken a Servant-maid, forsooth! you are jealous if she but looks (and then I began to Water) at a poor P—a—a—rson in his Pu—u—u—lpit, and then out burst a Flood of Tears.

My Dear, said he, for Heaven's sake dry your Eyes, and don't let him be a Witness of your Tears, which I should be sorry to think might be imputed to my Unkindness; I have already given you some Proofs that I am not jealous of this Parson; I will now give you a very strong one: For I will mount my Horse, and you shall take *Williams* into the Coach. You may be sure, this Motion pleased me, yet I pretended to make as light of it as possible, and told him, I was sorry his Behaviour had made some such glaring Instance necessary to the perfect clearing my Character.

He soon came up to Mr *Williams*, who had attempted to ride off, but was prevented by one of our Horsemen, whom my Husband sent to stop him. When we met, my Husband asked him how he did with a very good-humoured Air, and told him he perceived he had found good Sport that Morning. He answered pretty moderate, Sir; for that he had found the three Hares tied on to the Saddle dead in a Ditch (winking on me at the same time) and added he was sorry there was such a Rot among them.

Well, says Mr *Booby*, if you please, Mr *Williams*, you shall come in and ride with my Wife. For my own part, I will mount on Horseback; for it is fine Weather, and besides, it doth not become me to loll in a Chariot, whilst a Clergyman rides on Horseback.

At which Words, Mr *Booby* leap'd out, and Mr *Williams* leap'd in, in an Instant, telling my Husband as he mounted, he was glad to see such a Reformation, and that if he continued his Respect to the Clergy, he might assure himself of Blessings from above.

It was now that the Airing began to grow pleasant to me. Mr *Williams*, who never had but one Fault, *viz.* that he generally smells of Tobacco, was now perfectly sweet; for he had for two Days together enjoined himself as a Penance, not to smoke till he had kissed my Lips. I will loosen you from that Obligation, says I, and observing my Husband looking another way, I gave him a charming Kiss, and then he asked me Questions concerning my Wedding-night; this actually made me blush: I vow I did not think it had been in him.

As he went along, he began to discourse very learnedly, and told me the Flesh and the Spirit were two distinct Matters, which had not the least relation to each other. That all immaterial Substances (those were his very Words)[10] such as Love, Desire, and so forth, were guided by the Spirit: But fine Houses, large Estates, Coaches, and dainty Entertainments were the Product of the Flesh. Therefore, says he, my Dear, you have two Husbands, one the Object of your Love, and to satisfy your Desire; the other the Object of your Necessity, and to furnish you with those other Conveniencies. (I am sure I remember every Word, for he repeated it three Times; O he is very good whenever I desire him to repeat a thing to me three times he always doth it!) as then the Spirit is preferable to the Flesh, so am I preferable to your other Husband, to whom I am antecedent in Time likewise. I say these things, my Dear, (said he) to satisfie your Conscience. A Fig for my Conscience, said I, when shall I meet you again in the Garden?

My Husband now rode up to the Chariot, and asked us how we did — I hate the Sight of him. Mr *Williams* answered very well, at your Service. They then talked of the Weather, and other things, I wished him gone again, every Minute; but all in vain, I had no more Opportunity of conversing with Mr *Williams*.

Well; at Dinner Mr *Booby* was very civil to Mr *Williams*, and told him he was sorry for what had happened, and would make him sufficient Amends, if in his power, and desired him to accept of a Note for fifty Pounds; which he was so *good* to receive, notwithstanding all that had past; and told Mr *Booby*, he hop'd he would be forgiven, and that he would pray for him.

We make a charming Fool of him, i'fackins; Times are finely altered, I have entirely got the better of him, and am resolved never to give him his Humour.

O how foolish it is in a Woman, who hath once got the Reins into her own Hand, ever to quit them again.

After Dinner Mr *Williams* drank the Church *et cætera*;[11] and smiled on me; when my Husband's Turn came, he drank *et cætera* and the Church; for which he was very severely rebuked by Mr *Williams*; it being a high Crime, it seems, to name any thing before the Church. I do not know what *Et cetera* is, but I believe it is something concerning chusing Pallament Men; for I asked if it was not a Health to Mr *Booby's* Borough, and Mr

Williams with a hearty Laugh answered, Yes, Yes, it is his Borough we mean.

I slipt out as soon as I could, hoping Mr *Williams* would finish the Squire, as I have heard him say he could easily do, and come to me; but it happened quite otherwise, for in about half an Hour, *Booby* came to me, and told me he had left Mr *Williams*, the Mayor of his Borough, and two or three Aldermen heartily at it, and asked me if I would go hear *Williams* sing a Catch,[12] which, added he, he doth to a Miracle.

Every Opportunity of seeing my dear *Williams*, was agreeable to me, which indeed I scarce had at this time; for when we returned, the whole Corporation were got together, and the Room was in a Cloud of Tobacco; Parson *Williams* was at the upper End of the Table, and he hath pure round cherry Cheeks, and his Face look'd all the World to nothing like the Sun in a Fog. If the Sun had a Pipe in his Mouth, there would be no Difference.

I began now to grow uneasy, apprehending I should have no more of Mr *Williams*'s Company that Evening, and not at all caring for my Husband, I advised him to sit down and drink for his Country with the rest of the Company; but he refused, and desired me to give him some Tea; swearing nothing made him so sick, as to hear a Parcel of Scoundrels, roaring forth the Principles of honest Men over their Cups, when, says he, I know most of them are such empty Blockheads, that they don't know their right Hand from their left; and that Fellow there, who hath talked so much of *Shipping*, at the left Side of the Parson, in whom they all place a Confidence, if I don't take care, will sell them to my Adversary.[13]

I don't know why I mention this Stuff to you; for I am sure I know nothing about *Pollitricks*, more than Parson *Williams* tells me; who says that the Court-side are in the right on't, and that every Christian ought to be on the same with the Bishops.[14]

When we had finished our Tea, we walked in the Garden till it was dark, and then my Husband proposed, instead of returning to the Company, (which I desired, that I might see Parson *Williams* again,) to sup in another Room by our selves, which, for fear of making him jealous, and considering too, that Parson *Williams* would be pretty far gone, I was obliged to consent to.

O! what a devilish thing it is, for a Woman to be obliged to go to bed to a spindle-shanked young Squire, she doth not like, when there is a jolly Parson in the same House she is fond of.

In the Morning I grew very peevish, and in the Dumps, notwithstanding all he could say or do to please me. I exclaimed against the Priviledge of Husbands, and vowed I would not be pulled and tumbled about. At last he hit on the only Method, which could have brought me into Humour, and proposed to me a Journey to *London*, within a few Days. This you may easily guess pleased me; for besides the Desire which I have of shewing my self forth, of buying fine Cloaths, Jewels, Coaches, Houses, and ten thousand other fine things, Parson *Williams* is, it seems, going thither too, to be *instuted*.[15]

O! what a charming Journey I shall have; for I hope to keep the dear Man in the Chariot with me all the way; and that foolish Booby *(for that is the Name Mr* Williams *hath set him) will ride on Horseback.*

So as I shall have an Opportunity of seeing you so shortly, I think I will mention no more Matters to you now. O I had like to have forgot one very material thing; which is that it will look horribly, for a Lady of my Quality and Fashion, to own such a Woman as you for my Mother. Therefore we must meet in private only, and if you will never claim me, nor mention me to any one, I will always allow you what is very handsome. Parson *Williams* hath greatly advised me in this; and says, he thinks I should do very well to lay out twenty Pounds, and set you up in a little Chandler's Shop: but you must remember all my Favours to you will depend on your Secrecy; for I am positively resolved, I will not be known to be your Daughter; and if you tell any one so, I shall deny it with all my Might, which Parson *Williams* says, I may do with a safe Conscience, being now a married Woman. So I rest

Your humble Servant,

SHAMELA.

P. S. The strangest Fancy hath enter'd into my *Booby*'s Head, that can be imagined. He is resolved to have a Book made about him and me; he proposed it to Mr *Williams*, and offered him a Reward for his Pains; but he says he never writ any thing of that kind, but will recommend my Husband, when he comes to Town, to a Parson *who does that Sort of Business for Folks*,[16] one who can make my Husband, and me, and Parson *Williams*, to be all great People; for he *can make black white*, it seems. Well, but they say my Name is to be altered, Mr *Williams* says the first Syllabub hath too comical a Sound, so it is to be changed into *Pamela*; I own I can't imagine what can be said; for to be sure I shan't confess any of my Secrets to them, and so I whispered Parson *Williams* about that, who answered me, I need not give my self any Trouble; for the Gentleman *who writes*

Lives, never asked more than a few Names of his Customers, and that he made all the rest out of his own Head; you mistake, Child, said he, if you apprehend any Truths are to be delivered. So far on the contrary, if you had not been acquainted with the Name, you would not have known it to be your own History. I have seen a *Piece of his Performance*, where the Person, whose Life was written, could he have risen from the Dead again, would not have even suspected he had been aimed at, unless by the Title of the Book, which was superscribed with his Name. Well, all these Matters are strange to me, yet I can't help laughing, to think I shall see my self in a printed Book.

So much for Mrs *Shamela*, or *Pamela*, which I have taken Pains to transcribe from the Originals, sent down by her Mother in a Rage, at the Proposal in her last Letter. The Originals themselves are in my hands, and shall be communicated to you, if you think proper to make them publick; and certainly they will have their Use. The Character of *Shamela*, will make young Gentlemen wary how they take the most fatal Step both to themselves and Families, by youthful, hasty and improper Matches; indeed, they may assure themselves, that all such Prospects of Happiness are vain and delusive, and that they sacrifice all the solid Comforts of their Lives, to a very transient Satisfaction of a Passion, which how hot so ever it be, will be soon cooled; and when cooled, will afford them nothing but Repentance.

Can any thing be more miserable, than to be despised by the whole World, and that must certainly be the Consequence; to be despised by the Person obliged, which it is more than probable will be the Consequence, and of which, we see an Instance in *Shamela*; and lastly to despise one's self, which must be the Result of any Reflection on so weak and unworthy a Choice.

As to the Character of Parson *Williams*, I am sorry it is a true one. Indeed those who do not know him, will hardly believe it so; but what Scandal doth it throw on the Order to have one bad Member, unless they endeavour to screen and protect him? In him you see a Picture of almost every Vice exposed in nauseous and odious Colours; and if a Clergyman would ask me by what Pattern he should form himself, I would say, Be the reverse of *Williams*: So far therefore he may be of use to the Clergy themselves, and though God forbid there should be many *Williams's* amongst them, you and I are too honest to pretend, that the Body wants no Reformation.

To say the Truth, I think no greater Instance of the contrary can be given than that which appears in your Letter. The confederating to cry up a nonsensical ridiculous Book, (I believe the most extensively so of any ever yet published,) and to be so weak and so wicked as to pretend to make it a Matter of Religion; whereas so far from having any moral Tendency, the Book is by no means innocent: For,

First, There are many lascivious Images in it, very improper to be laid before the Youth of either Sex.[17]

2dly, Young Gentlemen are here taught, that to marry their Mother's Chambermaids, and to indulge the Passion of Lust, at the Expence of Reason and Common Sense, is an Act of Religion, Virtue, and Honour; and, indeed the surest Road to Happiness.[18]

3dly, All Chambermaids are strictly enjoyned to look out after their Masters; they are taught to use little Arts to that purpose:[19] And lastly, are countenanced in Impertinence to their Superiors, and in betraying the Secrets of Families.

4thly, In the Character of Mrs *Jewkes* Vice is rewarded; whence every Housekeeper may learn the Usefulness of pimping and bawding from her Master.[20]

5thly, In Parson *Williams*, who is represented as a faultless Character, we see a busy Fellow, intermeddling with the private Affairs of his Patron, whom he is very ungratefully forward to expose and condemn on every Occasion.[21]

Many more Objections might, if I had Time or Inclination, be made to this Book; but I apprehend, what hath been said is sufficient to persuade you of the use which may arise from publishing an Antidote to this Poison. I have therefore sent you the Copies of these Papers, and if you have Leisure to communicate them to the Press, I will transmit you the Originals, tho' I assure you, the Copies are exact.

I shall only add, that there is not the least Foundation for any thing which is said of Lady *Davers*, or any of the other Ladies; all that is merely to be imputed to the Invention of the Biographer. I have particularly enquired after Lady *Davers*, and dont hear Mr *Booby* hath such a Relation, or that there is indeed any such Person existing.[22] I am,

> *Dear Sir,*
>> *Most faithfully and respectfully,*
>>> *Your humble Servant,*
>>>> J. OLIVER.

Parson TICKLETEXT *to Parson* OLIVER.

Dear SIR,

I have read over the History of *Shamela*, as it appears in those authentick Copies you favour'd me with, and am very much ashamed of the Character, which I was hastily prevailed on to give that Book. I am equally angry with the pert Jade herself, and with the Author of her Life: For I scarce know yet to whom I chiefly owe an Imposition, which hath been so general, that if Numbers could defend me from Shame, I should have no Reason to apprehend it.

As I have your implied Leave to publish, what you so kindly sent me, I shall not wait for the Originals, as you assure me the Copies are exact, and as I am really impatient to do what I think a serviceable Act of Justice to the World.

Finding by the End of her last Letter, that the little Hussy was in Town, I made it pretty much my Business to enquire after her, but with no effect hitherto: As soon as I succeed in this Enquiry, you shall hear what Discoveries I can learn. You will pardon the Shortness of this Letter, as you shall be troubled with a much longer very soon: And believe me,

Dear Sir,

Your most faithful Servant,
THO. TICKLETEXT.

P. S. Since I writ, I have a certain Account, that Mr *Booby* hath caught his Wife in bed with *Williams*; hath turned her off, and is prosecuting him in the spiritual Court.

FINIS

JOSEPH ANDREWS

THE
HISTORY
OF THE
ADVENTURES
OF
JOSEPH ANDREWS,
And of his FRIEND
Mr. *ABRAHAM ADAMS*.

Written in Imitation of
The *Manner* of CERVANTES,
Author of *Don Quixote*.

IN TWO VOLUMES.

VOL. I.

LONDON:

Printed for A. MILLAR, over-against
St. *Clement's Church*, in the *Strand*.
M.DCC.XLII.

PREFACE

As it is possible the mere English Reader[1] may have a different Idea of Romance with the Author of these little Volumes;[2] and may consequently expect a kind of Entertainment, not to be found, nor which was even intended, in the following Pages; it may not be improper to premise a few Words concerning this kind of Writing, which I do not remember to have been hitherto attempted in our Language.

The EPIC as well as the DRAMA is divided into Tragedy, and Comedy. *Homer*, who was the Father of this Species of Poetry, gave us a Pattern of both these, tho' that of the latter kind is entirely lost; which *Aristotle* tells us, bore the same Relation to Comedy which his *Iliad* bears to Tragedy.[3] And perhaps, that we have no more Instances of it among the Writers of Antiquity, is owing to the Loss of this great Pattern, which, had it survived, would have found its Imitators, equally with the other Poems of this great Original.

And farther, as this Poetry may be Tragic or Comic, I will not scruple to say it may be likewise either in Verse or Prose: for tho' it wants one particular, which the Critic enumerates in the constituent Parts of an Epic Poem, namely Metre; yet, when any kind of Writing contains all its other Parts, such as Fable, Action, Characters, Sentiments, and Diction, and is deficient in Metre only;[4] it seems, I think, reasonable to refer it to the Epic; at least, as no Critic hath thought proper to range it under any other Head, nor to assign it a particular Name to itself.

Thus the *Telemachus* of the Arch-Bishop of *Cambray*[5] appears to me of the Epic Kind, as well as the *Odyssey* of *Homer*; indeed, it is much fairer and more reasonable to give it a Name common with that Species from which it differs only in a single Instance, than to confound it with those which it resembles in no other. Such are those voluminous Works commonly called *Romances*, namely, *Clelia*, *Cleopatra*, *Astræa*, *Cassandra*, the *Grand Cyrus*,[6] and innumerable others which contain, as I apprehend, very little Instruction or Entertainment.

Now a comic Romance is a comic Epic-Poem in Prose; differing from Comedy, as the serious Epic from Tragedy: its Action being more extended and comprehensive; containing a much larger Circle of Incidents, and introducing a greater variety of Characters. It differs from the serious Romance in its Fable and Action, in this; that as in the one these are grave and solemn, so in the other they are light and ridiculous: it differs in its Characters, by introducing Persons of inferiour Rank, and consequently of inferiour Manners, whereas the grave Romance sets the highest before us; lastly in its Sentiments and Diction; by preserving the Ludicrous instead of the Sublime. In the Diction I think, Burlesque itself may be sometimes admitted; of which many Instances will occur in this Work, as in the Descriptions of the Battles, and some other Places, not necessary to be pointed out to the Classical Reader; for whose Entertainment those Parodies or Burlesque Imitations are chiefly calculated.

But tho' we have sometimes admitted this in our Diction, we have carefully excluded it from our Sentiments and Characters: for there it is never properly introduced, unless in Writings of the Burlesque kind, which this is not intended to be. Indeed, no two Species of Writing can differ more widely than the Comic and the Burlesque: for as the latter is ever the Exhibition of what is monstrous and unnatural, and where our Delight, if we examine it, arises from the surprizing Absurdity, as in appropriating the Manners of the highest to the lowest, or *è converso*; so in the former, we should ever confine ourselves strictly to Nature, from the just Imitation of which, will flow all the Pleasure we can this way convey to a sensible Reader. And perhaps, there is one Reason, why a Comic Writer should of all others be the least excused for deviating from Nature, since it may not be always so easy for a serious Poet to meet with the Great and the Admirable; but Life every where furnishes an accurate Observer with the Ridiculous.

I have hinted this little, concerning Burlesque; because, I have often heard that Name given to Performances, which have been truly of the Comic kind, from the Author's having sometimes admitted it in his Diction only; which as it is the Dress of Poetry, doth like the Dress of Men establish Characters, (the one of the whole Poem, and the other of the whole Man,) in vulgar Opinion, beyond any of their greater Excellencies: But surely, a certain Drollery in Style, where the Characters and Sentiments are perfectly natural, no more constitutes the Burlesque, than an empty Pomp and Dignity of Words, where every thing else is mean and low, can entitle any Performance to the Appellation of the true Sublime.

And I apprehend, my Lord *Shaftesbury*'s Opinion of mere Burlesque agrees with mine, when he asserts, 'There is no such Thing to be found in the Writings of the Antients.'[7] But perhaps, I have less Abhorrence than he professes for it: and that not because I have had some little Success on the Stage this way;[8] but rather, as it contributes more to exquisite Mirth and Laughter than any other; and these are probably more wholesome Physic for the Mind, and conduce better to purge away Spleen, Melancholy and ill Affections, than is generally imagined. Nay, I will appeal to common Observation, whether the same Companies are not found more full of Good-Humour and Benevolence, after they have been sweeten'd for two or three Hours with Entertainments of this kind, than when soured by a Tragedy or a grave Lecture.

But to illustrate all this by another Science, in which, perhaps, we shall see the Distinction more clearly and plainly: Let us examine the Works of a Comic History-Painter, with those Performances which the *Italians* call *Caricatura*; where we shall find the true Excellence of the former to consist in the exactest Copy of Nature; insomuch, that a judicious Eye instantly rejects any thing *outré*; any Liberty which the Painter hath taken with the Features of that *Alma Mater*.[9] — Whereas in the *Caricatura* we allow all Licence. Its Aim is to exhibit Monsters not Men; and all Distortions and Exaggerations whatever are within its proper Province.

Now what *Caricatura* is in Painting, Burlesque is in Writing; and in the same manner the Comic Writer and Painter correlate to each other. And here I shall observe, that as in the former, the Painter seems to have the Advantage; so it is in the latter infinitely on the side of the Writer: for the *Monstrous* is much easier to paint than describe, and the *Ridiculous* to describe than paint.

And tho' perhaps this latter Species doth not in either Science so strongly affect and agitate the Muscles as the other; yet it will be owned, I believe, that a more rational and useful Pleasure arises to us from it. He who should call the Ingenious *Hogarth*[10] a Burlesque Painter, would, in my Opinion, do him very little Honour: for sure it is much easier, much less the Subject of Admiration, to paint a Man with a Nose, or any other Feature of a preposterous Size, or to expose him in some absurd or monstrous Attitude, than to express the Affections of Men on Canvas. It hath been thought a vast Commendation of a Painter, to say his Figures *seem to breathe*; but surely, it is a much greater and nobler Applause, *that they appear to think*.

But to return — The Ridiculous only, as I have before said, falls within my Province in the present Work. —— Nor will some Explanation of this Word be thought impertinent by the Reader, if he considers how wonderfully[11] it hath been mistaken, even by Writers who have profess'd it: for to what but such a Mistake, can we attribute the many Attempts to ridicule the blackest Villanies; and what is yet worse, the most dreadful Calamities? What could exceed the Absurdity of an Author, who should write *the Comedy of* Nero, *with the merry Incident of ripping up his Mother's Belly;*[12] or what would give a greater Shock to Humanity, than an Attempt to expose the Miseries of Poverty and Distress to Ridicule? And yet, the Reader will not want much Learning to suggest such Instances to himself.

Besides, it may seem remarkable, that *Aristotle*, who is so fond and free of Definitions, hath not thought proper to define the Ridiculous, Indeed, where he tells us it is proper to Comedy, he hath remarked that Villany is not its Object: but he hath not, as I remember, positively asserted what is.[13] Nor doth the *Abbé Bellegarde*, who hath writ a Treatise on this Subject,[14] tho' he shews us many Species of it, once trace it to its Fountain.

The only Source of the true Ridiculous (as it appears to me) is Affectation. But tho' it arises from one Spring only, when we consider the infinite Streams into which this one branches, we shall presently cease to admire at[15] the copious Field it affords to an Observer. Now Affectation proceeds from one of these two Causes; Vanity, or Hypocrisy: for as Vanity puts us on affecting false Characters, in order to purchase Applause; so Hypocrisy sets us on an Endeavour to avoid Censure by concealing our Vices under an Appearance of their opposite Virtues. And tho' these two Causes are often confounded, (for they require some Difficulty in distinguishing;) yet, as they proceed from very different Motives, so they are as clearly distinct in their Operations: for indeed, the Affectation which arises from Vanity is nearer to Truth than the other; as it hath not that violent Repugnancy of Nature to struggle with, which that of the Hypocrite hath. It may be likewise noted, that Affectation doth not imply an absolute Negation of those Qualities which are affected: and therefore, tho', when it proceeds from Hypocrisy, it be nearly allied to Deceit; yet when it comes from Vanity only, it partakes of the Nature of Ostentation: for instance, the Affectation of Liberality in a vain Man, differs visibly from the same Affectation in the Avaricious; for tho' the vain Man is not what he would appear, or hath not the Virtue he affects, to the degree he would be thought to have it; yet it sits less aukwardly on him than on the avaricious Man, who is the very Reverse of what he would *seem* to be.

From the Discovery of this Affectation arises the Ridiculous — which always strikes the Reader with Surprize and Pleasure; and that in a higher and stronger Degree when the Affectation arises from Hypocrisy, than when from Vanity: for to discover any one to be the exact Reverse of what he affects, is more surprizing, and consequently more ridiculous, than to find him a little deficient in the Quality he desires the Reputation of. I might observe that our *Ben Johnson*,[16] who of all Men understood the *Ridiculous* the best, hath chiefly used the hypocritical Affectation.

Now from Affectation only, the Misfortunes and Calamities of Life, or the Imperfections of Nature, may become the Objects of Ridicule. Surely he hath a very ill-framed Mind, who can look on Ugliness, Infirmity, or Poverty, as ridiculous in themselves: nor do I believe any Man living who meets a dirty Fellow riding through the Streets in a Cart, is struck with an Idea of the Ridiculous from it; but if he should see the same Figure descend from his Coach and Six, or bolt from his Chair[17] with his Hat under his Arm, he would then begin to laugh, and with justice. In the same manner, were we to enter a poor House, and behold a wretched Family shivering with Cold and languishing with Hunger, it would not incline us to Laughter, (at least we must have very diabolical Natures, if it would:) but should we discover there a Grate, instead of Coals, adorned with Flowers, empty Plate or China Dishes on the Side-board, or any other Affectation of Riches and Finery either on their Persons or in their Furniture; we might then indeed be excused, for ridiculing so fantastical an Appearance. Much less are natural Imperfections the Objects of Derision: but when Ugliness aims at the Applause of Beauty, or Lameness endeavours to display Agility; it is then that these unfortunate Circumstances, which at first moved our Compassion, tend only to raise our Mirth.

The Poet carries this very far;

> *None are for being what they are in Fault,*
> *But for not being what they would be thought.*[18]

Where if the Metre would suffer the Word *Ridiculous* to close the first Line, the Thought would be rather more proper. Great Vices are the proper Objects of our Detestation, smaller Faults of our Pity: but Affectation appears to me the only true Source of the Ridiculous.

But perhaps it may be objected to me, that I have against my own Rules introduced Vices, and of a very black Kind into this Work. To which I shall answer: First, that it is very difficult to pursue a Series of human Actions and keep clear from them. Secondly, That the Vices to be found here, are rather the accidental Consequences of some human Frailty, or Foible, than causes habitually existing in the Mind. Thirdly,

That they are never set forth as the Objects of Ridicule but Detestation. Fourthly, That they are never the principal Figure at that Time on the Scene; and lastly, they never produce the intended Evil.

Having thus distinguished *Joseph Andrews* from the Productions of Romance Writers on the one hand, and Burlesque Writers on the other, and given some few very short Hints[19] (for I intended no more) of this Species of writing, which I have affirmed to be hitherto unattempted in our Language; I shall leave to my good-natur'd Reader to apply my Piece to my Observations, and will detain him no longer than with a Word concerning the Characters in this Work.

And here I solemnly protest, I have no Intention to vilify or asperse any one: for tho' every thing is copied from the Book of Nature, and scarce a Character or Action produced which I have not taken from my own Observations and Experience, yet I have used the utmost Care to obscure the Persons by such different Circumstances, Degrees, and Colours, that it will be impossible to guess at them with any degree of Certainty; and if it ever happens otherwise, it is only where the Failure characterized is so minute, that it is a Foible only which the Party himself may laugh at as well as any other.

As to the Character of *Adams*,[20] as it is the most glaring in the whole, so I conceive it is not to be found in any Book now extant. It is designed a Character of perfect Simplicity; and as the Goodness of his Heart will recommend him to the Good-natur'd; so I hope it will excuse me to the Gentlemen of his Cloth; for whom, while they are worthy of their sacred Order, no Man can possibly have a greater Respect. They will therefore excuse me, notwithstanding the low Adventures in which he is engaged, that I have made him a Clergyman; since no other Office could have given him so many Opportunities of displaying his worthy Inclinations.

THE CONTENTS

BOOK II

BOOK III

BOOK IV

THE HISTORY OF THE ADVENTURES OF
JOSEPH ANDREWS, AND HIS FRIEND
MR ABRAHAM ADAMS

BOOK I

CHAPTER I

Of writing Lives in general, and particularly of Pamela; *with a Word
by the bye of* Colley Cibber *and others.*

It is a trite but true Observation, that Examples work more forcibly on
the Mind than Precepts: And if this be just in what is odious and blameable,
it is more strongly so in what is amiable and praise-worthy. Here Emulation
most effectually operates upon us, and inspires our Imitation in an irresistible manner. A good Man therefore is a standing Lesson to all his
Acquaintance, and of far greater use in that narrow Circle than a good
Book.

But as it often happens that the best Men are but little known, and
consequently cannot extend the Usefulness of their Examples a great way;
the Writer may be called in aid to spread their History farther, to present
the amiable Pictures to those who have not the Happiness of knowing the
Originals; and by communicating such valuable Patterns to the World,
may perhaps do a more extensive Service to Mankind than the Person
whose Life originally afforded the Pattern.

In this Light I have always regarded those Biographers who have
recorded the Actions of great and worthy Persons of both Sexes. Not to
mention those antient Writers which of late days are little read, being
written in obsolete, and as they are generally thought, unintelligible
Languages; such as *Plutarch, Nepos,*[1] and others which I heard of in my
Youth, our own Language affords many of excellent Use and Instruction,
finely calculated to sow the Seeds of Virtue in Youth, and very easy to be
comprehended by Persons of moderate Capacity. Such are the History
of *John* the Great, who, by his brave and heroic Actions against Men
of large and athletic Bodies, obtained the glorious Appellation of the
Giant-killer; that of an Earl of *Warwick*, whose Christian Name was *Guy*;
the Lives of *Argalus* and *Parthenia*, and above all, the History of those seven

worthy Personages, the Champions of Christendom.[2] In all these, Delight is mixed with Instruction,[3] and the Reader is almost as much improved as entertained.

But I pass by these and many others, to mention two Books lately published, which represent an admirable Pattern of the Amiable in either Sex. The former of these which deals in Male-Virtue, was written by the great Person himself, who lived the Life he hath recorded, and is by many thought to have lived such a Life only in order to write it. The other is communicated to us by an Historian who borrows his Lights, as the common Method is, from authentic Papers and Records.[4] The Reader, I believe, already conjectures, I mean, the Lives of Mr *Colley Cibber*,[5] and of Mrs[6] *Pamela Andrews*. How artfully doth the former, by insinuating that he *escaped* being promoted to the highest Stations in Church and State, teach us a Contempt of worldly Grandeur! how strongly doth he inculcate an absolute Submission to our Superiors! Lastly, how completely doth he arm us against so uneasy, so wretched a Passion as the Fear of Shame; how clearly doth he expose the Emptiness and Vanity of that Fantom, Reputation![7]

What the Female Readers are taught by the Memoirs of Mrs *Andrews*, is so well set forth in the excellent Essays or Letters prefixed to the second and subsequent Editions of that Work,[8] that it would be here a needless Repetition. The authentic History with which I now present the public is an Instance of the great Good that Book is likely to do, and of the Prevalence of Example which I have just observed since it will appear that it was by keeping the excellent Pattern of his Sister's Virtues before his Eyes, that Mr *Joseph Andrews* was chiefly enabled to preserve his Purity in the midst of such great Temptations; I shall only add, that this Character of Male-Chastity, tho' doubtless as desirable, as becoming in one Part of the human Species, as in the other, is almost the only Virtue which the great Apologist hath not given himself for the sake of giving the Example to his Readers.

CHAPTER II

Of Mr Joseph Andrews *his Birth, Parentage, Education, and great
Endowments, with a Word or two concerning Ancestors.*

Mr *Joseph Andrews*, the Hero of our ensuing History, was esteemed to be
the only Son of Gaffar and Gammer[1] *Andrews*, and Brother to the illustrious
Pamela, whose Virtue is at present so famous. As to his Ancestors, we have
searched with great Diligence, but little Success; being unable to trace
them farther than his Great Grandfather, who, as an elderly Person in
the Parish remembers to have heard his Father say, was an excellent
Cudgel-player. Whether he had any Ancestors before this, we must leave
to the Opinion of our Curious Reader, finding nothing of sufficient
Certainty to relie on. However, we cannot omit inserting an Epitaph
which an ingenious Friend of ours hath communicated:

> *Stay Traveller, for underneath this Pew*
> *Lies fast asleep that merry Man* Andrew;
> *When the last Day's great Sun shall gild the Skies,*
> *Then he shall from his Tomb get up and rise.*
> *Be merry while thou can'st: for surely thou*
> *Shall shortly be as sad as he is now.*

The Words are almost out of the Stone with Antiquity. But it is needless
to observe, that *Andrew* here is writ without an *s*, and is besides a Christian
Name. My Friend moreover conjectures this to have been the Founder
of that Sect of laughing Philosophers, since called *Merry Andrews*.[2]

To wave therefore a Circumstance, which, tho' mentioned in conformity
to the exact Rules of Biography, is not greatly material; I proceed to things
of more consequence. Indeed it is sufficiently certain, that he had as many
Ancestors, as the best Man living; and perhaps, if we look five or six hundred Years backwards, might be related to some Persons of very great Figure
at present, whose Ancestors within half the last Century are buried in as
great Obscurity. But suppose for Argument's sake we should admit that he
had no Ancestors at all, but had sprung up, according to the modern Phrase,
out of a Dunghill, as the *Athenians* pretended they themselves did from the
Earth,[3] would not this * *Autokopros* have been justly entitled to all the Praise

* In *English*, sprung from a Dunghill.

arising from his own Virtues? Would it not be hard, that a Man who hath no Ancestors should therefore be render'd incapable of acquiring Honour, when we see so many who have no Virtues, enjoying the Honour of their Forefathers? At ten Years old (by which time his Education was advanced to Writing and Reading) he was bound an Apprentice, according to the Statute,[4] to Sir *Thomas Booby*,[5] an Uncle of Mr *Booby*'s by the Father's side. Sir *Thomas* having then an Estate in his own hands, the young *Andrews* was at first employed in what in the Country they call *keeping Birds*. His Office was to perform the Part the Antients assigned to the God *Priapus*,[6] which Deity the Moderns call by the Name of *Jack-o'Lent*:[7] but his Voice being so extremely musical, that it rather allured the Birds than terrified them, he was soon transplanted from the Fields into the Dog-kennel, where he was placed under the Huntsman, and made what Sportsmen term a *Whipper-in*.[8] For this Place likewise the Sweetness of his Voice disqualified him: the Dogs preferring the Melody of his chiding to all the alluring Notes of the Huntsman, who soon became so incensed at it, that he desired Sir *Thomas* to provide otherwise for him; and constantly laid every Fault the Dogs were at, to the Account of the poor Boy, who was now transplanted to the Stable. Here he soon gave Proofs of Strength and Agility, beyond his Years, and constantly rode the most spirited and vicious Horses to water with an Intrepidity which surprised every one. While he was in this Station, he rode several Races for Sir *Thomas*, and this with such Expertness and Success, that the neighbouring Gentlemen frequently solicited the Knight, to permit little *Joey* (for so he was called) to ride their Matches. The best Gamesters, before they laid their Money, always enquired which Horse little *Joey* was to ride, and the Betts were rather proportioned by the Rider than by the Horse himself; especially after he had scornfully refused a considerable Bribe to play booty[9] on such an Occasion. This extremely raised his Character,[10] and so pleased the Lady *Booby*, that she desired to have him (being now seventeen Years of Age)[11] for her own Foot-boy.

Joey was now preferred from the Stable to attend on his Lady; to go on her Errands, stand behind her Chair, wait at her Tea-table, and carry her Prayer-Book to Church, at which Place, his Voice gave him an Opportunity of distinguishing himself by singing Psalms: he behaved likewise in every other respect so well at divine Service, that it recommended him to the Notice of Mr *Abraham Adams* the Curate;[12] who took an Opportunity one day, as he was drinking a Cup of Ale in Sir *Thomas*'s Kitchin, to ask the young Man several Questions concerning Religion; with his Answers to which he was wonderfully pleased.

CHAPTER III

Of Mr Abraham Adams *the Curate, Mrs* Slipslop *the*
Chambermaid, and others.

Mr *Abraham Adams* was an excellent Scholar. He was a perfect Master of the
Greek and *Latin* Languages; to which he added a great Share of Knowledge
in the Oriental Tongues, and could read and translate *French*, *Italian* and
Spanish. He had applied many Years to the most severe Study, and had
treasured up a Fund of Learning rarely to be met with in a University. He
was besides a Man of good Sense, good Parts, and good Nature;[1] but was
at the same time as entirely ignorant of the Ways of this World, as an Infant
just entered into it could possibly be. As he had never any Intention to
deceive, so he never suspected such a Design in others. He was generous,
friendly and brave to an Excess; but Simplicity was his Characteristic: he
did, no more than Mr *Colley Cibber*, apprehend any such Passions as Malice
and Envy to exist in Mankind,[2] which was indeed less remarkable in a
Country Parson than in a Gentleman who hath past his Life behind the
Scenes, a Place which hath been seldom thought the School of Innocence;
and where a very little Observation would have convinced the great
Apologist, that those Passions have a real Existence in the human Mind.

His Virtue and his other Qualifications, as they rendered him equal to
his Office, so they made him an agreeable and valuable Companion, and
had so much endeared and well recommended him to a Bishop; that at
the Age of Fifty, he was provided with a handsome Income of twenty-three
Pounds a Year; which however, he could not make any great Figure with:
because he lived in a dear Country,[3] and was a little incumbered with a
Wife and six Children.

It was this Gentleman, who having, as I have said, observed the singular
Devotion of young *Andrews*, had found means to question him, concerning
several Particulars; as how many Books there were in the New Testament?
which were they? how many Chapters they contained? and such like; to
all which Mr *Adams* said,[4] he answer'd much better than *Sir Thomas*, or
two other neighbouring Justices of the Peace could probably have done.

Mr *Adams* was wonderfully sollicitous to know at what Time, and by
what Opportunity the Youth became acquainted with these Matters: *Joey*
told him, that he had very early learnt to read and write by the Goodness
of his Father, who, though he had not Interest enough to get him into a

Charity School,[5] because a Cousin of his Father's Landlord did not vote on the right side for a Church-warden in a Borough-Town, yet had been himself at the Expence of Sixpence a Week for his Learning. He told him likewise, that ever since he was in Sir *Thomas's* Family, he had employed all his Hours of Leisure in reading good Books; that he had read the Bible, the *Whole Duty of Man*, and *Thomas à Kempis*; and that as often as he could, without being perceived, he had studied a great good Book which lay open in the Hall Window where he had read, *as how the Devil carried away half a Church in Sermon-time, without hurting one of the Congregation*; and *as how a Field of Corn ran away down a Hill with all the Trees upon it, and covered another Man's Meadow*. This sufficiently assured Mr *Adams*, that the good Book meant could be no other than *Baker's* Chronicle.[6]

The Curate, surprized to find such Instances of Industry and Application in a young Man, who had never met with the least Encouragement, asked him, if he did not extremely regret the want of a liberal Education, and the not having been born of Parents, who might have indulged his Talents and Desire of Knowledge? To which he answered, 'He hoped he had profited somewhat better from the Books he had read, than to lament his Condition in this World. That for his part, he was perfectly content with the State to which he was called, that he should endeavour to improve his Talent, which was all required of him, but not repine at his own Lot, nor envy those of his Betters.'[7] 'Well said, my Lad,' reply'd the Curate, 'and I wish some who have read many more good Books, nay and some who have written good Books themselves, had profited so much by them.'

Adams had no nearer Access to Sir *Thomas*, or my Lady, than through the Waiting-Gentlewoman: For Sir *Thomas* was too apt to estimate Men merely by their Dress, or Fortune; and my Lady was a Woman of Gaiety, who had been bless'd with a Town-Education, and never spoke of any of her Country Neighbours, by any other Appellation than that of *The Brutes*. They both regarded the Curate as a kind of Domestic only, belonging to the Parson of the Parish,[8] who was at this time at variance with the Knight; for the Parson had for many Years lived in a constant State of Civil War, or, which is perhaps as bad, of Civil Law, with Sir *Thomas* himself and the Tenants of his Manor. The Foundation of this Quarrel was a Modus,[9] by setting which aside, an Advantage of several Shillings *per Annum* would have accrued to the Rector: but he had not yet been able to ac-complish his Purpose; and had reaped hitherto nothing better from the Suits than the Pleasure (which he used indeed frequently to say was no small one) of reflecting that he had utterly undone many of the poor

Tenants, tho' he had at the same time greatly impoverish'd himself.

Mrs *Slipslop*[10] the Waiting-Gentlewoman; being herself the Daughter of a Curate, preserved some Respect for *Adams*; she professed great Regard for his Learning, and would frequently dispute with him on Points of Theology; but always insisted on a Deference to be paid to her Understanding, as she had been frequently at *London*, and knew more of the World than a Country Parson could pretend to.

She had in these Disputes a particular Advantage over *Adams*: for she was a mighty Affecter of hard Words, which she used in such a manner, that the Parson, who durst not offend her by calling her Words in question, was frequently at some loss to guess her meaning, and would have been much less puzzled by an *Arabian* Manuscript.

Adams therefore took an Opportunity one day, after a pretty long Discourse with her on the *Essence*, (or, as she pleased to term it, the *Incense*) of Matter, to mention the Case of young *Andrews*; desiring her to recommend him to her Lady as a Youth very susceptible of Learning, and one whose Instruction in *Latin* he would himself undertake; by which means he might be qualified for a higher Station than that of a Footman: and added, she knew it was in his Master's power easily to provide for him in a better manner. He therefore desired, that the Boy might be left behind under his Care.

'La, Mr *Adams*,' said Mrs *Slipslop*, 'do you think my Lady will suffer any *Preambles* about any such Matter? She is going to *London* very *concisely*, and I am *confidous* would not leave *Joey* behind her on any account; for he is one of the genteelest young Fellows you may see in a Summer's Day, and I am *confidous* she would as soon think of parting with a Pair of her *Grey*-Mares; for she values herself as much on one as the other.' *Adams* would have interrupted, but she proceeded: 'And why is *Latin* more *necessitous* for a Footman than a Gentleman? It is very proper that you Clergymen must learn it, because you can't preach without it: but I have heard Gentlemen say in *London*, that it is fit for nobody else. I am *confidous* my Lady would be angry with me for mentioning it, and I shall draw myself into no such *Delemy*.' At which words her Lady's Bell rung, and Mr *Adams* was forced to retire; nor could he gain a second Opportunity with her before their *London* Journey, which happen'd a few Days afterwards. However, *Andrews* behaved very thankfully and gratefully to him for his intended Kindness, which he told him he never would forget, and at the same time received from the good Man many Admonitions concerning the Regulation of his future Conduct, and his Perseverance in Innocence and Industry.

CHAPTER IV

What happened after their Journey to London.

No sooner was young *Andrews* arrived at *London*, than he began to scrape an Acquaintance with his party-colour'd Brethren,[1] who endeavour'd to make him despise his former Course of Life. His Hair was cut after the newest Fashion, and became his chief Care. He went abroad with it all the Morning in Papers, and drest it out in the Afternoon; they could not however teach him to game, swear, drink, nor any other genteel Vice the Town abounded with. He applied most of his leisure Hours to Music, in which he greatly improved himself, and became so perfect a Connoisseur in that Art, that he led the Opinion of all the other Footmen at an Opera, and they never condemned or applauded a single Song contrary to his Approbation or Dislike. He was a little too forward in Riots at the Play-Houses and Assemblies;[2] and when he attended his Lady at Church (which was but seldom) he behaved with less seeming Devotion than formerly: however, if he was outwardly a pretty Fellow, his Morals remained entirely uncorrupted, tho' he was at the same time smarter and genteeler, than any of the Beaus in Town, either in or out of Livery.

His Lady, who had often said of him that *Joey* was the handsomest and genteelest Footman in the Kingdom, but that it was pity he wanted Spirit, began now to find that Fault no longer; on the contrary, she was frequently heard to cry out, *Aye, there is some Life in this Fellow*. She plainly saw the Effects which the Town-Air hath on the soberest Constitutions. She would now walk out with him into *Hyde-Park* in a Morning, and when tired, which happened almost every Minute, would lean on his Arm, and converse with him in great Familiarity. Whenever she stept out of her Coach she would take him by the Hand, and sometimes, for fear of stumbling, press it very hard; she admitted him to deliver Messages at her Bed-side in a Morning, leer'd at him at Table, and indulged him in all those innocent Freedoms which Women of Figure may permit without the least sully of their Virtue.

But tho' their Virtue remains unsullied, yet now and then some small Arrows will glance on the Shadow of it, their Reputation; and so it fell out to Lady *Booby*, who happened to be walking Arm in Arm with *Joey* one Morning in *Hyde-Park*, when Lady *Tittle* and Lady *Tattle* came accidentally by in their Coach. *Bless me*, says Lady *Tittle*, *can I believe my*

Eyes? Is that Lady Booby*? Surely*, says *Tattle. But what makes you surprized? Why is not that her Footman*, reply'd *Tittle? At which Tattle* laughed and cryed, *An old Business, I assure you, is it possible you should not have heard it? The whole Town hath known it this half Year.* The Consequence of this Interview was a Whisper through a hundred Visits, which were separately performed by the two Ladies* the same Afternoon, and might have had a mischievous Effect, had it not been stopt by two fresh Reputations which were published[3] the Day afterwards, and engrossed the whole Talk of the Town.

But whatever Opinion or Suspicion the scandalous Inclination of Defamers might entertain of Lady *Booby*'s innocent Freedoms, it is certain they made no Impression on young *Andrews*, who never offered to encroach beyond the Liberties which his Lady allowed him. A Behaviour which she imputed to the violent Respect he preserved for her, and which served only to heighten a something she began to conceive, and which the next Chapter will open a little farther.

CHAPTER V

The Death of Sir Thomas Booby, *with the affectionate and mournful Behaviour of his Widow, and the great Purity of* Joseph Andrews.

At this Time, an Accident happened which put a stop to these agreeable Walks, which probably would have soon puffed up the Cheeks of Fame,[1] and caused her to blow her brazen Trumpet through the Town; and this was no other than the Death of Sir *Thomas Booby*, who departing his Life, left his disconsolate Lady confined to her House as closely as if she herself had been attacked by some violent Disease. During the first six Days the poor Lady admitted none but Mrs *Slipslop* and three Female Friends who made a Party at Cards: but on the seventh she ordered *Joey*, whom for a good Reason we shall hereafter call JOSEPH,[2] to bring up her Tea-kettle. The Lady being in Bed, call'd *Joseph* to her, bad him sit down, and having accidentally laid her hand on him, she asked him, *if he had never been in Love? Joseph* answered, with some Confusion, it was time enough for one so young as himself to think on such things. As young as you are, reply'd

---

* It may seem an Absurdity that *Tattle* should visit, as she actually did, to spread a known Scandal: but the Reader may reconcile this, by supposing with me, that, notwithstanding what she says, this was her first Acquaintance with it.

the Lady, I am convinced you are no Stranger to that Passion; 'Come *Joey*,' says she, 'tell me truly, who is the happy Girl whose Eyes have made a Conquest of you?' *Joseph* returned, that all Women he had ever seen were equally indifferent to him. 'O then,' said the Lady, 'you are a general Lover. Indeed you handsome Fellows, like handsome Women, are very long and difficult in fixing: but yet you shall never persuade me that your Heart is so insusceptible of Affection; I rather impute what you say to your Secrecy, a very commendable Quality, and what I am far from being angry with you for. Nothing can be more unworthy in a young Man than to betray any Intimacies with the Ladies.' *Ladies! Madam*, said *Joseph*, *I am sure I never had the Impudence to think of any that deserve that Name.* 'Don't pretend to too much modesty,' said she, 'for that sometimes may be impertinent: but pray, answer me this Question, Suppose a Lady should happen to like you, suppose she should prefer you to all your Sex, and admit you to the same Familiarities as you might have hoped for, if you had been born her equal, are you certain that no Vanity could tempt you to discover her? Answer me honestly, *Joseph*; Have you so much more Sense and so much more Virtue than you handsome young Fellows generally have, who make no scruple of sacrificing our dear Reputation to your Pride, without considering the great Obligation we lay on you, by our Condescension and Confidence? Can you keep a Secret, my *Joey?*' 'Madam,' says he, 'I hope your Ladyship can't tax me with ever betraying the Secrets of the Family, and I hope, if you was to turn me away, I might have that Character of you.' 'I don't intend to turn you away, *Joey*,' said she, and sighed, 'I am afraid it is not in my power.' She then raised herself a little in her Bed, and discovered[3] one of the whitest necks that ever was seen; at which *Joseph* blushed. 'La!' says she, in an affected Surprize, 'what am I doing? I have trusted my self with a Man alone, naked in Bed; suppose you should have any wicked Intentions upon my Honour, how should I defend myself?' *Joseph* protested that he never had the least evil Design against her. 'No,' says she, 'perhaps you may not call your Designs wicked, and perhaps they are not so.' – He swore they were not. 'You misunderstand me,' says she, 'I mean if they were against my Honour they may not be wicked, but the World calls them so. But then, say you, the World will never know any thing of the Matter, yet would not that be trusting to your Secrecy? Must not my Reputation be then in your power? Would you not then be my Master?' *Joseph* begged her Ladyship to be comforted, for that he would never imagine the least wicked thing against her, and that he had rather die a thousand Deaths[4] than give her any Reason to suspect him. 'Yes,' said she, 'I must have Reason to suspect you. Are you not a Man? and without Vanity I may pretend to some Charms. But perhaps you may fear I should prosecute you; indeed I hope you do, and yet Heaven knows I should never have the Confidence to appear before a Court of Justice, and you know, *Joey*, I am of a forgiving Temper. Tell me *Joey*, don't you think I should forgive you?' 'Indeed Madam,' says *Joseph*, 'I will never do any thing to disoblige your Ladyship.' 'How,' says she, 'do you think it would not disoblige me then? Do you think I would willingly suffer you?' 'I don't understand you, Madam,' says *Joseph*. 'Don't you?' said she, 'then you are either a Fool or pretend to be so; I find I was mistaken in you, so get you down Stairs, and never let me see your Face again: your pretended Innocence cannot impose on me.' 'Madam,' said *Joseph*, 'I would not have your Ladyship think any Evil of me. I have always endeavoured to be a dutiful Servant both to you and my Master.' 'O thou Villain,' answered my Lady, 'Why didst thou mention the Name of that dear Man, unless to torment me, to bring his precious Memory to my Mind, (*and then she burst into a Fit of Tears.*) Get thee from my Sight, I shall never endure thee more.' At which Words she turned away from him, and *Joseph* retreated from the Room in a most disconsolate Condition, and writ that Letter which the Reader will find in the next Chapter.

CHAPTER VI

How Joseph Andrews *writ a Letter to his Sister* Pamela.

TO MRS *PAMELA ANDREWS*, LIVING WITH SQUIRE *BOOBY*.

'*Dear Sister,*

'Since I received your Letter of your good Lady's Death, we have had a Misfortune of the same kind in our Family. My worthy Master, Sir *Thomas*, died about four Days ago,[1] and what is worse, my poor Lady is certainly gone distracted. None of the Servants expected her to take it so to heart, because they quarrelled almost every day of their Lives: but no more of that, because you know, *Pamela*, I never loved to tell the Secrets of my Master's Family;[2] but to be sure you must have known they never loved one another, and I have heard her Ladyship wish his Honour dead above a thousand times: but no body knows what it is to lose a Friend 'till they have lost him.[3]

'Don't tell any body what I write, because I should not care to have Folks say I discover what passes in our Family: but if it had not been so great a Lady, I should have thought she had had a mind to me. Dear *Pamela*, don't tell any body: but she ordered me to sit down by her Bed-side, when she was in naked Bed;[4] and she held my Hand, and talked exactly as a Lady does to her Sweetheart in a Stage-Play, which I have seen in *Covent-Garden*,[5] while she wanted him to be no better than he should be.

'If Madam be mad, I shall not care for staying long in the Family: so I heartily wish you could get me a Place either at the Squire's, or some other neighbouring Gentleman's, unless it be true that you are going to be married to Parson *Williams*,[6] as Folks talk, and then I should be very willing to be his Clerk: for which you know I am qualified, being able to read, and to set a Psalm.

'I fancy, I shall be discharged very soon; and the Moment I am, unless I hear from you, I shall return to my old Master's Country-Seat, if it be only to see Parson *Adams*, who is the best Man in the World. *London* is a bad Place, and there is so little good Fellowship, that next-door Neighbours don't know one another. Pray give my Service to all Friends that enquire for me; so I rest

Your Loving Brother,
Joseph Andrews.'

As soon as *Joseph* had sealed and directed this Letter, he walked down Stairs, where he met Mrs *Slipslop*, with whom we shall take this Opportunity to bring the Reader a little better acquainted. She was an antient maiden Gentlewoman of about Forty-five Years of Age, who having made a small Slip in her Youth had continued a good Maid ever since. She was not at this time remarkably handsome; being very short, and rather too corpulent in Body, and somewhat red, with the Addition of Pimples in the Face. Her Nose was likewise rather too large, and her Eyes too little; nor did she resemble a Cow so much in her Breath, as in two brown Globes which she carried before her; one of her Legs was also a little shorter than the other, which occasioned her to limp as she walked. This fair Creature had long cast the Eyes of Affection on *Joseph*, in which she had not met with quite so good Success as she probably wished, tho' besides the Allurements of her native Charms, she had given him Tea, Sweetmeats, Wine, and many other Delicacies, of which by keeping the Keys, she had the absolute Command. *Joseph* however, had not returned the least Gratitude to all these Favours, not even so much as a Kiss; tho' I would not insinuate she was so easily to be satisfied: for surely then he would have been highly blameable. The truth is, she arrived at an Age when she thought she might indulge herself in any Liberties with a Man, without the danger of bringing a third Person into the World to betray them. She imagined, that by so long a Self-denial, she had not only made amends for the small Slip of her Youth above hinted at: but had likewise laid up a Quantity of Merit to excuse any future Failings. In a word, she resolved to give a loose to her amorous Inclinations, and pay off the Debt of Pleasure which she found she owed herself, as fast as possible.

With these Charms of Person, and in this Disposition of Mind, she encountered poor *Joseph* at the Bottom of the Stairs, and asked him if he would drink a Glass of something good this Morning. *Joseph*, whose Spirits were not a little cast down, very readily and thankfully accepted the Offer; and together they went into a Closet,[7] where having delivered him a full Glass of Ratifia,[8] and desired him to sit down, Mrs *Slipslop* thus began:

'Sure nothing can be a more simple *Contract* in a Woman, than to place her Affections on a Boy. If I had ever thought it would have been my Fate, I should have wished to die a thousand Deaths rather than live to see that Day. If we like a Man, the lightest Hint *sophisticates*. Where a Boy *proposes* upon us to break through all the *Regulations* of Modesty, before we can make any *Oppression* upon him.' *Joseph*, who did not understand a Word she said, answered, '*Yes Madam*; — ' 'Yes Madam!' reply'd Mrs *Slipslop* with some Warmth, 'Do you intend to *result* my Passion? Is it not enough, ungrateful as you are, to make no Return to all the Favours I have done you: but you must treat me with *Ironing?* Barbarous Monster! how have I deserved that my Passion should be *resulted* and treated with *Ironing?*' 'Madam,' answered *Joseph*, 'I don't understand your hard Words: but I am certain, you have no Occasion to call me ungrateful: for so far from intending you any Wrong, I have always loved you as well as if you had been my own Mother.' 'How, Sirrah!' says Mrs *Slipslop* in a Rage: 'Your own Mother! Do you *assinuate* that I am old enough to be your Mother? I don't know what a Stripling may think: but I believe a Man would *refer* me to any Green-Sickness[9] silly Girl *whatsomdever*: but I ought to despise you rather than be angry with you, for *referring* the Conversation of Girls to that of a Woman of Sense.' 'Madam,' says *Joseph*, 'I am sure I have always valued the Honour you did me by your Conversation; for I know you are a Woman of Learning.' 'Yes but, *Joseph*,' said she a little softened by the Compliment to her Learning, 'If you had a Value for me, you certainly would have found some Method of shewing it me; for I am *convicted* you must see the Value I have for you. Yes, *Joseph*, my Eyes whether I would or no, must have declared a Passion I cannot conquer. —— Oh! *Joseph!* ——'

As when a hungry Tygress, who long had traversed the Woods in fruitless search, sees within the Reach of her Claws a Lamb, she prepared to leap on her Prey; or as a voracious Pike, of immense Size, surveys through the liquid Element a Roach or Gudgeon which cannot escape her Jaws, opens them wide to swallow the little Fish: so did Mrs *Slipslop* prepare to lay her violent amorous Hands on the poor *Joseph*, when luckily her Mistress's Bell rung, and delivered the intended Martyr from her Clutches. She was obliged to break off abruptly, and defer the Execution of her Purpose to some other Time. We shall therefore return to the Lady *Booby*, and give our Reader some Account of her Behaviour, after she was left by *Joseph* in a Temper of Mind not greatly different from that of the inflamed *Slipslop*.

CHAPTER VII

Sayings of wise Men. A Dialogue between the Lady and her Maid, and a Panegyric or rather Satire on the Passion of Love, in the sublime Style.

It is the Observation of some antient Sage, whose Name I have forgot, that Passions operate differently on the human Mind, as Diseases on the Body, in proportion to the Strength or Weakness, Soundness or Rottenness of the one and the other.

We hope therefore, a judicious Reader will give himself some Pains to observe, what we have so greatly laboured to describe, the different Operations of this Passion of Love in the gentle and cultivated Mind of the Lady *Booby*, from those which it effected in the less polished and coarser Disposition of Mrs *Slipslop*.

One other Philosopher, whose Name also at present escapes my Memory, hath somewhere said, that Resolutions taken in the Absence of the beloved Object are very apt to vanish in its Presence; on both which wise Sayings the following Chapter may serve as a Comment.

No sooner had *Joseph* left the Room in the Manner we have before related, than the Lady, enraged at her Disappointment, began to reflect with Severity on her Conduct. Her Love was now changed to Disdain, which Pride assisted to torment her. She despised herself for the Meanness[1] of her Passion, and *Joseph* for its ill Success. However, she had now got the better of it in her own Opinion, and determined immediately to dismiss the Object. After much tossing and turning in her Bed, and many Soliloquies, which, if we had no better Matter for our Reader, we would give him; she at last rung the Bell as above-mentioned, and was presently attended by Mrs *Slipslop*, who was not much better pleased with *Joseph*, than the Lady herself.

Slipslop, said Lady *Booby*, *when did you see* Joseph? The poor Woman was so surprized at the unexpected Sound of his Name, at so critical a time, that she had the greatest Difficulty to conceal the Confusion she was under from her Mistress, whom she answered nevertheless, with pretty good Confidence, though not entirely void of Fear of Suspicion, that she had not seen him that Morning. 'I am afraid,' said Lady *Booby*, 'he is a wild young Fellow.' 'That he is,' said *Slipslop*, 'and a wicked one too. To my knowledge he games, drinks, swears and fights eternally: besides he is horribly *indicted* to Wenching.' 'Ay!' said the Lady! 'I never heard that of him.' 'O Madam,' answered the other, 'he is so lewd a Rascal that if your Ladyship keeps him much longer, you will not have one Virgin in your House except myself. And yet I can't conceive what the Wenches see in him, to be so foolishly fond as they are: in my Eyes he is as ugly a Scarecrow as I ever *upheld*.' 'Nay,' said the Lady, 'the Boy is well enough.' — 'La Ma'am,' cries *Slipslop*, 'I think him the *ragmaticallest* Fellow in the Family.' 'Sure, *Slipslop*,' says she, 'you are mistaken: but which of the Women do you most suspect?' 'Madam,' says *Slipslop*, 'there is *Betty*[2] the Chamber-Maid, I am almost *convicted*, is with Child by him.' 'Ay!' says the Lady, 'then pray pay her her Wages instantly. I will keep no such Sluts in my Family. And as for *Joseph*, you may discard him too.' 'Would your Ladyship have him paid off immediately?' cries *Slipslop*, 'for perhaps, when *Betty* is gone, he may mend; and really the Boy is a good Servant, and a strong healthy *luscious* Boy enough.' 'This Morning,' answered the Lady with some Vehemence. 'I wish Madam,' cries *Slipslop*, 'your Ladyship would be so good as to try him a little longer.' 'I will not have my Commands disputed,' said the Lady; 'sure you are not fond of him yourself.' 'I Madam?' cries *Slipslop*, reddening, if not blushing, 'I should be sorry to think your Ladyship had any reason to *respect* me of Fondness for a Fellow; and if it be your Pleasure, I shall fulfil it with as much *reluctance* as possible.' 'As little, I suppose you mean,' said the Lady; 'and so about it instantly.' Mrs *Slipslop* went out, and the Lady had scarce taken two turns before she fell to knocking and ringing with great Violence. *Slipslop*, who did not travel post-haste, soon returned, and was countermanded as to *Joseph*, but ordered to send *Betty* about her Business without delay. She went out a second time with much greater alacrity than before; when the Lady began immediately to accuse herself of Want of Resolution, and to apprehend the Return of her Affection with its pernicious Consequences: she therefore applied herself again to the Bell, and resummoned Mrs *Slipslop* into her Presence; who again returned, and was told by her Mistress, that she had consider'd better of the Matter, and was absolutely resolved to turn away *Joseph*; which she ordered her to do immediately. *Slipslop*, who knew the Violence of her Lady's Temper, and would not venture her Place for any *Adonis* or *Hercules* in the Universe, left her a third time; which she had no sooner done, than the little God *Cupid*, fearing he had not yet done the Lady's Business, took a fresh Arrow with the sharpest Point out of his Quiver, and shot it directly into her Heart: in other and plainer Language, the Lady's Passion got the better of her Reason. She called back *Slipslop* once more, and told her, she had resolved to see the Boy, and examine him herself; therefore bid her send him up. This wavering in her Mistress's Temper probably put something into the Waiting-Gentlewoman's Head, not necessary to mention to the sagacious Reader.

Lady *Booby* was going to call her back again, but could not prevail with herself. The next Consideration therefore was, how she should behave to *Joseph* when he came in. She resolved to preserve all the Dignity of the Woman of Fashion to her Servant, and to indulge herself in this last View of *Joseph* (for that she was most certainly resolved it should be) at his own Expence, by first insulting, and then discarding him.

O Love, what monstrous Tricks dost thou play with thy Votaries of both Sexes! How dost thou deceive them, and make them deceive themselves! Their Follies are thy Delight! Their Sighs make thee laugh, and their Pangs are thy Merriment!

Nor the Great *Rich*,[3] who turns Men into Monkeys, Wheelbarrows, and whatever else best humours his Fancy, hath so strangely metamorphosed the human Shape; nor the Great *Cibber*,[4] who confounds all Number, Gender, and breaks through every Rule of Grammar at his Will, hath so distorted the *English* Language, as thou dost metamorphose and distort the human Senses.

Thou puttest out our Eyes, stoppest up our Ears, and takest away the

power of our Nostrils; so that we can neither see the largest Object, hea
the loudest Noise, nor smell the most poignant Perfume. Again, when thou
pleasest, thou can'st make a Mole-hill appear as a Mountain; a *Jew's*-Harp
sound like a Trumpet; and a Dazy smell like a Violet. Thou can'st make
Cowardice brave, Avarice generous, Pride humble, and Cruelty tender-
hearted. In short, thou turnest the Heart of Man inside-out, as a Juggler
doth a Petticoat, and bringest whatsoever pleaseth thee out from it. If there
be any one who doubts all this, let him read the next Chapter.

CHAPTER VIII

*In which, after some very fine Writing, the History goes on, and relates
the Interview between the Lady and* Joseph; *where the latter hath set
an Example, which we despair of seeing followed by his Sex, in this
vicious Age.*

Now the Rake *Hesperus*[1] had called for his Breeches, and having well
rubbed his drowsy Eyes, prepared to dress himself for all Night; by whose
Example his Brother Rakes on Earth likewise leave those Beds, in which
they had slept away the Day. Now *Thetis* the good Housewife began to
put on the Pot in order to regale the good Man *Phœbus*,[2] after his daily
Labours were over. In vulgar Language, it was in the Evening when *Joseph*
attended his Lady's Orders.

But as it becomes us to preserve the Character of this Lady, who is the
Heroine of our Tale; and as we have naturally a wonderful Tenderness
for that beautiful Part of the human Species, called the Fair Sex; before we
discover too much of her Frailty to our Reader, it will be proper to give him
a lively Idea of that vast Temptation, which overcame all the Efforts of a
modest and virtuous Mind; and then we humbly hope this Good-nature
will rather pity than condemn the Imperfection of human Virtue.

Nay, the Ladies themselves will, we hope, be induced, by considering
the uncommon Variety of Charms, which united in this young Man's
Person, to bridle their rampant Passion for Chastity, and be at least as
mild as their violent Modesty and Virtue will permit them, in censuring
the Conduct of a Woman, who, perhaps, was in her own Disposition as
chaste as those pure and sanctified Virgins, who, after a Life innocently
spent in the Gaieties of the Town, begin about Fifty to attend twice *per
diem* at the polite Churches and Chapels, to return Thanks for the Grace

which preserved them formerly amongst Beaus, from Temptations perhaps less powerful than what now attacked the Lady *Booby*.

Mr *Joseph Andrews* was now in the one and twentieth Year of his Age. He was of the highest Degree of middle Stature. His Limbs were put together with great Elegance and no less Strength. His Legs and Thighs were formed in the exactest Proportion. His Shoulders were broad and brawny, but yet his Arms hung so easily, that he had all the Symptoms of Strength without the least clumsiness. His Hair was of a nut-brown Colour, and was displayed in wanton³ Ringlets down his Back. His Forehead was high, his Eyes dark, and as full of Sweetness as of Fire. His Nose a little inclined to the Roman. His Teeth white and even. His Lips full, red, and soft. His Beard was only rough on his Chin and upper Lip; but his Cheeks, in which his Blood glowed, were overspread with a thick Down. His Countenance had a Tenderness joined with a Sensibility⁴ inexpressible. Add to this the most perfect Neatness in his Dress, and an Air, which to those who have not seen many Noblemen, would give an Idea of Nobility.

Such was the Person who now appeared before the Lady. She viewed him some time in Silence, and twice or thrice before she spake, changed her Mind as to the manner in which she should begin. At length, she said to him, '*Joseph*, I am sorry to hear such Complaints against you; I am told you behave so rudely to the Maids, that they cannot do their Business in quiet; I mean those who are not wicked enough to hearken to your Solicitations. As to others, they may not perhaps call you rude: for there are wicked Sluts who make one ashamed of one's own Sex; and are as ready to admit any nauseous Familiarity as Fellows to offer it; nay, there are such in my Family: but they shall not stay in it; that impudent Trollop, who is with Child by you, is discharged by this time.'

As a Person who is struck through the Heart with a Thunderbolt, looks extremely surprised, nay and perhaps is so too —— Thus the poor *Joseph* received the false Accusation of his Mistress; he blushed and looked confounded, which she misinterpreted to be Symptoms of his Guilt, and thus went on:

'Come hither, *Joseph*: another Mistress might discard you for these Offences; But I have a Compassion for your Youth, and if I could be certain you would be no more guilty —— Consider, Child, (*laying her Hand carelessly upon his*) you are a handsome young Fellow, and might do better; you might make your Fortune —.' 'Madam,' said *Joseph*, 'I do assure your Ladyship, I don't know whether any Maid in the House is

Man or Woman ———.' 'Oh fie! *Joseph*,' answer'd the Lady, 'don't commit another Crime in denying the Truth. I could pardon the first; but I hate a Lyar.' 'Madam,' cries *Joseph*, 'I hope your Ladyship will not be offended at my asserting my Innocence: and by all that is Sacred, I have never offered more than Kissing.' 'Kissing!' said the Lady, with great Discomposure of Countenance, and more Redness in her Cheeks, than Anger in her Eyes, 'do you call that no Crime? Kissing, *Joseph*, is but a Prologue to a Play. Can I believe a young Fellow of your Age and Complexion will be content with Kissing? No, *Joseph*, there is no Woman who grants that but will grant more, and I am deceived greatly in you, if you would not put her closely to it. What would you think, *Joseph*, if I admitted you to kiss me?' *Joseph* reply'd, 'He would sooner die than have any such Thought.' 'And yet, *Joseph*,' returned she, 'Ladies have admitted their Footmen to such Familiarities; and Footmen, I confess to you, much less deserving them; Fellows without half your Charms: for such might almost excuse the Crime. Tell me, therefore, *Joseph*, if I should admit you to such Freedom, what would you think of me? – tell me freely.' 'Madam;' said *Joseph*, 'I should think your Ladyship condescended a great deal below yourself.' 'Pugh!' said she, 'that I am to answer to myself: but would not you insist on more? Would you be contented with a Kiss? Would not your Inclinations be all on fire rather by such a Favour?' 'Madam,' said *Joseph*, 'if they were, I hope I should be able to controll them, without suffering them to get the better of my Virtue.' — You have heard, Reader, Poets talk of the *Statue of Surprize*;[5] you have heard likewise, or else you have heard very little, how Surprize made one of the Sons of *Crœsus* speak tho' he was dumb.[6] You have seen the Faces, in the Eighteen-penny Gallery, when through the Trap-Door, to soft or no Musick, Mr *Bridgewater*, Mr *William Mills*,[7] or some other of ghostly Appearance, hath ascended with a Face all pale with Powder, and a Shirt all bloody with Ribbons; but from none of these, nor from *Phidias*, or *Praxiteles*,[8] if they should return to Life — no, not from the inimitable Pencil of my Friend *Hogarth*, could you receive such an Idea of Surprize, as would have entered in at your Eyes, had they beheld the Lady *Booby*, when those last Words, issued out from the Lips of *Joseph*. — 'Your Virtue! (said the Lady recovering after a Silence of two Minutes) I shall never survive it. Your Virtue! Intolerable Confidence! Have you the Assurance to pretend,[9] that when a Lady demeans herself to throw aside the Rules of Decency, in order to honour you with the highest Favour in her power, your Virtue should resist her Inclination? That when she had conquer'd her own Virtue, she should find an Obstruction in yours?' 'Madam,' said *Joseph* 'I can't see why her having no Virtue should be a Reason against my having any: Or why, because I am a Man, or because I am poor, my Virtue must be subservient to her Pleasures.' 'I am out of patience,' cries the Lady: 'Did ever Mortal hear of a Man's Virtue! Did ever the greatest, or the gravest Men pretend to any of this Kind! Will Magistrates who punish Lewdness, or Parsons, who preach against it, make any scruple of committing it? And can a Boy, a Stripling, have the Confidence to talk of his Virtue?' 'Madam,' says *Joseph*, 'that Boy is the Brother of *Pamela*, and would be ashamed, that the Chastity of his Family, which is preserved in her, should be stained in him. If there are such Men as your Ladyship mentions, I am sorry for it, and I wish they had an Opportunity of reading over those Letters, which my Father hath sent me of my Sister *Pamela*'s, nor do I doubt but such an Example would amend them.'[10] 'You impudent Villain,' cries the Lady in a Rage, 'do you insult me with the Follies of my Relation, who hath exposed himself all over the Country upon your Sister's account? a little Vixen, whom I have always wondered my late Lady *John Booby* ever kept in her House. Sirrah! get out of my sight, and prepare to set out this Night, for I will order you your Wages immediately, and you shall be stripped and turned away. —' 'Madam,' says *Joseph*, 'I am sorry I have offended your Ladyship, I am sure I never intended it.' 'Yes, Sirrah,' cries she, 'you have had the Vanity to misconstrue the little innocent Freedom I took in order to try, whether what I had heard was true. O' my Conscience, you have had the Assurance to imagine, I was fond of you myself.' *Joseph* answered, he had only spoke out of Tenderdess for his Virtue; at which Words she flew into a violent Passion, and refusing to hear more, ordered him instantly to leave the Room.

He was no sooner gone, than she burst forth into the following Exclamation: 'Whither does this violent Passion hurry us? What Meannesses do we submit to from its Impulse? Wisely we resist its first and least Approaches; for it is then only we can assure ourselves the Victory. No Woman could ever safely say, *so far only will I go*. Have I not exposed myself to the Refusal of my Footman? I cannot bear the Reflection.' Upon which she applied herself to the Bell, and rung it with infinite more Violence than was necessary; the faithful *Slipslop* attending near at hand: To say the truth, she had conceived a Suspicion at her last Interview with her Mistress; and had waited ever since in the Antichamber, having carefully applied her Ears to the Key-Hole during the whole time, that the preceding Conversation passed between *Joseph* and the Lady.

CHAPTER IX

What passed between the Lady and Mrs Slipslop, *in which we prophesy there are some Strokes which every one will not truly comprehend at the first Reading.*

'*Slipslop*,' said the Lady, 'I find too much Reason to believe all thou hast told me of this wicked *Joseph*; I have determined to part with him instantly; so go you to the Steward, and bid him pay him his Wages.' *Slipslop*, who had preserved hitherto a Distance to her Lady, rather out of Necessity than Inclination, and who thought the Knowledge of this Secret had thrown down all Distinction between them, answered her Mistress very pertly, 'She wished she knew her own Mind; and that she was certain she would call her back again, before she was got half way down stairs.' The Lady replied, 'she had taken a Resolution, and was resolved to keep it.' 'I am sorry for it,' cried *Slipslop*; 'and if I had known you would have punished the poor Lad so severely, you should never have heard a *Particle* of the Matter. Here's a Fuss indeed, about nothing.' 'Nothing!' returned my Lady; 'Do you think I will countenance Lewdness in my House?' 'If you will turn away every Footman,' said *Slipslop*, 'that is a lover of the Sport, you must soon open the Coach-Door yourself, or get a Sett of *Mophrodites*[1] to wait upon you; and I am sure I hated the Sight of them even singing in an Opera.' 'Do as I bid you,' says my Lady, 'and don't shock my Ears with your beastly Language.' 'Marry-come-up,' cries *Slipslop*, 'People's Ears are sometimes the nicest[2] Part about them.'

The Lady, who began to admire[3] the new Style in which her Waiting-Gentlewoman delivered herself, and by the Conclusion of her Speech, suspected somewhat of the Truth, called her back, and desired to know what she meant by that extraordinary degree of Freedom in which she thought proper to indulge her Tongue. 'Freedom!' says *Slipslop*, 'I don't know what you call Freedom, Madam; Servants have Tongues as well as their Mistresses.' 'Yes, and saucy ones too,' answered the Lady: 'but I assure you I shall bear no such Impertinence.' 'Impertinence! I don't know that I am impertinent,' says *Slipslop*. 'Yes indeed you are,' cries my Lady; 'and unless you mend your Manners, this House is no Place for you.' 'Manners!' cries *Slipslop*, 'I never was thought to want Manners *nor Modesty neither*; and for Places, there are more Places than one; and I know what I know.' 'What do you know, Mistress?' answered the Lady. 'I am not obliged to tell that to every body,' says *Slipslop*, 'any more than I am obliged to keep it a Secret.' 'I desire you would provide yourself,'[4] answered the Lady. 'With all my heart,' replied the Waiting-Gentlewoman; and so departed in a passion, and slapped the Door after her.

The Lady too plainly perceived that her Waiting-Gentlewoman knew more than she would willingly have had her acquainted with; and this she imputed to *Joseph*'s having discovered to her what past at the first Interview. This therefore blew up her Rage against him, and confirmed her in a Resolution of parting with him.

But the dismissing Mrs *Slipslop* was a Point not so easily to be resolved upon: she had the utmost Tenderness for her Reputation, as she knew on that depended many of the most valuable Blessings of Life; particularly Cards, making Court'sies in public Places, and above all, the Pleasure of demolishing the Reputations of others, in which innocent Amusement she had an extraordinary Delight. She therefore determined to submit to any Insult from a Servant, rather than run a Risque of losing the Title to so many great Privileges.

She therefore sent for her Steward, Mr *Peter Pounce*; and ordered him to pay *Joseph* his Wages, to strip off his Livery and turn him out of the House that Evening.

She then called *Slipslop* up, and after refreshing her Spirits with a small Cordial which she kept in her Closet, she began in the following manner:

'*Slipslop*, why will you, who know my passionate Temper, attempt to provoke me by your Answers? I am convinced you are an honest Servant, and should be very unwilling to part with you. I believe likewise, you have found me an indulgent Mistress on many Occasions, and have as little Reason on your side to desire a Change. I can't help being surprized therefore, that you will take the surest Method to offend me. I mean repeating my Words, which you know I have always detested.'

The prudent Waiting-Gentlewoman had duly weighed the whole Matter, and found on mature Deliberation, that a good Place in Possession was better than one in Expectation; as she found her Mistress therefore inclined to relent, she thought proper also to put on some small Condescension;[5] which was as readily accepted: and so the Affair was reconciled, all Offences forgiven, and a Present of a Gown and Petticoat made her as an Instance of her Lady's future Favour.

She offered once or twice to speak in favour of *Joseph*: but found her Lady's Heart so obdurate, that she prudently dropt all such Efforts. She considered there were more Footmen in the House, and some as stout Fellows, tho' not quite so handsome as *Joseph*: besides the Reader hath already seen her tender Advances had not met with the Encouragement she might have reasonably expected. She thought she had thrown away a great deal of Sack and Sweet-meats[6] on an ungrateful Rascal; and being a little inclined to the Opinion of that female Sect, who hold one lusty young Fellow to be near as good as another lusty young Fellow, she at last gave up *Joseph* and his Cause, and with a Triumph over her Passion highly commendable, walked off with her Present, and with great Tranquillity paid a visit to a Stone-Bottle, which is of sovereign Use to a Philosophical Temper.

She left not her Mistress so easy. The poor Lady could not reflect, without Agony, that her dear Reputation was in the power of her Servants. All her Comfort, as to *Joseph* was, that she hoped he did not understand her Meaning; at least, she could say for herself, she had not plainly express'd any thing to him; and as to Mrs *Slipslop*, she imagined she could bribe her to Secrecy.

But what hurt her most was, that in reality she had not so entirely conquered her Passion; the little God lay lurking in her Heart, tho' Anger and Disdain so hood-winked her, that she could not see him. She was a thousand times on the very Brink of revoking the Sentence she had passed against the poor Youth. Love became his Advocate, and whispered many things in his favour. Honour likewise endeavoured to vindicate his Crime, and Pity to mitigate his Punishment; on the other side, Pride and Revenge spoke as loudly against him, and thus the poor Lady was tortured with Perplexity; opposite Passions distracting and tearing her Mind different Ways.

So have I seen, in the Hall of *Westminster*, where Serjeant *Bramble* hath been retained on the right Side, and Serjeant *Puzzle* on the left;[7] the Balance of Opinion (so equal were their Fees) alternately incline to either Scale. Now *Bramble* throws in an Argument, and *Puzzle*'s Scale strikes the Beam; again, *Bramble* shares the like Fate, overpowered by the Weight of *Puzzle*. Here *Bramble* hits, there *Puzzle* strikes; here one has you, there t'other has you; 'till at last all becomes one Scene of Confusion in the tortured Minds of the Hearers; equal Wagers are laid on the Success, and neither Judge nor Jury can possibly make any thing of the Matter; all Things are so enveloped by the careful Serjeants in Doubt and Obscurity.

Or as it happens in the Conscience, where Honour and Honesty pull one way, and a Bribe and Necessity another. — If it was only our present Business to make Similies, we could produce many more to this Purpose: but a Simile (as well as a Word) to the Wise. We shall therefore see a little after our Hero, for whom the Reader is doubtless in some pain.

CHAPTER X

Joseph *writes another Letter: His Transactions with Mr* Peter Pounce, *&c. with his Departure from Lady* Booby.

The disconsolate *Joseph* would not have had an Understanding sufficient for the principal Subject of such a Book as this, if he had any longer misunderstood the Drift of his Mistress; and indeed that he did not discern it sooner, the Reader will be pleased to apply to an Unwillingness in him to discover what he must condemn in her as a Fault. Having therefore quitted her Presence, he retired into his own Garret, and entered himself into an Ejaculation[1] on the numberless Calamities which attended Beauty, and the Misfortune it was to be handsomer than one's Neighbours.

He then sat down and addressed himself to his Sister *Pamela*, in the following Words:

'*Dear Sister Pamela*,

'Hoping you are well, what News have I to tell you! O *Pamela*, my Mistress is fallen in love with me – That is, what great Folks call falling in love, she has a mind to ruin me; but I hope, I shall have more Resolution and More Grace[2] than to part with my Virtue to any Lady upon Earth.

'Mr *Adams* hath often told me, that Chastity is as great a Virtue in a Man as in a Woman. He says he never knew any more than his Wife, and I shall endeavour to follow his Example. Indeed, it is owing entirely to his excellent Sermons and Advice, together with your Letters, that I have been able to resist a Temptation, which he says no Man complies with, but he repents in this World, or is damned for it in the next; and why should I trust to Repentance on my Death-Bed, since I may die in my sleep? What fine things are good Advice and good Examples! But I am glad she turned me out of the Chamber as she did: for I had once almost forgotten every Word Parson *Adams* had ever said to me.

'I don't doubt, dear Sister, but you will have Grace to preserve your Virtue against all Trials; and I beg you earnestly to pray, I may be enabled to preserve mine: for truly, it is very severely attacked by more than one: but, I hope I shall copy your Example, and that of *Joseph*, my Name's-sake; and maintain my Virtue against all Temptations.'

Joseph had not finished his Letter, when he was summoned down stairs by Mr *Peter Pounce*, to receive his Wages: for, besides that out of eight Pounds a Year, he allowed his Father and Mother four, he had been obliged, in order to furnish himself with musical Instruments, to apply to the Generosity of the aforesaid *Peter*, who, on urgent Occasions, used to advance the Servants their Wages: not before they were due, but before they were payable; that is, perhaps, half a Year after they were due, and this at the moderate *Premiums* of fifty *per Cent*[3] or a little more; by which charitable Methods, together with lending Money to other People, and even to his own Master and Mistress, the honest Man had, from nothing, in a few Years amassed a small Sum of twenty thousand Pounds or thereabouts.

Joseph having received his little Remainder of Wages, and having stript off his Livery, was forced to borrow a Frock[4] and Breeches of one of the Servants: (for he was so beloved in the Family, that they would all have lent him any thing) and being told by *Peter*, that he must not stay a Moment longer in the House than was necessary to pack up his Linnen, which he easily did in a very narrow Compass; he took a melancholy Leave of his Fellow-Servants, and set out at Seven in the Evening.

He had proceeded the length of two or three Streets, before he absolutely determined with himself, whether he should leave the town that Night, or procuring a Lodging, wait till the Morning. At last, the Moon shining very bright, helped him to come to a Resolution of beginning his Journey immediately, to which likewise he had some other Inducements which the Reader, without being a Conjurer, cannot possibly guess, 'till we have given him those hints, which it may be now proper to open.

CHAPTER XI

Of several new Matters not expected.

It is an Observation sometimes made, to indicate our Idea of a simple Fellow, *That he is easily to be seen through*: Nor do I believe it a more improper Denotation of a simple Book. Instead of applying this to any particular Performance, we chuse rather to remark the contrary in this History, where the Scene opens itself by small degrees, and he is a sagacious Reader who can see two Chapters before him.

For this reason, we have not hitherto hinted a Matter which now seems necessary to be explained; since it may be wondered at, first, that *Joseph* made such extraordinary haste out of Town, which hath been already shewn; and secondly, which will be now shewn, that instead of proceeding to the Habitation of his Father and Mother, or to his beloved Sister *Pamela*, he chose rather to set out full speed to the Lady *Booby*'s Country Seat, which he had left on his Journey to *London*.

Be it known then, that in the same Parish where this Seat stood, there lived a young Girl whom *Joseph* (tho' the best of Sons and Brothers) longed more impatiently to see than his Parents or his Sister. She was a poor Girl, who had been formerly bred up in Sir *John*'s Family;[1] whence a little before the Journey to *London*, she had been discarded by Mrs *Slipslop* on account of her extraordinary Beauty: for I never could find any other reason.

This young Creature (who now lived with a Farmer in the Parish) had been always beloved by *Joseph*, and returned his Affection. She was two Years only younger than our Hero. They had been acquainted from their Infancy, and had conceived a very early liking for each other, which had grown to such a degree of Affection, that Mr *Adams* had with much ado prevented them from marrying; and persuaded them to wait, 'till a few Years Service and Thrift had a little improved their Experience, and enabled them to live comfortably together.

They followed this good Man's Advice; as indeed his Word was little less than a Law in his Parish: for as he had shewn his Parishioners by a uniform Behaviour of thirty-five Years duration, that he had their Good entirely at heart; so they consulted him on every Occasion, and very seldom acted contrary to his Opinion.

Nothing can be imagined more tender than was the parting between these two Lovers. A thousand Sighs heaved the Bosom of *Joseph*; a thousand Tears distilled from the lovely Eyes of *Fanny*, (for that was her Name,) tho' her Modesty would only suffer her to admit his eager Kisses, her violent Love made her more than passive in his Embraces; and she often pulled him to her Breast with a soft Pressure, which, tho' perhaps it would not have squeezed an Insect to death, caused more Emotion in the Heart of *Joseph*, than the closest *Cornish* Hug could have done.[2]

The Reader may perhaps wonder, that so fond a Pair should during a Twelve-month's Absence never converse with one another; indeed there was but one Reason which did, or could have prevented them; and this was, that poor *Fanny* could neither write nor read, nor could she be prevailed upon to transmit the Delicacies of her tender and chaste Passion, by the Hands of an *Amanuensis*.

They contented themselves therefore with frequent Enquiries after each other's Health, with a mutual Confidence in each other's Fidelity, and the Prospect of their future Happiness.

Having explained these Matters to our Reader, and, as far as possible, satisfied all his Doubts, we return to honest *Joseph*, whom we left just set out on his Travels by the Light of the Moon.

Those who have read any Romance or Poetry antient or modern, must have been informed, that Love hath Wings; by which they are not to understand, as some young Ladies by mistake have done, that a Lover can fly: the Writers, by this ingenious Allegory, intending to insinuate no more, than that Lovers do not march like Horse-Guards; in short, that they put the best Leg foremost, which our lusty Youth, who could walk with any Man, did so heartily on this Occasion, that within four Hours, he reached a famous House of Hospitality well known to the Western Traveller. It presents you a Lion on the Sign-Post: and the Master, who was christened *Timotheus*, is commonly called plain *Tim*.[3] Some have conceived that he hath particularly chosen the Lion for his Sign, as he doth in Countenance greatly resemble that magnanimous Beast, tho' his Disposition favours more of the Sweetness of the Lamb. He is a Person well received among all sorts of Men, being qualified to render himself agreeable to any; as he is well versed in History and Politicks, hath a smattering in Law and Divinity, cracks a good Jest, and plays wonderfully well on the *French* Horn.

A violent Storm of Hail forced *Joseph* to take Shelter in this Inn, where he remembered Sir *Thomas* had dined in his way to Town. *Joseph* had no sooner seated himself by the Kitchen-Fire, than *Timotheus*, observing his

Livery, began to condole the loss of his late Master; who was, he said, his very particular and intimate Acquaintance, with whom he had cracked many a merry Bottle, aye many a dozen in his Time. He then remarked that all those Things were over now, all past, and just as if they had never been; and concluded with an excellent Observation on the Certainty of Death, which his Wife said was indeed very true. A Fellow now arrived at the same Inn with two Horses, one of which he was leading farther down into the Country to meet his Master; these he put into the Stable, and came and took his Place by *Joseph*'s Side, who immediately knew him to be the Servant of a neighbouring Gentleman, who used to visit at their House.

This Fellow was likewise forced in by the Storm; for he had Orders to go twenty Miles farther that Evening, and luckily on the same Road which *Joseph* himself intended to take. He therefore embraced this Opportunity of complimenting his Friend with his Master's Horses, (notwithstanding he had received express commands to the contrary) which was readily accepted; and so after they had drank a loving Pot, and the Storm was over, they set out together.

CHAPTER XII

Containing many surprizing Adventures, which Joseph Andrews met with on the Road, scarce credible by those who have never travelled in a Stage-Coach.[1]

Nothing remarkable happened on the Road, 'till their arrival at the Inn, whither the Horses were ordered: where they came about two in the Morning. The Moon then shone very bright, and *Joseph* making his Friend a present of a Pint of Wine, and thanking him for the favour of his Horse, notwithstanding all Entreaties to the contrary, proceeded on his Journey on foot.

He had not gone above two Miles, charmed with the hopes of shortly seeing his beloved *Fanny*, when he was met by two Fellows in a narrow Lane, and ordered to stand and deliver. He readily gave them all the Money he had, which was somewhat less than two Pounds; and told them he hoped they would be so generous as to return him a few Shillings, to defray his Charges on his way home.

One of the Ruffians answered with an Oath, *Yes, we'll give you something presently: but first strip and be d—n'd to you.* —— *Strip*, cry'd the other, *or I'll blow your Brains to the Devil. Joseph*, remembring that he had borrowed his Coat and Breeches of a Friend; and that he should be ashamed of making any Excuse for not returning them, reply'd, he hoped they would not insist on his Clothes, which were not worth much, but consider the Coldness of the Night. *You are cold, are you, you Rascal!* says one of the Robbers, *I'll warm you with a Vengeance*; and, damning his Eyes, snapt a Pistol at his Head: which he had no sooner done, than the other levell'd a Blow at him with his Stick, which *Joseph*, who was expert at Cudgel-playing, caught with his, and returned the Favour so successfully on his Adversary, that he laid him sprawling at his Feet, and at the same Instant received a Blow from behind, with the Butt-end of a Pistol from the other Villain, which felled him to the Ground, and totally deprived him of his Senses.

The Thief, who had been knocked down, had now recovered himself; and both together fell to be-labouring poor *Joseph* with their Sticks, till they were convinced they had put an end to his miserable Being: They then stript him entirely naked, threw him into a Ditch, and departed with their Booty.

The poor Wretch, who lay motionless a long time, just began to recover his Senses as a Stage-Coach came by. The Postillion hearing a Man's Groans, stopt his Horses, and told the Coachman, He was certain there was a *dead* Man lying in the Ditch, for he heard him groan. 'Go on, Sirrah,' says the Coachman, 'we are confounded late, and have no time to look after dead Men.' A Lady, who heard what the Postillion said, and likewise heard the Groan, called eagerly to the Coachman, To stop and see what was the matter. Upon which he bid the Postillion alight, and look into the Ditch. He did so, and returned, 'That there was a Man sitting upright as naked as ever he was born.' —— 'O *J—sus*,' cry'd the Lady, 'A naked Man! Dear Coachman, drive on and leave him.' Upon this the Gentlemen got out of the Coach; and *Joseph* begged them, to have Mercy upon him: For that he had been robbed, and almost beaten to death. 'Robbed,' cries an old Gentleman; 'Let us make all the haste imaginable, or we shall be robbed too.' A young Man, who belonged to the Law answered, 'He wished they had past by without taking any Notice: But that now they might be proved to have been *last in his Company*, if he should die, they might be called to some account for his Murder. He therefore thought it adviseable to save the poor Creature's Life, for their own sakes, if possible; at least, if he died, to prevent the Jury's finding *that they fled for it.*[2] He was therefore *of Opinion*, to take the Man into the Coach, and carry him to the next Inn.' The Lady insisted, 'That he should not come into the Coach. That if they lifted him in, she would herself alight: for she had rather stay in that Place to all Eternity, than ride with a naked Man.' The Coachman objected, 'That he could not suffer him to be taken in, unless somebody would pay a Shilling for his Carriage the four Miles.' Which the two Gentlemen refused to do; but the Lawyer, who was afraid of some Mischief happening to himself if the Wretch was left behind in that Condition, saying, No Man could be too cautious in these Matters, and that he remembered very extraordinary Cases in the Books, threatned the Coachman, and bid him deny taking him up at his Peril; for that if he died, he should be indicted for his Murder, and if he lived, and brought an Action against him, he would willingly take a Brief in it. These Words had a sensible Effect on the Coachman, who was well acquainted with the Person who spoke them; and the old Gentleman abovementioned, thinking the naked Man would afford him frequent Opportunities of shewing his Wit to the Lady, offered to join with the Company in giving a Mug of Beer for his Fare; till partly alarmed by the Threats of the one, and partly by the Promises of the other, and being perhaps *a little* moved with Compassion at the poor Creature's Condition, who stood bleeding and shivering with the Cold, he at length agreed; and *Joseph* was now advancing to the Coach, where seeing the Lady, who held the Sticks of her Fan before her Eyes, he absolutely refused, miserable as he was, to enter, unless he was furnished with sufficient Covering, to prevent giving the least Offence to Decency. So perfectly modest was this young Man: such mighty Effects had the spotless Example of the amiable *Pamela*, and the excellent Sermons of Mr *Adams* wrought upon him.

Though there were several Great Coats about the Coach, it was not easy to get over this Difficulty which *Joseph* had started. The two Gentlemen complained they were cold, and could not spare a Rag; the Man of Wit saying, with a Laugh, *that Charity began at home*; and the Coachman, who had two great Coats spread under him, refused to lend either, lest they should be made bloody; the Lady's Footman desired to be excused for the same Reason, which the Lady herself, notwithstanding her Abhorrence of a naked Man, approved: and it is more than probable, poor *Joseph*, who obstinately adhered to his modest Resolution, must have perished, unless the Postillion, (a Lad who hath been since transported for robbing a Hen-roost) had voluntarily stript off a great Coat, his only Garment, at the same time swearing a great Oath, (for which he was rebuked by the

Passengers) 'That he would rather ride in his Shirt all his Life, than suffer a Fellow-Creature to lie in so miserable a Condition.'

Joseph, having put on the great Coat, was lifted into the Coach, which now proceeded on its Journey. He declared himself almost dead with the Cold, which gave the Man of Wit an occasion to ask the Lady, if she could not accommodate him with a Dram. She answered with some Resentment, 'She wondered at his asking her such a Question;' but assured him, 'She never tasted any such thing.'

The Lawyer was enquiring into the Circumstances of the Robbery, when the Coach stopt, and one of the Ruffians, putting a Pistol in, demanded their Money of the Passengers; who readily gave it them; and the Lady, in her Fright, delivered up a little silver Bottle, of about a half-pint Size, which, the Rogue clapping it to his Mouth, and drinking her Health, declared held some of the best *Nantes*³ he had ever tasted: this the Lady afterwards assured the Company was the Mistake of her Maid, for that she had ordered her to fill the Bottle with *Hungary* Water.⁴

As soon as the Fellows were departed, the Lawyer, who had, it seems, a Case of Pistols in the Seat of the Coach, informed the Company, that if it had been Day-light, and he could have come at his Pistols, he would not have submitted to the Robbery; he likewise set forth, that he had often met Highwaymen when he travelled on horseback, but none ever durst attack him; concluding, that if he had not been more afraid for the Lady than for himself, he should not have now parted with his Money so easily.

As Wit is generally observed to love to reside in empty Pockets; so the Gentleman, whose Ingenuity we have above remark'd, as soon as he had parted with his Money, began to grow wonderfully facetious. He made frequent Allusions to *Adam* and *Eve*, and said many excellent things on Figs and Fig-Leaves; which perhaps gave more Offence to *Joseph* than to any other in the Company.

The Lawyer likewise made several very pretty Jests, without departing from his Profession. He said, 'If *Joseph* and the Lady were alone, he would be the more capable of making a *Conveyance* to her, as his *Affairs* were not *fettered* with any *Incumbrance*; he'd warrant, he soon suffered a *Recovery* by a Writ of *Entry*, which was the proper way to create *Heirs in Tail*; that for his own part, he would engage to make so *firm a Settlement* in a Coach, that there should be no Danger of an *Ejectment*;'⁵ with an Inundation of the like Gibbrish, which he continued to vent till the Coach arrived at an Inn, where one Servant-Maid only was up in readiness to attend the

Coachman, and furnish him with cold Meat and a Dram. *Joseph* desired to alight, and that he might have a Bed prepared for him, which the Maid readily promised to perform; and being a good-natur'd Wench, and not so squeamish as the Lady had been, she clapt a large Faggot on the Fire, and furnishing *Joseph* with a great Coat belonging to one of the Hostlers, desired him to sit down and warm himself, whilst she made his Bed. The Coachman, in the mean time, took an Opportunity to call up a Surgeon, who lived within a few Doors: after which, he reminded his Passengers how late they were, and after they had taken Leave of *Joseph*, hurried them off as fast as he could.

The Wench soon got *Joseph* to bed, and promised to use her Interest to borrow him a Shirt; but imagined, as she afterwards said, by his being so bloody, that he must be a dead Man: she ran with all speed to hasten the Surgeon, who was more than half drest, apprehending that the Coach had been overturned and some Gentleman or Lady hurt. As soon as the Wench had informed him at his Window, that it was a poor foot Passenger who had been stripped of all he had, and almost murdered; he chid her for disturbing him so early, slipped off his Clothes again, and very quietly returned to bed and to sleep.

Aurora[6] now began to shew her blooming Cheeks over the Hills, whilst ten Millions of feathered Songsters, in jocund Chorus, repeated Odes a thousand times sweeter than those of our *Laureate*, and sung both *the Day and the Song;*[7] when the Master of the Inn, Mr *Tow-wouse*,[8] arose, and learning from his Maid an Account of the Robbery, and the Situation of his poor naked Guest, he shook his Head, and cried, *Good-lack-a-day!* and then ordered the Girl to carry him one of his own Shirts.

Mrs *Tow-wouse* was just awake, and had stretched out her Arms in vain to fold her departed Husband, when the Maid entered the Room. 'Who's there, *Betty*?' 'Yes Madam.' 'Where's your Master?' 'He's without, Madam; he hath sent me for a Shirt to lend a poor naked Man, who hath been robbed and murdered.' 'Touch one, if you dare, you Slut,' said Mrs *Tow-wouse*, 'your Master is a pretty sort of a Man to take in naked Vagabonds, and clothe them with his own Clothes. I shall have no such Doings. — If you offer to touch any thing, I will throw the Chamber-Pot at your Head. Go, send your Master to me.' 'Yes Madam,' answered *Betty*. As soon as he came in, she thus began: 'What the Devil do you mean by this, Mr *Tow-wouse*? Am I to buy Shirts to lend to a sett of scabby Rascals?' 'My Dear,' said Mr *Tow-wouse*, 'this is a poor Wretch.' 'Yes,' says she, 'I know it is a poor Wretch, but what the Devil have we to do with poor Wretches? The Law makes us provide for too many already. We shall have thirty or forty poor Wretches in red Coats⁹ shortly.' 'My Dear,' cries *Tow-wouse*, 'this Man hath been robbed of all he hath.' 'Well then,' says she, 'where's his Money to pay his Reckoning? Why doth not such a Fellow go to an Ale-house?¹⁰ I shall send him packing as soon as I am up, I assure you.' 'My Dear,' said he, 'common Charity won't suffer you to do that.' 'Common Charity, a F—t!' says she, 'Common Charity teaches us to provide for ourselves, and our Families; and I and mine won't be ruined by your Charity, I assure you.' 'Well,' says he, 'my Dear, do as you will when you are up, you know I never contradict you.' 'No,' says she, 'if the Devil was to contradict me, I would make the House too hot to hold him.'

With such like Discourses they consumed near half an Hour, whilst *Betty* provided a Shirt from the Hostler, who was one of her Sweethearts, and put it on poor *Joseph*. The Surgeon had likewise at last visited him, had washed and drest his Wounds, and was now come to acquaint Mr *Tow-wouse*, that his Guest was in such extreme danger of his Life, that he scarce saw any hopes of his Recovery. — 'Here's a pretty Kettle of Fish,' cries Mrs *Tow-wouse*, 'you have brought upon us! We are like to have a Funeral at our own expence.' *Tow-wouse*, (who notwithstanding his Charity, would have given his Vote as freely as he ever did at an Election, that any other House in the Kingdom, should have had quiet Possession of his Guest) answered, 'My Dear, I am not to blame: he was brought hither by the Stage-Coach; and *Betty* had put him to bed before I was stirring.' 'I'll *Betty* her,' says she — At which, with half her Garments on, the other half under her Arm, she sallied out in quest of the unfortunate *Betty*, whilst *Tow-wouse* and the Surgeon went to pay a Visit to poor *Joseph*, and enquire into the Circumstance of this melancholy Affair.

CHAPTER XIII

What happened to Joseph *during his Sickness at the Inn, with the curious Discourse between him and Mr* Barnabas *the Parson of the Parish.*

As soon as *Joseph* had communicated a particular History of the Robbery, together with a short Account of himself, and his intended Journey, he asked the Surgeon, If he apprehended him to be in any Danger: To which the Surgeon very honestly answered, 'He feared he was; for that his Pulse was very exalted and feverish, and if his Fever should prove more than *Symptomatick*,[1] it would be impossible to save him. '*Joseph*, fetching a deep Sigh, cried, '*Poor* Fanny, *I would I could have lived to see thee! but* G—'s *Will be done.*'

The Surgeon then advised him, 'If he had any worldly Affairs to settle, that he would do it as soon as possible; for though he hoped he might recover, yet he thought himself obliged to acquaint him he was in great danger, and if the malign Concoction of his Humours should cause a suscitation of his Fever,[2] he might soon grow delirious, and incapable to make his Will.' *Joseph* answered, 'That it was impossible for any Creature in the Universe to be in a poorer Condition than himself: for since the Robbery, he had not one thing of any kind whatever, which he could call his own.' *I had,* said he, *a poor little Piece of Gold which they took away, that would have been a Comfort to me in all my Afflictions; but surely,* Fanny, *I want nothing to remind me of thee. I have thy dear Image in my Heart, and no Villain can ever tear it thence.*

Joseph desired Paper and Pens to write a Letter, but they were refused him; and he was advised to use all his Endeavours to compose himself. They then left him; and Mr *Tow-wouse* sent to a Clergyman to come and administer his good Offices to the Soul of poor *Joseph*, since the Surgeon despaired of making any successful Applications to his Body.

Mr *Barnabas*[3] (for that was the Clergyman's Name) came as soon as sent for, and having first drank a Dish of Tea with the Landlady, and afterwards a Bowl of Punch with the Landlord, he walked up to the Room where *Joseph* lay: but, finding him asleep, returned to take the other Sneaker;[4] which when he had finished, he again crept softly up to the Chamber-Door, and, having opened it, heard the Sick Man talking to himself in the following manner:

'O most adorable *Pamela!* most virtuous Sister! whose Example could alone enable me to withstand all the Temptations of Riches and Beauty, and to preserve my Virtue pure and chaste, for the Arms of my dear *Fanny*, if it had pleased Heaven that I should ever have come unto them. What Riches, or Honours, or Pleasures can make us amends for the Loss of Innocence? Doth not that alone afford us more Consolation, than all worldly Acquisitions? What but Innocence and Virtue could give any Comfort to such a miserable Wretch as I am? Yet these can make me prefer this sick and painful Bed to all the Pleasures I should have found in my Lady's. These can make me face Death without Fear; and though I love my *Fanny* more than ever Man loved a Woman; these can teach me to resign myself to the Divine Will without repining. O thou delightful charming Creature, would Heaven have indulged thee to my Arms, the poorest, humblest State would have been a Paradise; I could have lived with thee in the lowest Cottage, without envying the Palaces, the Dainties, or the Riches of any Man breathing. But I must leave thee, leave thee for ever, my dearest Angel, I must think of another World, and I heartily pray thou may'st meet Comfort in this.' — *Barnabas* thought he had heard enough; so down stairs he went, and told *Tow-wouse* he could do his Guest no Service: for that he was very light-headed, and had uttered nothing but a Rhapsody of Nonsense all the time he stayed in the Room.

The Surgeon returned in the Afternoon, and found his Patient in a higher Fever, as he said, than when he left him, though not delirious: for notwithstanding Mr *Barnabas*'s Opinion, he had not been once out of his Senses since his arrival at the Inn.

Mr *Barnabas* was again sent for, and with much difficulty prevailed on to make another Visit. As soon as he entered the Room, he told *Joseph*, 'He was come to pray by him, and to prepare him for another World: In the first place therefore, he hoped he had repented of all his Sins?' *Joseph* answered, 'He hoped he had: but there was one thing which he knew not whether he should call a Sin; if it was, he feared he should die in the Commission of it, and that was the Regret of parting with a young Woman, whom he loved as tenderly as he did his Heart-strings?' *Barnabas* bad him be assured, that 'any Repining at the Divine Will, was one of the greatest Sins he could commit; that he ought to forget all carnal Affections, and think of better things.' *Joseph* said, 'That neither in this World nor the next, he could forget his *Fanny*, and that the Thought, however grievous, of parting from her for ever, was not half so tormenting, as the Fear of what she would suffer when she knew his Misfortune.' *Barnabas* said, 'That such Fears argued a Diffidence and Despondence very criminal; that he must divest himself of all human Passion, and fix his Heart above.' *Joseph* answered, 'That was what he desired to do, and should be obliged to him, if he would enable him to accomplish it.' *Barnabas* replied, 'That must be done by Grace.' *Joseph* besought him to discover how he might attain it. *Barnabas* answered, 'By Prayer and Faith.' He then questioned him concerning his Forgiveness of the Thieves. *Joseph* answered, 'He feared, that was more than he could do: for nothing would give him more Pleasure than to hear they were taken.' 'That,' cries *Barnabas*, 'is for the sake of Justice.' 'Yes,' said *Joseph*, 'but if I was to meet them again, I am afraid I should attack them, and kill them too, if I could.' 'Doubtless,' answered

Barnabas, 'it is lawful to kill a Thief: but can you say, you forgive them as a Christian ought?' *Joseph* desired to know what that Forgiveness was. 'That is,' answered *Barnabas*, 'to forgive them as — as — it is to forgive them as —— in short, it is to forgive them as a Christian.' *Joseph* reply'd, 'He forgave them as much as he could.' 'Well, well,' said *Barnabas*, 'that will do.' He then demanded of him, 'if he remembered any more Sins unrepented of; and if he did, he desired him to make haste and repent of them as fast as he could: that they might repeat over a few Prayers together.' *Joseph* answered, 'He could not recollect any great Crimes he had been guilty of, and that those he had committed, he was sincerely sorry for.' *Barnabas* said that was enough, and then proceeded to Prayer with all the expedition he was master of: Some Company then waiting for him below in the Parlour, where the Ingredients for Punch were all in Readiness; but no one would squeeze the Oranges 'till he came.

Joseph complained he was dry, and desired a little Tea; which *Barnabas* reported to Mrs *Tow-wouse*, who answered, 'She had just done drinking it, and could not be slopping all day;' but ordered *Betty* to carry him up some Small Beer.[5]

Betty obeyed her Mistress's Commands; but *Joseph*, as soon as he had tasted it, said, he feared it would increase his Fever, and that he longed very much for Tea: To which the good-natured *Betty* answered, he should have Tea, if there was any in the Land; she accordingly went and bought him some herself, and attended him with it; where we will leave her and *Joseph* together for some time, to entertain the Reader with other Matters.

CHAPTER XIV

Being very full of Adventures, which succeeded each other at the Inn.

It was now the Dusk of the Evening, when a grave Person rode into the Inn, and committing his Horse to the Hostler, went directly into the Kitchin, and having called for a Pipe of Tobacco, took his place by the Fire-side; where several other Persons were likewise assembled.

The Discourse ran altogether on the Robbery which was committed the Night before, and on the poor Wretch, who lay above in the dreadful Condition, in which we have already seen him. Mrs *Tow-wouse* said, 'She wondered what the devil *Tom Whipwell* meant by bringing such Guests to her House, when there were so many Ale-houses on the Road proper for their Reception? But she assured him, if he died, the Parish should be at the Expence of the Funeral.' She added, 'Nothing would serve the Fellow's Turn but Tea, she would assure him.' *Betty*, who was just returned from her charitable Office, answered, she believed he was a Gentleman, for she never saw a finer Skin in her Life. 'Pox on his Skin,' replied Mrs *Tow-wouse*, 'I suppose, that is all we are like to have for the Reckoning. I desire no such Gentlemen should ever call at the *Dragon*;' (which it seems was the Sign of the Inn.)

The Gentleman lately arrived discovered a great deal of Emotion at the Distress of this poor Creature, whom he observed not to be fallen into the most compassionate Hands. And indeed, if Mrs *Tow-wouse* had given no Utterance to the Sweetness of her Temper, Nature had taken such Pains in her Countenance, that *Hogarth* himself never gave more Expression to a Picture.

Her Person was short, thin, and crooked. Her Forehead projected in the middle, and thence descended in a Declivity to the Top of her Nose, which was sharp and red, and would have hung over her Lips, had not Nature turned up the end of it. Her Lips were two Bits of Skin, which, whenever she spoke, she drew together in a Purse. Her Chin was peeked,[1] and at the upper end of that Skin, which composed her Cheeks, stood two Bones, that almost hid a Pair of small red Eyes. Add to this, a Voice most wonderfully adapted to the Sentiments it was to convey, being both loud and hoarse.

It is not easy to say, whether the Gentleman had conceived a greater Dislike for his Landlady, or Compassion for her unhappy Guest. He enquired very earnestly of the Surgeon, who was now come into the Kitchin, Whether he had any hopes of his Recovery? he begged him, to use all possible means towards it, telling him, 'it was the duty of Men of all Professions, to apply their Skill *gratis* for the Relief of the Poor and Necessitous.' The Surgeon answered, 'he should take proper care: but he defied all the Surgeons in *London* to do him any good.' 'Pray, Sir,' said the Gentleman, 'What are his Wounds?' —— 'Why, do you know any thing of Wounds?' says the Surgeon, (winking upon Mrs *Tow-wouse*.) 'Sir, I have a small smattering in Surgery,' answered the Gentleman. 'A smattering, — ho, ho, ho!' said the Surgeon, 'I believe it is a smattering indeed.'

The Company were all attentive, expecting to hear the Doctor, who was what they call a dry Fellow, expose the Gentleman.

He began therefore with an Air of Triumph: 'I suppose, Sir, you have travelled.' 'No really, Sir,' said the Gentleman. 'Ho! then you have practised in the Hospitals perhaps.' —— 'No, Sir.' 'Hum! not that neither? Whence, Sir, then, if I may be so bold to enquire, have you got your Knowledge in Surgery?' 'Sir,' answered the Gentleman, 'I do not pretend to much; but, the little I know I have from Books.' 'Books!' cries the Doctor. —— 'What, I suppose you have read *Galen* and *Hippocrates!*' 'No, Sir,' said the Gentleman. 'How! you understand Surgery,' answers the Doctor, 'and not read *Galen* and *Hippocrates?*' 'Sir,' cries the other, 'I believe there are many Surgeons who have never read these Authors.' 'I believe so too,' says the Doctor, 'more shame for them: but thanks to my Education, I have them by heart, and very seldom go without them both in my Pocket.' 'They are pretty large Books,' said the Gentleman.[2] 'Aye,' said the Doctor, 'I believe I know how large they are better than you,' (at which he fell a winking, and the whole Company burst into a Laugh.)

The Doctor pursuing his Triumph, asked the Gentleman, 'if he did not understand Physick as well as Surgery.' 'Rather better,' answered the Gentleman. 'Aye, like enough,' cries the Doctor, with a wink. 'Why, I know a little of Physick too.' 'I wish I knew half so much,' said *Tow-wouse*, 'I'd never wear an Apron again.' 'Why, I believe, Landlord,' cries the Doctor, there are few Men, tho' I say it, within twelve Miles of the Place, that handle a Fever better. — *Veniente accurrite Morbo:*[3] That is my Method. — I suppose Brother, you understand *Latin?*' 'A little,' says the Gentleman. 'Aye, and *Greek* now I'll warrant you: *Ton dapomibominos poluflosboio Thalasses.*[4] But I have almost forgot these things, I could have repeated *Homer* by heart once.' — 'Ifags! the Gentleman has caught a *Traytor*,'[5] says Mrs *Tow-wouse*; at which they all fell a laughing.

The Gentleman, who had not the least affection for joking, very contentedly suffered the Doctor to enjoy his Victory; which he did with no small Satisfaction: and having sufficiently sounded his Depth, told him, 'he was thoroughly convinced of his great Learning and Abilities; and that he would be obliged to him, if he would let him know his opinion of his Patient's Case above stairs.' 'Sir,' says the Doctor, 'his Case is that of a dead Man — The Contusion on his Head has *perforated* the *internal Membrane* of the *Occiput*, and *divellicated* that *radical* small *minute* invisible *Nerve*, which *coheres* to the *Pericranium*; and this was attended with a Fever at first *symptomatick*, then *pneumatick*,[6] and he is at length *grown deliruus*, or delirious, as the Vulgar express it.'

He was proceeding in this learned manner, when a mighty Noise interrupted him. Some young Fellows in the Neighbourhood had taken one of the Thieves, and were bringing him into the Inn. *Betty* ran up Stairs with this News to *Joseph*; who begged they might search for a little piece of broken Gold, which had a Ribband tied on it, and which he could swear to amongst all the Hoards of the richest Man in the Universe.

Notwithstanding the Fellow's persisting in his Innocence, the Mob were very busy in searching him, and presently, among other things, pulled out the Piece of Gold just mentioned; which *Betty* no sooner saw, than she laid violent hands on it, and conveyed it up to *Joseph*, who received it with raptures of Joy, and hugging it in his Bosom declared, *he could now die contented*.

Within a few Minutes afterwards, came in some other Fellows, with a Bundle which they had found in a Ditch; and which was indeed the Clothes which had been stripped off from *Joseph*, and the other things they had taken from him.

The Gentleman no sooner saw the Coat, than he declared he knew the Livery; and if it had been taken from the poor Creature above stairs, desired he might see him; for that he was very well acquainted with the Family to whom that Livery belonged.

He was accordingly conducted up by *Betty*: but what, Reader, was the surprize on both sides, when he saw *Joseph* was the Person in Bed; and when *Joseph* discovered the Face of his good Friend Mr *Abraham Adams*.

It would be impertinent to insert a Discourse which chiefly turned on the relation of Matters already well known to the Reader: for as soon as the Curate had satisfied *Joseph* concerning the perfect Health of his *Fanny*, he was on his side very inquisitive into all the Particulars which had produced this unfortunate Accident.

To return therefore to the Kitchin, where a great variety of Company were now assembled from all the Rooms of the House, as well as the Neighbourhood: so much delight do Men take in contemplating the Countenance of a Thief:

Mr *Tow-wouse* began to rub his Hands with pleasure, at seeing so large an Assembly; who would, he hoped, shortly adjourn into several Apartments, in order to discourse over the Robbery; and drink a Health to all honest Men: but Mrs *Tow-wouse*, whose Misfortune it was commonly to see things a little perversly, began to rail at those who brought the Fellow into her House; telling her Husband, 'they were very likely to thrive, who kept a House of Entertainment for Beggars and Thieves.'

The Mob had now finished their search; and could find nothing about the Captive likely to prove any Evidence: for as to the Clothes, tho' the Mob were very well satisfied with that Proof; yet, as the Surgeon observed, they could not convict him, because they were not found in his Custody; to which *Barnabas* agreed: and added, that these were *Bona Waviata*, and belonged to the Lord of the Manor.[7]

'How,' says the Surgeon, 'do you say these Goods belong to the Lord of the Manor?' 'I do,' cried *Barnabas*. 'Then I deny it,' says the Surgeon. 'What can the Lord of the Manor have to do in the Case? Will any one attempt to persuade me that what a Man finds is not his own?' 'I have heard,' (says an old Fellow in the Corner) 'Justice *Wise-one* say, that if every Man had his right, whatever is found belongs to the King of *London*.' 'That may be true,' says *Barnabas*, 'in some sense: for the Law makes a difference between things stolen, and things found: for a thing may be stolen that never is found; and a thing may be found that never was stolen. Now Goods that are both stolen and found are *Waviata*; and they belong to the Lord of the Manor.' 'So the Lord of the Manor is the Receiver of stolen Goods:' (says the Doctor) at which there was a universal Laugh, being first begun by himself.

While the Prisoner, by persisting in his Innocence, had almost (as there was no Evidence against him) brought over *Barnabas*, the Surgeon, *Tow-wouse*, and several others to his side; *Betty* informed them, that they had over-looked a little Piece of Gold, which she had carried up to the Man in bed; and which he offered to swear to amongst a Million, aye, amongst ten Thousand. This immediately turned the Scale against the Prisoner; and every one now concluded him guilty. It was resolved therefore, to keep him secured that Night, and early in the Morning to carry him before a Justice.

CHAPTER XV

Shewing how Mrs Tow-wouse *was a little mollified; and how officious Mr* Barnabas *and the Surgeon were to prosecute the Thief: With a Dissertation accounting for their Zeal; and that of many other Persons not mentioned in this History.*

Betty told her Mistress, she believed the Man in Bed was a greater Man than they took him for: for besides the extreme Whiteness of his Skin, and the Softness of his Hands; she observed a very great Familiarity between the Gentleman and him; and added, she was certain they were intimate Acquaintance, if not Relations.

This somewhat abated the severity of Mrs *Tow-wouse*'s Countenance. She said, 'God forbid she should not discharge the Duty of a Christian, since the poor Gentleman was brought to her House. She had a natural Antipathy to Vagabonds: but could pity the Misfortunes of a Christian as soon as another. '*Tow-wouse* said, 'If the Traveller be a Gentleman, tho' he hath no Money about him now, we shall most likely be paid hereafter; so you may begin to score[1] whenever you will.' Mrs *Tow-wouse* answered, 'Hold your simple Tongue, and don't instruct me in my Business. I am sure I am sorry for the Gentleman's Misfortune with all my heart, and I hope the Villain who hath used him so barbarously will be hanged. *Betty*, go, see what he wants. G— forbid he should want any thing in my House.'

Barnabas and the Surgeon went up to *Joseph*, to satisfy themselves concerning the piece of Gold. *Joseph* was with difficulty prevailed upon to shew it them; but would by no Entreaties be brought to deliver it out of his own Possession. He, however, attested this to be the same which had been taken from him; and *Betty* was ready to swear to the finding it on the Thief.

The only Difficulty that remained, was how to produce this Gold before the Justice: for as to carrying *Joseph* himself, it seemed impossible; nor was there any greater likelihood of obtaining it from him: for he had fastened it with a Ribband to his Arm, and solemnly vowed, that nothing but irresistible Force should ever separate them; in which Resolution, Mr *Adams*, clenching a Fist rather less than the Knuckle of an Ox, declared he would support him.

A Dispute arose on this Occasion concerning Evidence, not very necessary to be related here; after which the Surgeon dress'd Mr *Joseph*'s Head; still persisting in the imminent Danger in which his Patient lay: but concluding with a very important Look, 'that he began to have some hopes; that he should send him a *Sanative soporiferous* Draught,[2] and would see him in the Morning.' After which *Barnabas* and he departed, and left Mr *Joseph* and Mr *Adams* together.

Adams informed *Joseph* of the occasion of this Journey which he was making to *London*, namely to publish three Volumes of Sermons; being encouraged, he said, by an Advertisement lately set forth by a Society of Booksellers, who proposed to purchase any Copies offered to them at a Price to be settled by two Persons:[3] but tho' he imagined he should get a considerable Sum of Money on this occasion, which his Family were in urgent need of; he protested, he would not leave *Joseph* in his present

Condition: finally, he told him, 'he had nine Shillings and three-pence half-penny in his Pocket, which he was welcome to use as he pleased.'

This Goodness of Parson *Adams* brought Tears into *Joseph*'s Eyes; he declared 'he had now a second Reason to desire Life, that he might shew his Gratitude to such a Friend.' *Adams* bad him 'be chearful, for that he plainly saw the Surgeon, besides his Ignorance, desired to make a Merit of curing him, tho' the Wounds in his Head, he perceived, were by no means dangerous; that he was convinced he had no Fever, and doubted not but he would be able to travel in a day or two.'

These Words infused a Spirit into *Joseph*; he said, 'he found himself very sore from the Bruises, but had no reason to think any of his Bones injured, or that he had received any Harm in his Inside; unless that he felt something very odd in his Stomach: but he knew not whether that might not arise from not having eaten one Morsel for above twenty-four Hours.' Being then asked, if he had any Inclination to eat, he answered in the Affirmative; then Parson *Adams* desired him to name what he had the greatest Fancy for; whether a poached Egg, or Chicken-broth: he answered 'he could eat both very well; but that he seemed to have the greatest Appetite for a piece of boiled Beef and Cabbage.'

Adams was pleased with so perfect a Confirmation that he had not the least Fever: but advised him to a lighter Diet, for that Evening. He accordingly eat either a Rabbit or a Fowl, I never could with any tolerable Certainty discover which; after this he was by Mrs *Tow-wouse*'s order conveyed into a better Bed, and equipped with one of her Husband's Shirts.

In the Morning early, *Barnabas* and the Surgeon came to the Inn, in order to see the Thief conveyed before the Justice. They had consumed the whole Night in debating what Measures they should take to produce the piece of Gold in Evidence against him: for they were both extremely zealous in the Business, tho' neither of them were in the least interested in the Prosecution; neither of them had ever received any private Injury from the Fellow, nor had either of them ever been suspected of loving the Publick well enough, to give them a Sermon or a Dose of Physick for nothing.

To help our Reader therefore as much as possible to account for this Zeal, we must inform him, that as this Parish was so unfortunate as to have no Lawyer in it; there had been a constant Contention between the two Doctors, spiritual and physical, concerning their Abilities in a Science, in which, as neither of them professed it, they had equal Pretensions to dispute each other's Opinions. These Disputes were carried on with great Contempt on both sides, and had almost divided the Parish; Mr *Tow-wouse* and one half of the Neighbours inclining to the Surgeon, and Mrs *Tow-wouse* with the other half to the Parson. The Surgeon drew his Knowledge from those inestimable Fountains, called the *Attorney's Pocket-Companion*, and Mr *Jacob's Law-Tables*; *Barnabas* trusted entirely to *Wood's Institutes*.[4] It happened on this Occasion, as was pretty frequently the Case, that these two learned Men differed about the sufficiency of Evidence: the Doctor being of opinion, that the Maid's Oath[5] would convict the Prisoner without producing the Gold; the Parson, *è contra, totis viribus*.[6] To display their Parts therefore before the Justice and the Parish was the sole Motive, which we can discover, to this Zeal, which both of them pretended to be for public Justice.

O Vanity! How little is thy Force acknowledged, or thy Operations discerned? How wantonly dost thou deceive Mankind under different Disguises? Sometimes thou dost wear the Face of Pity, sometimes of Generosity: nay, thou hast the Assurance even to put on those glorious Ornaments which belong only to heroick Virtue. Thou odious, deformed Monster! whom Priests have railed at, Philosophers despised, and Poets ridiculed: Is there a Wretch so abandoned as to own thee for an Acquaintance in public? yet, how few will refuse to enjoy thee in private? nay, thou art the Pursuit of most Men through their Lives. The greatest Villanies are daily practised to please thee: nor is the meanest Thief below, or the greatest Hero above thy notice. Thy Embraces are often the sole Aim and sole Reward of the private Robbery, and the plundered Province. It is, to pamper up thee, thou Harlot, that we attempt to withdraw from others what we do not want, or to withhold from them what they do. All our Passions are thy Slaves. Avarice itself is often no more than thy Hand-maid, and even Lust thy Pimp. The Bully Fear, like a Coward, flies before thee, and Joy and Grief hide their Heads in thy Presence.

I know thou wilt think, that whilst I abuse thee, I court thee; and that thy Love hath inspired me to write this sarcastical Panegyrick on thee: but thou art deceived, I value thee not of a farthing; nor will it give me any Pain, if thou should'st prevail on the Reader to censure this Digression as errant Nonsense: for know to thy Confusion, that I have introduced thee for no other Purpose than to lengthen out a short Chapter; and so I return to my History.

CHAPTER XVI

The Escape of the Thief. Mr Adams's *Disappointment. The Arrival
of two very extraordinary Personages, and the Introduction of Parson*
Adams *to Parson* Barnabas.

Barnabas and the Surgeon being returned, as we have said, to the Inn, in
order to convey the Thief before the Justice, were greatly concerned to
find a small Accident had happened which somewhat disconcerted them;
and this was no other than the Thief's Escape, who had modestly withdrawn himself by Night, declining all Ostentation, and not chusing, in
imitation of some great Men, to distinguish himself at the Expence of
being pointed at.

When the Company had retired the Evening before, the Thief was
detained in a Room where the Constable, and one of the young Fellows
who took him, were planted as his Guard. About the second Watch, a
general Complaint of Drowth was made both by the Prisoner and his
Keepers. Among whom it was at last agreed, that the Constable should
remain on Duty, and the young Fellow should call up the Tapster; in
which Disposition the latter apprehended not the least Danger, as the
Constable was well armed, and could besides easily summon him back
to his Assistance, if the Prisoner made the least Attempt to gain his Liberty.

The young Fellow had not long left the Room, before it came into the
Constable's Head, that the Prisoner might leap on him by surprize, and
thereby, preventing him on the use of his Weapons, especially the long
Staff in which he chiefly confided, might reduce the Success of a Struggle
to an equal Chance. He wisely therefore, to prevent this Inconvenience,
slipt out of the Room himself and locked the Door, waiting without with
his Staff in his Hand, ready lifted to fell the unhappy Prisoner, if by ill
Fortune he should attempt to break out.

But human Life, as hath been discovered by some great Man or other,
(for I would by no means be understood to affect the Honour of making
any such Discovery) very much resembles a Game at *Chess:*[1] for as in the
latter, while a Gamester is too attentive to secure himself very strongly
on one side the Board, he is apt to leave an unguarded Opening on the
other; so doth it often happen in Life; and so did it happen on this
Occasion: for whilst the cautious Constable with such wonderful Sagacity
had possessed himself of the Door, he most unhappily forgot the Window.

The Thief who played on the other side, no sooner perceived this Opening, than he began to move that way; and finding the Passage easy, he took with him the young Fellow's Hat; and without any Ceremony, stepped into the Street, and made the best of his Way.

The young Fellow returning with a double Mug of Strong Beer, was a little surprized to find the Constable at the Door: but much more so, when, the Door being opened, he perceived the Prisoner had made his Escape, and which way: he threw down the Beer, and without uttering any thing to the Constable, except a hearty Curse or two, he nimbly leapt out at the Window, and went again in pursuit of his Prey: being very unwilling to lose the Reward[2] which he had assured himself of.

The Constable hath not been discharged of Suspicion on this account: It hath been said, that not being concerned in the taking the Thief, he could not have been entitled to any part of the Reward, if he had been convicted; that the Thief had several Guineas in his Pocket; that it was very unlikely he should have been guilty of such an Oversight; that his Pretence for leaving the Room was absurd: that it was his constant Maxim, that a wise Man never refused Money on any Conditions; that at every Election, he always had sold his Vote to both Parties, &c.

But notwithstanding these and many other such Allegations, I am sufficiently convinced of his Innocence; having been positively assured of it, by those who received their Informations from his own Mouth; which, in the Opinion of some Moderns, is the best and indeed only Evidence.

All the Family were now up, and with many others assembled in the Kitchin, where Mr *Tow-wouse* was in some Tribulation; the Surgeon having declared, that by Law, he was liable to be indicted for the Thief's Escape, as it was out of his House: He was a little comforted however by Mr *Barnabas*'s Opinion, that as the Escape was by Night, the Indictment would not lie.[3]

Mrs *Tow-wouse* delivered herself in the following Words: 'Sure never was such Fool as my Husband! would any other Person living have left a Man in the Custody of such a drunken, drowsy Blockhead as *Tom Suckbribe*;' (which was the Constable's Name) 'and if he could be indicted without any harm to his Wife and Children, I should be glad of it.' (Then the Bell rung in *Joseph*'s Room) 'Why *Betty*, *John Chamberlain*, where the Devil are you all? Have you no Ears, or no Conscience, not to tend the Sick better? — See what the Gentleman wants; why don't you go yourself, Mr *Tow-wouse?* but any one may die for you; you have no more feeling than a Deal-Board. If a Man lived a Fortnight in your House without spending a Penny, you would never put him in mind of it. See whether he drinks Tea or Coffee for Breakfast.' 'Yes, my Dear,' cry'd *Tow-wouse*. She then asked the Doctor and Mr *Barnabas* what Morning's Draught they chose, who answered, they had a Pot of *Syder-and*,[4] at the Fire; which we will leave them merry over, and return to *Joseph*.

He had rose pretty early this Morning: but tho' his Wounds were far from threatning any danger, he was so sore with the Bruises, that it was impossible for him to think of undertaking a Journey yet; Mr *Adams* therefore, whose Stock was visibly decreased with the Expences of Supper and Breakfast, and which could not survive that Day's Scoring, began to consider how it was possible to recruit it. At last he cry'd, 'He had luckily hit on a sure Method, and though it would oblige him to return himself home together with *Joseph*, it mattered not much.' He then sent for *Tow-wouse*, and taking him into another Room, told him, 'He wanted to borrow three Guineas, for which he would put ample Security into his Hands.' *Tow-wouse* who expected a Watch, or Ring, or something of double the Value, answered, 'He believed he could furnish him.' Upon which *Adams* pointing to his Saddle-Bag told him with a Face and Voice full of Solemnity, 'that there were in that Bag no less than nine Volumes of Manuscript Sermons, as well worth a hundred Pound as a Shilling was worth twelve Pence, and that he would deposite one of the Volumes in his Hands by way of Pledge; not doubting but that he would have the Honesty to return it on his Repayment of the Money: for otherwise he must be a very great loser, seeing that every Volume would at least bring him ten Pounds, as he had been informed by a neighbouring Clergyman in the Country: for,' said he, 'as to my own part, having never yet dealt in Printing, I do not pretend to ascertain the exact Value of such things.'

Tow-wouse, who was a little surprized at the Pawn, said (and not without some Truth) 'That he was no Judge of the Price of such kind of Goods: and as for Money he really was very short.' *Adams* answered, 'Certainly he would not scruple to lend him three Guineas, on what was undoubtedly worth at least ten.' The Landlord replied, 'He did not believe he had so much Money in the House, and besides he was to make up a Sum.[5] He was very confident the Books were of much higher Value, and heartily sorry it did not suit him.' He then cry'd out, *Coming Sir!* though no body called; and ran down Stairs without any Fear of breaking his Neck.

Poor *Adams* was extremely dejected at this Disappointment, nor knew he what farther Stratagem to try. He immediately apply'd to his Pipe, his constant Friend and Comfort in his Afflictions; and leaning over the Rails, he devoted himself to Meditation, assisted by the inspiring Fumes of Tobacco.

He had on a Night-Cap drawn over his Wig, and a short great Coat, which half covered his Cassock; a Dress which, added to something comical enough in his Countenance, composed a Figure likely to attract the Eyes of those who were not over-given to Observation.

Whilst he was smoaking his Pipe in this Posture, a Coach and Six, with a numerous Attendance, drove into the Inn. There alighted from the Coach a young Fellow, and a Brace of Pointers, after which another young Fellow leapt from the Box, and shook the former by the hand, and both, together with the Dogs, were instantly conducted by Mr *Tow-wouse* into an Apartment; whither as they passed, they entertained themselves with the following short facetious Dialogue.

'You are a pretty Fellow for a Coachman, *Jack!*' says he from the Coach, 'you had almost overturned us just now.' 'Pox take you,' says the Coachman, 'if I had only broke your Neck, it would have been saving somebody else the trouble: but I should have been sorry for the Pointers.' 'Why you Son of a B——,' answered the other, 'if no body could shoot better than you, the Pointers would be of no use.' 'D——n me,' says the Coachman, 'I will shoot with you, five Guineas a Shot.' 'You be hang'd,' says the other, 'for five Guineas you shall shoot at my A——.' 'Done,' says the Coachman, 'I'll pepper you better than ever you was peppered by *Jenny Bouncer*.'[6] 'Pepper your Grand-mother,' says the other, 'here's *Tow-wouse* will let you shoot at him for a Shilling a time.' 'I know his Honour better,' cries *Tow-wouse*, 'I never saw a surer shot at a Partridge. Every Man misses now and then; but if I could shoot half as well as his Honour, I would desire no better Livelihood than I could get by my Gun.' 'Pox on you,' said the Coachman, 'you demolish more Game now than your Head's worth. There's a Bitch, *Tow-wouse*, by G—— she never *blinked** a Bird in her Life.' 'I have a Puppy, not a Year old, shall hunt with her for a hundred,' cries the other Gentleman. 'Done,' says the Coachman, 'but you will be pox'd before you make the Bett. If you have a mind for a Bett,' cries the Coachman, 'I will match my spotted Dog with your white Bitch for a hundred, play or pay.'[7] 'Done,' says the other, 'and I'll run *Baldface* against *Slouch* with you for another.' 'No,' cries he from the Box, 'but I'll venture *Miss Jenny* against *Baldface*, or *Hannibal* either.' 'Go

---

* To *blink* is a Term used to signify the Dog's passing by a Bird without pointing at it.

to the Devil,' cries he from the Coach, 'I will make every Bett your own way, to be sure! I will match *Hannibal* with *Slouch* for a thousand, if you dare, and I say done first.'

They were now arrived, and the Reader will be very contented to leave them, and repair to the Kitchin, where *Barnabas*, the Surgeon, and an Exciseman were smoking their Pipes over some *Syder-and*, whither the Servants, who attended the two noble Gentlemen we have just seen alight, were now arrived.

'*Tom*,' cries one of the Footmen, 'there's Parson *Adams* smoking his Pipe in the Gallery.' 'Yes,' says *Tom*, 'I pulled off my Hat to him, and the Parson spoke to me.'

'Is the Gentleman a Clergyman then?' says *Barnabas*, (for his Cassock had been tied up when first he arrived.) 'Yes, Sir,' answered the Footman, 'and one there be but few like.' 'Ay,' said *Barnabas*, 'if I had known it sooner, I should have desired his Company; I would always shew a proper Respect for the Cloth; but what say you, Doctor, shall we adjourn into a Room, and invite him to take part in a Bowl of Punch?'

This Proposal was immediately agreed to, and executed; and Parson *Adams* accepting the Invitation; much Civility passed between the two Clergymen, who both declared the great Honour they had for the Cloth. They had not been long together before they entered into a Discourse on small Tithes,[8] which continued a full Hour, without the Doctor or the Exciseman's having one Opportunity to offer a Word.

It was then proposed to begin a general Conversation, and the Exciseman opened on foreign Affairs: but a Word unluckily dropping from one of them introduced a Dissertation on the Hardships suffered by the inferiour Clergy;[9] which after a long Duration, concluded with bringing the three Volumes of Sermons on the Carpet.[10]

Barnabas greatly discouraged poor *Adams*; he said, 'The Age was so wicked, that no body read Sermons: Would you think it, Mr *Adams*, (said he) I once intended to print a Volume of Sermons myself, and they had the Approbation of two or three Bishops: but what do you think a Bookseller offered me?' 'Twelve Guineas perhaps' (cried *Adams*.) 'Not Twelve Pence, I assure you,' answered *Barnabas*, 'nay the Dog refused me a Concordance in Exchange. — At last, I offered to give him the printing them, for the sake of dedicating them to that very Gentleman who just now drove his own Coach into the Inn, and I assure you he had the Impudence to refuse my Offer: by which means I lost a good Living, that was afterwards given away in exchange for a Pointer, to one who ——

but I will not say any thing against the Cloth. So you may guess, Mr *Adams*, what you are to expect; for if Sermons would have gone down, I believe —— I will not be vain: but to be concise with you, three Bishops said, they were the best that ever were writ: but indeed there are a pretty moderate number printed already, and not all sold yet.' —— 'Pray Sir,' said *Adams*, 'to what do you think the Numbers may amount?' 'Sir,' answered *Barnabas*, 'a Bookseller told me he believed five thousand Volumes at least.' 'Five thousand!' quoth the Surgeon, 'what can they be writ upon? I remember, when I was a Boy, I used to read one *Tillotson*'s Sermons;[11] and I am sure, if a Man practised half so much as is in one of those Sermons, he will go to Heaven.' 'Doctor,' cried *Barnabas*, 'you have a prophane way of talking, for which I must reprove you. A Man can never have his Duty too frequently inculcated into him. And as for *Tillotson*, to be sure he was a good Writer, and said things very well: but Comparisons are odious, another Man may write as well as he —— I believe there are some of my Sermons,' —— and then he apply'd the Candle to his Pipe. —— 'And I believe there are some of my Discourses,' cries *Adams*, 'which the Bishops would not think totally unworthy of being printed; and I have been informed, I might procure a very large Sum (indeed an immense one) on them.' 'I doubt that;' answered *Barnabas*: 'however, if you desire to make some Money of them, perhaps you may sell them by advertising *The Manuscript Sermons of a Clergyman lately deceased, all warranted Originals, and never printed*. And now I think of it, I should be obliged to you, if there be ever a Funeral one among them, to lend it me: for I am this very day to preach a Funeral Sermon, for which I have not penned a Line, though I am to have a double Price.' *Adams* answered, 'He had but one, which he feared would not serve his purpose, being sacred to the Memory of a Magistrate, who had exerted himself very singularly in the Preservation of the Morality of his Neighbours, insomuch, that he had neither Ale-house, nor lewd Woman in the Parish where he lived.' —— 'No,' replied *Barnabas*, 'that will not do quite so well; for the Deceased, upon whose Virtues I am to harangue, was a little too much addicted to Liquor, and publickly kept a Mistress. —— I believe I must take a common Sermon, and trust to my Memory to introduce something handsome on him.' —— 'To your Invention rather,' (said the Doctor) 'your Memory will be apter to put you out: for no Man living remembers any thing good of him.'

With such kind of spiritual Discourse, they emptied the Bowl of Punch, paid their Reckoning, and separated: *Adams* and the Doctor went up to

Joseph; Parson *Barnabas* departed to celebrate the aforesaid Deceased, and the Exciseman descended into the Cellar to gage the Vessels.[12]

Joseph was now ready to sit down to a Loin of Mutton, and waited for Mr *Adams*, when he and the Doctor came in. The Doctor having felt his Pulse, and examined his Wounds, declared him much better, which he imputed to *that Sanative soporiferous Draught*, a Medicine, 'whose Virtues,' he said, 'were never to be sufficiently extolled:' And great indeed they must be, if *Joseph* was so much indebted to them as the Doctor imagined, since nothing more than those Effluvia, which escaped the Cork, could have contributed to his Recovery: for the Medicine had stood untouched in the Window ever since its arrival.

Joseph passed that day and the three following with his Friend *Adams*, in which nothing so remarkable happened as the swift Progress of his Recovery. As he had an excellent Habit of Body,[13] his Wounds were now almost healed, and his Bruises gave him so little uneasiness, that he pressed Mr *Adams* to let him depart, told him he should never be able to return sufficient Thanks for all his Favours; but begged that he might no longer delay his Journey to *London*.

Adams, notwithstanding the Ignorance, as he conceived it, of Mr *Towwouse*, and the Envy (for such he thought it) of Mr *Barnabas*, had great Expectations from his Sermons: seeing therefore *Joseph* in so good a way, he told him he would agree to his setting out the next Morning in the Stage-Coach, that he believed he should have sufficient after the Reckoning paid, to procure him one Day's Conveyance in it, and afterwards he would be able to get on, on foot, or might be favoured with a lift in some Neighbour's Waggon, especially as there was then to be a Fair in the Town whither the Coach would carry him, to which Numbers from his Parish resorted. — And as to himself, he agreed to proceed to the great City.

They were now walking in the Inn-Yard, when a fat, fair, short Person, rode in, and alighting from his Horse went directly up to *Barnabas*, who was smoking his Pipe on a Bench. The Parson and the Stranger shook one another very lovingly by the Hand, and went into a Room together.

The Evening now coming on, *Joseph* retired to his Chamber, whither the good *Adams* accompanied him; and took this Opportunity to expatiate on the great Mercies God had lately shewn him, of which he ought not only to have the deepest inward Sense; but likewise to express outward Thankfulness for them. They therefore fell both on their Knees, and spent a considerable time in Prayer and Thanksgiving.

They had just finished, when *Betty* came in and told Mr *Adams*, Mr *Barnabas* desired to speak to him on some Business of Consequence below Stairs. *Joseph* desired, if it was likely to detain him long, he would let him know it, that he might go to bed, which *Adams* promised, and in that Case, they wished one another good Night.

CHAPTER XVII

A pleasant Discourse between the two Parsons and the Bookseller,
which was broke off by an unlucky Accident happening in the Inn,
which produced a Dialogue between Mrs Tow-wouse *and her*
Maid of no gentle kind.

As soon as *Adams* came into the Room, Mr *Barnabas* introduced him to the Stranger, who was, he told him, a Bookseller,[1] and would be as likely to deal with him for his Sermons as any Man whatever. *Adams*, saluting the Stranger, answered *Barnabas*, that he was very much obliged to him, that nothing could be more convenient, for he had no other Business to the great City, and was heartily desirous of returning with the young Man who was just recovered of his Misfortune. He then snapt his Fingers (as was usual with him) and took two or three turns about the Room in an Extasy. —— And to induce the Bookseller to be as expeditious as possible, as likewise to offer him a better Price for his Commodity, he assured him, their meeting was extremely lucky to himself: for that he had the most pressing Occasion for Money at that time, his own being almost spent, and having a Friend then in the same Inn who was just recovered from some Wounds he had received from Robbers, and was in a most indigent Condition. 'So that nothing,' says he, 'could be so opportune, for the supplying both our Necessities, as my making an immediate Bargain with you.'

As soon as he had seated himself, the Stranger began in these words; 'Sir, I do not care absolutely to deny engaging in what my Friend Mr *Barnabas* recommends: but Sermons are mere Drugs.[2] The Trade is so vastly stocked with them, that really unless they come out with the Name of *Whitfield* or *Westley*,[3] or some other such great Man, as a Bishop, or those sort of People, I don't care to touch, unless now it was a Sermon preached on the 30*th of January*, or we could say in the Title Page, published at the *earnest Request* of the Congregation, or the Inhabitants:[4] but truly for a dry Piece of Sermons, I had rather be excused; especially as my Hands are so full at present. However, Sir, as Mr *Barnabas* mentioned them to me, I will, if you please, take the Manuscript with me to Town, and send you my Opinion of it in a very short time.'

O, said *Adams*, if you desire it, I will read two or three Discourses as a Specimen. This *Barnabas*, who loved Sermons no better than a Grocer doth Figs, immediately objected to, and advised *Adams* to let the Bookseller have his Sermons; telling him, if he gave him a Direction, he might be certain of a speedy Answer: Adding, he need not scruple trusting them in his Possession. No, said the Bookseller, if it was a Play that had been acted twenty Nights together,[5] I believed it would be safe.

Adams did not at all relish the last Expression; he said, he was sorry to hear Sermons compared to Plays. 'Not by me, I assure you,' cry'd the Bookseller, 'though I don't know whether the licensing Act[6] may not shortly bring them to the same footing: but I have formerly known a hundred Guineas given for a Play ———.' 'More shame for those who gave it,' cry'd *Barnabas*. 'Why so?' said the Bookseller, 'for they got hundreds by it.' 'But is there no difference between conveying good or ill Instructions to Mankind?' said *Adams*; 'would not an honest Mind rather lose Money by the one, than gain it by the other?' 'If you can find any such, I will not be their Hinderance,' answered the Bookseller, 'but I think those Persons who get by preaching Sermons, are the properest to lose by printing them: for my part, the Copy that sells best, will be always the best Copy in my Opinion; I am no Enemy to Sermons but because they don't sell: for I would as soon print one of *Whitfield*'s, as any Farce whatever.'

'Whoever prints such Heterodox Stuff, ought to be hanged,' says *Barnabas*. 'Sir,' said he, turning to *Adams*, 'this Fellow's Writings (I know not whether you have seen them) are levelled at the Clergy. He would reduce us to the Example of the Primitive Ages forsooth! and would insinuate to the People, that a Clergyman ought to be always preaching and praying. He pretends to understand the Scripture literally, and would make Mankind believe, that the Poverty and low Estate, which was recommended to the Church in its Infancy, and was only temporary Doctrine adapted to her under-Persecution, was to be preserved in her flourishing and established State.[7] Sir, the Principles of *Toland*, *Woolston*, and all the Free-Thinkers,[8] are not calculated to do half the Mischief, as those professed by this Fellow and his Followers.'

'Sir,' answered *Adams*, 'if Mr *Whitfield* had carried his Doctrine no farther than you mention, I should have remained, as I once was, his Well-Wisher. I am myself as great an Enemy to the Luxury and Splendour of the Clergy as he can be. I do not, more than he, by the flourishing Estate of the Church, understand the Palaces, Equipages, Dress, Furniture, rich Dainties, and vast Fortunes of her Ministers. Surely those things, which savour so strongly of this World, become not the Servants of one who professed his Kingdom was not of it:[9] but when he began to call Nonsense and Enthusiasm to his Aid, and to set up the detestable Doctrine of Faith against good Works, I was his Friend no longer; for surely, that Doctrine was coined in Hell, and one would think none but the Devil himself could have the Confidence to preach it. For can any thing be more derogatory to the Honour of God, than for Men to imagine that the All-wise Being will hereafter say to the Good and Virtuous, *Notwithstanding the Purity of thy Life, notwithstanding that constant Rule of Virtue and Goodness in which you walked upon Earth, still as thou didst not believe every thing in the true Orthodox manner, thy want of Faith shall condemn thee?* Or on the other side, can any Doctrine have a more pernicious Influence on Society than a Persuasion, that it will be a good Plea for the Villain at the last day; *Lord, it is true I never obeyed one of thy Commandments, yet punish me not, for I believe them all?* 'I suppose, Sir,' said the Bookseller, 'your Sermons are of a different Kind.' 'Ay, Sir,' said *Adams*, 'the contrary, I thank Heaven, is inculcated in almost every Page, or I should belye my own Opinion, which hath always been, that a virtuous and good *Turk*, or Heathen, are more acceptable in the sight of their Creator, than a vicious and wicked Christian, tho' his Faith was as perfectly Orthodox as St *Paul*'s himself.'
— 'I wish you Success,' says the Bookseller, 'but must beg to be excused, as my Hands are so very full at present; and indeed I am afraid, you will find a Backwardness in the Trade, to engage in a Book which the Clergy would be certain to cry down.' 'God forbid,' says *Adams*, 'any Books should be propagated which the Clergy would cry down: but if you mean by the Clergy, some few designing factious Men, who have it at heart to establish some favourite Schemes at the Price of the Liberty of Mankind, and the very Essence of Religion, it is not in the power of such Persons to decry any Book they please; witness that excellent Book called, *A Plain Account of the Nature and End of the Sacrament*; a Book written (if I may venture on the Expression) with the Pen of an Angel, and calculated to restore the true Use of Christianity, and of that Sacred Institution: for what could

tend more to the noble Purposes of Religion, than frequent cheerful Meetings among the Members of a Society in which they should in the Presence of one another, and in the Service of the supreme Being, make Promises of being good, friendly and benevolent to each other? Now this excellent Book was attacked by a Party, but unsuccessfully.'[10] At these Words *Barnabas* fell a ringing with all the Violence imaginable, upon which a Servant attending, he bid him 'bring a Bill immediately: for that he was in Company, for aught he knew, with the Devil himself; and he expected to hear the Alcoran, the *Leviathan*, or *Woolston* commended,[11] if he staid a few Minutes longer.' *Adams* desired, 'as he was so much moved at his mentioning a Book, which he did without apprehending any possibility of Offence, that he would be so kind to propose any Objections he had to it, which he would endeavour to answer.' 'I propose Objections!' said *Barnabas*, 'I never read a Syllable in any such wicked Book; I never saw it in my Life, I assure you.' —— *Adams* was going to answer, when a most hideous uproar began in the Inn. Mrs *Tow-wouse*, Mr *Tow-wouse*, and *Betty*, all lifting up their Voices together: but Mrs *Tow-wouse*'s Voice, like a Bass Viol in a Concert, was clearly and distinctly distinguished among the rest, and was heard to articulate the following Sounds. —— 'O you damn'd Villain, is this the Return to all the Care I have taken of your Family? This the Reward of my Virtue? Is this the manner in which you behave to one who brought you a Fortune, and preferred you to so many Matches, all your Betters? To abuse my Bed, my own Bed, with my own Servant: but I'll maul the Slut, I'll tear her nasty Eyes out; was ever such a pitiful Dog, to take up with such a mean Trollop? If she had been a Gentle-woman like myself, it had been some excuse, but a beggarly saucy dirty Servant-Maid. Get you out of my House, you Whore.' To which, she added another Name, which we do not care to stain our Paper with. — It was a monosyllable, beginning with a B——, and indeed was the same, as if she had pronounced the Words, *She Dog*. Which Term, we shall, to avoid Offence, use on this Occasion, tho' indeed both the Mistress and Maid uttered the above-mentioned B—, a Word extremely disgustful to Females of the lower sort. *Betty* had borne all hitherto with Patience, and had uttered only Lamentations: but the last Appellation stung her to the Quick, 'I am a Woman as well as yourself,' she roared out, 'and no She-dog, and if I have been a little naughty, I am not the first; if I have been no better than I should be,' cries she sobbing, 'that's no Reason you

should call me out of my Name; my Be—Betters are wo—worse than me.'
'Huzzy, huzzy,' says Mrs *Tow-wouse*, 'have you the Impudence to answer
me? Did I not catch you, you saucy —' and then again repeated the
terrible word so odious to female Ears. 'I can't bear that Name,' answered
Betty, 'if I have been wicked, I am to answer for it myself in the other
World, but I have done nothing that's unnatural, and I will go out of your
House this Moment: for I will never be called *She Dog*, by any Mistress
in *England*.' Mrs *Tow-wouse* then armed herself with the Spit: but was
prevented from executing any dreadful Purpose by Mr *Adams*, who
confined her Arms with the Strength of a Wrist which *Hercules* would not
have been ashamed of. Mr *Tow-wouse* being caught, as our Lawyers express
it, with the Manner,[12] and having no Defence to make, very prudently
withdrew himself, and *Betty* committed herself to the Protection of the
Hostler, who, though she could not conceive him pleased with what
had happened, was in her Opinion rather a gentler Beast than her
Mistress.

Mrs *Tow-wouse*, at the Intercession of Mr *Adams*, and finding the Enemy
vanished, began to compose herself, and at length recovered the usual
Serenity of her Temper, in which we will leave her, to open to the Reader
the Steps which led to a Catastrophe, common enough, and comical
enough too, perhaps in modern History, yet often fatal to the Repose and
Well-being of Families, and the Subject of many Tragedies, both in Life
and on the Stage.

CHAPTER XVIII

The History of Betty *the Chambermaid, and an Account of what
occasioned the violent Scene in the preceding Chapter.*

Betty, who was the Occasion of all this Hurry, had some good Qualities.
She had Good-nature, Generosity and Compassion, but unfortunately
her Constitution was composed of those warm Ingredients, which, though
the Purity of Courts or Nunneries might have happily controuled them,
were by no means able to endure the ticklish Situation of a Chamber-maid
at an Inn, who is daily liable to the Sollicitations of Lovers of all Com-
plexions; to the dangerous Addresses of fine Gentlemen of the Army, who
sometimes are obliged to reside with them a whole Year together; and

above all are exposed to the Caresses of Footmen, Stage-Coachmen, and Drawers;[1] all of whom employ the whole Artillery of kissing, flattering, bribing, and every other Weapon which is to be found in the whole Armory of Love, against them.

Betty, who was about one and twenty, had now lived three years in this dangerous Situation, during which she had escaped pretty well. An Ensign of Foot was the first Person who made an Impression on her Heart; he did indeed raise a Flame in her, which required the Care of a Surgeon to cool.

While she burnt for him, several others burnt for her. Officers of the Army, young Gentlemen travelling the Western Circuit,[2] in-—offensive Squires, and some of graver Character were set afire by her Charms!

At length, having perfectly recovered the Effects of her first unhappy Passion, she seemed to have vowed a State of perpetual Chastity. She was long dead to all the Sufferings of her Lovers, till one day at a neighbouring Fair, the Rhetorick of *John* the Hostler, with a new Straw Hat, and a Pint of Wine, made a second Conquest over her.

She did not however feel any of those Flames on this Occasion, which had been the Consequence of her former Amour; nor indeed those other ill Effects, which prudent young Women very justly apprehend from too absolute an Indulgence to the pressing Endearments of their Lovers. This latter, perhaps, was a little owing to her not being entirely constant to *John*, with whom she permitted *Tom Whipwell* the Stage-Coachman, and now and then a handsome young Traveller, to share her Favours.

Mr *Tow-wouse* had for some time cast the languishing Eyes of Affection on this young Maiden. He had laid hold on every Opportunity of saying tender things to her, squeezing her by the Hand, and sometimes of kissing her Lips: for as the Violence of his Passion had considerably abated to Mrs *Tow-wouse*; so like Water, which is stopt from its usual Current in one Place, it naturally sought a vent in another. Mrs *Tow-wouse* is thought to have perceived this Abatement, and probably it added very little to the natural Sweetness of her Temper: for tho' she was as true to her Husband, as the Dial to the Sun, she was rather more desirous of being shone on, as being more capable of feeling his Warmth.

Ever since *Joseph*'s arrival, *Betty* had conceived an extraordinary Liking to him, which discovered itself more and more, as he grew better and better; 'till that fatal Evening when, as she was warming his Bed, her Passion grew to such a Height, and so perfectly mastered both her

Modesty and her Reason, that after many fruitless Hints and sly Insinuations, she at last threw down the Warming-Pan, and embracing him with great Eagerness swore he was the handsomest Creature she had ever seen.

Joseph in great Confusion leapt from her, and told her, he was sorry to see a young Woman cast off all Regard to Modesty: but she had gone too far to recede, and grew so very indecent, that *Joseph* was obliged, contrary to his Inclination, to use some Violence to her, and taking her in his Arms, he shut her out of the Room, and locked the Door.

How ought Man to rejoice, that his Chastity is always in his own power, that if he hath sufficient Strength of Mind, he hath always a competent Strength of Body to defend himself: and cannot, like a poor weak Woman, be ravished against his Will!

Betty was in the most violent Agitation at this Disappointment. Rage and Lust pulled her Heart, as with two Strings, two different Ways; one Moment she thought of stabbing *Joseph*, the next, of taking him in her Arms, and devouring him with Kisses; but the latter Passion was far more prevalent. Then she thought of revenging his Refusal on herself: but whilst she was engaged in this Meditation, happily Death presented himself to her in so many Shapes of drowning, hanging, poisoning, &c. that her distracted Mind could resolve on none. In this Perturbation of Spirit, it accidentally occurred to her Memory, that her Master's Bed was not made, she therefore went directly to his Room; where he happened at that time to be engaged at his Bureau. As soon as she saw him, she attempted to retire: but he called her back, and taking her by the hand, squeezed her so tenderly, at the same time whispering so many soft things into her Ears, and, then pressed her so closely with his Kisses, that the vanquished Fair-One, whose Passions were already raised, and which were not so whimsically capricious that one Man only could lay them, though perhaps, she would have rather preferred that one: The vanquished Fair-one quietly submitted, I say, to her Master's Will, who had just attained the Accomplishment of his Bliss, when Mrs *Tow-wouse* unexpectedly entered the Room, and caused all that Confusion which we have before seen, and which it is not necessary at present to take any farther Notice of: Since without the Assistance of a single Hint from us, every Reader of any Speculation,[3] or Experience, though not married himself, may easily conjecture, that it concluded with the Discharge of *Betty*, the Submission of Mr *Tow-wouse*, with some things to be performed on his side by way of Gratitude for his Wife's Goodness in being reconciled to him, with many hearty Promises never to offend any more in the like manner: and lastly, his quietly and contentedly bearing to be reminded of his Transgressions, as a kind of Penance, once or twice a Day, during the Residue of his Life.

The End of the First Book

THE HISTORY OF THE ADVENTURES OF
JOSEPH ANDREWS, AND HIS FRIEND
MR ABRAHAM ADAMS

BOOK II

CHAPTER I

Of Divisions in Authors.

There are certain Mysteries or Secrets in all Trades from the highest to
the lowest, from that of *Prime Ministring* to this of *Authoring*, which are
seldom discovered, unless to Members of the same Calling. Among those
used by us Gentlemen of the latter Occupation, I take this of dividing our
Works into Books and Chapters to be none of the least considerable. Now
for want of being truly acquainted with this Secret, common Readers
imagine, that by this Art of dividing, we mean only to swell our Works
to a much larger Bulk than they would otherwise be extended to. These
several Places therefore in our Paper, which are filled with our Books and
Chapters, are understood as so much Buckram, Stays, and Stay-tape in
a Taylor's Bill, serving only to make up the Sum Total, commonly found
at the Bottom of our first Page, and of his last.

But in reality the Case is otherwise, and in this, as well as all other
Instances, we consult the Advantage of our Reader, not our own; and
indeed many notable Uses arise to him from this Method: for first, those
little Spaces between our Chapters may be looked upon as an Inn or
Resting-Place, where he may stop and take a Glass, or any other Refreshment, as it pleases him.[1] Nay, our fine Readers will, perhaps, be scarce
able to travel farther than through one of them in a Day. As to those
vacant Pages which are placed between our Books, they are to be regarded
as those Stages, where, in long Journeys, the Traveller stays some time to
repose himself, and consider of what he hath seen in the Parts he hath
already past through; a Consideration which I take the Liberty to recommend a little to the Reader: for however swift his Capacity may be, I
would not advise him to travel through these Pages too fast: for if he doth,
he may probably miss the seeing some curious Productions of Nature
which will be observed by the slower and more accurate Reader. A

Volume without any such Places of Rest resembles the Opening of Wilds or Seas, which tires the Eye and fatigues the Spirit when entered upon.

Secondly, What are the Contents prefixed to every Chapter, but so many Inscriptions over the Gates of Inns (to continue the same Metaphor,) informing the Reader what Entertainment he is to expect, which if he likes not, he may travel on to the next: for in Biography, as we are not tied down to an exact Concatenation equally with other Historians; so a Chapter or two (for Instance this I am now writing) may be often passed over without any Injury to the Whole. And in these Inscriptions I have been as faithful as possible, not imitating the celebrated *Montagne*, who promises you one thing and gives you another;[2] nor some Title-Page Authors, who promise a great deal, and produce nothing at all.

There are, besides these more obvious Benefits, several others which our Readers enjoy from this Art of dividing; tho' perhaps most of them too mysterious to be presently understood, by any who are not initiated into the Science of *Authoring*. To mention therefore but one which is most obvious, it prevents spoiling the Beauty of a Book by turning down its Leaves, a Method otherwise necessary to those Readers, who, (tho' they read with great Improvement and Advantage) are apt, when they return to their Study, after half an Hour's Absence, to forget where they left off.

These Divisions have the Sanction of great Antiquity. *Homer* not only divided his great Work into twenty-four Books, (in Compliment perhaps to the twenty-four Letters to which he had very particular Obligations)[3] but, according to the Opinion of some very sagacious Critics, hawked them all separately, delivering only one Book at a Time, (probably by Subscription).[4] He was the first Inventor of the Art which hath so long lain dormant, of publishing by Numbers; an Art now brought to such Perfection, that even Dictionaries are divided and exhibited piece-meal to the Publick; nay, one Bookseller hath (*to encourage Learning and ease the Public*) contrived to give them a Dictionary in this divided Manner, for only fifteen Shillings more than it would have cost entire.[5]

Virgil hath given us his Poem in twelve Books, an Argument of his Modesty; for by that doubtless he would insinuate that he pretends to no more than half the Merit of the *Greek*: for the same Reason, our *Milton* went originally no farther than ten; 'till being puffed up by the Praise of his Friends, he put himself on the same footing with the *Roman* Poet.[6]

I shall not however enter so deep into this Matter as some very learned Criticks have done; who have with infinite Labour and acute Discernment discovered what Books are proper for Embellishment, and what require

Simplicity only, particularly with regard to Similies, which I think are now generally agreed to become any Book but the first.

I will dismiss this Chapter with the following Observation: That it becomes an Author generally to divide a Book, as it doth a Butcher to joint his Meat, for such Assistance is of great Help to both the Reader and the Carver. And now having indulged myself a little, I will endeavour to indulge the Curiosity of my Reader, who is no doubt impatient to know what he will find in the subsequent Chapters of this Book.

CHAPTER II

A surprising Instance of Mr Adams*'s short Memory, with the unfortunate Consequences which it brought on* Joseph.

Mr *Adams* and *Joseph* were now ready to depart different ways, when an Accident determined the former to return with his Friend, which *Towwouse, Barnabas*, and the Bookseller had not been able to do. This Accident was, that those Sermons, which the Parson was travelling to *London* to publish, were, O my good Reader, left behind; what he had mistaken for them in the Saddle-Bags being no other than three Shirts, a pair of Shoes, and some other Necessaries, which Mrs *Adams*, who thought her Husband would want Shirts more than Sermons on his Journey, had carefully provided him.

This Discovery was now luckily owing to the Presence of *Joseph* at the opening the Saddle-Bags; who having heard his Friend say, he carried with him 9 Volumes of Sermons, and not being of that Sect of Philosophers, who can reduce all the Matter of the World into a Nut-shell, seeing there was no room for them in the Bags, where the Parson had said they were deposited, had the Curiosity to cry out, 'Bless me, Sir, where are your Sermons?' The Parson answer'd, 'There, there Child, there they are, under my Shirts.' Now it happened that he had taken forth his last Shirt, and the Vehicle remained visibly empty. 'Sure, Sir,' says *Joseph*, 'there is nothing in the Bags.' Upon which *Adams* starting, and testifying some surprize, cry'd, 'Hey! fie, fie upon it; they are not here sure enough. Ay, they are certainly left behind.'

Joseph was greatly concerned at the Uneasiness which he apprehended his Friend must feel from this Disappointment: he begged him to pursue his Journey, and promised he would himself return with the Books to him, with the utmost Expedition. 'No, thank you, Child,' answered *Adams*, 'it shall not be so. What would it avail me, to tarry in the Great City, unless I had my Discourses with me, which are, *ut ita dicam*,[1] the sole Cause, the *Aitia monotate*[2] of my Peregrination. No, Child, as this Accident hath happened, I am resolved to return back to my Cure, together with you; which indeed my Inclination sufficiently leads me to. This Disappointment may, perhaps, be intended for my Good.' He concluded with a Verse out of *Theocritus*, which signifies no more than, *that sometimes it rains and sometimes the Sun shines.*[3]

Joseph bowed with Obedience, and Thankfulness for the Inclination which the Parson express'd of returning with him; and now the Bill was called for, which, on Examination, amounted within a Shilling to the Sum Mr *Adams* had in his Pocket. Perhaps the Reader may wonder how he was able to produce a sufficient Sum for so many Days: that he may not be surprized therefore, it cannot be unnecessary to acquaint him, that he had borrowed a Guinea of a Servant belonging to the Coach and Six, who had been formerly one of his Parishioners, and whose Master, the Owner of the Coach, then lived within three Miles of him: for so good was the Credit of Mr *Adams*, that even Mr *Peter* the Lady *Booby*'s Steward would have lent him a Guinea with very little Security.

Mr *Adams* discharged the Bill, and they were both setting out, having agreed *to ride and tie*: a Method of travelling much used by Persons who have but one Horse between them, and is thus performed. The two Travellers set out together, one on horseback, the other on foot: Now as it generally happens that he on horseback outgoes him on foot, the Custom is, that when he arrives at the Distance agreed on, he is to dismount, tie the Horse to some Gate, Tree, Post, or other thing, and then proceed on foot; when the other comes up to the Horse, he unties him, mounts and gallops on, 'till having passed by his Fellow-Traveller, he likewise arrives at the Place of tying. And this is that Method of Travelling so much in use among our prudent Ancestors, who knew that Horses had Mouths as well as Legs, and that they could not use the latter without being at the Expence of suffering the Beasts themselves to use the former. This was the Method in use in those Days: when, instead of a Coach and Six, a Member of Parliament's Lady used to mount a Pillion behind her Husband; and a grave Serjeant at Law condescended to amble to *Westminster* on an easy Pad,[4] with his Clerk kicking his Heels behind him.

Adams was now gone some Minutes, having insisted on *Joseph*'s beginning the Journey on horseback, and *Joseph* had his Foot in the Stirrup, when the Hostler presented him a Bill for the Horse's Board during his Residence at the Inn. *Joseph* said Mr *Adams* had paid all; but this Matter being referred to Mr *Tow-wouse* was by him decided in favour of the Hostler, and indeed with Truth and Justice: for this was a fresh Instance of that shortness of Memory which did not arise from want of Parts, but that continual Hurry in which Parson *Adams* was always involved.

Joseph was now reduced to a Dilemma which extremely puzzled him. The Sum due for Horse-meat was twelve Shillings, (for *Adams* who had borrowed the Beast of his Clerk, had ordered him to be fed as well as they could feed him) and the Cash in his Pocket amounted to Sixpence, (for *Adams* had divided the last Shilling with him.) Now, tho' there have been some ingenious Persons who have contrived to pay twelve Shillings with Sixpence, *Joseph* was not one of them. He had never contracted a Debt in his Life, and was consequently the less ready at an Expedient to extricate himself. *Tow-wouse* was willing to give him Credit 'till next time, to which Mrs *Tow-wouse* would probably have consented (for such was *Joseph*'s Beauty, that it had made some Impression even on that Piece of Flint which that good Woman wore in her Bosom by way of heart.) *Joseph* would have found therefore, very likely, the Passage free, had he not, when he honestly discovered the Nakedness of his Pockets, pulled out that little Piece of Gold which we have mentioned before. This caused Mrs *Tow-wouse*'s Eyes to water; she told *Joseph*, she did not conceive a Man could want Money whilst he had Gold in his Pocket. *Joseph* answered, he had such a Value for that little Piece of Gold, that he would not part with it for a hundred times the Riches which the greatest Esquire in the County was worth. 'A pretty Way indeed,' said Mrs *Tow-wouse*, 'to run in debt, and then refuse to part with your Money, because you have a Value for it. I never knew any Piece of Gold of more Value than as many Shillings as it would change for.' 'Not to preserve my Life from starving, nor to redeem it from a Robber, would I part with this dear Piece,' answered *Joseph*. 'What (says Mrs *Tow-wouse*) I suppose, it was given you by some vile Trollop, some Miss[5] or other; if it had been the Present of a virtuous Woman, you would not have had such a Value for it. My Husband is a Fool if he parts with the Horse, without being paid for him.' 'No, no, I can't part with the Horse indeed, till I have the Money,' cried *Tow-wouse*. A Resolution highly commended by a Lawyer then in the Yard, who declared Mr *Tow-wouse* might justify the Detainer.[6]

As we cannot therefore at present get Mr *Joseph* out of the Inn, we shall leave him in it, and carry our Reader on after Parson *Adams*, who, his

Mind being perfectly at ease, fell into a Contemplation on a Passage in
Æschylus,[7] which entertained him for three Miles together, without suffering
him once to reflect on his Fellow-Traveller.

At length having spun out this Thread, and being now at the Summit
of a Hill, he cast his Eyes backwards, and wondered that he could not see
any sign of *Joseph*. As he left him ready to mount the Horse, he could not
apprehend any Mischief had happened, neither could he suspect that he
had miss'd his Way, it being so broad and plain: the only Reason which
presented itself to him, was, that he had met with an Acquaintance who
had prevailed with him to delay some time in Discourse.

He therefore resolved to proceed slowly forwards, not doubting but
that he should be shortly overtaken, and soon came to a large Water,
which filling the whole Road, he saw no Method of passing unless by
wading through, which he accordingly did up to his Middle; but was no
sooner got to the other Side, than he perceived, if he had looked over the
Hedge, he would have found a Foot-Path capable of conducting him
without wetting his Shoes.

His Surprize at *Joseph*'s not coming up grew now very troublesome: he
began to fear he knew not what, and as he determined, to move no farther;
and, if he did not shortly overtake him, to return back; he wished to find
a House of publick Entertainment where he might dry his Clothes and
refresh himself with a Pint: but seeing no such (for no other Reason than
because he did not cast his Eyes a hundred Yards forwards) he sat himself
down on a Stile, and pulled out his *Æschylus*.

A fellow passing presently by, *Adams* asked him, if he could direct him
to an Alehouse. The Fellow who had just left it, and perceived the House
and Sign to be within sight, thinking he had jeered him, and being of a
morose Temper, bad him *follow his Nose and be d———n'd*. *Adams* told him
he was a *saucy Jackanapes*; upon which the Fellow turned about angrily:
but perceiving *Adams* clench his Fist he thought proper to go on without
taking any farther notice.

A Horseman following immediately after, and being asked the same
Question, answered, Friend, there is one within a Stone's-Throw; I believe
you may see it before you. *Adams* lifting up his Eyes, cry'd, I protest and
so there is; and thanking his Informer, proceeded directly to it.

CHAPTER III

*The Opinion of two Lawyers concerning the same Gentleman, with
Mr Adams's Enquiry into the Religion of his Host.*

He had just entered the House, had called for his Pint and seated himself,
when two Horsemen came to the Door, and fastening their Horses to the
Rails, alighted. They said there was a violent Shower of Rain coming on,
which they intended to weather there, and went into a little Room by
themselves, not perceiving Mr *Adams*.

One of these immediately asked the other, if he had seen a more comical
Adventure a great while? Upon which the other said, 'he doubted whether
by Law, the Landlord could justify detaining the Horse for his Corn and
Hay.' But the former answered, 'Undoubtedly he can:[1] it is an adjudged
Case, and I have known it tried.'

Adams, who tho' he was, as the Reader may suspect, a little inclined to
Forgetfulness, never wanted more than a Hint to remind him, over-hearing
their Discourse, immediately suggested to himself that this was his own
Horse, and that he had forgot to pay for him, which upon enquiry, he
was certified of by the Gentlemen; who added, that the Horse was likely
to have more Rest than Food, unless he was paid for.

The poor Parson resolved to return presently to the Inn, tho' he knew
no more than *Joseph*, how to procure his Horse his Liberty: he was however
prevailed on to stay under Covert, 'till the Shower which was now very
violent, was over.

The three Travellers then sat down together over a Mug of good Beer;
when *Adams*, who had observed a Gentleman's House as he passed along
the Road, enquired to whom it belonged: one of the Horsemen had no
sooner mentioned the Owner's Name, than the other began to revile him
in the most opprobrious Terms. The *English* Language scarce affords a
single reproachful Word, which he did not vent on this Occasion. He
charged him likewise with many particular Facts.[2] He said, — 'he no
more regarded a Field of Wheat when he was hunting, than he did the
High-way; that he had injured several poor Farmers by trampling their
Corn under his Horse's Heels; and if any of them begged him with the
utmost Submission to refrain, his Horse-whip was always ready to do
them justice.' He said, 'that he was the greatest Tyrant to the Neighbours
in every other Instance, and would not suffer a Farmer to keep a Gun,

tho' he might justify it by Law;[3] and in his own Family so cruel a Master, that he never kept a Servant a Twelve-month. In his Capacity as a Justice,' continued he, 'he behaves so partially, that he commits or acquits just as he is in the humour, without any regard to Truth or Evidence: The Devil may carry any one before him for me; I would rather be tried before some Judges than be a Prosecutor before him: If I had an Estate in the Neighbourhood, I would sell it for half the Value, rather than live near him.' *Adams* shook his Head, and said, 'he was sorry such Men were suffered to proceed with Impunity, and that Riches could set any Man above Law.' The Reviler a little after retiring into the Yard, the Gentleman, who had first mentioned his Name to *Adams*, began to assure him, 'that his Companion was a prejudiced Person. It is true,' says he, 'perhaps, that he may have sometimes pursued his Game over a Field of Corn, but he hath always made the Party ample Satisfaction; that so far from tyrannizing over his Neighbours, or taking away their Guns, he himself knew several Farmers not qualified, who not only kept Guns, but killed Game with them. That he was the best of Masters to his Servants, and several of them had grown old in his Service. That he was the best Justice of Peace in the Kingdom, and to his certain knowledge had decided many difficult Points, which were referred to him, with the greatest Equity, and the highest Wisdom. And he verily believed, several Persons would give a Year's Purchase[4] more for an Estate near him, than under the Wings of any other great Man.' He had just finished his Encomium, when his Companion returned and acquainted him the Storm was over. Upon which, they presently mounted their Horses and departed.

Adams, who was in the utmost Anxiety at those different Characters of the same Person, asked his Host if he knew the Gentleman: for he began to imagine they had by mistake been speaking of two several Gentlemen. 'No, no, Master!' answered the Host, a shrewd cunning Fellow, 'I know the Gentleman very well of whom they have been speaking, as I do the Gentlemen who spoke of him. As for riding over other Men's Corn, to my knowledge he hath not been on horseback these two Years. I never heard he did any Injury of that kind; and as to making Reparation, he is not so free of his Money as that comes to neither. Nor did I ever hear of his taking away any Man's Gun; nay, I know several who have Guns in their Houses: but as for killing Game with them, no Man is stricter; and I believe he would ruin any who did. You heard one of the Gentlemen say, he was the worst Master in the World, and the other that he is the best: but as for my own part, I know all his Servants, and never heard from any of them that he was either one or the other. — ' 'Aye! aye!' says *Adams*, 'and how doth he behave as a Justice, pray?' 'Faith, Friend,' answered the Host, 'I question whether he is in the Commission:[5] the only Cause I have heard he hath decided a great while, was one between those very two Persons who just went out of this House; and I am sure he determined that justly, for I heard the whole matter.' 'Which did he decide it in favour of,' quoth *Adams*? 'I think I need not answer that Question,' cried the Host, 'after the different Characters you have heard of him. It is not my Business to contradict Gentlemen, while they are drinking in my House: but I knew neither of them spoke a Syllable of Truth.' 'God forbid!' (said *Adams*,) 'that Men should arrive at such a Pitch of Wickedness, to be-lye the Character of their Neighbour from a little private Affection, or what is infinitely worse, a private Spite. I rather believe we have mistaken them, and they mean two other Persons: for there are many Houses on the Road.' 'Why prithee, Friend,' cries the Host, 'dost thou pretend never to have told a lye in thy Life?' 'Never a malicious one, I am certain,' answered *Adams*; 'nor with a Design to injure the Reputation of any Man living.' 'Pugh, malicious! no, no,' replied the Host; 'not malicious with a Design to hang a Man, or bring him into Trouble: but surely out of love to one's self, one must speak better of a Friend than an Enemy.' 'Out of love to your self, you should confine your self to Truth,' says *Adams*, 'for by doing otherwise, you injure the noblest Part of yourself, your immortal Soul. I can hardly believe any Man such an Idiot to risque the Loss of that by any trifling Gain, and the greatest Gain in this World is but Dirt in comparison of what shall be revealed hereafter.' Upon which the Host taking up the Cup, with a Smile drank a Health to Hereafter: adding, 'he was for something present.' 'Why,' says *Adams* very gravely, 'Do not you believe in another World?' To which the Host answered, 'yes, he was no Atheist.' 'And you believe you have an immortal Soul,' cries *Adams*. He answered, 'God forbid he should not.' 'And Heaven and Hell?' said the Parson. The Host then bid him 'not to prophane: for those were things not to be mentioned nor thought of but in Church.' *Adams* asked him, 'why he went to Church, if what he learned there had no Influence on his Conduct in Life?' 'I go to Church,' answered the Host, 'to say my Prayers and behave godly.' 'And dost not thou,' cry'd *Adams*, 'believe what thou hearest at Church?' 'Most part of it, Master,' returned the Host. 'And dost not thou then tremble,' cries *Adams*, 'at the

Thought of eternal Punishment?' 'As for that, Master,' said he, 'I never once thought about it: but what signifies talking about matters so far off? The Mug is out, shall I draw another?'

Whilst he was gone for that purpose, a Stage-Coach drove up to the Door. The Coachman coming into the House, was asked by the Mistress, what Passengers he had in his Coach? A Parcel of *Squinny-gut* B——s, (says he) I have a good mind to overturn them; you won't prevail upon them to drink any thing I assure you. *Adams* asked him, if he had not seen a young Man on horse-back on the Road, (describing *Joseph*.) Aye, said the Coachman, a Gentlewoman in my Coach that is his Acquaintance redeemed him and his Horse; he would have been here before this time, had not the Storm driven him to shelter. God bless her, said *Adams* in a Rapture; nor could he delay walking out to satisfy himself who this charitable Woman was; but what was his surprize, when he saw his old acquaintance, Madam *Slipslop*? Her's indeed was not so great, because she had been informed by *Joseph*, that he was on the Road. Very civil were the Salutations on both sides; and Mrs *Slipslop* rebuked the Hostess for denying the Gentleman to be there when she asked for him: but indeed the poor Woman had not erred designedly: for Mrs *Slipslop* asked for a Clergyman; and she had unhappily mistaken *Adams* for a Person travelling to a neighbouring Fair with the Thimble and Button,[6] or some other such Operation; for he marched in a swinging great, but short, white Coat with black Buttons, a short Wig, and a Hat, which so far from having a black Hatband, had nothing black, about it.

Joseph was now come up, and Mrs *Slipslop* would have had him quit his Horse to the Parson, and come himself into the Coach: but he absolutely refused, saying he thanked Heaven he was well enough recovered to be very able to ride, and added, he hoped he knew his Duty better than to ride in a Coach while Mr *Adams* was on horseback.

Mrs *Slipslop* would have persisted longer, had not a Lady in the Coach put a short End to the Dispute, by refusing to suffer a Fellow in a Livery to ride in the same Coach with herself: so it was at length agreed that *Adams* should fill the vacant Place in the Coach, and *Joseph* should proceed on horseback.

They had not proceeded far before Mrs *Slipslop*, addressing herself to the Parson, spoke thus: 'There hath been a strange Alteration in our Family, Mr *Adams*, since Sir *Thomas*'s Death.' 'A strange Alteration indeed!' says *Adams*, 'as I gather from some Hints which have dropped from *Joseph*.' 'Aye,' says she, 'I could never have believed it, but the longer one lives in the World, the more one sees. So *Joseph* hath given you Hints.' — 'But of what Nature, will always remain a perfect Secret with me,' cries the Parson; 'he forced me to promise before he would communicate any thing. I am indeed concerned to find her Ladyship behave in so unbecoming a manner. I always thought her in the main, a good Lady, and should never have suspected her of Thoughts so unworthy a Christian, and with a young Lad her own Servant.' 'These things are no Secrets to me, I assure you,' cries *Slipslop*; 'and I believe, they will be none any where shortly: for ever since the Boy's Departure she hath behaved more like a mad Woman than any thing else.' 'Truly, I am heartily concerned,' says *Adams*, 'for she was a good sort of a Lady; indeed I have often wished she had attended a little more constantly at the Service, but she hath done a great deal of Good in the Parish.' 'O Mr *Adams*!' says *Slipslop*. 'People that don't see all, often know nothing. Many Things have been given away in our Family, I do assure you, without her knowledge. I have heard you say in the Pulpit, we ought not to brag: but indeed I can't avoid saying, if she had kept the Keys herself, the Poor would have wanted many a Cordial which I have let them have. As for my late Master, he was as worthy a Man as ever lived, and would have done infinite Good if he had not been controlled: but he loved a quiet Life, Heavens rest his Soul! I am confident he is there, and enjoys a quiet Life, which some Folks would not allow him here.' *Adams* answered, 'he had never heard this before, and was mistaken, if she herself,' (for he remembered she used to commend her Mistress and blame her Master) 'had not formerly been of another Opinion.' 'I don't know,' (replied she,) 'what I might once think: but now I am *confidous* Matters are as I tell you: The World will shortly see who hath been deceived; for my part I say nothing, but that it is *wondersome* how some People can carry all things with a grave Face.'

Thus Mr *Adams* and she discoursed: 'till they came opposite to a great House which stood at some distance from the Road; a Lady in the Coach spying it, cry'd, yonder lives the unfortunate *Leonora*, if one can justly call a Woman unfortunate whom we must own at the same time guilty, and the Author of her own Calamity. This was abundantly sufficient to awaken the Curiosity of Mr *Adams*, as indeed it did that of the whole Company, who jointly solicited the Lady to acquaint them with *Leonora*'s History, since it seemed, by what she had said, to contain something remarkable.

The Lady, who was perfectly well bred, did not require many Entreaties, and having only wished their Entertainment might make amends for the Company's Attention, she began in the following manner.

CHAPTER IV

The History of Leonora, *or the Unfortunate Jilt.*

Leonora was the Daughter of a Gentleman of Fortune; she was tall and well-shaped, with a Sprightliness in her Countenance, which often attracts beyond more regular Features joined with an insipid Air; nor is this kind of Beauty less apt to deceive than allure; the Good-Humour which it indicates, being often mistaken for Good-Nature, and the Vivacity for true Understanding.

Leonora, who was now at the Age of Eighteen, lived with an Aunt of her's in a Town in the North of *England.* She was an extreme Lover of Gaiety, and very rarely missed a Ball or any other publick Assembly; where she had frequent Opportunities of satisfying a greedy Appetite of Vanity with the Preference which was given her by the Men to almost every other Woman present.

Among many young Fellows who were particular in their Gallantries towards her, *Horatio* soon distinguished himself in her Eyes beyond all his Competitors; she danced with more than ordinary Gaiety when he happened to be her Partner; neither the Fairness of the Evening nor the Musick of the Nightingale, could lengthen her Walk like his Company. She affected no longer to understand the Civilities of others: whilst she inclined so attentive an Ear to every Compliment of *Horatio,* that she often smiled even when it was too delicate for her Comprehension.

'Pray, Madam,' says *Adams,* 'who was this Squire *Horatio*?'

Horatio, says the Lady, was a young Gentleman of a good Family, bred to the Law, and had been some few Years called to the Degree of a Barrister. His Face and Person were such as the Generality allowed handsome: but he had a Dignity in his Air very rarely to be seen. His Temper was of the saturnine Complexion,[1] but without the least Taint of Moroseness. He had Wit and Humour with an Inclination to Satire, which he indulged rather too much.

This Gentleman, who had contracted the most violent Passion for *Leonora,* was the last Person who perceived the Probability of its Success. The whole Town had made the Match for him, before he himself had drawn a Confidence from her Actions sufficient to mention his Passion to her; for it was his Opinion, (and perhaps he was there in the right) that it is highly impolitick to talk seriously of Love to a Woman before you have made such a Progress in her Affections, that she herself expects and desires to hear it.

But whatever Diffidence the Fears of a Lover may create, which are apt to magnify every Favour conferred on a Rival, and to see the little Advances towards themselves through the other End of the Perspective;[2] it was impossible that *Horatio*'s Passion should so blind his Discernment, as to prevent his conceiving Hopes from the Behaviour of *Leonora*; whose Fondness for him was now as visible to an indifferent Person in their Company, as his for her.

. 'I never knew any of these forward Sluts come to good,' (says the Lady, who refused *Joseph*'s Entrance into the Coach,) 'nor shall I wonder at any thing she doth in the Sequel.'

The Lady proceeded in her Story thus: It was in the Midst of a gay Conversation in the Walks one Evening, when *Horatio* whispered *Leonora*, that he was desirous to take a Turn or two with her in private; for that he had something to communicate to her of great Consequence. 'Are you sure it is of Consequence?' said she, smiling. —— 'I hope,' answered he, 'you will think so too, since the whole future Happiness of my Life must depend on the Event.'

Leonora, who very much suspected what was coming, would have deferred it 'till another Time: but *Horatio*, who had more than half conquered the Difficulty of speaking by the first Motion, was so very importunate, that she at last yielded, and leaving the rest of the Company, they turned aside into an unfrequented Walk.

They had retired far out of the sight of the Company, both maintaining a strict Silence. At last *Horatio* made a full Stop, and taking *Leonora*, who stood pale and trembling, gently by the Hand, he fetched a deep Sigh, and then looking on her Eyes with all the Tenderness imaginable, he cried out in a faltering Accent; 'O *Leonora*! is it necessary for me to declare to you on what the future Happiness of my Life must be founded! Must I say, there is something belonging to you which is a Bar to my Happiness, and which unless you will part with, I must be miserable?' 'What can that be?' replied *Leonora*. — 'No wonder,' said he, 'you are surprized, that I should make an Objection to any thing which is yours, yet sure you may guess, since it is the only one which the Riches of the World, if they were mine, should purchase of me. — O it is that which you must part with, to bestow all the rest! Can *Leonora*, or rather will she doubt longer? —— Let me then whisper it in her Ears, —— It is your Name, Madam. It is by parting with that, by your Condescension to be for ever mine, which must at once prevent me from being the most miserable, and will render me the happiest of Mankind.' *Leonora*, covered with Blushes, and with as angry a Look as she could possibly put on, told him, 'that had she suspected what his Declaration would have been, he should not have decoyed her from her Company; that he had so surprized and frighted her, that she begged him to convey her back as quick as possible;' which he, trembling very near as much as herself, did.

'More Fool he,' cried *Slipslop*, 'it is a sign he knew very little of our *Sect*.' 'Truly, Madam,' said *Adams*, 'I think you are in the right, I should have insisted to know a piece of her Mind, when I had carried matters so far.' But Mrs *Grave-airs* desired the Lady to omit all such fulsome Stuff in her Story: for that it made her sick.

Well then, Madam, to be as concise as possible, said the Lady, many Weeks had not pass'd after this Interview, before *Horatio* and *Leonora* were what they call on a good footing together. All Ceremonies except the last were now over; the Writings were now drawn,[3] and every thing was in the utmost forwardness preparative to the putting *Horatio* in possession of all his Wishes. I will if you please repeat you a Letter from each of them which I have got by heart, and which will give you no small Idea of their Passion on both sides.

Mrs *Grave-airs* objected to hearing these Letters: but being put to the Vote, it was carried against her by all the rest in the Coach; Parson *Adams* contending for it with the utmost Vehemence.

HORATIO *to* LEONORA

How vain, most adorable Creature, is the Pursuit of Pleasure in the absence of an Object to which the Mind is entirely devoted, unless it have some Relation to that Object! I was last Night condemned to the Society of Men of Wit and Learning, which, however agreeable it might have formerly been to me, now only gave me a Suspicion that they imputed my Absence in Conversation to the true Cause. For which Reason, when your Engagements forbid me the extatic Happiness of seeing you, I am always desirous to be alone; since my Sentiments for *Leonora* are so delicate, that I cannot bear the Apprehension of another's prying into those delightful Endearments with which the warm Imagination of a Lover will sometimes indulge him, and which I suspect my Eyes then betray. To fear this Discovery of our Thoughts, may perhaps appear too ridiculous a Nicety to Minds, not susceptible of all the Tendernesses of this delicate Passion. And surely we shall suspect there are few such, when we consider that it requires every human Virtue to exert itself in its full Extent. Since the Beloved whose Happiness it ultimately respects, may give us charming Opportunities of being brave in her Defence, generous to her Wants, compassionate to her Afflictions, grateful to her Kindness, and, in the same manner, of exercising every other Virtue, which he who would not do to any Degree, and that with the utmost Rapture, can never deserve the Name of a Lover: It is therefore with a View to the delicate Modesty of your Mind that I cultivate it so purely in my own, and it is that which will sufficiently suggest to you the Uneasiness I bear from those Liberties which Men to whom the World allow Politeness will sometimes give themselves on these Occasions.

Can I tell you with what Eagerness I expect the Arrival of that blest Day, when I shall experience the Falshood of a common Assertion that the greatest human Happiness consists in Hope? A Doctrine which no Person had ever stronger Reason to believe than myself at present, since none ever tasted such Bliss as fires my Bosom with the Thoughts of spending my future Days with such a Companion, and that every Action of my Life will have the glorious Satisfaction of conducing to your Happiness.

*Leonora *to* Horatio

The Refinement of your Mind has been so evidently proved, by every Word and Action ever since I had first the Pleasure of knowing you, that I thought it impossible my Good Opinion of *Horatio* could have been heightened by any additional Proof of Merit. This very Thought was my Amusement when I received your last Letter, which, when I opened, I confess I was surprized to find the delicate Sentiments expressed there, so far exceeded what I thought could come even from you, (altho' I know all the generous Principles human Nature is capable of, are centered in your Breast) that Words cannot paint what I feel on the Reflection, that my Happiness shall be the ultimate End of all your Actions.

Oh *Horatio*! what a Life must that be, where the meanest domestic

---

* This Letter was written by a young Lady on reading the former.⁴

Cares are sweetened by the pleasing Consideration that the Man on Earth who best deserves, and to whom you are most inclined to give your Affections, is to reap either Profit or Pleasure from all you do! In such a Case, Toils must be turned into Diversions, and nothing but the unavoidable Inconveniences of Life can make us remember that we are mortal.

If the solitary Turn of your Thoughts, and the Desire of keeping them undiscovered, makes even the Conversation of Men of Wit and Learning tedious to you, what anxious Hours must I spend who am condemned by Custom to the Conversation of Women, whose natural Curiosity leads them to pry into all my Thoughts, and whose Envy can never suffer *Horatio*'s Heart to be possessed by any one without forcing them into malicious Designs, against the Person who is so happy as to possess it: but indeed, if ever Envy can possibly have any Excuse, or even Alleviation, it is in this Case, where the Good is so great, that it must be equally natural to all to wish it for themselves, nor am I ashamed to own it: and to your Merit, *Horatio*, I am obliged, that prevents my being in that most uneasy of all the Situations I can figure in my Imagination of being led by Inclination to love the Person whom my own Judgment forces me to condemn.

Matters were in so great forwardness between this fond Couple, that the Day was fixed for their Marriage, and was now within a Fortnight, when the Sessions chanced to be held for that County in a Town about twenty Miles distance from that which is the Scene of our Story. It seems, it is usual for the young Gentlemen of the Bar to repair to these Sessions, not so much for the sake of Profit, as to shew their Parts and learn the Law of the Justices of Peace: for which purpose one of the wisest and gravest of all the Justices is appointed Speaker or Chairman, as they modestly call it, and he reads them a Lecture, and instructs them in the true Knowledge of the Law.

'You are here guilty of a little Mistake,' says *Adams*, 'which if you please I will correct; I have attended at one of these Quarter Sessions,[5] where I observed the Counsel taught the Justices, instead of learning any thing of them.'

It is not very material, said the Lady: hither repaired *Horatio*, who as he hoped by his Profession to advance his Fortune, which was not at present very large, for the sake of his dear *Leonora*, he resolved to spare no Pains, nor lose any Opportunity of improving or advancing himself in it.

The same Afternoon in which he left the Town, as *Leonora* stood at her

Window, a Coach and Six passed by: which she declared to be the completest, genteelest, prettiest Equipage she ever saw; adding these remarkable Words, *O I am in love with that Equipage!* which, tho' her Friend *Florella* at that time did not greatly regard, she hath since remembered.

In the Evening an Assembly was held, which *Leonora* honoured with her Company: but intended to pay her dear *Horatio* the Compliment of refusing to dance in his Absence.

O Why have not Women as good Resolution to maintain their Vows, as they have often good Inclinations in making them!

The Gentleman who owned the Coach and Six, came to the Assembly. His Clothes were as remarkably fine as his Equipage could be. He soon attracted the Eyes of the Company; all the Smarts,[6] all the Silk Waistcoats with Silver and Gold Edgings, were eclipsed in an instant.

'Madam,' said *Adams*, 'if it be not impertinent, I should be glad to know how this Gentleman was drest.'

Sir, answered the Lady, I have been told, he had on a Cut-Velvet Coat of a Cinnamon Colour, lined with a Pink Satten, embroidered all over with Gold; his Waistcoat, which was Cloth of Silver, was embroidered with Gold, likewise. I cannot be particular as to the rest of his Dress: but it was all in the *French* Fashion, for *Bellarmine*[7] (that was his Name) was just arrived from *Paris*.

This fine Figure did not more entirely engage the Eyes of every Lady in the Assembly, than *Leonora* did his. He had scarce beheld her, but he stood motionless and fixed as a Statue, or at least would have done so, if Good-Breeding had permitted him. However, he carried it so far before he had power to correct himself, that every Person in the Room easily discovered where his Admiration was settled. The other Ladies began to single out their former Partners, all perceiving who would be *Bellarmine's* Choice; which they however endeavoured, by all possible means, to prevent: Many of them saying to *Leonora*, 'O Madam, I suppose we shan't have the pleasure of seeing you dance To-Night;' and then crying out in *Bellarmine's* hearing, 'O *Leonora* will not dance, I assure you; her Partner is not here.' One maliciously attempted to prevent her, by sending a disagreeable Fellow to ask her, that so she might be obliged either to dance with him, or sit down: but this Scheme proved abortive.

Leonora saw herself admired by the fine Stranger, and envied by every Woman present. Her little Heart began to flutter within her, and her Head was agitated with a convulsive Motion; she seemed as if she would speak to several of her Acquaintance, but had nothing to say: for as she would not mention her present Triumph, so she could not disengage her Thoughts one moment from the Contemplation of it: She had never tasted any thing like this Happiness. She had before known what it was to torment a single Woman; but to be hated and secretly cursed by a whole Assembly, was a Joy reserved for this blessed Moment. As this vast Profusion of Ecstacy had confounded her Understanding, so there was nothing so foolish as her Behaviour; she played a thousand childish Tricks, distorted her Person into several Shapes, and her Face into several Laughs, without any Reason. In a word, her Carriage was as absurd as her Desires, which were, to affect an Insensibility of the Stranger's Admiration, and at the same time a Triumph from that Admiration over every Woman in the Room.

In this Temper of Mind, *Bellarmine*, having enquired who she was, advanced to her, and with a low Bow, begged the Honour of dancing with her, which she with as low a Curt'sy immediately granted. She danced with him all Night, and enjoyed perhaps the highest Pleasure, which she was capable of feeling.

At these Words, *Adams* fetched a deep Groan, which frighted the Ladies, who told him, 'they hoped he was not ill.' He answered, 'he groaned only for the Folly of *Leonora*.'

Leonora retired, (continued the Lady) about Six in the Morning, but not to Rest. She tumbled and tossed in her Bed, with very short Intervals of Sleep, and those entirely filled with Dreams of the Equipage and fine Clothes she had seen, and the Balls, Operas and Ridotto's,[8] which had been the Subject of their Conversation.

In the Afternoon, *Bellarmine*, in the dear Coach and Six, came to wait on her. He was indeed charmed with her Person, and was, on Enquiry, so well pleased with the Circumstances of her Father, (for he himself notwithstanding all his Finery, was not quite so rich as a *Crœsus* or an *Attălus*.)[9] '*Attălus*,' says Mr *Adams*, 'but pray how came you acquainted with these Names?' The Lady smiled at the Question, and proceeded — He was so pleased, I say, that he resolved to make his Addresses to her directly. He did so accordingly, and that with so much warmth and briskness, that he quickly baffled her weak Repulses, and obliged the Lady to refer him to her Father, who, she knew, would quickly declare in favour of a Coach and Six.

Thus, what *Horatio* had by Sighs and Tears, Love and Tenderness, been so long obtaining, the *French-English Bellarmine* with Gaiety and Gallantry possessed himself of in an instant. In other words, what Modesty had employed a full Year in raising, Impudence demolished in 24 Hours.

Here *Adams* groaned a second time, but the Ladies, who began to smoke[10] him, took no Notice.

From the Opening of the Assembly 'till the End of *Bellarmine*'s Visit, *Leonora* had scarce once thought of *Horatio*: but he now began, tho' an unwelcome Guest, to enter into her Mind. She wished she had seen the charming *Bellarmine* and his charming Equipage before Matters had gone so far. 'Yet, why,' (says she) 'should I wish to have seen him before, or what signifies it that I have seen him now? Is not *Horatio* my Lover? almost my Husband? Is he not as handsome, nay handsomer than *Bellarmine*? Aye, but *Bellarmine* is the genteeler and the finer Man; yes, that he must be allowed. Yes, yes, he is that certainly. But did not I no longer ago than yesterday love *Horatio* more than all the World? aye, but yesterday I had not seen *Bellarmine*. But doth not *Horatio* doat on me, and may he not in despair break his Heart if I abandon him? Well, and hath not *Bellarmine* a Heart to break too? Yes, but I promised *Horatio* first; but that was poor *Bellarmine*'s Misfortune, if I had seen him first, I should certainly have preferred him. Did not the dear Creature prefer me to every Woman in the Assembly, when every She was laying out for him? When was it in *Horatio*'s power to give me such an Instance of Affection? Can he give me an Equipage or any of those Things which *Bellarmine* will make me Mistress of? How vast is the difference between being the Wife of a poor Counsellor, and the Wife of one of *Bellarmine*'s Fortune! If I marry *Horatio*, I shall triumph over no more than one Rival: but by marrying *Bellarmine*, I shall be the Envy of all my Acquaintance. What Happiness! — But can I suffer *Horatio* to die? for he hath sworn he cannot survive my Loss: but perhaps he may not die; if he should, can I prevent it? Must I sacrifice myself to him? besides, *Bellarmine* may be as miserable for me too.' She was thus arguing with herself, when some young Ladies called her to the Walks, and a little relieved her Anxiety for the present.

The next Morning *Bellarmine* breakfasted with her in presence of her Aunt, whom he sufficiently informed of his Passion for *Leonora*; he was no sooner withdrawn, than the old Lady began to advise her Niece on this Occasion. — 'You see, Child,' (says she) 'what Fortune hath thrown in your way, and I hope you will not withstand your own Preferments.' *Leonora* sighing, 'begged her not to mention any such thing, when she knew her Engagements to *Horatio*.' 'Engagements to a Fig,' cry'd the Aunt, 'you should thank Heaven on your Knees that you have it yet in your power to break them. Will any Woman hesitate a Moment, whether she shall ride in a Coach or walk on Foot all the Days of her Life? — But

Bellarmine drives six, and *Horatio* not even a Pair.' 'Yes, but, Madam, what will the World say?' answered *Leonora*; 'will not they condemn me?' 'The World is always on the side of Prudence,' cries the Aunt, 'and would surely condemn you if you sacrificed your Interest to any Motive whatever. O, I know the World very well, and you shew your own Ignorance, my Dear, by your Objection. O' my Conscience the World is wiser. I have lived longer in it than you, and I assure you there is not any thing worth our Regard besides Money: nor did I ever know one Person who married from other Considerations, who did not afterwards heartily repent it. Besides, if we examine the two Men, can you prefer a sneaking[11] Fellow, who hath been bred at a University, to a fine Gentleman just come from his Travels? — All the World must allow *Bellarmine* to be a fine Gentleman, positively a fine Gentleman, and a handsome Man. —' 'Perhaps, Madam, I should not doubt, if I knew how to be handsomely off with the other.' 'O leave that to me,' says the Aunt. 'You know your Father hath not been acquainted with the Affair. Indeed, for my part, I thought it might do well enough, not dreaming of such an Offer: but I'll disengage you, leave me to give the Fellow an Answer. I warrant you shall have no farther Trouble.'

Leonora was at length satisfied with her Aunt's Reasoning; and, *Bellarmine* supping with her that Evening, it was agreed he should the next Morning go to her Father and propose the Match, which she consented should be consummated at his Return.

The Aunt retired soon after Supper, and the Lovers being left together, *Bellarmine* began in the following manner: 'Yes, Madam, this Coat I assure you was made at *Paris*, and I defy the best *English* Taylor even to imitate it. There is not one of them can cut, Madam, they can't cut. If you observe how this Skirt is turned, and this Sleeve, a clumsy *English* Rascal can do nothing like it. — Pray how do you like my Liveries?' *Leonora* answered, 'she thought them very pretty.' 'All *French*,' says he, 'I assure you, except the Great Coats; I never trust any thing more than a Great Coat to an *Englishman*; you know one must encourage our own People what one can, especially as, before I had a Place, I was in the Country Interest, he, he, he! but for myself, I would see the dirty Island at the bottom of the Sea, rather than wear a single Rag of *English* Work about me; and I am sure after you have made one Tour to *Paris*, you will be of the same Opinion with regard to your own Clothes. You can't conceive what an Addition a *French* Dress would be to your Beauty; I positively assure you, at the first Opera I saw since I came over, I mistook the *English* Ladies for Chambermaids, he, he, he!'[12]

With such sort of polite Discourse did the gay *Bellarmine* entertain his beloved *Leonora*, when the Door opened on a sudden, and *Horatio* entered the Room; 'tis impossible to express the Surprize of *Leonora*.

'Poor Woman,' says Mrs *Slipslop*, 'what a terrible *Quandary* she must be in!' 'Not at all,' says Miss *Grave-airs*, 'such Sluts can never be confounded.' 'She must have then more than *Corinthian* Assurance,' said *Adams*; 'ay, more than *Lais* herself.'[13]

A long Silence, continued the Lady, prevailed in the whole Company: If the familiar Entrance of *Horatio* struck the greatest Astonishment into *Bellarmine*, the unexpected Presence of *Bellarmine* no less surprized *Horatio*. At length *Leonora* collecting all the Spirits she was Mistress of, addressed herself to the latter, and pretended to wonder at the Reason of so late a Visit. 'I should, indeed,' answered he, 'have made some Apology for disturbing you at this Hour, had not my finding you in Company assured me I do not break in on your Repose.' *Bellarmine* rose from his Chair, traversed the Room in a Minuet Step, and humm'd an Opera Tune, while *Horatio* advancing to *Leonora* ask'd her in a Whisper, if that Gentleman was not a Relation of her's; to which she answered with a Smile, or rather Sneer, 'No, he is no Relation of mine yet;' adding, 'she could not guess the Meaning of his Question.' *Horatio* told her softly, 'it did not arise from Jealousy.' 'Jealousy!' cries she, 'I assure you; — it would be very strange in a common Acquaintance to give himself any of those Airs.' These Words a little surprized *Horatio*, but before he had time to answer, *Bellarmine* danced up to the Lady, and told her, 'he feared he interrupted some Business between her and the Gentleman.' 'I can have no Business,' said she, 'with the Gentleman, nor any other, which need be any Secret to you.'

'You'll pardon me,' said *Horatio*, 'if I desire to know who this Gentleman is, who is to be intrusted with all our Secrets.' 'You'll know soon enough,' cries *Leonora*, 'but I can't guess what Secrets can ever pass between us of such mighty Consequence.' 'No Madam!' cries *Horatio*, 'I'm sure you would not have me understand you in earnest.' 'It's indifferent to me,' says she, 'how you understand me; but I think so unseasonable a Visit is difficult to be understood at all, at least when People find one engaged, though one's Servants do not deny one,[14] one may expect a well-bred Person should soon take the Hint.' 'Madam,' said *Horatio*, 'I did not imagine any Engagement with a Stranger, as it seems this Gentleman is, would have made my Visit impertinent, or that any such Ceremonies were to be preserved between persons in our Situation.' 'Sure you are in

a Dream,' says she, 'or would persuade me that I am in one. I know no
pretensions a common Acquaintance can have to lay aside the Ceremonies
of Good-Breeding.' 'Sure,' said he, 'I am in a Dream; for it is impossible
I should be really esteemed a common Acquaintance by *Leonora*, after
what has passed between us!' 'Passed between us! Do you intend to affront
me before this Gentleman?' 'D——n me, affront the Lady,' says *Bellarmine*,
cocking his Hat and strutting up to *Horatio*, 'does any Man dare affront
this Lady before me, d——n me?' 'Harkee, Sir,' says *Horatio*, 'I would advise
you to lay aside that fierce Air; for I am mightily deceived, if this Lady
has not a violent Desire to get your Worship a good drubbing.' 'Sir,' said
Bellarmine, 'I have the Honour to be her Protector, and d——n me, if I
understand your Meaning.' 'Sir,' answered *Horatio*, 'she is rather your
Protectress: but give yourself no more Airs, for you see I am prepared for
you,' (shaking his Whip at him.) 'Oh! *Serviteur tres humble*,' says *Bellarmine*,
'*Je Vous entend parfaitement bien*.'[15] At which time the Aunt, who had heard
of *Horatio*'s Visit, entered the Room, and soon satisfied all his Doubts. She
convinced him that he was never more awake in his Life, and that nothing
more extraordinary had happened in his three days Absence, than a small
Alteration in the Affections of *Leonora*: who now burst into Tears, and
wondered what Reason she had given him to use her in so barbarous a
manner. *Horatio* desired *Bellarmine* to withdraw with him: but the Ladies
prevented it by laying violent Hands on the latter; upon which, the former
took his Leave without any great Ceremony, and departed, leaving the
Lady with his Rival to consult for his Safety, which *Leonora* feared her
Indiscretion might have endangered: but the Aunt comforted her with
Assurances, that *Horatio* would not venture his Person against so accomplished a Cavalier as *Bellarmine*, and that being a Lawyer, he would seek
Revenge in his own way, and the most they had to apprehend from him
was an Action.[16]

They at length therefore agreed to permit *Bellarmine* to retire to his
Lodgings, having first settled all Matters relating to the Journey which he
was to undertake in the Morning, and their Preparations for the Nuptials
at his return.

But alas! as wise Men have observed, the Seat of Valour is not the
Countenance, and many a grave and plain Man, will, on a just Provocation,
betake himself to that mischievous Metal, cold Iron; while Men of a fiercer
Brow, and sometimes with that Emblem of Courage, a Cockade, will
more prudently decline it.

Leonora was waked in the Morning, from a Visionary Coach and Six,

.with the dismal Account, that *Bellarmine* was run through the Body by *Horatio*, that he lay languishing at an Inn, and the Surgeons had declared the Wound mortal. She immediately leap'd out of the Bed, danced about the Room in a frantic manner, tore her Hair and beat her Breast in all the Agonies of Despair; in which sad Condition her Aunt, who likewise arose at the News, found her. The good old Lady applied her utmost Art to comfort her Niece. She told her, 'while there was Life, there was Hope: but that if he should die, her Affliction would be of no service to *Bellarmine*, and would only expose herself, which might probably keep her some time without any future Offer; that as Matters had happened, her wisest way would be to think no more of *Bellarmine*, but to endeavour to reconcile herself to *Horatio*.' 'Speak not to me,' cry'd the disconsolate *Leonora*, 'is it not owing to me, that poor *Bellarmine* has lost his Life? have not these cursed Charms' (at which Words she looked stedfastly in the Glass,) 'been the Ruin of the most charming Man of this Age? Can I ever bear to contemplate my own Face again?' (with her Eyes still fixed on the Glass.) 'Am I not the Murderess of the finest Gentleman? No other Woman in the Town could have made any Impression on him.' 'Never think of Things past,' cries the Aunt, 'think of reconciling yourself to *Horatio*.' 'What Reason,' said the Niece, 'have I to hope he would forgive me? no, I have lost him as well as the other, and it was your wicked Advice which was the Occasion of all; you seduced me, contrary to my Inclinations, to abandon poor *Horatio*,' at which Words she burst into Tears; 'you prevailed upon me, whether I would or no, to give up my Affections for him; had it not been for you, *Bellarmine* never would have entered into my Thoughts; had not his Addresses been backed by your Persuasions, they never would have made any Impression on me; I should have defied all the Fortune and Equipage in the World; but it was you, it was you, who got the better of my Youth and Simplicity, and forced me to lose my dear *Horatio* for ever.'

The Aunt was almost borne down with this Torrent of Words, she however rallied all the Strength she could, and drawing her Mouth up in a Purse, began: 'I am not surprized, Niece, at this Ingratitude. Those who advise young Women for their Interest, must always expect such a Return: I am convinced my Brother will thank me for breaking off your Match with *Horatio* at any rate.' 'That may not be in your power yet,' answered *Leonora*; 'tho' it is very ungrateful in you to desire or attempt it, after the Presents you have received from him.' (For indeed true it is, that many Presents, and some pretty valuable ones, had passed from *Horatio* to the old Lady: but as true it is, that *Bellarmine* when he breakfasted with her and her Niece, had complimented her with a Brilliant from his Finger, of much greater Value than all she had touched of the other.)

The Aunt's Gall was on float[17] to reply, when a Servant brought a Letter into the Room; which *Leonora* hearing it came from *Bellarmine*, with great Eagerness opened, and read as follows:

Most Divine Creature,

The wound which I fear you have heard I received from my Rival, is not like to be so fatal as those shot into my Heart, which have been fired from your Eyes, *tout-brilliant*. Those are the only Cannons by which I am to fall: for my Surgeon gives me Hopes of being soon able to attend your *Ruelle*;[18] 'till when, unless you would do me an Honour which I have scarce the *Hardiesse* to think of, your Absence will be the greatest Anguish which can be felt by,

MADAM,
Avec tout le respecte *in the World,*
Your most Obedient, most Absolute
Devoté,

BELLARMINE.

As soon as *Leonora* perceived such Hopes of *Bellarmine*'s Recovery, and that the Gossip Fame had, according to Custom, so enlarged his Danger, she presently abandoned all further Thoughts of *Horatio*, and was soon reconciled to her Aunt, who received her again into Favour, with a more Christian Forgiveness than we generally meet with. Indeed it is possible she might be a little alarmed at the Hints which her Niece had given her concerning the Presents. She might apprehend such Rumours, should they get abroad, might injure a Reputation, which by frequenting Church twice a day, and preserving the utmost Rigour and Strictness in her Countenance and Behaviour for many Years, she had established.

Leonora's Passion returned now for *Bellarmine* with greater Force after its small Relaxation than ever. She proposed to her Aunt to make him a Visit in his Confinement, which the old Lady, with great and commendable Prudence advised her to decline: 'For,' says she, 'should any Accident intervene to prevent your intended Match, too forward a Behaviour with this Lover may injure you in the Eyes of others. Every Woman 'till she is married ought to consider of and provide against the Possibility of the Affair's breaking off.' *Leonora* said, 'she should be indifferent to whatever might happen in such a Case: for she had now so absolutely placed her Affections on this dear Man (so she called him) that, if it was her misfortune to lose him, she should for ever abandon all Thoughts of Mankind.' She therefore resolved to visit him, notwithstanding all the prudent Advice of her Aunt to the contrary, and that very Afternoon executed her Resolution.

The Lady was proceeding in her Story, when the Coach drove into the Inn where the Company were to dine, sorely to the dissatisfaction of Mr *Adams*, whose Ears were the most hungry Part about him; he being, as the Reader may perhaps guess, of an insatiable Curiosity, and heartily desirous of hearing the End of this Amour, tho' he professed he could scarce wish Success to a Lady of so inconstant a Disposition.

CHAPTER V

A dreadful Quarrel which happened at the Inn where the Company dined, with its bloody Consequences to Mr Adams.[1]

As soon as the Passengers had alighted from the Coach, Mr *Adams*, as was his Custom, made directly to the Kitchin, where he found *Joseph* sitting by the Fire and the Hostess anointing his Leg: for the Horse which Mr *Adams* had borrowed of his Clerk, had so violent a Propensity to kneeling, that one would have thought it had been his Trade as well as his Master's: nor would he always give any notice of such his Intention; he was often found on his Knees, when the Rider least expected it. This Foible however was of no great Inconvenience to the Parson, who was accustomed to it, and as his Legs almost touched the Ground when he bestrode the Beast, had but a little way to fall, and threw himself forward on such Occasions with so much dexterity, that he never received any Mischief; the Horse and he frequently rolling many Paces distance, and afterwards both getting up and meeting as good Friends as ever.

Poor *Joseph*, who had not been used to such kind of Cattle, tho' an excellent Horseman, did not so happily disengage himself: but falling with his Leg under the Beast, received a violent Contusion, to which the good Woman was, as we have said, applying a warm Hand with some camphirated Spirits[2] just at the time when the Parson entered the Kitchin.

He had scarce express'd his Concern for *Joseph*'s Misfortune, before the Host likewise entered. He was by no means of Mr *Tow-wouse*'s gentle

Disposition, and was indeed perfect Master of his House and every thing in it but his Guests.

This surly Fellow, who always proportioned his Respect to the Appearance of a Traveller, from *God bless your Honour*, down to plain *Coming presently*, observing his Wife on her Knees to a Footman, cried out, without considering his Circumstances, 'What a Pox is the Woman about? why don't you mind the Company in the Coach? Go and ask them what they will have for Dinner?' 'My Dear,' says she, 'you know they can have nothing but what is at the Fire, which will be ready presently; and really the poor young Man's Leg is very much bruised.' At which Words, she fell to chafing more violently than before: the Bell then happening to ring, he damn'd his Wife, and bid her go in to the Company, and not stand rubbing there all day: for he did not believe the young Fellow's Leg was so bad as he pretended; and if it was, within twenty Miles he would find a Surgeon to cut it off. Upon these Words, *Adams* fetched two Strides across the Room; and snapping his Fingers over his Head muttered aloud, He would excommunicate such a Wretch for a Farthing; for he believed the Devil had more Humanity. These Words occasioned a Dialogue between *Adams* and the Host, in which there were two or three sharp Replies, 'till *Joseph* bad the latter know how to behave himself to his Betters. At which the Host, (having first strictly surveyed *Adams*) scornfully repeating the word *Betters*, flew into a Rage, and telling *Joseph* he was as able to walk out of his House as he had been to walk into it, offered to lay violent Hands on him; which perceiving, *Adams* dealt him so sound a Compliment over his Face with his Fist, that the Blood immediately gushed out of his Nose in a Stream. The Host being unwilling to be out-done in Courtesy, especially by a Person of *Adams*'s Figure, returned the Favour with so much Gratitude, that the Parson's Nostrils likewise began to look a little redder than usual. Upon which he again assailed his Antagonist, and with another stroke laid him sprawling on the Floor.

The Hostess, who was a better Wife than so surly a Husband deserved, seeing her Husband all bloody and stretched along, hastened presently to his assistance, or rather to revenge the Blow which to all appearance was the last he would ever receive; when, lo! a Pan full of Hog's-Blood, which unluckily stood on the Dresser, presented itself first to her Hands. She seized it in her Fury, and without any Reflection discharged it into the Parson's Face, and with so good an Aim, that much the greater part first saluting his Countenance, trickled thence in so large a current down his Beard, and over his Garments, that a more horrible Spectacle was hardly to be seen or even imagined. All which was perceived by Mrs *Slipslop*, who entered the Kitchin at that Instant. This good Gentlewoman, not being of a Temper so extremely cool and patient as perhaps was required to ask many Questions on this Occasion; flew with great Impetuosity at the Hostess's Cap, which, together with some of her Hair, she plucked from her Head in a moment, giving her at the same time several hearty Cuffs in the Face, which by frequent Practice on the inferiour Servants, she had learned an excellent Knack of delivering with a good Grace. Poor *Joseph* could hardly rise from his Chair; the Parson was employed in wiping the Blood from his Eyes, which had intirely blinded him, and the Landlord was but just beginning to stir, whilst Mrs *Slipslop* holding down the Landlady's Face with her Left Hand, made so dextrous a use of her Right, that the poor Woman began to roar in a Key, which alarmed all the Company in the Inn.

There happened to be in the Inn at this time, besides the Ladies who arrived in the Stage-Coach, the two Gentlemen who were present at Mr *Tow-wouse*'s when *Joseph* was detained for his Horse's Meat, and whom we have before mentioned, to have stopt at the Alehouse with *Adams*. There was likewise a Gentleman just returned from his Travels to *Italy*; all whom the horrid Outcry of Murder, presently brought into the Kitchin, where the several Combatants were found in the Postures already described.

It was now no difficulty to put an end to the Fray, the Conquerors being satisfied with the Vengeance they had taken, and the Conquered having no Appetite to renew the Fight. The principal Figure, and which engaged the Eyes of all, was *Adams*, who was all over covered with Blood, which the whole Company concluded to be his own; and consequently imagined him no longer for this World. But the Host, who had now recovered from his Blow, and was risen from the Ground, soon delivered them from this Apprehension, by damning his Wife, for wasting the Hog's Puddings, and telling her all would have been very well if she had not intermeddled like a B—— as she was; adding, he was very glad the Gentlewoman had paid her, tho' not half what she deserved. The poor Woman had indeed fared much the worst, having, besides the unmerciful Cuffs received, lost a Quantity of Hair which Mrs *Slipslop* in Triumph held in her left Hand.

The Traveller, addressing himself to Miss *Grave-airs*, desired her not to be frighten'd; for here had been only a little Boxing, which he said to their *Disgracia* the *English* were *accustomata* to; adding, it must be however a Sight somewhat strange to him, who was just come from *Italy*, the *Italians* not being addicted to the *Cuffardo*, but *Bastonza*, says he. He then went up to *Adams*, and telling him he looked like the Ghost of *Othello*, bid him *not shake his gory Locks at him, for he could not say he did it*.[3] *Adams* very innocently answered, *Sir, I am far from accusing you*. He then returned to the Lady, and cried, I find the bloody Gentleman is *uno insipido del nullo senso. Damnata di me*, if I have seen such a *spectaculo*[4] in my way from *Viterbo*.

One of the Gentlemen having learnt from the Host the Occasion of this Bustle, and being assured by him that *Adams* had struck the first Blow, whispered in his Ear; He'd warrant he would *recover*. 'Recover! Master,' said the Host, smiling: 'Yes, yes, I am not afraid of dying with a Blow or two neither; I am not such a Chicken as that.' Pugh! said the Gentleman, I mean you will recover Damages, in that Action which undoubtedly you intend to bring, as soon as a Writ can be returned from *London*;[5] for you look like a Man of too much Spirit and Courage to suffer any one to beat you without bringing your Action against him: He must be a scandalous Fellow indeed, who would put up a Drubbing whilst the Law is open to revenge it; besides, he hath drawn Blood from you and spoiled your Coat, and the Jury will give Damages for that too. An excellent new Coat upon my Word, and now not worth a Shilling!

I don't care, continued he, to intermeddle in these Cases:[6] but you have a Right to my Evidence; and if I am sworn, I must speak the Truth. I saw you sprawling on the Floor, and the Blood gushing from your Nostrils. You may take your own Opinion; but was I in your Circumstances, every Drop of my Blood should convey an Ounce of Gold into my Pocket: remember I don't advise you to go to Law, but if your Jury were Christians, they must give swinging Damages, that's all. 'Master,' cry'd the Host, scratching his Head, 'I have no stomach to Law, I thank you. I have seen enough of that in the Parish, where two of my Neighbours have been at Law about a House, 'till they have both lawed themselves into a Goal.'[7] At which Words he turned about, and began to enquire again after his Hog's Puddings, nor would it probably have been a sufficient Excuse for his Wife that she spilt them in his Defence, had not some Awe of the Company, especially of the *Italian* Traveller, who was a Person of great Dignity, with-held his Rage. Whilst one of the above-mentioned Gentlemen was employed, as we have seen him, on the behalf of the Landlord, the other was no less hearty on the side of Mr *Adams*, whom he advised to bring his Action immediately. He said the Assault of the Wife was in Law the Assault of the Husband; for they were but one Person;[8] and he was liable to pay Damages, which he said must be considerable, where so bloody a Disposition appeared. *Adams* answered, if it was true that they were but one Person he had assaulted the Wife; for he was sorry to own he had struck the Husband the first Blow. I am sorry you own it too, cries the Gentleman; for it could not possibly appear to the Court: for here was no Evidence present but the lame Man in the Chair, whom I suppose to be your Friend, and would consequently say nothing but what made for you. How, Sir, says *Adams*, do you take me for a Villain, who would prosecute Revenge in cold Blood, and use unjustifiable Means to obtain it? If you knew me and my Order, I should think you affronted both. At the word Order, the Gentleman stared, (for he was too bloody to be of any modern Order of Knights,) and turning hastily about, said, every Man knew his own Business.

Matters being now composed, the Company retired to their several Apartments, the two Gentlemen congratulating each other on the Success of their good Offices, in procuring a perfect Reconciliation between the contending Parties; and the Traveller went to his Repast, crying, as the Italian Poet says,

> '*Je voi* very well, *que tutta e pace*,
> So send up Dinner, good *Boniface*.'⁹

The Coachman began now to grow importunate with his Passengers, whose Entrance into the Coach was retarded by Miss *Grave-airs* insisting, against the Remonstrances of all the rest, that she would not admit a Footman into the Coach: for poor *Joseph* was too lame to mount a Horse. A young Lady, who was, as it seems, an Earl's Grand-Daughter, begged it with almost Tears in her Eyes; Mr *Adams* prayed, and Mrs *Slipslop* scolded, but all to no purpose. She said, 'she would not demean herself to ride with a Footman: that there were Waggons on the Road: that if the Master of the Coach desired it, she would pay for two Places: but would suffer no such Fellow to come in.' 'Madam,' says *Slipslop*, 'I am sure no one can refuse another coming into a Stage-Coach.' 'I don't know, Madam,' says the Lady, 'I am not much used to Stage-Coaches, I seldom travel in them.' 'That may be, Madam,' replied *Slipslop*, 'very good People do, and some People's Betters, for aught I know.' Miss *Grave-airs* said, 'some Folks might sometimes give their Tongues a liberty, to some People that were their Betters, which did not become them: for her part, she was not used to converse with Servants.' *Slipslop* returned, 'some People kept no Servants to converse with: for her part, she thanked

Heaven, she lived in a Family where there were a great many; and had more under her own command, than any paultry little Gentlewoman in the Kingdom.' Miss *Grave-airs* cry'd, 'she believed, her Mistress would not encourage such Sauciness to her Betters.' 'My Betters,' says *Slipslop*, 'who is my Betters, pray?' 'I am your Betters,' answered Miss *Grave-airs*, 'and I'll acquaint your Mistress.' — At which Mrs *Slipslop* laughed aloud, and told her, 'her Lady was one of the great Gentry, and such little paultry Gentlewomen, as some Folks who travelled in Stage-Coaches, would not easily come at her.'

This smart Dialogue between some People, and some Folks, was going on at the Coach-Door, when a solemn Person riding into the Inn, and seeing Miss *Grave-airs*, immediately accosted her with 'Dear Child, how do you?' She presently answered, 'O! Papa, I am glad you have overtaken me.' 'So am I,' answered he: 'for one of our Coaches is just at hand; and there being room for you in it, you shall go no farther in the Stage, unless you desire it.' 'How can you imagine I should desire it?' says she; so bidding *Slipslop*, 'ride with her Fellow, if she pleased;' she took her Father by the Hand, who was just alighted, and walked with him into a Room.

Adams instantly asked the Coachman in a Whisper, if he knew who the Gentleman was? The Coachman answered, he was now a Gentleman, and kept his Horse and Man: but Times are altered, Master, said he, I remember, when he was no better born than myself. Aye! aye! says *Adams*. My Father drove the Squire's Coach, answered he, when that very Man rode Postilion: but he is now his Steward, and a great Gentleman. *Adams* then snapped his Fingers, and cry'd, he thought *she was some such Trollop*.

Adams made haste to acquaint Mrs *Slipslop* with this good News, as he imagined it; but it found a Reception different from what he expected. That prudent Gentlewoman, who despised the Anger of Miss *Grave-airs*, whilst she conceived her the Daughter of a Gentleman of small Fortune, now she heard her Alliance with the upper Servants of a great Family in her Neighbourhood, began to fear her Interest with the Mistress. She wished she had not carried the Dispute so far, and began to think of endeavouring to reconcile herself to the young Lady before she left the Inn; when luckily, the Scene at *London*, which the Reader can scarce have forgotten, presented itself to her Mind, and comforted her with such Assurance, that she no longer apprehended any Enemy with her Mistress.

Every thing being now adjusted, the Company entered the Coach, which was just on its Departure, when one Lady recollected she had left her Fan, a second her Gloves, a third a Snuff-Box, and a fourth a

Smelling-Bottle behind her; to find all which, occasioned some Delay, and much swearing of the Coachman.

As soon as the Coach had left the Inn, the Women all together fell to the Character of Miss *Grave-airs*, whom one of them declared she had suspected to be some low Creature from the beginning of their Journey; and another affirmed had not even the Looks of a Gentlewoman; a third warranted she was no better than she should be, and turning to the Lady who had related the Story in the Coach, said, 'Did you ever hear, Madam, any thing so prudish as her Remarks? Well, deliver me from the Censoriousness of such a Prude.' The fourth added, 'O Madam! all these Creatures are censorious: but for my part, I wonder where the Wretch was bred; indeed I must own I have seldom conversed with these mean kind of People, so that it may appear stranger to me; but to refuse the general Desire of a whole Company, hath something in it so astonishing, that, for my part, I own I should hardly believe it, if my own Ears had not been Witnesses to it.' 'Yes, and so handsome a young Fellow,' cries *Slipslop*, 'the Woman must have no Compassion in her, I believe she is more of a *Turk* than a Christian; I am certain if she had any Christian Woman's Blood in her Veins, the Sight of such a young Fellow must have warm'd it. Indeed there are some wretched, miserable old Objects that turn one's Stomach, I should not wonder if she had refused such a one; I am as nice as herself, and should have cared no more than herself for the Company of *stinking* old Fellows: but hold up thy Head, *Joseph*, thou art none of those, and she who hath not *Compulsion* for thee is a *Myhummetan*, and I will maintain it.' This Conversation made *Joseph* uneasy, as well as the Ladies: who perceiving the Spirits which Mrs *Slipslop* was in, (for indeed she was not a Cup too low) began to fear the Consequence; one of them therefore desired the Lady to conclude the Story — 'Ay Madam,' said *Slipslop*, 'I beg your Ladyship to give us that Story you *commensated* in the Morning;' which Request that well-bred Woman immediately complied with.

CHAPTER VI

Conclusion of the Unfortunate Jilt.

Leonora having once broke through the Bounds which Custom and Modesty impose on her Sex, soon gave an unbridled Indulgence to her Passion. Her Visits to *Bellarmine* were more constant as well as longer, than his Surgeon's; in a word, she became absolutely his Nurse, made his Water-gruel, administred him his Medicines, and, notwithstanding the prudent Advice of her Aunt to the contrary, almost intirely resided in her wounded Lover's Apartment.

The Ladies of the Town began to take her Conduct under consideration; it was the chief Topick of Discourse at their Tea-Tables, and was very severely censured by the most part; especially by *Lindamira*, a Lady whose discreet and starch Carriage, together with a constant Attendance at Church three times a day, had utterly defeated many malicious Attacks on her own Reputation: for such was the Envy that *Lindamira's* Virtue had attracted, that notwithstanding her own strict Behaviour and strict Enquiry into the Lives of others, she had not been able to escape being the Mark of some Arrows herself which however did her no Injury; a Blessing perhaps owed by her to the Clergy, who were her chief male Companions, and with two or three of whom she had been barbarously and unjustly calumniated.

'Not so unjustly neither perhaps,' says *Slipslop*, 'for the Clergy are Men as well as other Folks.'

The extreme Delicacy of *Lindamira's* Virtue was cruelly hurt by these Freedoms which *Leonora* allowed herself; she said, 'it was an Affront to her Sex; that she did not imagine it consistent with any Woman's Honour to speak to the Creature, or to be seen in her Company; and that, for her part, she should always refuse to dance at an Assembly with her, for fear of Contamination, by taking her by the Hand.'

But to return to my Story: As soon as *Bellarmine* was recovered, which was somewhat within a Month from his receiving the Wound, he set out, according to Agreement, for *Leonora's* Father's, in order to propose the Match and settle all Matters with him touching Settlements, and the like.

A little before his Arrival, the old Gentleman had received an Intimation of the Affair by the following Letter; which I can repeat *verbatim*, and which they say was written neither by *Leonora* nor her Aunt, tho' it was in a Woman's Hand. The Letter was in these Words:

'*SIR*,

'I am sorry to acquaint you that your Daughter *Leonora* hath acted one of the basest, as well as most simple Parts with a young Gentleman to whom she had engaged herself, and whom she hath (pardon the Word) jilted for another of inferiour Fortune, notwithstanding his superiour Figure. You may take what Measures you please on this Occasion; I have performed what I thought my Duty, as I have, tho' unknown to you, a very great Respect for your Family.'

The old Gentleman did not give himself the trouble to answer this kind Epistle, nor did he take any notice of it after he had read it, 'till he saw *Bellarmine*. He was, to say the truth, one of those Fathers who look on Children as an unhappy Consequence of their youthful Pleasures; which as he would have been delighted not to have had attended them, so was he no less pleased with any opportunity to rid himself of the Incumbrance. He pass'd in the World's Language as an exceeding good Father, being not only so rapacious as to rob and plunder all Mankind to the utmost of his power, but even to deny himself the Conveniencies and almost Necessaries of Life; which his Neighbours attributed to a desire of raising immense Fortunes for his Children: but in fact it was not so, he heaped up Money for its own sake only, and looked on his Children as his Rivals, who were to enjoy his beloved Mistress, when he was incapable of possessing her, and which he would have been much more charmed with the Power of carrying along with him: nor had his Children any other Security of being his Heirs, than that the Law would constitute them such without a Will, and that he had not Affection enough for any one living to take the trouble of writing one.

To this Gentleman came *Bellarmine* on the Errand I have mentioned. His Person, his Equipage, his Family and his Estate seemed to the Father to make him an advantageous Match for his Daughter; he therefore very readily accepted his Proposals: but *Bellarmine* when he imagined the principal Affair concluded, and began to open the incidental Matters of Fortune; the old Gentleman presently changed his Countenance, saying, 'he resolved never to marry his Daughter on a *Smithfield* Match;[1] that whoever had Love for her to take her, would, when he died, find her Share of his Fortune in his Coffers: but he had seen such Examples of

Undutifulness happen from the too early Generosity of Parents, that he had made a Vow never to part with a Shilling whilst he lived.' He commended the Saying of *Solomon*,[2] *he that spareth the Rod, spoileth the Child*: but added, 'he might have likewise asserted, that *he that spareth the Purse, saveth the Child*.' He then ran into a Discourse on the Extravagance of the Youth of the Age; whence he launched into a Dissertation on Horses, and came at length to commend those *Bellarmine* drove. That fine Gentleman, who at another Season would have been well enough pleased to dwell a little on that Subject, was now very eager to resume the Circumstance of Fortune. He said, 'he had a very high value for the young Lady, and would receive her with less than he would any other whatever; but that even his Love to her made some Regard to worldly Matters necessary; for it would be a most distracting Sight for him to see her, when he had the Honour to be her Husband, in less than a Coach and Six.' The old Gentleman answer'd, 'Four will do, Four will do;' and then took a turn from Horses to Extravagance, and from Extravagance to Horses, till he came round to the Equipage again, whither he was no sooner arrived, than *Bellarmine* brought him back to the Point; but all to no purpose, he made his Escape from that Subject in a Minute, till at last the Lover declared, 'that in the present Situation of his Affairs it was impossible for him, though he loved *Leonora* more than *tout le monde*, to marry her without any Fortune.' To which the Father answered, 'he was sorry then his Daughter must lose so valuable a Match; that if he had an Inclination at present, it was not in his power to advance a Shilling: that he had had great Losses and been at great Expences on Projects, which, though he had great Expectation from them, had yet produced him nothing: that he did not know what might happen hereafter, as on the Birth of a Son, or such Accident, but he would make no promise, or enter into any Article: for he would not break his Vow for all the Daughters in the World.'

In short, Ladies, to keep you no longer in suspense, *Bellarmine* having tried every Argument and Persuasion which he could invent, and finding them all ineffectual, at length took his leave, but not in order to return to *Leonora*; he proceeded directly to his own Seat, whence after a few Days stay, he returned to *Paris*, to the great delight of the *French*, and the honour of the *English* Nation.

But as soon as he arrived at his home, he presently dispatched a Messenger, with the following Epistle to *Leonora*.

'*Adorable* and *Charmante*,

'I am sorry to have the Honour to tell you I am not the *heureux* Person destined for your divine Arms. Your Papa hath told me so with a *Politesse* not often seen on this side *Paris*. You may perhaps guess his manner of refusing me — *Ah mon Dieu!* You will certainly believe me, Madam, incapable of my self delivering this *triste* Message: Which I intend to try the *French* Air to cure the Consequences of — *Ah jamais! Cœur! Ange!* — *Ah Diable!* — If your Papa obliges you to a Marriage, I hope we shall see you at *Paris*, till when the Wind that flows from thence will be the warmest *dans le Monde*: for it will consist almost entirely of my Sighs. *Adieu, ma Princesse! Ah L'Amour!*

BELLARMINE'

I shall not attempt, Ladies, to describe *Leonora*'s Condition when she received this Letter. It is a Picture of Horrour, which I should have as little pleasure in drawing as you in beholding. She immediately left the Place, where she was the Subject of Conversation and Ridicule, and retired to that House I shewed you when I began the Story, where she hath ever since led a disconsolate Life, and deserves perhaps Pity for her Misfortunes more than our Censure, for a Behaviour to which the Artifices of her Aunt very probably contributed, and to which very young Women are often rendered too liable, by that blameable Levity in the Education of our Sex.

'If I was inclined to pity her,' said a young Lady in the Coach, 'it would be for the Loss of *Horatio*; for I cannot discern any Misfortune in her missing such a Husband as *Bellarmine*.'

'Why I must own,' says *Slipslop*, 'the Gentleman was a little false-hearted: but *howsumever* it was hard to have two Lovers, and get never a Husband at all — But pray, Madam, what became of *Ourasho*?'

He remains, said the Lady, still unmarried, and hath applied himself so strictly to his Business, that he hath raised I hear a very considerable Fortune. And what is remarkable, they say, he never hears the name of *Leonora* without a Sigh, nor hath ever uttered one Syllable to charge her with her ill Conduct towards him.

CHAPTER VII

A very short Chapter, in which Parson Adams *went a great Way.*

The Lady having finished her Story received the Thanks of the Company, and now *Joseph* putting his Head out of the Coach, cried out, 'Never believe me, if yonder be not our Parson *Adams* walking along without his Horse.' 'On my Word, and so he is,' says *Slipslop*; 'and as sure as Two-pence, he hath left him behind at the Inn.' Indeed, true it is, the Parson had exhibited a fresh Instance of his Absence of Mind: for he was so pleased with having got *Joseph* into the Coach, that he never once thought of the Beast in the Stable; and finding his Legs as nimble as he desired, he sallied out brandishing a Crabstick, and had kept on before the Coach, mending and slackening his Pace occasionally, so that he had never been much more or less than a Quarter of a Mile distant from it.

Mrs *Slipslop* desired the Coachman to overtake him, which he attempted, but in vain: for the faster he drove, the faster ran the Parson, often crying out, *Aye, aye, catch me if you can*: 'till at length the Coachman swore he would as soon attempt to drive after a Greyhound; and giving the Parson two or three hearty Curses, he cry'd, Softly, softly Boys, to his Horses, which the civil Beasts immediately obeyed.

But we will be more courteous to our Reader than he was to Mrs *Slipslop*, and leaving the Coach and its Company to pursue their Journey, we will carry our Reader on after Parson *Adams*, who stretched forwards without once looking behind him, 'till having left the Coach full three Miles in his Rear, he came to a Place, where, by keeping the extremest Track to the Right, it was just barely possible for a human Creature to miss his Way. This Track however did he keep, as indeed he had a wonderful Capacity at these kinds of bare Possibilities; and travelling in it about three Miles over the Plain, he arrived at the Summit of a Hill, whence looking a great way backwards, and perceiving no Coach in sight, he sat himself down on the Turf, and pulling out his *Æschylus* determined to wait here for its Arrival.

He had not sat long here, before a Gun going off very near, a little startled him; he looked up, and saw a Gentleman within a hundred Paces taking up a Partridge, which he had just shot.

Adams stood up, and presented a Figure to the Gentleman which would have moved Laughter in many: for his Cassock had just again fallen down below his great Coat, that is to say, it reached his Knees; whereas, the Skirts of his great Coat descended no lower than half way down his Thighs: but the Gentleman's Mirth gave way to his Surprize, at beholding such a Personage in such a Place.

Adams advancing to the Gentleman told him he hoped he had good Sport; to which the other answered, very little. 'I see, Sir,' says *Adams*, 'you have *smote* one Partridge:' To which the Sportsman made no Reply, but proceeded to charge his Piece.

Whilst the Gun was charging, *Adams* remained in Silence, which he at last broke, by observing that it was a delightful Evening. The Gentleman, who had at first sight conceived a very distasteful Opinion of the Parson, began, on perceiving a Book in his Hand, and smoking likewise the Information of the Cassock, to change his Thoughts, and made a small Advance to Conversation on his side, by saying, Sir, *I suppose you are not one of these Parts?*

Adams immediately told him, No; that he was a Traveller, and invited by the Beauty of the Evening and the Place to repose a little, and amuse himself with reading. 'I may as well repose myself too,' said the Sportsman; 'for I have been out this whole Afternoon, and the Devil a Bird have I seen 'till I came hither.'

'Perhaps then the Game is not very plenty hereabouts,' cries *Adams*. 'No, Sir,' said the Gentleman, 'the Soldiers, who are quartered in the Neighbourhood, have killed it all.'[1] 'It is very probable,' cries *Adams*, 'for Shooting is their Profession.' 'Ay, shooting the Game,' answered the other, 'but I don't see they are so forward to shoot our Enemies. I don't like that Affair of *Carthagena*;[2] if I had been there, I believe I should have done otherguess things, d—n me; what's a Man's Life when his Country demands it; a Man who won't sacrifice his Life for his Country deserves to be hanged, d—n me.' Which Words he spoke with so violent a Gesture, so loud a Voice, so strong an Accent, and so fierce a Countenance, that he might have frightned a Captain of Trained-Bands[3] at the Head of his Company; but Mr *Adams* was not greatly subject to Fear, he told him intrepidly that he very much approved his Virtue, but disliked his Swearing, and begged him not to addict himself to so bad a Custom, without which he said he might fight as bravely as *Achilles* did. Indeed he was charm'd with this Discourse, he told the Gentleman he would willingly have gone many Miles to have met a Man of his generous Way of thinking; that if he pleased to sit down, he should be greatly delighted to commune with him: for tho' he was a Clergyman, he would himself be ready, if thereto called, to lay down his Life for his Country.

The Gentleman sat down and *Adams* by him, and then the latter began, as in the following Chapter, a Discourse which we have placed by itself, as it is not only the most curious in this, but perhaps in any other Book.

CHAPTER VIII

*A notable Dissertation, by Mr Abraham Adams; wherein that
Gentleman appears in a political Light.*

'I do assure you, Sir,' says he, taking the Gentleman by the Hand, 'I am heartily glad to meet with a Man of your Kidney: for tho' I am a poor Parson, I will be bold to say, I am an honest Man, and would not do an ill Thing to be made a Bishop: Nay, tho' it hath not fallen in my way to offer so noble a Sacrifice, I have not been without Opportunities of suffering for the sake of my Conscience, I thank Heaven for them; for I have had Relations, tho' I say it, who made some Figure in the World; particularly a Nephew, who was a Shopkeeper, and an Alderman of a Corporation. He was a good Lad, and was under my Care when a Boy, and I believe would do what I bad him to his dying Day. Indeed, it looks like extreme Vanity in me, to affect being a Man of such Consequence, as to have so great an Interest in an Alderman; but others have thought so too, as manifestly appeared by the Rector, whose Curate I formerly was, sending for me on the Approach of an Election, and telling me if I expected to continue in his Cure, that I must bring my Nephew to vote for one Colonel *Courtley*, a Gentleman whom I had never heard Tidings of 'till that Instant. I told the Rector, I had no power over my Nephew's Vote, (God forgive me for such Prevarication!) that I supposed he would give it according to his Conscience, that I would by no means endeavour to influence him to give it otherwise. He told me it was in vain to equivocate: that he knew I had already spoke to him in favour of Esquire *Fickle* my Neighbour, and indeed it was true I had: for it was at a Season when the *Church was in Danger*,[1] and when all good Men expected they knew not what would happen to us all. I then answered boldly, If he thought I had given my Promise, he affronted me, in proposing any Breach of it. Not to be too prolix: I persevered, and so did my Nephew, in the Esquire's Interest, who was chose chiefly through his Means, and so I lost my Curacy. Well, Sir, but do you think the Esquire ever mentioned a Word of the Church? *Ne verbum quidem, ut ita dicam*;[2] within two Years he got a Place, and hath ever since lived in *London*; where I have been informed, (but G— forbid I should believe that) that he never so much as goeth to Church. I remained, Sir, a considerable Time without any Cure, and lived a full Month on one Funeral Sermon, which I preached on the indisposition of a Clergyman: but this by the Bye. At last, when Mr *Fickle* got his Place, Colonel *Courtly* stood again; and who should make Interest for him, but Mr *Fickle* himself: that very identical Mr *Fickle*, who had formerly told me, the Colonel was an Enemy to both the Church and State, had the Confidence to sollicite my Nephew for him, and the Colonel himself offered me to make me Chaplain to his Regiment, which I refused in favour of Sir *Oliver Hearty*, who told us, he would sacrifice every thing to his Country: and I believe he would, except his Hunting, which he stuck so close to, that in five Years together, he went but twice up to Parliament; and one of those Times, I have been told, never was within sight of the House. However, he was a worthy Man, and the best Friend I ever had: for by his Interest with a Bishop, he got me replaced into my Curacy, and give me eight Pounds out of his own Pocket to buy me a Gown and Cassock, and furnish my House. He had our Interest while he lived, which was not many Years. On his Death, I had fresh Applications made to me; for all the World knew the Interest I had in my good Nephew, who now was a leading Man in the Corporation; and Sir *Thomas Booby*, buying the Estate which had been Sir *Oliver*'s, proposed himself a Candidate. He was then a young Gentleman just come from his Travels;[3] and it did me good to hear him discourse on Affairs, which for my part I knew nothing of. If I had been Master of a thousand Votes, he should have had them all. I engaged my Nephew in his Interest, and he was elected, and a very fine Parliament-Man he was. They tell me he made Speeches of an Hour long; and I have been told very fine ones: but he could never persuade the Parliament to be of his Opinion. — *Non omnia possumus omnes.*[4] He promised me a Living, poor Man; and I believe I should have had it, but an Accident happened; which was, that my Lady had promised it before unknown to him. This indeed I never heard 'till afterwards: for my Nephew, who died about a Month before the Incumbent, always told me I might be assured of it. Since that Time, Sir *Thomas*, poor Man, had always so much Business, that he never could find Leisure to see me. I believe it was partly my Lady's fault too: who did not think my Dress good enough for the Gentry at her Table. However, I must do him the Justice to say, he never was ungrateful; and I have always found his Kitchin, and his Cellar too, open to me; many a time after Service on a *Sunday*, for I preach at four Churches, have I recruited my Spirits with a Glass of his Ale. Since my Nephew's Death, the Corporation is in other hands; and I am not a Man of that Consequence I was formerly. I have now no longer any Talents[5] to lay out in the Service of my Country; and to whom nothing is given, of him can nothing be required. However, on all proper Seasons, such as the Approach of an Election, I throw a suitable Dash or two into my Sermons; which I have the pleasure to hear is not disagreeable to Sir *Thomas*, and the other honest Gentlemen my Neighbours, who have all promised me these five Years, to procure an Ordination for a Son of mine, who is now near Thirty, hath an infinite Stock of Learning, and is, I thank Heaven, of an unexceptionable Life; tho', as he was never at an University, the Bishop refuses to ordain him.[6] Too much Care cannot indeed be taken in admitting any to the sacred Office; tho' I hope he will never act so as to be a Disgrace to any Order: but will serve his God and his Country to the utmost of his power, as I have endeavoured to do before him; nay, and will lay down his Life whenever called to that purpose. I am sure I have educated him in those Principles; so that I have acquitted my Duty, and shall have nothing to answer for on that account: but I do not distrust him; for he is a good Boy; and if Providence should throw it in his way, to be of as much consequence in a public Light, as his Father once was, I can answer for him, he will use his Talents as honestly as I have done.'

CHAPTER IX

In which the Gentleman descants on Bravery and heroic Virtue, 'till an unlucky Accident puts an end to the Discourse.[1]

The Gentleman highly commended Mr *Adams* for his good Resolutions, and told him, 'he hoped his Son would tread in his Steps;' adding, 'that if he would not die for his Country, he would not be worthy to live in it; I'd make no more of shooting a Man that would not die for his Country, than ——

'Sir,' said he, 'I have disinherited a Nephew who is in the Army, because he would not exchange his Commission, and go to the *West-Indies*. I believe the Rascal is a Coward, tho' he pretends to be in love forsooth. I would have all such Fellows hanged, Sir, I would have them hanged.' *Adams* answered, 'that would be too severe: That Men did not make themselves; and if Fear had too much Ascendance in the Mind, the Man was rather to be pitied than abhorred: That Reason and Time might teach him to subdue it.' He said, 'a Man might be a Coward at one time, and brave at another. *Homer*,' says he, 'who so well understood and copied Nature, hath taught us this Lesson; for *Paris* fights, and *Hector* runs away:[2] nay, we have a mighty Instance of this in the History of later Ages, no longer ago, than the 705th Year of *Rome*, when the Great *Pompey*,[3] who had won so many Battles, and been honoured with so many Triumphs, and of whose Valour, several Authors, especially *Cicero* and *Paterculus*, have formed such Elogiums; this very *Pompey* left the Battle of *Pharsalia* before he had lost it, and retreated to his Tent, where he sat like the most pusillanimous Rascal in a Fit of Despair, and yielded a Victory, which was to determine the Empire of the World, to *Cæsar*. I am not much travelled in the History of modern Times, that is to say, these last thousand Years: but those who are, can, I make no question, furnish you with parallel Instances.' He concluded therefore, that had he taken any such hasty Resolutions against his Nephew, he hoped he would consider better and retract them. The Gentleman answered with great Warmth, and talked much of Courage and his Country, 'till perceiving it grew late, he asked *Adams*, 'what Place he intended for that Night?' He told him, 'he waited there for the Stage-Coach.' 'The Stage-Coach! Sir,' said the Gentleman, 'they are all past by long ago. You may see the last yourself, almost three Miles before us.' 'I protest and so they are,' cries *Adams*, 'then I must make haste and follow them.' The Gentleman told him, 'he would hardly be able to overtake them; and that if he did not know his Way, he would be in danger of losing himself on the Downs; for it would be presently dark; and he might ramble about all Night, and perhaps, find himself farther from his Journey's End in the Morning than he was now. He advised him therefore to accompany him to his House, which was very little out of his way,' assuring him, 'that he would find some Country-Fellow in his Parish, who would conduct him for Sixpence to the City, where he was going.' *Adams* accepted this Proposal, and on they travelled, the Gentleman renewing his Discourse on Courage, and the Infamy of not being ready at all times to sacrifice our Lives to our Country. Night overtook them much about the same time as they arrived near some Bushes: whence, on a sudden, they heard the most violent Shrieks imaginable in a female

Voice. *Adams* offered to snatch the Gun out of his Companion's Hand. 'What are you doing?' said he. 'Doing!' says *Adams*, 'I am hastening to the Assistance of the poor Creature whom some Villains are murdering.' 'You are not mad enough, I hope,' says the Gentleman, trembling: 'Do you consider this Gun is only charged with Shot, and that the Robbers are most probably furnished with Pistols loaded with Bullets? This is no Business of ours; let us make as much haste as possible out of the way, or we may fall into their hands ourselves.' The Shrieks now encreasing, *Adams* made no Answer, but snapt his Fingers, and brandishing his Crabstick, made directly to the Place whence the Voice issued; and the Man of Courage made as much Expedition towards his own Home, whither he escaped in a very short time without once looking behind him: where we will leave him, to contemplate his own Bravery, and to censure the want of it in others; and return to the good *Adams*, who, on coming up to the Place whence the Noise proceeded, found a Woman struggling with a Man, who had thrown her on the Ground, and had almost over-power'd her. The great Abilities of Mr *Adams* were not necessary to have formed a right Judgment of this Affair, on the first sight. He did not therefore want the Entreaties of the poor Wretch to assist her, but lifting up his Crabstick, he immediately levelled a Blow at that Part of the Ravisher's Head, where, according to the Opinion of the Ancients, the Brains of some persons are deposited, and which he had undoubtedly let forth, had not Nature, (who, as wise Men have observed, equips all Creatures with what is most expedient for them) taken a provident Care, (as she always doth with those she intends for Encounters) to make this part of the Head three times as thick as those of ordinary Men, who are designed to exercise Talents which are vulgarly called rational, and for whom as Brains are necessary, she is obliged to leave some room for them in the Cavity of the Skull: whereas, those Ingredients being entirely useless to Persons of the heroic Calling, she hath an Opportunity of thickening the Bone, so as to make it less subject to any Impression or liable to be cracked or broken; and indeed, in some who are predestined to the Command of Armies and Empires, she is supposed sometimes to make that Part perfectly solid.

As a Game-Cock when engaged in amorous Toying with a Hen, if perchance he espies another Cock at hand, immediately quits his Female, and opposes himself to his Rival; so did the Ravisher, on the Information of the Crabstick, immediately leap from the Woman, and hasten to assail the Man. He had no Weapons but what Nature had furnished him with.

However, he clenched his Fist, and presently darted it at that Part of *Adams*'s Breast where the Heart is lodged. *Adams* staggered at the Violence of the Blow, when throwing away his Staff, he likewise clenched that Fist, which we have before commemorated, and would have discharged it full in the Breast of his Antagonist, had he not dexterously caught it with his left Hand, at the same time darting his Head, (which some modern Heroes, of the lower Class, use like the Battering-Ram of the Ancients, for a Weapon of Offence; another Reason to admire the Cunningness of Nature, in composing it of those impenetrable Materials) dashing his Head, I say, into the Stomach of *Adams*, he tumbled him on his Back, and not having any regard to the Laws of Heroism, which would have restrained him from any farther Attack on his Enemy, 'till he was again on his Legs, he threw himself upon him, and laying hold on the Ground with his left Hand, he with his right belaboured the Body of *Adams* 'till he was weary, and indeed, 'till he concluded (to use the Language of fighting) *that he had done his Business*; or, in the Language of Poetry, *that he had sent him to the Shades below*; in plain *English, that he was dead*.

But *Adams*, who was no Chicken, and could bear a drubbing as well as any boxing Champion in the Universe, lay still only to watch his Opportunity; and now perceiving his Antagonist to pant with his Labours, he exerted his utmost Force at once, and with such Success, that he overturned him and became his Superiour; when fixing one of his Knees in his Breast, he cried out in an exulting Voice, *It is my turn now*: and after a few Minutes constant Application, he gave him so dextrous a Blow just under his Chin, that the Fellow no longer retained any Motion, and *Adams* began to fear he had struck him once too often; for he often asserted, 'he should be concerned to have the Blood of even the Wicked upon him.'

Adams got up, and called aloud to the young Woman, —— 'Be of good cheer, Damsel,' said he, 'you are no longer in danger of your Ravisher, who, I am terribly afraid, lies dead at my Feet; but G— forgive me what I have done in defence of Innocence.' The poor Wretch, who had been some time in recovering Strength enough to rise, and had afterwards, during the Engagement, stood trembling, being disabled by Fear, even from running away, hearing her Champion was victorious, came up to him, but not without Apprehensions, even of her Deliverer; which, however, she was soon relieved from, by his courteous Behaviour and gentle Words. They were both standing by the Body, which lay motionless on the Ground, and which *Adams* wished to see stir much more than the Woman did, when he earnestly begged her to tell him 'by what Misfortune she came, at such a time of Night, into so lonely a Place?' She acquainted him, 'she was travelling towards *London*, and had accidentally met with the Person from whom he had delivered her, who told her he was likewise on his Journey to the same Place, and would keep her Company: an Offer which, suspecting no harm, she had accepted; that he told her, they were at a small distance from an Inn where she might take up her Lodging that Evening, and he would shew her a nearer way to it than by following the Road. That if she had suspected him, (which she did not, he spoke so kindly to her,) being alone on these Downs in the dark, she had no human Means to avoid him; that therefore she put her whole Trust in Providence, and walk'd on, expecting every Moment to arrive at the Inn; when, on a sudden, being come to those Bushes, he desired her to stop, and after some rude Kisses, which she resisted, and some Entreaties, which she rejected, he laid violent hands on her, and was attempting to execute his wicked Will, when, she thanked G——, he timely came up and prevented him.' *Adams* encouraged her for saying, she had put her whole Trust in Providence, and told her 'He doubted not but Providence had sent him to her Deliverance, as a Reward for that Trust. He wished indeed he had not deprived the wicked Wretch of Life, but G——'s Will be done;' he said, 'he hoped the Goodness of his Intention would excuse him in the next World, and he trusted in her Evidence to acquit him in this.' He was then silent, and began to consider with himself, whether it would be properer to make his Escape, or to deliver himself into the hands of Justice; which Meditation ended, as the Reader will see in the next Chapter.

CHAPTER X

Giving an Account of the Strange Catastrophe[1] of the preceding Adventure, which drew poor Adams *into fresh Calamities; and who the Woman was who owed the Preservation of her Chastity to his victorious Arm.*

The Silence of *Adams*, added to the Darkness of the Night, and Loneliness of the Place, struck dreadful Apprehensions into the poor Woman's Mind: She began to fear as great an Enemy in her Deliverer, as he had delivered her from; and as she had not Light enough to discover the Age of *Adams*, and the Benevolence visible in his Countenance, she suspected he had used her as some very honest Men have used their Country; and had rescued her out of the hands of one Rifler, in order to rifle her himself. Such were the Suspicions she drew from his Silence: but indeed they were ill-grounded. He stood over his vanquished Enemy,[2] wisely weighing in his Mind the Objections which might be made to either of the two Methods of proceeding mentioned in the last Chapter, his Judgment sometimes inclining to the one, and sometimes to the other; for both seemed to him so equally adviseable, and so equally dangerous, that probably he would have ended his Days, at least two or three of them, on that very Spot, before he had taken any Resolution: At length he lifted up his Eyes, and spied a Light at a distance, to which he instantly addressed himself with *Heus tu*,[3] *Traveller, heus tu!* He presently heard several Voices, and perceived the Light approaching toward him. The Persons who attended the Light began some to laugh, others to sing, and others to hollow, at which the Woman testified some Fear, (for she had concealed her Suspicions of the Parson himself,) but *Adams* said, 'Be of good cheer, Damsel, and repose thy Trust in the same Providence, which hath hitherto protected thee, and never will forsake the Innocent.' These People who now approached were no other, Reader, than a Set of young Fellows, who came to these Bushes in pursuit of a Diversion which they call *Bird-baiting*. This, if thou art ignorant of it (as perhaps if thou hast never travelled beyond *Kensington, Islington, Hackney*, or the *Borough*,[4] thou mayst be) I will inform thee is performed by holding a large Clap-Net[5] before a Lantern, and at the same time, beating the Bushes: for the Birds, when they are disturbed from their Places of Rest, Roost, immediately make to the Light, and so are enticed within the Net. *Adams* immediately told them, what had happened, and desired them, 'to hold the Lantern to the Face of the Man on the ground, for he feared he had *smote* him fatally.' But indeed his Fears were frivolous, for the Fellow, though he had been stunned by the last Blow he received, had long since recovered his Senses, and finding himself quit of *Adams*, had listened attentively to the Discourse between him and the young Woman; for whose Departure he had patiently waited, that he might likewise withdraw himself, having no longer hopes of succeeding in his Desires, which were moreover almost as well cooled by Mr *Adams*, as they could have been by the young Woman herself, had he obtained his utmost Wish. This Fellow, who had a Readiness at improving any Accident, thought he might now play a better part than that of a dead Man; and accordingly, the moment the Candle was held to his Face, he leapt up, and laying hold on *Adams*, cried out, 'No, Villain, I am not dead, though you and your wicked Whore might well think me

so, after the barbarous Cruelties you have exercised on me. Gentlemen,'
said he, 'you are luckily come to the Assistance of a poor Traveller, who
would otherwise have been robbed and murdered by this vile Man and
Woman, who led me hither out of my way from the High-Road, and
both falling on me have used me as you see.' *Adams* was going to answer,
when one of the young Fellows, cry'd, 'D——n them, let's carry them both
before the Justice.' The poor Woman began to tremble, and *Adams* lifted
up his Voice, but in vain. Three or four of them laid hands on him, and
one holding the Lantern to his Face, they all agreed, *he had the most villainous
Countenance* they ever beheld, and an Attorney's Clerk who was of the
Company declared, *he was sure he had remembered him at the Bar.* As to the
Woman, her Hair was dishevelled in the Struggle, and her Nose had bled,
so that they could not perceive whether she was handsome or ugly: but
they said her Fright plainly discovered her Guilt. And searching her
Pockets, as they did those of *Adams* for Money, which the Fellow said he
had lost, they found in her Pocket a Purse with some Gold in it, which
abundantly convinced them, especially as the Fellow offered to swear to
it. Mr *Adams* was found to have no more than one Halfpenny about him.
This the Clerk said, 'was a great Presumption that he was an old Offender,
by cunningly giving all the Booty to the Woman.' To which all the rest
readily assented.

This Accident promising them better Sport, than what they had proposed, they quitted their Intention of catching Birds, and unanimously
resolved to proceed to the Justice with the Offenders. Being informed
what a desperate Fellow *Adams* was, they tied his Hands behind him, and
having hid their Nets among the Bushes, and the Lantern being carried
before them, they placed the two Prisoners in their Front, and then began
their March: *Adams* not only submitting patiently to his own Fate, but
comforting and encouraging his Companion under her Sufferings.

Whilst they were on their way, the Clerk informed the rest, that this
Adventure would prove a very beneficial one: for that they would be all
entitled to their Proportions of 80 *l*.[6] for apprehending the Robbers. This
occasion'd a Contention concerning the Parts which they had severally
born in taking them; one insisting, 'he ought to have the greatest Share,
for he had first laid his Hands on *Adams*;' another claiming a superiour
Part for having first held the Lantern to the Man's Face, on the Ground,
by which, he said, 'the whole was discovered.' The Clerk claimed four
fifths of the Reward, for having proposed to search the Prisoners; and
likewise the carrying them before the Justice: he said indeed, 'in strict

Justice he ought to have the whole.' These Claims however they at last consented to refer to a future Decision, but seem'd all to agree that the Clerk was intitled to a Moiety. They then debated what Money should be allotted to the young Fellow, who had been employed only in holding the Nets. He very modestly said, 'that he did not apprehend any large Proportion would fall to his share; but hoped they would allow him something: he desired them to consider, that they had assigned their Nets to his Care, which prevented him from being as forward as any in laying hold of the Robbers, (for so these innocent People were called;) that if he had not occupied the Nets, some other must; concluding however that he should be contented with the smallest Share imaginable, and should think that rather their Bounty than his Merit.' But they were all unanimous in excluding him from any Part whatever, the Clerk particularly swearing, 'if they gave him a Shilling, they might do what they pleased with the rest; for he would not concern himself with the Affair.' This Contention was so hot, and so totally engaged the Attention of all the Parties, that a dextrous nimble Thief, had he been in Mr *Adams*'s situation, would have taken care to have given the Justice no Trouble that Evening. Indeed it required not the Art of a *Shepherd* to escape,[7] especially as the Darkness of the Night would have so much befriended him: but *Adams* trusted rather to his Innocence than his Heels, and without thinking of Flight, which was easy, or Resistance (which was impossible, as there were six lusty young Fellows, besides the Villain himself, present) he walked with perfect Resignation the way they thought proper to conduct him.

Adams frequently vented himself in Ejaculations during their Journey; at last poor *Joseph Andrews* occurring to his Mind, he could not refrain sighing forth his Name, which being heard by his Companion in Affliction, she cried, with some Vehemence, 'Sure I should know that Voice, you cannot certainly, Sir, be Mr *Abraham Adams*?' 'Indeed Damsel,' says he, 'that is my Name; there is something also in your Voice, which persuades me I have heard it before.' 'La, Sir,' says she, 'don't you remember poor *Fanny*?' 'How *Fanny*!' answered *Adams*, 'indeed I very well remember you; what can have brought you hither?' 'I have told you Sir,' replied she, 'I was travelling towards *London*; but I thought you mentioned *Joseph Andrews*, pray what is become of him?' 'I left him, Child, this Afternoon,' said *Adams*, 'in the Stage-Coach, in his way towards our Parish, whither he is going to see you.' 'To see me? La, Sir,' answered *Fanny*, 'sure you jeer me; what should he be going to see me for?' 'Can you ask that?' replied *Adams*. 'I hope *Fanny* you are not inconstant; I assure you he deserves much better of you.' 'La! Mr *Adams*,' said she, 'what is Mr *Joseph* to me? I am sure I never had any thing to say to him, but as one Fellow-Servant might to another.' 'I am sorry to hear this,' said *Adams*, 'a vertuous Passion for a young Man, is what no Woman need be ashamed of. You either do not tell me Truth, or you are false to a very worthy Man.' *Adams* then told her what had happened at the Inn, to which she listened very attentively; and a Sigh often escaped from her, notwithstanding her utmost Endeavours to the contrary, nor could she prevent herself from asking a thousand Questions, which would have assured any one but *Adams*, who never saw farther into People than they desired to let him, of the Truth of a Passion she endeavoured to conceal. Indeed the Fact was, that this poor Girl having heard of *Joseph*'s Misfortune by some of the Servants belonging to that Coach, which we have formerly mentioned to have stopped at the Inn while the poor Youth was confined to his Bed, that instant abandoned the Cow she was milking, and taking with her a little Bundle of Clothes under her Arm, and all the Money she was worth in her own Purse, without consulting any one, immediately set forward, in pursuit of One, whom, notwithstanding her Shyness to the Parson, she loved with inexpressible Violence,[8] though with the purest and most delicate Passion. This Shyness therefore, as we trust it will recommend her Character to all our Female Readers, and not greatly surprize such of our Males as are well acquainted with the younger part of the other Sex, we shall not give our selves any trouble to vindicate.

CHAPTER XI

What happened to them while before the Justice. A Chapter very full of Learning.

Their Fellow-Travellers were so engaged in the hot Dispute concerning the Division of the Reward for apprehending these innocent People, that they attended very little to their Discourse. They were now arrived at the Justice's House, and sent one of his Servants in to acquaint his Worship, that they had taken two Robbers, and brought them before him. The Justice, who was just returned from a Fox-Chace, and had not yet finished his Dinner, ordered them to carry the Prisoners into the Stable, whither they were attended by all the Servants in the House, and all the People of the Neighbourhood, who flock'd together to see them with as much

Curiosity as if there was something uncommon to be seen, or that a Rogue did not look like other People.

The Justice being now in the height of his Mirth and his Cups, bethought himself of the Prisoners, and telling his Company he believed they should have good Sport in their Examination, he ordered them into his Presence. They had no sooner entered the Room, than he began to revile them, saying, 'that Robberies on the Highway were now grown so frequent, that People could not sleep safely in their Beds, and assured them they both should be made Examples of at the ensuing Assizes.' After he had gone on some time in this manner, he was reminded by his Clerk, 'that it would be proper to take the Deposition of the Witnesses against them.' Which he bid him do, and he would light his Pipe in the mean time. Whilst the Clerk was employed in writing down the Depositions of the Fellow who had pretended to be robbed, the Justice employed himself in cracking Jests on poor *Fanny*, in which he was seconded by all the Company at Table. One asked, 'whether she was to be indicted for a *Highwayman*?' Another whispered in her Ear, 'if she had not provided herself a great Belly,[1] he was at her service.' A third said, 'he warranted she was a Relation of *Turpin*.' To which one of the Company, a great Wit, shaking his Head and then his Sides, answered, 'he believed she was nearer related to *Turpis*;'[2] at which there was an universal Laugh. They were proceeding thus with the poor Girl, when somebody smoaking the Cassock, peeping forth from under the Great Coat of *Adams*, cried out, 'What have we here, a Parson?' 'How, Sirrah,' says the Justice, 'do you go a robbing in the Dress of a Clergyman? let me tell you, your Habit will not entitle you to the *Benefit of the Clergy*.'[3] 'Yes,' said the witty Fellow, 'he will have one Benefit of Clergy, he will be exalted above the Heads of the People;' at which there was a second Laugh. And now the witty Spark, seeing his Jokes take, began to rise in Spirits; and turning to *Adams*, challenged him to *cap* Verses,[4] and provoking him by giving the first Blow, he repeated,

Molle meum levibus cord est vilebile Telis.[5]

Upon which *Adams*, with a Look full of ineffable Contempt, told him, he deserved scourging for his Pronuntiation. The witty Fellow answered, 'What do you deserve, Doctor, for not being able to answer the first time? Why I'll give you one you Blockhead — with an *S*?

Si licet, ut fulvum spectatur in igdibus haurum.[6]

'What can'st not with an *M* neither? Thou art a pretty Fellow for a Parson — Why did'st not steal some of the Parson's *Latin* as well as his Gown?' Another at the Table then answered, 'if he had, you would have been too hard for him; I remember you at the College a very Devil at this Sport, I have seen you catch a fresh Man: for no body that knew you, would engage with you.' 'I have forgot those things now,' cried the Wit. 'I believe I could have done pretty well formerly. — Let's see, what did I end with — an *M* again — ay —

Mars, Bacchus, Apollo, virorum.[7]

I could have done it at once.' —— 'Ah! evil betide you, and so you can now,' said the other, 'no body in this County will undertake you.' *Adams* could hold no longer; 'Friend,' said he, 'I have a Boy not above eight Years old, who would instruct thee, that the last Verse runs thus:

Ut sunt Divorum, Mars, Bacchus, Apollo, virorum.'

'I'll hold thee a Guinea of that,' said the Wit, throwing the Money on the Table. —— 'And I'll go your halves,' cries the other.' 'Done,' answered *Adams*, but upon applying to his Pocket, he was forced to retract, and own he had no Money about him; which set them all a laughing, and confirmed the Triumph of his Adversary, which was not moderate, any more than the Approbation he met with from the whole Company, who told *Adams* he must go a little longer to School, before he attempted to attack that Gentleman in *Latin*.

The Clerk having finished the Depositions, as well of the Fellow himself, as of those who apprehended the Prisoners, delivered them to the Justice; who having sworn the several Witnesses, without reading a Syllable, ordered his Clerk to make the *Mittimus*.[8]

Adams then said, 'he hoped he should not be condemned unheard.' 'No, no,' cries the Justice, 'you will be asked what you have to say for yourself, when you come on your Trial, we are not trying you now; I shall only commit you to Goal: if you can prove your Innocence at *Size*, you will be found *Ignoramus*,[9] and so no Harm done.' 'Is it no Punishment, Sir, for an innocent Man to lie several Months in Goal?' cries *Adams*: 'I beg you would at least hear me before you sign the *Mittimus*.' 'What signifies all you can say?' says the Justice, 'is it not here in black and white against you? I must tell you, you are a very impertinent Fellow, to take up so much of my time. —— So make haste with his *Mittimus*.'

The Clerk now acquainted the Justice, that among other suspicious things, as a Penknife, &c. found in *Adams*'s Pocket, they had discovered a Book written, as he apprehended, in Ciphers: for no one could read a Word in it. 'Ay,' says the Justice, 'this Fellow may be more than a common Robber, he may be in a Plot against the Government. — Produce the Book.' Upon which the poor Manuscript of *Æschylus*, which *Adams* had transcribed with his own Hand, was brought forth; and the Justice looking at it, shook his Head, and turning to the Prisoner, asked the Meaning of those Ciphers. 'Ciphers!' answer'd *Adams*, 'it is a Manuscript of *Æschylus*.' 'Who? who?' said the Justice. *Adams* repeated, '*Æschylus*.' 'That is an outlandish Name,' cried the Clerk. 'A fictitious Name rather, I believe,' said the Justice. One of the Company declared it looked very much like *Greek*. '*Greek*!' said the Justice, 'why 'tis all Writing.' 'Nay,' says the other, 'I don't positively say it is so: for it is a very long time since I have seen any *Greek*. There's one,' says he, turning to the Parson of the Parish, who was present, 'will tell us immediately.' The Parson taking up the Book, putting on his Spectacles and Gravity together, muttered some Words to himself, and then pronounced aloud —— 'Ay indeed it is a *Greek* Manuscript, a very fine piece of Antiquity. I make no doubt but it was stolen from the same Clergyman from whom the Rogue took the Cassock.' 'What did the Rascal mean by his *Æschylus*?' says the Justice. 'Pooh!' answered the Doctor with a contemptuous Grin, 'do you think that Fellow knows any thing of this Book? *Æschylus*! ho! ho! ho! I see now what it is. — A Manuscript of one of the Fathers.[10] I know a Nobleman who would give a great deal of Money for such a Piece of Antiquity. — Ay, ay, Question and Answer. The Beginning is the Catechism in *Greek*. —— Ay, — Ay, — *Pollaki toi* —— What's your Name?'[11] —— 'Ay, what's your Name?' says the Justice to *Adams*, who answered, 'It is *Æschylus*, and I will maintain it.' —— 'O it is,' says the Justice, 'make Mr *Æschylus* his *Mittimus*. I will teach you to banter me with a false Name.'

One of the Company having looked stedfastly at *Adams*, asked him, 'if he did not know Lady *Booby*?' Upon which *Adams* presently calling him to mind, answered in a Rapture, 'O Squire, are you there? I believe you will inform his Worship I am innocent.' 'I can indeed say,' replied the Squire, 'that I am very much surprized to see you in this Situation;' and then addressing himself to the Justice, he said, 'Sir, I assure you Mr *Adams* is a Clergyman as he appears, and a Gentleman of a very good Character. I wish you would enquire a little farther into this Affair: for I am convinced of his Innocence.' 'Nay,' says the Justice, 'if he is a Gentleman, and you are sure he is innocent, I don't desire to commit him, not I; I will commit the Woman by herself, and take your Bail for the Gentleman; look into the Book, Clerk, and see how it is to take Bail; come — and make the *Mittimus* for the *Woman* as fast as you can.' 'Sir,' cries *Adams*, 'I assure you she is as innocent as myself.' 'Perhaps,' said the Squire, 'there may be some Mistake; pray let us hear Mr *Adams*'s Relation.' 'With all my heart,' answered the Justice, 'and give the Gentleman a Glass to whet his Whistle before he begins. I know how to behave myself to Gentlemen as well as another. No body can say I have committed a Gentleman since I have been in the Commission.' *Adams* then began the Narrative, in which, though he was very prolix, he was uninterrupted, unless by several *Hums* and *Ha*'s of the Justice, and his Desire to repeat those Parts which seemed to him most material. When he had finished, the Justice, who, on what the Squire had said, believed every Syllable of his Story on his bare Affirmation, notwithstanding the Depositions on Oath to the contrary, began to let loose several *Rogues and Rascals* against the Witness, whom he ordered to stand forth, but in vain: the said Witness, long since finding what turn Matters were like to take, had privily withdrawn, without attending the Issue. The Justice now flew into a violent Passion, and was hardly prevailed with not to commit the innocent Fellows who had been imposed on as well as himself. He swore, 'they had best find out the Fellow who was guilty of Perjury, and bring him before him within two Days, or he would bind them all over to their good Behaviour.' They all promised to use their best Endeavours to that purpose, and were dismissed. Then the Justice insisted, that Mr *Adams* should sit down and take a Glass with him; and the Parson of the Parish delivered him back the Manuscript without saying a Word; nor would *Adams*, who plainly discerned his Ignorance, expose it. As for *Fanny*, she was, at her own Request, recommended to the Care of a Maid-Servant of the House, who helped her to new dress, and clean herself.

The Company in the Parlour had not been long seated, before they were alarmed with a horrible Uproar from without, where the Persons who had apprehended *Adams* and *Fanny*, had been regaling, according to the Custom of the House, with the Justice's Strong Beer. These were all fallen together by the Ears, and were cuffing each other without any Mercy. The Justice himself sallied out, and with the Dignity of his Presence, soon put an end to the Fray. On his return into the Parlour, he reported, 'That the Occasion of the Quarrel, was no other than a Dispute, to whom, if *Adams* had been convicted, the greater Share of the Reward for apprehending him had belonged.' All the Company laughed at this, except

Adams, who taking his Pipe from his Mouth, fetched a deep Groan, and said, he was concerned to see so litigious a Temper in Men. That he remembered a Story something like it in one of the Parishes where his Cure lay: 'There was,' continued he, 'a Competition between three young Fellows, for the Place of the Clerk, which I disposed of, to the best of my Abilities, according to Merit: that is, I gave it to him who had the happiest Knack at setting a Psalm. The Clerk was no sooner established in his Place than a Contention began between the two disappointed Candidates, concerning their Excellence, each contending, on whom, had they two been the only Competitors, my Election would have fallen. This Dispute frequently disturbed the Congregation, and introduced a Discord into the Psalmody, 'till I was forced to silence them both. But alas, the litigious Spirit could not be stifled; and being no longer able to vent itself in singing, it now broke forth in fighting. It produced many Battles, (for they were very near a Match;) and, I believe, would have ended fatally, had not the Death of the Clerk given me an Opportunity to promote one of them to his Place; which presently put an end to the Dispute, and entirely reconciled the contending Parties.' *Adams* then proceeded to make some Philosophical Observations on the Folly of growing warm in Disputes, in which neither Party is interested. He then applied himself vigorously to smoaking; and a long Silence ensued, which was at length broken by the Justice; who began to sing forth his own Praises, and to value himself exceedingly on his nice Discernment in the Cause, which had lately been before him. He was quickly interrupted by Mr *Adams*, between whom and his Worship a Dispute now arose, whether he ought not, in strictness of Law, to have committed him, the said *Adams*; in which the latter maintained he ought to have been committed, and the Justice as vehemently held he ought not. This had most probably produced a Quarrel, (for both were very violent and positive in their Opinions) had not *Fanny* accidentally heard, that a young Fellow was going from the Justice's House, to the very Inn where the Stage-Coach in which *Joseph* was, put up. Upon this News, she immediately sent for the Parson out of the Parlour. *Adams*, when he found her resolute to go, (tho' she would not own the Reason, but pretended she could not bear to see the Faces of those who had suspected her of such a Crime,) was as fully determined to go with her; he accordingly took leave of the Justice and Company, and so ended a Dispute, in which the Law seemed shamefully to intend to set a Magistrate and a Divine together by the ears.

CHAPTER XII

A very delightful Adventure, as well to the Persons concerned as to the good-natur'd Reader.

Adams, *Fanny*, and the Guide, set out together, about one in the Morning, the Moon then just being risen. They had not gone above a Mile, before a most violent Storm of Rain obliged them to take shelter in an Inn, or rather Alehouse; where *Adams* immediately procured himself a good Fire, a Toast and Ale,[1] and a Pipe, and began to smoke with great Content, utterly forgetting every thing that had happened.

Fanny sat likewise down by the Fire; but was much more impatient at the Storm. She presently engaged the Eyes of the Host, his Wife, the Maid of the House, and the young Fellow who were their Guide; they all conceived they had never seen any thing half so handsome: and indeed, Reader, if thou art of an amorous Hue, I advise thee to skip over the next Paragraph; which to render our History perfect, we are obliged to set down, humbly hoping, that we may escape the Fate of *Pygmalion*:[2] for if it should happen to us or to thee to be struck with this Picture, we should be perhaps in as helpless a Condition as *Narcissus*; and might say to ourselves, *Quid petis est nusquam.*[3] Or if the finest Features in it should set Lady ———'s Image before our Eyes, we should be still in as bad Situation, and might say to our Desires, *Cælum ipsum petimus stultitia.*[4]

Fanny was now in the nineteenth Year of her Age; she was tall and delicately shaped; but not one of those slender young Women, who seem rather intended to hang up in the Hall of an Anatomist, than for any other Purpose. On the contrary she was so plump, that she seemed bursting through her tight Stays, especially in the Part which confined her swelling Breasts. Nor did her Hips want the Assistance of a Hoop to extend them. The exact Shape of her Arms, denoted the Form of those Limbs which she concealed; and tho' they were a little redden'd by her Labour, yet if her Sleeve slipt above her Elbow, or her Handkerchief discovered any part of her Neck, a Whiteness appeared which the finest *Italian* Paint would be unable to reach. Her Hair was of a Chesnut Brown, and Nature had been extremely lavish to her of it, which she had cut, and on *Sundays* used to curl down her Neck in the modern Fashion. Her Forehead was high, her Eye-brows arched, and rather full than otherwise. Her Eyes black and sparkling; her Nose, just inclining to the *Roman*; her

Lips red and moist, and her Under-Lip, according to the Opinion of the Ladies, too pouting. Her Teeth were white, but not exactly even. The Small-Pox had left only one Mark on her Chin, which was so large, it might have been mistaken for a Dimple, had not her left Cheek produced one so near a Neighbour to it, that the former served only for a Foil to the latter. Her Complexion was fair, a little injured by the Sun, but overspread with such a Bloom, that the finest Ladies would have exchanged all their White for it: add to these, a Countenance in which tho' she was extremely bashful, a Sensibility appeared almost incredible; and a Sweetness, whenever she smiled, beyond either Imitation or Description. To conclude all, she had a natural Gentility, superior to the Acquisition of Art, and which surprised all who beheld her.

This lovely Creature was sitting by the Fire with *Adams*, when her Attention was suddenly engaged by a Voice from an inner Room, which sung the following Song:

The SONG

> *Say*, Chloe,[5] *where must the Swain stray*
>   *Who is by thy Beauties undone,*
> *To wash their Remembrance away,*
>   *To what distant* Lethe[6] *must run?*
> *The Wretch who is sentenc'd to die,*
>   *May escape and leave Justice behind;*
> *From his Country perhaps he may fly,*
>   *But O can he fly from his Mind!*
>
> *O Rapture! unthought of before,*
>   *To be thus of* Chloe *possest;*
> *Nor she, nor no Tyrant's hard Power,*
>   *Her Image can tear from my Breast.*
> *But felt not* Narcissus *more Joy,*
>   *With his Eyes he beheld his lov'd Charms?*
> *Yet what he beheld, the fond Boy*
>   *More eagerly wish'd in his Arms.*

How can it thy dear Image be,
 Which fills thus my Bosom with Woe?
Can aught bear Resemblance to thee,
 Which Grief and not Joy can bestow?
This Counterfeit snatch from my Heart,
 Ye Pow'rs, tho' with Torment I rave,
Tho' mortal will prove the fell Smart,
 I then shall find rest in my Grave.

Ah! see the dear Nymph o'er the Plain,
 Comes smiling and tripping along,
A thousand Loves dance in her Train,
 The Graces around her all throng.
To meet her soft Zephyrus[7] *flies,*
 And wafts all the Sweets from the Flow'rs;
Ah Rogue! whilst he kisses her Eyes,
 More Sweets from her Breath he devours.

My Soul, whilst I gaze, is on fire,
 But her Looks were so tender and kind,
My Hope almost reach'd my Desire,
 And left lame Despair far behind.
Transported with Madness I flew,
 And eagerly seiz'd on my Bliss;
Her Bosom but half she withdrew,
 But half she refus'd my fond Kiss.

Advances like these made me bold,
 I whisper'd her, Love, —— *we're alone,*
The rest let Immortals unfold,
 No Language can tell but their own.
Ah Chloe *expiring, I cry'd,*
 How long I thy Cruelty bore?
Ah! Strephon,[8] *she blushing reply'd,*
 You ne'er was so pressing before.

Adams had been ruminating all this Time on a Passage in *Æschylus*, without attending in the least to the Voice, tho' one of the most melodious that ever was heard; when casting his Eyes on *Fanny*, he cried out, 'Bless us, you look extremely pale.' Pale! Mr *Adams*, says she, O Jesus! and fell backwards in her Chair. *Adams* jumped up, flung his *Æschylus* into the

Fire, and fell a roaring to the People of the House for Help. He soon summon'd every one into the Room, and the Songster among the rest: But, O Reader, when this Nightingale, who was no other than *Joseph Andrews* himself, saw his beloved *Fanny* in the Situation we have described her, can'st thou conceive the Agitations of his Mind? If thou can'st not, wave that Meditation to behold his Happiness, when clasping her in his Arms, he found Life and Blood returning into her Cheeks; when he saw her open her beloved Eyes, and heard her with the softest Accent whisper, 'Are you *Joseph Andrews*?' 'Art thou my *Fanny*?' he answered eagerly, and pulling her to his Heart he imprinted numberless Kisses on her Lips, without considering who were present.

If Prudes are offended at the Lusciousness of this Picture, they may take their Eyes off from it, and survey Parson *Adams* dancing about the Room in a Rapture of Joy. Some Philosophers may perhaps doubt, whether he was not the happiest of the three; for the Goodness of his Heart enjoyed the Blessings which were exulting in the Breasts of both the other two, together with his own. But we shall leave such Disquisitions as too deep for us, to those who are building some favourite Hypotheses, which they will refuse no Metaphysical Rubbish to erect, and support: for our part, we give it clearly on the side of *Joseph*, whose Happiness was not only greater than the Parson's, but of longer Duration: for as soon as the first Tumults of *Adams*'s Rapture were over, he cast his Eyes towards the Fire, where *Æschylus* lay expiring; and immediately rescued the poor Remains, to-wit, the Sheep-skin Covering of his dear Friend, which was the Work of his own Hands, and had been his inseparable Companion for upwards of thirty Years.

Fanny had no sooner perfectly recovered herself, than she began to restrain the Impetuosity of her Transports; and reflecting on what she had done and suffered in the Presence of so many, she was immediately covered with Confusion; and pushing *Joseph* gently from her, she begged him to be quiet: nor would admit of either Kiss or Embrace any longer. Then seeing Mrs *Slipslop*, she curt'sied, and offered to advance to her; but that high Woman would not return her Curt'sies; but casting her Eyes another way, she immediately withdrew into another Room, muttering as she went, she wondered *who the Creature was*.

CHAPTER XIII

A Dissertation concerning high People and low People, with Mrs
Slipslop*'s Departure in no very good Temper of Mind, and the evil*
Plight in which she left Adams *and his Company.*

It will doubtless seem extremely odd to many Readers, that Mrs *Slipslop*, who had lived several Years in the same House with *Fanny*, should in a short Separation utterly forget her. And indeed the truth is, that she remembered her very well. As we would not willingly therefore, that any thing should appear unnatural in this our History, we will endeavour to explain the Reasons of her Conduct; nor do we doubt being able to satisfy the most curious Reader, that Mrs *Slipslop* did not in the least deviate from the common Road in this Behaviour; and indeed, had she done otherwise, she must have descended below herself, and would have very justly been liable to Censure.

Be it known then, that the human Species are divided into two sorts of People, to wit, *High* People and *Low* People. As by High People, I would not be understood to mean Persons literally born higher in their Dimensions than the rest of the Species, nor metaphorically those of exalted Characters or Abilities; so by Low People I cannot be construed to intend the Reverse. High People signify no other than People of Fashion, and low People those of no Fashion. Now this Word *Fashion*, hath by long use lost its original Meaning, from which at present it gives us a very different Idea: for I am deceived, if by Persons of Fashion, we do not generally include a Conception of Birth and Accomplishments superior to the Herd of Mankind; whereas in reality, nothing more was originally meant by a Person of Fashion, than a Person who drest himself in the Fashion of the Times; and the Word really and truly signifies no more at this day. Now the World being thus divided into People of Fashion, and People of no Fashion, a fierce Contention arose between them, nor would those of one Party, to avoid Suspicion, be seen publickly to speak to those of the other; though they often held a very good Correspondence in private. In this Contention, it is difficult to say which Party succeeded: for whilst the People of Fashion seized several Places to their own use, such as Courts, Assemblies, Operas, Balls, &c. the People of no Fashion, besides one Royal Place called his Majesty's Bear-Garden,[1] have been in constant Possession of all Hops, Fairs, Revels, &c. Two Places have been agreed to be divided between them, namely the Church and the Play-House; where they segregate themselves from each other in a remarkable Manner: for as the People of Fashion exalt themselves at Church over the Heads of the People of no Fashion; so in the Play-House they abase themselves in the same degree under their Feet.[2] This Distinction I have never met with any one able to account for; it is sufficient, that so far from looking on each other as Brethren in the Christian Language, they seem scarce to regard each other as of the same Species. This the Terms *strange Persons*, *People one does not know*, *the Creature*, *Wretches*, *Beasts*, *Brutes*, and many other Appellations evidently demonstrate; which Mrs *Slipslop* having often heard her Mistress use, thought she had also a Right to use in her turn: and perhaps she was not mistaken; for these two Parties, especially those bordering nearly on each other, to wit the lowest of the High, and the highest of the Low, often change their Parties according to Place and Time; for those who are People of Fashion in one place, are often People of no Fashion in another: And with regard to Time, it may not be unpleasant to survey the Picture of Dependance like a kind of Ladder; as for instance early in the Morning arises the Postillion, or some other Boy which great Families no more than great Ships are without, and falls to brushing the Clothes, and cleaning the Shoes of *John* the Footman, who being drest himself, applies his Hands to the same Labours for Mr *Second-hand* the Squire's Gentleman; the Gentleman in the like manner, a little later in the Day, attends the Squire; the Squire is no sooner equipped, than he attends the Levee of my Lord; which is no sooner over, than my Lord himself is seen at the Levee of the Favourite, who after his Hour of Homage is at an end, appears himself to pay Homage to the Levee of his Sovereign. Nor is there perhaps, in this whole Ladder of Dependance, any one Step at a greater distance from the other, than the first from the second: so that to a Philosopher the Question might only seem whether you would chuse to be a great Man at six in the Morning, or at two in the Afternoon. And yet there are scarce two of these, who do not think the least Familiarity with the Persons below them a Condescension, and if they were to go one Step farther, a Degradation.

And now, Reader, I hope thou wilt pardon this long Digression, which seemed to me necessary to vindicate the great Character of Mrs *Slipslop*, from what low People, who have never seen high People, might think an Absurdity: but we who know them, must have daily found very high Persons know us in one Place and not in another, To-day, and not To-morrow; all which, it is difficult to account for, otherwise than I have here endeavour'd; and perhaps, if the Gods, according to the Opinion of some, made Men only to laugh at them,[3] there is no part of our Behaviour which answers the End of our Creation better than this.

But to return to our History: *Adams*, who knew no more of all this than the Cat which sat on the Table, imagining Mrs *Slipslop*'s Memory had been much worse than it really was, followed her into the next Room, crying out, 'Madam *Slipslop*, here is one of your old Acquaintance: Do but see what a fine Woman she is grown since she left Lady *Booby*'s Service.' 'I think I *reflect* something of her,' answered she with great Dignity, 'but I can't remember all the inferior Servants in our Family.' She then proceeded to satisfy *Adams*'s Curiosity, by telling him, 'when she arrived at the Inn, she found a Chaise ready for her; that her Lady being expected very shortly in the Country, she was obliged to make the utmost haste, and in *Commensuration* of *Joseph*'s Lameness, she had taken him with her; and lastly, that the excessive *Virulence* of the Storm had driven them into the House where he found them.' After which, she acquainted *Adams* with his having left his Horse, and exprest some Wonder at his having stray'd so far out of his Way, and at meeting him, as she said, 'in the Company of that Wench, who she feared was no better than she should be.'

The Horse was no sooner put into *Adams*'s Head, but he was immediately driven out by this Reflection on the Character of *Fanny*. He protested, 'he believed there was not a chaster Damsel in the Universe. I heartily wish, I heartily wish,' cry'd he, (snapping his Fingers) 'that all her Betters were as good.' He then proceeded to inform her of the Accident of their meeting; but when he came to mention the Circumstance of delivering her from the Rape, she said, 'she thought him properer for the Army than the Clergy: that it did not become a Clergyman to lay violent Hands on any one, that he should have rather prayed that she might be strengthened.' *Adams* said, 'he was very far from being ashamed of what he had done;' she replied, 'want of Shame was not the *Currycuristick* of a Clergyman.' This Dialogue might have probably grown warmer, had not *Joseph* opportunely entered the Room, to ask leave of Madam *Slipslop* to introduce *Fanny*: but she positively refused to admit any such Trollops; and told him, 'she would have been burnt before she would have suffered him to get into a Chaise with her; if she had once *respected* him of having his Sluts way-laid on the Road for him;' adding, 'that Mr *Adams* acted a very pretty Part, and she did not doubt but to see him a Bishop.' He made the best Bow he could, and cried out, 'I thank you, Madam, for that Right Reverend Appellation, which I shall take all honest Means to deserve.'

'Very honest Means,' returned she with a Sneer, 'to bring good People together.' At these Words, *Adams* took two or three Strides a-cross the Room, when the Coachman came to inform Mrs *Slipslop*, 'that the Storm was over, and the Moon shone very bright.' She then sent for *Joseph*, who was sitting without with his *Fanny*; and would have had him gone with her: but he peremptorily refused to leave *Fanny* behind; which threw the good Woman into a violent Rage. She said, 'she would inform her Lady what Doings were carrying on, and did not doubt, but she would rid the Parish of all such People;' and concluded a long Speech full of Bitterness and very hard Words, with some Reflections on the Clergy, not decent to repeat: at last finding *Joseph* unmoveable, she flung herself into the Chaise, casting a Look at *Fanny* as she went, not unlike that which *Cleopatra* gives *Octavia* in the Play.[4] To say the truth, she was most disagreeably disappointed by the Presence of *Fanny*; she had from her first seeing *Joseph* at the Inn, conceived Hopes of something which might have been accomplished at an Alehouse as well as a Palace; indeed it is probable, Mr *Adams* had rescued more than *Fanny* from the Danger of a Rape that Evening.

When the Chaise had carried off the enraged *Slipslop*; *Adams*, *Joseph* and *Fanny* assembled over the Fire; where they had a great deal of innocent Chat, pretty enough; but as possibly it would not be very entertaining to the Reader, we shall hasten to the Morning; only observing that none of them went to bed that Night. *Adams*, when he had smoked three Pipes, took a comfortable Nap in a great Chair, and left the Lovers, whose Eyes were too well employed to permit any Desire of shutting them, to enjoy by themselves during some Hours, an Happiness which none of my Readers, who have never been in love, are capable of the least Conception of, tho' we had as many Tongues as *Homer* desired[5] to describe it with, and which all true Lovers will represent to their own Minds without the least Assistance from us.

Let it suffice then to say, that *Fanny* after a thousand Entreaties at last gave up her whole Soul to *Joseph*, and almost fainting in his Arms, with a Sigh infinitely softer and sweeter too, than any *Arabian* Breeze, she whispered to his Lips, which were then close to hers, 'O *Joseph*, you have won me; I will be yours for ever.' *Joseph*, having thanked her on his Knees, and embraced her with an Eagerness, which she now almost returned, leapt up in a Rapture, and awakened the Parson, earnestly begging him, 'that he would that Instant join their Hands together.' *Adams* rebuked him for his Request, and told him, 'he would by no means consent to any thing contrary to the Forms of the Church, that he had no Licence, nor indeed would he advise him to obtain one. That the Church had prescribed a Form, namely the Publication of Banns, with which all good Christians ought to comply, and to the Omission of which, he attributed the many Miseries which befel great Folks in Marriage; concluding, *As many as are joined together otherwise than G——'s Word doth allow, are not joined together by G——, neither is their Matrimony lawful.*[6] *Fanny* agreed with the Parson, saying to *Joseph* with a Blush, 'she assured him she would not consent to any such thing, and that she wondred at his offering it.' In which Resolution she was comforted, and commended by *Adams*; and *Joseph* was obliged to wait patiently till after the third Publication of the Banns, which however, he obtained the Consent of *Fanny* in the Presence of *Adams* to put in at their Arrival.

The Sun had been now risen some Hours, when *Joseph* finding his Leg surprisingly recovered, proposed to walk forwards; but when they were all ready to set out, an Accident a little retarded them. This was no other than the Reckoning which amounted to seven Shillings; no great Sum if we consider the immense Quantity of Ale which Mr *Adams* poured in. Indeed they had no Objection to the Reasonableness of the Bill, but many to the Probability of paying it; for the Fellow who had taken poor *Fanny*'s Purse, had unluckily forgot to return it. So that the Account stood thus:

Mr *Adams* and Company Dr.[7]	o	7	o
In Mr *Adams*'s Pocket,	o	o	6½
In Mr *Joseph*'s,	o	o	o
In Mrs *Fanny*'s,	o	o	o
Balance	o	6	5½

They stood silent some few Minutes, staring at each other, when *Adams* whipt out on his Toes, and asked the Hostess 'if there was no Clergyman in that Parish?' She answered, 'there was.' 'Is he wealthy?' replied he; to which she likewise answered in the Affirmative. *Adams* then snapping his Fingers returned overjoyed to his Companions, crying out, '*Eureka, Eureka*;' which not being understood, he told them in plain *English* 'they need give themselves no trouble; for he had a Brother in the Parish, who would defray the Reckoning, and that he would just step to his House and fetch the Money, and return to them instantly.'

CHAPTER XIV

An Interview between Parson Adams *and Parson* Trulliber.

Parson *Adams* came to the House of Parson *Trulliber*,[1] whom he found stript into his Waistcoat, with an Apron on, and a Pail in his Hand, just come from serving his Hogs; for Mr *Trulliber* was a Parson on *Sundays*, but all the other six might more properly be called a Farmer.[2] He occupied a small piece of Land of his own, besides which he rented a considerable deal more. His Wife milked his Cows, managed his Dairy, and followed the Markets with Butter and Eggs. The Hogs fell chiefly to his care, which he carefully waited on at home, and attended to Fairs; on which occasion he was liable to many Jokes, his own Size being with much Ale rendered little inferior to that of the Beasts he sold. He was indeed one of the largest Men you should see, and could have acted the Part of Sir *John Falstaff* without stuffing. Add to this, that the Rotundity of his Belly was considerably increased by the shortness of his Stature, his Shadow ascending very near as far in height when he lay on his Back, as when he stood on his Legs. His Voice was loud and hoarse, and his Accents extremely broad; to complete the whole, he had a Stateliness in his Gait, when he walked, not unlike that of a Goose, only he stalked slower.

Mr *Trulliber* being informed that somebody wanted to speak with him, immediately slipt off his Apron, and clothed himself in an old Night-Gown,[3] being the Dress in which he always saw his Company at home. His Wife who informed him of Mr *Adams*'s Arrival, had made a small Mistake; for she had told her Husband, 'she believed here was a Man come for some of his Hogs.' This Supposition made Mr *Trulliber* hasten with the utmost expedition to attend his Guest; he no sooner saw *Adams*, than not in the least doubting the Cause of his Errand to be what his Wife had imagined, he told him, 'he was come in very good time; that he expected a Dealer that very Afternoon;' and added, 'they were all pure and fat, and upwards of 20 Score a-piece.' *Adams* answered, 'he believed he did not know him.' 'Yes, yes,' cried *Trulliber*, 'I have seen you often at *Fair*; why, we have dealt before now mun, I warrant you; yes, yes,' cries he, 'I remember thy Face very well, but won't mention a word more till you have seen them, tho' I have never sold thee a Flitch of such Bacon as is now in the Stye.' Upon which he laid violent hands on *Adams*, and dragged him into the Hogs-Stye, which was indeed but two Steps from his Parlour Window. They were no sooner arrived there than he cry'd out, 'Do but handle them, step in, Friend, art welcome to handle them whether dost buy or no.' At which words opening the Gate, he pushed *Adams* into the Pig-Stye, insisting on it, that he should handle them, before he would talk one word with him. *Adams*, whose natural Complacence was beyond any artificial, was obliged to comply before he was suffered to explain himself, and laying hold on one of their Tails, the unruly Beast gave such a sudden spring, that he threw poor *Adams* all along in the Mire. *Trulliber* instead of assisting him to get up, burst into a Laughter, and entering the Stye, said to *Adams* with some contempt, *Why, dost not know how to handle a Hog?* and was going to lay hold of one himself; but *Adams*, who thought he had carried his Complacence far enough, was no sooner on his Legs, than he escaped out of the Reach of the Animals, and cried out, *Nihil habeo cum Porcis*:[4] 'I am a Clergyman, Sir, and am not come to buy Hogs.' *Trulliber* answered, 'he was sorry for the Mistake; but that he must blame his Wife;' adding, 'she was a Fool, and always committed Blunders.' He then desired him to walk in and clean himself, that he would only fasten up the Stye and follow him. *Adams* desired leave to dry his Great Coat, Wig, and Hat by the Fire, which *Trulliber* granted. Mrs *Trulliber* would have brought him a Bason of Water to wash his Face, but her Husband bid her be quiet like a Fool as she was, or she would commit more Blunders, and then directed *Adams* to the Pump. While *Adams* was thus employed, *Trulliber* conceiving no great Respect for the Appearance of his Guest, fastened the Parlour-Door, and now conducted him into the Kitchin; telling him, he believed a Cup of Drink would do him no harm, and whispered his Wife to draw a little of the worst Ale. After a short Silence, *Adams* said, 'I fancy, Sir, you already perceive me to be a Clergyman.' 'Ay, ay,' cries *Trulliber* grinning; 'I perceive you have some Cassock; I will not venture to *caale* it a whole one.' *Adams* answered, 'it was indeed none of the best; but he had the misfortune to tear it about ten Years ago in passing over a Stile.' Mrs *Trulliber* returning with the Drink, told her Husband 'she fancied the Gentleman was a Traveller, and that he would be glad to eat a bit.' *Trulliber* bid her 'hold her impertinent Tongue;' and asked her 'if Parsons used to travel without Horses?' adding, 'he supposed the Gentleman had none by his having no Boots on.' 'Yes, Sir, yes,' says *Adams*, 'I have a Horse, but I have left him behind me.' 'I am glad to hear you have one,' says *Trulliber*, 'for I assure you, I don't love to see Clergymen on foot; it is not seemly nor suiting the Dignity of the Cloth.' Here *Trulliber* made a long Oration on the Dignity of the Cloth (or rather Gown) not much worth relating, till his Wife had spread the Table and set a Mess of Porridge on it for his Breakfast. He then said to *Adams*, 'I don't know, Friend, how you came to *caale* on me; however, as you are here, if you think proper to eat a Morsel, you may.' *Adams* accepted the Invitation, and the two Parsons sat down together, Mrs *Trulliber* waiting behind her Husband's Chair, as was, it seems, her custom. *Trulliber* eat heartily, but scarce put any thing in his Mouth without finding fault with his Wife's Cookery. All which the poor Woman bore patiently. Indeed she was so absolute an Admirer of her Husband's Greatness and Importance, of which she had frequent Hints from his own Mouth, that she almost carried her Adoration to an opinion of his Infallibility. To say the truth, the Parson had exercised her more ways than one; and the pious Woman had so well edified by her Husband's Sermons, that she had resolved to receive the good things of this World together with the bad. She had indeed been at first a little contentious; but he had long since got the better, partly by her love for *this*, partly by her fear of *that*, partly by her Religion, partly by the Respect he paid himself, and partly by that which he received from the Parish: She had, in short, absolutely submitted, and now worshipped her Husband as *Sarah* did *Abraham*, calling him (not Lord but) Master.[5] Whilst they were at Table, her Husband gave her a fresh Example of his Greatness; for as she had just delivered a Cup of Ale to *Adams*, he snatched it out of his Hand, and crying out, *I caal'd vurst*, swallowed down the Ale. *Adams* denied it, and it was referred to the Wife, who tho' her Conscience was on the side of *Adams*, durst not give it against her Husband. Upon which he said, 'No, Sir, no, I should not have been so rude to have taken it from you, if you had *caal'd vurst*; but I'd have you know I'm a better Man than to suffer the best He in the Kingdom to drink before me in my own House, when I *caale vurst*.'

As soon as their Breakfast was ended, *Adams* began in the following manner: 'I think, Sir, it is high time to inform you of the business of my Embassy. I am a Traveller, and am passing this way in company with two young People, a Lad and a Damsel, my Parishioners, towards my own Cure: we stopt at a House of Hospitality in the Parish, where they directed me to you, as having the Cure.' — 'Tho' I am but a Curate,' says *Trulliber*, 'I believe I am as warm[6] as the Vicar himself, or perhaps the Rector of the next Parish too; I believe I could buy them both.' 'Sir,' cries *Adams*, 'I rejoice thereat. Now, Sir, my Business is, that we are by various Accidents stript of our Money, and are not able to pay our Reckoning, being seven Shillings. I therefore request you to assist me with the Loan of those seven Shillings, and also seven Shillings more, which peradventure I shall return to you; but if not, I am convinced you will joyfully embrace such an Opportunity of laying up a Treasure in a better Place than any this World affords.'[7]

Suppose a Stranger, who entered the Chambers of a Lawyer, being imagined a Client, when the Lawyer was preparing his Palm for the Fee, should pull out a Writ against him. Suppose an Apothecary, at the Door of a Chariot containing some great Doctor of eminent Skill, should, instead of Directions to a Patient, present him with a Potion for himself. Suppose a Minister should, instead of a good round Sum, treat my Lord —— or Sir —— or. Esq; —— with a good Broomstick. Suppose a civil Companion, or a led Captain[8] should, instead of Virtue, and Honour, and Beauty, and Parts, and Admiration, thunder Vice and Infamy, and Ugliness, and Folly, and Contempt, in his Patron's Ears. Suppose when a Tradesman first carries in his Bill, the Man of Fashion should pay it; or suppose, if he did so, the Tradesman should abate what he had overcharged on the Supposition of waiting. In short — suppose what you will, you never can nor will suppose any thing equal to the Astonishment which seized on *Trulliber*, as soon as *Adams* had ended his Speech. A while he rolled his Eyes in Silence, sometimes surveying *Adams*, then his Wife, then casting them on the Ground, then lifting them to Heaven. At last, he burst forth in the following Accents. 'Sir, I believe I know where to lay my little Treasure up as well as another; I thank G— if I am not so warm as some, I am content; that is a Blessing greater than Riches; and he to whom that is given need ask no more. To be content with a little is greater than to possess the World, which a Man may possess without being so. Lay up my Treasure! what matters where a Man's Treasure is, whose Heart is in the Scriptures?[9] there is the Treasure of a Christian.' At these Words the Water ran from *Adams*'s Eyes; and catching *Trulliber* by the Hand, in a Rapture, 'Brother,' says he, 'Heavens bless the Accident by which I came to see you; I would have walked many a Mile to have communed with you, and, believe me, I will shortly pay you a second Visit: but my Friends, I fancy, by this time, wonder at my stay, so let me have the Money immediately.' *Trulliber* then put on a stern Look, and cried out, 'Thou dost not intend to rob me?'[10] At which the Wife, bursting into Tears, fell on her Knees and roared out, 'O dear Sir, for Heavens sake don't rob my Master, we are but poor People.' 'Get up for a Fool as thou art, and go about thy Business,' said *Trulliber*, 'dost think the Man will venture his Life? he is a Beggar and no Robber.' 'Very true indeed,' answered *Adams*. 'I wish, with all my heart, the Tithing-Man[11] was here,' cries *Trulliber*, 'I would have thee punished as a Vagabond for thy Impudence. Fourteen Shillings indeed! I won't give thee a Farthing. I believe thou art no more a Clergyman than the Woman there, (pointing to his Wife) but if thou art, dost deserve to have thy Gown stript over thy Shoulders, for running about the Country in such a manner.' 'I forgive your Suspicions,' says *Adams*, 'but suppose I am not a Clergyman, I am nevertheless thy Brother, and thou, as a Christian, much more as a Clergyman, art obliged to relieve my Distress.' 'Dost preach to me,' replied *Trulliber*, 'dost pretend to instruct me in my Duty?' 'Ifacks, a good Story,' cries Mrs *Trulliber*, 'to preach to my Master.' 'Silence, Woman,' cries *Trulliber*, 'I would have thee know, Friend,' (addressing himself to *Adams*) 'I shall not learn my Duty from such as thee; I know what Charity is, better than to give to Vagabonds.' 'Besides, if we were inclined, the Poors Rate[12] obliges us to give so much Charity,' cries the Wife. 'Pugh! thou art a Fool; Poors Reate! hold thy Nonsense,' answered *Trulliber*, and then turning to *Adams*, he told him, 'he would give him nothing.' 'I am sorry,' answered *Adams*, 'that you do know what Charity is, since you practise it no better; I must tell you, if you trust to your Knowledge for your Justification, you will find yourself deceived, though you should add Faith to it without good Works.' 'Fellow,' cries *Trulliber*, 'Dost thou speak against Faith in my House? Get out of my Doors, I will no longer remain under the same Roof with a Wretch who speaks wantonly of Faith and the Scriptures.' 'Name not the Scriptures,' says *Adams*. 'How, not name the Scriptures! Do you disbelieve the Scriptures?' cries *Trulliber*. 'No, but you do,' answered *Adams*, 'if I may reason from your Practice: for their Commands are so explicit, and their Rewards and Punishments so immense, that it is impossible a Man should stedfastly believe without obeying. Now, there is no Command more express, no Duty more frequently enjoined than Charity. Whoever therefore is void of Charity, I make no scruple of pronouncing that he is no Christian.'[13] 'I would not advise thee,' (says *Trulliber*) 'to say that I am no Christian; I won't take it of you: for I believe I am as good a Man as thyself;' (and indeed, though he was now rather too corpulent for athletic Exercises, he had in his Youth been one of the best Boxers and Cudgel-players in the County.) His Wife seeing him clench his Fist, interposed, and begged him not to fight, but shew himself a true Christian, and take the Law of him. As nothing could provoke *Adams* to strike, but an absolute Assault on himself or his Friend; he smiled at the angry Look and Gestures of *Trulliber*, and telling him, he was sorry to see such Men in Orders, departed without further Ceremony.

CHAPTER XV

An Adventure, the Consequence of a new Instance which Parson Adams gave of his Forgetfulness.

When he came back to the Inn, he found *Joseph* and *Fanny* sitting together. They were so far from thinking his Absence long, as he had feared they would, that they never once miss'd or thought of him. Indeed I have been often assured by both, that they spent these Hours in a most delightful Conversation: but as I never could prevail on either to relate it, so I cannot communicate it to the Reader.

Adams acquainted the Lovers with the ill Success of his Enterprize. They were all greatly confounded, none being able to propose any Method of departing, 'till *Joseph* at last advised calling in the Hostess, and desiring her to trust them; which *Fanny* said she despaired of her doing, as she was one of the sourest-fac'd Women she had ever beheld.

But she was agreeably disappointed; for the Hostess was no sooner asked the Question than she readily agreed; and with a Curt'sy and Smile, wished them a good Journey. However, lest *Fanny*'s Skill in Physiognomy should be called in question, we will venture to assign one Reason, which might probably incline her to this Confidence and Good-Humour. When *Adams* said he was going to visit his Brother, he had unwittingly imposed on *Joseph* and *Fanny*; who both believed he had meant his natural Brother, and not his Brother in Divinity; and had so informed the Hostess on her Enquiry after him. Now Mr *Trulliber* had by his Professions of Piety, by his Gravity, Austerity, Reserve, and the Opinion of his great Wealth, so great an Authority in his Parish, that they all lived in the utmost Fear and Apprehension of him. It was therefore no wonder that the Hostess, who knew it was in his Option whether she should ever sell another Mug of Drink, did not dare to affront his supposed Brother by denying him Credit.

They were now just on their Departure, when *Adams* recollected he had left his Great Coat and Hat at Mr *Trulliber*'s. As he was not desirous of renewing his Visit, the Hostess herself, having no Servant at home, offered to fetch it.

This was an unfortunate Expedient: for the Hostess was soon undeceived in the Opinion she had entertained of *Adams*, whom *Trulliber* abused in the grossest Terms, especially when he heard he had had the Assurance to pretend to be his near Relation.

At her Return therefore, she entirely changed her Note. She said, 'Folks might be ashamed of travelling about and pretending to be what they were not. That Taxes were high, and for her part, she was obliged to pay for what she had; she could not therefore possibly, nor she would not trust any body, no not her own Father. That Money was never scarcer, and she wanted to make up a Sum. That she expected therefore they should pay their Reckoning before they left the House.'

Adams was now greatly perplexed: but as he knew that he could easily have borrowed such a Sum in his own Parish, and as he knew he would have lent it himself to any Mortal in Distress; so he took fresh Courage, and sallied out all round the Parish, but to no purpose; he returned as pennyless as he went, groaning and lamenting, that it was possible in a Country professing Christianity, for a Wretch to starve in the midst of his Fellow-Creatures who abounded.

Whilst he was gone, the Hostess who stayed as a sort of Guard with *Joseph* and *Fanny*, entertained them with the Goodness of Parson *Trulliber*; and indeed he had not only a very good Character, as to other Qualities, in the Neighbourhood, but was reputed a Man of great Charity: for tho' he never gave a Farthing, he had always that Word in his Mouth.

Adams was no sooner returned the second time, than the Storm grew exceeding high, the Hostess declaring among other things, that if they offered to stir without paying her, she would soon overtake them with a Warrant.

Plato or *Aristotle*, or somebody else hath said, THAT WHEN THE MOST EXQUISITE CUNNING FALLS, CHANCE OFTEN HITS THE MARK, AND THAT BY MEANS THE LEAST EXPECTED. *Virgil* expresses this very boldly:

> *Turne quod optanti Divûm promittere nemo*
> *Auderet, volvenda Dies en attulit ultro.*[1]

I would quote more great Men if I could: but my Memory not permitting me, I will proceed to exemplify these Observations by the following Instance.

There chanced (for *Adams* had not Cunning enough to contrive it) to be at that time in the Alehouse, a Fellow, who had been formerly a Drummer in an *Irish* Regiment, and now travelled the Country as a Pedlar. This Man having attentively listened to the Discourse of the Hostess, at last took *Adams* aside, and asked him what the Sum was for which they were detained. As soon as he was informed, he sighed and said, 'he was sorry it was so much: for that he had no more than six Shillings and Sixpence in his Pocket, which he would lend them with all his heart.' *Adams* gave a Caper, and cry'd out, 'It would do: for that he had Sixpence himself.' And thus these poor People, who could not engage the Compassion of Riches and Piety, were at length delivered out of their Distress by the Charity of a poor Pedlar.

I shall refer it to my Reader, to make what Observations he pleases on this Incident: it is sufficient for me to inform him, that after *Adams* and his Companions had returned him a thousand Thanks, and told him where he might call to be repaid, they all sallied out of the House without any Compliments from their Hostess, or indeed without paying her any; *Adams* declaring, he would take particular Care never to call there again, and she on her side assuring them she wanted no such Guests.

CHAPTER XVI

A very curious Adventure, in which Mr Adams *gave a much greater Instance of the honest Simplicity of his Heart than of his Experience in the Ways of this World.*

Our Travellers had walked about two Miles from that Inn, which they had more Reason to have mistaken for a Castle, than Don *Quixote* ever had any of those in which he sojourned; seeing they had met with such Difficulty in escaping out of its Walls; when they came to a Parish, and beheld a Sign of Invitation hanging out. A Gentleman sat smoaking a Pipe at the Door; of whom *Adams* enquired the Road, and received so courteous and obliging an Answer, accompanied with so smiling a Countenance, that the good Parson, whose Heart was naturally disposed to Love and Affection, began to ask several other Questions; particularly the Name of the Parish, and who was the Owner of a large House whose Front they then had in prospect. The Gentleman answered as obligingly as before; and as to the House, acquainted him it was his own. He then proceeded in the following manner: 'Sir, I presume by your Habit you are a Clergyman: and as you are travelling on foot, I suppose a Glass of good Beer will not be disagreeable to you; and I can recommend my Landlord's within, as some of the best in all this County. What say you, you will halt a little and let us take a Pipe together? there is no better Tobacco in the Kingdom.' This Proposal was not displeasing to *Adams*, who had allayed his Thirst that Day, with no better Liquor than what Mrs *Trulliber*'s Cellar had produced; and which was indeed little superior either in Richness or Flavour to that which distilled from those Grains her generous Husband bestowed on his Hogs. Having therefore abundantly thanked the Gentleman for his kind Invitation, and bid *Joseph* and *Fanny* follow him, he entered the Alehouse, where a large Loaf and Cheese and a Pitcher of Beer, which truly answered the Character given of it, being set before them, the three Travellers fell to eating with Appetites infinitely more voracious than are to be found at the most exquisite Eating-Houses in the Parish of *St James's*.

The Gentleman expressed great Delight in the hearty and chearful Behaviour of *Adams*; and particularly in the Familiarity with which he conversed with *Joseph* and *Fanny*, whom he often called his Children, a Term, he explain'd to mean no more than his Parishioners; saying, he looked on all those whom God had entrusted to his Cure, to stand to him in that Relation. The Gentleman shaking him by the Hand, highly applauded those Sentiments. 'They are indeed,' says he, 'the true Principles of a Christian Divine; and I heartily wish they were universal: but on the contrary, I am sorry to say the Parson of our Parish instead of esteeming his poor Parishioners as a part of his Family, seems rather to consider them as not of the same Species with himself. He seldom speaks to any unless some few of the richest of us; nay indeed, he will not move his Hat to the others. I often laugh when I behold him on *Sundays* strutting along the Church-Yard, like a Turky-Cock, through Rows of his Parishioners; who bow to him with as much Submission and are as unregarded as a Sett of servile Courtiers by the proudest Prince in *Christendom*. But if such temporal Pride is ridiculous, surely the spiritual is odious and detestable: if such a puffed up empty human Bladder, strutting in princely Robes, justly moves one's Derision; surely in the Habit of a Priest it must raise our Scorn.'

'Doubtless,' answer'd *Adams*, 'your Opinion is right; but I hope such Examples are rare. The Clergy whom I have the honour to know, maintain a different Behaviour; and you will allow me, Sir, that the Readiness, which too many of the Laity show to condemn the Order, may be one reason of their avoiding too much Humility.' 'Very true indeed,' says the Gentleman; 'I find, Sir, you are a Man of excellent Sense, and am happy in this Opportunity of knowing you: perhaps our accidental meeting may not be disadvantageous to you neither. At present, I shall only say to you, that the Incumbent of this Living is old and infirm; and that it is in my Gift. Doctor, give me your Hand; and assure yourself of it at his Decease.' *Adams* told him, 'he was never more confounded in his Life, than at his utter Incapacity to make any return to such noble and unmerited Generosity.' 'A mere Trifle, Sir,' cries the Gentleman, 'scarce worth your Acceptance; a little more than three hundred a Year. I wish it was double the Value for your sake.' *Adams* bowed, and cried from the Emotions of his Gratitude; when the other asked him, 'if he was married, or had any Children, besides those in the spiritual Sense he had mentioned.' 'Sir,' replied the Parson, 'I have a Wife and six at your service.' 'That is unlucky,' says the Gentleman; 'for I would otherwise have taken you into my own House as my Chaplain: however, I have another in the Parish, (for the Parsonage-House is not good enough) which I will furnish for you. Pray does your Wife understand a Dairy?' 'I can't profess she does,' says *Adams*. 'I am sorry for it,' quoth the Gentleman; 'I would have given you half a dozen Cows, and very good Grounds to have maintained them.'[1] 'Sir,' said *Adams*, in an Ecstacy, 'you are too liberal; indeed you are.' 'Not at all,' cries the Gentleman, 'I esteem Riches only as they give me an opportunity of doing Good; and I never saw one whom I had a greater Inclination to serve.' At which Words he shook him heartily by the Hand, and told him he had sufficient room in his House to entertain him and his Friends. *Adams* begged he might give him no such Trouble, that they could be very well accommodated in the House where they were; forgetting they had not a Sixpenny Piece among them. The Gentleman would not be denied; and informing himself how far they were; travelling, he said it was too long a Journey to take on foot, and begged that they would favour him, by suffering him to lend them a Servant and Horses; adding withal, that if they would do him the pleasure of their Company only two days, he would furnish them with his Coach and Six. *Adams* turning to *Joseph*, said, How lucky is this Gentleman's goodness to you, who I am afraid would be scarce able to hold out on your lame Leg; and then addressing the Person who made him these liberal Promises, after much bowing, he cried out, 'Blessed be the Hour which first introduced me to a Man of your Charity: you are indeed a Christian of the true primitive kind, and an honour to the Country wherein you live. I would willingly have taken a Pilgrimage to the holy Land to have beheld you: for the Advantages which we draw from your Goodness, give me little pleasure, in comparison of what I enjoy for your own sake; when I consider the Treasures you are by these means laying up for your self in a Country that passeth not away. We will therefore, most generous Sir, accept your Goodness, as well the Entertainment you have so kindly offered us at your House this Evening, as the Accommodation of your Horses To-morrow Morning.' He then began to search for his Hat, as did *Joseph* for his; and both they and *Fanny* were in order of Departure, when the Gentleman stopping short, and seeming to meditate by himself for the space of about a Minute, exclaimed thus: 'Sure never any thing was so unlucky; I have forgot that my House-Keeper was gone abroad, and hath locked up all my Rooms; indeed I would break them open for you, but shall not be able to furnish you with a Bed; for she has likewise put away all my Linnen. I am glad it entered into my Head before I had given you the trouble of walking there; besides, I believe you will find better accommodations here than you expect. Landlord, you can provide good Beds for these People, can't you?' 'Yes and please your Worship,' cries the Host, 'and such as no Lord or Justice of the Peace in the Kingdom need be ashamed to lie in.' 'I am heartily sorry,' says the Gentleman, 'for this Disappointment. I am resolved I will never suffer her to carry away the Keys again.' 'Pray, Sir, let it not make you uneasy,' cries *Adams*, 'we shall do very well here; and the Loan of your Horses is a Favour, we shall be incapable of making any Return to.' 'Ay!' said the Squire, 'the Horses shall attend you here at what Hour in the Morning you please.' And now after many Civilities too tedious to enumerate, many Squeezes by the Hand, with most affectionate Looks and Smiles on each other, and after appointing the Horses at seven the next Morning, the Gentleman took his Leave of them, and departed to his own House. *Adams* and his Companions returned to the Table, where the Parson smoaked another Pipe, and then they all retired to Rest.

Mr *Adams* rose very early and called *Joseph* out of his Bed, between whom a very fierce Dispute ensued, whether *Fanny* should ride behind *Joseph*, or behind the Gentleman's Servant; *Joseph* insisting on it, that he was perfectly recovered, and was as capable of taking care of *Fanny*, as any other Person could be. But *Adams* would not agree to it, and declared he would not trust her behind him; for that he was weaker than he imagined himself to be.

This Dispute continued a long time, and had begun to be very hot, when a Servant arrived from their good Friend, to acquaint them, that he was unfortunately prevented from lending them any Horses; for that his Groom had, unknown to him, put his whole Stable under a Course of Physick.

This Advice presently struck the two Disputants dumb; *Adams* cried out, 'Was ever any thing so unlucky as this poor Gentleman? I protest I am more sorry on his account than my own. You see, *Joseph*, how this good-natur'd Man is treated by his Servants; one locks up his Linnen, another physicks his Horses; and I suppose by his being at this House last Night, the Butler had locked up his Cellar. Bless us! how Good-nature is used in this World! I protest I am more concerned on his account than my own.' 'So am not I,' cries *Joseph*; 'not that I am much troubled about walking on foot; all my Concern is, how we shall get out of the House; unless God sends another Pedlar to redeem us. But certainly, this Gentleman has such an Affection for you, that he would lend you a larger Sum than we owe here; which is not above four or five Shillings.' 'Very true, Child,' answered *Adams*; 'I will write a Letter to him, and will even venture to sollicit him for three Half-Crowns; there will be no harm in having two or three Shillings in our Pockets; as we have full forty Miles to travel, we may possibly have occasion for them.'

Fanny being now risen, *Joseph* paid her a Visit, and left *Adams* to write his Letter, which having finished, he dispatched a Boy with it to the Gentleman, and then seated himself by the Door, lighted his Pipe, and betook himself for Meditation.

The Boy staying longer than seemed to be necessary, *Joseph* who with *Fanny* was now returned to the Parson, expressed some Apprehensions, that the Gentleman's Steward had locked up his Purse too. To which *Adams* answered, 'It might very possibly be; and he should wonder at no Liberties which the Devil might put into the Head of a wicked Servant to take with so worthy a Master:' but added, 'that as the Sum was so small so noble a Gentleman would be easily able to procure it in the Parish; tho' he had it not in his own Pocket. Indeed,' says he, 'if it was four or five Guineas, or any such large Quantity of Money, it might be a different Matter.'

They were now sat down to Breakfast over some Toast and Ale, when the Boy returned; and informed them, that the Gentleman was not at home. 'Very well,' cries *Adams*; 'but why, Child, did you not stay 'till his return? Go back again, my good Boy, and wait for his coming home: he cannot be gone far, as his Horses are all sick; and besides, he had no Intention to go abroad; for he invited us to spend this Day and To-morrow at his House. Therefore, go back, Child, and tarry 'till his return home.' The Messenger departed, and was back again with great Expedition; bringing an Account, that the Gentleman was gone a long Journey, and would not be at home again this Month. At these Words, *Adams* seemed greatly confounded, saying, 'This must be a sudden Accident, as the Sickness or Death of a Relation, or some such unforeseen Misfortune;' and then turning to *Joseph* cried, 'I wish you had reminded me to have borrowed this Money last Night.' *Joseph* smiling, answered, 'he was very much deceived, if the Gentleman would not have found some Excuse to avoid lending it. I own,' says he, 'I was never much pleased with his professing so much Kindness for you at first sight: for I have heard the Gentlemen of our Cloth in *London* tell many such Stories of their Masters. But when the Boy brought the Message back of his not being at home, I presently knew what would follow; for whenever a Man of Fashion doth not care to fulfil his Promises, the Custom is, to order his Servants that he will never be at home to the Person so promised. In *London* they call it *denying him*. I have myself denied Sir *Thomas Booby* above a hundred times; and when the Man hath danced Attendance for about a Month, or sometimes longer, he is acquainted in the end, that the Gentleman is gone out of Town, and could do nothing in the Business.' 'Good Lord!' says *Adams*; 'what Wickedness is there in the Christian World? I profess, almost equal to what I have read of the *Heathens*. But surely, *Joseph*, your Suspicions of this Gentleman must be unjust; for, what a silly Fellow must he be, who would do the Devil's Work for nothing? and can'st thou tell me any Interest he could possibly propose to himself by deceiving us in his Professions?' 'It is not for me,' answered *Joseph*, 'to give Reasons for what Men do, to a Gentleman of your Learning.' 'You say right,' quoth *Adams*; 'Knowledge of Men is only to be learnt from Books, *Plato* and *Seneca*[2] for that; and those are Authors, I am afraid, Child, you never read.' 'Not I, Sir, truly,' answered *Joseph*; 'all I know is, it is a Maxim among the Gentlemen of our Cloth, that those Masters who promise the most perform the least; and I have often heard them say, they have found the largest Vails[3] in those Families where they were not promised any. But, Sir, instead of considering any farther these Matters, it would be our wisest way to contrive some Method of getting out of this House: for the generous Gentleman, instead of doing us any Service, hath left us the whole Reckoning to pay.' *Adams* was going to answer, when their Host came in; and with a kind of Jeering-Smile said, 'Well, Masters! the Squire hath not sent his Horses for you yet. Laud help me! how easily some Folks make Promises!' 'How!' says *Adams*, 'have you ever known him do any thing of this kind before?' 'Aye marry have I,' answered the Host; 'it is no business of mine, you know, Sir, to say any thing to a Gentleman to his face: but now he is not here, I will assure you, he hath not his Fellow within the three next Market-Towns. I own, I could not help laughing, when I heard him offer you the Living; for thereby hangs a good Jest. I thought he would have offered you my House next; for one is no more his to dispose of than the other.' At these Words, *Adams* blessing himself, declared, 'he had never read of such a Monster; but what vexes me most,' says he, 'is, that he hath decoyed us into running up a long Debt with you, which we are not able to pay; for we have no Money about us; and what is worse, live at such a distance, that if you should trust us, I am afraid you would lose your Money, for want of our finding any Conveniency of sending it.' 'Trust you, Master!' says the Host, 'that I will with all my heart; I honour the Clergy too much to deny trusting one of them for such a Trifle; besides, I like your fear of never paying me. I have lost many a Debt in my Life-time; but was promised to be paid them all in a very short time. I will score this Reckoning for the Novelty of it. It is the first I do assure you of its kind. But what say you, Master, shall we have t'other Pot before we part? It will waste but a little Chalk more; and if you never pay me a Shilling, the Loss will not ruin me.' *Adams* liked the Invitation very well; especially as it was delivered with so hearty an Accent.

—— He shook his Host by the Hand, and thanking him, said, 'he would tarry another Pot, rather for the Pleasure of such worthy Company than for the Liquor;' adding, 'he was glad to find some Christians left in the Kingdom; for that he almost began to suspect that he was sojourning in a Country inhabited only by *Jews* and *Turks*.'

The kind Host produced the Liquor, and *Joseph* with *Fanny* retired into the Garden; where while they solaced themselves with amorous Discourse, *Adams* sat down with his Host; and both filling their Glasses and lighting their Pipes, they began that Dialogue which the Reader will find in the next Chapter.

CHAPTER XVII

A Dialogue between Mr Abraham Adams *and his Host, which
by the Disagreement in their Opinions seemed to threaten an unlucky
Catastrophe, had it not been timely prevented by the Return of
the Lovers.*

'Sir,' said the Host, 'I assure you, you are not the first to whom our Squire hath promised more than he hath performed. He is so famous for this Practice, that his Word will not be taken for much by those who know him. I remember a young Fellow whom he promised his Parents to make an Exciseman. The poor People, who could ill afford it, bred their Son to Writing and Accounts, and other Learning, to qualify him for the Place; and the Boy held up his Head above his Condition with these Hopes; nor would he go to plough, nor do any other kind of Work; and went constantly drest as fine as could be, with two clean *Holland*[1] Shirts a Week, and this for several Years; 'till at last he followed the Squire up to *London*, thinking there to mind him of his Promises: but he could never get sight of him. So that being out of Money and Business, he fell into evil Company, and wicked Courses; and in the end came to a Sentence of Transportation, the News of which broke the Mother's Heart. I will tell you another true Story of him: There was a Neighbour of mine, a Farmer, who had two Sons whom he bred up to the Business. Pretty Lads they were; nothing would serve the Squire, but that the youngest must be made a Parson. Upon which he persuaded the Father to send him to School, promising, that he would afterwards maintain him at the University; and when he was of a proper Age, give him a Living. But after the Lad had been seven Years at School, and his Father brought him to the Squire with a Letter from his Master, that he was fit for the University; the Squire, instead of minding his Promise, or sending him thither at his Expence, only told his Father, that the young Man was a fine Scholar; and it was pity he could not afford to keep him at *Oxford* for four or five Years more, by which Time, if he could get him a Curacy, he might have him ordained. The Farmer said, "he was not a Man sufficient to do any such thing." "Why then," answered the Squire; "I am very sorry you have given him so much Learning; for if he cannot get his living by that, it will rather spoil him for any thing else; and your other Son who can hardly write his Name, will do more at plowing and sowing, and is in a better Condition than he:" and indeed so it proved; for the poor Lad not finding Friends to maintain him in his Learning, as he had expected; and being unwilling to work, fell to drinking, though he was a very sober Lad before; and in a short time, partly with Grief, and partly with good Liquor, fell into a Consumption and died. Nay, I can tell you more still: There was another, a young Woman, and the handsomest in all this Neighbourhood, whom he enticed up to *London*, promising to make her a Gentlewoman to one of your Women of Quality: but instead of keeping his Word, we have since heard, after having a Child by her himself, she became a common Whore; then kept a Coffee-House in *Covent-Garden*, and a little after died of the *French* Distemper[2] in a Goal. I could tell you many more Stories: but how do you imagine he served me myself? You must know, Sir, I was bred a Sea-faring Man, and have been many Voyages; 'till at last I came to be Master of a Ship myself, and was in a fair Way of making a Fortune, when I was attacked by one of those cursed *Guarda-Costas*, who took our Ships before the Beginning of the War;[3] and after a Fight wherein I lost the greater part of my Crew, my Rigging being all demolished, and two Shots received between Wind and Water, I was forced to strike.[4] The Villains carried off my Ship, a Brigantine of 150 Tons, a pretty Creature she was, and put me, a Man, and a Boy, into a little bad Pink,[5] in which with much ado, we at last made *Falmouth*; tho' I believe the *Spaniards* did not imagine she could possibly live a Day at Sea. Upon my return hither, where my Wife who was of this Country then lived, the Squire told me, he was so pleased with the Defence I had made against the Enemy, that he did not fear getting me promoted to a Lieutenancy of a Man of War, if I would accept of it, which I thankfully assured him I would. Well, Sir, two or three Years past, during which, I had many repeated Promises, not only from the Squire, but (as he told me) from the Lords of the Admiralty. He never returned from *London*, but I was assured I might be satisfied now, for I was certain of the first Vacancy; and what surprizes me still, when I reflect on it, these Assurances were given me with no less Confidence, after so many Disappointments, than at first. At last, Sir, growing weary and somewhat suspicious after so much delay, I wrote to a Friend in *London*, who I knew had some Acquaintance at the best House in the Admiralty; and desired him to back the Squire's Interest: for indeed, I feared he had sollicited the Affair with more Coldness than he pretended. — And what Answer do you think my Friend sent me? —— Truly, Sir, he acquainted me, that the Squire had never mentioned my Name at the Admiralty in his Life; and unless I had much faithfuller Interest, advised me to give over my Pretensions, which I immediately did; and with the Concurrence of my Wife, resolved to set up an Alehouse, where you are heartily welcome: and so my Service to you; and may the Squire, and all such sneaking Rascals go to the Devil together.' 'Oh fie!' says *Adams*; 'Oh fie! He is indeed a wicked Man; but G— will, I hope, turn his Heart to Repentance. Nay, if he could but once see the Meanness of this detestable Vice; would he but once reflect that he is one of the most scandalous as well as pernicious Lyars; sure he must despise himself to so intolerable a degree, that it would be impossible for him to continue a Moment in such a Course. And to confess the Truth, notwithstanding the Baseness of this Character, which he hath too well deserved, he hath in his Countenance sufficient Symptoms of that *bona Iudoles*, that Sweetness of Disposition which furnishes out a good Christian.' 'Ah! Master, Master,' (says the Host,) 'if you had travelled as far as I have, and conversed with the many Nations where I have traded, you would not give any Credit to a Man's Countenance. Symptoms in his Countenance, quotha! I would look there perhaps to see whether a Man had had the Small-Pox, but for nothing else!' He spoke this with so little regard to the Parson's Observation, that it a good deal nettled him; and taking the Pipe hastily from his Mouth, he thus answered: — 'Master of mine, perhaps I have travelled a great deal farther than you without the Assistance of a Ship. Do you imagine sailing by different Cities or Countries is travelling? No.

Cælum non Animum mutant qui trans mare currunt.[6]

'I can go farther in an Afternoon, than you in a Twelve-Month. What, I suppose you have seen the Pillars of *Hercules*, and perhaps the Walls of *Carthage*. Nay, you may have heard *Scylla*, and seen *Charybdis*; you may have entered the Closet where *Archimedes* was found at the taking *Syracuse*. I suppose you have sailed among the *Cyclades*, and passed the famous Streights which take their name from the unfortunate *Helle*, whose Fate is sweetly described by *Apollonius Rhodius*; you have past the very Spot, I conceive, where *Dædalus* fell into that Sea, his waxen Wings being melted by the Sun; you have traversed the *Euxine* Sea, I make no doubt; nay, you may have been on the Banks of the *Caspian*, and called at *Colchis*, to see if there is ever another Golden Fleece.'[7] — 'Not I truly, Master,' answered the Host, 'I never touched at any of these Places.' 'But I have been at all these,' replied *Adams*. 'Then I suppose,' cries the Host, 'you have been at the *East Indies*, for there are no such, I will be sworn, either in the *West* or the *Levant*.'[8] 'Pray where's the *Levant*,' quoth *Adams*, 'that should be in the *East Indies* by right.' — 'Oh ho! you are a pretty Traveller,' cries the Host, 'and not know the *Levant*. My service to you, Master; you must not talk of these things with me! you must not tip us the Traveller;[9] it won't go here.' 'Since thou art so dull to misunderstand me still,' quoth *Adams*, 'I will inform thee; the travelling I mean is in Books, the only way of travelling by which any Knowledge is to be acquired. From them I learn what I asserted just now, that Nature generally imprints such a Portraiture of the Mind in the Countenance, that a skilful Physiognomist will rarely be deceived. I presume you have never read the Story of *Socrates*[10] to this purpose, and therefore I will tell it you. A certain Physiognomist asserted of *Socrates*, that he plainly discovered by his Features that he was a Rogue in his Nature. A Character so contrary to the Tenour of all this great Man's Actions, and the generally received Opinion concerning him, incensed the Boys of *Athens* so that they threw Stones at the Physiognomist, and would have demolished him for his Ignorance, had not *Socrates* himself prevented them by confessing the Truth of his Observations, and acknowledging that tho' he corrected his Disposition by Philosophy, he was indeed naturally as inclined to Vice as had been predicated of him. Now, pray resolve me, — How should a Man know this Story, if he had not read it?' 'Well Master,' said the Host, 'and what signifies it whether a Man knows it or no? He who goes abroad, as I have done, will always have opportunities enough of knowing the World, without troubling his head with *Socrates*, or any such Fellows.' —— 'Friend,' cries *Adams*, 'if a Man would sail round the World, and anchor in every Harbour of it, without Learning, he would return home as ignorant as he went out.' 'Lord help you,' answered the Host, 'there was my Boatswain, poor Fellow! he could scarce either write or read, and yet he would navigate a Ship with any Master of a Man of War; and a very pretty knowledge of Trade he had too.' 'Trade,' answered *Adams*, 'as *Aristotle* proves in his first Chapter of Politics, is below a Philosopher, and unnatural as it is managed now.'[11] The Host look'd stedfastly at *Adams*, and after a Minute's silence asked him 'if he was one of the Writers of the *Gazetteers*?[12] for I have heard,' says he, 'they are writ by Parsons.' '*Gazetteers*!' answered *Adams*, 'What is that?' 'It is a dirty News-Paper,' replied the Host, 'which hath been given away all over the Nation for these many Years to abuse Trade and honest Men, which I would not suffer to lie on my Table, tho' it hath been offered me for nothing.' 'Not I truly,' said *Adams*, 'I never write any thing but Sermons, and I assure you I am no Enemy to Trade, whilst it is consistent with Honesty; nay, I have always looked on the

Tradesman, as a very valuable Member of Society, and perhaps inferior to none but the Man of Learning.' 'No, I believe he is not, nor to him neither,' answered the Host. 'Of what use would Learning be in a Country without Trade? What would all your Parsons do to clothe your Backs and feed your Bellies? Who fetches you your Silks and your Linens, and your Wines, and all the other Necessaries of Life? I speak chiefly with regard to the Sailors.' 'You should say the Extravagancies of Life,' replied the Parson, 'but admit they were the Necessaries, there is something more necessary than Life it self, which is provided by Learning; I mean the Learning of the Clergy. Who clothes you with Piety, Meekness, Humility, Charity, Patience, and all the other Christian Virtues? Who feeds your Souls with the Milk of brotherly Love, and diets them with all the dainty Food of Holiness, which at once cleanses them of all impure carnal Affections, and fattens them with the truly rich Spirit of Grace? — Who doth this?' 'Ay, who indeed!' cries the Host; 'for I do not remember ever to have seen any such Clothing or such Feeding. And so in the mean time, Master, my service to you.' *Adams* was going to answer with some severity, when *Joseph* and *Fanny* returned, and pressed his Departure so eagerly, that he would not refuse them; and so grasping his Crabstick, he took leave of his Host, (neither of them being so well pleased with each other as they had been at their first sitting down together) and with *Joseph* and *Fanny*, who both exprest much Impatience, departed; and now all together renewed their Journey.

The End of the First Volume

BOOK III

CHAPTER I

Matter prefatory in Praise of Biography.

Notwithstanding the Preference which may be vulgarly given to the Authority of those Romance-Writers, who intitle their Books, the History of *England*, the History of *France*, of *Spain*, &c. it is most certain, that Truth is only to be found in the Works of those who celebrate the Lives of Great Men, and are commonly called Biographers, as the others should indeed be termed Topographers or Chorographers: Words which might well mark the Distinction between them; it being the Business of the latter chiefly to describe Countries and Cities, which, with the Assistance of Maps, they do pretty justly, and may be depended upon: But as to the Actions and Characters of Men, their Writings are not quite so authentic, of which there needs no other Proof than those eternal Contradictions, occurring between two Topographers who undertake the History of the same Country: For instance, between my Lord *Clarendon* and Mr *Whitlock*, between Mr *Echard* and *Rapin*,[1] and many others; where Facts being set forth in a different Light, every Reader believes as he pleases, and indeed the more judicious and suspicious very justly esteem the whole as no other than a Romance, in which the Writer hath indulged a happy and fertile Invention. But tho' these widely differ in the Narrative of Facts; some ascribing Victory to the one, and others to the other Party: Some representing the same Man as a Rogue, while others give him a great and honest Character, yet all agree in the Scene where the Fact is supposed to have happened; and where the Person, who is both a Rogue, and an honest Man, lived. Now with us Biographers the Case is different, the Facts we deliver may be relied on, tho' we often mistake the Age and Country wherein they happened: For tho' it may be worth the Examination of Critics, whether the Shepherd *Chrysostom*, who, as *Cervantes* informs us, died for Love of the fair *Marcella*, who hated him, was ever in *Spain*, will any one doubt but that such a silly Fellow hath really existed? Is there in the World such a Sceptic as to disbelieve the Madness of *Cardenio*, the Perfidy of *Ferdinand*, the impertinent Curiosity of *Anselmo*, the Weakness of *Camilla* the irresolute Friendship of *Lothario*;[2] tho' perhaps as to the Time and Place where those several Persons lived, that good Historian may be deplorably deficient: But the most known Instance of this kind is in the true History of *Gil-Blas*, where the inimitable Biographer hath made a notorious Blunder in the Country of Dr *Sanglardo*, who used his Patients as a Vintner doth his Wine-Vessels, by letting out their Blood, and filling them up with Water. Doth not every one, who is the least versed in Physical History, know that *Spain* was not the Country in which this Doctor lived? The same Writer hath likewise erred in the Country of his Archbishop, as well as that of those great Personages whose Understandings were too sublime to taste any thing but Tragedy, and in many others.[3] The same Mistakes may likewise be observed in *Scarron*, the *Arabian Knights*, the History of *Marianne* and *Le Paisan Parvenu*,[4] and perhaps some few other Writers of this Class, whom I have not read, or do not at present recollect; for I would by no means be thought to comprehend those Persons of surprizing Genius, the Authors of immense Romances, or the modern Novel and *Atalantis* Writers;[5] who without any Assistance from Nature or History, record Persons who never were, or will be, and Facts which never did nor possibly can happen: Whose Heroes are of their own Creation, and their Brains the Chaos whence all their Materials are collected. Not that such Writers deserve no Honour; so far otherwise, that perhaps they merit the highest: for what can be nobler than to be as an Example of the wonderful Extent of human Genius. One may apply to them what *Balzac* says of *Aristotle*, that they are *a second Nature*;[6] for they have no Communication with the first; by which Authors of an inferiour Class, who cannot stand alone, are obliged to support themselves as with Crutches; but these of whom I am now speaking, seem to be possessed of *those Stilts*, which the excellent *Voltaire* tells us in his Letters *carry the Genius far off, but with an irregular Pace*.[7] Indeed, far out of the sight of the Reader,

Beyond the Realm of Chaos and old Night.[8]

But, to return to the former Class, who are contented to copy Nature, instead of forming Originals from the confused heap of Matter in their own Brains; Is not such a Book as that which records the Achievements of the renowned Don *Quixote*, more worthy the Name of a History than even *Mariana*'s:[9] for whereas the latter is confined to a particular Period of Time, and to a particular Nation; the former is the History of the World in general, at least that Part which is polished by Laws, Arts and Sciences; and of that from the time it was first polished to this day; nay and forwards, as long as it shall so remain.

I shall now proceed to apply these Observations to the Work before us; for indeed I have set them down principally to obviate some Constructions, which the Good-nature of Mankind, who are always forward to see their Friend's Virtues recorded, may put to particular parts. I question not but several of my Readers will know the Lawyer in the Stage-Coach, the Moment they hear his Voice. It is likewise odds, but the Wit and the Prude meet with some of their Acquaintance, as well as all the rest of my Characters. To prevent therefore any such malicious Applications, I declare here once for all, I describe not Men, but Manners; not an Individual, but a Species. Perhaps it will be answered, Are not the Characters then taken from Life? To which I answer in the Affirmative; nay, I believe I might aver, that I have writ little more than I have seen. The Lawyer is not only alive, but hath been so these 4000 Years, and I hope G— will indulge his Life as many yet to come. He hath not indeed confined himself to one Profession, one Religion, or one Country; but when the first mean selfish Creature appeared on the human Stage, who made Self the Centre of the whole Creation; would give himself no Pain, incur no Danger, advance no Money to assist, or preserve his Fellow-Creatures; then was our Lawyer born; and whilst such a Person as I have described, exists on Earth, so long shall he remain upon it. It is therefore doing him little Honour, to imagine he endeavours to mimick some little obscure Fellow, because he happens to resemble him in one particular Feature, or perhaps in his Profession; whereas his Appearance in the World is calculated for much more general and noble Purposes; not to expose one pitiful Wretch, to the small and contemptible Circle of his Acquaintance; but to hold the Glass to thousands in their Closets, that they may contemplate their Deformity, and endeavour to reduce it, and thus by suffering private Mortification may avoid public Shame. This places the Boundary between, and distinguishes the Satirist from the Libeller; for the former privately corrects the Fault for the Benefit of the Person, like a Parent; the latter publickly exposes the Person himself, as an Example to others, like an Executioner.

There are besides little Circumstances to be considered, as the Drapery of a Picture which tho' Fashion varies at different Times, the Resemblance of the Countenance is not by those means diminished. Thus, I believe, we may venture to say, Mrs *Tow-wouse* is coeval with our Lawyer, and tho' perhaps during the Changes, which so long an Existence must have passed through, she may in her Turn have stood behind the Bar at an Inn, I will not scruple to affirm, she hath likewise in the Revolution of Ages sat on a Throne. In short where extreme Turbulency of Temper, Avarice, and an Insensibility of human Misery, with a Degree of Hypocrisy, have united in a female Composition, Mrs *Tow-wouse* was that Woman; and where a good Inclination eclipsed by a Poverty of Spirit and Under-standing, hath glimmer'd forth in a Man, that Man hath been no other than her sneaking Husband.

I shall detain my Reader no longer than to give him one Caution more of an opposite kind: For as in most of our particular Characters we mean not to lash Individuals, but all of the like sort; so in our general Descriptions, we mean not Universals, but would be understood with many Exceptions: For instance, in our Description of high People, we cannot be intended to include such, as whilst they are an Honour to their high Rank, by a well-guided Condescension, make their Superiority as easy as possible, to those whom Fortune hath chiefly placed below them. Of this number I could name a Peer[10] no less elevated by Nature than by Fortune, who whilst he wears the noblest Ensigns of Honour on his Person, bears the truest Stamp of Dignity on his Mind, adorned with Greatness, enriched with Knowledge, and embelished with Genius. I have seen this Man relieve with Generosity, while he hath conversed with Freedom, and be to the same Person a Patron and a Companion. I could name a Commoner[11] raised higher above the Multitude by superiour Talents, than is in the power of his Prince to exalt him; whose Behaviour to those he hath obliged is more amiable than the Obligation itself, and who is so great a Master of Affability, that if he could divest himself of an inherent Greatness in his Manner, would often make the lowest of his Acquaintance forget who was the Master of that Palace, in which they are so courteously entertained. These are Pictures which must be, I believe, known: I declare they are taken from the Life, nor are intended to exceed it. By those high People therefore whom I have described, I mean a Sett of Wretches, who while they are a Disgrace to their Ancestors, whose Honours and Fortunes they inherit, (or perhaps a greater to their Mother, for such Degeneracy is scarce credible) have the Insolence to treat those with disregard, who have been equal to the Founders of their own Splendor. It is, I fancy, impossible to conceive a Spectacle more worthy of our Indignation, than that of a Fellow who is not only a Blot in the Escutcheon of a great Family, but a Scandal to the human Species, maintaining a supercilious Behaviour to Men who are an Honour to their Nature, and a Disgrace to their Fortune.

And now, Reader, taking these Hints along with you, you may, if you please, proceed to the Sequel of this our true History.

CHAPTER II

A Night-Scene, wherein several wonderful Adventures befel Adams *and his Fellow-Travellers.*[1]

It was so late when our Travellers left the Inn or Ale-house, (for it might be called either) that they had not travelled many Miles before Night overtook them, or met them, which you please. The Reader must excuse me if I am not particular as to the Way they took; for as we are now drawing near the Seat of the *Boobies*; and as that is a ticklish Name, which malicious Persons may apply according to their evil Inclinations to several worthy Country 'Squires, a Race of Men whom we look upon as entirely inoffensive, and for whom we have an adequate Regard, we shall lend no assistance to any such malicious Purposes.

Darkness had now overspread the Hemisphere, when *Fanny* whispered *Joseph*, 'that she begged to rest herself a little, for that she was so tired, she could walk no farther.' *Joseph* immediately prevailed with Parson *Adams*, who was as brisk as a Bee, to stop. He had no sooner seated himself, than he lamented the loss of his dear *Æschylus*; but was a little comforted, when reminded, that if he had it in his possession, he could not see to read.

The Sky was so clouded, that not a Star appeared. It was indeed, according to *Milton*, Darkness visible.[2] This was a Circumstance however very favourable to *Joseph*; for *Fanny*, not suspicious of being overseen by *Adams*, gave a loose to her Passion, which she had never done before; and reclining her Head on his Bosom, threw her Arm carelessly round him, and suffered him to lay his Cheek close to hers. All this infused such Happiness into *Joseph*, that he would not have changed his Turf for the finest Down in the finest Palace in the Universe.

Adams sat at some distance from the Lovers, and being unwilling to disturb them, applied himself to Meditation; in which he had not spent much time, before he discovered a Light at some distance, that seemed approaching towards him. He immediately hailed it, but to his Sorrow and Surprize it stopped for a moment and then disappeared. He then called to *Joseph*, asking him, 'if he had not seen the Light.' *Joseph* answered, 'he had.' 'And did you not mark how it vanished?' (returned he) 'tho' I am not afraid of Ghosts, I do not absolutely disbelieve them.'

He then entered into a Meditation on those unsubstantial Beings, which was soon interrupted, by several Voices which he thought almost at his Elbow, tho' in fact they were not so extremely near. However, he could distinctly hear them agree on the Murder of any one they met. And a little after heard one of them say, 'he had killed a dozen since that day Fortnight.'

Adams now fell on his Knees, and committed himself to the Care of Providence; and poor *Fanny*, who likewise heard those terrible Words, embraced *Joseph* so closely, that had not he, whose Ears were also open, been apprehensive on her account, he would have thought no danger which threatned only himself too dear a Price for such Embraces.

Joseph now drew forth his Penknife, and *Adams* having finished his Ejaculations, grasped his Crabstick, his only Weapon, and coming up to *Joseph* would have had him quit *Fanny*, and place her in their Rear: But his Advice was fruitless, she clung closer to him, not at all regarding the Presence of *Adams*, and in a soothing Voice declared, 'she would die in his Arms.' *Joseph* clasping her with inexpressible Eagerness, whispered her, 'that he preferred Death in hers, to Life out of them.' *Adams* brandishing his Crabstick, said, 'he despised Death as much as any Man,' and then repeated aloud,

> '*Est hic, est animus lucis contemptor, & illum,*
> '*Qui vita bene credat emi quo tendis, Honorem.*'[3]

Upon this the Voices ceased for a moment, and then one of them called out, 'D—n you, who is there?' To which *Adams* was prudent enough to make no Reply; and of a sudden he observed half a dozen Lights, which seemed to rise all at once from the Ground, and advance briskly towards him. This he immediately concluded to be an Apparition, and now beginning to conceive that the Voices were of the same kind, he called out, 'In the Name of the L—d what would'st thou have?' He had no sooner spoke, than he heard one of the Voices cry out, 'D—n them, here they come;' and soon after heard several hearty Blows, as if a number of Men had been engaged at Quarterstaff. He was just advancing towards the Place of Combat, when *Joseph* catching him by the Skirts, begged him that they might take the Opportunity of the dark, to convey away *Fanny* from the Danger which threatned her. He presently complied, and *Joseph* lifting up *Fanny*, they all three made the best of their way; and without looking behind them or being overtaken, they had travelled full two Miles, poor *Fanny* not once complaining of being tired, when they saw far off several Lights scattered at a small distance from each other, and at the same time found themselves on the Descent of a very steep Hill. *Adams*'s Foot slipping, he instantly disappeared which greatly frightned both *Joseph* and *Fanny*; indeed, if the Light had permitted them to see it, they would scarce have refrained laughing to see the Parson rolling down the Hill, which he did from top to bottom, without receiving any harm. He then hollowed as loud as he could, to inform them of his safety, and relieve them from the Fears which they had conceived for him. *Joseph* and *Fanny* halted some time, considering what to do; at last they advanced a few Paces, where the Declivity seemed least steep; and then *Joseph* taking his *Fanny* in his Arms, walked firmly down the Hill, without making a false step, and at length landed her at the bottom, where *Adams* soon came to them.

Learn hence, my fair Countrywomen, to consider your own Weakness, and the many Occasions on which the Strength of a Man may be useful to you; and duly weighing this, take care, that you match not yourselves with the spindle-shanked Beaus and Petit Maîtres[4] of the Age, who instead of being able, like *Joseph Andrews*, to carry you in lusty Arms through the rugged ways and downhill Steeps of Life, will rather want to support their feeble Limbs with your Strength and Assistance.

Our Travellers now moved forwards, whither the nearest Light presented itself, and having crossed a common Field, they came to a Meadow, whence they seemed to be at a very little distance from the Light, when, to their grief, they arrived at the Banks of a River. *Adams* here made a full stop, and declared he could swim, but doubted how it was possible to get *Fanny* over; to which *Joseph* answered, 'if they walked along its Banks they might be certain of soon finding a Bridge, especially as by the number of Lights they might be assured a Parish was near.' 'Odso, that's true indeed,' said *Adams*, 'I did not think of that.' Accordingly, *Joseph*'s Advice being taken, they passed over two Meadows, and came to a little Orchard, which led them to a House. *Fanny* begged of *Joseph* to knock at the Door, assuring him, 'she was so weary that she could hardly stand on her Feet.' *Adams* who was foremost performed this Ceremony, and the Door being immediately opened, a plain kind of Man appeared at it; *Adams* acquainted him, 'that they had a young Woman with them, who was so tired with her Journey, that he should be much obliged to him, if he would suffer her to come in and rest herself.' The Man, who saw *Fanny* by the Light of the Candle which he held in his Hand, perceiving her innocent and modest Look, and having no Apprehensions from the civil Behaviour of *Adams*, presently answer'd, that the young Woman was very welcome to rest herself in his House, and so were her Company. He then ushered them into a very decent Room, where his Wife was sitting at a Table; she immediately rose up, and assisted them in setting forth Chairs, and desired them to sit down, which they had no sooner done, than the Man of the House asked them if they would have any thing to refresh themselves with? *Adams* thanked him, and answered, he should be obliged to him for a Cup of his Ale, which was likewise chosen by *Joseph* and *Fanny*. Whilst he was gone to fill a very large Jugg with this Liquor, his Wife told *Fanny* she seemed greatly fatigued, and desired her to take something stronger than Ale; but she refused, with many thanks, saying it was true, she was very much tired, but a little Rest she hoped would restore her. As soon as the Company were all seated, Mr *Adams*, who had filled himself with Ale, and by publick Permission had lighted his Pipe; turned to the Master of the House, asking him, 'if evil Spirits did not use to walk in that Neighbourhood?' To which receiving no answer, he began to inform him of the Adventure which they had met with on the Downs; nor had he proceeded far in his Story, when somebody knocked very hard at the Door. The Company expressed some Amazement, and *Fanny* and the good Woman turned pale; her Husband went forth, and whilst he was absent, which was some time, they all remained silent looking at one another, and heard several Voices discoursing pretty loudly. *Adams* was fully persuaded that Spirits were abroad, and began to meditate some Exorcisms; *Joseph* a little inclined to the same Opinion: *Fanny* was more afraid of Men, and the good Woman herself began to suspect her Guests, and imagined those without were Rogues belonging to their Gang. At length the Master of the House returned, and laughing, told *Adams* he had discovered his Apparition; that the Murderers were Sheep-stealers, and the twelve Persons murdered were no other than twelve Sheep. Adding that the Shepherds had got the better of them, had secured two, and were proceeding with them to a Justice of Peace. This Account greatly relieved the Fears of the whole Company; but *Adams* muttered to himself, 'He was convinced of the truth of Apparitions for all that.'

They now sat chearfully round the Fire, 'till the Master of the House having survey'd his Guests, and conceiving that the Cassock, which having fallen down, appeared under *Adams*'s Great-Coat, and the shabby Livery on *Joseph Andrews*, did not well suit with the Familiarity between them, began to entertain some suspicions, not much to their Advantage: addressing himself therefore to *Adams*, he said, 'he perceived he was a Clergyman by his Dress, and supposed that honest Man was his Footman.' 'Sir,' answer'd *Adams*, 'I am a Clergyman at your Service; but as to that young Man, whom you have rightly termed honest, he is at present in no body's Service, he never lived in any other Family than that of Lady *Booby*, from whence he was discharged, I assure you, for no Crime.' *Joseph* said, 'he did not wonder the Gentleman was surprized to see one of Mr *Adams*'s Character condescend to so much goodness with a poor Man.' 'Child,' said *Adams*, 'I should be ashamed of my Cloth, if I thought a poor Man, who is honest, below my notice or my familiarity. I know not how those who think otherwise, can profess themselves followers and servants of him who made no distinction, unless, peradventure, by preferring the Poor to the Rich. Sir,' said he, addressing himself to the Gentleman, 'these two poor young People are my Parishioners, and I look on them and love them as my Children. There is something singular enough in their History, but I have not now time to recount it.' The Master of the House, notwithstanding the Simplicity which discover'd itself in *Adams*, knew too much of the World to give a hasty Belief to Professions. He was not yet quite certain that *Adams* had any more of the Clergyman in him than his Cassock. To try him therefore further, he asked him, 'if Mr *Pope* had lately published any thing new?' *Adams* answer'd, 'he had heard great Commendations of that Poet, but that he had never read, nor knew any of his Works.' 'Ho! ho!' says the Gentleman to himself, 'have I caught you?' 'What,' said he, 'have you never seen his *Homer*?'[5] *Adams* answer'd, 'he had never read any Translation of the Classicks.' 'Why truly,' reply'd the Gentleman, 'there is a Dignity in the *Greek* Language which I think no modern Tongue can reach.' 'Do you understand *Greek*, Sir?' said *Adams* hastily. 'A little, Sir,' answered the Gentleman. 'Do you know, Sir,' cry'd *Adams*, 'where I can buy an *Æschylus* an unlucky Misfortune lately happened to mine.' *Æschylus* was beyond the Gentleman, tho' he knew him very well by Name; he therefore returning back to *Homer*, asked *Adams* 'what Part of the *Iliad* he thought most excellent.' *Adams* return'd, 'His Question would be properer, what kind of Beauty was the chief in Poetry, for that *Homer* was equally excellent in them all.

'And indeed,' continued he, 'what *Cicero* says of a complete Orator, may well be applied to a great Poet. He *ought to comprehend all Perfections*,[6] *Homer* did this in the most excellent degree; it is not without Reason therefore that the Philosopher, in the 22d Chapter of his *Poeticks*, mentions him by no other Appellation than that of *The Poet*:[7] He was the Father of the Drama, as well as the Epic: Not of Tragedy only, but of Comedy also; for his *Margites*, which is deplorably lost, bore, says *Aristotle*, the same Analogy to Comedy, as his *Odyssey* and *Iliad* to Tragedy.[8] To him therefore we owe *Aristophanes*,[9] as well as *Euripides*, *Sophocles*, and my poor *Æschylus*. But if you please we will confine ourselves (at least for the present) to the *Iliad*, his noblest Work; tho' neither *Aristotle*, nor *Horace* give it the Preference, as I remember, to the *Odyssey*. First then as to his Subject, can any thing be more simple, and at the same time be more noble? He is rightly praised by the first of those judicious Critics, for not chusing the whole War,[10] which, tho' he says, it hath a compleat Beginning and End, would have been too great for the Understanding to comprehend at one View. I have therefore often wondered why so correct a Writer as *Horace* should in his Epistle to *Lollius* call him the *Trojani Belli Scriptorem*.[11] Secondly, his Action, termed by *Aristotle Pragmaton Systasis*;[12] is it possible for the Mind of Man to conceive an Idea of such perfect Unity, and at the same time so replete with Greatness? And here I must observe what I do not remember to have seen noted by any, the *Harmotton*,[13] that agreement of his Action to his Subject: For as the Subject is Anger, how agreeable is his Action, which is War? from which every Incident arises, and to which every Episode immediately relates. Thirdly, His Manners, which *Aristotle* places second in his Description of the several Parts of Tragedy, and which he says are included in the Action;[14] I am at a loss whether I should rather admire the Exactness of his Judgment in the nice Distinction, or the Immensity of his Imagination in their Variety. For, as to the former of these, how accurately is the sedate, injured Resentment of *Achilles* distinguished from the hot insulting Passion of *Agamemnon*? How widely doth the brutal Courage of *Ajax* differ from the amiable Bravery of *Diomedes*; and the Wisdom of *Nestor*, which is the Result of long Reflection and Experience, from the Cunning of *Ulysses*, the Effect of Art and Subtilty only. If we consider their Variety, we may cry out with *Aristotle* in his 24th Chapter, that no Part of this divine Poem is destitute of Manners.[15] Indeed I might affirm, that there is scarce a Character in human Nature untouched in some part or other. And as there is no Passion which he is not able to describe, so is there none in his Reader which he cannot raise. If he hath any superior Excellence to the rest, I have been inclined to fancy it is in the Pathetick. I am sure I never read with dry Eyes, the two Episodes, where *Andromache* is introduced, in the former lamenting the Danger, and in the latter the Death of *Hector*.[16] The Images are so extremely tender in these, that I am convinced, the Poet had the worthiest and best Heart imaginable. Nor can I help observing how short *Sophocles* falls of the Beauties of the Original, in that Imitation of the dissuasive Speech of *Andromache*, which he hath put into the Mouth of *Tecmessa*.[17] And yet *Sophocles* was the greatest Genius who ever wrote Tragedy, nor have any of his Successors in that Art, that is to say, neither *Euripides* nor *Seneca* the Tragedian[18] been able to come near him. As to his Sentiments and Diction, I need say nothing; the former are particularly remarkable for the utmost Perfection on that Head, namely Propriety; and as to the latter, *Aristotle*, whom doubtless you have read over and over, is very diffuse.[19] I shall mention but one thing more, which that great Critic in his Division of Tragedy calls *Opsis*, or the Scenery,[20] and which is as proper to the Epic as to the Drama, with this difference, that in the former it falls to the share of the Poet, and in the latter to that of the Painter. But did ever Painter imagine a Scene like that in the 13th and 14th *Iliads*? where the Reader sees at one View the Prospect of *Troy*, with the Army drawn up before it; the *Grecian* Army, Camp, and Fleet, *Jupiter* sitting on Mount *Ida*, with his Head wrapt in a Cloud, and a Thunderbolt in his Hand looking towards *Thrace*; *Neptune* driving through the Sea, which divides on each side to permit his Passage, and then seating himself on Mount *Samos*: The Heavens open'd, and the Deities all seated on their Thrones. This is Sublime! This is Poetry!' *Adams* then rapt out a hundred *Greek* Verses, and with such a Voice, Emphasis and Action, that he almost frighten'd the Women; and as for the Gentleman, he was so far from entertaining any further suspicion of *Adams*, that he now doubted whether he had not a Bishop in his House. He ran into the most extravagant Encomiums on his Learning, and the Goodness of his Heart began to dilate to all the Strangers. He said he had great Compassion for the poor young Woman, who looked pale and faint with her Journey; and in truth he conceived a much higher Opinion of her Quality than it deserved. He said, he was sorry he could not accommodate them all: But if they were contented with his Fire-side, he would sit up with the Men, and the young Woman might, if she pleased, partake his Wife's Bed, which he advis'd her to; for that they must walk upwards of a Mile to any House of Entertainment, and that not very good neither. *Adams*, who liked his Seat, his Ale, his Tobacco and his Company, persuaded *Fanny* to accept this kind Proposal, in which Sollicitation he was seconded by *Joseph*. Nor was she very difficultly prevailed on; for she had slept little the last Night, and nor at all the preceding, so that Love itself was scarce able to keep her Eyes open any longer. The Offer therefore being kindly accepted, the good Woman produced every thing eatable in her House on the Table, and the Guests being heartily invited, as heartily regaled themselves, especially Parson *Adams*. As to the other two, they were Examples of the Truth of that physical[21] Observation, that Love, like other sweet Things, is no Whetter of the Stomach.

Supper was no sooner ended, than *Fanny* at her own Request retired, and the good Woman bore her Company. The Man of the House, *Adams*, and *Joseph* who would modestly have withdrawn had not the Gentleman insisted on the contrary, drew round the Fire-side, where *Adams*, (to use his own Words) replenished his Pipe, and the Gentleman produced a Bottle of excellent Beer, being the best Liquor in his House.

The modest Behaviour of *Joseph*, with the Gracefulness of his Person, the Character which *Adams* gave of him, and the Friendship he seemed to entertain for him, began to work on the Gentleman's Affections, and raised in him a Curiosity to know the Singularity which *Adams* had mentioned in his History. This Curiosity *Adams* was no sooner informed of, than with *Joseph*'s Consent, he agreed to gratify it, and accordingly related all he knew, with as much Tenderness as was possible for the Character of Lady *Booby*; and concluded with the long, faithful and mutual Passion between him and *Fanny*, not concealing the Meanness of her Birth and Education. These latter Circumstances entirely cured a Jealousy[22] which had lately risen in the Gentleman's Mind, that *Fanny* was the Daughter of some Person of Fashion, and that *Joseph* had run away with her, and *Adams* was concerned in the Plot. He was now enamour'd of his Guests, drank their Healths with great Cheerfulness, and return'd many Thanks to *Adams*, who had spent much Breath; for he was a circumstantial Teller of a Story.

Adams told him it was now in his power to return that Favour; for his extraordinary Goodness, as well as that Fund of Literature he was Master of,* which he did not expect to find under such a Roof, had raised in him

---

* The Author hath by some been represented to have made a Blunder here: For *Adams* had indeed shewn some Learning, (say they) perhaps all the Author had; but the Gentleman hath shewn none, unless his Approbation of Mr *Adams* be such: But surely it would be preposterous in him to call it so. I have however, notwithstanding this Criticism which I am told came from the Mouth of a great Orator,[23] in a public Coffee-House, left this Blunder as it stood in the first Edition. I will not have the Vanity to apply to any thing in this Work, the Observation which M. *Dacier* makes in her Preface to her *Aristophanes*: *Je tiens pour une Maxime constante qu'une Beauté médiocre plait plus généralement qu'une Beauté sans défaut.*[24] Mr *Congreve* hath made such another Blunder in his *Love for Love*, where *Tattle* tells Miss *Prue*, *She should admire him as much for the Beauty he commends in her, as if he himself was possess of it.*[25]

more Curiosity than he had ever known. Therefore, said he, if it be not too troublesome, Sir, your History, if you please.

The Gentleman answered, he could not refuse him what he had so much Right to insist on; and after some of the common Apologies, which are the usual Preface to a Story, he thus began.

CHAPTER III

In which the Gentleman relates the History of his Life.

Sir, I am descended of a good Family, and was born a Gentleman. My Education was liberal, and at a public School, in which I proceeded so far as to become Master of the *Latin*, and to be tolerably versed in the *Greek* Language. My Father died when I was sixteen, and left me Master of myself. He bequeathed me a moderate Fortune, which he intended I should not receive till I attained the Age of twenty-five: For he constantly asserted that was full early enough to give up any Man entirely to the Guidance of his own Discretion. However, as this Intention was so obscurely worded in his Will, that the Lawyers advised me to contest the Point with my Trustees, I own I paid so little Regard to the Inclinations of my dead Father, which were sufficiently certain to me, that I followed their Advice, and soon succeeded: For the Trustees did not contest the Matter very obstinately on their side. 'Sir,' said *Adams*, 'may I crave the Favour of your Name?' The Gentleman answer'd, 'his Name was *Wilson*,' and then proceeded.

I stay'd a very little while at School after his Death; for being a forward Youth, I was extremely impatient to be in the World: For which I thought my Parts, Knowledge, and Manhood thoroughly qualified me. And to this early Introduction into Life, without a Guide, I impute all my future Misfortunes; for besides the obvious Mischiefs which attend this, there is one which hath not been so generally observed. The first Impression which Mankind receives of you, will be very difficult to eradicate. How unhappy, therefore, must it be to fix your Character in Life, before you can possibly know its Value, or weigh the Consequences of those Actions which are to establish your future Reputation?

A little under seventeen I left my School and went to *London*, with no more than six Pounds in my Pocket. A great Sum as I then conceived; and which I was afterwards surprized to find so soon consumed.

The Character I was ambitious of attaining, was that of a fine Gentleman; the first Requisites to which, I apprehended were to be supplied by a Taylor, a Periwig-maker, and some few more Tradesmen, who deal in furnishing out the human Body. Notwithstanding the Lowness of my Purse, I found Credit with them more easily than I expected, and was soon equipped to my Wish. This I own then agreeably surprized me; but I have since learn'd, that it is a Maxim among many Tradesmen at the polite End of the Town to deal as largely as they can, reckon as high as they can, and arrest as soon as they can.

The next Qualifications, namely Dancing, Fencing, Riding the great Horse,[1] and Musick, came into my Head: But as they required Expence and Time; I comforted myself with regard to Dancing, that I had learned a little in my Youth, and could walk a Minuet genteelly enough; as to Fencing, I thought my Good-humour would preserve me from the Danger of a Quarrel; as to the Horse, I hoped it would not be thought of; and for Musick, I imagined I could easily acquire the Reputation of it; for I had heard some of my School-fellows pretend to Knowledge in Operas, without being able to sing or play on the Fiddle.

Knowledge of the Town seemed another Ingredient; this I thought I should arrive at by frequenting public Places. Accordingly I paid constant Attendance to them all; by which means I was soon Master of the fashionable Phrases, learn'd to cry up the fashionable Diversions, and knew the Names and Faces of the most fashionable Men and Women.

Nothing now seemed to remain but an Intrigue, which I was resolved to have immediately; I mean the Reputation of it; and indeed I was so successful, that in a very short time I had half a dozen with the finest Women in Town.

At these Words *Adams* fetched a deep Groan, and then blessing himself, cry'd out, *Good Lord! What wicked Times these are?*

Not so wicked as you imagine, continued the Gentleman; for I assure you, they were all Vestal Virgins for any thing which I knew to the contrary. The Reputation of Intriguing with them was all I sought, and was what I arrived at: and perhaps I only flattered myself even in that; for very probably the Persons to whom I shewed their Billets, knew as well as I, that they were Counterfeits, and that I had written them to myself.

'*WRITE Letters to yourself!*' said *Adams* staring!

O Sir, answer'd the Gentleman, *It is the very Error of the Times.* Half our modern Plays have one of these Characters in them.[2] It is incredible the

Pains I have taken, and the absurd Methods I employed to traduce the Character of Women of Distinction. When another had spoken in Raptures of any one, I have answered, 'D—n her, she! We shall have her at *H——d*'s³ very soon.' When he hath reply'd, 'he thought her virtuous,' I have answered, 'Ay, thou wilt always think a Woman virtuous, till she is in the Streets; but you and I, *Jack* or *Tom*, (turning to another in Company) know better.' At which I have drawn a Paper out of my Pocket, perhaps a Taylor's Bill, and kissed it, crying at the same time, *By Gad I was once fond of her.*

'Proceed, if you please, but do not swear any more,' said *Adams*.

Sir, said the Gentleman, I ask your Pardon. Well, Sir, in this Course of Life I continued full three Years. —— 'What Course of Life,' answer'd *Adams*; 'I do not remember you have yet mentioned any.' —— Your Remark is just, said the Gentleman smiling, I should rather have said, in this Course of doing nothing. I remember some time afterwards I wrote the Journal of one Day, which would serve, I believe, as well for any other, during the whole Time; I will endeavour to repeat it to you.

In the Morning I arose, took my great Stick, and walked out in my green Frock with my Hair in Papers, (*a Groan from* Adams) and sauntered about till ten.

Went to the Auction; told Lady —— she had a dirty Face; laughed heartily at something Captain — said; I can't remember what, for I did not very well hear it; whispered Lord —; bowed to the Duke of ——; and was going to bid for a Snuff-box; but did not, for fear I should have had it.

From	2 to 4, drest myself.	A Groan.
	4 to 6, dined.	A Groan.
	6 to 8, Coffee-house.	
	8 to 9, *Drury-Lane* Play-house.	
	9 to 10, *Lincoln's-Inn-Fields*.⁴	
	10 to 12, Drawing-Room.	A great Groan.

At all which Places nothing happened worth Remark. At which *Adams* said with some Vehemence, 'Sir, this is below the Life of an Animal, hardly above Vegetation; and I am surprized what could lead a Man of your Sense into it.' What leads us into more Follies than you imagine, Doctor, answered the Gentleman; Vanity: For as contemptible a Creature as I was, and I assure you, yourself cannot have more Contempt for such a Wretch than I now have, I then admir'd myself, and should have despised a Person of your present Appearance (you will pardon me) with all your Learning, and those excellent Qualities which I have remarked in you. *Adams* bowed, and begged him to proceed. After I had continued two Years in this Course of Life, said the Gentleman, an Accident happened which obliged me to change the Scene. As I was one day at *St James*'s Coffee-House,[5] making very free with the Character of a young Lady of Quality, an Officer of the Guards who was present, thought proper to give me the lye. I answered, I might possibly be mistaken; but I intended to tell no more than the Truth. To which he made no Reply, but by a scornful Sneer. After this I observed a strange Coldness in all my Acquaintance; none of them spoke to me first, and very few returned me even the Civility of a Bow. The Company I used to dine with, left me out, and within a Week I found myself in as much Solitude at *St James*'s, as if I had been in a Desart. An honest elderly Man, with a great Hat and long Sword, at last told me, he had a Compassion for my Youth, and therefore advised me to shew the World I was not such a Rascal as they thought me to be. I did not at first understand him: But he explained himself, and ended with telling me, if I would write a Challenge to the Captain, he would out of pure Charity go to him with it. 'A very charitable Person truly!' cried *Adams*. I desired till the next Day, continued the Gentleman, to consider on it, and retiring to my Lodgings, I weighed the Consequences on both sides as fairly as I could. On the one, I saw the Risk of this Alternative, either losing my own Life, or having on my hands the Blood of a Man with whom I was not in the least angry. I soon determined that the Good which appeared on the other, was not worth this Hazard. I therefore resolved to quit the Scene, and presently retired to the *Temple*,[6] where I took Chambers. Here I soon got a fresh Sett of Acquaintance, who knew nothing of what had happened to me. Indeed they were not greatly to my Approbation; for the Beaus of the *Temple* are only the Shadows of the others. They are the Affectation of Affectation. The Vanity of these is still more ridiculous, if possible, than of the others. Here I met with smart Fellows who drank with Lords they did not know, and intrigued with Women they never saw. *Covent-Garden* was now the farthest Stretch of my Ambition, where I shone forth in the Balconies at the Play-houses, visited Whores, made Love to Orange-Wenches, and damned Plays. This Career was soon put a stop to by my Surgeon, who convinced me of the Necessity of confining myself to my Room for a Month. At the End of which, having had Leisure to reflect, I resolved to quit all further Conversation with Beaus and Smarts of every kind, and to avoid, if possible, any Occasion of returning to this Place of Confinement. 'I think,' said *Adams*, 'the Advice of a Month's Retirement and Reflection was very proper; but I should rather have expected it from a Divine than a Surgeon.' The Gentleman smiled at *Adams*'s Simplicity, and without explaining himself farther on such an odious Subject went on thus: I was no sooner perfectly restored to Health, than I found my Passion for Women, which I was afraid to satisfy as I had done, made me very uneasy; I determined therefore to keep a Mistress. Nor was I long before I fixed my Choice on a young Woman, who had before been kept by two Gentlemen, and to whom I was recommended by a celebrated Bawd. I took her home to my Chambers, and made her a Settlement, during Cohabitation. This would perhaps have been very ill paid: However, she did not suffer me to be perplexed on that account; for before Quarter-day,⁷ I found her at my Chambers in too familiar Conversation with a young Fellow who was drest like an Officer, but was indeed a City Apprentice. Instead of excusing her Inconstancy, she rapped out half a dozen Oaths, and snapping her Fingers at me, swore she scorned to confine herself to the best Man in *England*. Upon this we parted, and the same Bawd presently provided her another Keeper. I was not so much concerned at our Separation, as I found within a Day or two I had Reason to be for our Meeting: For I was obliged to pay a second Visit to my Surgeon. I was now obliged to do Penance for some Weeks, during which Time I contracted an Acquaintance with a beautiful young Girl, the Daughter of a Gentleman, who after having been 40 Years in the Army, and in all the Campaigns under the Duke of *Marlborough*,⁸ died a Lieutenant on Half-pay; and had left a Widow with this only Child, in very distrest Circumstances: They had only a small Pension from the Government, with what little the Daughter could add to it by her Work; for she had great Excellence at her Needle. This Girl was, at my first Acquaintance with her, sollicited in Marriage by a young Fellow in good Circumstances. He was Apprentice to a Linen-draper, and had a little Fortune sufficient to set up his Trade. The Mother was greatly pleased with this Match, as indeed she had sufficient Reason. However, I soon prevented it. I represented him in so low a Light to his Mistress, and made so good an Use of Flattery, Promises, and Presents, that, not to dwell longer on this Subject than is necessary, I prevailed with the poor Girl, and convey'd her away from her Mother! In a word, I debauched her. — (At which Words, *Adams* started up, fetched three Strides cross the Room, and then replaced himself in his Chair.) You are not more affected with this Part

of my Story than myself: I assure you it will never be sufficiently repented of in my own Opinion: But if you already detest it, how much more will your Indignation be raised when you hear the fatal Consequences of this barbarous, this villainous Action? If you please therefore, I will here desist.
—— 'By no means,' cries *Adams*, 'Go on, I beseech you, and Heaven grant you may sincerely repent of this and many other things you have related.' — I was now, continued the Gentleman, as happy as the Possession of a fine young Creature, who had a good Education, and was endued with many agreeable Qualities, could make me. We lived some Months with vast Fondness together, without any Company or Conversation more than we found in one another: But this could not continue always; and tho' I still preserved a great Affection for her, I began more and more to want the Relief of other Company, and consequently to leave her by degrees, at last, whole Days to herself. She failed not to testify some Uneasiness on these Occasions, and complained of the melancholy Life she led; to remedy which, I introduced her into the Acquaintance of some other kept Mistresses, with whom she used to play at Cards, and frequent Plays and other Diversions. She had not lived long in this Intimacy, before I perceived a visible Alteration in her Behaviour; all her Modesty and Innocence vanished by degrees, till her Mind became thoroughly tainted. She affected the Company of Rakes, gave herself all manner of Airs, was never easy but abroad, or when she had a Party at my Chambers. She was rapacious of Money, extravagant to Excess, loose in her Conversation; and if ever I demurred to any of her Demands, Oaths, Tears, and Fits, were the immediate Consequences. As the first Raptures of Fondness were long since over, this Behaviour soon estranged my Affections from her; I began to reflect with pleasure that she was not my Wife, and to conceive an Intention of parting with her, of which having given her a Hint, she took care to prevent me the Pains of turning her out of doors, and accordingly departed herself, having first broken open my Escrutore, and taken with her all she could find, to the Amount of about 200 *l.* In the first Heat of my Resentment, I resolved to pursue her with all the Vengeance of the Law: But as she had the good Luck to escape me during that Ferment, my Passion afterwards cooled, and having reflected that I had been the first Aggressor, and had done her an Injury for which I could make her no Reparation, by robbing her of the Innocence of her Mind; and hearing at the same time that the poor old Woman her Mother had broke her Heart, on her Daughter's Elopement from her, I, concluding myself her Murderer, ('As you very well might,' cries *Adams*,

with a Groan;) was pleased that God Almighty had taken this Method of punishing me, and resolved quietly to submit to the Loss. Indeed I could wish I had never heard more of the poor Creature, who became in the end an abandoned Profligate; and after being some Years a common Prostitute, at last ended her miserable Life in *Newgate*. — Here the Gentleman fetched a deep Sigh, which Mr *Adams* echo'd very loudly, and both continued silent looking on each other for some Minutes. At last the Gentleman proceeded thus: I had been perfectly constant to this Girl, during the whole Time I kept her: But she had scarce departed before I discovered more Marks of her Infidelity to me, than the Loss of my Money. In short, I was forced to make a third Visit to my Surgeon, out of whose hands I did not get a hasty Discharge.

I now forswore all future Dealings with the Sex, complained loudly that the Pleasure did not compensate the Pain, and railed at the beautiful Creatures, in as gross Language as *Juvenal* himself formerly reviled them in.[9] I looked on all the Town-harlots with a Detestation not easy to be conceived, their Persons appeared to me as painted Palaces inhabited by Disease and Death: Nor could their Beauty make them more desirable Objects in my Eyes, than Gilding could make me covet a Pill, or golden Plates a Coffin. But tho' I was no longer the absolute Slave, I found some Reasons to own myself still the Subject of Love. My Hatred for Women decreased daily; and I am not positive but Time might have betrayed me again to some common Harlot, had I not been secured by a Passion for the charming *Saphira*; which having once entered upon, made a violent Progress in my Heart. *Saphira* was Wife to a Man of Fashion and Gallantry, and one who seemed, I own, every way worthy of her Affections, which however he had not the Reputation of having. She was indeed a *Coquette achevée*.[10] 'Pray Sir,' says *Adams*, 'What is a Coquette? I have met with the Word in *French* Authors, but never could assign any Idea to it. I believe it is the same with *une Sotte*, Anglicé *a Fool*.' Sir, answer'd the Gentleman, perhaps you are not much mistaken: but as it is a particular kind of Folly, I will endeavour to describe it. Were all Creatures to be ranked in the Order of Creation, according to their Usefulness, I know few Animals that would not take place of a Coquette; nor indeed hath this Creature much Pretence to any thing beyond Instinct; for tho' sometimes we might imagine it was animated by the Passion of Vanity, yet far the greater part of its Actions fall beneath even that low Motive; For instance, several absurd Gestures and Tricks, infinitely more foolish than what can be observed in the most ridiculous Birds and Beasts, and which would persuade the Beholder that the silly Wretch was aiming at our Contempt. Indeed its Characteristick is Affectation, and this led and governed by Whim only: for as Beauty, Wisdom, Wit, Good-nature, Politeness and Health are sometimes affected by this Creature; so are Ugliness, Folly, Nonsense, Ill-nature, Ill-breeding and Sickness likewise put on by it in their Turn. Its Life is one constant Lye, and the only Rule by which you can form any Judgment of them is, that they are never what they seem. If it was possible for a Coquette to love (as it is not, for if ever it attains this Passion, the Coquette ceases instantly) it would wear the Face of Indifference if not of Hatred to the beloved Object; you may therefore be assured, when they endeavour to persuade you of their liking, that they are indifferent to you at least. And indeed this was the Case of my *Saphira*, who no sooner saw me in the number of her Admirers, than she gave me what is commonly called Encouragement; she would often look at me, and when she perceived me meet her Eyes, would instantly take them off, discovering at the same time as much Surprize and Emotion as possible. These Arts failed not of the Success she intended; and as I grew more particular to her than the rest of her Admirers, she advanced in proportion more directly to me than to the others. She affected the low Voice, Whisper, Lisp, Sigh, Start, Laugh, and many other Indications of Passion, which daily deceive thousands. When I play'd at Whisk[11] with her, she would look earnestly at me, and at the same time lose Deal or revoke; then burst into a ridiculous Laugh, and cry, La! I can't imagine what I was thinking of. To detain you no longer, after I had gone through a sufficient Course of Gallantry, as I thought, and was thoroughly convinced I had raised a violent Passion in my Mistress; I sought an Opportunity of coming to an Eclaircissement[12] with her. She avoided this as much as possible, however great Assiduity at length presented me one. I will not describe all the Particulars of this Interview; let it suffice, that till she could no longer pretend not to see my Drift, she first affected a violent Surprize, and immediately after as violent a Passion: She wondered what I had seen in her Conduct, which could induce me to affront her in this manner: And breaking from me the first Moment she could, told me, I had no other way to escape the Consequence of her Resentment, than by never seeing, or at least speaking to her more. I was not contented with this Answer; I still pursued her, but to no purpose, and was at length convinced that her Husband had the sole Possession of her Person, and that neither he nor any other had made any Impression on her Heart. I was taken off from following this *Ignis Fatuus* by some Advances which were made me by the Wife of a Citizen,[13] who tho' neither very young nor handsome, was yet too agreeable to be rejected by my amorous Constitution. I accordingly soon satisfy'd her, that she had not cast away her Hints on a barren or cold Soil; on the contrary, they instantly produced her an eager and desiring Lover. Nor did she give me any Reason to complain; she met the Warmth she had raised with equal Ardour. I had no longer a Coquette to deal with, but one who was wiser than to prostitute the noble Passion of Love to the ridiculous Lust of Vanity. We presently understood one another; and as the Pleasures we sought lay in a mutual Gratification, we soon found and enjoyed them. I thought myself at first greatly happy in the possession of this new Mistress, whose Fondness would have quickly surfeited a more sickly Appetite, but it had a different Effect on mine; she carried my Passion higher by it than Youth or Beauty had been able: But my Happiness could not long continue uninterrupted. The Apprehensions we lay under from the Jealousy of her Husband, gave us great Uneasiness. 'Poor Wretch! I pity him,' cry'd *Adams*. He did indeed deserve it, said the Gentleman, for he loved his Wife with great Tenderness, and I assure you it is a great Satisfaction to me that I was not the Man who first seduced her Affections from him. These Apprehensions appeared also too well grounded; for in the End he discovered us, and procur'd Witnesses of our Caresses. He then prosecuted me at Law, and recovered 3000 *l.* Damages, which much distressed my Fortune to pay: and what was worse, his Wife being divorced, came upon my hands. I led a very uneasy Life with her; for besides that my Passion was now much abated, her excessive Jealousy was very troublesome. At length Death rid me of an Inconvenience, which the Consideration of my having been the Author of her Misfortunes, would never suffer me to take any other Method of discarding.

I now bad adieu to Love, and resolved to pursue other less dangerous and expensive Pleasures. I fell into the Acquaintance of a Sett of jolly Companions, who slept all Day and drank all Night: Fellows who might rather be said to consume Time than to live. Their best Conversation was nothing but Noise: Singing, Hollowing, Wrangling, Drinking, Toasting, Sp—wing,[14] Smoking, were the chief Ingredients of our Entertainment. And yet bad as these were, they were more tolerable than our graver Scenes, which were either excessive tedious Narratives of dull common Matters of Fact, or hot Disputes about trifling Matters, which commonly ended in a Wager. This Way of Life the first serious Reflection put a period to, and I became Member of a Club frequented by young Men of great Abilities. The Bottle was now only called in the Assistance of our Conversation, which rolled on the deepest Points of Philosophy. These Gentlemen were engaged in a Search after Truth,[15] in the Pursuit of which they threw aside all the Prejudices of Education, and governed themselves only by the infallible Guide of Human Reason.[16] This great Guide, after having shewn them the Falshood of that very antient but simple Tenet, that there is such a Being as a Deity in the Universe, helped them to establish in his stead a certain *Rule of Right*,[17] by adhering to which they all arrived at the utmost Purity of Morals. Reflection made me as much delighted with this Society, as it had taught me to despise and detest the former. I began now to esteem myself a Being of a higher Order than I had ever before conceived, and was the more charmed with this Rule of Right, as I really found in my own Nature nothing repugnant to it. I held in utter Contempt all Persons who wanted any other Inducement to Virtue besides her intrinsick Beauty and Excellence; and had so high an Opinion of my present Companions, with regard to their Morality, that I would have trusted them with whatever was nearest and dearest to me. Whilst I was engaged in this delightful Dream, two or three Accidents happen'd successively, which at first much surprized me. For, one of our greatest Philosophers, or *Rule of Right-men*, withdrew himself from us, taking with him the Wife of one of his most intimate Friends. Secondly, Another of the same Society left the Club without remembring to take leave of his Bail.[18] A third having borrowed a Sum of Money of me, for which I received no Security, when I asked him to repay it, absolutely denied the Loan. These several Practices, so inconsistent with our golden Rule, made me begin to suspect its Infallibility; but when I communicated my Thoughts to one of the Club, he said 'there was nothing absolutely good or evil in itself; that Actions were denominated good or bad by the Circumstances of the Agent.[19] That possibly the Man who ran away with his Neighbour's Wife might be one of very good Inclinations, but over-prevailed on by the Violence of an unruly Passion, and in other Particulars might be a very worthy Member of Society: That if the Beauty of any Woman created in him an Uneasiness, he had a Right from Nature to relieve himself;' with many other things, which I then detested so much, that I took Leave of the Society that very Evening, and never returned to it again. Being now reduced to a State of Solitude, which I did not like, I became a great Frequenter of the Play-houses, which indeed was always my favourite Diversion, and most Evenings past away two or three Hours behind the Scenes, where I met with several Poets, with whom I made

Engagements at the Taverns. Some of the Players were likewise of our Parties. At these Meetings we were generally entertain'd by the Poets with reading their Performances, and by the Players with repeating their Parts: Upon which Occasions, I observed the Gentleman who furnished our Entertainment, was commonly the best pleased of the Company; who, tho' they were pretty civil to him to his Face, seldom failed to take the first Opportunity of his Absence to ridicule him. Now I made some Remarks, which probably are too obvious to be worth relating. 'Sir,' says *Adams*, 'your Remarks if you please.' First then, says he, I concluded that the general Observation, that Wits are most inclined to Vanity, is not true. Men are equally vain of Riches, Strength, Beauty, Honours, *&c.* But, these appear of themselves to the Eyes of the Beholders, whereas the poor Wit is obliged to produce his Performance to shew you his Perfection, and on his Readiness to do this that vulgar Opinion I have before mentioned is grounded: But doth not the Person who expends vast Sums in the Furniture of his House, or the Ornaments of his Person, who consumes much Time, and employs great Pains in dressing himself, or who thinks himself paid for Self-Denial, Labour, or even Villany by a Title or a Ribbon, sacrifice as much to Vanity as the poor Wit, who is desirous to read you his Poem or his Play? My second Remark was, that Vanity is the worst of Passions, and more apt to contaminate the Mind than any other: For as Selfishness is much more general than we please to allow it, so it is natural to hate and envy those who stand between us and the Good we desire. Now in Lust and Ambition these are few; and even in Avarice we find many who are no Obstacles to our Pursuits; but the vain Man seeks Preeminence; and every thing which is excellent or praise-worthy in another, renders him the Mark of his Antipathy. *Adams* now began to fumble in his Pockets, and soon cried out, 'O la! I have it not about me.' —— Upon this the Gentleman asking him what he was searching for, he said he searched after a Sermon, which he thought his Master-piece, against Vanity. 'Fie upon it, fie upon it,' cries he, 'why do I ever leave that Sermon out of my Pocket; I wish it was within five Miles, I would willingly fetch it, to read it to you.' The Gentleman answered, that there was no need, for he was cured of the Passion. 'And for that very Reason,' quoth *Adams*, 'I would read it, for I am confident you would admire it: Indeed, I have never been a greater Enemy to any Passion than that simple one of Vanity.' The Gentleman smiled, and proceeded —— From this Society I easily past to that of the Gamesters, where nothing remarkable happened, but the finishing my Fortune, which those

Gentlemen soon helped me to the End of. This opened Scenes of Life hitherto unknown; Poverty and Distress with their horrid Train of Duns, Attorneys, Bailiffs, haunted me Day and Night. My Clothes grew shabby, my Credit bad, my Friends and Acquaintance of all kinds cold. In this Situation the strangest Thought imaginable came into my Head; and what was this, but to write a Play? for I had sufficient Leisure; Fear of Bailiffs confined me every Day to my Room; and having always had a little Inclination and something of a Genius that way, I set myself to work, and within few Months produced a Piece of five Acts, which was accepted of at the Theatre. I remembered to have formerly taken Tickets of other Poets for their Benefits long before the Appearance of their Performances,[20] and resolving to follow a Precedent, which was so well suited to my present Circumstances; I immediately provided myself with a large Number of little Papers. Happy indeed would be the State of Poetry, would these Tickets pass current at the Bakehouse, the Ale-House, and the Chandler's-Shop: But alas! far otherwise; no Taylor will take them in Payment for Buckram, Stays, Stay-tape; nor no Bailiff for Civility-Money. They are indeed no more than a Passport to beg with, a Certificate that the Owner wants five Shillings, which induces well-disposed Christians to Charity. I now experienced what is worse than Poverty, or rather what is the worst Consequence of Poverty, I mean Attendance and Dependance on the Great. Many a Morning have I waited Hours in the cold Parlours of Men of Quality, where after seeing the lowest Rascals in Lace and Embroidery, the Pimps and Buffoons in Fashion admitted, I have been sometimes told on sending in my Name, that my Lord could not possibly see me this Morning: A sufficient Assurance that I should never more get entrance into that House. Sometimes I have been at last admitted, and the great Man hath thought proper to excuse himself, by telling me he was *tied up*. '*Tied up*,' says *Adams*, 'pray what's that?' Sir, says the Gentleman, the Profit which Booksellers allowed Authors for the best Works, was so very small, that certain Men of Birth and Fortune some Years ago, who were the Patrons of Wit and Learning, thought fit to encourage them farther, by entring into voluntary Subscriptions for their Encouragement.[21] Thus *Prior*, *Rowe*, *Pope*, and some other Men of Genius, received large Sums for their Labours from the Public. This seemed so easy a Method of getting Money, that many of the lowest Scriblers of the Times ventured to publish their Works in the same Way; and many had even the Assurance to take in Subscriptions for what was never writ nor intended. Subscriptions in this manner growing infinite, and a kind of Tax on the Public; some

Persons finding it not so easy a Task to discern good from bad Authors, or to know what Genius was worthy Encouragement, and what was not, to prevent the Expence of Subscribing to so many, invented a Method to excuse themselves from all Subscriptions whatever; and this was to receive a small Sum of Money in consideration of giving a large one if ever they subscribed; which many have done, and many more have pretended to have done, in order to silence all Sollicitation. The same Method was likewise taken with Play-house Tickets, which were no less a public Grievance; and this is what they called being *tied up* from subscribing. 'I can't say but the Term is apt enough, and somewhat typical,' said *Adams*; 'for a Man of large Fortune, who ties himself up, as you call it, from the Encouragement of Men of Merit, ought to be tied up in reality.' Well, Sir, says the Gentleman, to return to my Story. Sometimes I have received a Guinea from a Man of Quality, given with as ill a Grace as Alms are generally to the meanest Beggar, and purchased too with as much Time spent in Attendance, as, if it had been spent in honest Industry, might have brought me more Profit with infinitely more Satisfaction. After about two Months spent in this disagreeable way with the utmost Mortification, when I was pluming my Hopes on the Prospect of a plentiful Harvest from my Play, upon applying to the Prompter to know when it came into Rehearsal, he informed me he had received Orders from the Managers to return me the Play again; for that they could not possibly act it that Season; but if I would take it and revise it against the next, they would be glad to see it again. I snatch'd it from him with great Indignation, and retired to my Room, where I threw myself on the Bed in a Fit of Despair —— 'You should rather haven thrown yourself on your Knees,' says *Adams*; 'for Despair is sinful.' As soon, continued the Gentleman, as I had indulged the first Tumult of my Passion, I began to consider coolly what Course I should take, in a Situation without Friends, Money, Credit or Reputation of any kind. After revolving many things in my Mind, I could see no other Possibility of furnishing myself with the miserable Necessaries of Life than to retire to a Garret near the Temple, and commence Hackney-writer to the Lawyers; for which I was well qualify'd, being an excellent Penman. This Purpose I resolved on, and immediately put it in execution. I had an Acquaintance with an Attorney who had formerly transacted Affairs for me, and to him I applied: But instead of furnishing me with any Business, he laugh'd at my Undertaking, and told me 'he was afraid I should turn his Deeds into Plays, and he should expect to see them on the Stage.' Not to tire you with Instances of this kind from others,

I found that *Plato* himself did not hold Poets in greater Abhorrence than these Men of Business do.[22] Whenever I durst venture to a Coffee-house, which was on *Sundays* only,[23] a Whisper ran round the Room, which was constantly attended with a Sneer —— *That's Poet Wilson*: for I know not whether you have observed it, but there is a Malignity in the Nature of Man, which when not weeded out, or at least covered by a good Education and Politeness, delights in making another uneasy or dissatisfied with himself. This abundantly appears in all Assemblies, except those which are filled by People of Fashion, and especially among the younger People of both Sexes, whose Birth and Fortunes place them just without the polite Circles; I mean the lower Class of the Gentry, and the higher of the mercantile World, who are in reality the worst bred part of Mankind. Well, Sir, whilst I continued in this miserable State, with scarce sufficient Business to keep me from starving, the Reputation of a Poet being my Bane, I accidentally became acquainted with a Bookseller, who told me it was a pity a Man of my Learning and Genius should be obliged to such a Method of getting his Livelihood; that he had a Compassion for me, and if I would engage with him, he would undertake to provide handsomely for me.' A Man in my Circumstances, as he very well knew, had no Choice. I accordingly accepted his Proposal with his Conditions, which were none of the most favourable, and fell to translating with all my Might. I had no longer reason to lament the want of Business; for he furnished me with so much, that in half a Year I almost writ myself blind. I likewise contracted a Distemper by my sedentary Life, in which no part of my Body was exercised but my right Arm, which rendered me incapable of writing for a long time. This unluckily happening to delay the Publication of a Work, and my last Performance not having sold well, the Bookseller declined any further Engagement, and aspersed me to his Brethren as a careless, idle Fellow. I had however, by having half-work'd and half-starv'd myself to death during the Time I was in his Service, amassed a few Guineas, with which I bought a Lottery-Ticket,[24] resolving to throw myself into Fortune's Lap, and try if she would make me amends for the Injuries she had done me at the Gaming-Table. This Purchase being made, left me almost pennyless; when, as if I had not been sufficiently miserable, a Bailiff in Woman's Clothes got Admittance to my Chamber, whither he was directed by the Bookseller. He arrested me at my Taylor's Suit, for thirty-five Pounds;[25] a Sum for which I could not procure Bail, and was therefore conveyed to his House, where I was locked up in an upper Chamber. I had now neither Health (for I was scarce recovered from my

Indisposition) Liberty, Money, or Friends; and had abandoned all Hopes, and even the Desire of Life. 'But this could not last long,' said *Adams*, 'for doubtless the Taylor released you the moment he was truly acquainted with your Affairs; and knew that your Circumstances would not permit you to pay him.' Oh, Sir, answered the Gentleman, he knew that before he arrested me; nay, he knew that nothing but Incapacity could prevent me paying my Debts; for I had been his Customer many Years, had spent vast Sums of Money with him, and had always paid most punctually in my prosperous Days: But when I reminded him of this, with Assurances that if he would not molest my Endeavours, I would pay him all the Money I could, by my utmost Labour and Industry, procure, reserving only what was sufficient to preserve me alive: He answered, His Patience was worn out; that I had put him off from time to time; that he wanted the Money; that he had put it into a Lawyer's hands; and if I did not pay him immediately, or find Security, I must lie in Goal and expect no Mercy. 'He may expect Mercy,' cries *Adams* starting from his Chair, 'where he will find none. How can such a Wretch repeat the Lord's Prayer, where the Word which is translated, I know not for what Reason, *Trespasses*, is in the Original *Debts*? And as surely as we do not forgive others their Debts when they are unable to pay them; so surely shall we ourselves be unforgiven, when we are in no Condition of paying.' He ceased, and the Gentleman proceeded. While I was in this deplorable Situation a former Acquaintance, to whom I had communicated my Lottery-Ticket, found me out, and making me a Visit with great Delight in his Countenance, shook me heartily by the Hand, and wished me Joy of my good Fortune: For, says he, your Ticket is come up a Prize of 3000 *l. Adams* snapt his Fingers at these Words in an Ecstasy of Joy; which however did not continue long: For the Gentleman thus proceeded. Alas! Sir, this was only a Trick of Fortune to sink me the deeper: For I had disposed of this Lottery-Ticket two Days before to a Relation, who refused lending me a Shilling without it, in order to procure myself Bread.[26] As soon as my Friend was acquainted with my unfortunate Sale, he began to revile me, and remind me of all the ill Conduct and Miscarriages of my Life. He said, 'I was one whom Fortune could not save, if she would; that I was now ruined without any Hopes of Retrieval, nor must expect any Pity from my Friends; that it would be extreme Weakness to compassionate the Misfortunes of a Man who ran headlong to his own Destruction.' He then painted to me in as lively Colours as he was able, the Happiness I should have now enjoyed, had I not foolishly disposed of my Ticket. I urg'd the Plea of Necessity: But he made no Answer to that, and began again to revile me, till I could bear it no longer, and desired him to finish his Visit. I soon exchanged the Bailiff's House for a Prison; where, as I had not Money sufficient to procure me a separate Apartment, I was crouded in with a great number of miserable Wretches, in common with whom I was destitute of every Convenience of Life, even that which all the Brutes enjoy, wholesome Air. In these dreadful Circumstances I applied by Letter to several of my old Acquaintance, and such to whom I had formerly lent Money without any great Prospect of its being returned, for their Assistance; but in vain. An Excuse instead of a Denial was the gentlest Answer I received. —— Whilst I languished in a Condition too horrible to be described, and which in a Land of Humanity, and, what is much more Christianity, seems a strange Punishment for a little Inadvertency and Indiscretion. Whilst I was in this Condition, a Fellow came one day into the Prison, and enquiring me out, deliver'd me the following Letter:

SIR,

My Father, to whom you sold your Ticket in the last Lottery, died the same Day in which it came up a Prize, as you have possibly heard, and left me sole Heiress of all his Fortune. I am so much touched with your present Circumstances, and the Uneasiness you must feel at having been driven to dispose of what might have made you happy, that I must desire your Acceptance of the inclosed, and am

Your humble Servant,
HARRIET HEARTY.

And what do you think was inclosed? 'I don't know,' cried *Adams*: 'Not less than a Guinea, I hope.' —— Sir, it was a Bank-Note for 200 *l.* —— '200 *l.*' says *Adams*, in a Rapture! — No less, I assure you, answered the Gentleman; a Sum I was not half so delighted with, as with the dear Name of the generous Girl that sent it me; and who was not only the best, but the handsomest Creature in the Universe; and for whom I had long had a Passion, which I never durst disclose to her. I kiss'd her Name a thousand times, my Eyes overflowing with Tenderness and Gratitude, I repeated — But not to detain you with these Raptures, I immediately acquired my Liberty, and having paid all my Debts, departed with upwards of fifty Pounds in my Pocket, to thank my kind Deliverer. She happened to be then out of Town, a Circumstance which, upon Reflection, pleased me; for by that means I had an Opportunity to appear before her in a more decent Dress. At her Return to Town within a Day or two, I threw myself at her Feet with the most ardent Acknowledgments, which she rejected with an unfeigned Greatness of Mind, and told me I could not oblige her more than by never mentioning, or if possible, thinking on a Circumstance which must bring to my Mind an Accident that might be grievous to me to think on. She proceeded thus: 'What I have done is in my own eyes a Trifle, and perhaps infinitely less than would have become me to do. And if you think of engaging in any Business, where a larger Sum may be serviceable to you, I shall not be over-rigid, either as to the Security or Interest.' I endeavoured to express all the Gratitude in my power to this Profusion of Goodness, tho' perhaps it was my Enemy, and began to afflict my Mind with more Agonies, than all the Miseries I had undergone; it affected me with severer Reflections than Poverty, Distress, and Prisons united had been able to make me feel: For, Sir, these Acts and Professions of Kindness, which were sufficient to have raised in a good Heart the most violent Passion of Friendship to one of the same, or to Age and Ugliness in a different Sex, came to me from a Woman, a young and beautiful Woman, one whose Perfections I had long known; and for whom I had long conceived a violent Passion, tho' with a Despair, which made me endeavour rather to curb and conceal, than to nourish or acquaint her with it. In short, they came upon me united with Beauty, Softness, and Tenderness, such bewitching Smiles —— O Mr *Adams*, in that Moment I lost myself, and forgetting our different Situations, nor considering what Return I was making to her Goodness, by desiring her who had given me so much, to bestow her All, I laid gently hold on her Hand, and conveying it to my Lips, I prest it with inconceivable Ardour; then lifting up my swimming Eyes, I saw her Face and Neck overspread with one Blush; she offered to withdraw her Hand, yet not so as to deliver it from mine, tho' I held it with the gentlest Force. We both stood trembling, her Eyes cast on the ground, and mine stedfastly fix'd on her. Good G——, what was then the Condition of my Soul! burning with Love, Desire, Admiration, Gratitude, and every tender Passion, all bent on one charming Object. Passion at last got the better of both Reason and Respect, and softly letting go her Hand, I offered madly to clasp her in my Arms; when a little recovering herself, she started from me, asking me with some Shew of Anger, 'If she had any Reason to expect this Treatment from me.' I then fell prostrate before her, and told her, 'If I had offended, my Life was absolutely in her power, which I would in any manner lose for her sake. Nay, Madam,' said I, 'you shall not be so ready to punish me, as I to suffer. I own my Guilt. I detest the Reflection that I would have sacrificed your Happiness to mine. Believe me, I sincerely repent my Ingratitude, yet believe me too, it was my Passion, my unbounded Passion for you, which hurried me so far; I have loved you long and tenderly; and the Goodness you have shewn me, hath innocently weighed down a Wretch undone before. Acquit me of all mean mercenary Views, and before I take my Leave of you for ever, which I am resolved instantly to do, believe me, that Fortune could have raised me to no height to which I could not have gladly lifted you. O curst be Fortune.' ——— 'Do not,' says she, interrupting me with the sweetest Voice, 'Do not curse Fortune, since she hath made me happy, and if she hath put your Happiness in my power, I have told you, you shall ask nothing in Reason which I will refuse.' 'Madam,' said I, 'you mistake me if you imagine, as you seem, my Happiness is in the Power of Fortune now. You have obliged me too much already; if I have any Wish, it is for some blest Accident, by which I may contribute with my Life to the least Augmentation of your Felicity. As for my self, the only Happiness I can ever have, will be hearing of your's; and if Fortune will make that complete, I will forgive her all her Wrongs to me.' 'You may, indeed,' answered she, smiling, 'For your own Happiness must be included in mine. I have long known your Worth; nay, I must confess,' said she, blushing, 'I have long discovered that Passion for me you profess, notwithstanding those Endeavours which I am convinced were unaffected, to conceal it; and if all I can give with Reason will not suffice, —— take Reason away, —— and now I believe you cannot ask me what I will deny.' — She uttered these Words with a Sweetness not to be imagined. I immediately started, my Blood which lay freezing at my Heart, rushed tumultuously through every Vein. I stood for a Moment silent, then flying to her, I caught her in my Arms, no longer resisting, —— and softly told her, she must give me then herself. — O Sir, — Can I describe her Look? She remained silent and almost motionless several Minutes. At last, recovering herself a little, she insisted on my leaving her, and in such a manner that I instantly obeyed: You may imagine, however, I soon saw her again. —— But I ask pardon, I fear I have detained you too long in relating the Particulars of the former Interview. 'So far otherwise,' said *Adams*, licking his Lips, 'that I could willingly hear it over again.' Well, Sir, continued the Gentleman, to be as concise as possible, within a Week she consented to make me the happiest of Mankind. We were married shortly after; and when I came to examine the Circumstances of my Wife's Fortune; (which I do assure you I was not presently at Leisure enough to do) I found it amounted to about six thousand Pounds, most part of which lay in Effects; for her Father had been a Wine-Merchant, and she seemed willing, if I liked it, that I should carry on the same Trade. I readily and too inconsiderately undertook it: For not having been bred up to the Secrets of the Business, and endeavouring to deal with the utmost Honesty and Uprightness, I soon found our Fortune in a declining Way, and my Trade decreasing by little and little: For my Wines which I never adulterated after their Importation, and were sold as neat as they came over, were universally decried by the Vintners, to whom I could not allow them quite as cheap as those who gained double the Profit by a less Price. I soon began to despair of improving our Fortune by these means; nor was I at all easy at the Visits and Familiarity of many who had been my Acquaintance in my Prosperity, but denied, and shunned me in my Adversity, and now very forwardly renewed their Acquaintance with me. In short, I had sufficiently seen, that the Pleasures of the World are chiefly Folly, and the Business of it mostly Knavery; and both, nothing better than Vanity: The Men of Pleasure tearing one another to pieces, from the Emulation of spending Money, and the Men of Business from Envy in getting it. My Happiness consisted entirely in my Wife, whom I loved with an inexpressible Fondness, which was perfectly returned; and my Prospects were no other than to provide for our growing Family; for she was now big of her second Child: I therefore took an Opportunity to ask her Opinion of entering into a retired Life, which after hearing my Reasons, and perceiving my Affection for it, she readily embraced. We soon put our small Fortune, now reduced under three thousand Pounds, into Money, with part of which we purchased this little Place, whither we retired soon after her Delivery, from a World full of Bustle, Noise, Hatred, Envy and Ingratitude, to Ease, Quiet, and Love. We have here liv'd almost twenty Years, with little other Conversation than our own, most of the Neighbourhood taking us for very strange People; the Squire of the Parish representing me as a Madman, and the Parson as a Presbyterian; because I will not hunt with the one, nor drink with the other. 'Sir,' says *Adams*, 'Fortune hath I think paid you all her Debts in this sweet Retirement.' Sir, replied the Gentleman, I am thankful to the great Author of all Things for the Blessings I here enjoy, I have the best of Wives, and three pretty Children, for whom I have the true Tenderness of a Parent; but no Blessings are pure in this World. Within three Years of my Arrival here I lost my eldest Son. *(Here he sighed bitterly.)* 'Sir,' says *Adams*, 'we must submit to Providence, and consider Death is common to all.' We must submit, indeed, answered the Gentleman; and if he had died, I could have borne the Loss with Patience: But alas! Sir, he was stolen away from my Door by some wicked travelling People whom they call *Gipsies*; nor could I ever with the most diligent Search recover him. Poor Child! he had the sweetest Look, the exact Picture of his Mother; at which some Tears unwittingly dropt from his Eyes, as did likewise from those of *Adams*, who always sympathized with his Friends on those Occasions. Thus, Sir, said the Gentleman, I have finished my Story, in which if I have been too particular, I ask your Pardon; and now, if you please, I will fetch you another Bottle; which Proposal the Parson thankfully accepted.

CHAPTER IV

A Description of Mr Wilson's *Way of Living. The tragical Adventure of the Dog, and other grave Matters.*

The Gentleman returned with the Bottle, and *Adams* and he sat some time silent, when the former started up and cried, '*No, that won't do.*' The Gentleman enquired into his Meaning; he answered, 'He had been considering that it was possible the late famous King *Theodore*[1] might have been that very Son whom he lost;' but added, 'that his Age could not answer that Imagination.' 'However,' says he, 'G— disposes all things for the best, and very probably he may be some Great Man, or Duke, and may one day or other revisit you in that Capacity.' The Gentleman answered, he should know him amongst ten thousand, for he had a Mark on his left Breast, of a Strawberry, which his Mother had given him by longing for that Fruit.

That beautiful young Lady, the *Morning*, now rose from her Bed, and with a Countenance blooming with fresh Youth and Sprightliness, like Miss* ——, with soft Dews hanging on her pouting Lips, began to take her early Walk over the eastern Hills; and presently after, that gallant Person the Sun stole softly from his Wife's Chamber to pay his Addresses to her; when the Gentleman ask'd his Guest if he would walk forth and survey his little Garden, which he readily agreed to, and *Joseph* at the same time awaking from a Sleep in which he had been two Hours buried, went with them. No Parterres,[2] no Fountains, no Statues embellished this

* *Whoever the Reader pleases.*

little Garden. Its only Ornament was a short Walk, shaded on each side by a Filbert Hedge, with a small Alcove at one end, whither in hot Weather the Gentleman and his Wife used to retire and divert themselves with their Children, who played in the Walk before them: But tho' Vanity had no Votary in this little Spot, here was variety of Fruit, and every thing useful for the Kitchin, which was abundantly sufficient to catch the Admiration of *Adams*, who told the Gentleman he had certainly a good Gardener. Sir, answered he, that Gardener is now before you; whatever you see here, is the Work solely of my own Hands. Whilst I am providing Necessaries for my Table, I likewise procure myself an Appetite for them. In fair Seasons I seldom pass less than six Hours of the twenty four in this Place, where I am not idle, and by these means I have been able to preserve my Health ever since my Arrival here without Assistance from Physick. Hither I generally repair at the Dawn, where I exercise myself whilst my Wife dresses her Children, and prepares our Breakfast, after which we are seldom asunder during the residue of the Day; for when the Weather will not permit them to accompany me here, I am usually within with them; for I am neither ashamed of conversing with my Wife, nor of playing with my Children: to say the Truth, I do not perceive that Inferiority of Understanding which the Levity of Rakes, the Dulness of Men of Business, or the Austerity of the Learned would persuade us of in Women. As for my Woman, I declare I have found none of my own Sex capable of making juster Observations on Life, or of delivering them more agreeably; nor do I believe any one possessed of a faithfuller or braver Friend. And sure as this Friendship is sweetened with more Delicacy and Tenderness, so is it confirmed by dearer Pledges than can attend the closest male Alliance: For what Union can be so fast, as our common Interest in the Fruits of our Embraces? Perhaps, Sir, you are not yourself a Father; if you are not, be assured you cannot conceive the Delight I have in my Little-Ones. Would you not despise me, if you saw me stretched on the Ground, and my Children playing round me? 'I should reverence the Sight,' quoth *Adams*, 'I myself am now the Father of six, and have been of eleven, and I can say I never scourged a Child of my own, unless as his School-master, and then have felt every Stroke on my own Posteriors. And as to what you say concerning Women. I have often lamented my own Wife did not understand *Greek*.' — The Gentleman smiled, and answered, he would not be apprehended to insinuate that his own had an Understanding above the Care of her Family, on the contrary, says he, my *Harriet* I assure you is a notable Housewife, and few Gentlemen's

House-keepers understand Cookery or Confectionary better; but these are Arts which she hath no great Occasion for now: however, the Wine you commended so much last Night at Supper, was of her own making, as is indeed all the Liquor in my House, except my Beer, which falls to my Province. ('And I assure you it is as excellent,' quoth *Adams*, 'as ever I tasted.') We formerly kept a Maid-Servant, but since my Girls have been growing up, she is unwilling to indulge them in Idleness; for as the Fortunes I shall give them will be very small, we intend not to breed them above the Rank they are likely to fill hereafter, nor to teach them to despise or ruin a plain Husband. Indeed I could wish a Man of my own Temper, and a retired Life, might fall to their Lot: for I have experienced that calm serene Happiness which is seated in Content, is inconsistent with the Hurry and Bustle of the World. He was proceeding thus, when the Little Things, being just risen, ran eagerly towards him, and asked him Blessing: They were shy to the Strangers, but the eldest acquainted her Father that her Mother and the young Gentlewoman were up, and that Breakfast was ready. They all went in, where the Gentleman was surprized at the Beauty of *Fanny*, who had now recovered herself from her Fatigue, and was entirely clean drest; for the Rogues who had taken away her Purse, had left her her Bundle. But if he was so much amazed at the Beauty of this young Creature, his Guests were no less charmed at the Tenderness which appeared in the Behaviour of Husband and Wife to each other, and to their Children, and at the dutiful and affectionate Behaviour of these to their Parents. These Instances pleased the well-disposed Mind of *Adams* equally with the Readiness which they exprest to oblige their Guests, and their Forwardness to offer them the best of every thing in their House; and what delighted him still more, was an Instance or two of their Charity: for whilst they were at Breakfast, the good Woman was called forth to assist her sick Neighbour, which she did with some Cordials made for the public Use; and the good Man went into his Garden at the same time, to supply another with something which he wanted thence, for they had nothing which those who wanted it were not welcome to. These good People were in the utmost Cheerfulness, when they heard the Report of a Gun, and immediately afterwards a little Dog, the Favourite of the eldest Daughter, came limping in all bloody, and laid himself at his Mistress's Feet: The poor Girl, who was about eleven Years old,[3] burst into Tears at the sight, and presently one of the Neighbours came in and informed them, that the young Squire, the Son of the Lord of the Manor, had shot him as he past by, swearing at the same time he would prosecute the Master of him for keeping a Spaniel; for that he had given Notice he would not suffer one in the Parish. The Dog, whom his Mistress had taken into her Lap, died in a few Minutes, licking her Hand. She exprest great Agony at his Loss, and the other Children began to cry for their Sister's Misfortune, nor could *Fanny* herself refrain. Whilst the Father and Mother attempted to comfort her, *Adams* grasped his Crab Stick, and would have sallied out after the Squire, had not *Joseph* withheld him. He could not however bridle his Tongue — He pronounced the Word *Rascal* with great Emphasis, said he deserved to be hanged more than a Highwayman, and wish'd he had the scourging him. The Mother took her Child, lamenting and carrying the dead Favourite in her Arms out of the Room, when the Gentleman said, this was the second time this Squire had endeavoured to kill the little Wretch, and had wounded him smartly once before, adding, he could have no Motive but Ill-nature; for the little thing, which was not near as big as one's Fist, had never been twenty Yards from the House in the six Years his Daughter had had it. He said he had done nothing to deserve this Usage: but his Father had too great a Fortune to contend with. That he was as absolute as any Tyrant in the Universe, and had killed all the Dogs, and taken away all the Guns in the Neighbourhood,[4] and not only that, but he trampled down Hedges, and rode over Corn and Gardens, with no more Regard than if they were the Highway. 'I wish I could catch him in my Garden,' said *Adams*; 'tho' I would rather forgive him riding through my House than such an ill-natur'd Act as this.'

The Cheerfulness of their Conversation being interrupted by this Accident, in which the Guests could be of no service to their kind Entertainer, and as the Mother was taken up in administring Consolation to the poor Girl, whose Disposition was too good hastily to forget the sudden Loss of her little Favourite, which had been fondling with her a few Minutes before; and as *Joseph* and *Fanny* were impatient to get home and begin those previous Ceremonies to their Happiness which *Adams* had insisted on, they now offered to take their Leave. The Gentleman importuned them much to stay Dinner: but when he found their Eagerness to depart, he summoned his Wife, and accordingly having performed all the usual Ceremonies of Bows and Curt'sies, more pleasant to be seen than to be related, they took their Leave, the Gentleman and his Wife heartily wishing them a good Journey, and they as heartily thanking them for their kind Entertainment. They then departed, *Adams* declaring that this was the Manner in which the People had lived in the Golden Age.

CHAPTER V

*A Disputation on Schools, held on the Road between Mr Abraham
Adams and* Joseph; *and a Discovery not unwelcome to them both.*

Our Travellers having well refreshed themselves at the Gentleman's
House, *Joseph* and *Fanny* with Sleep, and Mr *Abraham Adams* with Ale and
Tobacco, renewed their Journey with great Alacrity; and, pursuing the
Road in which they were directed, travelled many Miles before they met
with any Adventure worth relating. In this Interval, we shall present our
Readers with a very curious Discourse, as we apprehend it, concerning
public Schools, which pass'd between Mr *Joseph Andrews* and Mr *Abraham
Adams.*

They had not gone far, before *Adams* calling to *Joseph,* asked him if he
had attended to the Gentleman's Story; he answered, to all the former
Part. 'And don't you think,' says he, 'he was a very unhappy Man in his
Youth?' 'A very unhappy Man indeed,' answered the other. '*Joseph*,' cries
Adams, screwing up his Mouth, 'I have found it; I have discovered the
Cause of all the Misfortunes which befel him. A public School, *Joseph,*
was the Cause of all the Calamities which he afterwards suffered. Public
Schools are the Nurseries of all Vice and Immorality. All the wicked
Fellows whom I remember at the University were bred at them. — Ah
Lord! I can remember as well as if it was but yesterday, a Knot of them;
they call them King's Scholars,[1] I forget why ——— very wicked Fellows!
Joseph, you may thank the Lord you were not bred at a public School,
you would never have preserved your Virtue as you have. The first Care
I always take, is of a Boy's Morals, I had rather he should be a Blockhead
than an Atheist or a Presbyterian. What is all the Learning of the World
compared to his immortal Soul? What shall a Man take in exchange for
his Soul! But the Masters of great Schools trouble themselves about no
such thing. I have known a Lad of eighteen at the University, who hath
not been able to say his Catechism; but for my own part, I always scourged
a Lad sooner for missing that than any other Lesson. Believe me, Child,
all that Gentleman's Misfortunes arose from his being educated at a public
School.'

'It doth not become me,' answer'd *Joseph,* 'to dispute any thing, Sir,
with you, especially a matter of this kind; for to be sure you must be
allowed by all the World to be the best Teacher of a School in all our

County.' 'Yes, that,' says *Adams*, 'I believe, is granted me; that I may without much Vanity pretend to ——— nay I believe I may go to the next County too ——— but *gloriari non est meum*.'² ——— 'However, Sir, as you are pleased to bid me speak,' says *Joseph*, 'you know, my late Master, Sir *Thomas Booby*, was bred at a public School, and he was the finest Gentleman in all the Neighbourhood. And I have often heard him say, if he had a hundred Boys he would breed them all at the same Place. It was his Opinion, and I have often heard him deliver it, that a Boy taken from a public School, and carried into the World, will learn more in one Year there, than one of a private Education will in five. He used to say, the School itself initiated him a great way, (I remember that was his very Expression) for great Schools are little Societies, where a Boy of any Observation may see in Epitome what he will afterwards find in the World at large.' '*Hinc illæ lachrymæ*;³ for that very Reason,' quoth *Adams*, 'I prefer a private School, where Boys may be kept in Innocence and Ignorance: for, according to that fine Passage in the Play of *Cato*, the only *English* Tragedy I ever read,

> *If Knowledge of the World must make Men Villains,*
> *May* Juba *ever live in Ignorance.*⁴

Who would not rather preserve the Purity of his Child, than wish him to attain the whole Circle of Arts and Sciences; which, by the bye, he may learn in the Classes of a private School? for I would not be vain, but I esteem myself to be second to none, *nulli secundum*, in teaching these things; so that a Lad may have as much Learning in a private as in a public Education.' 'And with Submission,' answered *Joseph*, 'he may get as much Vice, witness several Country Gentlemen, who were educated within five Miles of their own Houses, and are as wicked as if they had known the World from their Infancy. I remember when I was in the Stable, if a young Horse was vicious in his Nature, no Correction would make him otherwise; I take it to be equally the same among Men: if a Boy be of a mischievous wicked Inclination, no School, tho' ever so private, will ever make him good; on the contrary, if he be of a righteous Temper, you may trust him to *London*, or wherever else you please, he will be in no danger of being corrupted. Besides, I have often heard my Master say, that the Discipline practised in public Schools was much better than that in private.' — 'You talk like a Jackanapes,' says *Adams*, 'and so did your Master. Discipline indeed! because one Man scourges twenty or thirty Boys more in a Morning than another, is he therefore a better Disciplinarian? I do presume to confer[5] in this Point with all who have taught from *Chiron*'s[6] time to this Day; and, if I was Master of six Boys only, I would preserve as good Discipline amongst them as the Master of the greatest School in the World. I say nothing, young Man; remember, I say nothing; but if Sir *Thomas* himself had been educated nearer home, and under the Tuition of somebody, remember, I name nobody, it might have been better for him —— but his Father must institute him in the Knowledge of the World. *Nemo mortalium omnibus horis sapit.*[7] *Joseph* seeing him run on in this manner asked pardon many times, assuring him he had no Intention to offend. 'I believe you had not, Child,' said he, 'and I am not angry with you: but for maintaining good Discipline in a School; for this,' —— And then he ran on as before, named all the Masters who are recorded in old Books, and preferred himself to them all. Indeed if this good Man had an Enthusiasm, or what the Vulgar call a Blind-side, it was this: He thought a Schoolmaster the greatest Character in the World, and himself the greatest of all Schoolmasters, neither of which Points he would have given up to *Alexander the Great* at the Head of his Army.[8]

Adams continued his Subject till they came to one of the beautifullest Spots of Ground in the Universe. It was a kind of natural Amphitheatre, formed by the winding of a small Rivulet, which was planted with thick Woods, and the Trees rose gradually above each other by the natural Ascent of the Ground they stood on; which Ascent, as they hid with their Boughs, they seemed to have been disposed by the most skilful Design of the Planter. The Soil was spread with a Verdure which no Paint could imitate, and the whole Place might have raised romantic Ideas in elder Minds than those of *Joseph* and *Fanny*, without the Assistance of Love.

Here they arrived about Noon, and *Joseph* proposed to *Adams* that they should rest a while in this delightful Place, and refresh themselves with some Provisions which the Good-nature of Mrs *Wilson* had provided them with. *Adams* made no Objection to the Proposal, so down they sat, and pulling out a cold Fowl, and a Bottle of Wine, they made a Repast with a Cheerfulness which might have attracted the Envy of more splendid Tables. I should not omit, that they found among their Provision a little Paper, containing a piece of Gold, which *Adams* imagining it had been put there by mistake, would have returned back, to deliver them; but he was at last convinced by *Joseph*, that Mr *Wilson* had taken this handsome way of furnishing them with a Supply for their Journey, on his having related the Distress which they had been in, when they were relieved by the Generosity of the Pedlar. *Adams* said, he was glad to see such an

Instance of Goodness, not so much for the Conveniency which it brought them, but for the sake of the Doer, whose Reward would be great in Heaven. He likewise comforted himself with a Reflection, that he should shortly have an Opportunity of returning it him; for the Gentleman was within a Week to make a Journey into *Somersetshire*, to pass through *Adams*'s Parish, and had faithfully promised to call on him: A Circumstance which we thought too immaterial to mention before; but which those who have as great an Affection for that Gentleman as ourselves will rejoice at, as it may give them Hopes of seeing him again. Then *Joseph* made a Speech on Charity, which the Reader if he is so disposed, may see in the next Chapter; for we scorn to betray him into any such Reading, without first giving him Warning.

CHAPTER VI

Moral Reflections by Joseph Andrews, *with the Hunting Adventure, and Parson* Adams*'s miraculous Escape.*[1]

I have often wondered, Sir, said *Joseph*, to observe so few Instances of Charity among Mankind; for tho' the Goodness of a Man's Heart did not incline him to relieve the Distresses of his Fellow-Creatures, methinks the Desire of Honour should move him to it. What inspires a Man to build fine Houses, to purchase fine Furniture, Pictures, Clothes, and other things at a great Expence, but an Ambition to be respected more than other People? Now would not one great Act of Charity, one Instance of redeeming a poor Family from all the Miseries of Poverty, restoring an unfortunate Tradesman by a Sum of Money to the means of procuring a Livelihood by his Industry, discharging an undone Debtor from his Debts or a Goal, or any such like Example of Goodness, create a Man more Honour and Respect than he could acquire by the finest House, Furniture, Pictures or Clothes that were ever beheld? For not only the Object himself, who was thus relieved, but all who heard the Name of such a Person must, I imagine, reverence him infinitely more than the Possessor of all those other things: which when we so admire, we rather praise the Builder, the Workman, the Painter, the Laceman, the Taylor, and the rest, by whose Ingenuity they are produced, than the Person who by his Money makes them his own. For my own part, when I have waited behind my Lady in a Room hung with fine Pictures, while I have been looking at them I have never once thought of their Owner, nor hath any one else, as I ever observed; for when it hath been asked whose Picture that was, it was never once answered, the Master's of the House, but *Ammyconni, Paul Varnish, Hannibal Scratchi,* or *Hogarthi*,[2] which I suppose were the Names of the Painters: but if it was asked, who redeemed such a one out of Prison? who lent such a ruined Tradesman Money to set up? who cloathed that Family of poor little Children? it is very plain, what must be the Answer. And besides, these great Folks are mistaken, if they imagine they get any Honour at all by these means; for I do not remember I have ever been with my Lady at any House where she commended the House or Furniture, but I have heard her at her return home make sport and jeer at whatever she had before commended: and I have been told by other Gentlemen in Livery, that it is the same in their Families: but I defy the wisest Man in the World to turn a true good Action into Ridicule.[3] I defy him to do it. He who should endeavour it, would be laughed at himself, instead of making others laugh. Nobody scarce doth any Good, yet they all agree in praising those who do. Indeed it is strange that all Men should consent in commending Goodness, and no Man endeavour to deserve that Commendation; whilst, on the contrary, all rail at Wickedness, and all are as eager to be what they abuse. This I know not the Reason of, but it is as plain as Daylight to those who converse in the World, as I have done these three Years. 'Are all the great Folks wicked then?' says *Fanny*. To be sure there are some Exceptions, answered *Joseph*. Some Gentlemen of our Cloth report charitable Actions done by their Lords and Masters, and I have heard 'Squire *Pope*, the great Poet, at my Lady's Table, tell Stories of a Man that lived at a Place called *Ross*, and another at the *Bath*, one *Al——Al——* I forget his Name, but it is in the Book of Verses.[4] This Gentleman hath built up a stately House too, which the 'Squire likes very well; but his Charity is seen farther than his House, tho' it stands on a Hill, ay, and brings him more Honour. It was his Charity that put him in the Book, where the 'Squire says he puts all those who deserve it; and to be sure, as he lives among all the great People, if there were any such, he would know them. —— This was all of Mr *Joseph Andrews*'s Speech which I could get him to recollect, which I have delivered as near as was possible in his own Words, with a very small Embellishment. But I believe the Reader hath not been a little surprized at the long Silence of Parson *Adams*, especially as so many Occasions offer'd themselves to exert his Curiosity and Observation. The truth is, he was fast asleep, and had so been from the beginning of the preceding Narrative: and indeed if the Reader considers that so many Hours had past since he had closed his Eyes, he will not wonder at his Repose, tho' even *Henley* himself, or as great an Orator (if any such be) had been in his *Rostrum* or Tub before him.'[5]

Joseph, who, whilst he was speaking, had continued in one Attitude, with his Head reclining on one side, and his Eyes cast on the Ground, no sooner perceived, on looking up, the Position of *Adams*, who was stretched on his Back, and snored louder than the usual braying of the Animal with long Ears; than he turned towards *Fanny*, and taking her by the Hand, began a Dalliance, which, tho' consistent with the purest Innocence and Decency, neither he would have attempted, nor she permitted before any Witness. Whilst they amused themselves in this harmless and delightful manner, they heard a Pack of Hounds approaching in full Cry towards them, and presently afterwards saw a Hare pop forth from the Wood, and crossing the Water, land within a few Yards of them in the Meadows. The Hare was no sooner on shore, than it seated itself on its hinder Legs, and listened to the Sound of the Pursuers. *Fanny* was wonderfully pleased with the little Wretch, and eagerly longed to have it in her Arms, that she might preserve it from the Dangers which seemed to threaten it:[6] but the sensible and human part of the Creation do not always aptly distinguish their Friends from their Foes; what wonder then if this silly Creature, the moment it beheld her, fled from the Friend who would have protected it, and traversing the Meadows again, past the little Rivulet on the opposite side. It was however so spent and weak, that it fell down twice or thrice in its way. This affected the tender Heart of *Fanny*, who exclaimed with Tears in her Eyes against the Barbarity of worrying a poor innocent defenceless Animal out of its Life, and putting it to the extremest Torture for Diversion. She had not much time to make Reflections of this kind, for on a sudden the Hounds rushed through the Wood, which resounded with their Throats, and the Throats of their *Retinue*, who *attended* on them on horseback. The Dogs now past the Rivulet, and pursued the Footsteps of the Hare; five Horsemen attempted to leap over, three of whom succeeded, and two were in the Attempt thrown from their Saddles into the Water; their Companions and their own Horses too proceeded after their Sport, and left their Friends and Riders to invoke the Assistance of Fortune, or employ the more active means of Strength, and Agility for their Deliverance. *Joseph* however was not so unconcerned on this Occasion; he left *Fanny* for a moment to herself, and ran to the Gentlemen, who were immediately on their Legs, shaking their Ears, and easily with the help of his Hand attained the Bank; (for the Rivulet was not at all deep) and without staying to thank their kind Assister, ran dripping across the Meadow, calling to their Brother Sportsmen to stop their Horses: but they heard them not.

The Hounds were now very little behind their poor reeling, staggering Prey, which fainting almost at every Step, crawled through the Wood, and had almost got round to the Place where *Fanny* stood, when it was overtaken by its Enemies; and being driven out of the Covert was caught, and instantly tore to pieces before *Fanny*'s Face, who was unable to assist it with any Aid more powerful than Pity; nor could she prevail on *Joseph*, who had been himself a Sportsman in his Youth, to attempt any thing contrary to the Laws of Hunting, in favour of the Hare, which he said was killed fairly.

The Hare was caught within a Yard or two of *Adams*, who lay asleep at some distance from the Lovers, and the Hounds in devouring it, and pulling it backwards and forwards, had drawn it so close to him, that some of them (by Mistake perhaps for the Hare's Skin) laid hold of the Skirts of his Cassock, others at the same time applying their Teeth to his Wig, which he had with a Handkerchief fastened to his Head; they began to pull him about; and had not the Motion of his Body had more effect on him than seemed to be wrought by the Noise, they must certainly have tasted his Flesh, which delicious Flavour might have been fatal to him: But being roused by these Tuggings, he instantly awaked, and with a Jerk delivering his Head from his Wig, he with most admirable Dexterity recovered his Legs, which now seemed the only Members he could entrust his Safety to. Having therefore escaped likewise from at least a third Part of his Cassock, which he willingly left as his *Exuviæ* [7] or Spoils to the Enemy, he fled with the utmost speed he could summon to his Assistance. Nor let this be any Detraction from the Bravery of his Character; let the Number of the Enemies, and the Surprize in which he was taken, be considered; and if there be any Modern so outrageously brave, that he cannot admit of Flight in any Circumstance whatever, I say (but I whisper that softly, and I solemnly declare, without any Intention of giving Offence to any brave Man in the Nation) I say, or rather I whisper that he is an ignorant Fellow, and hath never read *Homer* nor *Virgil*, nor knows he any thing of *Hector* or *Turnus*;[8] nay, he is unacquainted with the History of some great Men living, who, tho' as brave as Lions, ay, as Tigers, have run away the Lord knows how far, and the Lord knows why, to the Surprize of their Friends, and the Entertainment of their Enemies. But if Persons of such heroick Disposition are a little offended at the Behaviour of *Adams*, we assure them they shall be as much pleased with what we shall immediately relate of *Joseph Andrews*. The Master of the Pack was just arrived, or, as the Sportsmen call it, *Come in*, when *Adams* set out, as we have before mentioned. This Gentleman was generally said to be a great Lover of Humour; but not to mince the matter, especially as we are upon this Subject, he was a great *Hunter of Men*:[9] Indeed he had hitherto followed the Sport only with Dogs of his own Species; for he kept two or three Couple of barking Curs for that Use only. However, as he thought he had now found a Man nimble enough, he was willing to indulge himself with other Sport, and accordingly crying out, *Stole away*, encouraged the Hounds to pursue Mr *Adams*, swearing it was the largest Jack-Hare he ever saw; at the same time hallooing and hooping as if a conquered Foe was flying before him; in which he was imitated by these two or three Couple of Human, or rather two-leg'd Curs on horseback which we have mentioned before.

Now thou, whoever thou art, whether a Muse, or by what other Name soever thou chusest to be called, who presidest over Biography, and hast inspired all the Writers of Lives in these our Times: Thou who didst infuse such wonderful Humour into the Pen of immortal *Gulliver*, who hast carefully guided the Judgment, whilst thou hast exalted the nervous manly Style of thy *Mallet*:[10] Thou who hadst no Hand in that Dedication, and Preface, or the Translations which thou wouldst willingly have struck out of the Life of *Cicero*:[11] Lastly, Thou who without the Assistance of the least Spice of Literature, and even against his Inclination, hast, in some Pages of his Book, forced *Colley Cibber* to write *English*;[12] do thou assist me in what I find my self unequal to. Do thou introduce on the Plain, the young, the gay, the brave *Joseph Andrews*, whilst Men shall view him with Admiration and Envy; tender Virgins with Love and anxious Concern for his Safety.

No sooner did *Joseph Andrews* perceive the Distress of his Friend, when first the quick-scenting Dogs attacked him, than he grasped his Cudgel[13] in his Right-hand, a Cudgel which his Father had of his Grandfather, to whom a mighty strong Man of *Kent*[14] had given it for a Present in that Day, when he broke three Heads on the Stage. It was a Cudgel of mighty Strength and wonderful Art, made by one of Mr *Deard*'s best Workmen,[15] whom no other Artificer can equal; and who hath made all those Sticks which the Beaus have lately walked with about the Park[16] in a Morning: But this was far his Master-piece; on its Head was engraved a Nose and Chin, which might have been mistaken for a Pair of Nut-crackers. The

Learned have imagined it designed to represent the *Gorgon*: but it was in fact copied from the Face of a certain long *English* Baronet of infinite Wit, Humour, and Gravity.[17] He did intend to have engraved here many Histories: As the first Night of Captain *B———*'s Play, where you would have seen Criticks in Embroidery transplanted from the Boxes to the Pit, whose ancient Inhabitants were exalted to the Galleries, where they played on Catcalls.[18] He did intend to have painted an Auction-Room, where Mr *Cock*[19] would have appeared aloft in his Pulpit, trumpeting forth the Praises of a *China* Bason; and with Astonishment wondering that *Nobody bids more for that fine, that superb ———*. He did intend to have engraved many other things, but was forced to leave all out for want of room.

No sooner had *Joseph* grasped this Cudgel in his Hands, than Lightning darted from his Eyes; and the heroick Youth, swift of Foot,[20] ran with the utmost speed to his Friend's Assistance. He overtook him just as *Rockwood* had laid hold of the Skirt of his Cassock, which being torn hung to the ground. Reader, we would make a Simile on this Occasion, but for two Reasons: The first is, it would interrupt the Description, which should be *rapid* in this Part; but that doth not weigh much, many Precedents occurring for such an Interruption: The second, and much the greater Reason is, that we could find no Simile adequate to our Purpose: For indeed, what Instance could we bring to set before our Reader's Eyes at once the Idea of Friendship, Courage, Youth, Beauty, Strength, and Swiftness; all which blazed in the Person of *Joseph Andrews*. Let those therefore that describe Lions and Tigers, and Heroes fiercer than both, raise their Poems or Plays with the Simile of *Joseph Andrews*, who is himself above the reach of any Simile.

Now *Rockwood* had laid fast hold on the Parson's Skirts, and stopt his Flight; which *Joseph* no sooner perceived, than he levelled his Cudgel at his Head, and laid him sprawling. *Jowler* and *Ringwood* then fell on his Great-Coat, and had undoubtedly brought him to the Ground, had not *Joseph*, collecting all his Force, given *Jowler* such a Rap on the Back, that quitting his hold he ran howling over the Plain: A harder Fate remained for thee, O *Ringwood*. *Ringwood* the best Hound that ever pursued a Hare, who never threw his Tongue but where the Scent was undoubtedly true; good at *trailing*; and *sure in a Highway*, no *Babler*, no *Over-runner*,[21] respected by the whole Pack, who, whenever he opened,[22] knew the Game was at hand. He fell by the Stroke of *Joseph*. *Thunder*, and *Plunder*, and *Wonder*, and *Blunder*, were the next Victims of his Wrath, and measured their Lengths on the Ground. Then *Fairmaid*, a Bitch which Mr *John Temple*[23] had bred up in his House, and fed at his own Table, and lately sent the

Squire fifty Miles for a present, ran fiercely at *Joseph*, and bit him by the Leg; no Dog was ever fiercer than she, being descended from an *Amazonian* Breed, and had worried Bulls in her own Country, but now waged an unequal Fight; and had shared the Fate of these we have mentioned before, had not *Diana*[24] (the Reader may believe it or not, as he pleases) in that instant interposed, and in the Shape of the Huntsman snatched her Favourite up in her Arms.

The Parson now faced about, and with his Crab-Stick felled many to the Earth, and scattered others, till he was attacked by *Cæsar* and pulled to the Ground; then *Joseph* flew to his Rescue, and with such Might fell on the Victor, that, O eternal Blot to his Name! *Cæsar* ran yelping away.

The Battle now raged with the most dreadful Violence, when lo the Huntsman, a Man of Years and Dignity, lifted his Voice, and called his Hounds from the Fight; telling them, in a Language they understood, that it was in vain to contend longer; for that Fate had decreed the Victory to their Enemies.

Thus far the Muse hath with her usual Dignity related this prodigious Battle, a Battle we apprehend never equalled by any Poet, Romance or Life-writer whatever, and having brought it to a Conclusion she ceased; we shall therefore proceed in our ordinary Style with the Continuation of this History. The Squire and his Companions, whom the Figure of *Adams* and the Gallantry of *Joseph* had at first thrown into a violent Fit of Laughter, and who had hitherto beheld the Engagement with more Delight than any Chace, Shooting-match, Race, Cock-fighting, Bull or Bear-baiting had ever given them, began now to apprehend the Danger of their Hounds, many of which lay sprawling in the Fields. The Squire therefore having first called his Friends about him, as Guards for Safety of his Person, rode manfully up to the Combatants, and summoning all the Terror he was Master of, into his Countenance, demanded with an authoritative Voice of *Joseph*, what he meant by assaulting his Dogs in that manner. *Joseph* answer'd with great Intrepidity, that they had first fallen on his Friend; and if they had belonged to the greatest Man in the Kingdom, he would have treated them in the same way; for whilst his Veins contained a single Droop of Blood, he would not stand idle by, and see that Gentleman (*pointing to* Adams) abused either by Man or Beast; and having so said, both he and *Adams* brandished their wooden Weapons, and put themselves into such a Posture, that the Squire and his Company thought proper to preponderate, before they offered to revenge the Cause of their four-footed Allies.

At this Instant *Fanny*, whom the Apprehension of *Joseph*'s Danger had alarmed so much, that forgetting her own, she had made the utmost Expedition, came up. The Squire and all the Horsemen were so surprized with her Beauty, that they immediately fixed both their Eyes and Thoughts solely on her, every one declaring he had never seen so charming a Creature. Neither Mirth nor Anger engaged them a Moment longer; but all sat in silent Amaze. The Huntsman only was free from her Attraction, who was busy in cutting the Ears of the Dogs,[25] and endeavouring to recover them to Life; in which he succeeded so well, that only two of no great Note remained slaughtered on the Field of Action. Upon this the Huntsman declared, ''Twas well it was no worse; for his part he could not blame the Gentleman, and wondered his Master would encourage the Dogs to hunt *Christians*; that it was the surest way to spoil them, to make them follow *Vermin* instead of sticking to a Hare.'

The Squire being informed of the little Mischief that had been done; and perhaps having more Mischief of another kind in his Head, accosted Mr *Adams* with a more favourable Aspect than before: he told him he was sorry for what had happened; that he had endeavoured all he could to prevent it the moment he was acquainted with his Cloth, and greatly commended the Courage of his Servant; for so he imagined *Joseph* to be. He then invited Mr *Adams* to Dinner, and desired the young Woman might come with him. *Adams* refused a long while; but the Invitation was repeated with so much Earnestness and Courtesy, that at length he was forced to accept it. His Wig and Hat, and other Spoils of the Field, being gathered together by *Joseph*, (for otherwise probably they would have been forgotten;) he put himself into the best Order he could; and then the Horse and Foot moved forward in the same Pace towards the Squire's House, which stood at a very little distance.

Whilst they were on the Road, the lovely *Fanny* attracted the Eyes of all; they endeavoured to outvie one another in Encomiums on her Beauty; which the Reader will pardon my not relating, as they had not any thing new or uncommon in them: So must he likewise my not setting down the many curious Jests which were made on *Adams*, some of them declaring that Parson-hunting was the best Sport in the World: Others commending his standing at Bay, which they said he had done as well as any Badger; with such like Merriment, which though it would ill become the Dignity of this History, afforded much Laughter and Diversion to the Squire, and his facetious Companions.

CHAPTER VII

A Scene of Roasting[1] *very nicely adapted to the present Taste and Times.*

They arrived at the Squire's House just as his Dinner was ready. A little Dispute arose on the account of *Fanny*, whom the Squire, who was a Batchelor, was desirous to place at his own Table; but she would not consent, nor would Mr *Adams* permit her to be parted from *Joseph*: so that she was at length with him consigned over to the Kitchin, where the Servants were ordered to make him drunk; a Favour which was likewise intended for *Adams*: which Design being executed, the Squire thought he should easily accomplish, what he had, when he first saw her, intended to perpetrate with *Fanny*.

It may not be improper, before we proceed farther, to open a little the Character of this Gentleman, and that of his Friends. The Master of this House then was a Man of a very considerable Fortune; a Batchelor, as we have said, and about forty Years of Age: he had been educated (if we may use the Expression) in the Country, and at his own Home, under the Care of his Mother and a Tutor, who had Orders never to correct him nor to compel him to learn more than he liked, which it seems was very little, and that only in his Childhood; for from the Age of fifteen he addicted himself entirely to Hunting and other rural Amusements, for which his Mother took care to equip him with Horses, Hounds, and all other Necessaries: and his Tutor endeavouring to ingratiate himself with his young Pupil, who would, he knew, be able handsomely to provide for him, became his Companion, not only at these Exercises, but likewise over a Bottle, which the young Squire had a very early Relish for. At the Age of twenty, his Mother began to think she had not fulfilled the Duty of a Parent; she therefore resolved to persuade her Son, if possible, to that which she imagined would well supply all that he might have learned at a publick School or University. This is what they commonly call *Travelling*; which, with the help of the Tutor who was fixed on to attend him, she easily succeeded in. He made in three Years the Tour of *Europe* as they term it, and returned home, well furnish'd with *French* Clothes, Phrases and Servants, with a hearty Contempt for his own Country; especially what had any Savour of the plain Spirit and Honesty of our Ancestors. His Mother greatly applauded herself at his Return; and now being Master of his own Fortune, he soon procured himself a Seat in Parliament, and was in the common Opinion one of the finest Gentlemen of his Age: But what distinguished him chiefly, was a strange Delight which he took in every thing which is ridiculous, odious, and absurd in his own Species; so that he never chose a Companion without one or more of these Ingredients, and those who were marked by Nature in the most eminent Degree with them, were most his Favourites: if he ever found a Man who either had not, or endeavoured to conceal these Imperfections, he took great pleasure in inventing Methods of forcing him into Absurdities, which were not natural to him, or in drawing forth and exposing those that were; for which purpose he was always provided with a Set of Fellows whom we have before called Curs; and who did indeed no great honour to the Canine Kind: Their Business was to hunt out and display every thing that had any Savour of the above mentioned Qualities, and especially in the gravest and best Characters: But if they failed in their Search, they were to turn even Virtue and Wisdom themselves into Ridicule for the Diversion of their Master and Feeder. The Gentlemen of Cur-like Disposition, who were now at his House, and whom he had brought with him from *London*, were an old Half-pay Officer, a Player, a dull Poet, a Quack-Doctor, a Scraping-Fiddler, and a lame *German* Dancing-Master.

As soon as Dinner was served, while Mr *Adams* was saying Grace, the Captain convey'd his Chair from behind him; so that when he endeavoured to seat himself, he fell down on the Ground; and thus compleated Joke the first, to the great Entertainment of the whole Company. The second Joke was performed by the Poet, who sat next him on the other side, and took an Opportunity, while poor *Adams* was respectfully drinking to the Master of the House, to overturn a Plate of Soup into his Breeches; which, with the many Apologies he made, and the Parson's gentle Answers, caused much Mirth in the Company. Joke the third was served up by one of the Waiting-men, who had been ordered to convey a Quantity of Gin into Mr *Adams*'s Ale, which he declaring to be the best Liquor he ever drank, but rather too rich of the Malt, contributed again to their Laughter. Mr *Adams*, from whom we had most of this Relation, could not recollect all the Jests of this kind practised on him, which the inoffensive Disposition of his own Heart made him slow in discovering; and indeed had it not been for the Information which we received from a Servant of the Family, this Part of our History, which we take to be none of the least curious, must have been deplorably imperfect; tho' we must own it probable, that some more Jokes were (as they call it) *cracked* during their Dinner; but we have by no means been able to come at the Knowledge of them. When Dinner was removed, the Poet began to repeat some Verses, which he said were made *extempore*. The following is a Copy of them, procured with the greatest difficulty.

An extempore *Poem on Parson* Adams.

> *Did ever Mortal such a Parson view;*
> *His Cassock old, his Wig not over-new?*
> *Well might the Hounds have him for Fox mistaken,*
> *In Smell more like to that than rusty Bacon**.[2]
> *But would it not make any Mortal stare,*
> *To see this Parson taken for a Hare?*
> *Could* Phœbus *err thus grossly, even he*
> *For a good Player might have taken thee.*

At which Words the Bard whip'd off the Player's Wig, and received the Approbation of the Company, rather perhaps for the Dexterity of his Hand than his Head. The Player, instead of retorting the Jest on the Poet, began to display his Talents on the same Subject. He repeated many Scraps of Wit out of Plays, reflecting on the whole Body of the Clergy, which were received with great Acclamations by all present. It was now the Dancing-Master's Turn to exhibit his Talents; he therefore addressing himself to *Adams* in broken *English*, told him, 'He was a Man ver well made for de Dance, and he suppose by his Walk, dat he had learn of some great Master. He said it was ver pretty Quality in Clergyman to dance;' and concluded with desiring him to dance a Minuet, telling him, 'his Cassock would serve for Petticoats; and that he would himself be his Partner.' At which Words, without waiting for an Answer, he pulled out his Gloves, and the Fiddler was preparing his Fiddle. The Company all offered the Dancing-Master Wagers that the Parson outdanced him, which he refused, saying, 'He believed so too; for he had never seen any Man in his Life who looked de Dance so well as de Gentleman:' He then stepped forwards to take *Adams* by the Hand, which the latter hastily withdrew, and at the same time clenching his Fist, advised him not to carry the Jest too far, for he would not endure being put upon. The

---

* All Hounds that will hunt Fox or other Vermin, will hunt a Piece of rusty Bacon trailed on the Ground.

Dancing-Master no sooner saw the Fist than he prudently retired out of its reach, and stood aloof mimicking *Adams*, whose Eyes were fixed on him, not guessing what he was at, but to avoid his laying hold on him, which he had once attempted. In the mean while, the Captain perceiving an Opportunity pinned a Cracker or Devil to the Cassock, and then lighted it with their little smoking Candle. *Adams* being a Stranger to this Sport, and believing he had been blown up in reality, started from his Chair, and jumped about the Room, to the infinite Joy of the Beholders, who declared he was the best Dancer in the Universe. As soon as the Devil had done tormenting him, and he had a little recovered his Confusion, he returned to the Table, and standing up in the Posture of one who intended to make a Speech, they all cried out, *Hear him, Hear him*; and he then spoke in the following manner: 'Sir, I am sorry to see one to whom Providence hath been so bountiful in bestowing his Favours, make so ill and ungrateful a Return for them; for tho' you have not insulted me yourself, it is visible you have delighted in those that do it, nor have once discouraged the many Rudenesses which have been shewn towards me; indeed towards yourself, if you rightly understood them; for I am your Guest, and by the Laws of Hospitality entitled to your Protection. One Gentleman hath thought proper to produce some Poetry upon me, of which I shall only say, that I had rather be the Subject than the Composer. He hath pleased to treat me with Disrespect as a Parson; I apprehend my Order is not the Object of Scorn, nor that I can become so, unless by being a Disgrace to it, which I hope Poverty will never be called. Another Gentleman indeed hath repeated some Sentences, where the Order itself is mentioned with Contempt. He says they are taken from Plays. I am sure such Plays are a Scandal to the Government which permits them, and cursed will be the Nation where they are represented. How others have treated me, I need not observe; they themselves, when they reflect, must allow the Behaviour to be as improper to my Years as to my Cloth. You found me, Sir, travelling with two of my Parishioners, (I omit your Hounds falling on me; for I have quite forgiven it, whether it proceeded from the Wantonness or Negligence of the Huntsman,) my Appearance might very well persuade you that your Invitation was an Act of Charity, tho' in reality we were well provided; yes, Sir, if we had had an hundred Miles to travel, we had sufficient to bear our Expences in a noble manner.' (At which Words he produced the half Guinea which was found in the Basket.) 'I do not shew you this out of Ostentation of Riches, but to convince you I speak Truth. Your seating me at your Table was an Honour which I did not ambitiously affect; when I was here, I endeavoured to behave towards you with the utmost Respect; if I have failed, it was not with Design, nor could I, certainly, so far be guilty as to deserve the Insults I have suffered. If they were meant therefore either to my Order or my Poverty (and you see I am not very poor) the Shame doth not lie at my door, and I heartily pray, that the Sin may be averted from yours.' He thus finished, and received a general Clap from the whole Company. Then the Gentleman of the House told him, 'he was sorry for what had happened; that he could not accuse him of any Share in it: That the Verses were, as himself had well observed, so bad, that he might easily answer them; and for the Serpent,[3] it was undoubtedly a very great Affront done him by the Dancing-Master, for which if he well threshed him, as he deserved, he should be very much pleased to see it;' (in which probably he spoke Truth). *Adams* answered, 'Whoever had done it, it was not his Profession to punish him that way; but for the Person whom he had accused, I am a Witness,' says he, 'of his Innocence, for I had my Eye on him all the while. Whoever he was, God forgive him, and bestow on him a little more Sense as well as Humanity.' The Captain answer'd with a surly Look and Accent, 'That he hoped he did not mean to reflect on him; d—n him, he had as much *Imanity* as another, and if any Man said he had not, he would convince him of his Mistake by cutting his Throat.' *Adams* smiling, said, 'He believed he had spoke right by Accident.' To which the Captain returned, 'What do you mean by my speaking right? if you was not a Parson, I would not take these Words; but your Gown protects you. If any Man who wears a Sword had said so much, I had pulled him by the Nose before this.' *Adams* replied, 'If he attempted any Rudeness to his Person, he would not find any Protection for himself in his Gown;' and clenching his Fist, declared he had threshed many a stouter Man. The Gentleman did all he could to encourage this warlike Disposition in *Adams*, and was in hopes to have produced a Battle: But he was disappointed; for the Captain made no other Answer than, 'It is very well you are a Parson,' and so drinking off a Bumper to old Mother Church, ended the Dispute.

Then the Doctor, who had hitherto been silent, and who was the gravest, but most mischievous Dog of all, in a very pompous Speech highly applauded what *Adams* had said; and as much discommended the Behaviour to him; he proceeded to Encomiums on the Church and Poverty; and lastly recommended Forgiveness of what had past to *Adams*, who immediately answered, 'That every thing was forgiven;' and in the Warmth of his Goodness he filled a Bumper of strong Beer, (a Liquor he preferred to Wine) and drank a Health to the whole Company, shaking the Captain and the Poet heartily by the Hand, and addressing himself with great Respect to the Doctor; who indeed had not laughed outwardly at any thing that past, as he had a perfect Command of his Muscles, and could laugh inwardly without betraying the least Symptoms in his Countenance. The Doctor now began a second formal Speech, in which he declaimed against all Levity of Conversation; and what is usually called Mirth. He said, 'There were Amusements fitted for Persons of all Ages and Degrees, from the Rattle to the discussing a Point of Philosophy, and that Men discovered themselves in nothing more than in the Choice of their Amusements; for,' says he, 'as it must greatly raise our Expectation of the future Conduct in Life of Boys, whom in their tender Years we perceive instead of Taw [4] or Balls, or other childish Play-things, to chuse, at their Leisure-Hours, to exercise their Genius in Contentions of Wit, Learning, and such like; so must it inspire one with equal Contempt of a Man, if we should discover him playing at Taw or other childish Play.' *Adams* highly commended the Doctor's Opinion, and said, 'He had often wondered at some Passages in ancient Authors, where *Scipio*, *Lælius*,[5] and other great Men were represented to have passed many Hours in Amusements of the most trifling kind.' The Doctor reply'd, 'He had by him an old *Greek* Manuscript where a favourite Diversion of *Socrates* was recorded.' 'Ay,' says the Parson eagerly, 'I should be most infinitely obliged to you for the Favour of perusing it.' The Doctor promised to send it him, and farther said, that he believed he could describe it. 'I think,' says he, 'as near as I can remember, it was this. There was a Throne erected, on one side of which sat a King, and on the other a Queen, with their Guards and Attendants ranged on both sides; to them was introduced an Ambassador, which Part *Socrates* always used to perform himself; and when he was led up to the Footsteps of the Throne, he addressed himself to the Monarchs in some grave Speech, full of Virtue and Goodness, and Morality, and such like. After which, he was seated between the King and Queen, and royally entertained. This I think was the chief part. —— Perhaps I may have forgot some Particulars; for it is long since I read it.' *Adams* said, 'It was indeed a Diversion worthy the Relaxation of so great a Man; and thought something resembling it should be instituted among our great Men, instead of Cards and other idle Passtime, in which he was informed they trifled away too much of their Lives.' He added, 'The Christian Religion was a nobler Subject for these Speeches than any *Socrates* could have invented.' The Gentleman of the House approved what Mr *Adams* said, and declared, 'he was resolved to perform the Ceremony this very Evening.' To which the Doctor objected, as no one was prepared with a Speech, 'unless,' said he (turning to *Adams* with a Gravity of Countenance which would have deceived a more knowing Man) 'you have a Sermon about you, Doctor.' — 'Sir,' says *Adams*, 'I never travel without one, for fear what may happen.' He was easily prevailed on by his worthy Friend, as he now called the Doctor, to undertake the Part of the Ambassador; so that the Gentleman sent immediate Orders to have the Throne erected; which was performed before they had drank two Bottles: And perhaps the Reader will hereafter have no great reason to admire the Nimbleness of the Servants. Indeed, to confess the Truth, the Throne was no more than this; there was a great Tub of Water provided, on each side of which were placed two Stools raised higher than the Surface of the Tub, and over the Whole was laid a Blanket; on these Stools were placed the King and Queen, namely, the Master of the House, and the Captain. And now the Ambassador was introduced, between the Poet and the Doctor, who having read his Sermon to the great Entertainment of all present, was led up to his Place, and being seated between their Majesties, they immediately rose up, when the Blanket wanting its Supports at either end, gave way, and soused *Adams* over Head and Ears in the Water;[6] the Captain made his Escape, but unluckily the Gentleman himself not being as nimble as he ought, *Adams* caught hold of him before he descended from his Throne, and pulled him in with him, to the entire secret Satisfaction of all the Company. *Adams* after ducking the Squire twice or thrice leapt out of the Tub, and looked sharp for the Doctor, whom he would certainly have convey'd to the same Place of Honour; but he had wisely withdrawn: he then searched for his Crab stick, and having found that, as well as his Fellow-Travellers, he declared he would not stay a moment longer in such a House. He then departed, without taking leave of his Host, whom he had exacted a more severe Revenge on, than he intended: For as he did not use sufficient care to dry himself in time, he caught a Cold by the Accident, which threw him into a Fever, that had like to have cost him his Life.

CHAPTER VIII

Which some Readers will think too short, and others too long.

Adams, and *Joseph,* who was no less enraged than his Friend, at the Treatment he met with, went out with their Sticks in their Hands; and carried off *Fanny,* notwithstanding the Opposition of the Servants, who did all, without proceeding to Violence, in their power to detain them. They walked as fast as they could, not so much from any Apprehension of being pursued, as that Mr *Adams* might by Exercise prevent any harm from the Water. The Gentleman who had given such Orders to his Servants concerning *Fanny,* that he did not in the least fear her getting away, no sooner heard that she was gone, than he began to rave, and immediately dispatched several with Orders, either to bring her back, or never return. The Poet, the Player, and all but the Dancing-Master and Doctor went on this Errand.

The Night was very dark, in which our Friends began their Journey; however they made such Expedition, that they soon arrived at an Inn, which was at seven Miles Distance. Here they unanimously consented to pass the Evening, Mr *Adams* being now as dry as he was before he had set out on his Embassy.

This Inn, which indeed we might call an Ale-house, had not the Words, *The New Inn,* been writ on the Sign, afforded them no better Provision than Bread and Cheese, and Ale; on which, however, they made a very comfortable Meal; for Hunger is better than a *French* Cook.

They had no sooner supped, than *Adams* returning Thanks to the Almighty for his Food, declared he had eat his homely Commons,[1] with much greater Satisfaction than his splendid Dinner, and exprest great Contempt for the Folly of Mankind, who sacrificed their Hopes of Heaven to the Acquisition of vast Wealth, since so much Comfort was to be found in the humblest State and the lowest Provision. Very true, Sir, says a grave Man who sat smoking his Pipe by the Fire, and who was a Traveller as well as himself. 'I have often been as much surprized as you are, when I consider the Value which Mankind in general set on Riches, since every day's Experience shews us how little is in their power; for what indeed truly desirable can they bestow on us? Can they give Beauty to the Deformed, Strength to the Weak, or Health to the Infirm? Surely if they could, we should not see so many ill-favoured Faces haunting the

Assemblies of the Great, nor would such numbers of feeble Wretches languish in their Coaches and Palaces. No, not the Wealth of a Kingdom can purchase any Paint, to dress pale Ugliness in the Bloom of that young Maiden, nor any Drugs to equip Disease with the Vigour of that young Man. Do not Riches bring us Sollicitude instead of Rest, Envy instead of Affection, and Danger instead of Safety? Can they prolong their own Possession, or lengthen his Days who enjoys them? So far otherwise, that the Sloth, the Luxury, the Care which attend them, shorten the Lives of Millions, and bring them with Pain and Misery, to an untimely Grave. Where then is their Value, if they can neither embellish, or strengthen our Forms, sweeten or prolong our Lives? Again —— Can they adorn the Mind more than the Body? Do they not rather swell the Heart with Vanity, puff up the Cheeks with Pride, shut our Ears to every Call of Virtue, and our Bowels to every Motive of Compassion!' 'Give me your Hand, Brother,' said *Adams* in a Rapture; 'for I suppose you are a Clergyman.' 'No truly,' answered the other, (indeed he was a Priest of the Church of *Rome*; but those who understand our Laws, will not wonder he was not over-ready to own it.)[2] 'Whatever you are,' cries *Adams*, 'you have spoken my Sentiments: I believe I have preached every Syllable of your Speech twenty times over: For it hath always appeared to me easier for a Cable Rope (which by the way is the true rendering of that Word we have translated *Camel*) to go through the Eye of a Needle, than for a rich Man to get into the Kingdom of Heaven.'[3] 'That, Sir,' said the other, 'will be easily granted you by Divines, and is deplorably true: But as the Prospect of our Good at a distance doth not so forcibly affect us, it might be of some Service to Mankind to be made thoroughly sensible, which I think they might be with very little serious Attention, that even the Blessings of this World, are not to be purchased with Riches. A Doctrine in my Opinion, not only metaphysically, but if I may so say, mathematically demonstrable; and which I have been always so perfectly convinced of, that I have a Contempt for nothing so much as for Gold.' *Adams* now began a long Discourse; but as most which he said occurs among many Authors, who have treated this Subject, I shall omit inserting it. During its Continuance *Joseph* and *Fanny* retired to Rest, and the Host likewise left the Room. When the *English* Parson had concluded, the *Romish* resumed the Discourse, which he continued with great Bitterness and Invective; and at last ended by desiring *Adams* to lend him eighteen Pence to pay his Reckoning; promising, if he never paid him, he might be assured of his Prayers. The good Man answered, that eighteen Pence would be too little to carry him any very long Journey; that he had half a Guinea in his Pocket, which he would divide with him. He then fell to searching his Pockets, but could find no Money: For indeed the Company with whom he dined, had past one Jest upon him: which we did not then enumerate, and had picked his Pocket of all that Treasure which he had so ostentatiously produced.

'Bless me,' cried *Adams*, 'I have certainly lost it, I can never have spent it. Sir, as I am a Christian I had a whole half Guinea in my Pocket this Morning, and have not now a single Halfpenny of it left. Sure the Devil must have taken it from me.' 'Sir,' answered the Priest smiling, 'You need make no Excuses; if you are not willing to lend me the Money, I am contented.' 'Sir,' cries *Adams*, 'if I had the greatest Sum in the World; ay, if I had ten Pounds about me, I would bestow it all to rescue any Christian from Distress. I am more vexed at my Loss on your account than my own. Was ever any thing so unlucky? because I have no Money in my Pocket, I shall be suspected to be no Christian.' 'I am more unlucky,' quoth the other, 'if you are as generous as you say: For really a Crown would have made me happy, and conveyed me in plenty to the Place I am going, which is not above twenty Miles off, and where I can arrive by to-morrow Night. I assure you I am not accustomed to travel Pennyless: But am just arrived in *England*, and we were forced by a Storm in our Passage to throw all we had overboard. I don't suspect but this Fellow will take my Word for the Trifle I owe him; but I hate to appear so mean as to confess myself without a Shilling to such People: For these, and indeed too many others know little Difference in their Estimation between a Beggar and a Thief.' However, he thought he should deal better with the Host that Evening than the next Morning; he therefore resolved to set out immediately, notwithstanding the Darkness; and accordingly as soon as the Host returned he communicated to him the Situation of his Affairs; upon which the Host scratching his Head, answered, 'Why, I do not know, Master, if it be so, and you have no Money, I must trust I think, tho' I had rather always have ready Money if I could; but, marry, you look like so honest a Gentleman, that I don't fear your paying me, if it was twenty times as much.' The Priest made no Reply, but taking leave of him and *Adams*, as fast as he could, not without Confusion, and perhaps with some Distrust of *Adams*'s Sincerity, departed.

He was no sooner gone than the Host fell a shaking his Head, and declared if he had suspected the Fellow had no Money, he would not have drawn him a single Drop of Drink; saying, he despaired of ever seeing his Face again; for that he looked like a confounded Rogue. 'Rabbit [4] the Fellow,' cries he, 'I thought by his talking so much about Riches, that he had a hundred Pounds at least in his Pocket.' *Adams* chid him for his Suspicions, which he said were not becoming a Christian; and then without reflecting on his Loss, or considering how he himself should depart in the Morning, he retired to a very homely Bed, as his Companions had before; however, Health and Fatigue gave them a sweeter Repose than is often in the power of Velvet and Down to bestow.

CHAPTER IX

Containing as surprizing and bloody Adventures as can be found in this, or perhaps any other authentick History.

It was almost Morning when *Joseph Andrews*, whose Eyes the Thoughts of his dear *Fanny* had opened, as he lay fondly meditating on that lovely Creature, heard a violent knocking at the Door over which he lay; he presently jumped out of Bed, and opening the Window, was asked if there were no Travellers in the House; and presently by another Voice, If two Men and a young Woman had not taken up their Lodgings there that Night. Tho' he knew not the Voices, he began to entertain a Suspicion of the Truth; for indeed he had received some Information from one of the Servants of the Squire's House, of his Design; and answered in the Negative. One of the Servants who knew the Host well, called out to him by his Name, just as he had opened another Window, and asked him the same Question; to which he answered in the Affirmative. O ho! said another; have we found you? And ordered the Host to come down and open his Door. *Fanny*, who was as wakeful as *Joseph*, no sooner heard all this, than she leap'd from her Bed, and hastily putting on her Gown and Petticoats, ran as fast as possible to *Joseph*'s Room, who then was almost drest; he immediately let her in, and embracing her with the most passionate Tenderness, bid her fear nothing: For he would die in her Defence. 'Is that a Reason why I should not fear,' says she, 'when I should lose what is dearer to me than the whole World?' *Joseph* then kissing her Hand, said he could almost thank the Occasion which had extorted from her a Tenderness she would never indulge him with before. He then ran and waked his Bedfellow *Adams*, who was yet fast asleep, notwithstanding many Calls from *Joseph*: But was no sooner made sensible of their Danger than he leaped from his Bed, without considering the Presence of *Fanny*, who hastily turned her Face from him, and enjoyed a double Benefit from the dark, which as it would have prevented any Offence to an Innocence less pure, or a Modesty less delicate, so it concealed even those Blushes which were raised in her.

Adams had soon put on all his Clothes but his Breeches, which in the Hurry he forgot; however, they were pretty well supplied by the length of his other Garments: And now the House-Door being opened, the Captain, the Poet, the Player, and three Servants came in. The Captain told the Host, that two Fellows who were in his House had run away with a young Woman, and desired to know in which Room she lay. The Host, who presently believed the Story, directed them, and instantly the Captain and Poet, jostling one another, ran up. The Poet who was the nimblest entering the Chamber first, searched the Bed and every other part, but to no purpose; the Bird was flown, as the impatient Reader, who might otherwise have been in pain for her, was before advertised. They then enquired where the Men lay, and were approaching the Chamber, when *Joseph* roared out in a loud Voice, that he would shoot the first Man who offered to attack the Door. The Captain enquired what Fire-Arms they had; to which the Host answered, he believed they had none; nay, he was almost convinced of it: For he had heard one ask the other in the Evening, what they should have done, if they had been overtaken when they had no Arms; to which the other answered, they would have defended themselves with their Sticks as long as they were able, and G— would assist a just Cause. This satisfied the Captain, but not the Poet, who prudently retreated down Stairs, saying it was his Business to record great Actions, and not to do them. The Captain was no sooner well satisfied that there were no Fire-Arms, than bidding Defiance to Gunpowder, and swearing he loved the Smell of it, he ordered the Servants to follow him, and marching boldly up, immediately attempted to force the Door, which the Servants soon helped him to accomplish. When it was opened, they discovered the Enemy drawn up three deep; *Adams* in the Front, and *Fanny* in the Rear. The Captain told *Adams*, that if they would go all back to the House again, they should be civilly treated: but unless they consented, he had Orders to carry the young Lady with him, whom there was great Reason to believe they had stolen from her Parents; for notwithstanding her Disguise, her Air, which she could not conceal, sufficiently discovered her Birth to be infinitely superiour to theirs. *Fanny* bursting into Tears, solemnly assured him he was mistaken; that she was a poor helpless

Foundling, and had no Relation in the World which she knew of; and throwing herself on her Knees, begged that he would not attempt to take her from her Friends, who she was convinced would die before they would lose her, which *Adams* confirmed with Words not far from amounting to an Oath. The Captain swore he had no leisure to talk, and bidding them thank themselves for what happened, he ordered the Servants to fall on, at the same time endeavouring to pass by *Adams* in order to lay hold on *Fanny*; but the Parson interrupting him, received a Blow from one of them, which without considering whence it came, he returned to the Captain, and gave him so dextrous a Knock in that part of the Stomach which is vulgarly called the Pit, that he staggered some Paces backwards. The Captain, who was not accustomed to this kind of play, and who wisely apprehended the Consequence of such another Blow, two of them seeming to him equal to a Thrust through the Body, drew forth his Hanger,[1] as *Adams* approached him, and was levelling a Blow at his Head, which would probably have silenced the Preacher for ever, had not *Joseph* in that Instant lifted up a certain huge Stone Pot of the Chamber with one Hand, which six Beaus could not have lifted with both,[2] and discharged it, together with the Contents, full in the Captain's Face. The uplifted Hanger dropped from his Hand, and he fell prostrate on the Floor *with a lumpish Noise, and his Halfpence rattled in his Pocket*;[3] the red Liquor which his Veins contained, and the white Liquor which the Pot contained, ran in one Stream down his Face and his Clothes. Nor had *Adams* quite escaped, some of the Water having in its Passage shed its Honours on his Head, and began to trickle down the Wrinkles or rather Furrows of his Cheeks, and when one of the Servants snatching a Mop out of a Pail of Water which had already done its Duty in washing the House, pushed it in the Parson's Face; yet could not he bear him down; for the Parson wresting the Mop from the Fellow with one Hand, with the other brought his Enemy as low as the Earth, having given him a Stroke over that part of the Face, where, in some Men of Pleasure, the natural and artificial Noses are conjoined.[4]

Hitherto Fortune seemed to incline the Victory on the Travellers side, when, according to her Custom, she began to shew the Fickleness of her Disposition: for now the Host entering the Field, or rather Chamber, of Battle, flew directly at *Joseph*, and darting his Head into his Stomach (for he was a stout Fellow, and an expert Boxer) almost staggered him; but *Joseph* stepping one Leg back, did with his left Hand so chuck him under the Chin that he reeled. The Youth was pursuing his Blow with his right Hand, when he received from one of the Servants such a Stroke with a

Cudgel on his Temples, that it instantly deprived him of Sense, and he measured his Length on the Ground.

Fanny rent the Air with her Cries, and *Adams* was coming to the assistance of *Joseph*: but the two Serving-Men and the Host now fell on him, and soon subdued him, tho' he fought like a Madman, and looked so black with the Impressions he had received from the Mop, that *Don Quixotte* would certainly have taken him for an inchanted *Moor*.[5] But now follows the most tragical Part; for the Captain was risen again, and seeing *Joseph* on the Floor, and *Adams* secured, he instantly laid hold on *Fanny*, and with the Assistance of the Poet and Player, who hearing the Battle was over, were now come up, dragged her, crying and tearing her Hair, from the Sight of her *Joseph*, and with a perfect Deafness to all her Entreaties, carried her down Stairs by Violence, and fastened her on the Player's Horse; and the Captain mounting his own, and leading that on which this poor miserable Wretch was, departed without any more Consideration of her Cries than a Butcher hath of those of a Lamb; for indeed his Thoughts were only entertained with the Degree of Favour which he promised himself from the Squire on the Success of this Adventure.

The Servants who were ordered to secure *Adams* and *Joseph* as safe as possible, that the Squire might receive no Interruption to his Design on poor *Fanny*, immediately by the Poet's Advice tied *Adams* to one of the Bed-posts, with his Hands behind him, as they did *Joseph* on the other side, as soon as they could bring him to himself; and then leaving them together, back to back, and desiring the Host not to set them at liberty, nor to go near them till he had farther Orders, they departed towards their Master; but happened to take a different Road from that which the Captain had fallen into.

CHAPTER X

A Discourse between the Poet and Player; of no other Use in this History, but to divert the Reader.

Before we proceed any farther in this Tragedy, we shall leave Mr *Joseph* and Mr *Adams* to themselves, and imitate the wise Conductors of the Stage; who in the midst of a grave Action entertain you with some excellent piece of Satire or Humour called a Dance.[1] Which Piece indeed is therefore danced, and not spoke, as it is delivered to the Audience by Persons whose thinking Faculty is by most People held to lie in their Heels; and to whom, as well as Heroes, who think with their Hands, Nature hath only given Heads for the sake of Conformity, and as they are of use in Dancing, to hang their Hats on.

The Poet addressing the Player, proceeded thus: 'As I was saying' (for they had been at this Discourse all the time of the Engagement, above Stairs) 'the Reason you have no good new Plays is evident; it is from your Discouragement of Authors. Gentlemen will not write, Sir, they will not write without the Expectation of Fame or Profit, or perhaps both. Plays are like Trees which will not grow without Nourishment; but like Mushrooms, they shoot up spontaneously, as it were, in a rich Soil. The Muses, like Vines, may be pruned, but not with a Hatchet. The Town like a peevish Child, knows not what it desires, and is always best pleased with a Rattle. A Farce-Writer hath indeed some Chance for Success; but they have lost all Taste for the Sublime. Tho' I believe one Reason of their Depravity is the Badness of the Actors. If a Man writes like an Angel, Sir, those Fellows know not how to give a Sentiment Utterance.' 'Not so fast,' says the Player, 'the modern Actors are as good at least as their Authors, nay, they come nearer their illustrious Predecessors, and I expect a *Booth* on the Stage again, sooner than a *Shakespear* or an *Otway*;[2] and indeed I may turn your Observation against you, and with Truth say, that the Reason no Authors are encouraged, is because we have no good new Plays.' 'I have not affirmed the contrary,' said the Poet, 'but I am surprized you grow so warm; you cannot imagine yourself interested in this Dispute, I hope you have a better Opinion of my Taste, than to apprehend I squinted at yourself. No, Sir, if we had six such Actors as you, we should soon rival the *Bettertons* and *Sandfords*[3] of former Times; for, without a Compliment to you, I think it impossible for any one to have excelled you in most of your Parts. Nay, it is solemn Truth, and I have heard many, and all great Judges, express as much; and you will pardon me if I tell you, I think every time I have seen you lately, you have constantly acquired some new Excellence, like a Snowball. You have deceived me in my Estimation of Perfection, and have outdone what I thought inimitable.' 'You are as little interested,' answer'd the Player, 'in what I have said of other Poets; for d—n me, if there are not manly Strokes, ay whole Scenes, in your last Tragedy, which at least equal *Shakespear*. There is a Delicacy of Sentiment, a Dignity of Expression in it, which I will own many of our Gentlemen did not do adequate Justice to. To confess the Truth, they are bad enough, and I pity an Author who is present at the

Murder of his Works.' —— 'Nay, it is but seldom that it can happen,' returned the Poet, 'the Works of most modern Authors, like dead-born Children, cannot be murdered. It is such wretched half-begotten, half-writ, lifeless, spiritless, low, groveling Stuff, that I almost pity the Actor who is oblig'd to get it by heart, which must be almost as difficult to remember as Words in a Language you don't understand.' 'I am sure,' said the Player, 'if the Sentences have little Meaning when they are writ, when they are spoken they have less. I know scarce one who ever lays an Emphasis right, and much less adapts his Action to his Character. I have seen a tender Lover in an Attitude of fighting with his Mistress, and a brave Hero suing to his Enemy with his Sword in his Hand —— I don't care to abuse my Profession, but rot me if in my Heart I am not inclined to the Poet's Side.' 'It is rather generous in you than just,' said the Poet; 'and tho' I hate to speak ill of any Person's Production; nay I never do it, nor will —— but yet to do Justice to the Actors, what could *Booth* or *Betterton* have made of such horrible Stuff as *Fenton*'s *Mariamne*, *Frowd*'s *Philotas*, or *Mallet*'s *Eurydice*,[4] or those low, dirty, last dying Speeches, which a Fellow in the City or *Wapping*, your *Dillo* or *Lillo*,[5] what was his Name, called Tragedies?' —— 'Very well, Sir,' says the Player, 'and pray what do you think of such Fellows as *Quin* and *Delane*, or that face-making Puppy young *Cibber*, that ill-looked Dog *Macklin*, or that saucy Slut Mrs *Clive*?[6] What work would they make with your *Shakespeares*, *Otways* and *Lees*? How would those harmonious Lines of the last come from their Tongues?

> —— *No more; for I disdain*
> *All Pomp when thou art by — far be the Noise*
> *Of Kings and Crowns from us, whose gentle Souls*
> *Our kinder Fates have steer'd another way.*
> *Free as the Forest Birds we'll pair together,*
> *Without rememb'ring who our Fathers were:*
> *Fly to the Arbors, Grots and flowry Meads,*
> *There in soft Murmurs interchange our Souls,*
> *Together drink the Crystal of the Stream,*
> *Or taste the yellow Fruit which Autumn yields.*
> *And when the golden Evening calls us home,*
> *Wing to our downy Nests and sleep till Morn.*[7]

'Or how would this Disdain of *Otway*,

> *Who'd be that foolish, sordid thing, call'd Man?*[8]

'Hold, hold, hold,' said the Poet, 'Do repeat that tender Speech in the third Act of my Play which you made such a Figure in.' — 'I would willingly,' said the Player, 'but I have forgot it.' — 'Ay, you was not quite perfect enough in it when you play'd it,' cries the Poet, 'or you would have had such an Applause as was never given on the Stage; an Applause I was extremely concerned for your losing.' —— 'Sure,' says the Player, 'if I remember, that was hiss'd more than any Passage in the whole Play.' —— 'Ay your speaking it was hiss'd,' said the Poet. 'My speaking it!' said the Player. —— 'I mean your not speaking it,' said the Poet. 'You was out, and then they hiss'd.' — 'They hiss'd, and then I was out, if I remember,' answer'd the Player; 'and I must say this for myself, that the whole Audience allowed I did your Part Justice, so don't lay the Damnation of your Play to my account.' 'I don't know what you mean by Damnation,' reply'd the Poet. 'Why you know it was acted but one Night,' cried the Player. 'No,' said the Poet, 'you and the whole Town had Enemies; the Pit were all my Enemies, Fellows that would cut my Throat, if the Fear of Hanging did not restrain them. All Taylors, Sir, all Taylors.' —— 'Why should the Taylors be so angry with you?' cries the Player. 'I suppose you don't employ so many in making your Clothes.' 'I admit your Jest,' answered the Poet, 'but you remember the Affair as well as myself; you know there was a Party in the Pit and Upper-Gallery, would not suffer it to be given out again; tho' much, ay infinitely, the Majority, all the Boxes in particular, were desirous of it; nay, most of the Ladies swore they never would come to the House till it was acted again —— Indeed I must own their Policy was good, in not letting it be given out a second time; for the Rascals knew if it had gone a second Night, it would have run fifty: for if ever there was Distress in a Tragedy — I am not fond of my own Performance; but if I should tell you what the best Judges said of it —— Nor was it entirely owing to my Enemies neither, that it did not succeed on the Stage as well as it hath since among the polite Readers; for you can't say it had Justice done it by the Performers.' —— 'I think,' answer'd the Player, 'the Performers did the Distress of it Justice: for I am sure we were in Distress enough, who were pelted with Oranges all the last Act; we all imagined it would have been the last Act of our Lives.'

The Poet, whose Fury was now raised, had just attempted to answer, when they were interrupted, and an end put to their Discourse by an Accident; which, if the Reader is impatient to know, he must skip over the next Chapter, which is a sort of Counterpart to this, and contains some of the best and gravest Matters in the whole Book, being a Discourse between Parson *Abraham Adams* and Mr *Joseph Andrews*.

CHAPTER XI

Containing the Exhortations of Parson Adams *to his Friend
in Affliction;*[1] *calculated for the Instruction and Improvement of
the Reader.*

Joseph no sooner came perfectly to himself, than perceiving his Mistress
gone, he bewailed her Loss with Groans, which would have pierced any
Heart but those which are possessed by some People, and are made of a
certain Composition not unlike Flint in its Hardness and other Properties;
for you may strike Fire from them which will dart through the Eyes, but
they can never distil one Drop of Water the same way. His own, poor
Youth, was of a softer Composition; and at those Words, *O my dear* Fanny*!*
O my Love! shall I never, never see thee more? his Eyes overflowed with Tears,
which would have become any thing but a Hero. In a word, his Despair
was more easy to be conceived than related. ——

Mr *Adams* after many Groans, sitting with his back to *Joseph*, began
thus in a sorrowful Tone: 'You cannot imagine, my good Child, that I
entirely blame these first Agonies of your Grief; for, when Misfortunes
attack us by Surprize, it must require infinitely more Learning than you
are master of to resist them: but it is the Business of a Man and a Christian
to summon Reason as quickly as he can to his Aid; and she will presently
teach him Patience and Submission. Be comforted, therefore, Child, I say
be comforted. It is true you have lost the prettiest, kindest, loveliest,
sweetest young Woman: One with whom you might have expected to
have lived in Happiness, Virtue and Innocence. By whom you might have
promised yourself many little Darlings, who would have been the Delight
of your Youth, and the Comfort of your Age. You have not only lost her,
but have reason to fear the utmost Violence which Lust and Power can
inflict upon her. Now indeed you may easily raise Ideas of Horror, which
might drive you to Despair.' —— 'O I shall run mad,' cries *Joseph*, 'O
that I could but command my Hands to tear my Eyes out and my Flesh
off.' —— 'If you would use them to such Purposes, I am glad you can't,'
answer'd *Adams*. 'I have stated your Misfortune as strong as I possibly
can; but on the other side, you are to consider you are a Christian, that
no Accident happens to us without the Divine Permission, and that it is
the Duty of a Man and a Christian to submit. We did not make ourselves;

but the same Power which made us, rules over us, and we are absolutely at his Disposal; he may do with us what he pleases, nor have we any Right to complain. A second Reason against our Complaint is our Ignorance; for as we know not future Events, so neither can we tell to what Purpose any Accident tends; and that which at first threatens us with Evil, may in the end produce our Good. I should indeed have said our Ignorance is twofold (but I have not at present time to divide properly) for as we know not to what purpose any Event is ultimately directed; so neither can we affirm from what Cause it originally sprung. You are a Man, and consequently a Sinner; and this may be a Punishment to you for your Sins; indeed in this Sense it may be esteemed as a Good, yea as the greatest Good, which satisfies the Anger of Heaven, and averts that Wrath which cannot continue without our Destruction. Thirdly, Our Impotency of relieving ourselves, demonstrates the Folly and Absurdity of our Complaints: for whom do we resist? or against whom do we complain, but a Power from whose Shafts no Armour can guard us, no Speed can fly? A Power which leaves us no Hope, but in Submission.' — 'O Sir,' cried *Joseph*, 'all this is very true, and very fine; and I could hear you all day, if I was not so grieved at Heart as now I am.' 'Would you take Physick,' says *Adams*, 'when you are well, and refuse it when you are sick? Is not Comfort to be administred to the Afflicted, and not to those who rejoice, or those who are at ease?' —— 'O you have not spoken one Word of Comfort to me yet,' returned Joseph. 'No!' cries *Adams*, 'What am I then doing? what can I say to comfort you?' — 'O tell me,' cries *Joseph*, 'that *Fanny* will escape back to my Arms, that they shall again inclose that lovely Creature, with all her Sweetness, all her untainted Innocence about her.' —— 'Why perhaps you may,' cries *Adams*; 'but I can't promise you what's to come. You must with perfect Resignation wait the Event; if she be restored to you again, it is your Duty to be thankful, and so it is if she be not: *Joseph*, if you are wise, and truly know your own Interest, you will peaceably and quietly submit to all the Dispensations of Providence; being thoroughly assured, that all the Misfortunes, how great soever, which happen to the Righteous, happen to them for their own Good. —— Nay, it is not your Interest only, but your Duty to abstain from immoderate Grief; which if you indulge, you are not worthy the Name of a Christian.'

—— He spoke these last Words with an Accent a little severer than usual; upon which *Joseph* begged him not to be angry, saying he mistook him, if he thought he denied it was his Duty; for he had known that long ago.

'What signifies knowing your Duty, if you do not perform it?' answer'd *Adams*. 'Your Knowledge increases your Guilt — O *Joseph*, I never thought you had this Stubbornness in your Mind.' *Joseph* replied, 'he fancied he misunderstood him, which I assure you,' says he, 'you do, if you imagine I endeavour to grieve; upon my Soul I don't.' *Adams* rebuked him for swearing, and then proceeded to enlarge on the Folly of Grief, telling him, all the wise Men and Philosophers, even among the Heathens, had written against it, quoting several Passages from *Seneca*,[2] and the *Consolation*, which tho' it was not *Cicero*'s,[3] was, he said, as good almost as any of his Works, and concluded all by hinting, that immoderate Grief in this Case might incense that Power which alone could restore him his *Fanny*. This Reason, or indeed rather the Idea which it raised of the Restoration of his Mistress, had more effect than all which the Parson had said before; and for a moment abated his Agonies: but when his Fears sufficiently set before his Eyes the Danger that poor Creature was in, his Grief returned again with repeated Violence, nor could *Adams* in the least asswage it; tho' it may be doubted in his Behalf, whether *Socrates* himself could have prevailed any better.

They remained some time in silence; and Groans and Sighs issued from them both, at length *Joseph* burst out into the following Soliloquy:

> *Yes, I will bear my Sorrows like a Man,*
> *But I must also feel them as a Man.*
> *I cannot but remember such things were,*
> *And were most dear to me* ———[4]

Adams asked him what Stuff that was he repeated? —— To which he answer'd they were some Lines he had gotten by heart out of a Play — 'Ay, there is nothing but Heathenism to be learn'd from Plays,' reply'd he —— 'I never heard of any Plays fit for a Christian to read, but *Cato* and the *Conscious Lovers*;[5] and I must own in the latter there are some things almost solemn enough for a Sermon.' But we shall now leave them a little, and enquire after the Subject of their Conversation.

CHAPTER XII

*More Adventures, which we hope will as much please as surprize
the Reader.*

Neither the facetious Dialogue which pass'd between the Poet and Player,
nor the grave and truly solemn Discourse of Mr *Adams*, will, we conceive,
make the Reader sufficient Amends for the Anxiety which he must have
felt on the account of poor *Fanny*, whom we left in so deplorable a
Condition. We shall therefore now proceed to the Relation of what
happened to that beautiful and innocent Virgin, after she fell into the
wicked Hands of the Captain.

The Man of War having convey'd his charming Prize out of the Inn a
little before Day, made the utmost Expedition in his power towards the
Squire's House, where this delicate Creature was to be offered up a
Sacrifice to the Lust of a Ravisher. He was not only deaf to all her
Bewailings and Entreaties on the Road, but accosted her Ears with
Impurities, which, having been never before accustomed to them, she
happily for herself very little understood. At last he changed this Note,
and attempted to sooth and mollify her, by setting forth the Splendor and
Luxury which would be her Fortune with a Man who would have the
Inclination, and Power too, to give her whatever her utmost Wishes could
desire; and told her he doubted not but she would soon look kinder on
him, as the Instrument of her Happiness, and despise that pitiful Fellow,
whom her Ignorance only could make her fond of. She answered, She
knew not whom he meant, she never was fond of any pitiful Fellow. 'Are
you affronted, Madam,' says he, 'at my calling him so? but what better
can be said of one in a Livery, notwithstanding your Fondness for him?'
She returned, That she did not understand him, that the Man had been
her Fellow-Servant, and she believed was as honest a Creature as any
alive; but as for Fondness for Men —— 'I warrant ye,' cries the Captain,
'we shall find means to persuade you to be fond; and I advise you to yield
to gentle ones; for you may be assured that it is not in your power by any
Struggles whatever to preserve your Virginity two Hours longer. It will
be your Interest to consent; for the Squire will be much kinder to you if
he enjoys you willingly than by force.' —— At which Words she began
to call aloud for Assistance (for it was now open Day) but finding none,
she lifted her Eyes to Heaven, and supplicated the Divine Assistance to

preserve her Innocence. The Captain told her, if she persisted in her
Vociferation, he would find a means of stopping her Mouth. And now
the poor Wretch perceiving no Hopes of Succour, abandoned herself to
Despair, and sighing out the Name of *Joseph! Joseph!* a River of Tears ran
down her lovely Cheeks, and wet the Handkerchief which covered her
Bosom. A Horseman now appeared in the Road, upon which the Captain
threatened her violently if she complained; however, the moment they
approached each other, she begged him with the utmost Earnestness to
relieve a distressed Creature, who was in the hands of a Ravisher. The
Fellow stopt at those Words: but the Captain assured him it was his Wife,
and that he was carrying her home from her Adulterer. Which so satisfied
the Fellow, who was an old one, (and perhaps a married one too) that he
wished him a good Journey, and rode on. He was no sooner past,
than the Captain abused her violently for breaking his Commands, and
threaten'd to gagg her; when two more Horsemen, armed with Pistols,
came into the Road just before them. She again sollicited their Assistance;
and the Captain told the same Story as before. Upon which one said to
the other —— 'That's a charming Wench! *Jack*; I wish I had been in
the Fellow's Place whoever he is.' But the other, instead of answering
him, cried out eagerly, 'Zounds, I know her:' and then turning to her
said, 'Sure you are not *Fanny Goodwill?*' — 'Indeed, indeed I am,' she
cry'd — 'O *John*, I know you now —— Heaven hath sent you to my
Assistance, to deliver me from this wicked Man, who is carrying me away
for his vile Purposes —— O for G—'s sake rescue me from him.' A
fierce Dialogue immediately ensued between the Captain and these two
Men, who being both armed with Pistols, and the Chariot which they
attended being now arrived, the Captain saw both Force and Stratagem
were vain, and endeavoured to make his Escape; in which however he
could not succeed. The Gentleman who rode in the Chariot, ordered it
to stop, and with an Air of Authority examined into the Merits of the
Cause; of which being advertised[1] by *Fanny*, whose Credit was confirmed
by the Fellow who knew her, he ordered the Captain, who was all bloody
from his Encounter at the Inn, to be conveyed as a Prisoner behind the
Chariot, and very gallantly took *Fanny* into it; for, to say the truth, this
Gentleman (who was no other than the celebrated Mr *Peter Pounce*, and
who preceded the Lady *Booby* only a few Miles, by setting out earlier in
the Morning) was a very gallant Person, and loved a pretty Girl better
than any thing, besides his own Money, or the Money of other People.

The Chariot now proceeded towards the Inn, which as *Fanny* was informed lay in their way, and where it arrived at that very time while the Poet and Player were disputing below Stairs, and *Adams* and *Joseph* were discoursing back to back above: just at that Period to which we brought them both in the two preceding Chapters, the Chariot stopt at the Door, and in an instant *Fanny* leaping from it, ran up to her *Joseph*. — O Reader, conceive if thou canst, the Joy which fired the Breasts of these Lovers on this Meeting; and, if thy own Heart doth not sympathetically assist thee in this Conception, I pity thee sincerely from my own: for let the hard-hearted Villain know this, that there is a Pleasure in a tender Sensation beyond any which he is capable of tasting.

Peter being informed by *Fanny* of the Presence of *Adams*, stopt to see him, and receive his Homage; for, as *Peter* was an Hypocrite, a sort of People whom Mr *Adams* never saw through, this paid that Respect to his Goodness which the other attributed to be paid to his Riches; and hence Mr *Adams* was so much his Favourite, that he once lent him four Pounds thirteen Shillings and Sixpence, to prevent his going to Goal, on no greater Security than a Bond and Judgment,[2] which probably he would have made no use of, tho' the Money had not been (as it was) paid exactly at the time.

It is not perhaps easy to describe the Figure of *Adams*; he had risen in such a Hurry, that he had on neither Breeches, Garters, nor Stockings; nor had he taken from his Head a red spotted Handkerchief, which by Night bound his Wig, turned inside out, around his Head. He had on his torn Cassock, and his Great-Coat; but as the remainder of his Cassock hung down below his Great-Coat; so did a small Stripe of white, or rather whitish Linnen appear below that; to which we may add the several Colours which appeared on his Face, where a long Piss-burnt Beard, served to retain the Liquor of the Stone Pot, and that of a blacker hue which distilled from the Mop. —— This Figure, which *Fanny* had delivered from his Captivity, was no sooner spied by *Peter*, than it disordered the composed Gravity of his Muscles; however he advised him immediately to make himself clean, nor would accept his Homage in that Pickle.

The Poet and Player no sooner saw the Captain in Captivity, than they began to consider of their own Safety, of which Flight presented itself as the only means; they therefore both of them mounted the Poet's Horse, and made the most expeditious Retreat in their power.

The Host, who well knew Mr *Pounce*, and the Lady *Booby*'s Livery, was not a little surprized at this change of the Scene, nor was his Confusion much helped by his Wife, who was now just risen, and having heard the

Account of what had past from him, comforted him with a decent Number of Fools and Blockheads, asked him why he did not consult her, and told him he would never leave following the nonsensical Dictates of his own Numscull, till she and her Family were ruined.

Joseph being informed of the Captain's Arrival, and seeing his *Fanny* now in Safety, quitted her a moment, and running down Stairs, went directly to him, and stripping off his Coat challenged him to fight; but the Captain refused, saying he did not understand Boxing. He then grasped a Cudgel in one Hand, and catching the Captain by the Collar with the other, he gave him a most severe Drubbing, and ended with telling him, he had now had some Revenge for what his dear *Fanny* had suffered.

When Mr *Pounce* had a little regaled himself with some Provision which he had in his Chariot, and Mr *Adams* had put on the best Appearance his Clothes would allow him, *Pounce* ordered the Captain into his Presence; for he said he was guilty of Felony, and the next Justice of Peace should commit him: but the Servants (whose Appetite for Revenge is soon satisfied) were sufficiently contented with the Drubbing which *Joseph* had inflicted on him, and which was indeed of no very moderate kind, and had suffered him to go off, which he did, threatening a severe Revenge against *Joseph*, which I have never heard he thought proper to take.

The Mistress of the House made her voluntary Appearance before Mr *Pounce*, and with a thousand Curt'sies told him, 'she hoped his Honour would pardon her Husband, who was a very *nonsense* Man, for the sake of his poor Family; that indeed if he could be ruined alone, she should be very willing of it, *for because as why*, his Worship very well knew he deserved it: but she had three poor small Children, who were not capable to get their own Living; and if her Husband was sent to Goal, they must all come to the Parish;[3] for she was a poor weak Woman, continually a breeding, and had no time to work for them. She therefore hoped his Honour would take it into his Worship's Consideration, and forgive her Husband this time; for she was sure he never intended any Harm to Man, Woman, or Child; and if it was not for that Block-Head of his own, the Man in some things was well enough; for she had had three Children by him in less than three Years, and was almost ready to cry out the fourth time.' She would have proceeded in this manner much longer, had not *Peter* stopt her Tongue, by telling her he had nothing to say to her Husband, nor her neither. So, as *Adams* and the rest had assured her of Forgiveness, she cried and curt'sied out of the Room.

Mr *Pounce* was desirous that *Fanny* should continue her Journey with him in the Chariot, but she absolutely refused, saying she would ride behind *Joseph*, on a Horse which one of Lady *Booby*'s Servants had equipped him with. But alas! when the Horse appeared, it was found to be no other than that identical Beast which Mr *Adams* had left behind him at the Inn, and which these honest Fellows who knew him had redeemed. Indeed whatever Horse they had provided for *Joseph*, they would have prevailed with him to mount none, no not even to ride before his beloved *Fanny*, till the Parson was supplied; much less would he deprive his Friend of the Beast which belonged to him, and which he knew the moment he saw, tho' *Adams* did not: however, when he was reminded of the Affair, and told that they had brought the Horse with them which he left behind, he answered — *Bless me! and so I did*.

Adams was very desirous that *Joseph* and *Fanny* should mount this Horse, and declared he could very easily walk home. 'If I walked alone,' says he, 'I would wage a Shilling, that the *Pedestrian* out-stripped the *Equestrian* Travellers: but as I intend to take the Company of a Pipe, peradventure I may be an Hour later.' One of the Servants whispered *Joseph* to take him at his Word, and suffer the old Put[4] to walk if he would: This Proposal was answered with an angry Look and a peremptory Refusal by *Joseph*, who catching *Fanny* up in his Arms, aver'd he would rather carry her home in that manner, than take away Mr *Adams*'s Horse, and permit him to walk on foot.

Perhaps, Reader, thou hast seen a Contest between two Gentlemen, or two Ladies quickly decided, tho' they have both asserted they would not eat such a nice Morsel, and each insisted on the other's accepting it; but in reality both were very desirous to swallow it themselves. Do not therefore conclude hence, that this Dispute would have come to a speedy Decision: for here both Parties were heartily in earnest, and it is very probable, they would have remained in the Inn-yard to this day, had not the good *Peter Pounce* put a stop to it; for finding he had no longer hopes of satisfying his old Appetite with *Fanny*, and being desirous of having some one to whom he might communicate his Grandeur, he told the Parson he would convey him home in his Chariot. This Favour was by *Adams*, with many Bows and Acknowledgments, accepted, tho' he afterwards said, 'he ascended the Chariot rather that he might not offend, than from any Desire of riding in it, for that in his heart he preferred the *Pedestrian* even to the *Vehicular* Expedition.' All matters being now settled, the Chariot in which rode *Adams* and *Pounce* moved forwards; and *Joseph*

271

having borrowed a Pillion from the Host, *Fanny* had just seated herself thereon, and had laid hold on the Girdle which her Lover wore for that purpose, when the wise Beast, who concluded that one at a time was sufficient, that two to one were odds, *&c.* discovered much Uneasiness at his double Load, and began to consider his hinder as his Fore-legs, moving the direct contrary way to that which is called forwards. Nor could *Joseph* with all his Horsemanship persuade him to advance: but without having any regard to the lovely Part of the lovely Girl which was on his Back, he used such Agitations, that had not one of the Men come immediately to her Assistance, she had in plain *English* tumbled backwards on the Ground. This Inconvenience was presently remedied by an Exchange of Horses, and then *Fanny* being again placed on her Pillion, on a better natured, and somewhat a better fed Beast, the Parson's Horse finding he had no longer Odds to contend with, agreed to march, and the whole Procession set forwards for *Booby-Hall*, where they arrived in a few Hours without any thing remarkable happening on the Road, unless it was a curious Dialogue between the Parson and the Steward; which, to use the Language of a late Apologist, a Pattern to all Biographers, *waits for the Reader in the next Chapter.*[5]

CHAPTER XIII

A curious Dialogue which passed between Mr Abraham Adams *and Mr* Peter Pounce, *better worth reading than all the Works of* Colley Cibber *and many others.*

The Chariot had not proceeded far, before Mr *Adams* observed it was a very fine Day. 'Ay, and a very fine Country too,' answered *Pounce*. 'I should think so more,' returned *Adams*, 'if I had not lately travelled over the *Downs*, which I take to exceed this and all other Prospects in the Universe.' 'A Fig for Prospects,' answered *Pounce*, 'one Acre here is worth ten there; and for my own part, I have no Delight in the Prospect of any Land but my own.' 'Sir,' said *Adams*, 'you can indulge yourself with many fine Prospects of that kind.' 'I thank God I have a little,' replied the other, 'with which I am content, and envy no Man: I have a little, Mr *Adams*, with which I do as much good as I can.' *Adams* answered, that Riches without Charity were nothing worth; for that they were only a Blessing to him who made them a Blessing to others. 'You and I,' said *Peter*, 'have different Notions of Charity. I own, as it is generally used, I do not like the Word, nor do I think it becomes one of us Gentlemen; it is a mean Parson-like Quality; though I would not infer many Parsons have it neither.' 'Sir,' said *Adams*, 'my Definition of Charity is a generous Disposition to relieve the Distressed.'[1] 'There is something in that Definition,' answered *Peter*, 'which I like well enough; it is, as you say, a Disposition — and does not so much consist in the Act as in the Disposition to do it; but alas, Mr *Adams*, Who are meant by the Distressed? Believe me, the Distresses of Mankind are mostly imaginary, and it would be rather Folly than Goodness to relieve them.' 'Sure, Sir,' replied *Adams*, 'Hunger and Thirst, Cold and Nakedness, and other Distresses which attend the Poor, can never be said to be imaginary Evils.' 'How can any Man complain of Hunger,' said *Peter*, 'in a Country where such excellent Sallads are to be gathered in almost every Field? or of Thirst, where every River and Stream produces such delicious Potations? And as for Cold and Nakedness, they are Evils introduced by Luxury and Custom. A Man naturally wants Clothes no more than a Horse or any other Animal, and there are whole Nations who go without them: but these are things perhaps which you, who do not know the World —' 'You will pardon me, Sir,' returned *Adams*; 'I have read of the *Gymnosophists*.'[2] 'A plague of your *Jehosaphats*,' cried *Peter*; 'the greatest Fault in our Constitution is the Provision made for the Poor, except that perhaps made for some others. Sir, I have not an Estate which doth not contribute almost as much again to the Poor as to the Land-Tax, and I do assure you I expect to come myself to the Parish in the end.' To which *Adams* giving a dissenting Smile, *Peter* thus proceeded: 'I fancy, Mr *Adams*, you are one of those who imagine I am a Lump of Money; for there are many who I fancy believe that not only my Pockets, but my whole Clothes, are lined with Bank Bills; but I assure you, you are all mistaken: I am not the Man the World esteems me. If I can hold my Head above Water, it is all I can. I have injured myself by purchasing. I have been too liberal of my Money. Indeed I fear my Heir will find my Affairs in a worse Situation than they are reputed to be. Ah! he will have reason to wish I had loved Money more and Land less.[3] Pray, my good Neighbour, where should I have that Quantity of Riches the World is so liberal to bestow on me? Where could I possibly, without I had stole it, acquire such a Treasure?' 'Why truly,' says *Adams*, 'I have been always of your Opinion; I have wondered as well as yourself with what Confidence they could report such things of you, which have to me appeared as mere Impossibilities; for you know, Sir, and I have often

273

heard you say it, that your Wealth is your own Acquisition, and can it be credible that in your short time you should have amassed such a heap of Treasure as these People will have you worth? Indeed had you inherited an Estate like Sir *Thomas Booby*, which had descended in your Family for many Generations, they might have had a colour for their Assertions.' 'Why, what do they say I am worth?' cries *Peter* with a malicious Sneer. 'Sir,' answered *Adams*, 'I have heard some aver you are not worth less than twenty thousand Pounds.' At which *Peter* frowned. 'Nay, Sir,' said *Adams*, 'you ask me only the Opinion of others, for my own part I have always denied it, nor did I ever believe you could possibly be worth half that Sum.' 'However, Mr *Adams*,' said he, squeezing him by the Hand, 'I would not sell them all I am worth for double that Sum; and as to what you believe, or they believe, I care not a Fig, no not a Fart. I am not poor because you think me so, nor because you attempt to undervalue me in the Country. I know the Envy of Mankind very well, but I thank Heaven I am above them. It is true my Wealth is of my own Acquisition. I have not an Estate like Sir *Thomas Booby*, that has descended in my Family through many Generations; but I know the Heirs of such Estates who are forced to travel about the Country like some People in torn Cassocks, and might be glad to accept of a pitiful Curacy for what I know. Yes, Sir, as shabby Fellows as yourself, whom no Man of my Figure, without that Vice of Good-nature about him, would suffer to ride in a Chariot with him.' 'Sir,' said *Adams*, 'I value not your Chariot of a Rush; and if I had known you had intended to affront me, I would have walked to the World's End on foot ere I would have accepted a place in it. However, Sir, I will soon rid you of that Inconvenience;' and so saying, he opened the Chariot-Door without calling to the Coachman, and leapt out into the High-way, forgetting to take his Hat along with him; which however Mr *Pounce* threw after him with great violence. *Joseph* and *Fanny* stopt to bear him Company the rest of the way, which was not above a Mile.

The End of the Third Book

THE HISTORY OF THE ADVENTURES OF
JOSEPH ANDREWS, AND HIS FRIEND
MR ABRAHAM ADAMS

BOOK IV

CHAPTER I

The Arrival of Lady Booby, *and the rest at* Booby-Hall.[1]

The Coach-and-six, in which Lady *Booby* rode, overtook the other Travellers as they entered the Parish. She no sooner saw *Joseph*, than her Cheeks glow'd with red, and immediately after became as totally pale. She had in her Surprize almost stopt her Coach; but recollected herself timely enough to prevent it. She entered the Parish amidst the ringing of Bells, and the Acclamations of the Poor, who were rejoiced to see their Patroness returned after so long an Absence, during which time all her Rents had been drafted to *London*, without a Shilling being spent among them, which tended not a little to their utter impoverishing; for if the Court would be severely missed in such a City as *London*, how much more must the Absence of a Person of great Fortune be felt in a little Country Village, for whose Inhabitants such a Family finds a constant Employment and Supply; and with the Offalls[2] of whose Table the infirm, aged, and infant Poor are abundantly fed, with a Generosity which hath scarce a visible Effect on their Benefactor's Pockets?

But if their Interest inspired so publick a Joy into every Countenance, how much more forcibly did the Affection which they bore Parson *Adams* operate upon all who beheld his Return? They flocked about him like dutiful Children round an indulgent Parent, and vyed with each other in Demonstrations of Duty and Love. The Parson on his side shook every one by the Hand, enquired heartily after the Healths of all that were absent, of their Children and Relations, and exprest a Satisfaction in his Face, which nothing but Benevolence made happy by its Objects could infuse.

Nor did *Joseph* and *Fanny* want a hearty Welcome from all who saw them. In short, no three Persons could be more kindly received, as indeed none ever more deserved to be universally beloved.

Adams carried his Fellow-Travellers home to his House, where he insisted on their partaking whatever his Wife, whom with his Children he found in Health and Joy, could provide. Where we shall leave them, enjoying perfect Happiness over a homely Meal, to view Scenes of greater Splendor but infinitely less Bliss.

Our more intelligent Readers will doubtless suspect by this second Appearance of Lady *Booby* on the Stage, that all was not ended by the Dismission of *Joseph*; and to be honest with them, they are in the right; the Arrow had pierced deeper than she imagined; nor was the Wound so easily to be cured. The Removal of the Object soon cooled her Rage, but it had a different Effect on her Love; that departed with his Person; but this remained lurking in her Mind with his Image. Restless, interrupted Slumbers, and confused horrible Dreams were her Portion the first Night. In the Morning, Fancy painted her a more delicious Scene; but to delude, not delight her: for before she could reach the promised Happiness, it vanished, and left her to curse, not bless the Vision.

She started from her Sleep, her Imagination being all on fire with the Phantom, when her Eyes accidentally glancing towards the Spot where yesterday the real *Joseph* had stood, that little Circumstance raised his Idea in the liveliest Colours in her Memory. Each Look, each Word, each Gesture rushed back on her Mind with Charms which all his Coldness could not abate. Nay, she imputed that to his Youth, his Folly, his Awe, his Religion, to every thing, but what would instantly have produced Contempt, want of Passion for the Sex; or, that which would have roused her Hatred, want of Liking to her.

Reflection then hurried her farther, and told her she must see this beautiful Youth no more, nay, suggested to her, that she herself had dismissed him for no other Fault, than probably that of too violent an Awe and Respect for herself; and which she ought rather to have esteemed a Merit, the Effects of which were besides so easily and surely to have been removed; she then blamed, she cursed the hasty Rashness of her Temper; her Fury was vented all on herself, and *Joseph* appeared innocent in her Eyes. Her Passion at length grew so violent that it forced her on seeking Relief, and now she thought of recalling him: But Pride forbad that, Pride which soon drove all softer Passions from her Soul, and represented to her the Meanness of him she was fond of. That Thought soon began to obscure his Beauties; Contempt succeeded next, and then Disdain, which presently introduced her Hatred of the Creature who had given her so much Uneasiness. These Enemies of *Joseph* had no sooner taken possession of her Mind, than they insinuated to her a thousand things in his Disfavour; every thing but Dislike of her Person; a Thought, which as it would have been intolerable to her, she checked the moment it endeavoured to arise. Revenge came now to her Assistance; and she considered her Dismission of him stript, and without a Character,[3] with the utmost Pleasure. She rioted in the several kinds of Misery, which her Imagination suggested to her, might be his Fate; and with a Smile composed of Anger, Mirth, and Scorn, viewed him in the Rags in which her Fancy had drest him.

Mrs *Slipslop* being summoned, attended her Mistress, who had now in her own Opinion totally subdued this Passion. Whilst she was dressing, she asked if that Fellow had been turned away according to her Orders. *Slipslop* answered, she had told her Ladyship so, (as indeed she had) —— 'And how did he behave?' replied the Lady. 'Truly Madam,' cries *Slipslop*, 'in such a manner that *infected* every body who saw him. The poor Lad had but little Wages to receive: for he constantly allowed his Father and Mother half his Income; so that when your Ladyship's Livery was stript off, he had not wherewithal to buy a Coat, and must have gone naked, if one of the Footmen had not *incommodated* him with one; and whilst he was standing in his Shirt, (and to say truth, he was an *amorous* Figure) being told your Ladyship would not give him a Character, he sighed, and said he had done nothing willingly to offend; that for his part he should always give your Ladyship a good Character where-ever he went; and he pray'd God to bless you; for you was the best of Ladies, tho' his Enemies had set you against him: I wish you had not turned him away; for I believe you have not a faithfuller Servant in the House.' —— 'How came you then,' replied the Lady, 'to advise me to turn him away?' 'I, Madam!' said *Slipslop*, 'I am sure you will do me the Justice to say, I did all in my power to prevent it; but I saw your Ladyship was angry; and it is not the business of us upper Servants to *hintorfear* on those occasions.' —— 'And was it not you, audacious Wretch,' cried the Lady, 'who made me angry? Was it not your Tittle-tattle, in which I believe you belyed the poor Fellow, which incensed me against him? He may thank you for all that hath happened; and so may I for the Loss of a good Servant, and one who probably had more Merit than all of you. Poor Fellow! I am charmed with his Goodness to his Parents. Why did not you tell me of that, but suffer me to dismiss so good a Creature without a Character? I see the Reason of your whole Behaviour now as well as your Complaint; you was jealous of the Wenches.' 'I jealous!' said *Slipslop*, 'I assure you I look upon myself as his Betters; I am not Meat for a Footman I hope.' These Words threw the Lady into a violent Passion, and she sent *Slipslop* from her Presence, who departed tossing her Nose and crying, 'Marry come up! there are some People more jealous than I, I believe.' Her Lady affected not to hear the Words, tho' in reality she did, and understood them too. Now ensued a second Conflict, so like the former, that it might savour of Repetition to relate it minutely. It may suffice to say, that Lady *Booby* found good Reason to doubt whether she had so absolutely conquered her Passion, as she had flattered herself; and in order to accomplish it quite, took a Resolution more common than wise, to retire immediately into the Country. The Reader hath long ago seen the Arrival of Mrs *Slipslop*, whom no Pertness could make her Mistress resolve to part with; lately, that of Mr *Pounce*, her Fore-runners; and lastly, that of the Lady herself.

The Morning after her Arrival being *Sunday*, she went to Church, to the great Surprize of every body, who wondered to see her Ladyship, being no very constant Churchwoman, there so suddenly upon her Journey. *Joseph* was likewise there; and I have heard it was remarked, that she fixed her Eyes on him much more than on the Parson; but this I believe to be only a malicious Rumour. When the Prayers were ended, Mr *Adams* stood up, and with a loud Voice pronounced: *I publish the Banns of Marriage between* Joseph Andrews *and* Frances Goodwill, *both of this Parish*, &c. Whether this had any Effect on Lady *Booby* or no, who was then in her Pew, which the Congregation could not see into, I could never discover: But certain it is, that in about a quarter of an Hour she stood up, and directed her Eyes to that part of the Church where the Women sat, and persisted in looking that way during the remainder of the Sermon, in so scrutinizing a manner, and with so angry a Countenance, that most of the Women were afraid she was offended at them.

The moment she returned home, she sent for *Slipslop* into her Chamber, and told her, she wondered what that impudent Fellow *Joseph* did in that Parish? Upon which *Slipslop* gave her an account of her meeting *Adams* with him on the Road, and likewise the Adventure with *Fanny*. At the relation of which, the Lady often changed her Countenance; and when she had heard all, she ordered Mr *Adams* into her Presence, to whom she behaved as the Reader will see in the next Chapter.

CHAPTER II

A Dialogue between Mr Abraham Adams *and the Lady* Booby.

Mr *Adams* was not far off; for he was drinking her Ladyship's Health below in a Cup of her Ale. He no sooner came before her, than she began in the following manner: 'I wonder, Sir, after the many great Obligations you have had to this Family,' (with all which the Reader hath, in the Course of this History, been minutely acquainted) 'that you will ungratefully show any Respect to a Fellow who hath been turned out of it for his Misdeeds. Nor doth it, I can tell you, Sir, become a Man of your Character, to run about the Country with an idle Fellow and Wench. Indeed, as for the Girl, I know no harm of her. *Slipslop* tells me she was formerly bred up in my House, and behaved as she ought, till she hankered after this Fellow, and he spoiled her. Nay, she may still perhaps do very well, if he will let her alone. You are therefore doing a monstrous thing, in endeavouring to procure a Match between these two People, which will be to the Ruin of them both.' — 'Madam,' says *Adams*, 'if your Ladyship will but hear me speak, I protest I never heard any harm of Mr *Joseph Andrews*; if I had, I should have corrected him for it: For I never have, nor will encourage the Faults of those under my Cure. As for the young Woman, I assure your Ladyship I have as good an Opinion of her as your Ladyship yourself, or any other can have. She is the sweetest-tempered, honestest, worthiest, young Creature; indeed as to her Beauty, I do not commend her on that account, tho' all Men allow she is the handsomest Woman, Gentle or Simple, that ever appeared in the Parish.' 'You are very impertinent,' says she, 'to talk such fulsome Stuff to me. It is mighty becoming truly in a Clergyman to trouble himself about handsome Women, and you have a delicate Judge of Beauty, no doubt. A Man who hath lived all his Life in such a Parish as this, is a rare Judge of Beauty. Ridiculous! Beauty indeed, —— a Country Wench a Beauty. —— I shall be sick whenever I hear Beauty mentioned again. —— And so this Wench is to stock the Parish with Beauties, I hope. —— But, Sir, our Poor is numerous enough already; I will have no more Vagabonds settled here.' 'Madam,' says *Adams*, 'your Ladyship is offended with me, I protest without any Reason. This Couple were desirous to consummate long ago, and I dissuaded them from it; nay, I may venture to say, I believe, I was the sole Cause of their delaying it.' 'Well,' says she, 'and you did very wisely and honestly too, notwithstanding she is the greatest Beauty in the Parish.'[1] —— 'And now, Madam,' continued he, 'I only perform my Office to Mr *Joseph*.' — 'Pray don't Mister such Fellows to me,' cries the Lady. 'He,' said the Parson, 'with the Consent of *Fanny*, before my Face, put in the Banns.' —— 'Yes', answered the Lady, 'I suppose the Slut is forward enough; *Slipslop* tells me how her Head runs on Fellows; that is one of her Beauties, I suppose. But if they have put in the Banns, I desire you will publish them no more without my Orders.' 'Madam,' cries *Adams*, 'if any one puts in sufficient Caution, and assigns a proper Reason against them, I am willing to surcease.' —— 'I tell you a Reason,' says she, 'he is a Vagabond, and he shall not settle here, and bring a Nest of Beggars into the Parish; it will make us but little Amends that they will be Beauties.' 'Madam,' answered *Adams*, 'with the utmost Submission to your Ladyship, I have been informed by Lawyer *Scout*, that any Person who serves a Year, gains a Settlement in the Parish where he serves.'[2] 'Lawyer *Scout*,' replied the Lady, 'is an impudent Coxcomb; I will have no Lawyer *Scout* interfere with me. I repeat to you again, I will have no more Incumbrances brought on us; so I desire you will proceed no farther.' 'Madam,' returned *Adams*, 'I would obey your Ladyship in every thing that is lawful; but surely the Parties being poor is no Reason against their marrying. G—d forbid there should be any such Law. The Poor have little Share enough of this World already; it would be barbarous indeed to deny them the common Privileges, and innocent Enjoyments which Nature indulges to the animal Creation.' 'Since you understand yourself no better,' cries the Lady, 'nor the Respect due from such as you to a Woman of my Distinction, than to affront my Ears by such loose Discourse, I shall mention but one short Word; It is my Orders to you, that you publish these Banns no more; and if you dare, I will recommend it to your Master, the Doctor, to discard you from his Service. I will, Sir, notwithstanding your poor Family; and then you and the greatest Beauty in the Parish may go and beg together.' 'Madam,' answered *Adams*, 'I know not what your Ladyship means by the Terms *Master* and *Service*. I am in the Service of a Master who will never discard me for doing my Duty: And if the Doctor (for indeed I have never been able to pay for a Licence)[3] thinks proper to turn me from my Cure, G— will provide me, I hope, another. At least, my Family as well as myself have Hands; and he will prosper, I doubt not, our Endeavours to get our Bread honestly with them. Whilst my Conscience is pure, I shall never fear what Man can do unto me.' —— 'I condemn my Humility,' said the Lady, 'for demeaning myself to converse with you so long. I shall take other Measures; for I see you are a Confederate with them. But the sooner you leave me, the better; and I shall give Orders that my Doors may no longer be open to you, I will suffer no Parsons who run about the Country with Beauties to be entertained here.' —— 'Madam,' said *Adams*, 'I shall enter into no Person's Doors against their Will: But I am assured, when you have enquired farther into this Matter, you will applaud, not blame my Proceeding; and so I humbly take my Leave:' Which he did with many Bows, or at least many Attempts at a Bow.

CHAPTER III

What past between the Lady and Lawyer Scout.

In the Afternoon the Lady sent for Mr *Scout*, whom she attacked most violently for intermeddling with her Servants, which he denied, and indeed with Truth; for he had only asserted accidentally, and perhaps rightly, that a Year's Service gained a Settlement; and so far he owned he might have formerly informed the Parson, and believed it was Law. 'I am resolved,' said the Lady, 'to have no discarded Servants of mine settled here; and so, if this be your Law, I shall send to another Lawyer.' *Scout* said, 'If she sent to a hundred Lawyers, not one nor all of them could alter the Law. The utmost that was in the power of a Lawyer, was to prevent the Law's taking effect; and that he himself could do for her Ladyship as well as any other: And I believe,' says he, 'Madam, your Ladyship not being conversant in these Matters hath mistaken a Difference: For I asserted only, that a Man who served a Year was settled. Now there is a matterial Difference between being settled in Law and settled in Fact; and as I affirmed generally he was settled, and Law is preferable to Fact, my Settlement must be understood in Law, and not in Fact! And suppose, Madam, we admit he was settled in Law, what use will they make of it, how doth that relate to Fact? He is not settled in Fact; and if he be not settled in Fact, he is not an Inhabitant; and if he is not an Inhabitant, he is not of this Parish; and then undoubtedly he ought not to be published here; for Mr *Adams* hath told me your Ladyship's Pleasure, and the Reason, which is a very good one, to prevent burdening us with the Poor; we have too many already; and I think we ought to have an Act to hang or transport half of them. If we can prove in Evidence, that he is not settled in Fact, it is another matter. What I said to Mr *Adams*, was on a Supposition that he was settled in Fact; and indeed if that was the Case, I should doubt.' —— 'Don't tell me your *Facts* and your *ifs*,' said the Lady, 'I don't understand your Gibberish: You take too much upon you, and are very impertinent in pretending to direct in this Parish, and you shall be taught better, I assure you, you shall. But as to the Wench, I am resolved she shall not settle here; I will not suffer such Beauties as these to produce Children for us to keep.' — 'Beauties indeed! your Ladyship is pleased to be merry,' — answered *Scout*. — 'Mr *Adams* described her so to me,' said the Lady. — 'Pray what sort of Dowdy is it, Mr *Scout*?' — 'The ugliest Creature almost I ever beheld, a poor dirty Drab,' your Ladyship never saw such a Wretch.' —— 'Well but, dear Mr *Scout*, let her be what she will, — these ugly Women will bring Children you know; so that we must prevent the Marriage.' — 'True, Madam,' replied *Scout*, 'for the subsequent Marriage co-operating with the Law, will carry Law into Fact. When a Man is married, he is settled in Fact; and then he is not removable.² I will see Mr *Adams*, and I make no doubt of prevailing with him. His only Objection is doubtless that he shall lose his Fee: but that being once made easy, as it shall be, I am confident no farther Objection will remain. No, no, it is impossible: but your Ladyship can't discommend his Unwillingness to depart with his Fee. Every Man ought to have a proper Value for his Fee. As to the matter in question, if your Ladyship pleases to employ me in it, I will venture to promise you Success. The Laws of this Land are not so vulgar, to permit a mean Fellow to contend with one of your Ladyship's Fortune. We have one sure Card, which is to carry him before Justice *Frolick*, who, upon hearing your Ladyship's Name, will commit him without any farther Questions. As for the dirty Slut, we shall have nothing to do with her: for if we get rid of the Fellow, the ugly Jade will ——' 'Take what Measures you please, good Mr *Scout*,' answered the Lady, 'but I wish you could rid the Parish of both; for *Slipslop* tells me such Stories of this Wench, that I abhor the Thoughts of her; and tho' you say she is such an ugly Slut, yet you know, dear Mr *Scout*, these forward Creatures who run after Men, will always find some as forward as themselves: So that, to prevent the Increase of Beggars, we must get rid of her.' —— 'Your Ladyship is very much in the right,' answered *Scout*, 'but I am afraid the Law is a little deficient in giving us any such Power of Prevention; however the Justice will stretch it as far as he is able, to oblige your Ladyship. To say truth, it is a great Blessing to the Country that he is in the Commission; for he hath taken several Poor off our hands, that the Law would never lay hold on. I know some Justices who make as much of committing a Man to *Bridewell*, as his Lordship at *Size* would of hanging him: But it would do a Man good to see his Worship our Justice commit a Fellow to *Bridewell*;[3] he takes so much pleasure in it: And when once we ha' un there, we seldom hear any more o' un. He's either starved or eat up by Vermin in a Month's time.' —— Here the Arrival of a Visitor put an end to the Conversation, and Mr *Scout* having undertaken the Cause, and promised it Success, departed.

This *Scout* was one of those Fellows, who without any Knowledge of the Law, or being bred to it, take upon them, in defiance of an Act of Parliament, to act as Lawyers in the Country,[4] and are called so. They are the Pests of Society, and a Scandal to a Profession, to which indeed they do not belong; and which owes to such kind of Rascallions the Ill-will which weak Persons bear towards it. With this Fellow, to whom a little before she would not have condescended to have spoken, did a certain Passion for *Joseph*, and the Jealousy and Disdain of poor innocent *Fanny*, betray the Lady *Booby*, into a familiar Discourse, in which she inadvertently confirmed many Hints, with which *Slipslop*, whose Gallant he was, had pre-acquainted him; and whence he had taken an Opportunity to assert those severe Falshoods of little *Fanny*, which possibly the Reader might not have been well able to account for, if we had not thought proper to give him this Information.

CHAPTER IV

A short Chapter, but very full of Matter; particularly the Arrival of
Mr Booby *and his Lady.*

All that Night and the next Day, the Lady *Booby* past with the utmost Anxiety; her Mind was distracted, and her Soul tossed up and down by many turbulent and opposite Passions. She loved, hated, pitied, scorned, admired, despised the same Person by Fits, which changed in a very short Interval. On *Tuesday* Morning, which happened to be a Holiday, she went to Church, where, to her surprize, Mr *Adams* published the Banns again with as audible a Voice as before. It was lucky for her, that as there was no Sermon, she had an immediate Opportunity of returning home, to vent her Rage, which she could not have concealed from the Congregation five Minutes; indeed it was not then very numerous, the Assembly consisting of no more than *Adams*, his Clerk, his Wife, the Lady, and one of her Servants. At her Return she met *Slipslop*, who accosted her in these Words: —— 'O Meam, what doth your Ladyship think? To be sure Lawyer *Scout* hath carried *Joseph* and *Fanny* both before the Justice. All the Parish are in Tears, and say they will certainly be hanged: For no body knows what it is for.' —— 'I suppose they deserve it,' says the Lady. 'What dost thou mention such Wretches to me?' —— 'O dear Madam,' answered *Slipslop*, 'is it not a pity such a *graceless* young Man should die a *virulent* Death? I hope the Judge will take *Commensuration* on his Youth. As for *Fanny*, I don't think it signifies much what becomes of her; and if poor *Joseph* hath done any thing, I could venture to swear she *traduced* him to it: Few Men ever come to *fragrant* Punishment, but by those nasty Creatures who are a Scandal to our *Sect.*' The Lady was no more pleased at this News, after a moment's Reflection, than *Slipslop* herself: For tho' she wished *Fanny* far enough, she did not desire the Removal of *Joseph*, especially with her. She was puzzled how to act, or what to say on this Occasion, when a Coach-and-six drove into the Court, and a Servant acquainted her with the Arrival of her Nephew *Booby* and his Lady. She ordered them to be conducted into a Drawing-Room, whither she presently repaired, having composed her Countenance as well as she could; and being a little satisfied that the Wedding would by these means be at least interrupted; and that she should have an Opportunity to execute any Resolution she might take, for which she saw herself provided with an excellent Instrument in *Scout*.

The Lady *Booby* apprehended her Servant had made a Mistake, when he had mentioned Mr *Booby*'s Lady; for she had never heard of his Marriage; but how great was her Surprize, when at her entering the Room, her Nephew presented his Wife to her, saying, 'Madam, this is that charming *Pamela*, of whom I am convinced you have heard so much.' The Lady received her with more Civility than he expected; indeed with the utmost: For she was perfectly polite, nor had any Vice inconsistent with Good-breeding. They past some little time in ordinary Discourse, when a Servant came and whispered Mr *Booby*, who presently told the Ladies he must desert them a little on some Business of Consequence; and as their Discourse during his Absence would afford little Improvement or Entertainment to the Reader, we will leave them for a while to attend Mr *Booby*.

CHAPTER V

Containing Justice Business: Curious Precedents of Depositions,
and other Matters necessary to be perused by all Justices of the Peace
and their Clerks.

The young Squire and his Lady were no sooner alighted from their Coach, than the Servants began to enquire after Mr *Joseph*, from whom they said their Lady had not heard a Word to her great Surprize, since he had left Lady *Booby*'s. Upon this they were instantly informed of what had lately happened, with which they hastily acquainted their Master, who took an immediate Resolution to go himself, and endeavour to restore his *Pamela* her Brother, before she even knew she had lost him.

The Justice, before whom the Criminals were carried, and who lived within a short Mile of the Lady's House, was luckily Mr *Booby*'s Acquaintance, by his having an Estate in his Neighbourhood. Ordering therefore his Horses to his Coach, he set out for the Judgment-Seat, and arrived when the Justice had almost finish'd his Business. He was conducted into a Hall, where he was acquainted that his Worship would wait on him in a moment; for he had only a Man and a Woman to commit to *Bridewell* first. As he was now convinced he had not a Minute to lose, he insisted on the Servants introducing him directly into the Room where the Justice was then executing his Office, as he called it. Being brought thither, and the first Compliments being past between the Squire and his Worship, the former asked the latter what Crime those two young People had been guilty of. 'No great Crime,' answered the Justice, 'I have only ordered them to *Bridewell* for a Month.' 'But what is their Crime?' repeated the Squire. 'Larceny, an't please your Honour,' said *Scout*. 'Ay,' says the Justice, 'a kind of felonious larcenous thing. I believe I must order them a little Correction too, a little Stripping and Whipping.' (Poor *Fanny*, who had hitherto supported all with the Thoughts of *Joseph*'s Company, trembled at that Sound; but indeed without reason, for none but the Devil himself would have executed such a Sentence on her.) 'Still,' said the Squire, 'I am ignorant of the Crime, the Fact I mean.' 'Why, there it is in Peaper,' answered the Justice, shewing him a Deposition, which in the Absence of his Clerk he had writ himself, of which we have with great Difficulty procured an authentick Copy; and here it follows *verbatim &* *literatim*.[1]

The Depusition of James Scout, *Layer, and* Thomas Trotter, *Yeoman, taken befor mee, on of his Magesty's Justasses of the Piece for* Zumersetshire.

'These Deponants saith, and first *Thomas Trotter* for himself saith, that on the   of this instant *October*, being Sabbath-Day, betwin the Ours of 2 and 4 in the Afternoon, he zeed *Joseph Andrews* and *Francis Goodwill* walk akross a certane Felde belunging to Layer *Scout*, and out of the Path which ledes thru the said Felde, and there he zede *Joseph Andrews* with a Nife cut one Hassel-Twig, of the value, as he believes, of 3 half pence, or thereabouts; and he saith, that the said *Francis Goodwill* was likewise walking on the Grass out of the said Path in the said Felde, and did receive and karry in her Hand the said Twig, and so was cumfarting, eading and abatting to the said *Joseph* therein. And the said *James Scout* for himself says, that he verily believes the said Twig to be his own proper Twig, *&c.*'

'*Jesu!*' said the Squire, 'would you commit two Persons to *Bridewell* for a Twig?' 'Yes,' said the Lawyer, 'and with great Lenity too; for if we had called it a young Tree they would have been both hanged.'[2] ——— 'Harkee,' (says the Justice, taking aside the Squire) 'I should not have been so severe on this Occasion, but Lady *Booby* desires to get them out of the Parish; so Lawyer *Scout* will give the Constable Orders to let them run away, if they please; but it seems they intend to marry together, and the Lady hath no other means, as they are legally settled there, to prevent their bringing an Incumbrance on her own Parish.' 'Well,' said the Squire, 'I will take care my Aunt shall be satisfied in this Point; and likewise I promise you, *Joseph* here shall never be any Incumbrance on her. I shall be obliged to you therefore, if, instead of *Bridewell*, you will commit them to my Custody.' ——— 'O to be sure, Sir, if you desire it,' answered the Justice; and without more ado, *Joseph* and *Fanny* were delivered over to Squire *Booby*, whom *Joseph* very well knew; but little guest how nearly he was related to him. The Justice burnt his *Mittimus*: The Constable was sent about his Business: The Lawyer made no Complaint for want of Justice; and the Prisoners, with exulting Hearts, gave a thousand Thanks to his Honour Mr *Booby*, who did not intend their Obligations to him should cease here; for ordering his Man to produce a Cloakbag which he had caused to be brought from Lady *Booby*'s on purpose, he desired the

Justice that he might have *Joseph* with him into a Room; where ordering his Servant to take out a Suit of his own Clothes, with Linnen and other Necessaries, he left *Joseph* to dress himself, who not yet knowing the Cause of all this Civility, excused his accepting such a Favour, as long as decently he could. Whilst *Joseph* was dressing, the Squire repaired to the Justice, whom he found talking with *Fanny*; for during the Examination she had lopped her Hat over her Eyes, which were also bathed in Tears, and had by that means concealed from his Worship what might perhaps have rendered the Arrival of Mr *Booby* unnecessary, at least for herself. The Justice no sooner saw her Countenance cleared up, and her bright Eyes shining through her Tears, than he secretly cursed himself for having once thought of *Bridewell* for her. He would willingly have sent his own Wife thither, to have had *Fanny* in her place. And conceiving almost at the same instant Desires and Schemes to accomplish them, he employed the Minutes whilst the Squire was absent with *Joseph*, in assuring her how sorry he was for having treated her so roughly before he knew her Merit; and told her, that since Lady *Booby* was unwilling that she should settle in her Parish, she was heartily welcome to his, where he promised her his Protection, adding, that he would take *Joseph* and her into his own Family, if she liked; which Assurance he confirmed with a Squeeze by the Hand. She thanked him very kindly, and said, 'She would acquaint *Joseph* with the Offer, which he would certainly be glad to accept; for that Lady *Booby* was angry with them both; tho' she did not know either had done any thing to offend her: but imputed it to Madam *Slipslop*, who had always been her Enemy.'

The Squire now returned, and prevented any farther Continuance of this Conversation; and the Justice out of a pretended Respect to his Guest, but in reality from an Apprehension of a Rival; (for he knew nothing of his Marriage) ordered *Fanny* into the Kitchin, whither she gladly retired; nor did the Squire, who declined the Trouble of explaining the whole matter, oppose it.

It would be unnecessary, if I was able, which indeed I am not, to relate the Conversation between these two Gentlemen, which rolled, as I have been informed, entirely on the Subject of Horse-racing. *Joseph* was soon drest in the plainest Dress he could find, which was a blue Coat and Breeches, with a Gold Edging, and a red Waistcoat with the same; and as this Suit, which was rather too large for the Squire, exactly fitted him; so he became it so well, and looked so genteel, that no Person would have doubted its being as well adapted to his Quality as his Shape; nor have

suspected, as one might when my Lord ——, or Sir ——, or Mr ——
appear in Lace or Embroidery, that the Taylor's Man wore those Clothes
home on his Back, which he should have carried under his Arm.

The Squire now took leave of the Justice, and calling for *Fanny*, made
her and *Joseph*, against their Wills, get into the Coach with him, which
he then ordered to drive to Lady *Booby*'s. —— It had moved a few Yards
only, when the Squire asked *Joseph*, if he knew who that Man was crossing
the Field; for, added he, I never saw one take such Strides before. *Joseph*
answered eagerly, 'O Sir, it is Parson *Adams*.' —— 'O la, indeed, and so
it is,' said *Fanny*; 'poor Man, he is coming to do what he could for us.
Well, he is the worthiest best natur'd Creature.' —— 'Ay,' said *Joseph*,
'God bless him; for there is not such another in the Universe.' —— 'The
best Creature living sure,' cries *Fanny*. 'Is he?' says the Squire, 'then I am
resolved to have the best Creature living in my Coach;' and so saying he
ordered it to stop, whilst *Joseph* at his Request hollowed to the Parson,
who well knowing his Voice, made all the haste imaginable, and soon
came up with them; he was desired by the Master, who could scarce
refrain from Laughter at his Figure, to mount into the Coach, which he
with many Thanks refused, saying he could walk by its side, and he'd
warrant he kept up with it; but he was at length over-prevailed on. The
Squire now acquainted *Joseph* with his Marriage; but he might have spared
himself that Labour; for his Servant, whilst *Joseph* was dressing, had
performed that Office before. He continued to express the vast Happiness
he enjoyed in his Sister, and the Value he had for all who belonged to
her. *Joseph* made many Bows, and exprest as many Acknowledgments;
and Parson *Adams*, who now first perceived *Joseph*'s new Apparel, burst
into Tears with Joy, and fell to rubbing his Hands and snapping his
Fingers, as if he had been mad.

They were now arrived at the Lady *Booby*'s, and the Squire desiring
them to wait a moment in the Court, walked in to his Aunt, and calling
her out from his Wife, acquainted her with *Joseph*'s Arrival; saying,
'Madam, as I have married a virtuous and worthy Woman, I am resolved
to own her Relations, and shew them all a proper Respect; I shall think
myself therefore infinitely obliged to all mine, who will do the same. It is
true her Brother hath been your Servant, but he is now become my Brother;
and I have one Happiness, that neither his Character, his Behaviour or
Appearance give me any reason to be ashamed of calling him so. In short,
he is now below, drest like a Gentleman, in which Light I intend he shall
hereafter be seen; and you will oblige me beyond Expression, if you will

admit him to be of our Party; for I know it will give great Pleasure to my Wife, tho' she will not mention it.'

This was a stroke of Fortune beyond the Lady *Booby*'s Hopes or Expectation; she answered him eagerly, 'Nephew, you know how easily I am prevailed on to do any thing which *Joseph Andrews* desires — Phoo, I mean which you desire me, and as he is now your Relation, I cannot refuse to entertain him as such.' The Squire told her, he knew his Obligation to her for her Compliance, and going three Steps, returned and told her — he had one more Favour, which he believed she would easily grant, as she had accorded him the former. 'There is a young Woman' — 'Nephew,' says she, 'don't let my Good-nature make you desire, as is too commonly the Case, to impose on me. Nor think, because I have with so much Condescension agreed to suffer your Brother-in-law to come to my Table, that I will submit to the Company of all my own Servants, and all the dirty Trollops in the Country.' 'Madam,' answer'd the Squire, 'I believe you never saw this young Creature. I never beheld such Sweetness and Innocence joined with such Beauty, and withal so genteel.' 'Upon my Soul, I won't admit her,' reply'd the Lady in a Passion; 'the whole World shan't prevail on me, I resent even the Desire as an Affront, and' — The Squire, who knew her Inflexibility, interrupted her, by asking Pardon, and promising not to mention it more. He then returned to *Joseph*, and she to *Pamela*. He took *Joseph* aside and told him, he would carry him to his Sister; but could not prevail as yet for *Fanny*. *Joseph* begged that he might see his Sister alone, and then be with his *Fanny*; but the Squire knowing the Pleasure his Wife would have in her Brother's Company, would not admit it, telling *Joseph* there would be nothing in so short an Absence from *Fanny*, whilst he was assured of her Safety; adding, he hoped he could not so easily quit a Sister whom he had not seen so long, and who so tenderly loved him — *Joseph* immediately complied; for indeed no Brother could love a Sister more; and recommending *Fanny*, who rejoiced that she was not to go before Lady *Booby*, to the Care of Mr *Adams*, he attended the Squire up stairs, whilst *Fanny* repaired with the Parson to his House, where she thought herself secure of a kind Reception.

CHAPTER VI

Of which you are desired to read no more than you like.

The Meeting between *Joseph* and *Pamela* was not without Tears of Joy on both sides; and their Embraces were full of Tenderness and Affection. They were however regarded with much more Pleasure by the Nephew than by the Aunt, to whose Flame they were Fewel only; and being assisted by the Addition of Dress, which was indeed not wanted to set off the lively Colours in which Nature had drawn Health, Strength, Comeliness, and Youth. In the Afternoon *Joseph*, at their Request, entertained them with an Account of his Adventures, nor could Lady *Booby* conceal her Dissatisfaction at those Parts in which *Fanny* was concerned, especially when Mr *Booby* launched forth into such rapturous Praises of her Beauty. She said, applying to her Niece, that she wondered her Nephew, who had pretended to marry for Love, should think such a Subject proper to amuse his Wife with: adding, that for her part, she should be jealous of a Husband who spoke so warmly in praise of another Woman. *Pamela* answer'd, indeed she thought she had cause; but it was an Instance of Mr *Booby*'s aptness to see more Beauty in Women than they were Mistresses of. At which Words both the Women fixed their Eyes on two Looking-Glasses; and Lady *Booby* replied that Men were in the general very ill Judges of Beauty; and then whilst both contemplated only their own Faces, they paid a cross Compliment to each other's Charms. When the Hour of Rest approached, which the Lady of the House deferred as long as decently she could, she informed *Joseph* (whom for the future we shall call Mr *Joseph*, he having as good a Title to that Appellation as many others, I mean that incontested one of good Clothes) that she had ordered a Bed to be provided for him, he declined this Favour to his utmost; for his Heart had long been with his *Fanny*; but she insisted on his accepting it, alledging that the Parish had no proper Accommodation for such a Person, as he was now to esteem himself. The Squire and his Lady both joining with her, Mr *Joseph* was at last forced to give over his Design of visiting *Fanny* that Evening, who on her side as impatiently expected him till Midnight, when in complacence to Mr *Adams*'s Family, who had sat up two Hours out of Respect to her, she retired to Bed, but not to sleep; the Thoughts of her Love kept her waking, and his not returning according to his Promise, filled her with Uneasiness; of which however she could not assign any other Cause than merely that of being absent from him.

Mr *Joseph* rose early in the Morning, and visited her in whom his Soul delighted. She no sooner heard his Voice in the Parson's Parlour, than she leapt from her Bed, and dressing herself in a few Minutes, went down to him. They past two Hours with inexpressible Happiness together, and then having appointed *Monday*, by Mr *Adams's* Permission, for their Marriage, Mr *Joseph* returned according to his Promise, to Breakfast at the Lady *Booby's*, with whose Behaviour since the Evening we shall now acquaint the Reader.

She was no sooner retired to her Chamber than she asked *Slipslop* what she thought of this wonderful Creature her Nephew had married. 'Madam!' said *Slipslop*, not yet sufficiently understanding what Answer she was to make. 'I ask you,' answered the Lady, 'what you think of the Dowdy, my Niece I think I am to call her?' *Slipslop*, wanting no further Hint, began to pull her to pieces, and so miserably defaced her, that it would have been impossible for any one to have known the Person. The Lady gave her all the Assistance she could, and ended with saying —— 'I think, *Slipslop*, you have done her Justice; but yet, bad as she is, she is an Angel compared to this *Fanny*.' *Slipslop* then fell on *Fanny*, whom she hack'd and hew'd in the like barbarous manner, concluding with an Observation that there was always something in those low-life Creatures which must eternally distinguish them from their Betters. 'Really,' said the Lady, 'I think there is one Exception to your Rule, I am certain you may guess who I mean.' — 'Not I, upon my word, Madam,' said *Slipslop*. — 'I mean a young Fellow; sure you are the dullest Wretch,' said the Lady —— 'O la, I am indeed —— Yes truly, Madam, he is an *Accession*,' answer'd *Slipslop*. —— 'Ay, is he not, *Slipslop*?' returned the Lady. 'Is he not so genteel that a Prince might without a Blush acknowledge him for his Son. His Behaviour is such that would not shame the best Education. He borrows from his Station a Condescension in every thing to his Superiors, yet unattended by that mean Servility which is called Good-Behaviour in such Persons. Every thing he doth hath no mark of the base Motive of Fear, but visibly shews some Respect and Gratitude, and carries with it the Persuasion of Love —— And then for his Virtues; such Piety to his Parents, such tender Affection to his Sister, such Integrity in his Friendship, such Bravery, such Goodness, that if he had been born a Gentleman, his Wife would have possest the most invaluable Blessing.'

—— 'To be sure, Ma'am,' says *Slipslop*. —— 'But as he is,' answered the Lady, 'if he had a thousand more good Qualities, it must render a Woman of Fashion contemptible even to be suspected of thinking of him, yes I should despise myself for such a Thought.' 'To be sure, Ma'am,' said *Slipslop*. 'And why to be sure?' reply'd the Lady; 'thou art always one's Echo. Is he not more worthy of Affection than a dirty Country Clown, tho' born of a Family as old as the Flood, or an idle worthless Rake, or little puisny[1] Beau of Quality? And yet these we must condemn ourselves to, in order to avoid the Censure of the World; to shun the Contempt of others, we must ally ourselves to those we despise; we must prefer Birth, Title and Fortune to real Merit. It is a Tyranny of Custom, a Tyranny we must comply with: For we People of Fashion are the Slaves of Custom.' —— 'Marry come up!' said *Slipslop*, who now well knew which Party to take, 'if I was a Woman of your Ladyship's Fortune and Quality, I would be a Slave to no body.' —— 'Me,' said the Lady, 'I am speaking, if a young Woman of Fashion who had seen nothing of the World should happen to like such a Fellow. — Me indeed; I hope thou dost not imagine' —— 'No, Ma'am, to be sure,' cried *Slipslop*. —— 'No! what no?' cried the Lady. 'Thou art always ready to answer, before thou hast heard one. So far I must allow he is a charming Fellow. Me indeed! No, *Slipslop*, all Thoughts of Men are over with me. —— I have lost a Husband, who —— but if I should reflect, I should run mad —— My future Ease must depend upon Forgetfulness. *Slipslop*, let me hear some of thy Nonsense to turn my Thoughts another way. What dost thou think of Mr *Andrews*?' 'Why I think,' says *Slipslop*, 'he is the handsomest most properest Man I ever saw; and if I was a Lady of the greatest Degree, it would be well for some Folks. Your Ladyship may talk of Custom if you please; but I am *confidous* there is no more Comparison between young Mr *Andrews*, and most of the young Gentlemen who come to your Ladyship's House in *London*; a Parcel of *Whipper-snapper* Sparks: I would sooner marry our old Parson *Adams*: Never tell me what People say, whilst I am happy in the Arms of him I love. Some Folks rail against other Folks, because other Folks have what some Folks would be glad of.' —— 'And so,' answered the Lady, 'if you was a Woman of Condition, you would really marry Mr *Andrews*.' —— 'Yes, I assure your Ladyship,' replied *Slipslop*, 'if he would have me.' —— 'Fool, Idiot,' cries the Lady, 'if he would have a Woman of Fashion! Is that a Question?' 'No truly, Madam,' said *Slipslop*, 'I believe it would be none, if *Fanny* was out of the way; and I am *confidous* if I was in your Ladyship's Place, and liked Mr *Joseph Andrews*, she should not stay in the Parish a moment. I am sure Lawyer *Scout* would send her packing if your Ladyship would but say the Word.' This last Speech of *Slipslop* raised a Tempest in the Mind of her Mistress. She feared *Scout* had betrayed her, or rather that she had betrayed herself. After some Silence and a double Change of her Complexion; first to pale and then to red, she thus spoke: 'I am astonished at the Liberty you give your Tongue. Would you insinuate, that I employed *Scout* against this Wench, on the account of the Fellow?' 'La Ma'am,' said *Slipslop*, frighted out of her Wits, 'I *assassinate* such a Thing!' 'I think you dare not,' answered the Lady, 'I believe my Conduct may defy Malice itself to assert so cursed a Slander. If I had ever discovered any Wantonness, any Lightness in my Behaviour: if I had followed the Example of some whom thou hast I believe seen, in allowing myself indecent Liberties, even with a Husband: But the dear Man who is gone' (*here she began to sob*) 'was he alive again,' (*then she produced Tears*) 'could not upbraid me with any one Act of Tenderness or Passion. No, *Slipslop*, all the time I cohabited with him, he never obtained even a Kiss from me, without my expressing Reluctance in the granting it. I am sure he himself never suspected how much I loved him.[2] —— Since his Death, thou knowest, tho' it is almost six Weeks (it wants but a Day) ago,[3] I have not admitted one Visitor, till this Fool my Nephew arrived. I have confined myself quite to one Party of Friends. —— And can such a Conduct as this fear to be arraigned? To be accused not only of a Passion which I have always despised, but of fixing it on such an Object, a Creature so much beneath my Notice.' —— 'Upon my word, Ma'am,' says *Slipslop*, 'I do not understand your Ladyship, nor know I any thing of the matter.' —— 'I believe indeed thou dost not understand me. —— Those are Delicacies which exist only in superior Minds; thy coarse Ideas cannot comprehend them. Thou art a low Creature, of the *Andrews* Breed, a Reptile of a lower Order, a Weed that grows in the common Garden of the Creation.' —— 'I assure your Ladyship,' says *Slipslop*, whose Passions were almost of as high an Order as her Lady's, 'I have no more to do with *Common Garden*[4] than other Folks. Really, your Ladyship talks of Servants as if they were not born of the Christian *Specious*. Servants have Flesh and Blood as well as Quality; and Mr *Andrews* himself is a Proof that they have as good, if not better. And for my own Part, I can't perceive my *Dears** are coarser than other People's; and I am sure, if Mr *Andrews* was a *Dear* of mine, I should not be ashamed of him in

---

* Meaning perhaps Ideas.

company with Gentlemen; for whoever hath seen him in his new Clothes, must confess he looks as much like a Gentleman as any body. Coarse, quotha! I can't bear to hear the poor young Fellow run down neither; for I will say this, I never heard him say an ill Word of any body in his Life. I am sure his Coarseness doth not lie in his Heart; for he is the best-natur'd Man in the World; and as for his Skin, it is no coarser than other People's, I am sure. His Bosom when a Boy was as white as driven Snow; and where it is not covered with Hairs, is so still. Ifaukins![5] if I was Mrs *Andrews*, with a hundred a Year, I should not envy the best She who wears a Head. A Woman that could not be happy with such a Man, ought never to be so: For if he can't make a Woman happy, I never yet beheld the Man who could. I say again I wish I was a great Lady for his sake, I believe when I had made a Gentleman of him, he'd behave so, that no body should *deprecate* what I had done; and I fancy few would venture to tell him he was no Gentleman to his Face, nor to mine neither.' At which Words, taking up the Candles, she asked her Mistress, who had been some time in her Bed, if she had any farther Commands; who mildly answered she had none; and telling her, she was a comical Creature, bid her Good-night.

CHAPTER VII

Philosophical Reflections, the like not to be found in any light French *Romance. Mr* Booby's *grave Advice to* Joseph, *and* Fanny's *Encounter with a Beau.*

Habit, my good Reader, hath so vast a Prevalence over the human Mind, that there is scarce any thing too strange or too strong to be asserted of it. The Story of the Miser, who from long accustoming to cheat others, came at last to cheat himself, and with great Delight and Triumph, picked his own Pocket of a Guinea, to convey to his Hoard, is not impossible or improbable. In like manner, it fares with the Practisers of Deceit, who from having long deceived their Acquaintance, gain at last a Power of deceiving themselves, and acquire that very Opinion (however false) of their own Abilities, Excellences and Virtues, into which they have for Years perhaps endeavoured to betray their Neighbours. Now, Reader, to apply this Observation to my present Purpose, thou must know, that as the Passion generally called Love, exercises most of the Talents of the

Female or fair World; so in this they now and then discover a small Inclination to Deceit; for which thou wilt not be angry with the beautiful Creatures, when thou hast considered, that at the Age of seven or something earlier, Miss is instructed by her Mother, that Master is a very monstrous kind of Animal, who will, if she suffers him to come too near her, infallibly eat her up, and grind her to pieces. That so far from kissing or toying with him of her own accord, she must not admit him to kiss or toy with her. And lastly, that she must never have any Affection towards him; for if she should, all her Friends in Petticoats would esteem her a Traitress, point at her, and hunt her out of their Society. These Impressions being first received, are farther and deeper inculcated by their School-mistresses and Companions; so that by the Age of Ten they have contracted such a Dread of, and Abhorrence of the above named Monster, that whenever they see him, they fly from him as the innocent Hare doth from the Greyhound. Hence to the Age of fourteen or fifteen they entertain a mighty Antipathy to Master; they resolve and frequently profess that they will never have any Commerce with him, and entertain fond Hopes of passing their Lives out of his reach, of the Possibility of which they have so visible an Example in their good Maiden Aunt. But when they arrive at this Period, and have now past their second Climacteric,[1] when their Wisdom grown riper, begins to see a little farther; and from almost daily falling in Master's way, to apprehend the great Difficulty of keeping out of it; and when they observe him look often at them, and sometimes very eagerly and earnestly too, (for the Monster seldom takes any notice of them till at this Age) they then begin to think of their Danger; and as they perceive they cannot easily avoid him, the wiser Part bethink themselves of providing by other Means for their Security. They endeavour by all the Methods they can invent to render themselves so amiable in his Eyes, that he may have no Inclination to hurt them; in which they generally succeed so well, that his Eyes, by frequent languishing, soon lessen their Idea of his Fierceness, and so far abate their Fears, that they venture to parley with him; and when they perceive him so different from what he hath been described, all Gentleness, Softness, Kindness, Tenderness, Fondness, their dreadful Apprehensions vanish in a moment; and now, (it being usual with the human Mind, to skip from one Extreme to its Opposite, as easily, and almost as suddenly, as a Bird from one Bough to another;) Love instantly succeeds to Fear: But as it happens to Persons who have in their Infancy been thoroughly frightned with certain no Persons called Ghosts, that they retain their Dread of those Beings, after they are convinced that there are no such things; so these young Ladies, tho' they no longer apprehend devouring, cannot so entirely shake off all that hath been instilled into them; they still entertain the Idea of that Censure which was so strongly imprinted on their tender Minds, to which the Declarations of Abhorrence they every day hear from their Companions greatly contribute. To avoid this Censure therefore, is now their only care; for which purpose they still pretend the same Aversion to the Monster: And the more they love him, the more ardently they counterfeit the Antipathy. By the continual and constant Practice of which Deceit on others, they at length impose on themselves, and really believe they hate what they love. Thus indeed it happened to Lady *Booby*, who loved *Joseph* long before she knew it; and now loved him much more than she suspected. She had indeed, from the time of his Sister's Arrival in the Quality of her Niece; and from the Instant she viewed him in the Dress and Character of a Gentleman, began to conceive secretly a Design which Love had concealed from herself, till a Dream betray'd it to her.

She had no sooner risen than she sent for her Nephew; when he came to her, after many Compliments on his Choice, she told him, 'He might perceive in her Condescension to admit her own Servant to her Table, that she looked on the Family of *Andrews* as his Relations, and indeed her's; that as he had married into such a Family, it became him to endeavour by all Methods to raise it as much as possible; at length she advised him to use all his Art to dissuade *Joseph* from his intended Match, which would still enlarge their Relation to Meanness and Poverty; concluding, that by a Commission in the Army,[2] or some other genteel Employment, he might soon put young Mr *Andrews* on the foot of a Gentleman; and that being once done, his Accomplishments might quickly gain him an Alliance, which would not be to their Discredit.'

Her Nephew heartily embraced this Proposal; and finding Mr *Joseph* with his Wife, at his Return to her Chamber, he immediately began thus: 'My Love to my dear *Pamela*, Brother, will extend to all her Relations; nor shall I shew them less Respect than if I had married into the Family of a Duke. I hope I have given you some early Testimonies of this, and shall continue to give you daily more. You will excuse me therefore, Brother, if my Concern for your Interest makes me mention what may be, perhaps, disagreeable to you to hear: But I must insist upon it, that if you have any Value for my Alliance or my Friendship, you will decline any Thoughts of engaging farther with a Girl, who is, as you are a Relation of mine, so much beneath you. I know there may be at first some Difficulty in your Compliance, but that will daily diminish; and you will in the end sincerely thank me for my Advice. I own, indeed, the Girl is handsome: but Beauty alone is a poor Ingredient, and will make but an uncomfortable Marriage.' 'Sir,' said *Joseph*, 'I assure you her Beauty is her least Perfection; nor do I know a Virtue which that young Creature is not possest of.' 'As to her Virtues,' answered *Mr Booby*, 'you can be yet but a slender Judge of them: But if she had never so many, you will find her Equal in these among her Superiors in Birth and Fortune, which now you are to esteem on a footing with yourself; at least I will take care they shall shortly be so, unless you prevent me by degrading yourself with such a Match, a Match I have hardly patience to think of; and which would break the Hearts of your Parents, who now rejoice in the Expectation of seeing you make a Figure in the World.' 'I know not,' replied *Joseph*, 'that my Parents have any Power over my Inclinations; nor am I obliged to sacrifice my Happiness to their Whim or Ambition: Besides, I shall be very sorry to see that the unexpected Advancement of my Sister, should so suddenly inspire them with this wicked Pride, and make them despise their Equals, I am resolved on no account to quit my dear *Fanny*, no, tho' I could raise her as high above her present Station as you have raised my Sister.' 'Your Sister, as well as myself,' said *Booby*, 'are greatly obliged to you for the Comparison: But, Sir, she is not worthy to be compared in Beauty to my *Pamela*; nor hath she half her Merit. And besides, Sir, as you civilly throw my Marriage with your Sister in my teeth, I must teach you the wide Difference between us; my Fortune enabled me to please myself; and it would have been as overgrown a Folly in me to have omitted it, as in you to do it.' 'My Fortune enables me to please myself likewise,' said *Joseph*; 'for all my Pleasure is centred in *Fanny*, and whilst I have Health, I shall be able to support her with my Labour in that Station to which she was born, and with which she is content.' 'Brother,' said *Pamela*, 'Mr *Booby* advises you as a Friend; and, no doubt, my Papa and Mamma will be of his Opinion, and will have great reason to be angry with you for destroying what his Goodness hath done, and throwing down our Family again, after he hath raised it. It would become you better, Brother, to pray for the Assistance of Grace against such a Passion, than to indulge it.' —— 'Sure, Sister, you are not in earnest; I am sure she is your Equal at least.' —— 'She was my Equal,' answered *Pamela*, 'but I am no longer *Pamela Andrews*, I am now this Gentleman's Wife, and as such am above her — I hope I shall never behave with an unbecoming Pride, but at the same time I shall always endeavour to know myself, and question not the Assistance of Grace to that purpose.' They were now summoned to Breakfast, and thus ended their Discourse for the present, very little to the Satisfaction of any of the Parties.

Fanny was now walking in an Avenue at some distance from the House, where *Joseph* had promised to take the first Opportunity of coming to her. She had not a Shilling in the World, and had subsisted ever since her Return entirely on the Charity of Parson *Adams*. A young Gentleman attended by many Servants, came up to her, and asked her if that was not the Lady *Booby*'s House before him? This indeed he well knew, but had framed the Question for no other Reason than to make her look up and discover if her Face was equal to the Delicacy of her Shape. He no sooner saw it, than he was struck with Amazement. He stopt his Horse, and swore she was the most beautiful Creature he ever beheld. Then instantly alighting, and delivering his Horse to his Servant, he rapt out half a dozen Oaths that he would kiss her; to which she at first submitted, begging he would not be rude: but he was not satisfied with the Civility of a Salute, nor even with the rudest Attack he could make on her Lips, but caught her in his Arms and endeavoured to kiss her Breasts, which with all her Strength she resisted; and as our Spark was not of the *Herculean* Race, with some difficulty prevented. The young Gentleman being soon out of breath in the Struggle, quitted her, and remounting his Horse called one of his Servants to him, whom he ordered to stay behind with her, and make her any Offers whatever, to prevail on her to return home with him in the Evening; and to assure her he would take her into Keeping. He then rode on with his other Servants, and arrived at the Lady's House, to whom he was a distant Relation, and was come to pay a Visit.

The trusty Fellow, who was employ'd in an Office he had been long accustomed to, discharged his Part with all the Fidelity and Dexterity imaginable; but to no purpose. She was entirely deaf to his Offers, and rejected them with the utmost Disdain. At last the Pimp, who had perhaps more warm Blood about him than his Master, began to sollicit for himself; he told her, tho' he was a Servant, he was a Man of some Fortune, which he would make her Mistress of —— and this without any Insult to her Virtue, for that he would marry her. She answer'd, if his Master himself, or the greatest Lord in the Land would marry her, she would refuse him. At last being weary with Persuasions, and on fire with Charms which would have almost kindled a Flame in the Bosom of an antient Philosopher, or modern Divine, he fastened his Horse to the Ground, and attacked her with much more Force than the Gentleman had exerted. Poor *Fanny* would have been able to resist his Rudeness a very short time, when the Deity who presides over chaste Love sent her *Joseph* to her Assistance. He no sooner came within sight, and perceived her struggling with a Man, than like a Cannon-Ball, or like Lightning, or any thing that is swifter, if any thing be, he ran towards her, and coming up just as the Ravisher had torn her Handkerchief from her Breast, before his Lips had touched that Seat of Innocence and Bliss, he dealt him so lusty a Blow in that part of his Neck which a Rope would have become with the utmost Propriety, that the Fellow staggered backwards, and perceiving he had to do with something rougher than the little, tender, trembling Hand of *Fanny*, he quitted her, and turning about saw his Rival, with Fire flashing from his Eyes, again ready to assail him; and indeed before he could well defend himself or return the first Blow, he received a second, which had it fallen on that part of the Stomach to which it was directed, would have been probably the last he would have had any occasion for; but the Ravisher lifting up his Hand, drove the Blow upwards to his Mouth, whence it dislodged three of his Teeth; and now not conceiving any extraordinary Affection for the Beauty of *Joseph*'s Person, nor being extremely pleased with this method of Salutation, he collected all his Force, and aimed a Blow at *Joseph*'s Breast, which he artfully parry'd with one Fist, so that it lost its Force entirely in Air. And stepping one Foot backward, he darted his Fist so fiercely at his Enemy, that had he not caught it in his Hand (for he was a Boxer of no inferiour Fame) it must have tumbled him on the Ground. And now the Ravisher meditated another Blow, which he aimed at that part of the Breast where the Heart is lodged; *Joseph* did not catch it as before, but so prevented its Aim, that it fell directly on his Nose, but with abated Force. *Joseph* then moving both Fist and Foot forwards at the same time, threw his Head so dextrously into the Stomach of the Ravisher, that he fell a lifeless Lump on the Field, where he lay many Minutes breathless and motionless.

When *Fanny* saw her *Joseph* receive a Blow in his Face, and Blood running in a Stream from him, she began to tear her Hair, and invoke all human and divine Power to his Assistance. She was not, however, long under this Affliction, before *Joseph* having conquered his Enemy, ran to her, and assured her he was not hurt; she then instantly fell on her Knees and thanked G—, that he had made *Joseph* the means of her Rescue, and at the same time preserved him from being injured in attempting it. She offered with her Handkerchief to wipe his Blood from his Face; but he seeing his Rival attempting to recover his Legs, turned to him and asked him if he had enough; to which the other answered he had; for he believed he had fought with the Devil, instead of a Man, and loosening his Horse, said he should not have attempted the Wench if he had known she had been so well provided for.

Fanny now begged *Joseph* to return with her to Parson *Adams*, and to promise that he would leave her no more; these were Propositions so agreeable to *Joseph*, that had he heard them he would have given an immediate Assent: but indeed his Eyes were now his only Sense; for you may remember, Reader, that the Ravisher had tore her Handkerchief from *Fanny*'s Neck, by which he had discovered such a Sight, that *Joseph* hath declared all the Statues he ever beheld were so much inferiour to it in Beauty, that it was more capable of converting a Man into a Statue, than of being imitated by the greatest Master of that Art. This modest Creature, whom no Warmth in Summer could ever induce to expose her Charms to the wanton Sun, a Modesty to which perhaps they owed their inconceivable Whiteness; had stood many Minutes bare-necked in the Presence of *Joseph*, before her Apprehension of his Danger, and the Horror of seeing his Blood would suffer her once to reflect on what concerned herself; till at last, when the Cause of her Concern had vanished, an Admiration at his Silence, together with observing the fixed Position of his Eyes, produced an Idea in the lovely Maid, which brought more Blood into her Face than had flowed from *Joseph*'s Nostrils. The snowy Hue of her Bosom was likewise exchanged to Vermillion at the instant when she clapped her Handkerchief round her Neck. *Joseph* saw the Uneasiness she suffered, and immediately removed his Eyes from an Object, in surveying which he had felt the greatest Delight which the Organs of Sight were capable of conveying to his Soul. So great was his Fear of offending her, and so truly did his Passion for her deserve the noble Name of Love.

Fanny being recovered from her Confusion, which was almost equalled by what *Joseph* had felt from observing it, again mentioned her Request; this was instantly and gladly complied with, and together they crossed two or three Fields, which brought them to the Habitation of Mr *Adams*.

CHAPTER VIII

A Discourse which happened between Mr Adams, *Mrs* Adams,
Joseph *and* Fanny; *with some Behaviour of Mr* Adams, *which will
be called by some few Readers, very low, absurd, and unnatural.*

The Parson and his Wife had just ended a long Dispute when the Lovers
came to the Door. Indeed this young Couple had been the Subject of the
Dispute; for Mrs *Adams* was one of those prudent People who never do
any thing to injure their Families, or perhaps one of those good Mothers
who would even stretch their Conscience to serve their Children. She had
long entertained hopes of seeing her eldest Daughter succeed Mrs *Slipslop*,
and of making her second Son an Exciseman by Lady *Booby*'s Interest.
These were Expectations she could not endure the Thoughts of quitting,
and was therefore very uneasy to see her Husband so resolute to oppose
the Lady's Intention in *Fanny*'s Affair. She told him, 'it behoved every
Man to take the first Care of his Family; that he had a Wife and six
Children, the maintaining and providing for whom would be Business
enough for him without intermeddling in other Folks Affairs; that he had
always preached up Submission to Superiours, and would do ill to give
an Example of the contrary Behaviour in his own Conduct; that if Lady
Booby did wrong, she must answer for it herself, and the Sin would not lie
at their door; that *Fanny* had been a Servant, and bred up in the Lady's
own Family, and consequently she must have known more of her than
they did, and it was very improbable if she had behaved herself well, that
the Lady would have been so bitterly her Enemy; that perhaps he was
too much inclined to think well of her because she was handsome, but
handsome Women were often no better than they should be; that G—
made ugly Women as well as handsome ones, and that if a Woman had
Virtue, it signified nothing whether she had Beauty or no.' For all which
Reasons she concluded, he should oblige the Lady and stop the future
Publication of the Banns. But all these excellent Arguments had no effect
on the Parson, who persisted in doing his Duty without regarding the
Consequence it might have on his worldly Interest; he endeavoured to
answer her as well as he could, to which she had just finished her Reply,
(for she had always the last Word every where but at Church) when *Joseph*
and *Fanny* entered their Kitchen, where the Parson and his Wife then sat
at Breakfast over some Bacon and Cabbage. There was a Coldness in the

Civility of Mrs *Adams*, which Persons of accurate Speculation[1] might have observed, but escaped her present Guests; indeed it was a good deal covered by the Heartiness of *Adams*, who no sooner heard that *Fanny* had neither eat nor drank that Morning, than he presented her a Bone of Bacon which he had just been gnawing, being the only Remains of his Provision, and then ran nimbly to the Tap, and produced a Mug of small Beer, which he called Ale, however it was the best in his House. *Joseph* addressing himself to the Parson, told him the Discourse which had past between Squire *Booby*, his Sister and himself, concerning *Fanny*: he then acquainted him with the Dangers whence he had rescued her, and communicated some Apprehensions on her account. He concluded, that he should never have an easy Moment till *Fanny* was absolutely his, and begged that he might be suffered to fetch a Licence, saying, he could easily borrow the Money. The Parson answered, that he had already given his Sentiments concerning a Licence, and that a very few Days would make it unnecessary. '*Joseph*,' says he, 'I wish this Haste doth not arise rather from your Impatience than your Fear; but as it certainly springs from one of these Causes, I will examine both. Of each of these therefore in their Turn; and first, for the first of these, namely, Impatience. Now, Child, I must inform you, that if in your purposed Marriage with this young Woman, you have no Intention but the Indulgence of carnal Appetites, you are guilty of a very heinous Sin. Marriage was ordained for nobler Purposes, as you will learn when you hear the Service provided on that Occasion read to you. Nay perhaps, if you are a good Lad, I shall give you a Sermon *gratis*, wherein I shall demonstrate how little Regard ought to be had to the Flesh on such Occasions. The Text will be, Child, *Matthew* the 5th, and Part of the 28th Verse, *Whosoever looketh on a Woman so as to lust after her*. The latter Part I shall omit, as foreign to my Purpose.[2] Indeed all such brutal Lusts and Affections are to be greatly subdued, if not totally eradicated, before the Vessel can be said to be consecrated to Honour. To marry with a View of gratifying those Inclinations is a Prostitution of that holy Ceremony, and must entail a Curse on all who so lightly undertake it. If, therefore, this Haste arises from Impatience, you are to correct, and not give way to it. Now as to the second Head which I proposed to speak to, namely, Fear: It argues a Diffidence highly criminal of that Power in which alone we should put our Trust, seeing we may be well assured that he is able not only to defeat the Designs of our Enemies, but even to turn their Hearts. Instead of taking therefore any unjustifiable or desperate means to rid ourselves of Fear, we should resort to Prayer only on these Occasions, and we may be then certain of obtaining what is best for us. When any Accident threatens us, we are not to despair, nor when it overtakes us, to grieve; we must submit in all things to the Will of Providence, and set our Affections so much on nothing here that we cannot quit it without Reluctance. You are a young Man, and can know but little of this World; I am older, and have seen a great deal. All Passions are criminal in their Excess, and even Love itself, if it is not subservient to our Duty, may render us blind to it. Had *Abraham* so loved his Son *Isaac*, as to refuse the Sacrifice required,[3] is there any of us who would not condemn him? *Joseph*, I know your many good Qualities, and value you for them: but as I am to render an Account of your Soul, which is committed to my Cure,[4] I cannot see any Fault without reminding you of it. You are too much inclined to Passion, Child, and have set your Affections so absolutely on this young Woman, that if G— required her at your hands, I fear you would reluctantly part with her. Now believe me, no Christian ought so to set his Heart on any Person or Thing in this World, but that whenever it shall be required or taken from him in any manner by Divine Providence, he may be able, peaceably, quietly, and contentedly to resign it.' At which Words one came hastily in and acquainted Mr *Adams* that his youngest Son was drowned. He stood silent a moment, and soon began to stamp about the Room and deplore his Loss with the bitterest Agony. *Joseph*, who was overwhelmed with Concern likewise, recovered himself sufficiently to endeavour to comfort the Parson; in which Attempt he used many Arguments that he had at several times remember'd out of his own Discourses both in private and publick, (for he was a great Enemy to the Passions, and preached nothing more than the Conquest of them by Reason and Grace) but he was not at leisure now to hearken to his Advice. 'Child, Child,' said he, 'do not go about Impossibilities. Had it been any other of my Children I could have born it with patience; but my little Prattler, the Darling and Comfort of my old Age —— the little Wretch to be snatched out of Life just at his Entrance into it; the sweetest, best-temper'd Boy, who never did a thing to offend me. It was but this Morning I gave him his first Lesson in *Quæ Genus*.[5] This was the very Book he learnt, poor Child! it is of no further use to thee now. He would have made the best Scholar, and have been an Ornament to the Church —— such Parts and such Goodness never met in one so young.' 'And the handsomest Lad too,' says Mrs *Adams*, recovering from a Swoon in *Fanny*'s Arms. —— 'My poor *Jacky*,[6] shall I never see thee more?' cries the Parson —— 'Yes, surely,' says *Joseph*, 'and in a better Place, you will meet again never to part more.' —— I believe the Parson did not hear these Words, for he paid little regard to them, but went on lamenting whilst the Tears trickled down into his Bosom. At last he cry'd out, 'Where is my little Darling?' and was sallying out, when to his great Surprize and Joy, in which I hope the Reader will sympathize, he met his Son in a wet Condition indeed, but alive, and running towards him. The Person who brought the News of his Misfortune, had been a little too eager, as People sometimes are, from I believe no very good Principle, to relate ill News; and seeing him fall into the River, instead of running to his Assistance, directly ran to acquaint his Father of a Fate which he had concluded to be inevitable, but whence the Child was relieved by the same poor Pedlar who had relieved his Father before from a less Distress. The Parson's Joy was now as extravagant as his Grief had been before; he kissed and embraced his Son a thousand times, and danced about the Room like one frantick; but as soon as he discovered the Face of his old Friend the Pedlar, and heard the fresh Obligation he had to him, what were his Sensations? not those which two Courtiers feel in one another's Embraces; not those with which a great Man receives the vile, treacherous Engines of his wicked Purposes; not those with which a worthless younger Brother wishes his elder Joy of a Son, or a Man congratulates his Rival on his obtaining a Mistress, a Place, or an Honour. —— No, Reader, he felt the Ebullition, the Overflowings of a full, honest, open Heart towards the Person who had conferred a real Obligation, and of which if thou can'st not conceive an Idea within, I will not vainly endeavour to assist thee.

When these Tumults were over, the Parson taking *Joseph* aside, proceeded thus —— 'No, *Joseph*, do not give too much way to thy Passions, if thou dost expect Happiness.' —— The Patience of *Joseph*, nor perhaps of *Job*, could bear no longer; he interrupted the Parson, saying, 'it was easier to give Advice than take it, nor did he perceive he could so entirely conquer himself, when he apprehended he had lost his Son, or when he found him recover'd.' —— 'Boy,' reply'd *Adams*, raising his Voice, 'it doth not become green Heads to advise grey Hairs — Thou art ignorant of the Tenderness of fatherly Affection; when thou art a Father thou wilt be capable then only of knowing what a Father can feel. No Man is obliged to Impossibilities, and the Loss of a Child is one of those great Trials where our Grief may be allowed to become immoderate.' 'Well, Sir,' cries *Joseph*, 'and if I love a Mistress as well as you your Child, surely her Loss would grieve me equally.' 'Yes, but such Love is Foolishness, and wrong in itself, and ought to be conquered,' answered *Adams*, 'it savours too much of the Flesh.' 'Sure, Sir,' says *Joseph*, 'it is not sinful to love my Wife, no not even to doat on her to Distraction!' 'Indeed but it is,' says *Adams*. 'Every man ought to love his Wife, no doubt; we are commanded so to do; but we ought to love her with Moderation and Discretion.' —— 'I am afraid I shall be guilty of some Sin, in spight of all my Endeavours,' says *Joseph*; 'for I shall love without any Moderation, I am sure.' —— 'You talk foolishly and childishly,' cries *Adams*. 'Indeed,' says Mrs *Adams*, who had listen'd to the latter part of their Conversation, 'you talk more foolishly yourself. I hope, my Dear, you will never preach any such Doctrine as that Husbands can love their Wives too well. If I knew you had such a Sermon in the House, I am sure I would burn it; and I declare if I had not been convinced you had loved me as well as you could, I can answer for myself I should have hated and despised you. Marry come up! Fine Doctrine indeed! A Wife hath a Right to insist on her Husband's loving her as much as ever he can; and he is a sinful Villain who doth not. Doth he not promise to love her, and to comfort her, and to cherish her, and all that? I am sure I remember it all, as well as if I had repeated it over but yesterday, and shall never forget it. Besides, I am certain you do not preach as you practise; for you have been a loving and a cherishing Husband to me, that's the truth on't; and why you should endeavour to put such wicked Nonsense into this young Man's Head, I cannot devise. Don't hearken to him, Mr *Joseph*, be as good a Husband as you are able, and love your Wife with all your Body and Soul too.' Here a violent Rap at the Door put an end to their Discourse, and produced a Scene which the Reader will find in the next Chapter.

CHAPTER IX

A Visit which the good Lady Booby *and her polite Friend paid to the Parson.*

The Lady *Booby* had no sooner had an Account from the Gentleman of his meeting a wonderful Beauty near her House, and perceived the Raptures with which he spoke of her, than immediately concluding it must be *Fanny*, she began to meditate a Design of bringing them better acquainted; and to entertain Hopes that the fine Clothes, Presents and Promises of his Youth, would prevail on her to abandon *Joseph*: She therefore proposed to her Company a Walk in the Fields before Dinner, when she led them towards Mr *Adams*'s House; and as she approached it, told them, if they pleased she would divert them with one of the most ridiculous Sights they had ever seen, which was an old foolish Parson, who, she said laughing, kept a Wife and six Brats on a Salary of about 20 Pounds a Year; adding, that there was not such another ragged Family in the Parish. They all readily agreed to this Visit, and arrived whilst Mrs *Adams* was declaiming, as in the last Chapter. Beau *Didapper*, which was the Name of the young Gentleman we have seen riding towards Lady *Booby*'s, with his Cane mimicked the Rap of a *London* Footman at the Door. The People within; namely, *Adams*, his Wife, and three Children, *Joseph*, *Fanny*, and the Pedlar, were all thrown into Confusion by this knock; but *Adams* went directly to the Door, which being opened, the Lady *Booby* and her Company walked in, and were received by the Parson with about two hundred Bows; and by his Wife with as many Curt'sies; the latter telling the Lady, 'She was ashamed to be seen in such a Pickle, and that her House was in such a Litter: But that if she had expected such an Honour from her Ladyship, she should have found her in a better manner.' The Parson made no Apologies, tho' he was in his Half-Cassock and a Flannel Night-Cap. He said, 'they were heartily welcome to his poor Cottage,' and turning to Mr *Didapper*, cried out, *Non mea renidet in Domo Lacunar.*[1] The Beau answer'd, 'He did not understand *Welch*;' at which the Parson stared, and made no Reply.

Mr *Didapper*, or Beau *Didapper*, was a young Gentleman of about four Foot five Inches in height. He wore his own Hair, tho' the Scarcity of it might have given him sufficient Excuse for a Periwig. His Face was thin and pale: The Shape of his Body and Legs none of the best; for he had very narrow Shoulders, and no Calf; and his Gait might more properly be called hopping than walking. The Qualifications of his Mind were well adapted to his Person. We shall handle them first negatively. He was not entirely ignorant: For he could talk a little *French*, and sing two or three *Italian* Songs: He had lived too much in the World to be bashful, and too much at Court to be proud: He seemed not much inclined to Avarice; for he was profuse in his Expences: Nor had he all the Features of Prodigality; for he never gave a Shilling: — No Hater of Women; for he always dangled after them; yet so little subject to Lust, that he had, among those who knew him best, the Character of great Moderation in his Pleasures. No Drinker of Wine; nor so addicted to Passion, but that a hot Word or two from an Adversary made him immediately cool.

Now, to give him only a Dash or two on the affirmative Side: 'Tho' he was born to an immense Fortune, he chose, for the pitiful and dirty Consideration of a Place of little consequence, to depend entirely on the Will of a Fellow, whom they call a Great-Man; who treated him with the utmost Disrespect, and exacted of him a plenary Obedience to his Commands; which he implicitly submitted to, at the Expence of his Conscience, his Honour, and of his Country in which he had himself so very large a Share.'[2] And to finish his Character; 'As he was entirely well satisfied with his own Person and Parts, so he was very apt to ridicule and laugh at any Imperfection in another.'[3] Such was the little Person or rather Thing that hopped after Lady *Booby* into Mr *Adams*'s Kitchin.

The Parson and his Company retreated from the Chimney-side, where they had been seated, to give room to the Lady and hers. Instead of returning any of the Curt'sies or extraordinary Civility of Mrs *Adams*, the Lady turning to Mr *Booby*, cried out, '*Quelle Bête! Quel Animal!*' And presently after discovering *Fanny* (for she did not need the Circumstance of her standing by *Joseph* to assure the Identity of her Person) she asked the Beau, 'Whether he did not think her a pretty Girl?' —— 'Begad, Madam,' answered he, ' 'tis the very same I met.' 'I did not imagine,' replied the Lady, 'you had so good a Taste.' 'Because I never liked you, I warrant,' cries the Beau. 'Ridiculous!' said she, 'you know you was always my Aversion.' 'I would never mention Aversion,' answer'd the Beau, 'with that Face;* dear Lady *Booby*, wash your Face before you mention Aversion, I beseech you.' He then laughed and turned about to coquette it with *Fanny*.

Mrs *Adams* had been all this time begging and praying the Ladies to sit down, a Favour which she had at last obtained. The little Boy to whom the Accident had happened, still keeping his Place by the Fire, was chid by his Mother for not being more mannerly: But Lady *Booby* took his part, and commending his Beauty, told the Parson he was his very Picture. She then seeing a Book in his Hand, asked, 'if he could read?' 'Yes,' cried *Adams*, 'a little *Latin*, Madam, he is just got into *Quæ Genus*.' —— 'A Fig for *quere genius*,' answered she, 'let me hear him read a little *English*.' —— '*Lege, Dick, Lege*,' said *Adams*: But the Boy made no Answer, till he saw the Parson knit his Brows; and then cried, 'I don't understand you, Father.' 'How, Boy,' says *Adams*, 'What doth *Lego* make in the imperative Mood?

* Lest this should appear unnatural to some Readers, we think proper to acquaint them, that it is taken *verbatim* from very polite Conversation.[4]

Legito, doth it not?' 'Yes,' answered *Dick*. —— 'And what besides,' says the Father. '*Lege*,' quoth the Son, after some hesitation. 'A good Boy,' says the Father: 'And now, Child, What is the *English* of *Lego*?' — To which the Boy, after long puzzling, answered, he could not tell. 'How,' cries *Adams* in a Passion, — 'What hath the Water washed away your Learning? Why, what is *Latin* for the *English* Verb *read*. Consider before you speak.' — The Child considered some time, and then the Parson cried twice or thrice, '*Le*—, *Le*—,' —— *Dick* answered, '*Lego*.' —— 'Very well; — and then, what is the *English*,' says the Parson, 'of the Verb *Lego*?' —— '*To read*,' cried *Dick*. —— 'Very well,' said the Parson, 'a good Boy, you can do well, if you will take pains. —— I assure your Ladyship he is not much above eight Years old, and is out of his *Propria quæ Maribus*[5] already. —— Come, *Dick*, read to her Ladyship;' —— which she again desiring, in order to give the Beau Time and Opportunity with *Fanny*, *Dick* began as in the following Chapter.

CHAPTER X

The History of two Friends, which may afford an useful Lesson to all those Persons, who happen to take up their Residence in married Families.

'*Leonard* and *Paul* were two Friends.' —— 'Pronounce it *Lennard*, Child,' cry'd the Parson. —— 'Pray, Mr *Adams*,' says Lady *Booby*, 'let your Son read without Interruption.' *Dick* then proceeded. '*Lennard* and *Paul* were two Friends, who having been educated together at the same School, commenced a Friendship which they preserved a long time for each other. It was so deeply fixed in both their Minds, that a long Absence, during which they had maintained no Correspondence, did not eradicate nor lessen it: But it revived in all its Force at their first Meeting, which was not till after fifteen Years Absence, most of which Time *Lennard* had spent in the *East-Indi-es*.' —— 'Pronounce it short *Indies*,' says *Adams*. —— 'Pray, Sir, be quiet,' says the Lady. — The Boy repeated — 'in the *East-Indies*, whilst *Paul* had served his King and Country in the Army. In which different Services, they had found such different Success, that *Lennard* was now married, and retired with a Fortune of thirty thousand Pound; and *Paul* was arrived to the Degree of a Lieutenant of Foot; and was not worth a single Shilling.

'The Regiment in which *Paul* was stationed, happened to be ordered into Quarters, within a small distance from the Estate which *Lennard* had purchased; and where he was settled. This latter, who was now become a Country Gentleman and a Justice of Peace, came to attend the Quarter-Sessions, in the Town where his old Friend was quartered, soon after his Arrival. Some Affair in which a Soldier was concerned, occasioned *Paul* to attend the Justices. Manhood, and Time, and the Change of Climate had so much altered *Lennard*, that *Paul* did not immediately recollect the Features of his old Acquaintance: But it was otherwise with *Lennard*. He knew *Paul* the moment he saw him; nor could he contain himself from quitting the Bench, and running hastily to embrace him. *Paul* stood at first a little surprized; but had soon sufficient Information from his Friend, whom he no sooner remembred, than he returned his Embrace with a Passion which made many of the Spectators laugh, and gave to some few a much higher and more agreeable Sensation.

'Not to detain the Reader with minute Circumstances, *Lennard* insisted on his Friend's returning with him to his House that Evening; which Request was complied with, and Leave for a Month's Absence for *Paul*, obtained of the commanding Officer.

'If it was possible for any Circumstance to give any addition to the Happiness which *Paul* proposed in this Visit, he received that additional Pleasure, by finding on his Arrival at his Friend's House, that his Lady was an old Acquaintance which he had formerly contracted at his Quarters; and who had always appeared to be of a most agreeable Temper. A Character she had ever maintained among her Intimates, being of that number, every Individual of which is called quite best sort of Woman in the World.

'But good as this Lady was, she was still a Woman; that is to say, an Angel and not an Angel — 'You must mistake, Child,' cries the Parson, 'for you read Nonsense.' 'It is so in the Book,' answered the Son. Mr *Adams* was then silenced by Authority, and *Dick* proceeded — 'For tho' her Person was of that kind to which Men attribute the Name of Angel, yet in her Mind she was perfectly Woman. Of which a great degree of Obstinacy gave the most remarkable, and perhaps most pernicious Instance.

'A Day or two past after *Paul*'s Arrival before any Instances of this appear'd; but it was impossible to conceal it long. Both she and her Husband soon lost all Apprehension from their Friend's Presence, and fell to their Disputes with as much Vigour as ever. These were still pursued with the utmost Ardour and Eagerness, however trifling the Causes were whence they first arose. Nay, however incredible it may seem, the little Consequence of the matter in Debate was frequently given as a Reason for the Fierceness of the Contention, as thus: *If you loved me, sure you would never dispute with me such a Trifle as this.* The Answer to which is very obvious; for the Argument would hold equally on both sides, and was constantly retorted with some Addition, as — *I am sure I have much more Reason to say so, who am in the right.* During all these Disputes, *Paul* always kept strict Silence, and preserved an even Countenance without shewing the least visible Inclination to either Party. One day, however, when Madam had left the Room in a violent Fury, *Lennard* could not refrain from referring his Cause to his Friend. Was ever any thing so unreasonable, says he, as this Woman? What shall I do with her? I doat on her to Distraction; nor have I any Cause to complain of more than this Obstinacy in her Temper; whatever she asserts she will maintain against all the Reason and Conviction[1] in the World. Pray give me your Advice. — First, says *Paul,* I will give my Opinion, which is flatly that you are in the wrong; for supposing she is in the wrong, was the Subject of your Contention anywise material? What signified it whether you was married in a red or yellow Waistcoat? for that was your Dispute. Now suppose she was mistaken, as you love her you say so tenderly, and I believe she deserves it, would it not have been wiser to have yielded, tho' you certainly knew yourself in the right, than to give either her or yourself any Uneasiness? For my own part, if ever I marry, I am resolved to enter into an Agreement with my Wife, that in all Disputes (especially about Trifles) that Party who is most convinced they are right, shall always surrender the Victory: by which means we shall both be forward to give up the Cause. I own, said *Lennard,* my dear Friend, shaking him by the Hand, there is great Truth and Reason in what you say; and I will for the future endeavour to follow your Advice. They soon after broke up the Conversation, and *Lennard* going to his Wife, asked her pardon, and told her his Friend had convinced him he had been in the wrong. She immediately began a vast Encomium on *Paul,* in which he seconded her, and both agreed he was the worthiest and wisest Man upon Earth. When next they met, which was at Supper, tho' she had promised not to mention what her Husband told her, she could not forbear casting the kindest and most affectionare Looks on *Paul,* and asked him with the sweetest Voice, whether she should help him to some Potted-Woodcock? — Potted Partridge, my Dear, you mean, says the Husband. My Dear, says she, I ask your Friend if he will eat any potted Woodcock; and I am sure I must know, who potted it. I think I should know too who shot them, reply'd the Husband, and I am convinced I have not seen a Woodcock this Year; however, tho' I know I am in the right I submit, and the potted Partridge is potted Woodcock, if you desire to have it so. It is equal to me, says she, whether it is one or the other; but you would persuade one out of one's Senses; to be sure you are always in the right in your own Opinion; but your Friend I believe knows which he is eating. *Paul* answered nothing, and the Dispute continued as usual the greatest part of the Evening. The next Morning the Lady accidentally meeting *Paul*, and being convinced he was her Friend, and of her side, accosted him thus: — I am certain, Sir, you have long since wonder'd at the Unreasonableness of my Husband. He is indeed in other respects a good sort of Man; but so positive, that no Woman but one of my complying Temper could possibly live with him. Why last Night now, was ever any Creature so unreasonable? —— I am certain you must condemn him. —— Pray answer me, was he not in the wrong? *Paul*, after a short Silence, spoke as follows: I am sorry, Madam, that as Good-manners obliges me to answer against my Will, so an Adherence to Truth forces me to declare myself of a different Opinion. To be plain and honest, you was entirely in the wrong; the Cause I own not worth disputing, but the Bird was undoubtedly a Partridge. O Sir, reply'd the Lady, I cannot possibly help your Taste. —— Madam, returned *Paul*, that is very little material; for had it been otherwise, a Husband might have expected Submission. —— Indeed! Sir, says she, I assure you! — Yes, Madam, cry'd he, he might from a Person of your excellent Understanding; and pardon me for saying such a Condescension would have shewn a Superiority of Sense even to your Husband himself. —— But, dear Sir, said she, why should I submit when I am in the right? — For that very Reason, answer'd he, it would be the greatest Instance of Affection imaginable: for can any thing be a greater Object of our Compassion than a Person we love, in the wrong? Ay, but I should endeavour, said she, to set him right. Pardon me, Madam, answer'd *Paul*, I will apply to your own Experience, if you ever found your Arguments had that effect. The more our Judgments err, the less we are willing to own it: for my own part, I have always observed the Persons who maintain the worst side in any Contest, are the warmest. Why, says she, I must confess there is Truth in what you say, and I will endeavour to practise it. The Husband then coming in, *Paul* departed. And *Lennard* approaching his Wife with an Air of Good-humour, told her he was sorry for their foolish Dispute the last Night: but he was now convinced of his Error. She answer'd smiling, she believed she owed his

Condescension to his Complacence;[2] that she was ashamed to think a Word had past on so silly an Occasion, especially as she was satisfy'd she had been mistaken. A little Contention follow'd, but with the utmost Good-will to each other, and was concluded by her asserting that *Paul* had thoroughly convinced her she had been in the wrong. Upon which they both united in the Praises of their common Friend.

'*Paul* now past his time with great Satisfaction; these Disputes being much less frequent as well as shorter than usual: but the Devil, or some unlucky Accident in which perhaps the Devil had no hand, shortly put an end to his Happiness. He was now eternally the private Referee of every Difference; in which after having perfectly as he thought established the Doctrine of Submission, he never scrupled to assure both privately that they were in the right in every Argument, as before he had follow'd the contrary Method. One day a violent Litigation happen'd in his Absence, and both Parties agreed to refer it to his Decision. The Husband professing himself sure the Decision would be in his favour, the Wife answer'd, he might be mistaken; for she believed his Friend was convinced how seldom she was to blame — and that if he knew all — The Husband reply'd — My Dear, I have no desire of any Retrospect, but I believe if you knew all too, you would not imagine my Friend so entirely on your side. Nay, says she, since you provoke me, I will mention one Instance. You may remember our Dispute about sending *Jacky* to School in cold Weather, which Point I gave up to you from mere Compassion, knowing myself to be in the right, and *Paul* himself told me afterwards, he thought me so. My Dear, replied the Husband, I will not scruple[3] your Veracity; but I assure you solemnly, on my applying to him, he gave it absolutely on my side, and said he would have acted in the same manner. They then proceeded to produce numberless other Instances, in all which *Paul* had, on Vows of Secrecy, given his Opinion on both sides. In the Conclusion, both believing each other, they fell severely on the Treachery of *Paul*, and agreed that he had been the occasion of almost every Dispute which had fallen out between them. They then became extremely loving, and so full of Condescension on both sides, that they vyed with each other in censuring their own Conduct, and jointly vented their Indignation on *Paul*, whom the Wife, fearing a bloody Consequence, earnestly entreated her Husband to suffer quietly to depart the next Day, which was the time fixed for his Return to Quarters, and then drop his Acquaintance.

'However ungenerous this Behaviour in *Lennard* may be esteemed, his Wife obtain'd a Promise from him (tho' with difficulty) to follow her

Advice; but they both exprest such unusual Coldness that day to *Paul*, that he, who was quick of Apprehension, taking *Lennard* aside, prest him so home, that he at last discovered the Secret. *Paul* acknowledged the Truth, but told him the Design with which he had done it — To which the other answer'd, he would have acted more friendly to have let him into the whole Design; for that he might have assured himself of his Secrecy. *Paul* reply'd, with some Indignation, he had given him a sufficient Proof how capable he was of concealing a Secret from his Wife. *Lennard* returned with some Warmth — He had more reason to upbraid him, for that he had caused most of the Quarrels between them by his strange Conduct, and might (if they had not discover'd the Affair to each other) have been the Occasion of their Separation. *Paul* then said' — But something now happen'd which put a stop to *Dick*'s Reading, and of which we shall treat in the next Chapter.

CHAPTER XI

In which the History is continued.

Joseph Andrews had borne with great Uneasiness the Impertinence of Beau *Didapper* to *Fanny*, who had been talking pretty freely to her, and offering her Settlements;[1] but the Respect to the Company had restrained him from interfering, whilst the Beau confined himself to the Use of his Tongue only; but the said Beau watching an Opportunity whilst the Ladies Eyes were disposed another way, offered a Rudeness to her with his Hands; which *Joseph* no sooner perceived than he presented him with so sound a Box on the Ear, that it conveyed him several Paces from where he stood. The Ladies immediately skreamed out, rose from their Chairs, and the Beau, as soon as he recovered himself, drew his Hanger, which *Adams* observing, snatched up the Lid of a Pot in his left Hand, and covering himself with it as with a Shield, without any Weapon of Offence, in his other Hand, stept in before *Joseph*, and exposed himself to the enraged Beau, who threatened such Perdition and Destruction, that it frighted the Women, who were all got in a huddle together, out of their Wits, even to hear his Denunciations of Vengeance. *Joseph* was of a different Complexion,[2] and begged *Adams* to let his Rival come on; for he had a good Cudgel in his Hand, and did not fear him. *Fanny* now fainted into Mrs *Adams*'s Arms, and the whole Room was in Confusion, when Mr *Booby* passing by *Adams*, who lay snug under the Pot-Lid, came up to *Didapper*, and insisted on his sheathing the Hanger, promising he should have Satisfaction; which *Joseph* declared he would give him, and fight him at any Weapon whatever. The Beau now sheathed his Hanger, and taking out a Pocket-Glass, and vowing Vengeance all the Time, he re-adjusted his Hair; the Parson deposited his Shield, and *Joseph* running to *Fanny*, soon brought her back to Life. Lady *Booby* chid *Joseph* for his Insult on *Didapper*; but he answered he would have attacked an Army in the same Cause. 'What Cause?' said the Lady. 'Madam,' answered *Joseph*, 'he was rude to that young Woman.' —— 'What,' says the Lady, 'I suppose he would have kissed the Wench; and is a Gentleman to be struck for such an Offer? I must tell you, *Joseph*, these Airs do not become you.' —— 'Madam,' said Mr *Booby*, 'I saw the whole Affair, and I do not commend my Brother; for I cannot perceive why he should take upon him to be this Girl's Champion.' —— 'I can commend him,' says *Adams*, 'he is a brave Lad; and it becomes any Man to be the Champion of the Innocent; and he must be the basest Coward, who would not vindicate a Woman with whom he is on the Brink of Marriage.' —— 'Sir,' says Mr *Booby*, 'my Brother is not a proper Match for such a young Woman as this.' —— 'No,' says Lady *Booby*, 'nor do you, Mr *Adams*, act in your proper Character, by encouraging any such Doings; and I am very much surprized you should concern yourself in it. I think your Wife and Family your properer Care.' —— 'Indeed, Madam, your Ladyship says very true,' answered Mrs *Adams*, 'he talks a pack of Nonsense, that the whole Parish are his Children. I am sure I don't understand what he means by it; it would make some Women suspect he had gone astray: but I acquit him of that; I can read Scripture as well as he; and I never found that the Parson was obliged to provide for other Folks Children; and besides, he is but a poor Curate, and hath little enough, as your Ladyship knows, for me and mine.' —— 'You say very well, Mrs *Adams*,' quoth the Lady *Booby*, who had not spoke a Word to her before, 'you seem to be a very sensible Woman; and I assure you, your Husband is acting a very foolish Part, and opposing his own Interest; seeing my Nephew is violently set against this Match: and indeed I can't blame him; it is by no means one suitable to our Family.' In this manner the Lady proceeded with Mrs *Adams*, whilst the Beau hopped about the Room, shaking his Head; partly from Pain, and partly from Anger; and *Pamela* was chiding *Fanny* for her Assurance,[3] in aiming at such a Match as her Brother. —— Poor *Fanny* answered only with her Tears, which had long since begun to wet her

Handkerchief; which *Joseph* perceiving, took her by the Arm, and wrapping it in his, carried her off, swearing he would own no Relation to any one who was an Enemy to her he loved more than all the World. He went out with *Fanny* under his left Arm, brandishing a Cudgel in his right, and neither Mr *Booby* nor the Beau thought proper to oppose him. Lady *Booby* and her Company made a very short stay behind him; for the Lady's Bell now summoned them to dress; for which they had just time before Dinner.

Adams seemed now very much dejected, which his Wife perceiving, began to apply some matrimonial Balsam. She told him he had Reason to be concerned; for that he had most probably ruined his Family with his Tricks: But perhaps he was grieved for the Loss of his two Children, *Joseph* and *Fanny*. His eldest Daughter went on: — 'Indeed Father, it is very hard to bring Strangers here to eat your Children's Bread out of their Mouths. — You have kept them ever since they came home; and for any thing I see to the contrary may keep them a Month longer: Are you obliged to give her Meat, tho's she was never so handsome? But I don't see she is so much handsomer than other People. If People were to be kept for their Beauty, she would scarce fare better than her Neighbours, I believe. —— As for Mr *Joseph*, I have nothing to say, he is a young Man of honest Principles, and will pay some time or other for what he hath: But for the Girl, —— Why doth she not return to her Place she ran away from? I would not give such a Vagabond Slut a Halfpenny, tho' I had a Million of Money; no, tho' she was starving.' 'Indeed but I would,' cries little *Dick*; 'and Father, rather than poor *Fanny* shall be starved, I will give her all this Bread and Cheese.' —— *(Offering what he held in his Hand.)* —— *Adams* smiled on the Boy, and told him he rejoiced to see he was a Christian; and that if he had a Halfpenny in his Pocket he would have given it him; telling him, it was his Duty to look upon all his Neighbours as his Brothers and Sisters, and love them accordingly. 'Yes, Papa,' says he, 'I love her better than my Sisters; for she is handsomer than any of them.' 'Is she so, Saucebox?' says the Sister, giving him a Box on the Ear, which the Father would probably have resented, had not *Joseph*, *Fanny*, and the Pedlar, at that Instant, returned together. —— *Adams* bid his Wife prepare some Food for their Dinner; she said, 'truly she could not, she had something else to do.' *Adams* rebuked her for disputing his Commands, and quoted many Texts of Scripture[4] to prove, *that the Husband is the Head of the Wife, and she is to submit and obey.* The Wife answered, 'it was Blasphemy to talk Scripture out of Church; that such things were very proper to be said in the Pulpit: but that it was prophane to talk them

315

in common Discourse.' *Joseph* told Mr *Adams* 'he was not come with any Design to give him or Mrs *Adams* any trouble; but to desire the Favour of all their Company to the *George* (an Alehouse in the Parish,) where he had bespoke a Piece of Bacon and Greens for their Dinner.' Mrs *Adams*, who was a very good sort of Woman, only rather too strict in Œconomicks,[5] readily accepted this Invitation, as did the Parson himself by her Example; and away they all walked together, not omitting little *Dick*, to whom *Joseph* gave a Shilling, when he heard of his intended Liberality to *Fanny*.

CHAPTER XII

Where the good-natur'd Reader will see something which will give him
no great Pleasure.

The Pedlar had been very inquisitive from the time he had first heard that the great House in this Parish belonged to the Lady *Booby*; and had learnt that she was the Widow of Sir *Thomas*, and that Sir *Thomas* had bought *Fanny*, at about the Age of three or four Years, of a travelling Woman; and now their homely but hearty Meal was ended, he told *Fanny*, he believed he could acquaint her with her Parents. The whole Company, especially she herself, started at this Offer of the Pedlar's —— He then proceeded thus, while they all lent their strictest Attention: 'Tho' I am now contented with this humble way of getting my Livelihood, I was formerly a Gentleman; for so all those of my Profession are called. In a word, I was a Drummer in an *Irish* Regiment of Foot. Whilst I was in this honourable Station, I attended an Officer of our Regiment into *England* a recruiting. In our March from *Bristol* to *Froome* (for since the Decay of the Woollen Trade, the clothing Towns have furnished the Army with a great number of Recruits)[1] we overtook on the Road a Woman who seemed to be about thirty Years old, or thereabouts, not very handsome; but well enough for a Soldier. As we came up to her, she mended her Pace, and falling into Discourse with our Ladies, (for every Man of the Party, namely, a Serjeant, two private Men, and a Drum, were provided with their Woman, except myself) she continued to travel on with us. I perceiving she must fall to my Lot, advanced presently to her, made Love to her in our military way, and quickly succeeded to my Wishes. We struck a Bargain within a Mile, and lived together as Man and Wife to her dying Day.' —— 'I suppose,' says *Adams* interrupting him, 'you were married with a Licence: For I don't see how you could contrive to have the Banns published while you were marching from Place to Place.' —— 'No, Sir,' said the Pedlar, 'we took a Licence to go to Bed together, without any Banns.' —— 'Ay, ay,' said the Parson, '*ex Necessitate*, a Licence may be allowable enough; but surely, surely, the other is the more regular and eligible Way.' —— The Pedlar proceeded thus; 'She returned with me to our Regiment, and removed with us from Quarters to Quarters, till at last, whilst we lay at *Galloway*, she fell ill of a Fever, and died. When she was on her Death-bed she called me to her, and crying bitterly, declared she could not depart this World without discovering a Secret to me, which she said was the only Sin which sat heavy on her Heart. She said she had formerly travelled in a Company of Gipsies, who had made a practice of stealing away Children; that for her own part, she had been only once guilty of the Crime; which she said she lamented more than all the rest of her Sins, since probably it might have occasioned the Death of the Parents: For, added she, it is almost impossible to describe the Beauty of the young Creature, which was about a Year and half old when I kidnapped it. We kept her (for she was a Girl) above two Years in our Company, when I sold her myself for three Guineas to Sir *Thomas Booby* in *Somersetshire*. Now, you know whether there are any more of that Name in this County.' —— 'Yes,' says *Adams*, 'there are several *Boobys* who are Squires, but I believe no Baronet now alive; besides it answers so exactly in every Point there is no room for Doubt; but you have forgot to tell us the Parents from whom the Child was stoln.' —— 'Their Name,' answer'd the Pedlar, 'was *Andrews*. They lived about thirty Miles from the Squire; and she told me, that I might be sure to find them out by one Circumstance; for that they had a Daughter of a very strange Name *Pamēla* or *Pamēla*;[2] some pronounced it one way, and some the other.' *Fanny*, who had changed Colour at the first mention of the Name, now fainted away; *Joseph* turned pale, and poor *Dicky* began to roar; the Parson fell on his Knees and ejaculated many Thanksgivings that this Discovery had been made before the dreadful Sin of Incest was committed; and the Pedlar was struck with Amazement, not being able to account for all this Confusion, the Cause of which was presently opened by the Parson's Daughter, who was the only unconcerned Person; (for the Mother was chaffing *Fanny*'s Temples, and taking the utmost care of her) and indeed *Fanny* was the only Creature whom the Daughter would not have pitied in her Situation; wherein, tho' we compassionate her ourselves, we shall leave her for a little while, and pay a short Visit to Lady *Booby*.

CHAPTER XIII

The History returning to the Lady Booby, gives some Account of the
terrible Conflict in her Breast between Love and Pride; with what
happened on the present Discovery.

The Lady sat down with her Company to Dinner; but eat nothing. As soon as her Cloth was removed, she whispered *Pamela*, that she was taken a little ill, and desired her to entertain her Husband and Beau *Didapper*. She then went up into her Chamber, sent for *Slipslop*, threw herself on the Bed, in the Agonies of Love, Rage, and Despair; nor could she conceal these boiling Passions longer, without bursting. *Slipslop* now approached her Bed, and asked how her Ladyship did; but instead of revealing her Disorder, as she intended, she entered into a long Encomium on the Beauty and Virtues of *Joseph Andrews*; ending at last with expressing her Concern, that so much Tenderness should be thrown away on so despicable an Object as *Fanny*. *Slipslop* well knowing how to humour her Mistress's Frenzy, proceeded to repeat, with Exaggeration if possible, all her Mistress had said, and concluded with a Wish, that *Joseph* had been a Gentleman, and that she could see her Lady in the Arms of such a Husband. The Lady then started from the Bed, and taking a Turn or two cross the Room, cry'd out with a deep Sigh, —— *Sure he would make any Woman happy.* —— 'Your Ladyship,' says she, 'would be the happiest Woman in the World with him. —— A fig for Custom and Nonsense. What *vails* what People say? Shall I be afraid of eating Sweetmeats, because People may say I have a sweet Tooth? If I had a mind to marry a Man, all the World should not hinder me. Your Ladyship hath no Parents to *tutelar* your *Infections*; besides he is of your Ladyship's Family now, and as good a Gentleman as any in the Country; and why should not a Woman follow her Mind as well as a Man? Why should not your Ladyship marry the Brother, as well as your Nephew the Sister. I am sure, if it was a *fragrant* Crime I would not persuade your Ladyship to it.' —— 'But, dear *Slipslop*,' answered the Lady, 'if I could prevail on myself to commit such a Weakness, there is that cursed *Fanny* in the way, whom the Idiot, O how I hate and despise him!' —— 'She, a little ugly Mynx,' cries *Slipslop*, 'leave her to me. — I suppose your Ladyship hath heard of *Joseph's fitting* with one of Mr *Didapper's* Servants about her; and his Master hath ordered them to carry her away by force this Evening. I'll take care they shall not want Assistance. I was talking with his Gentleman, who was below just when your Ladyship sent for me.' —— 'Go back,' says the Lady *Booby*, 'this Instant; for I expect Mr *Didapper* will soon be going. Do all you can; for I am resolved this Wench shall not be in our Family; I will endeavour to return to the Company; but let me know as soon as she is carried off.' *Slipslop* went away, and her Mistress began to arraign her Conduct in the following Manner:

'What am I doing? How do I suffer this Passion to creep imperceptibly upon me! How many Days are past since I could have submitted to ask myself the Question? —— Marry a Footman! Distraction! Can I afterwards bear the Eyes of my Acquaintance? But I can retire from them; retire with one in whom I propose more Happiness than the World without him can give me! Retire —— to feed continually on Beauties, which my inflamed Imagination sickens with eagerly gazing on; to satisfy every Appetite, every Desire, with their utmost Wish. —— Ha! and do I doat thus on a Footman! I despise, I detest my Passion. —— Yet why? Is he not generous, gentle, kind? —— Kind to whom, to the meanest Wretch, a Creature below my Consideration. Doth he not? —— Yes, he doth prefer her; curse his Beauties, and the little low Heart that possesses them; which can barely descend to this despicable Wench, and be ungratefully deaf to all the Honours I do him. —— And can I then love this Monster? No, I will tear his Image from my Bosom, tread on him, spurn him. I will have those pitiful Charms which now I despise, mangled in my sight; for I will not suffer the little Jade I hate to riot in the Beauties I contemn. No, tho' I despise him myself; tho' I would spurn him from my Feet, was he to languish at them, no other should taste the Happiness I scorn. Why do I say Happiness? To me it would be Misery. — To sacrifice my Reputation, my Character, my Rank in Life, to the Indulgence of a mean and a vile Appetite. — How I detest the Thought! How much more exquisite is the Pleasure resulting from the Reflection of Virtue and Prudence, than the faint Relish of what flows from Vice and Folly! Whither did I suffer this improper, this mad Passion to hurry me, only by neglecting to summon the Aids of Reason to my Assistance? Reason, which hath now set before me my Desires in their proper Colours, and immediately helped me to expel them. Yes, I thank Heaven and my Pride, I have now perfectly conquered this unworthy Passion; and if there was no Obstacle in its way, my Pride would disdain any Pleasures which could be the Consequence of so base, so mean, so vulgar' — *Slipslop* returned at this Instant in a violent Hurry, and with the utmost Eagerness, cry'd out, — 'O, Madam, I have strange News. *Tom* the Footman is just come from the *George*; where it seems *Joseph* and the rest of them are a *jinketting*; and he says, there is a strange Man who hath discovered that *Fanny* and *Joseph* are Brother and Sister.' —— 'How, *Slipslop*,' cries the Lady in a Surprize. —— 'I had not time, Madam,' cries *Slipslop*, 'to enquire about *Particles*, but *Tom* says, it is most certainly true.'

This unexpected Account entirely obliterated all those admirable Reflections which the supreme Power of Reason had so wisely made just before. In short, when Despair, which had more share in producing the Resolutions of Hatred we have seen taken, began to retreat, the Lady hesitated a Moment, and then forgetting all the Purport of her Soliloquy, dismissed her Woman again, with Orders to bid *Tom* attend her in the Parlour, whither she now hastened to acquaint *Pamela* with the News. *Pamela* said, she could not believe it: For she had never heard that her Mother had lost any Child, or that she had ever had more than *Joseph* and herself. The Lady flew into a violent Rage with her, and talked of Upstarts and disowning Relations, who had so lately been on a level with her. *Pamela* made no answer: But her Husband, taking up her Cause, severely reprimanded his Aunt for her Behaviour to his Wife; he told her, if it had been earlier in the Evening, she should not have staid a Moment longer in her House; that he was convinced, if this young Woman could be proved her Sister, she would readily embrace her as such; and he himself would do the same: He then desired the Fellow might be sent for, and the young Woman with him; which Lady *Booby* immediately ordered, and thinking proper to make some Apology to *Pamela* for what she had said, it was readily accepted, and all things reconciled.

The Pedlar now attended, as did *Fanny*, and *Joseph* who would not quit her; the Parson likewise was induced, not only by Curiosity, of which he had no small Portion, but his Duty, as he apprehended it, to follow them: for he continued all the way to exhort them, who were now breaking their Hearts, to offer up Thanksgivings, and be joyful for so miraculous an Escape.

When they arrived at *Booby-Hall*, they were presently called into the Parlour, where the Pedlar repeated the same Story he had told before, and insisted on the Truth of every Circumstance; so that all who heard him were extremely well satisfied of the Truth, except *Pamela*, who imagined, as she had never heard either of her Parents mention such an Accident, that it must be certainly false; and except the Lady *Booby*, who suspected the Falshood of the Story, from her ardent Desire that it should be true; and

Joseph, who feared its Truth, from his earnest Wishes that it might prove false.

Mr *Booby* now desired them all to suspend their Curiosity and absolute Belief or Disbelief, till the next Morning, when he expected old Mr *Andrews* and his Wife to fetch himself and *Pamela* home in his Coach, and then they might be certain of certainly knowing the Truth or Falshood of this Relation; in which he said, as there were many strong Circumstances to induce their Credit, so he could not perceive any Interest the Pedlar could have in inventing it, or in endeavouring to impose such a Falshood on them.

The Lady *Booby*, who was very little used to such Company, entertained them all, *viz.* Her Nephew, his Wife, her Brother and Sister, the Beau, and the Parson, with great Good-humour at her own Table. As to the Pedlar, she ordered him to be made as welcome as possible, by her Servants. All the Company in the Parlour, except the disappointed Lovers, who sat sullen and silent, were full of Mirth: For Mr *Booby* had prevailed on *Joseph* to ask Mr *Didapper*'s pardon; with which he was perfectly satisfied. Many Jokes past between the Beau and the Parson, chiefly on each other's Dress; these afforded much Diversion to the Company. *Pamela* chid her Brother *Joseph* for the Concern which he exprest at discovering a new Sister. She said, if he loved *Fanny* as he ought, with a pure Affection, he had no Reason to lament being related to her. — Upon which *Adams* began to discourse on *Platonic* Love; whence he made a quick Transition to the Joys in the next World, and concluded with strongly asserting that there was no such thing as Pleasure in this. At which *Pamela* and her Husband smiled on one another.

This happy Pair proposing to retire (for no other Person gave the least Symptom of desiring Rest) they all repaired to several Beds provided for them in the same House; nor was *Adams* himself suffered to go home, it being a stormy Night. *Fanny* indeed often begged she might go home with the Parson; but her Stay was so strongly insisted on, that she at last, by *Joseph*'s Advice, consented.

CHAPTER XIV

Containing several curious Night-Adventures,[1] *in which Mr Adams*
fell into many Hair-breadth 'Scapes, partly owing to his Goodness, and
partly to his Inadvertency.

About an Hour after they had all separated (it being now past three in
the Morning) Beau *Didapper*, whose Passion for *Fanny* permitted him not
to close his Eyes, but had employed his Imagination in Contrivances how
to satisfy his Desires, at last hit on a Method by which he hoped to effect
it. He had ordered his Servant to bring him word where *Fanny* lay, and
had received his Information; he therefore arose, put on his Breeches and
Night-gown, and stole softly along the Gallery which led to her Apartment;
and being come to the Door, as he imagined it, he opened it with the
least Noise possible, and entered the Chamber. A Savour now invaded
his Nostrils which he did not expect in the Room of so sweet a young
Creature, and which might have probably had no good effect on a cooler
Lover. However, he groped out the Bed with difficulty; for there was not
a Glimpse of Light, and opening the Curtains, he whispered in *Joseph*'s
Voice (for he was an excellent Mimick)[2] '*Fanny*, my Angel, I am come to
inform thee that I have discovered the Falshood of the Story we last Night
heard. I am no longer thy Brother, but thy Lover; nor will I be delayed
the Enjoyment of thee one Moment longer. You have sufficient Assurances
of my Constancy not to doubt my marrying you, and it would be want
of Love to deny me the possession of thy Charms.' —— So saying, he
disencumbered himself from the little Clothes he had on, and leaping into
Bed, embraced his Angel, as he conceived her, with great Rapture. If he
was surprized at receiving no Answer, he was no less pleased to find his
Hug returned with equal Ardour. He remained not long in this sweet
Confusion; for both he and his Paramour presently discovered their
mutual Deceit. Indeed it was no other than the accomplished *Slipslop*
whom he had engaged; but tho' she immediately knew the Person whom
she had mistaken for *Joseph*, he was at a loss to guess at the Representative
of *Fanny*. He had so little seen or taken notice of this Gentlewoman, that
Light itself would have afforded him no Assistance in his Conjecture.
Beau *Didapper* no sooner had perceived his Mistake, than he attempted
to escape from the Bed with much greater haste than he had made to it;
but the watchful *Slipslop* prevented him. For that prudent Woman being

disappointed of those delicious Offerings which her Fancy had promised her Pleasure, resolved to make an immediate Sacrifice to her Virtue. Indeed she wanted an Opportunity to heal some Wounds which her late Conduct had, she feared, given her Reputation; and as she had a wonderful Presence of Mind, she conceived the Person of the unfortunate Beau to be luckily thrown in her way to restore her Lady's Opinion of her impregnable Chastity. At that instant therefore, when he offered to leap from the Bed, she caught fast hold of his Shirt, at the same time roaring out, 'O thou Villain! who hast attacked my Chastity, and I believe ruined me in my Sleep; I will swear a Rape against thee, I will prosecute thee with the utmost Vengeance.' The Beau attempted to get loose, but she held him fast, and when he struggled, she cry'd out, 'Murther! Murther! Rape! Robbery! Ruin!' At which Words Parson *Adams*, who lay in the next Chamber, wakeful and meditating on the Pedlar's Discovery, jumped out of Bed, and without staying to put a rag of Clothes on, hastened into the Apartment whence the Cries proceeded. He made directly to the Bed in the dark, where laying hold of the Beau's Skin (for *Slipslop* had torn his Shirt almost off) and finding his Skin extremely soft, and hearing him in a low Voice begging *Slipslop* to let him go, he no longer doubted but this was the young Woman in danger of ravishing, and immediately falling on the Bed, and laying hold on *Slipslop*'s Chin, where he found a rough Beard, his Belief was confirmed; he therefore rescued the Beau, who presently made his Escape, and then turning towards *Slipslop*, received such a Cuff on his Chops, that his Wrath kindling instantly, he offered to return the Favour so stoutly, that had poor *Slipslop* received the Fist, which in the dark past by her and fell on the Pillow, she would most probably have given up the Ghost. —— *Adams* missing his Blow, fell directly on *Slipslop*, who cussed and scratched as well as she could; nor was he behind-hand with her, in his Endeavours, but happily the Darkness of the Night befriended her —— She then cry'd she was a Woman; but *Adams* answered she was rather the Devil, and if she was, he would grapple with him; and being again irritated by another Stroke on his Chops, he gave her such a Remembrance in the Guts, that she began to roar loud enough to be heard all over the House. Adams then seizing her by the Hair (for her Double-clout[3] had fallen off in the Scuffle) pinned her Head down to the Bolster, and then both called for Lights together. The Lady *Booby*, who was as wakeful as any of her Guests, had been alarmed from the beginning; and, being a Woman of a bold Spirit, she slipt on a Night-gown, Petticoat and Slippers, and taking a Candle, which always burnt in her Chamber, in her Hand, she walked undauntedly to *Slipslop*'s Room; where she entred just at the instant as *Adams* had discovered, by the two Mountains which *Slipslop* carried before her, that he was concerned with a Female. He then concluded her to be a Witch, and said he fancied those Breasts gave suck to a Legion of Devils. *Slipslop* seeing Lady *Booby* enter the Room, cried, *Help! or I am ravished*, with a most audible Voice, and *Adams* perceiving the Light, turned hastily and saw the Lady (as she did him) just as she came to the Feet of the Bed, nor did her Modesty, when she found the naked Condition of *Adams*,[4] suffer her to approach farther. —— She then began to revile the Parson as the wickedest of all Men, and particularly railed at his Impudence in chusing her House for the Scene of his Debaucheries, and her own Woman for the Object of his Bestiality. Poor *Adams* had before discovered the Countenance of his Bedfellow, and now first recollecting he was naked, he was no less confounded than Lady *Booby* herself, and immediately whipt under the Bed-clothes, whence the chaste *Slipslop* endeavoured in vain to shut him out. Then putting forth his Head, on which, by way of Ornament, he wore a Flannel Nightcap, he protested his Innocence, and asked ten thousand Pardons of Mrs *Slipslop* for the Blows he had struck her, vowing he had mistaken her for a Witch. Lady *Booby* then, casting her Eyes on the Ground, observed something sparkle with great Lustre, which, when she had taken it up, appeared to be a very fine pair of Diamond Buttons for the Sleeves. A little farther she saw lie the Sleeve itself of a Shirt with laced Ruffles. 'Heyday!' says she, 'what is the meaning of this?' —— 'O, Madam,' says *Slipslop*, 'I don't know what hath happened, I have been so terrified. Here may have been a dozen Men in the Room.' 'To whom belongs this laced Shirt and Jewels?' says the Lady. —— 'Undoubtedly,' cries the Parson, 'to the young Gentleman whom I mistook for a Woman on coming into the Room, whence proceeded all the subsequent Mistakes; for if I had suspected him for a Man, I would have seized him had he been another *Hercules*, tho' indeed he seems rather to resemble *Hylas*.'[5] He then gave an account of the Reason of his rising from Bed, and the rest, till the Lady came into the Room; at which, and the Figures of *Slipslop* and her Gallant, whose Heads only were visible at the opposite Corners of the Bed, she could not refrain from Laughter, nor did *Slipslop* persist in accusing the Parson of any Motions towards a Rape. The Lady therefore desired him to return to his Bed as soon as she was departed, and then ordering *Slipslop* to rise and attend her in her own Room, she returned herself thither. When she was gone, *Adams* renewed his Petitions for

Pardon to Mrs *Slipslop*, who with a most Christian Temper, not only forgave, but began to move with much Courtesy towards him, which he taking as a Hint to be gone, immediately quitted the Bed, and made the best of his way towards his own; but unluckily instead of turning to the right, he turned to the left, and went to the Apartment where *Fanny* lay, who (as the Reader may remember) had not slept a wink the preceding Night, and who was so hagged out[6] with what had happen'd to her in the Day, that notwithstanding all Thoughts of her *Joseph*, she was fallen into so profound a Sleep, that all the Noise in the adjoining Room had not been able to disturb her. *Adams* groped out the Bed, and turning the Clothes down softly, a Custom Mrs *Adams* had long accustomed him to, crept in, and deposited his Carcase on the Bedpost, a Place which that good Woman had always assigned him.

As the Cat or Lapdog of some lovely Nymph for whom ten thousand Lovers languish, lies quietly by the side of the charming Maid, and ignorant of the Scene of Delight on which they repose, meditates the future Capture of a Mouse, or Surprizal of a Plate of Bread and Butter: so *Adams* lay by the side of *Fanny*, ignorant of the Paradise to which he was so near, nor could the Emanation of Sweets which flowed from her Breath, overpower the Fumes of Tobacco which played in the Parson's Nostrils. And now Sleep had not overtaken the good Man, when *Joseph*, who had secretly appointed *Fanny* to come to her at the break of Day, rapped softly at the Chamber-Door, which when he had repeated twice, *Adams* cry'd, *Come in, whoever you are*. *Joseph* thought he had mistaken the Door, tho' she had given him the most exact Directions; however, knowing his Friend's Voice, he opened it, and saw some female Vestments lying on a Chair. *Fanny* waking at the same instant, and stretching out her Hand on *Adams*'s Beard, she cry'd out, —— 'O Heavens! where am I?' 'Bless me! where am I?' said the Parson. Then *Fanny* skreamed, *Adams* leapt out of Bed, and *Joseph* stood, as the Tragedian calls it, like the *Statue of Surprize*.[7] '*How came she into my Room?*' cry'd *Adams*. '*How came you into hers?*' cry'd *Joseph*, in an Astonishment. 'I know nothing of the matter,' answered *Adams*, 'but that she is a Vestal for me. As I am a Christian, I know not whether she is a Man or Woman. He is an Infidel who doth not believe in Witchcraft. They as surely exist now as in the days of *Saul*.[8] My Clothes are bewitched away too, and *Fanny*'s brought into their place.' For he still insisted he was in his own Apartment; but *Fanny* denied it vehemently, and said his attempting to persuade *Joseph* of such a Falshood, convinced her of his wicked Designs. 'How!' said *Joseph*, in a Rage, 'hath he offered any

Rudeness to you?' —— She answered, she could not accuse him of more than villainously stealing to Bed to her, which she thought Rudeness sufficient, and what no Man would do without a wicked Intention. *Joseph*'s great Opinion of *Adams* was not easily to be staggered, and when he heard from *Fanny* that no Harm had happened, he grew a little cooler; yet still he was confounded, and as he knew the House, and that the Women's Apartments were on this side Mrs *Slipslop*'s Room, and the Men's on the other, he was convinced that he was in *Fanny*'s Chamber. Assuring *Adams*, therefore, of this Truth, he begged him to give some Account how he came there. *Adams* then, standing in his Shirt, which did not offend *Fanny* as the Curtains of the Bed were drawn, related all that had happened, and when he had ended, *Joseph* told him, it was plain he had mistaken, by turning to the right instead of the left. 'Odso!' cries *Adams*, 'that's true, as sure as Sixpence, you have hit on the very thing.' He then traversed the Room, rubbing his Hands, and begged *Fanny*'s pardon, assuring her he did not know whether she was Man or Woman. That innocent Creature firmly believing all he said, told him, she was no longer angry, and begged *Joseph* to conduct him into his own Apartment, where he should stay himself, till she had put her Clothes on. *Joseph* and *Adams* accordingly departed, and the latter soon was convinced of the Mistake he had committed; however, whilst he was dressing himself, he often asserted he believed in the Power of Witchcraft notwithstanding, and did not see how a Christian could deny it.

CHAPTER XV

The Arrival of Gaffar and Gammar Andrews, *with another Person, not much expected; and a perfect Solution of the Difficulties raised by the Pedlar.*

As soon as *Fanny* was drest, *Joseph* returned to her, and they had a long Conversation together, the Conclusion of which was, that if they found themselves to be really Brother and Sister, they vowed a perpetual Celibacy, and to live together all their days, and indulge a *Platonick* Friendship for each other.

The Company were all very merry at Breakfast, and *Joseph* and *Fanny* rather more cheerful than the preceding Night. The Lady *Booby* produced the Diamond Button, which the Beau most readily owned, and alledged that he was very subject to walk in his Sleep. Indeed he was far from being ashamed of his Amour, and rather endeavoured to insinuate that more than was really true had past between him and the fair *Slipslop*.

Their Tea was scarce over, when News came of the Arrival of old Mr *Andrews* and his Wife. They were immediately introduced and kindly received by the Lady *Booby*, whose Heart went now pit-a-pat, as did those of *Joseph* and *Fanny*. They felt perhaps little less Anxiety in this Interval than *Œdipus* himself whilst his Fate was revealing.[1]

Mr *Booby* first open'd the Cause, by informing the old Gentleman that he had a Child in the Company more than he knew of, and taking *Fanny* by the Hand, told him, this was that Daughter of his who had been stolen away by Gypsies in her Infancy. Mr *Andrews*, after expressing some Astonishment, assured his Honour that he had never lost a Daughter by Gypsies, nor ever had any other Children than *Joseph* and *Pamela*. These Words were a Cordial to the two Lovers; but had a different effect on Lady *Booby*. She ordered the Pedlar to be called, who recounted his Story as he had done before. —— At the end of which, old Mrs *Andrews* running to *Fanny*, embraced her, crying out, *She is, she is my Child*. The Company were all amazed at this Disagreement between the Man and his Wife; and the Blood had now forsaken the Cheeks of the Lovers, when the old Woman turning to her Husband, who was more surprized than all the rest, and having a little recovered her own Spirits, delivered herself as follows. 'You may remember, my Dear, when you went a Serjeant to *Gibraltar* you left me big with Child, you staid abroad you know upwards of three Years. In your Absence I was brought to bed, I verily believe of this Daughter, whom I am sure I have reason to remember, for I suckled her at this very Breast till the Day she was stolen from me. One Afternoon, when the Child was about a Year, or a Year and half old, or thereabouts, two Gipsy Women came to the Door, and offered to tell my Fortune. One of them had a Child in her Lap; I shewed them my Hand, and desired to know if you was ever to come home again, which I remember as well as if it was but yesterday, they faithfully promised me you should —— I left the Girl in the Cradle, and went to draw them a Cup of Liquor, the best I had; when I returned with the Pot (I am sure I was not absent longer than whilst I am telling it to you) the Women were gone. I was afraid they had stolen something, and looked and looked, but to no purpose, and Heaven knows I had very little for them to steal. At last hearing the Child cry in the Cradle, I went to take it up —— but *O the living!* how was I surprized to find, instead of my own Girl that I had put into the Cradle, who was as fine a fat thriving Child as you shall see in a Summer's Day, a poor sickly Boy, that did not seem to have an Hour to live. I ran out, pulling my Hair off, and crying like any mad after the Women, but never could hear a Word of them from that Day to this. When I came back, the poor Infant (which is our *Joseph* there, as stout as he now stands) lifted up its Eyes upon me so piteously, that to be sure, notwithstanding my Passion, I could not find in my heart to do it any mischief. A Neighbour of mine happening to come in at the same time, and hearing the Case, advised me to take care of this poor Child, and G— would perhaps one day restore me my own. Upon which I took the Child up, and suckled it to be sure, all the World as if it had been born of my own natural Body. And as true as I am alive, in a little time I loved the Boy all to nothing as if it had been my own Girl. —— Well, as I was saying, Times growing very hard, I having two Children, and nothing but my own Work, which was little enough, G— knows, to maintain them, was obliged to ask Relief of the Parish; but instead of giving it me, they removed me, by Justices Warrants,[2] fifteen Miles to the Place where I now live, where I had not been long settled before you came home. *Joseph* (for that was the Name I gave him myself —— the Lord knows whether he was baptized or no, or by what Name) *Joseph*, I say, seemed to me to be about five Years old when you returned; for I believe he is two or three Years older than our Daughter here; (for I am thoroughly convinced she is the same) and when you saw him you said he was a chopping Boy,[3] without ever minding his Age; and so I seeing you did not suspect any thing of the matter, thought I might e'en as well keep it to myself, for fear you should not love him as well as I did. And all this is veritably true, and I will take my Oath of it before any Justice in the Kingdom.'

The Pedlar, who had been summoned by the Order of Lady *Booby*, listened with the utmost Attention to Gammar *Andrews*'s Story, and when she had finished, asked her if the supposititious Child had no Mark on its Breast? To which she answered, 'Yes, he had as fine a Strawberry as ever grew in a Garden.' This *Joseph* acknowledged, and unbuttoning his Coat, at the Intercession of the Company, shewed to them. 'Well,' says Gaffar *Andrews*, who was a comical sly old Fellow, and very likely desired to have no more Children, than he could keep, 'you have proved, I think, very plainly that this Boy doth not belong to us; but how are you certain that the Girl is ours?' The Parson then brought the Pedlar forward, and desired him to repeat the Story which he had communicated to him the preceding

Day at the Alehouse; which he complied with, and related what the Reader, as well as Mr *Adams*, hath seen before. He then confirmed, from his Wife's Report, all the Circumstances of the Exchange, and of the Strawberry on *Joseph*'s Breast. At the Repetition of the word Strawberry, *Adams*, who had seen it without any Emotion, started, and cry'd, *Bless me! something comes into my Head.* But before he had time to bring any thing out, a Servant called him forth. When he was gone, the Pedlar assured *Joseph*, that his Parents were Persons of much greater Circumstances than those he had hitherto mistaken for such; for that he had been stolen from a Gentleman's House, by those whom they call Gypsies, and had been kept by them during a whole Year, when looking on him as in a dying Condition, they had exchanged him for the other healthier Child, in the manner before related. He said, as to the Name of his Father, his Wife had either never known or forgot it; but that she had acquainted him he lived about forty Miles from the Place where the Exchange had been made, and which way, promising to spare no Pains in endeavouring with him to discover the Place.

But Fortune, which seldom doth good or ill, or makes Men happy or miserable by halves, resolved to spare him this Labour. The Reader may please to recollect, that Mr *Wilson* had intended a Journey to the West, in which he was to pass through Mr *Adams*'s Parish, and had promised to call on him. He was now arrived at the Lady *Booby*'s Gates for that purpose, being directed thither from the Parson's House, and had sent in the Servant whom we have above seen call Mr *Adams* forth. This had no sooner mentioned the Discovery of a stolen Child, and had uttered the word Strawberry, than Mr *Wilson*, with Wildness in his Looks, and the utmost Eagerness in his Words, begged to be shewed into the Room, where he entered without the least Regard to any of the Company but *Joseph*, and embracing him with a Complexion all pale and trembling, desired to see the Mark on his Breast; the Parson followed him capering, rubbing his Hands, and crying out, *Hic est quem quæris, inventus est, &c.*[4] *Joseph* complied with the Request of Mr *Wilson*, who no sooner saw the Mark, than abandoning himself to the most extravagant Rapture of Passion, he embraced *Joseph*, with inexpressible Extasy, and cried out in Tears of Joy, *I have discovered my Son, I have him again in my Arms. Joseph* was not sufficiently apprized yet, to taste the same Delight with his Father, (for so in reality he was;) however, he returned some Warmth to his Embraces: But he no sooner perceived from his Father's Account, the Agreement of every Circumstance, of Person, Time, and Place, than he threw himself at his feet, and embracing his Knees, with Tears begged his Blessing, which was given with much Affection, and received with such Respect, mixed with such Tenderness on both sides, that it affected all present: But none so much as Lady *Booby*, who left the Room in an Agony, which was but too much perceived, and not very charitably accounted for by some of the Company.

CHAPTER XVI

Being the last. In which this true History is brought to a happy Conclusion.

Fanny was very little behind her *Joseph*, in the Duty she exprest towards her Parents; and the Joy she evidenced in discovering them. Gammar *Andrews* kiss'd her, and said she was heartily glad to see her: But for her part she could never love any one better than *Joseph*. Gaffar *Andrews* testified no remarkable Emotion, he blessed and kissed her, but complained bitterly, that he wanted his Pipe, not having had a Whiff that Morning.

Mr *Booby*, who knew nothing of his Aunt's Fondness, imputed her abrupt Departure to her Pride, and Disdain of the Family into which he was married; he was therefore desirous to be gone with the utmost Celerity: And now, having congratulated Mr *Wilson* and *Joseph* on the Discovery, he saluted *Fanny*, called her Sister, and introduced her as such to *Pamela*, who behaved with great Decency on the Occasion.

He now sent a Message to his Aunt, who returned, that she wished him a good Journey; but was too disordered to see any Company: He therefore prepared to set out, having invited Mr *Wilson* to his House, and *Pamela* and *Joseph* both so insisted on his complying, that he at last consented, having first obtained a Messenger from Mr *Booby*, to acquaint his Wife with the News; which, as he knew it would render her completely happy, he could not prevail on himself to delay a moment in acquainting her with.

The Company were ranged in this manner. The two old People with their two Daughters rode in the Coach, the Squire, Mr *Wilson*, *Joseph*, Parson *Adams*, and the Pedlar proceeded on horseback.

In their way *Joseph* informed his Father of his intended Match with *Fanny*; to which, tho' he expressed some Reluctance at first, on the Eagerness of his Son's Instances he consented, saying if she was so good a Creature as she appeared, and he described her, he thought the Disadvantages of Birth and Fortune might be compensated. He however insisted on the Match being deferred till he had seen his Mother; in which *Joseph* perceiving him positive, with great Duty obeyed him, to the great delight of Parson *Adams*, who by these means saw an Opportunity of fulfilling the Church Forms, and marrying his Parishioners without a Licence.

Mr *Adams* greatly exulting on this Occasion, (for such Ceremonies were Matters of no small moment with him) accidentally gave Spurs to his Horse, which the generous Beast disdaining, for he was high of Mettle, and had been used to more expert Riders than the Gentleman who at present bestrode him: for whose Horsemanship he had perhaps some Contempt, immediately ran away full speed, and played so many antic Tricks, that he tumbled the Parson from his Back; which *Joseph* perceiving, came to his Relief. This Accident afforded infinite Merriment to the Servants, and no less frighted poor *Fanny*, who beheld him as he past by the Coach; but the Mirth of the one, and Terror of the other were soon determined,[1] when the Parson declared he had received no Damage.

The Horse having freed himself from his unworthy Rider, as he probably thought him, proceeded to make the best of his way; but was stopped by a Gentleman and his Servants, who were travelling the opposite way; and were now at a little distance from the Coach. They soon met; and as one of the Servants delivered *Adams* his Horse, his Master hailed him, and *Adams* looking up, presently recollected he was the Justice of Peace before whom he and *Fanny* had made their Appearance. The Parson presently saluted him very kindly; and the Justice informed him, that he had found the Fellow who attempted to swear against him and the young Woman the very next day, and had committed him to *Salisbury* Goal, where he was charged with many Robberies.

Many Compliments having past between the Parson and the Justice, the latter proceeded on his Journey, and the former having with some disdain refused *Joseph*'s Offer of changing Horses; and declared he was as able a Horseman as any in the Kingdom, remounted his Beast; and now the Company again proceeded, and happily arrived at their Journey's End, Mr *Adams* by good Luck, rather than by good Riding, escaping a second Fall.

The Company arriving at Mr *Booby*'s House, were all received by him in the most courteous, and entertained in the most splendid manner, after the Custom of the old *English* Hospitality, which is still preserved in some very few Families in the remote Parts of *England*. They all past that Day with the utmost Satisfaction; it being perhaps impossible to find any Set of People more solidly and sincerely happy. *Joseph* and *Fanny* found means to be alone upwards of two Hours, which were the shortest but the sweetest imaginable.

In the Morning, Mr *Wilson* proposed to his Son to make a Visit with him to his Mother; which, notwithstanding his dutiful Inclinations, and a longing Desire he had to see her, a little concerned him as he must be obliged to leave his *Fanny*: But the Goodness of Mr *Booby* relieved him; for he proposed to send his own Coach and six for Mrs *Wilson*, whom *Pamela* so very earnestly invited, that Mr *Wilson* at length agreed with the Entreaties of Mr *Booby* and *Joseph*, and suffered the Coach to go empty for his Wife.

On *Saturday* Night the Coach return'd with Mrs *Wilson*, who added one more to this happy Assembly. The Reader may imagine much better and quicker too than I can describe, the many Embraces and Tears of Joy which succeeded her Arrival. It is sufficient to say, she was easily prevailed with to follow her Husband's Example, in consenting to the Match.

On *Sunday* Mr *Adams* performed the Service at the Squire's Parish Church, the Curate of which very kindly exchanged Duty, and rode twenty Miles to the Lady *Booby*'s Parish, so to do; being particularly charged not to omit publishing the Banns, being the third and last Time.

At length the happy Day arrived, which was to put *Joseph* in the possession of all his Wishes. He arose and drest himself in a neat, but plain Suit of Mr *Booby*'s, which exactly fitted him; for he refused all Finery; as did *Fanny* likewise, who could be prevailed on by *Pamela* to attire herself in nothing richer than a white Dimity Night-Gown. Her Shift indeed, which *Pamela* presented her, was of the finest Kind, and had an Edging of Lace round the Bosom; she likewise equipped her with a Pair of fine white Thread Stockings,[2] which were all she would accept; for she wore one of her own short round-ear'd Caps, and over it a little Straw Hat, lined with Cherry-coloured Silk, and tied with a Cherry-coloured Ribbon. In this Dress she came forth from her Chamber, blushing and breathing Sweets; and was by *Joseph*, whose Eyes sparkled Fire, led to Church, the whole Family attending, where Mr *Adams* performed the Ceremony; at which nothing was so remarkable, as the extraordinary and unaffected Modesty of *Fanny*, unless the true Christian Piety of *Adams*, who publickly rebuked Mr *Booby* and *Pamela* for laughing in so sacred a Place, and so solemn an Occasion. Our Parson would have done no less to the highest

Prince on Earth: For tho' he paid all Submission and Deference to his Superiors in other Matters, where the least Spice of Religion intervened, he immediately lost all Respect of Persons. It was his Maxim, That he was a Servant of the Highest, and could not, without departing from his Duty, give up the least Article of his Honour, or of his Cause, to the greatest earthly Potentate. Indeed he always asserted, that Mr *Adams* at Church with his Surplice on, and Mr *Adams* without that Ornament, in any other place, were two very different Persons.

When the Church Rites were over, *Joseph* led his blooming Bride back to Mr *Booby*'s (for the Distance was so very little, they did not think proper to use a Coach) the whole Company attended them likewise on foot; and now a most magnificent Entertainment was provided, at which Parson *Adams* demonstrated an Appetite surprizing, as well as surpassing every one present. Indeed the only Persons who betrayed any Deficiency on this Occasion, were those on whose account the Feast was provided. They pampered their Imaginations with the much more exquisite Repast which the Approach of Night promised them; the Thoughts of which filled both their Minds, tho' with different Sensations; the one all Desire, while the other had her Wishes tempered with Fears.

At length, after a Day past with the utmost Merriment, corrected by the strictest Decency; in which, however, Parson *Adams*, being well filled with Ale and Pudding, had given a Loose to more Facetiousness than was usual to him: The happy, the blest Moment arrived, when *Fanny* retired with her Mother, her Mother-in-law, and her Sister. She was soon undrest; for she had no Jewels to deposite in their Caskets, nor fine Laces to fold with the nicest Exactness. Undressing to her was properly discovering, not putting off Ornaments: For as all her Charms were the Gifts of Nature, she could divest herself of none. How, Reader, shall I give thee an adequate Idea of this lovely young Creature! the Bloom of Roses and Lillies might a little illustrate her Complexion, or their Smell her Sweetness: but to comprehend her entirely, conceive Youth, Health, Bloom, Beauty, Neatness, and Innocence in her Bridal-Bed; conceive all these in their utmost Perfection, and you may place the charming *Fanny*'s Picture before your Eyes.

Joseph no sooner heard she was in Bed, than he fled with the utmost Eagerness to her. A Minute carried him into her Arms, where we shall leave this happy Couple to enjoy the private Rewards of their Constancy; Rewards so great and sweet, that I apprehend *Joseph* neither envied the noblest Duke, nor *Fanny* the finest Duchess that Night.

The third Day, Mr *Wilson* and his Wife, with their Son and Daughter returned home; where they now live together in a State of Bliss scare ever equalled. Mr *Booby* hath with unprecedented Generosity given *Fanny* a Fortune of two thousand Pound, which *Joseph* hath laid out in a little Estate in the same Parish with his Father, which he now occupies, (his Father having stock'd it for him;) and *Fanny* presides, with most excellent Management in his Dairy; where, however, she is not at present very able to bustle much, being, as Mr *Wilson* informs me in his last Letter, extremely big with her first Child.

Mr *Booby* hath presented Mr *Adams* with a Living of one hundred and thirty Pounds a Year. He at first refused it, resolving not to quit his Parishioners, with whom he hath lived so long: But on recollecting he might keep a Curate at this Living, he hath been lately inducted into it.

The Pedlar, besides several handsome Presents both from Mr *Wilson* and Mr *Booby*, is, by the latter's Interest, made an Excise-man; a Trust which he discharges with such Justice, that he is greatly beloved in his Neighbourhood.

As for the Lady *Booby*, she returned to *London* in a few days, where a young Captain of Dragoons, together with eternal Parties at Cards, soon obliterated the Memory of *Joseph*.

Joseph remains blest with his *Fanny*, whom he doats on with the utmost Tenderness, which is all returned on her side. The Happiness of this Couple is a perpetual Fountain of Pleasure to their fond Parents; and what is particularly remarkable, he declares he will imitate them in their Retirement; nor will be prevailed on by any Booksellers, or their Authors, to make his Appearance in *High-Life*.[3]

FINIS

NOTES

In the preparation of these notes, I have found the excellent Wesleyan and Norton editions particularly useful. Where I have taken over annotations, I have acknowledged the editors as Battestin and Goldberg. All Biblical references are to the Authorized Version; Shakespeare references are to Stanley Wells and Gary Taylor, general eds., *The Complete Oxford Shakespeare*. Classical quotations have been checked against the texts in the Loeb Classical Library and all translations are derived from this series, unless otherwise indicated.

Battestin	Martin C. Battestin, ed., *Joseph Andrews*, The Wesleyan Edition of the Works of Henry Fielding (Clarendon Press, Oxford, 1967).
Don Quixote	Miguel de Cervantes Saavedra, *The Life and Achievements of the Renown'd Don Quixote*, translated by several hands, supervised by Peter Motteux, revised by John Ozell (London, 1725).
Goldberg	Homer Goldberg, ed., Henry Fielding, *Joseph Andrews, with Shamela and Related Writings*, Norton Critical Edition (W. W. Norton & Company, New York, 1987).
Johnson	Samuel Johnson, *A Dictionary of the English Language* (London, 1755).
OED	*The Shorter Oxford English Dictionary*, C. T. Onions, ed., 3rd ed. (Oxford University Press, Oxford, 1972).
Partridge	Eric Partridge, *The Penguin Dictionary of Historical Slang*, abridged by Jacqueline Simpson (Penguin Books, Harmondsworth, 1972).
Wood, *Institute*	Thomas Wood, *An Institute of the Laws of England*, 5th ed. (London, 1734).

SHAMELA

TITLE PAGE

p. 3 ll. 7–8 *FALSHOODS . . . MISREPRSENTATIONS*. These typographical errors were not corrected in the second edition.

p. 3 l. 11 *Politician*. Schemer.

p. 3 ll. 18–19 *exact Copies . . . the Editor*. This was Richardson's claim, too; he did not subscribe himself the author of the work in any lifetime edition.

p. 3 l. 20 *Necessary . . . all FAMILIES*. A conflation of the claim in the first introductory letter of the second edition of *Pamela* that 'there will not be a Family without it' (p. xiv) and the caption 'Necessary For All Families' which appeared on the title page of the popular religious handbook, *The Whole Duty of Man, Laid down in a Plain and Familiar Way for the use of All, but Especially the Meanest Reader*, attributed to Richard Allestree, royalist divine and Provost of Eton (first published in 1658, but much reprinted).

p. 3 l. 21 *CONNY KEYBER*. A conflation of the names of two people: Colley Cibber and Dr Conyers Middleton, both of whom had recently published 'lives' (see Introduction); for Cibber, see *Joseph Andrews*, I, i, *n*. 5, below. Cibber (pronounced with a hard c) was sometimes spelt in satires Keiber, or Keyber, alluding to his Danish origins. Conny puns on Conyers, 'cony' (a simpleton or dupe) and 'cunny' (the female pudenda).

DEDICATION

1. *To Miss Fanny, &c.* Another complex compression of allusions. Lord Fanny was Pope's derogatory nickname for the bisexual John, Lord Hervey, Baron Ickworth (1696–1743), the dedicatee of Conyers Middleton's *History of the Life of Marcus Tullius Cicero* (published February 1741). (For Hervey, see *Joseph Andrews*, IV, ix, *n*. 2, below.) Fanny, short for Frances, was a popular name in the eighteenth century; it was probably already a slang term for the female pudenda, although Partridge dates this usage from John Cleland's obscene *Fanny Hill* (1749). (Fielding's choice of this name for Joseph's true love might be a sort of anti-pun.) Fielding's '*&c.*' underlines the sexual suggestion (cf. Tickletext's 'a poor Girl's little, *&c.*', below), while also mocking the formality of Middleton's address: 'To the Right Honourable John Lord Hervey, Lord Keeper of His Majesty's Privy Seal'. Fielding brilliantly parodies Middleton's dedication paragraph for paragraph. The mockery of the dedication and of Hervey continues in *Joseph Andrews*, III, iv; IV, ix, xi, xiv; cf. Alexander Pope, *The Dunciad* (1743), IV, 103–4.

2. *Dr Woodward.* Middleton praised Hervey's temperance in diet which supposedly aided his study; Fielding couples this with an allusion to *The State of Physic and Diseases* (1718), by the eccentric virtuoso Dr John Woodward, FRS (1665–1738). Woodward was not alone in suggesting that luxury in diet was responsible for physical ills, but his extravagant assertion that all social evils, including stupidity, partisanship and atheism, were attributable to 'the New Cookery' was much mocked.

3. *Mr Nash . . . your Mamma.* Richard 'Beau' Nash (1674–1762), leader of fashion and Master of Ceremonies in Bath. Hervey's mother was a lady of the bedchamber to Queen Caroline. Under cover of descriptions of fashionable society, the suggestion is that Hervey's mother introduced him to court intrigues at an early age, and that he attempted a political balancing act: Fanny's dancing in the ballroom parallels Middleton's description of Hervey's activities in Parliament, where he maintained 'the rights of the people, yet asserting the prerogative of the Crown; measuring them both by the equal balance of the laws'. Fielding asserts that he 'leaned too much to one side'.

4. *Sonnets, and sprightly Compositions.* Middleton praises 'the sprightly compositions of various kinds, with which Your Lordship has often entertained' the Kingdom; they included verses attacking Pope, and pamphlets defending the much-derided Sir Robert Walpole (1676–1745), Prime Minister, 1721–42.

LETTERS TO THE EDITOR

1. *The Editor to Himself.* Richardson prefixed *Pamela* with a preface in the voice of an anonymous editor praising the book's moral usefulness. The first edition was also preceded by letters of 'puffery' from two of Richardson's friends, one by Jean Baptiste de Freval, the other probably by William Webster; it had previously appeared in Webster's *Weekly Miscellany*, 11 October 1740, urging the author to publish (alluded to in 'out with it'). The second edition added an introduction including enthusiastic letters and a poem by another of Richardson's friends, Aaron Hill (1685–1750), and a list of objections raised by 'an anonymous Gentleman' (p. xxi) which anticipate many of the criticisms Fielding himself makes. Hill was then drafted in to answer these objections in some crassly eulogistic letters which the 'editor' dubs *'some of the most beautiful letters that have been written in any Language'* (p. xxii).

2. *it will do more good than the C—y . . . World.* C—y, i.e., clergy. A travesty of Pope's comment that *Pamela* 'will do more good than many volumes of sermons'.

3. *Who is he . . . Book?* cf. 'Pray, Who is he, Dear Sir? and where, and how, has he been able to hide, hitherto, such an encircling and all-mastering Spirit?' (introduction to *Pamela*, 2nd ed., p. xvii); parodied again in Tickletext's letter, below.

4. *he must be doubtless . . . to Perfection but Virtue.* cf. the author 'I am convinc'd, has one of the best, and most generous Hearts, of Mankind: because, mis-measuring *other* Minds, by *His Own*, he can draw Every thing to Perfection, but *Wickedness*' (introduction to *Pamela*, 2nd ed., p. xviii).

5. *his Honour*. An ironic nickname for Walpole.

PARSON TICKLETEXT TO PARSON OLIVER

1. *Tickletext*. A colloquial name for a parson, possibly with bawdy implications, or suggesting that he misreads the Scriptures. There is a Parson Tickletext in Fielding's *Grub-Street Opera* (written 1731; first published 1755).

2. *The Pulpit . . . Letter to our whole Body*. Dr Benjamin Slocock, who also wrote to Richardson in praise of *Pamela*, recommended the novel from his pulpit in St Saviour's church, Southwark, shortly after its publication. *his L[ordshi]p*. Edmund Gibson (1669–1748), Bishop of London, wrote notable 'pastoral letters' against Deists, Methodists and other dangers to the Church.

3. *Grace*. Pamela frequently appeals to Grace. Defined by Johnson as the 'Favourable influence of God on the human mind', Grace was a key term in the Evangelical or Methodist movement of the 1730s led by George Whitefield (1714–70) and Charles (1707–80) and John (1703–91) Wesley. The Calvinist Whitefield, even more than the Wesleys, maintained that God bestowed saving Grace on the Elect, or those who had faith in him, regardless of works (good deeds). Fielding asserted that this inward-looking doctrine sanctioned immorality; he repeatedly attacked Whitefield and dwells on the opposition between faith and works in *Shamela*, letters V, IX, and *Joseph Andrews*, I, xvii; II, xiv.

4. *SOUL of Religion . . . without any Covering*. Throughout this letter, Fielding closely parodies *Pamela*'s prefatory letters, reorganizing paragraphs, exploiting innuendos, taking sentiments out of context and exposing the blatant absurdity of the correspondents' praise by quoting verbatim. *Soul of Religion . . . Morality*: quoted verbatim from *Pamela*, 2nd ed., p. xvi. *There is an Ease . . . without any Covering*: cf. 'there is an *Ease*, a *natural Air*, a dignify'd *Simplicity*, and measured Fullness, in it, that, resembling *Life*, outglows it! He hath reconciled the *Pleasing* to the *Proper*. The *Thought* is every-where exactly *cloath'd* by the *Expression*: And becomes its Dress as roundly, and as close, as *Pamela* her Country habit . . . And so, dear Sir, it will be always found. —— When modest Beauty seeks to hide itself by casting off the *Pride of Ornament*, it but displays itself without a *Covering*: And so, becoming more distinguished, by its Want of *Drapery*, grows *stronger* from its *purpos'd Weakness*' (*Pamela*, 2nd ed., pp. xx–xxi).

5. *I have done . . . every Page of it*. Quoted verbatim from *Pamela*, 2nd ed., p. xvi.

6. *Little Book . . . like thyself*. cf. 'Little Book, charming PAMELA! face the World, and never doubt of finding Friends and Admirers, not only in thine own Country, but far from Home . . .' (*Pamela*, 2nd ed., p. ix, signed J[ean] B[aptiste] D[e] F[reval]).

7. *But, now I think of it, who is the Author . . . all-mastering Spirit.* cf. 'Pray, Who is he, Dear Sir? and where, and how, has he been able to hide, hitherto, such an encircling and all-mastering Spirit?' (introduction to *Pamela*, 2nd ed., p. xvii).

8. *he possesses every Quality . . . compared it to.* Quoted verbatim from *Pamela*, 2nd ed., p. xvii, except for one crucial change: '(a poor Girl's little, innocent, Story)' in the original becomes the bawdy '(a poor Girls's little, *&c.*)' – a suggestion of where the appeal of Pamela's story lay for the male reader; cf. 'Fanny, *&c.*', above, and 'I do not know what *Et cetera* is', below. The mustard seed in the good book is an allusion to Matthew 13.31–2: 'The kingdom of heaven is like to a grain of mustard seed, which a man took, and sowed in his field: Which indeed is the least of all seeds: but when it is grown, it is the greatest among herbs, and becometh a tree, so that the birds of the air come and lodge in the branches thereof.'

9. *To be short . . . Restraint.* cf. 'It will live on, through Posterity, with such unbounded Extent of Good consequences, that Twenty Ages to come may be Better and Wiser, for its Influence . . . And, let me abominate the contemptible *Reserves of mean-spirited Men*, who while they but *hesitate* their Esteem, with Restraint, can be fluent and uncheck'd in their *Envy* . . . I WAS thinking, just now, as I return'd from a *Walk* in the *Snow*, on that *Old Roman Policy*, of Exemptions in Favour of Men, who had given a few, bodily, Children to the Republick. — What superior Distinction ought *our* Country to find (but that *Policy* and *We* are at Variance) for Reward of this *Father, of Millions of* MINDS, which are to owe new Formation to the future Effect of his Influence!' (*Pamela*, 2nd ed., pp. xviii–xix).

10. *As soon as you . . . read it to them.* Hill claimed to have read the manuscript three times and to have read it out loud to 'Audiences, where the *Tears* were applausively eloquent' (*Pamela*, 2nd ed., p. xxx). Richardson presented *Pamela* to Hill's daughters, Astraea and Minerva. The nature of the lessons it would teach daughters and servantmaids was a matter of concern for Richardson's other correspondent, 'the anonymous Gentleman', as for Fielding.

11. *the Fourth edition.* The second edition of *Pamela* was published in February 1741, the third in March and the fourth in May of that year. *Shamela* was published in April 1741.

PARSON OLIVER TO PARSON TICKLETEXT

1. *C—ly C—b–r by G—.* Colley Cibber by God.

2. *As for Honour to the Clergy . . . walking in it.* This paragraph possibly alludes to the Bangorian controversy; see *Joseph Andrews*, I, xvii, *n.* 10, below.

3. *Who that is . . . his hands on.* Another allusion to Middleton's eulogy of Hervey.

4. *The Instruction which it conveys . . . our Sons.* At the beginning and end of *Pamela*, Richardson sets out the lessons which can be learnt from it, a practice inverted by Parson Oliver.

5. *Author's Professions . . . Epilogue.* Presumably a reference to the theatrical practice of following a bawdy comedy with a hypocritical epilogue.

6. *Jade.* Hussy.

7. *Her Father . . . the Custom-house.* Unlike Pamela's 'poor but honest' parents, Shamela's mother is a prostitute and her father a blackguard. After a criminal indictment, he served with the turncoat Scottish regiments who fought on the Dutch side in the Anglo-Dutch Wars (1665–7, 1672–4), then worked as a stool-pigeon, informing against those who dodged the financial restrictions imposed by the 1736 Gin Act (9 George II, chapter 23). Addiction to cheap gin ruined the lives of many of the urban poor, but the government's campaign against it was highly unpopular.

LETTER I

1. *Henrietta Maria . . . Pepper-Box . . . Drury-Lane.* Shamela's mother is named after the wife of Charles I, but her address signals prostitution: Drury Lane, to the east of Covent Garden, was notorious for its brothels (*Coulstin's-Court*, *Wild Street*, *Short's Gardens*, and *Queen Street* were also in the vicinity); Fan suggests Fanny, or perhaps coquetry; 'peppered' was a slang term for venereal disease.

2. *Put.* Fool, especially a country bumpkin.

3. *Bannio.* i.e., *bagno*, Italian for bath; like the modern *sauna*, it suggests a brothel.

4. *the Old House.* The Theatre Royal in Drury Lane; a parody of Pamela's longing to be in her old home.

LETTER V

1. *Mr Whitefield . . . Dealings with him.* For the Evangelical preacher, Whitefield, see Tickletext's letter, *n.* 3, above. *A Short Account of God's Dealings with the Reverend Mr George Whitefield* (1740) is his spiritual autobiography. Pamela reported that she reads good books as often as she has leisure (letter IV).

LETTER VI

1. *Rochester's Poems.* The poems of the infamous Restoration libertine John Wilmot, Second Earl of Rochester (1647–80), were often frankly sexual.

2. *Saucy Chops, Boldface.* Mr B occasionally calls Pamela rude names, but Fielding orchestrates them into a string of invectives here and in letter X.

3. *upon my Fackins.* 'Upon my faith', a mild oath.

4. *snapt my Fingers.* A characteristic gesture of Abraham Adams too (see *Joseph Andrews*, I, v).

5. *Odsbobs.* From 'ods bodikins': God's little body.

6. *Lavender Water, and Hartshorn.* Fainting remedies, smelling salts.

7. *by Heaven, I know not whether you are a Man . . . Breasts.* After his second rape attempt, Mr B assures Pamela, 'I know not, I declare beyond this lovely Bosom, your Sex' (*Pamela*, 2nd ed., 276).

8. *i'cod.* A form of 'egad', or 'in God'. These oaths may be parodying Pamela's frequent invocations of God, complained about by Richardson's anonymous correspondent, who cited the biblical injunction 'be not righteous over-much' (Ecclesiastes 7.16) (*Pamela*, 2nd ed., p. xxi).

LETTER IX

1. *Tube.* Tobacco pipe.

2. *Incumbents . . . Gift. Incumbent*: 'The holder of an ecclesiastical benefice' (*OED*); *Cure*: 'The spiritual charge of parishioners . . . hence a parish' (*OED*). The Williams family have been for successive generations parsons of a parish of which the Boobys are patrons. Williams hopes Mr Booby will present him with a second 'living', Mr Squeeze-Tithes's 'benefice' or parish. At the end of *Joseph Andrews*, Mr Booby presents Adams with a rich living (IV, xvi). See *Joseph Andrews*, II, viii for another view of how this system works.

3. *Ingenium Versatile.* 'Versatile disposition', probably an ironic allusion to Livy's description of Cato (Livy, 39, 40, 5).

4. *Indeed, a Contempt of the Clergy . . . the Times.* A subject of serious concern to Fielding at this time; see his articles on the subject in *The Champion*, 29 March, 5 April, 19 April 1740.

5. *Be not Righteous over-much.* This text (Ecclesiastes 7.16), cited to encourage Richardson to tone down Pamela's sanctimoniousness, was a key text in the Methodist controversy. The Reverend Joseph Trapp preached an anti-Methodist sermon entitled *The Nature, Folly, Sin, and Danger of Being Righteousness Overmuch; with a Particular View to Doctrines and Practices of Certain Modern Enthusiasts* (1739), and Fielding quoted it in his exhortation to the clergy in *The Champion*, 5 April 1740. Williams perverts its sense, using it as a licence for immorality.

LETTER X

1. *old Scratch.* The Devil.

2. *the Statue of Lamentations.* i.e., the Statute of Limitations (21 James I, chapter 16), according to which, actions for the recovery of debt had to be brought within six years.

3. *paw.* Obscene.

4. *How sweet is Revenge . . . a Sinner.* cf. 'Revenge is certainly the most luscious morsel that the devil can put into the sinner's mouth', a phrase from the *Sermons* (1715 ed., II, 391) of Robert South (1633–1716), a divine much admired by Fielding; he also used this saying in *The Mock Doctor* (1732), and *The Champion*, 2 February 1740.

LETTER XII

1. *five Shifts, one Sham. Shift*: an undergarment; *sham*: a false sleeve to put over a dirty or plain shirt; both words are probably puns on deception. Richardson's Pamela makes a similar inventory of her clothes before her departure (*Pamela*, letter XXXIX).

2. *as, A full Answer ... Orfus and Eurydice*. A catalogue of literature unsound morally, religiously and aesthetically; Fielding also strikes at many of these targets in *Joseph Andrews*. *A full Answer ...* is probably Thomas Bowyer's *A True Account of the Nature, End, and Efficacy of the Sacrament of the Lord's Supper; Being a Full Answer to the Plain Account* (1736), one of the replies to Hoadly's *Plain Account of the Nature and End of the Sacrament of the Lord's Supper* (1735) (see *Joseph Andrews*, I, xvii). *The Whole Duty*, see note to title page above, and *Joseph Andrews*, I, iii, below. Shamela has torn out one of the three branches of the duty of man, leaving only 'Man's Duty to God' and 'to Ourselves'. *The Third Volume of the Atalantis* is a reference to *Secret Memoirs and Manners of several Persons of Quality of both Sexes. From the New Atalantis* (1709), a scandalous *roman à clef* libelling the Whigs, by the Tory propagandist Mary Delerivière Manley (1663–1724) (see also *Joseph Andrews*, III, i). Goldberg argues that Fielding might have had in mind a Pamela-like story that opens volume III. *Venus in the Cloyster* (first published 1683, translated from the French in 1724 by Robert Samber): the notorious publisher, Edmund Curll, was prosecuted for publishing this pornographic work. Derided in *The Champion*, 21 February 1740, 24 May 1740, *Orpheus and Eurydice*, a play by Lewis Theobald (1688–1744), the hero of Pope's *Dunciad* (1728), was staged in 1740 by John Rich (1682?–1761), for more mockery of whom, see *Joseph Andrews*, I, vii.

3. *Potestas*. 'Power', possibly punning on sexual potency.

4. *Nil conscire ... culpæ*. 'To have no guilt at heart, no wrongdoing to turn us pale' (Horace, *Epistles*, 1, 1, 61).

5. *Nothing moves one ... in Distress*. A reference to Lucy Lockit's mock-heroic lament as her villainous lover, Macheath, is about to be hanged in John Gay's *The Beggar's Opera* (1728), III, xv.

6. *a blue Camblet Coat ... a Paduasoy Waistcoat*. The first is a 'strong corded or *gros-grain* fabric' (*OED*), and the second, a name for 'orig. A costly eastern fabric, subseq. for substitutes, made of various combinations of wool, silk, hair' (*OED*).

7. *Lease*. i.e., a leash of three hounds.

8. *Higler*. 'An itinerant dealer; esp. a carrier or huckster who buys up poultry and dairy produce, and supplies in exchange petty commodities from the shops in town' (*OED*).

9. *No, no, I am the Hare . . . the Motive.* The hare is a traditional symbol of lust. For this image, cf. *Tom Jones*, XI, x: 'the Virtue of a young Lady is, in the World, in the same Situation with a poor Hare, which is certain, whenever it ventures abroad, to meet its Enemies: For it can hardly meet any other.'

10. *That all immaterial Substances . . . very Words.* A contradiction in terms made familiar by the philosophers Descartes and Locke. This is possibly a specific allusion to George Cheyne's *Philosophical Conjectures on the Original of the Animal Body* (1740); Fielding mocked his jargon in *The Champion*, 17 May, 12 June 1740. He also uses the phrase in *A Journey from this World to the Next*, I, i, and in 'An Essay on Nothing', in *Miscellanies* (1743).

11. *et cætera.* See dedication, *n.* 1, above.

12. *Catch.* A round.

13. *and that Fellow there . . . my Adversary.* A political allegory. The Opposition had recently tried to remove Walpole from office, but the vote collapsed; one Opposition figure, William Shippen (1673–1743), left before the vote, taking his supporters with him, and was thus suspected of taking a bribe from Walpole. The Opposition sat on the left of the Speaker in the House of Commons.

14. *who says that the Court-side . . . the Bishops.* Walpole packed the House of Lords with bishops loyal to his Court Party.

15. *instuted.* i.e., instituted, that is, officially appointed by the bishop to Squeeze –Tithe's living.

16. *a Parson who does that Sort of Business for Folks.* This parson has not been identified convincingly. The candidates are Conyers Middleton and Thomas Birch, who wrote lots of biographies for the English version of Pierre Bayle's *General Dictionary* (1734–41).

17. *First, There are . . . either Sex.* cf. the title page of *Pamela* which proclaims it to be addressed to 'the YOUTH of BOTH SEXES' and 'entirely divested of those Images, which . . . tend to *inflame* the Minds they should *instruct*'. From here to the end, Fielding parodies the list of morals drawn by the 'editor' of *Pamela* by adapting phrases from Richardson's book, as he did in Parson Oliver's letter at the start.

18. *2dly, Young Gentlemen are . . . Happiness.* cf. 'First, then, in the Character of the GENTLEMAN, may be seen . . . an edifying lesson . . . for the use of such as are born to large Fortunes; and who may be taught, by his Example, the inexpressible Difference between the Hazards and Remorse which attend a profligate Course of Life; and the Pleasures which flow from virtuous Love, and virtuous Actions' (*Pamela*, 2nd ed., II, 392).

19. *3dly, All Chambermaids . . . little Arts to that purpose.* The 'editor' praises the innocence Pamela 'preserved throughout all her Stratagems and Contrivances to save herself from Violation' (*Pamela*, 2nd ed., II, 395).

20. *4thly, In the Character of Mrs Jewkes . . . her Master.* Richardson's anonymous correspondent complains that Mrs Jewkes is not dismissed, but the 'editor' insists that 'The UPPER SERVANTS of great Families may, from the odious Character of Mrs *Jewkes*, and the amiable ones of Mrs *Jervis*, Mr *Longan*, &c. learn what to avoid, and what to chuse, to make themselves valued and esteemed by all who know them' (*Pamela*, 2nd ed., II, 393).

21. *5thly, In Parson Williams . . . every Occasion.* Richardson claimed that the clergy will in the end be 'even *more* valued for a Conduct that gave Offense while the Violence of Passion lasted, than if they had merely stooped to flatter or sooth the Vices of the Great' (*Pamela*, 2nd ed., I, xxii).

22. *I have particularly enquired after Lady Davers . . . any such Person existing.* When Richardson's correspondent complained that Mr B's sister's passionate behaviour was unnatural, Aaron Hill replied that he could point out 'a Dozen or two of *Quality Originals*, from whom (with the Exception perhaps of her Wit) one wou'd swear the Author had taken her Copy' (*Pamela*, 2nd ed., I, xxiv).

JOSEPH ANDREWS

PREFACE

1. *mere English Reader.* Someone who only reads English; not necessarily pejorative.

2. *a different Idea of Romance with the Author of these little Volumes.* Fielding is contrasting the huge and extravagant romances of, for example, La Calprenède and Mlle de Scudery, which he names below, with his more modest work, which was originally publishing in two duodecimo volumes.

3. *Homer, who was the Father . . . to Tragedy.* Throughout his preface, Fielding relates his practice to Aristotle's *Poetics*; composed in the fourth century BC, this analytical account of Greek literature, especially tragedy and epic, bore great authority in the eighteenth century, and Aristotle's descriptions acquired the force of precepts. Aristotle attributes to Homer a lost satirical epic, called *Margites* after its hero (a *margos* or fool), which he says marks out 'the main lines of comedy, since he made his drama not out of personal satire but out of the laughable as such. His *Margites* indeed provides an analogy: as are the *Iliad* and *Odyssey* to our tragedies, so is the *Margites* to our comedies.' (*Poetics*, 4, 10–12).

4. *for tho' it wants one particular . . . in Metre only.* See Aristotle, *Poetics*, 6, 24.

5. *Thus the Telemachus . . . Cambray.* Les Avantures de Télémaque fils d'Ulysse (1699), available in two English translations, was a popular prose epic concerning the education of a prince, written by the French theologian François de Salignac de la Mothe-Fénelon (1651–1715). Fénelon was appointed Archbishop of Cambrai in 1695.

6. *Clelia, Cleopatra, Astraea, Cassandra, the Grand Cyrus*. Fashionable multi-volume French romances with chivalric characters and improbable plots: *Clélie*, 10 vols. (1654–60), and *Artamène, ou le Grand Cyrus*, 10 vols. (1649–53), were by Mlle Madeleine de Scudéry (1607–1701); *Cassandre*, 10 vols. (1644–50), and *Cléopâtre*, 12 vols. (1647–56), were by Gauthier de Costes de la Calprenède (1614–63); *Astrée*, 5 parts (1607–28), was by Honoré d'Urfé (1567–1625). They were all available in English translations.

7. *And I apprehend, my Lord Shaftesbury . . . Antients*. Anthony Ashley Cooper, third earl of Shaftesbury (1671–1713), remarked that buffoonery and burlesque flourish under tyranny: ' 'Tis for this reason, I verily believe, that the Antients discover so little of this Spirit, and that there is hardly such a thing found as mere Burlesque in any Authors of the politer Ages' (*Sensus Communis: An Essay on the Freedom of Wit and Humour*, 5th ed. (1732; first published 1709, later included in *Characteristicks* (1711)) part 1, sections 4 and 5, I, 73. See also III, iii, *n*. 17 and III, vi, *n*. 3, below.

8. *I have had some little Success on the Stage this way*. Fielding's name did not appear on the title page until the 3rd edition (1743), but he seems to have expected people to know that *Joseph Andrews* was by the author of such successful burlesques as *Tom Thumb* (1730), *The Covent-Garden Tragedy* (1732), and *Tumble-Down Dick; or, Phaeton in the Suds* (1736).

9. *Alma Mater*. 'Literally: bounteous mother, used of schools or universities with the sense that they are foster mothers to their *alumni*' (*OED*).

10. *the Ingenious Hogarth*. A good friend of Fielding, William Hogarth (1697–1764), the 'Comic History-Painter' referred to above, repaid the compliment by referring to this passage in his *Characters and Caricaturas* (1743). His famous series of paintings and engravings, such as *The Harlot's Progress* (1732), *The Rake's Progress* (1733–5), and *Marriage à la Mode* (1745), are close to Fielding's spirit in their depiction of folly and vice. The reader is also referred to Hogarth in *Tom Jones* I, xi; II, iii; III, vi.

11. *wonderfully*. Astonishingly.

12. *the Comedy of Nero, with the merry Incident of ripping up his Mother's Belly*. In AD 59, when the Roman emperor Nero (AD 37–68) sent assassins to kill his mother, Agrippina, she symbolically proffered her womb to the blow (Tacitus, *Annals*, 14, 8). Fielding also refers to the incident in *The Jacobite's Journal* (26 March 1748).

13. *Besides, it may seem remarkable, that Aristotle . . . what is*. 'Comedy . . . is a representation of inferior people, not indeed in the full sense of the word bad, but the laughable [ridiculous] is a species of the base or ugly. It consists in some blunder or ugliness that does not cause pain or disaster, an obvious example being the comic mask which is ugly and distorted but not painful' (Aristotle, *Poetics*, 5, 1–2).

14. *the Abbé Bellegarde, who hath writ a Treatise on this Subject.* Jean Baptiste Morvan de Bellegarde (1648–1734), *Réflexions sur le ridicule, et sur les moyens de l'éviter* (1696). Fielding praises him in *The Covent-Garden Journal* (18 and 25 July 1752).

15. *admire at.* Wonder at.

16. *Ben Johnson.* i.e. Ben Jonson (1572–1637), a poet and dramatist greatly admired by Fielding.

17. *Chair.* Sedan chair.

18. *None are for being . . . be thought.* From William Congreve (1670–1729), 'Of Pleasing; An Epistle to Sir Richard Temple', II, 63–4. The preceding lines are also relevant: 'Affect not any thing in Nature's Spite./ Baboons and Apes ridiculous we find;/ For what? For ill-resembling Human-kind.'

19. *Hints.* Fielding continues these 'hints' in his preface to his sister Sarah's novel, *David Simple* (1744).

20. *the Character of Adams.* Battestin suggests that the Parson is drawn from Fielding's friend, the learned and absent-minded Dorsetshire curate William Young (1702?–57).

BOOK I

CHAPTER I

1. *Plutarch, Nepos.* Plutarch (*c.*AD 46–120), celebrated Greek philosopher and biographer, author of the *Parallel Lives* of famous Greeks and Romans; Cornelius Nepos (*c.*99–*c.*24 BC), Roman historian, author of *De Viris Illustribus*; both were noted for their ethical approach to character.

2. *Such are the History of John . . . Champions of Christendom.* Fielding is alluding to *The History of Jack and the Giants*, *The History of Guy, Earl of Warwick*, *The Unfortunate Lovers: The History of Argalus and Parthenia*, and *The Most Famous History of the Seven Champions of Christendom* (i.e. the patron saints of England, Scotland, Wales, Ireland, France, Spain and Italy). These were chapbooks, or cheap popular retellings of romances and folktales.

3. *Delight is mixed with Instruction.* An ironic allusion to Horace's precept that literature should be '*utile et dulce*' (see *Ars Poetica*, 333–46).

4. *authentic Papers and Records.* Richardson pretended that *Pamela, or Virtue Rewarded* (1740) comprised actual letters and journals which he, anonymously, edited.

5. *Colley Cibber.* Colley Cibber (1671–1757), hero of Alexander Pope's *Dunciad* (1743 ed.), theatre manager, actor and playwright, created poet laureate in 1730; he was closely involved in Fielding's theatrical career, first as an ally (he produced and acted in Fielding's first play, *Love in Several Masques* (1728)), and then as an enemy. The publication in 1740 of Cibber's pretentious and politically loaded autobiography *An Apology for the Life of Mr Colley Cibber, Comedian, and Late Patentee of the Theatre-Royal. With an Historical View of the Stage during his Own Time. Written* *by Himself*, in grand quarto and octavo editions, provoked Fielding for a number of reasons. Not only was Cibber self-important, boasting about how Providence had rescued him from preferments in Church and State for a career on the stage (2nd ed., iii, 47–52), he complacently parades his own stupidity, hypocrisy and bad writing. Furthermore, his political opinions were bound to annoy Fielding. Dismissing Fielding as 'a broken Wit' and 'a mad poet' who attempted to assassinate Walpole's reputation, Cibber launched a lengthy defence of the Stage Licensing Act (1737) which drove Fielding from the theatre. Fielding retaliated in a series of attacks from *The Author's Farce* (1734), through *The Champion* (see, for example, 22, 29 April and 3, 6, 17 May 1740), to *Shamela*, to *The Journal of a Voyage to Lisbon* (1755). See I, vii, *n.* 4, below.

6. *Mrs.* Short for Mistress, a title applied to single as well as married women at this time.

7. *How artfully doth the former . . . Fantom, Reputation.* cf. Cibber's *Apology*: 'I am now come to that Crisis of my Life, when Fortune seem'd to be at a Loss what she should do with me. Had she favour'd my Father's first Designation of me, he might then, perhaps, have had as sanguine Hopes of my being a Bishop, as I afterwards conceived of my being a General, when I first took Arms, at the Revolution. Nay after that, I had a third Chance too, equally as good, of becoming an Under-propper of the State' (*An Apology for the Life . . . Written by Himself*, 2nd ed., iii, 47).

8. *the excellent Essays or Letters prefixed to the second and subsequent Editions of that Work.* There were 14 pages of 'puffery' prefixed to the first edition of *Pamela*; 24 more pages of extravagant praise were added in the second edition. Fielding also mocks this self-promotion and self-righteousness in *Shamela*, above, and I, viii, below.

CHAPTER II

1. *Gaffar and Gammer*: From Godfather and Godmother, rustic terms of respect for older people of low rank, but by Fielding's time sometimes used contemptuously.

2. *Merry Andrews.* 'A buffoon; a zany; a jack-pudding' (Johnson).

3. *as the Athenians pretended they themselves did from the Earth.* The ancient Athenians claimed to be *autocthones* (literally, 'sprung from the earth'), i.e. the original inhabitants, and traced their ancestry back to the legendary kings Cecrops and Erectheus, sons of Gaia, the earth goddess.

4. *Apprentice, according to the Statute.* Reference to an act of 1563, 5 Elizabeth, chapter 4, commonly known as the 'Statute of Apprentices'. According to Battestin, one could not be bound as an apprentice before the age of twelve, but according to Goldberg, a boy might be apprenticed in husbandry at the age of ten.

5. *Sir Thomas Booby.* In the first edition, Fielding is inconsistent about the name of Joseph's master, calling him sometimes Thomas and sometimes John. (John is the name of his brother, Mr Booby's father.) In the second edition he corrected some but not all of these slips. In this Penguin edition, his name has been corrected to Thomas throughout.

6. *Priapus.* In Greek mythology, the son of Dionysus and Aphrodite, Priapus was the god of fertility and the guardian deity of gardens. He was represented by a phallus, or by a grotesque little figure with an enormous penis; his statue was placed in gardens, probably to encourage fruitfulness, but also as a kind of scarecrow. (See also Fielding's short novel, *The Life and Death of Jonathan Wild the Great*, I, iii.)

7. *Jack-o'Lent.* A scarecrow figure used as the target in a West Country throwing game played on Ash Wednesday.

8. *Whipper-in.* 'A huntsman's assistant who keeps the hounds from straying by driving them back into the pack with a whip' (*OED*).

9. *play booty.* 'To play falsely; covertly to help one's apparent opponent' (Partridge).

10. *Character.* Reputation.

11. *seventeen Years of Age.* Joseph's biblical prototype was 17 when he was sold to Potiphar (Genesis 37.2, 36).

12. *Abraham Adams the Curate.* Fielding's choice of biblical names is significant but ambiguous. Battestin argues that Abraham had become a symbol of 'the good man' and that Adam carried associations of primitive simplicity (*Moral Basis*, chapter 3). But simplicity could imply foolishness: an Abra(ha)m man was a lunatic or 'pseudo-madman seeking alms', and a 'Jack Adams', 'a fool' (Partridge). A curate could be a parish priest; in Adams's case it means a 'clergyman hired to perform the duties of another' (Johnson).

CHAPTER III

1. *good Nature.* See Fielding's essay on Good Nature in *The Champion*, 27 March 1749.

2. *he did, no more than Mr Colley Cibber, apprehend any such passions as Malice and Envy to exist in Mankind.* cf. Cibber's *Apology*: 'My Ignorance, and want of Jealousy of Mankind has been so strong, that it is with Reluctance I even yet believe any Person, I am acquainted with, can be capable of Envy, Malice, or Ingratitude . . .' (2nd ed., i, 7).

3. *that at the Age of Fifty . . . a handsome Income . . . dear Country.* Country means county here. In 1713 an act of parliament set the scale of stipends for licensed curates at £20–£50 per annum, and a scheme known as Queen Anne's Bounty was established to raise the value of poor livings. The effect on the poor of rising costs in the provinces was a recurring topic in Opposition newspapers in 1741. See I, xvi, *n.* 9, below.

4. *Adams said.* In the fourth edition, Fielding inserted the word 'privately' to make Adams seem less critical of his social superior; critics had complained about Pamela's impertinence.

5. *Charity School.* The most significant of the eighteenth-century Charity Schools were those founded by the Society for the Promotion of Christian Knowledge (SPCK, est. 1699). They provided free uniforms, religious education and instruction in reading, writing and arithmetic, along with some vocational training for children of the poor. While motivated by religious and philanthropic impulses, they were broadly political as they were part of a wide-scale project to reform manners and morals, and thus to improve the stability of society. They were also narrowly political in that, being under the management of lay trustees and governors, the common practices of influence and patronage played a role.

6. *that he had read . . . the Whole Duty of Man . . . Thomas à Kempis . . . Baker's Chronicle.* Fielding links three very popular books of different sorts to suggest the range of influences on the credulous country boy. *The Whole Duty of Man, Laid Down in a Plain and Familiar Way for the Use of All, but Especially the Meanest Reader* (1658), probably by Richard Allestree, was one of the most popular devotional texts of the period and would have been read aloud to Fielding as a student at Eton; Thomas à Kempis, or Thomas Hemerker of Kempen (1380–1471), an Augustinian Monk, was the supposed author of *De Imitatio Christi* (*The Imitation of Christ*); Sir Richard Baker (*c.*1568–1645) was the author of *A Chronicle of the Kings of England from the Time of the Romans Government unto the Raigne of our Soveraigne Lord King Charles* (1643; updated by later hands), a favourite book of Fielding's. Joseph has in mind the 'Casualties' (natural disasters and other extraordinary events) listed at the end of the accounts of the reigns of Henry IV and Elizabeth I. In 1583 during an earthquake in Dorsetshire, 'A field of three Acres . . . with the Trees and Fences, moved from its place, and passed over another Field . . . and there stayed' (Baker, *A Chronicle of the Kings of England* . . . , 118).

7. *He hoped he had profited . . . his Betters.* Joseph alludes to the parable of the talents (Matthew 25.14ff.) and may be specifically following the moral advice of *The Whole Duty of Man* (see III, *n*. 6, above) in resting contented with his lot in life; the same advice was frequently issued from the pulpit.

8. *the Curate as a kind of Domestic only, belonging to the Parson of the Parish.* Curates were often in an insecure position; though appointed by the bishop, they were paid a fixed stipend by the incumbent of the benefice to officiate in his stead, and could easily be dismissed.

9. *Modus.* i.e. *modus decimandi*, 'a money payment in lieu of tithe' (*OED*). The rector wished to have this arrangement set aside because, the value of the payment being fixed, it would, in effect, decrease over the years as the value of the parishioners' produce increased. A popular handbook, *The Clergyman's Vade-Mecum*, 6th ed. (1731), advises incumbents that a modus 'in the Opinion of good Lawyers, be recovered by an action of Debt', but it is difficult to have them set aside (250).

10. *Mrs Slipslop.* This name has interesting associations; according to Johnson, 'slipslop' means 'Bad liquor. A low word formed by reduplication of *slop*.' It was also used by the humorist Ned Ward (1667–1731) to mean 'soft drinks' and 'kissing' (Partridge).

CHAPTER IV

1. *party-colour'd Brethren.* Referring to the variegated liveries worn by footmen.
2. *Riots at the Play-Houses and Assemblies.* Revelry. According to Goldberg, 'After holding seats below for their employers, footmen were admitted free to the upper gallery. When the management of Drury Lane tried to withdraw this privilege in 1737, a riot by three hundred footmen ensued. Assemblies were large social gatherings at which footmen attended on their masters.'
3. *published.* Johnson, s.v. 'To publish': 'To discover to mankind; to make generally and openly known; . . . to divulge.'

CHAPTER V

1. *the Cheeks of Fame.* This image of the goddess Fame blowing her trumpet is probably an allusion to the *Aeneid*, 4, 173–97, where the monstrous Fame (Rumour) broadcasts a scandalous account of Dido's liaison with Aeneas (though Virgil's Rumour does not have cheeks and a trumpet).
2. *JOSEPH.* An allusion to his biblical namesake and exemplar of chastity who resisted the advances of Potiphar's wife (Genesis 39.7–20). Partridge states that by the nineteenth century, the name was used ironically in the term 'fancy Joseph': 'a harlot's "boy" or bully'.
3. *discovered.* Disclosed, revealed.
4. *die . . . Deaths.* A cliché, but perhaps also an echo of Pamela's claim: 'I will die a thousand deaths rather than be dishonoured in any way' (letter III).

CHAPTER VI

1. *four Days ago.* Seven days, according to the previous chapter.
2. *never loved to tell the Secrets of my Master's Family.* In *Shamela*, Parson Oliver argues that *Pamela* teaches chambermaids to betray the secrets of their families.
3. *no body knows what it is to lose a Friend 'till they have lost him.* As Fielding's parody of Richardson's style in *Shamela* indicates, Pamela was given to uttering such moral sententiae.
4. *in naked Bed.* Originally this phrase meant 'a bed in which the occupant slept entirely naked; later used with reference to the removal of ordinary wearing apparel' (*OED*).

5. *a Stage-Play, which I have seen in Covent-Garden*. Probably an allusion to George Lillo's *The London Merchant* (1731), which Fielding greatly admired (see III, x, *n*. 5, below). This didactic tragedy ends with the execution of the apprentice George Barnwell for murder, a crime he was led to by the wicked lady of pleasure, Millwood, who first seduced him by questioning him about love and 'accidentally' laying her hand on his (I, v), as Lady Booby does in I, v, and I, viii. Brean Hammond suggests that this seduction might also be an ironic reworking of the plot of Eliza Haywood's romantic novella, *Philidore and Placentia* (1727), especially 175–6 (see '*Hackney for Bread*' (Oxford, 1997), 284–6).

6. *Parson Williams*. To conceal his intentions, Mr B claims that Pamela is to marry his chaplain, Mr Williams. Fielding exploits this relationship much further in *Shamela*.

7. *Closet*. A small private room.

8. *Ratifia*. 'A cordial or liqueur flavoured with almonds, or peach-, apricot-, or cherry-kernels' (*OED*).

9. *Green-Sickness*. 'An aenemic disease which mostly affects young women about the age of puberty and gives a pale or greenish tinge to the complexion' (*OED*).

CHAPTER VII

1. *Meanness*. Baseness or sordidness.

2. *Betty*. A generic name for chambermaids.

3. *the Great Rich*. John Rich (1682?–1761). As manager from 1714 of the theatre in Lincoln's Inn Fields, and then from 1732 as manager of the New Theatre in Covent Garden, Rich was famous for staging popular afterpieces and interludes, and spectacular pantomimes with alternating tragic and comic scenes. In the character of 'Lun' the Harlequin, he effected burlesque transformations, like those referred to here. Both Fielding and Pope satirized his monstrous inversions of order; see *Pasquin* (1736), *Tumble-Down Dick* (1736), *The Champion*, 22 April, 3 May, 24 May 1740, *Tom Jones*, V, i; cf. Pope, *The Dunciad* (1728), III, 252–64.

4. *the Great Cibber*. In *The Champion*, Fielding repeatedly attacked Cibber for his poor command of English; on 17 May 1740, he arraigned him on the charge of murdering the English language with 'a certain Weapon called a Goose-quill'. See also *The Champion* for 22, 29 April and 3, 6 May 1740.

CHAPTER VIII

1. *Hesperus*. The evening star.

2. *Now Thetis the good Housewife . . . the good Man Phœbus*. Thetis, Greek sea goddess, was married against her will to the mortal Peleus. Phœbus, meaning bright, is the name given to the Greek sun god Apollo. Goldberg notes that this domestic arrangement is anticipated in Matthew Prior's poem 'A Better Answer to Chloe Jealous' (1718), 17–20.

3. *wanton.* Luxuriant.

4. *Sensibility.* A key term in the eighteenth century, approximately meaning sensitivity.

5. *the Statue of Surprize.* A common verbal trope and physical pose in heroic drama; one of many allusions to theatrical conventions in *Joseph Andrews*. Battestin identifies parallels for this image in Ovid, *Metamorphoses*, 3, 418–19; Shakespeare, *Richard III*, III, vii, 24–6; Lewis Theobald, *Persian Princess*, IV, ii; Edward Young, *Busiris*, IV.

6. *how Surprize made one of the Sons of Cræsus speak tho' he was dumb.* According to Herodotus (*History*, 1, 85), when a Persian soldier was about to kill Cræsus (*c.*560–*c.*546 BC), the last king of Lydia, his mute son was shocked into crying out 'Man, do not kill Cræsus!', saving his father's life and regaining the power of speech.

7. *Mr Bridgewater, Mr William Mills.* Roger Bridgewater (d. 1754) often appeared as the ghost in *Hamlet* 'honest Billy' Mills (d. 1750) often played Banquo in *Macbeth*; both acted in Fielding's plays, Mills taking the part of the ghost of Tom Thumb's father, Gaffer, in *The Tragedy of Tragedies* (1732). Fielding also compliments them in *The Jacobite's Journal*, 23 April 1748, and *Tom Jones*, VII, i.

8. *Phidias, or Praxiteles.* Fielding compliments his friend Hogarth by associating him with two ancient Athenian sculptors (Phidias, fifth century BC; Praxiteles, fourth century BC), often referred to as master artists, though none of their work survives.

9. *Have you the Assurance to pretend.* i.e., the confidence or impudence to claim.

10. *Letters, which my Father hath sent me of my Sister Pamela's, nor do I doubt but such an Example would amend them.* At the beginning and end of *Pamela*, Richardson, in the guise of the editor, outlines the moral improvement which will accrue to the reader of Pamela's letters. Fielding also mocks these claims at the beginning and end of *Shamela*.

CHAPTER IX

1. *Mophrodites.* Hermaphrodites, a term applied loosely to any effeminate man; Addison used the term for a catamite (see *OED*, s.v. Hermaphrodite). Slipslop means here the *castrati*, male sopranos, who played the lead roles in the Italian operas which were then in vogue.

2. *nicest.* Most fastidious.

3. *admire.* Wonder at.

4. *provide yourself.* i.e., make ready to leave Lady Booby's service.

5. *Condescension.* 'Voluntary submission to equality with inferiors' (Johnson).

6. *Sack and Sweet-meats. Sack*: 'A kind of sweet wine, now brought chiefly from the Canaries' (Johnson). *Sweetmeats*: sweet food such as sugared cakes, candied fruits, sugared nuts, etc.

7. *So have I seen, in the Hall of Westminster . . . Serjeant Bramble . . . Serjeant Puzzle. Hall of Westminster*: the chief law court of England until the nineteenth century. *Serjeant*: 'A member of a superior order of barristers (abolished in 1880), from which until 1873 the Common Law judges were always chosen' (*OED*). *Bramble* and *Puzzle* are colloquial names for lawyers, the first suggesting that he will entangle you like a bramble, the second suggesting a confused understanding of the law.

CHAPTER X

1. *Ejaculation*. An emotional exclamation.

2. *Grace*. See *Shamela*, Parson Tickletext to Parson Oliver, *n.* 3, above.

3. *moderate Premiums of fifty per Cent*. Pounce charges ten times the allowable rate of interest, which was fixed at five per cent by an act of 1713 (12 Anne, chapter 16). Fielding has in mind the notoriously greedy moneylender, his neighbour Peter Walter (1664?–1746), steward to the Duke of Newcastle. See III, xiii, *n.* 3, below.

4. *Frock*. i.e., frockcoat.

CHAPTER XI

1. *Sir Thomas's Family*. In the 1st and 2nd editions Fielding calls Fanny's master 'John'. This error would place Fanny in the same household as Pamela. There are other inconsistencies of detail hereabouts: Adams was said to be 50 years old in I, iii, but now is said to have been curate for 35 years; Joseph was stripped of his livery in I, x, but is recognized by it in I, xiv.

2. *Cornish Hug*. According to Brewer's *Dictionary of Phrase and Fable*, 'The Cornishmen were famous wrestlers, and tried to throttle their antagonist with a particular lock, called the Cornish Hug'.

3. *It presents you a Lion . . . Tim*. Probably a reference to Timothy Harris (d. 1748), keeper of the Red Lion Inn, Egham, Surrey, on the Basingstoke–Salisbury road. He was praised in *Tom Jones*, VIII, viii, as a publican of 'good Taste'.

CHAPTER XII

1. *Containing many Surprizing Adventures . . . Stage-Coach*. Fielding continues his examination of charity in this reworking of the parable of the Good Samaritan (Luke 10.30–7).

2. *they fled for it.* 'Flight for any Crime Committed . . . implies Guilt; for that no Man not Guilty should fly from, or be afraid of Justice . . . the Offender is to forfeit all his Goods and Chattels . . . notwithstanding his Acquittal' (Giles Jacob, *The Common Law Common-Placed* (1726), 227, s.v. 'Flight').

3. *Nantes.* French brandy.

4. *Hungary Water.* Used as a remedy for fainting and hysteria, it was 'a distilled water, denominated from a queen of Hungary, for whose use it was first prepared; . . . made of rosemary flowers infused in rectified spirit of wine, and thus distilled' (*OED*, citing Chambers' *Cyclopædia*, 1727–41).

5. . . . *a Conveyance to her . . . any Incumbrance . . . Recovery by a Writ of Entry . . . Heirs in Tail . . . no Danger of an Ejectment.* Bawdy quibbles on the jargon of real property law. They are defined by the *OED* as follows: *conveyance*: 'The transference of property (*esp.* real property) from one person to another by any lawful act . . .'; *incumbrance*: 'A burden on property: "A claim, lien, liability attached to property; as a mortgage, a registered judgment, etc." '; *recovery*: 'The fact or procedure of gaining possession of some property or right by a . . . judgment of court; *spec.* The process . . . by which an entailed state was commonly transferred from one party to another'; *heir in tail*: 'the person who succeeds or is entitled to succeed to an entailed estate by virtue of the deed of entail . . .'; *ejectment*: 'The act or process of ejecting a person from his holding'.

6. *Aurora.* Dawn, daughter of Hyperion, sister of Helios the sun, and Selene the moon.

7. *repeated Odes a thousand times sweeter than those of our Laureate, and sung both the Day and the Song.* The odes which Cibber as poet laureate (from 1730) composed for occasions such as the New Year and the King's birthday were famously inane and much mocked. Fielding alludes here to his previous parody of a Cibberian New Year ode: 'Then sing the Day,/ And sing the Song;/ And thus be merry/ All Day long' (*The Historical Register for the Year 1736*, I, i). In his *Apology*, Cibber himself blithely admitted that his first schoolboy ode was not much better than Fielding's travesty (2nd ed., i, 29).

8. *Tow-wouse.* The name may pun on 'touze': 'to abuse or mistreat' (Partridge); or 'touzle': 'to pull about roughly' (*OED*), as in tousled hair.

9. *poor Wretches in red Coats.* Soldiers were often billeted in inns and alehouses because there were few barracks in Britain; innkeepers were compelled by law to give them beer, board and lodging for only four pence per day.

10. *Ale-house.* A humble drinking establishment, distinguished from a tavern, where wine was sold, and an inn, primarily established to feed and lodge travellers.

CHAPTER XIII

1. *Symptomatick.* 'Of the nature of, or constituting, a symptom of disease; *spec.* applied to a secondary disease or morbid state arising from and accompanying a primary one' (*OED*, citing this passage).

2. *the malign Concoction of his Humours should cause a suscitation of his Fever.* The idea that the body was composed of four humours (blood, yellow bile, black bile and phlegm), on whose correct balance health depended, can be traced back to Hippocrates (*c.*460–*c.*377 BC). The doctrine survived into the eighteenth century though it had by then been challenged by progressive theorists. The point of Fielding's satire is that the surgeon employs this jargon ignorantly but is able to bamboozle most clients. *Concoction* is actually the healthy 'ripening' of the disease; *suscitation* is his cant word for resuscitation or revival.

3. *Barnabas.* The biblical Barnabas was a charitable man whose name was interpreted as 'the son of consolation'; see Acts 4.24, 11.24. He sold all his possessions and donated the proceeds to the apostles; the religious order of Barnabites renounced all worldly goods. The ironic resonances of the clergyman's name became clear in I, vii.

4. *Sneaker.* A small bowl of punch.

5. *Small Beer.* Weak or inferior brew.

CHAPTER XIV

1. *Her Chin was peeked.* A minor textual crux: the first and second editions read 'pecked', the third and fourth 'picked', while the fifth reads 'peeked'. Whether the differences suggest changing authorial intentions or compositorial myopia, the idea probably is that her chin is pointed. While this Penguin edition generally follows the second edition, in this instance it goes with the fifth.

2. *'What, I suppose you have read Galen and Hippocrates . . . They are pretty large Books,' said the Gentleman.* As the tone of this exchange suggests, the canting doctor probably has not read the works of the fathers of western medicine, Hippocrates and Galen (AD *c.*130–200). There is little agreement about what they actually wrote. Their collected works in Greek and Latin, published in folio, would not fit in his pocket, but there were several pocket-sized editions of selections such as Hippocrates' *Aphorisms* or Galen's *Ars Medica* in existence in the eighteenth century. Surgeons, unlike physicians, who studied medicine at university, tended to acquire their knowledge as apprentices; both surgeons and physicians were encouraged to improve their knowledge through travel.

3. *Veniente accurrite Morbo.* Criticizing laziness and bad habits, Persius declares: 'It is too late to call for hellebore when the skin is already swollen and diseased; meet the malady on its way, and then what need to promise big mountainous

fees to Craterus?' (Horace, *Satires*, 3, 6–65; Craterus was a doctor in Horace's second *Satire*). The phrase should read '*venienti occurite morbo*'; the first edition read '*occurite*'. The change to '*accurrite*' in the second, if deliberate, compounds the impression of the doctor's ignorance and hypocrisy: he does little to treat Joseph's injuries. cf. *Tom Jones*, V, vii, and *Jonathan Wild*, I, iii.

4. *Ton dapomibominos . . . Thalasses.* The doctor conflates two unrelated formulaic phrases from the *Iliad*: '*Ton dapomibominos*' (answering him), and '*poluflosboio Thalasses*' (of the loud sounding sea).

5. *Ifags . . . caught a Traytor. Ifags*: a corruption of the trivial oath 'by my faith', or 'in faith'. *Caught a Traytor* is presumably a corruption of the phrase 'caught a Tartar' ('Unexpectedly to meet one's superior; to be hoist by one's own petard' (Partridge)); the mistake is either a printer's error not corrected by Fielding, or is intended as a malapropism on Mrs Tow-wouse's part.

6. *Occiput . . . divellicated . . . coheres . . . Pericranium . . . symptomatick . . . pneumatick.* A confused mixture of jargon and ignorance: *Occiput*: 'The hinder part of the head' (Johnson); *divellicated*: 'pulled to pieces' (*OED*; cf. *Tom Jones*, VII, xiii); *coheres*: in error for adheres; *Pericranium*: 'the membrane that covers the skull' (Johnson); *symptomatick*: a morbid state arising from the primary one; *pneumatick*: pertaining to the respiratory system.

7. *and added, that these were Bona Waviata . . . the Lord of the Manor.* The amateur lawyer, Barnabas, who 'trusted entirely to *Wood's Institutes*' (see I, xv, *n.* 4, below), distinguishes between the old principle of 'finders keepers' and the legal situation with regard to lost and stolen goods. See Thomas Wood, *An Institute of the Laws of England*, 5th ed. (1734), II, ii, 213: '*Waifs (Bona Waviata)* are Goods which are stolen and waived upon Pursuit (for Fear of being Apprehended) by the Thief in his Flight, and upon that Account forfeited to the Lord of the Manor. The Reason of this Forfeiture is as a Punishment of the Owner of the Goods, for not Pursuing and Bringing the Thief to be Attainted. If the Thief had not the Goods in Possession upon Pursuit, there is no Forfeiture; and then the Owner may seise them where He finds them, without any fresh Pursuit.'

CHAPTER XV

1. *to score.* To keep a tally of charges.

2. *Sanative soporiferous Draught.* A potion to promote healing and sleep.

3. *a Society of Booksellers, who proposed to purchase any Copies offered to them at a Price to be settled by two Persons.* Founded in 1741 by Thomas Osborne, a friend of Richardson's, 'the Society of Booksellers for promoting of Learning, by purchasing of Manuscripts, Copies, &c. Design'd for the Press' advertised that they would buy manuscripts approved by 'two Persons of Judgment, to be nominated one by the Author, the other by the Society', who would also determine the

price. Their advertisement appeared in *The Champion*, from 4 March to 8 August 1741. Booksellers meant publishers, see I, xvi, below.

4. *the Attorney's Pocket-Companion . . . Mr Jacob's Law-Tables . . . Wood's Institutes.* The surgeon characteristically relies on popular handbooks which do not provide a level of knowledge adequate for the professional: *The Attorney's Pocket Companion* (1733) by John Mallory, and Giles Jacob's *The Statute-Law Common-plac'd: or a General Table to the Statutes* (1719), and perhaps *The Common Law Common-Placed* (1726). A prolific compiler, Jacob also produced the more reliable *New Law Dictionary* (1729). For Fielding's opinion of Jacob, see *The Champion*, 25 December 1739 and 12 February 1740. Barnabas trusts to the more scholarly and comprehensive textbook *An Institute of the Laws of England* (1720) by Thomas Wood, a copy of which Fielding possessed and annotated for his own use.

5. *the Maid's Oath.* The question of evidence is complex, but the doctor in this instance is correct: 'The Testimony of one single *Evidence* is sufficient for the King in all Causes, except for Treason; where there must be two Witnesses . . . In all other Criminal Matters, one *Evidence* is enough; and to a Jury one Witness is sufficient' (Jacob, *New Law Dictionary*, s.v. 'Evidence'). Wood states that servants can be witnesses (Wood, *Institute*, 598), but Jacob adds a caution: 'the Credit of Servants is left to the Jury' (*Common Law*, s.v. 'Witnesses', 484).

6. *è contra, totis viribus.* 'With all his strength to the contrary'.

CHAPTER XVI

1. *But human Life . . . a Game at Chess.* A commonplace, but Fielding may have had in mind Cervantes, *Don Quixote*, II, xii; Richard Braithwaite, *The English Gentleman* (1630), 111; or Abraham Cowley, *Destiny*.

2. *Reward.* By the statute 4 & 5 William and Mary, chapter 8, 'He who Apprehends and Prosecutes a *Highway-Man* to Conviction, shall . . . Receive . . . Forty Pounds . . . with His Horse, Furniture, Arms, Money, and other Goods taken with Him; not taking away the Rights of any Persons claiming the same, from whom they were taken' (Wood, *Institute*, II, i, 373).

3. *as the Escape was by Night, the Indictment would not lie.* Although Tow-wouse is not an official gaoler, he could be held responsible for the escape of a prisoner lawfully detained on his premises. If a gaoler voluntarily permits a prisoner to escape, he is guilty of felony and is esteemed guilty of the offence for which the prisoner was committed; if the gaoler is negligent, he is guilty of a misdemeanour (see Wood, *Institute*, 75–9; 350–1). However, the case is not clear-cut: the prisoner has not been legally indicted, but it is also not certain that Tow-wouse would be exonerated because the escape was by night.

4. *Syder-and.* A hot drink made of cider and brandy, spices and sugar.

5. *to make up a Sum.* i.e., pay a sum of money by a certain date; the same excuse is used by the hostess in II, xv, below.

6. *I'll pepper you better than ever you was peppered by Jenny Bouncer.* 'Playing on two meanings of "pepper" – to pelt with shot, and to infect with venereal disease' (Goldberg).

7. *play or pay.* 'A bet requiring the bettor to pay if his contender does not appear for the match' (Goldberg).

8. *small Tithes.* The tax raised to support the clergy, consisting of 10 per cent of profits; the great tithes were raised on major agricultural produce, and the small tithes on lesser products and profits from labour.

9. *the Hardships suffered by the inferiour Clergy.* The lower clergy – curates, parsons and priests – as distinct from bishops. While the wealth of some clerics aroused criticism, the poverty of the lower clergy could sometimes lead to abuses such as poor education, an inability to provide charitable support or the taking of paid employment, which brought the clergy into contempt. The contempt of the clergy was a subject of concern to Fielding (see *The Champion*, 29 March, 5, 12, 19 April 1740). Battestin suggests an allusion to Thomas Stackhouse's *The Miseries and Great Hardships of the Inferior Clergy* (1722), which was reissued about the time Fielding was writing *Joseph Andrews*. An act of Parliament had instituted a system known as Queen Anne's Bounty which raised revenue to provide a minimum income of £20–£50 for curates, but it did not wipe out clerical poverty. (Adams's stipend is £23 p.a., and on that he has to support a wife and six children.)

10. *the three Volumes of Sermons on the Carpet.* Fielding is inconsistent about the number of volumes: there are three in I, xv, but nine in I, xvi and II, ii; *on the Carpet*: under consideration (from the heavy cloth covering a council table).

11. *Tillotson's Sermons.* John Tillotson (1630–94), Archbishop of Canterbury (1691–4), was the epitome of the Latitudinarian divines who, by stressing the importance of morality and good works (rather than original sin, justification by faith, and dogmatic zeal), directed the Church of England on a moderate, rational and optimistic course after the violently schismatic Interregnum. A distinguished preacher in London and at the Court of William and Mary, Tillotson wrote his sermons in a clear and easy style and was widely read and imitated. His sermons, published in 14 volumes (1696–1704), were sold posthumously for 2,500 guineas. Moderation was the watchword of the Latitudinarians, although, because they were more sympathetic to the Dissenters who inherited the Puritan tradition, they were unfairly accused by the High Church party of heresy. Whitefield attacked Tillotson in his first *Journal* (1739) as a mere moralist because of his emphasis on good works; however, he adhered more to the sacred mysteries than later Latitudinarians such as Benjamin Hoadly. The self-serving Barnabas, who has already shown he does not understand love and forgiveness, and has professed the importance of Grace and Faith (I, xiii), would be no admirer of Tillotson's sermons.

12. *gage the Vessels.* Assess the quantity of beer and ale liable for tax.

13. *Habit of Body.* 'Bodily condition or constitution' (*OED*).

CHAPTER XVII

1. *a Bookseller*. 'Fielding may have had in mind either of the two prominent booksellers who published *Pamela*. Charles Rivington (1688–1742) brought out many religious works, including the earliest sermons of George Whitefield . . . On the other hand, the physical description . . . rare for an incidental character – fits Thomas Osborne (d. 1767)' (Goldberg).

2. *Drugs*. 'A commodity which is no longer in demand, and so is unsaleable' (*OED*).

3. *Whitfield or Westley*. George Whitefield (1714–70), the son of an innkeeper, and John Wesley (1703–91) and his brother Charles (1707–88), the sons of a High Church clergyman, were influential evangelists who led the religious revival which became known as the Methodist movement. United in their opposition to worldliness in the Church of England, including the Latitudinarians' emphasis on good works, they insisted that salvation could not be earned by sinful man, but came only through faith in Christ's redeeming Grace. They later separated over Whitefield's Calvinistic bias, including his belief in predestination, and his provocative sermonizing. Their stress on spiritual rebirth, inward holiness, and the outward manifestations of the workings of the spirit were reminiscent of the Enthusiasm or zeal of the religious radicals of the seventeenth century. Along with their appeal to the lower classes and to women, and the fact that they established chapels in converted sheds in the Grub Street regions of the City, their flamboyant (and often open-air) preaching was bound to attract the attention of Augustan satirists.

4. *a Sermon preached on the 30th of January, or we could say in the Title Page, published at the earnest Request of the Congregation, or the Inhabitants*. Like the claim '*Manuscript Sermons of a Clergyman lately-deceased . . .*' (see I, xvi, above), these are common promotional devices. 30 January was the anniversary of the execution of Charles I (1649) and was usually occasion for a political sermon.

5. *a Play that had been acted twenty Nights together*. As plays were rarely performed for more than a few nights in a row, this would have been a very profitable work for the bookseller.

6. *the licensing Act*. Passed in 1737, the Licensing Act, particularly directed against Fielding's satirical plays, closed all unlicensed theatres (including Fielding's Little Theatre in the Haymarket) and demanded that all new plays be submitted to the Lord Chamberlain for censorship.

7. *Sir, said he . . . her flourishing and established State*. Whitefield maintained a controversy with defenders of the Church of England concerning the proper degrees of poverty and piety of clergymen. In a series of articles in *The Champion* (mentioned I, xvi, *n*. 9, above), Fielding discussed abuses of and abuses by the clergy and, like Adams, agreed with Whitefield insofar as he maintained that the clergy should not 'make a Trade of Divinity' (*The Champion*, 5 April 1740).

Fielding steers a middle way between the insistence that the clergy do not profit by their office and the Methodists' insistence on clerical poverty. On the one hand, many Anglican bishops died rich; on the other, many Methodist preachers lived in a state of near starvation until the Methodist Conference (1752, 1763) decided that preachers and their families should be given basic financial support. See the note to the key phrase 'Be not Righteous over-much' in *Shamela*, letter IX, *n*. 5, above.

8. *Toland, Woolston, and all the Free-Thinkers*. 'Free-thinker' was a term adopted in the late seventeenth and early eighteenth centuries by a loose grouping of radical philosophers who submitted religion and morality to the test of reason. It quickly became a dirty word. Johnson defines it 'A Libertine; a contemner of religion' because, as Fielding elaborates in III, iii below, free-thinking was said to lead to free-living. Deists like John Toland (1670–1722) and Thomas Woolston (1670–1733), who rejected revelation (i.e., the scriptures and miracles) and organized religion and accused the priesthood of mystification, were stigmatized as atheists, even though they still believed in a deity; however, there were many Anglicans who approved of the Deists' notion of Natural Religion. Toland was prosecuted for his *Christianity Not Mysterious* (1696) in which he maintained the infallibility of human reason; Woolston was found guilty of blasphemy for his *Discourses on the Miracles of our Saviour* (1727–9) and died in prison. See III, iii, *n*. 15, below.

9. *his Kingdom was not of it*. Quote from John 18.36.

10. *witness that excellent Book . . . but unsuccessfully*. Fielding may have Benjamin Hoadly (1676–1761), the Low Church Bishop of Winchester, in mind throughout this passage. Hoadly argued that the virtuous heathen could be saved. His provocative treatise, *A Plain Account of the Nature and End of the Sacrament of the Lord's Supper* (1735), was a demystifying account of the Eucharist. Fielding may also be alluding to an earlier debate, 'The Bangorian Controversy' (so-called because Hoadly was then Bishop of Bangor). Hoadly's sermon on the text 'My Kingdom is not of this World' (John 18.36), delivered in March 1717, was condemned as an attack on the authority of the church by High Church Tories and 'Non-Jurors' (those who refused to swear allegiance to the Hanoverian succession). Hence Adams's outburst against the 'few designing factious men'. Shamela's favourite books include two attacks on Hoadly: *A True Account of the Nature, End, and Efficacy of the Sacrament of the Lord's Supper* (1736) by Thomas Bowyer and Whitefield's *A Short Account of God's Dealings with the Reverend Mr George Whitefield* (1740). They demonstrate that to his opponents, Hoadly's rationalism was difficult to distinguish from Deism, as Barnabas's response immediately implies. Fielding, however, held Hoadly in high regard and praised him in *Of True Greatness* (1741) and *Tom Jones*, II, vii.

11. *the Alcoran, the Leviathan, or Woolston*. The Alcoran (*Koran*), the sacred book of Islam, *The Leviathan: or the Matter, Form, and Power of a Commonwealth, Ecclesiastical and Civil* (1651) by Thomas Hobbes (1588–1679), and Thomas Woolston (see *n*. 8 above), were all decried by the Church for blasphemy, impiety and so forth.

12. *being caught, as our Lawyers express it, with the Manner.* 'To be *Taken with the Manner*, is where a Thief having stolen any Thing, is taken with the same about him, as it were in his *Hands*; which is called *Flagrante delicto*' (Jacob, *New Law Dictionary*, s.v. 'Manner'). Compare *The Covent-Garden Journal*, 28 October 1752.

CHAPTER XVIII

1. *Drawers.* 'A tapster at a tavern' (*OED*).
2. *Western Circuit.* One of the eight districts (six in England, two in Wales) through which itinerant judges would travel twice a year to try cases at the court of assizes.
3. *Speculation.* Perception.

BOOK II

CHAPTER I

1. *an Inn or Resting-Place, where he may stop and take a Glass, or any other Refreshment, as it pleases him.* Fielding employs Dryden's image of 'two inns' meaning the two extremities of literary style, in his preface to *The Tragedy of Tragedies, or the Life and Death of Tom Thumb the Great* (1731). He develops the idea of reading as a journey and the author as provider of refreshment in the introductory chapters to *Tom Jones*, especially I, i; II, i; III, i; IV, i; XVIII, i. The Sterne scholar Tom Keymer suggests that Sterne parodies this image in *The Life and Opinions of Tristram Shandy* (1759–67), VI, i.
2. *the celebrated Montague, who promises you one thing and gives you another.* The *Essais* (1580) of Michel Eyquem de Montaigne (1533–92) frequently stray from the subject indicated by their titles. Fielding, who read Charles Cotton's 1738 translation, pays tribute to Montaigne's digressive method in *The Champion*, 31 May 1740.
3. *Homer not only divided his great Work into twenty-four Letters ... very particular Obligations.* Homer's poems the *Iliad* and the *Odyssey* were divided (probably by a later hand) into 24 books designated by the letters of the Greek alphabet.
4. *but, according to the Opinion of some very sagacious Critics ... probably by Subscription.* An allusion to the recent debate between, for example, Mme Dacier and Henry Felton on the one hand and René Rapin and Richard Bentley on the other, as to whether Homer's poems were composed as organic wholes or assembled from fragments and separate works by a later editor. That Fielding favoured the former view is suggested by Adams's discussion of Homer (see III, ii, below; cf. *A Journey from this World to the Next* (1743), I, viii, and *Tom Jones*, VIII, i). He also tilts at Alexander Pope, whose translation of the *Iliad* was published in

five instalments (1715–20) by the lucrative method of subscription publication, whereby authors issued proposals and subscribers paid in advance of publication.

5. *He was the first Inventor . . . it would have cost entire.* While mimicking the jargon of booksellers' advertisements, and the practice which became popular in the 1730s of publishing large books in instalments ('numbers'), Fielding may have in mind here a specific work. According to Battestin, the only dictionary published by an individual bookseller at this time was Robert James's *Medicinal Dictionary,* published by Richardson's friend Thomas Osborne in unusually expensive parts. Proposals were issued in June 1741 and it began to appear in January 1742.

6. *for the same Reason, our Milton . . . the Roman Poet. Paradise Lost* was first published in 1667 in 10 books; the second edition (1674) comprised 12 books because the longest (7 and 10) were divided in two.

CHAPTER II

1. *ut ita dicam.* Latin for 'so to speak'.

2. *Aitia monotate.* Greek for 'sole cause'.

3. *He concluded with a Verse out of Theocritus . . . the Sun shines.* Corydon comforts Battus on the loss of his lover with the words, 'Good luck comes with another morn; while there's life here's hope; rain one day, shine the next' (Theocritus, *Idyll,* 4, 41–3).

4. *an easy Pad.* A slow-paced horse.

5. *Miss.* A kept mistress or whore.

6. *Detainer.* The withholding of another's possessions, here to constrain them to pay a debt.

7. *Æschylus.* Greek tragic poet (c.525–456 BC) who supposedly wrote about 90 plays. However, only seven survive, the best known of which are *Prometheus Bound* and the *Oresteia.*

CHAPTER III

1. *Undoubtedly he can.* The gentleman is correct; see Jacob, *New Law Dictionary,* s.v. 'Inns'.

2. *Facts.* Actions cognizable in law; evil deeds, crimes.

3. *would not suffer a Farmer to keep a Gun, tho' he might justify it by Law.* A series of statutes restricted the hunting of game and the ownership of guns and dogs for that purpose. According to Jacob, 'Lords of Manors may authorize Game-keepers to seise Guns, dogs, &c. of unqualified Persons. Persons qualified to keep Guns, &c. are such as have £100 *per Annum* of inheritance, or for Life, or Lease for Ninety-nine Years of £150 *per Annum*' (22 & 23 Charles 2, chapter 25) (*Statute-Law Common-plac'd,* s.v. 'Game').

4. *Purchase.* The annual return or rent from land.

5. *in the Commission.* i.e., a Justice of the Peace.

6. *Thimble and Button.* A trick played by a conman, or 'thimble-rigger': bystanders were challenged to wager under which thimble a pea was hidden.

CHAPTER IV

1. *saturnine Complexion.* A sluggish, cold and gloomy temperament.

2. *Perspective.* Telescope.

3. *the Writings were now drawn.* 'The legal papers stipulating the marital property settlement were prepared' (Goldberg).

4. *This Letter was written . . . the former.* Fielding is probably referring here to his sister Sarah (1710–68), for whose first and most famous novel, *The Adventures of David Simple* (1744), he wrote a preface.

5. *Quarter Sessions.* Justices of the Peace presided over Quarter Sessions, courts lasting two or three days, held to try small offences four times a year in every county. Though they were supposed to be dignified affairs, attended by all the legal hierarchy, Wood records that special or petty sessions were sometimes held in an inn 'for the more speedy Dispatch of Business in the Neighbourhood' (Wood, *Institute*, IV, i, 483).

6. *Smarts.* Elegant young men about town, or those affecting that air.

7. *Bellarmine.* Fielding used this name once before for a fop. In *The Champion*, 7 February 1740, a young man called Bellarmine tricks Amanda, a rich widow, into thinking he loves her, but when they marry spends all her money and dumps her.

8. *Ridotto's.* A fashionable entertainment featuring music and dancing.

9. *a Crœsus or an Attālus.* Crœsus was the last king of Lydia, reigning 560–546 BC (see I, viii, *n*. 6, above). Attalus was the name of three successive kings of Pergamum whose reigns spanned the years 241–133 BC. All four increased the wealth and glory of their kingdoms; Crœsus was legendary for his personal fortune, supposedly due to the gold-bearing sands of the Pactolus, but actually derived from commercial enterprise; Attalus III bequeathed his kingdom to Rome and became a byword for largesse in Latin poetry (see Horace, *Odes*, 1, 2, 12, and 2, 18, 5–6). As Parson Adams hints, it would have been unusual for the lady to have known this because women rarely received a classical education.

10. *smoke.* To suspect, with the extended sense to ridicule (see Partridge, s.v. 'Smoke').

11. *sneaking.* Mean, contemptible.

12. *'All French,' says he . . . I mistook the English Ladies for Chambermaids, he, he, he.* The phrase 'before I had a Place, I was in the Country Interest' was added in the 2nd edition – a sign of Fielding's changing political allegiances. He had supported the Country Interest, or Patriots, when they were in opposition, but now they were in power, they were proving as corrupt as Walpole's ministry. ('Place' means government appointment.) The decline of the English woollen industry as an indirect result of Walpole's policies had been a concern of the Country Party when in opposition; the wearing of French clothes was therefore held to be unpatriotic.

13. *more than Corinthian Assurance, said Adams; ay, more than Lais herself.* The ancient Greek trading city of Corinth was famous for its luxury and licentiousness; there were three legendary courtesans named Lais, two of whom lived in Corinth.

14. *one's Servants do not deny one.* Fielding explains the process of 'denying' in II, xvi, below.

15. *Serviteur tres humble . . . Je Vous entend parfaitement bien.* Your very humble servant . . . I understand you perfectly well.

16. *Action.* Lawsuit.

17. *The Aunt's Gall was on float.* i.e., she was angry; the term derives from the old system of humours.

18. *Ruelle.* 'A bedroom, where ladies of fashion in the seventeenth and eighteenth centuries, especially in France, held a morning reception of persons of distinction; hence, a reception of this kind' (*OED*).

CHAPTER V

1. *A dreadful Quarrel . . . bloody Consequences to Mr Adams.* Based on 'The Dreadful Battle betwixt Don Quixote and Certain Wine-Skins', *Don Quixote*, I, iv, viii. First published in two parts in Spanish (1605, 1615), *Don Quixote* was available in several English translations; Fielding probably read the translation 'by several hands', supervised by Peter Motteux, revised by John Ozell (1725). Fielding's departures from his model are highly significant. See, for example, Stephen Gilman, 'On Henry Fielding's Reception of *Don Quijote*' in Ian Michael and Richard A. Cardwell, eds., *Medieval and Renaissance Stories* (1986), 27–38.

2. *camphirated Spirits.* Spirits infused with a bitter oil distilled from plants such as *camphora officinarum*. They seem to have been used for their cooling properties; in Sterne's *Tristram Shandy*, Walter makes his brother some breeches from camphorated cerecloth to quell his lust (VI, xxxvi).

3. *Ghost of Othello, bid him not shake his gory Locks at him, for he could not say he did it.* The traveller has mixed up his Shakespeare. Macbeth says to the ghost of Banquo, 'Thou canst not say I did it. Never shake/ Thy gory locks at me' (*Macbeth*, III, iv, 49–50).

4. *Disgracia . . . accustomata . . . Cuffardo . . . Bastonza . . . uno insipido del nullo senso. Damnata di me . . . spectaculo.* Goldberg points out that the gentleman garbles his Italian as well as his Shakespeare, often simply Italianizing English words: '*Disgracia*' for *disgrazia*, '*accustomata*' for *abituata*, '*Cuffardo*' from cuff; '*Bastonza*' (which I have corrected from '*Bastanza*' in the 2nd edition) is derived from *bastone* (cudgel); he says '*Damnata*' instead of *dannato*, and, with Slipslop-like pretension, confuses two senses of 'dull', substituting *insipido* (tasteless, flat) for *insipiente* (ignorant, foolish).

5. *as soon as a Writ can be returned from London.* 'To initiate a lawsuit, the plaintiff had to obtain a writ from the Court of Chancery directing the sheriff of the county to order the defendant's appearance in court' (Goldberg).

6. *I don't care, continued he, to intermeddle in these Cases.* For intermeddling in a case in which he has no interest, or 'an Unlawful upholding of Quarrels against Justice', a lawyer could be charged with the crime of maintenance (Wood, *Institute*, III, iii, 418).

7. *Goal.* Gaol; presumably debtors' prison.

8. *they were but one Person.* According to Wood, 'the *Husband* and *Wife* are accounted to be but *one Person* in Law' (Wood, *Institute*, 59). In some cases, e.g. debt, treason and murder, the wife could be indicted without her husband, but in other cases where the wife had done wrong or had been wronged, they had to stand trial together and damages had to be given for or against the husband.

9. *Boniface.* A generic name for a landlord of a country tavern, originally the name of the jovial innkeeper in George Farquhar's *The Beaux' Stratagem* (1707).

CHAPTER VI

1. *a Smithfield Match.* A marriage for money (named after the London meat market).

2. *the Saying of Solomon.* cf. 'He that spareth his rod hateth his son: but he that loveth him chasteneth him betimes', Proverbs 13.24.

CHAPTER VII

1. *the Soldiers, who are quartered in the Neighbourhood, have killed it all.* According to statutes 4 & 5 William & Mary, chapter 23, 'soldiers killing Game without Leave, [have] to forfeit £5 an Officer, and 10 shillings a Soldier' (Jacob, *Statue-Law Common-plac'd*, s.v. 'Game', 206).

2. *that Affair of Carthagena.* The British attack in spring 1741 against this Spanish stronghold in the West Indies, led by General Wentworth, failed because of poor leadership and ill-trained troops. The Patriot opposition capitalized on the failure. For example, *The Craftsman* of 1 August 1741 criticized Walpole for sending raw recruits to battle while maintaining a standing army at home in order to intimidate the electorate.

3. *Trained-Bands.* Civilian militia.

CHAPTER VIII

1. *the Church was in Danger.* This episode demonstrates how easily Adams's innocence and poverty are taken advantage of by those in power as he is exploited first by one faction, then another. 'The Church was in Danger' was a common complaint in the early eighteenth century, but most often voiced by the High Church party in response to increasing doctrinal latitude, tolerance of Dissenters and declining church attendance, and at particular crises such as union with Scotland (1707). It was last invoked with urgency as an anti-ministerial slogan in the election of 1722.

2. *Ne verbum quidem, ut ita dicem.* Latin for 'not even a word, so to speak'.

3. *his Travels.* i.e., the Grand Tour, the European tour thought essential to complete a gentleman's education – or ruin his morals.

4. *Non omnia possumus omnes.* 'Not all things can we all do' (Virgil, *Eclogues*, 8, 63); a favourite motto of Fielding's, apparently proverbial.

5. *Talents.* For the parable of the master who bestows talents (coins) on his servants to see how they will make use of them, see Matthew 25.14–30: '*to whom nothing is given . . .*' cf. Luke 12.48: 'For unto whomsoever much is given, of him much shall be required.'

6. *as he was never at an University, the Bishop refuses to ordain him.* A university degree was not obligatory for ordination, but, according to *The Clergyman's Vade-Mecum*, no one should be admitted to a benefice worth more than £30 p.a. unless he was a Bachelor of Divinity or a licenced preacher (54). Furthermore, ' 'Tis entirely at the Bishop's Discretion, whether he will admit one to the Order of Priest, or Deacon; nor is he obliged to give any reason for his Refusal' (52).

CHAPTER IX

1. *In which the Gentleman descants . . . the Discourse.* Modelled on *Don Quixote*, I, i, iv, in which the knight rescues a servant who is being beaten, and causes more problems than he solves.

2. *Paris fights, and Hector runs away.* Paris, whose abduction of Helen initiated the Trojan war, is accused of being cowardly by the Trojan hero Hector (*Iliad*, 3, 40–59; 6, 326–33); yet Paris fights with the Greek warrior Diomedes (*Iliad*, 11, 370–95), and Hector twice retreats in battle (*Iliad*, 16, 588; 17, 129 ff.), and finally flies in fear from Achilles (*Iliad*, 22, 136–213).

3. *the Great Pompey.* The Roman general and statesman Pompey (106–48 BC) was eulogized by Cicero ('On the Manilian Law') and Paterculus (*Roman History*, 2, 29), yet when Caesar's cavalry charged in the battle of Pharsalia in 48 BC, he crumbled (see Plutarch, *Life of Pompey*, 72).

CHAPTER X

1. *Catastrophe.* A term from classical literary criticism, catastrophe is defined by the *OED* as 'the change which produces the final event of a dramatic piece; the dénouement'.

2. *The Silence of Adams . . . vanquished Enemy.* This passage was added in the 2nd ed., after Walpole's fall from office in February 1742. Like the revision to Bellarmine's speech in II, iii, it is a sign of Fielding's disillusionment with the behaviour of some leaders of the Country Party who, once they came into power, arguably rifled their country after rescuing her.

3. *Heus tu.* 'Ho there!'

4. *Kensington, Islington, Hackney, or the Borough.* Districts formerly on the fringes of London; Southwark, to the south, was traditionally called 'the Borough'.

5. *Clap-Net.* 'A kind of Net so constructed that it can be suddenly shut by pulling a string' (*OED*, citing this passage).

6. *80 l.* See I, xvi, *n.* 2, above.

7. *Shepherd.* A reference to Jack Shepherd (1702–24), a robber and highwayman, notorious for his repeated escapes from prison. He was celebrated in popular literature; Defoe, for example, published two accounts of his exploits.

8. *Violence.* Force, intensity or vehemence; it is one of Fielding's favourite terms (see David Nokes, *Henry Fielding: 'Joseph Andrews'* (1987), 51–4).

CHAPTER XI

1. *a great Belly.* 'Pregnant women condemned to death could plead their condition in hopes that the sentence would be mitigated or deferred' (Battestin).

2. *Turpin . . . Turpis.* Dick Turpin (1705–39), famous highwayman, hanged shortly before the composition of *Joseph Andrews*. *Turpis*: Latin for 'foul' or 'disgraceful'.

3. *Benefit of the Clergy.* 'Originally the privilege allowed to clergymen of exemption from trial by a secular court; modified and extended later to everyone who could read . . . Abolished in 1827' (*OED*). The literacy test involved reading the opening of Psalm 51 ('Have mercy upon me, O God, according to thy loving kindness . . .') which became known as the 'neck verse'. By the eighteenth century, this benefit was limited to a very narrow range of offences and highway robbery was not one of them.

4. *to cap Verses.* 'to reply to [a verse] quoted with another that begins with the final or initial letter of the first' (*OED*).

5. *Molle meum . . . Telis.* A misquotation of Ovid, *Heroides*, 15, 79: '*molle meum levibusque cor est violabile telis*' ('Tender is my heart, and easily pierced by the light shaft'). This, and the subsequent garbled phrases are, as every schoolboy would have known, taken from a Latin textbook which Fielding would have studied at Eton. Known as *Lily's Grammar, A short Introduction of Grammar*, was based on the textbook of the scholar and humanist William Lily (*c.*1468–1523). All the 'witty Fellow's' anotations are taken from part 2 of this work.

6. *Si licet . . . haurum.* A misquotation of Ovid, *Tristia*, 1, 5, 25–6: '*scilicet ut fulvum spectatur in ignibus aurum,/ tempore sic duro est inspicienda fides*' (' 'Tis clear that as tawny gold is tested in the flames so loyalty must be proved in time of stress').

7. *Mars, Bacchus . . . virorum.* The wit makes a pig's ear out of a phrase which was used to teach the gender of nouns; Adams correctly quotes it below: '*Propria quae maribus tribuntur, mascula dicas:/ Ut sunt Divorum; Mars, Bacchus, Apollo: vivorum;/ Ut Cato, Vigilius: fluviorum; ut Tibris, Orontes:/ Mensium; ut, October: ventorum; ut, Notus, Auster.*' ('Proper names that are assigned to the male kind you may call masculines,/ As are those of Gods: Mars, Bacchus, Apollo; of men,/ like Cato, Virgil; or rivers, like the Tiber, Orontes;/ Of months; like October; of winds; like Notus, Auster.')

8. *Mittimus.* 'A warrant by which a justice commits an offender to prison' (Johnson).

9. *Size . . . Ignoramus. Size*, i.e., assizes, from *assideo*, to sit together. *Ignoramus*: 'When the *Grand Jury* find the Bill of Indictment, They write on the Back of the Bill *Billa Vera*. But if they think it a Groundless Accusation, They Endorse *Ignoramus*; and then the Party is discharged without further Answer' (Wood, *Institute*, IV, v, 623).

10. *one of the Fathers.* The Church Fathers, a group of ecclesiastical writers from about the fourth to the eighth century AD who have carried particular authority in the Christian church because of their piety and orthodox doctrines.

11. *Pollaki toi —— What's your Name?* Probably a phrase from a Greek text book, not from Æschylus; 'What is your name?' is the opening of the Anglican catechism, a text written in English in the sixteenth century, not in Greek by one of the Church Fathers.

CHAPTER XII

1. *Toast and Ale.* 'Bread dried and put into liquor' (Johnson).

2. *Pygmalion.* Legendary king of Cyprus, who made an ivory statue of a maiden, fell in love with her and prayed to Venus to bring her to life (Ovid, *Metamorphoses*, 10, 243–97).

3. *Quid petis est nusquam.* Ovid's narrator exclaims, 'What you seek is nowhere,' when Narcissus, punished by Nemesis for spurning Echo and others who desire him, falls in love with his own reflection (*Metamorphoses*, 3, 433).

4. *Cælum ipsum petimus stultitia.* 'Heaven itself we seek in our folly' (Horace, *Odes*, 1, 3, 38).

5. *Chloe.* Generic name for a pastoral lover.

6. *Lethe.* Meaning 'oblivion', the Greek name for the river in the underworld; the dead drank its waters and forgot their past lives.

7. *Zephyrus.* The personification of the west wind in Greek mythology.

8. *Strephon.* Another generic name for a pastoral lover, see above.

CHAPTER XIII

1. *Bear-Garden.* The Bear-Garden in Hockley-in-the-Hole, Clerkenwell, London, was famous for bear-baiting, dog-fighting, cudgel-playing and other rough sports.

2. *Two Places have been agreed to be divided between them, namely the Church and the Play-House . . . under their Feet.* In church, the gentry sat in raised pews; in the theatre, 'low' types, such as apprentices and footmen, sat in the cheaper upper galleries while the rich and fashionable sat below them in boxes and the stalls.

3. *if the Gods. . . made Men only to laugh at them.* A version of the philosophy of Epicurus (b. 341 BC), popular with Freethinkers.

4. *not unlike that which Cleopatra gives Octavia in the Play.* A reference to John Dryden's *All for Love* (1678); in fact, it is Octavia rather than Cleopatra who leaves the stage, in act III.

5. *as many Tongues as Homer desired.* Homer claims that without the aid of the muses, he could not tell of the Greek heroes 'not though ten tongues were mine and ten mouths and a voice unwearying' (*Iliad*, 2, 489–90). Pope translates this as 'To count them all, demands a thousand Tongues,/ A Throat of Brass, and Adamantine Lungs' (*Iliad*, 2, 580–1), and Fielding settles on a hundred in *Jonathan Wild*, IV, ix.

6. *he would by no means consent to any thing contrary to the Forms of the Church . . . neither is their Matrimony Lawful.* Before the Marriage Act of 1753 there were several more or less informal ways of tying the knot, but only two established procedures for marrying within the Church of England: it was necessary either to proclaim the banns at three services in the parish church, or to obtain a special licence issued by a bishop – a method used more commonly by the upper than the lower classes. Pamela and Mr B marry by special licence to prevent Lady Davers interfering. Adams quotes from 'The Form of the Solemnization of Matrimony' in *The Book of Common Prayer* to underline his argument.

7. *Dr. Debtor.* In II, x, Adams has 'no more than one Halfpenny about him'.

CHAPTER XIV

1. *Trulliber.* A name derived from the phrase 'tripes and trullibubs', meaning entrails, hence 'a jeering nickname for a fat man' (Partridge); also from 'tro-lubber': 'a husbandman, a day-labourer' (Grose, *A Provincial Glossary*).

2. *a Farmer.* The clergy, as Fielding pointed out in *The Champion* (12 April 1740), were forbidden by law (21 Henry VIII, chapter 13) from farming or selling land so that 'nothing might prevent them from discharging their Duties to the Souls of Men'. Gordon Rupp states, however, that 'Most country parsons had their glebe of several acres', and some bishops had extensive estates (*Religion in England, 1688–1791* (Oxford, 1986), 494).

3. *Night-Gown*. Dressing gown.

4. *Nihil habeo cum Porcis*. 'I have nothing to do with pigs.'

5. *as Sarah did Abraham, calling him (not Lord but) Master*. See 1 Peter 3.6: 'Even as Sara obeyed Abraham, calling him lord'. Pamela calls Mr B 'Master' even after their marriage.

6. *warm*. Rich.

7. *laying up a Treasure in a better Place than any this World affords*. A message reiterated at many points in the New Testament, see, for example, Matthew 6.19–21, 19.21.

8. *led Captain*. 'An humble dependent in a great family, who for a precarious subsistence and distant hopes of preferment suffers every kind of indignity, and is the butt of every species of joke or ill humour' (Grose).

9. *what matters where a Man's Treasure is, whose Heart is in the Scriptures*. Trulliber counters Adams with another common scriptural sentiment; see, for example, Matthew 6.21, Luke 6.45.

10. *Thou dost not intend to rob me?* The frequent distrust – or the excuses for abuse – with which Adams is met might be related to the fact that thieves and conmen sometimes disguised themselves as clergymen to win the confidence of their victims, a trick known as 'preaching the parson'. Fielding refers to one such trickster, Roger Johnson, in *Jonathan Wild*, IV, iii.

11. *Tithing-Man*. The parish constable.

12. *Poors Rate*. 'A rate or assessment for the relief or support of the poor' (*OED*). The inadequacy of the support the Poor Law system offered the poor was intended to discourage them from applying for it.

13. *Whoever therefore is void of Charity . . . no Christian*. Fielding continues his dramatization of the differences between faith and works by recalling St Paul's words: 'And though I have the gift of prophecy, and understand all mysteries, and all knowledge; and though I have all faith, so that I could remove mountains, and have not charity, I am nothing' (1 Corinthians 13.2). Fielding also insists that the clergy are especially bound to offer charity in *The Champion*, 5 April 1740.

CHAPTER XV

1. *Turne quod . . . attulit ultro*. 'Turnus, that which no god had dared to promise to thy prayers, lo, the circling hour has brought unasked!' (Virgil, *Aeneid*, 9, 6–7).

CHAPTER XVI

1. *half a dozen Cows, and very good Grounds to have maintained them*. Adams ought to disapprove of these offers of farms and plural benefices; the fact that he does not refuse them, and later accepts a second living (see IV, xvi), suggests either that he is inconsistent, or that such practices were commonly acceptable.

2. *Seneca*. Lucius Annaeus Seneca (*c*.4 BC–AD 65), Roman Stoic philosopher. Fielding's educated readers would have noticed the ironic disparity between the ethical standards Seneca maintained in his moral writings and tragedies and his failure to live in accordance with his principles. He was banished for his intimacy with the daughter of his patron, Emperor Claudius, then condoned Claudius's murder and became tutor to his successor, the savage Emperor Nero. He died by his own hand.

3. *Vails*. Tips, especially those given to a servant by a visitor on his departure; they could form a large part of a servant's income.

CHAPTER XVII

1. *Holland*. 'Fine linen made in Holland' (Johnson).

2. *the French Distemper*. Slang term for venereal disease.

3. *those cursed Guarda-Costas, who took our Ships before the Beginning of the War*. Spanish coastguard vessels zealously enforced the ban against English trafficking in Spanish waters. In 1731 they pillaged a vessel in the West Indies and cut off the captain's ear, an incident which eventually forced Walpole's reluctant government to declare war against Spain in 1739. The war, initially known as the War of Jenkins's Ear, lasted until 1748.

4. *to strike*. To lower the flag and sails as a salute or, as here, a sign of surrender.

5. *Pink*. 'A term applied to vessels of various sizes, apparently in this case a small flat-bottomed coastal sailer unsuited for the open sea' (Goldberg).

6. *Cœlum non Animum . . . mare currunt*. 'They change their clime, not their mind, who rush across the sea' (Horace, *Epistles*, I, 11, 27).

7. *What, I suppose you have seen the Pillars of Hercules . . . Golden Fleece*. Adams runs through some of the mythical and historical people and places he has encountered in his reading of the classics; his recall is not perfect. *Pillars of Hercules*: the headlands bounding the straits of Gibraltar, anciently known as Calpe and Abyla, which were supposed to be the pillars marking the end of the world, erected by Hercules in his tenth labour. *Carthage*: Phoenician city on the north coast of Africa, founded by Dido, and destroyed in the third Punic war (146 BC). *Scylla* and *Charybdis*: a rock and a whirlpool – a pair of hazards for those sailing between Sicily and Italy; according to legend, Scylla was a ghastly man-eating monster and Charybdis swallowed and regurgitated the sea thrice daily.

Archimedes . . . Syracuse: Archimedes (*c*.287–211 BC), while intent on a mathematical problem, was killed by Roman soldiers at the sacking of Syracuse. *Cyclades*: group of islands in the Aegean sea, off the coast of the Peloponnesus. *Helle . . . Apollonius Rhodius . . . Caspian . . . Colchis . . . Golden Fleece*: Helle gave her name to the sea (the Hellespont, now the Dardanelles) into which she fell from the back of the winged and golden-fleeced ram on which she and her brother were escaping from their murderous stepmother, Ino. Her brother, Phryxus, when he reached Colchis on the Euxine or Black Sea (not the Caspian as Adams has it), sacrificed the ram to Zeus. It was the object of the quest of Jason and the Argonauts recounted in the *Argonautica* by Apollonius the Rhodian (*c*.295–*c*.230 BC). *Dædalus*: Dædalus fashioned the wings by means of which he and his son escaped from the Cretan Minotaur, but it was Icarus who flew too near the sun and fell into the sea which bears his name.

8. *Levant*. Derived from the French for sunrise, the Levant was a term applied at this time to the eastern Mediterranean, although it had also been used to signify the Orient, as Adams deduces from its etymology.

9. *tip us the Traveller*. 'To exaggerate, to romance, as a traveller is apt to do' (Partridge, citing Fielding).

10. *the Story of Socrates*. The story is told by Cicero in *Tusculan Disputations* (4, 37, 80); Fielding refers to it again in 'An Essay on the Knowledge of the Characters of Men' (1743).

11. *Trade, answered Adams . . . it is managed now*. Aristotle endorses the pursuit of wealth to furnish necessities, but argues that trade for the mere acquisition of riches 'is justly discredited (for it is not in accordance with nature, but involves men's taking things from one another)' (*Politics*, 1, 3, 23). Furthermore, 'whereas the theory of such matters is a liberal study, the practical pursuit of them is narrowing' (1, 4, 1). Later he claims that 'it is easy for philosophers to be rich if they choose, but this is not what they care about' (1, 4, 5). However, Fielding generally praised honest tradesmen for their contribution to the nation.

12. *Gazetteers*. *The Daily Gazetteer*, printed by Richardson from 1735 to 1746, was Walpole's principal propaganda rag. It numbered clergymen among its contributors and Fielding repeatedly attacked it.

BOOK III

CHAPTER I

1. *For instance, between my Lord Clarendon . . . Rapin*. The partisan spirit of the Civil War and its aftermath was reflected in the controversial histories of the period. Fielding owned these leading examples of works written from a Tory perspective: *The True Historical Narrative of the Rebellion and Civil Wars in England* (1702–18), by Edward Hyde, earl of Clarendon (1609–74), and *The History of England* (1707–

18), by Laurence Eachard (1670?–1730). The following books with a Whig slant could also be found in his library: Bulstrode Whitelocke (1605–75), *Memorials of the English Affairs from the Beginning of the Reign of Charles I to the Happy Restoration of King Charles II* (1682) and Nicholas Tindal's translation of Paul de Rapin de Thoyras (1661–1725), *Histoire d'Angleterre* (1723–5).

2. *Chrysostom . . . Marcella . . . Cardenio . . . Ferdinand . . . Anselmo . . . Camilla . . . Lothario.* Characters in the interpolated tales in *Don Quixote*; for Chrysostom and Marcella, see I, ii; I, iv–vi; for Cardenio and Ferdinand, see I, iii; I, ix, ff.; for Anselmo, Camilla and Lothario, see I, iv; I, vi–viii.

3. *But the most known Instance of this kind is in the true History of Gil-Blas . . . in many others.* See Alain René Le Sage (1668–1747), *L'Histoire de Gil Blas de Santillane* (1715, 1724, 1735): Dr Sangrado appears in II, iii–v (his name appears incorrectly as *Sanglado* in the 2nd ed.); the Archbishop of Granada in VII, ii–iv; the 'great Personages' are the members of the salon of the Marchioness de Chaves who condemn witty and humorous works (IV, viii).

4. *Scarron, the Arabian Nights, the History of Marianne and Le Paisan Parvenu.* Fielding continues his survey of popular fiction: Paul Scarron (1610–60), *Roman Comique* (1651–7); *Arabian Nights Entertainment* (1st pub. 1705–8, many subsequent editions), translated from the French of Antoine Galland, was the first European collection of these oriental tales; *La Vie de Marianne* (1731–41) and *Le Paysan parvenu* (1734–6) are both by Pierre Carlet de Chamblain de Marivaux (1688–1763).

5. *the Authors of immense Romances, or the modern Novel and Atalantis Writers.* For 'immense Romances', see preface, n. 2, above. By 'the modern Novel' Fielding probably means short amatory prose fictions such as those by Aphra Behn (1640–89), Jane Barker (fl. 1688–1726), Eliza Haywood (1693–1756) or Mary Delarivière Manley (1663–1724), author of many scandalous novels including *Secret Memoirs and Manners of Several Persons of Quality, of both Sexes. From the New Atalantis, an Island in the Mediterranean* (1709). Fielding uses *New Atalantis* as an index of character in other works, see *Shamela*, letter XII, above, *Tom Jones*, XI, vii, *The Champion*, 26 April 1740, *The Pleasures of the Town* (1730), *Amelia*, VIII, v, and the preface of *The Journal of a Voyage to Lisbon.*

6. *Balzac says of Aristotle, that they are a second Nature.* Discussing hyperbolical compliments, Jean-Louis Guez de Balzac (1597–1654) cites a philosopher who called Aristotle 'VNE SECONDE NATURE' (see *Deux Discours envoyez à Rome, à monsieur le cardinal Bentivoglio* (1627)).

7. *those Stilts, which the excellent Voltaire tells us in his Letters carry the Genius far off, but with an irregular Pace.* Voltaire was highly critical of English tragedy; see *Letters concerning the English Nation*, trans. J. Lockman (1733), letter XVIII, 178.

8. *Beyond the Realm of Chaos and old Night.* cf. Milton, *Paradise Lost*, I, 541–3: 'A shout that tore Hell's Concave, and beyond/ Frighted the reign of *Chaos* and old Night.'

9. *Mariana's. Historia general de España* (1601; first pub. in Latin, 1592) by Juan de

Mariana (1536–1632). Fielding owned a copy of John Steevens' English translation (1699).

10. *a Peer.* Probably Fielding's patron, Philip Dormer Stanhope, fourth earl of Chesterfield (1694–1773), leader of the Opposition against Walpole, and author of the famous letters to his son (1774).

11. *a Commoner.* Ralph Allen (1693–1764), philanthropist, patron and friend of Pope and Fielding. In 1741, both of them visited Prior Park, near Bath, the 'Palace' he built with the fortune he had made from devising a new system of post roads. Fielding dedicated *Amelia* to him, and he was the model for Squire Allworthy in *Tom Jones.*

CHAPTER II

1. *A Night-Scene . . . Fellow-Travellers.* This and the next two chapters are loosely based on *Don Quixote*, II, xvi–xviii.

2. *Darkness visible.* cf. the description of hell in Milton, *Paradise Lost*, I, 63.

3. *Est hic, est animus . . . Honorem.* 'Here, here is a soul that scorns the light [i.e. life], and counts that fame, where to thou strivest, cheaply bought with a life' (Virgil, *Aeneid*, 9, 205–6). With these words Euryalus responds to his friend Nisus's courageous resolve to do battle. Fielding has '*illum*' for '*istum*' in the original, an immaterial change.

4. *spindle-shanked Beaus and Petit Maîtres.* Skinny-legged fops.

5. *if Mr Pope had lately published . . . his Homer.* Fielding had a high opinion of Pope's celebrated translations, or rather versions, of the *Iliad* (6 vols. (1715–20)) and the *Odyssey* (5 vols. (1725–6), translated with William Broome and Elijah Fenton). In *Amelia*, VIII, v, he criticizes Pope's accuracy.

6. *what Cicero says of a complete Orator, may well be applied to a great Poet; He ought to comprehend all Perfections.* See Cicero, *De Oratore*, I, 6, 20: 'in my opinion, no man can be an orator complete in all points of merit, who has not attained a knowledge of all important subjects and arts'.

7. *It is not without Reason therefore . . . that of The Poet.* See Aristotle, *Poetics*, 22, 9.

8. *for his Margites, which is deplorably lost . . . to Tragedy.* See *Poetics*, 4, 12, and compare the preface to *Joseph Andrews*. There are many similarities between the sentiments of Adams and of his creator Fielding, including their preference for the *Iliad*, which is alluded to many times in this novel.

9. *Aristophanes.* Greek comic dramatist (*c.*445–*c.*380 BC) whose works, e.g. *The Wasps, The Birds, Lysistrata* and *The Frogs*, caricature public figures and deal with topical issues.

10. *He is rightly praised by the first of those judicious Critics, for not chusing the whole War.* See Aristotle, *Poetics*, 23, 5.

11. *Trojani Belli Scriptorem.* 'Writer of the Trojan War' (Horace, *Epistles*, I, 2, 1).

12. *termed by Aristotle Pragmaton Systasis.* 'By "plot" I mean here the arrangement of the incidents' (Aristotle, *Poetics*, 6, 12). Adams follows quite closely the six constituent parts of tragedy identified by Aristotle in *Poetics*, 6: plot, character, diction, thought, spectacle and song; however, he gives greater importance to character and spectacle than does Aristotle.

13. *Harmotton*. 'Appropriateness' or 'propriety'; Aristotle uses the term with reference to character (*Poetics*, 15, 4).

14. *Thirdly, His Manners . . . included in the Action*. See Aristotle, *Poetics*, 6, 12–14, 19. 'Manners' would now be translated as 'character'.

15. *Aristotle in his 24th Chapter, that no Part of this divine Poem is destitute of Manners*. 'Homer after a brief prelude at once brings in a man or a woman or some other character, never without character, but all having character of their own' (Aristotle, *Poetics*, 24, 14). Aristotle is here praising Homer for seldom speaking in his own voice.

16. *where Andromache is introduced, in the former lamenting the Danger, and in the latter the Death of Hector*. See *Iliad*, 6, 407–39, and 24, 723–45.

17. *Nor can I help observing . . . Mouth of Tecmessa*. See Sophocles' tragedy *Ajax*, 485–524.

18. *Seneca the Tragedian*. See II, xvi, n. 2, above. Adams distinguishes between the tragedian and his father, the rhetorician.

19. *As to his Sentiments . . . very diffuse*. Aristotle discusses diction and thought (sentiment) in *Poetics*, 19–22, and later asserts that Homer's works 'surpass all other poems in diction and thought' (24, 3), but could be said to be diffuse.

20. *Opsis, or the Scenery*. Usually translated 'spectacle'; Aristotle argues that it is much less important in tragedy than the plot (see *Poetics*, 6, 9, 6, 28–9; cf. 14, 1).

21. *physical*. Medical.

22. *Jealousy*. Suspicion.

23. *a great Orator*. Possibly John 'Orator' Henley, see III.vi, n. 5, below.

24. *Je tiens pour une Maxime constante qu'une Beauté médiocre plaît plus généralement qu'une Beauté sans défaut*. 'It is my constant maxim that a moderate beauty pleases more generally than a faultless one', said Mme Anne Lefèvre Dacier (1654–1720) in her preface to her translation, *Le Plutus et les Nuées d'Aristophane* (1684). Fielding's French has been silently corrected for this Penguin edition.

25. *Mr Congreve hath made . . . were possest of it*. In Congreve, *Love for Love* (1695), II, ii, the beau, Tattle, instructs the simple Miss Prue how to respond to lovers: 'If I tell you you are handsome, you must deny it, and say I flatter you. But you must think yourself more charming than I speak you: and like me for the beauty which I say you have, as much as if I had it myself'.

CHAPTER III

1. *Riding the great Horse*. 'The horse used in battle and tournament' (*OED*, s.v. 'Horse'). Also, colloquially, to put on airs.

2. *WRITE Letters to Yourself . . . Characters in them.* Fielding employed this device in *The Old Debauchees* (1732), I, ix. The most famous instance occurs in Congreve's *The Way of the World* (1700), I, i. It may also be an allusion to an anecdote concerning the Revd William Young (1702?–57), Fielding's friend and neighbour, who may have served as a model for Adams. In order to gain leave from his duties, Young is supposed to have written himself a letter of invitation, but the absent-minded parson presented this letter unopened to his patron.

3. *at H——d's.* i.e., Mother Haywood's fashionable brothel in Covent Garden.

4. *Lincoln's-Inn-Fields.* Site of John Rich's theatre.

5. *St James's Coffee-House.* Situated near St James's Palace, a fashionable resort for Guards officers and Whigs.

6. *the Temple.* The Inner and Middle Temples, between Fleet Street and the Thames, two of the Inns of Court; Fielding studied law at the Middle Temple in 1737–9.

7. *Quarter-day.* 'One of the four days in the year [Lady Day, 25 March; Midsummer Day, 24 June; Michaelmas, 29 September; and Christmas Day], on which rent or interest is paid' (Johnson).

8. *the Duke of Marlborough.* The hero of the Whigs, John Churchill, first Duke of Marlborough (1650–1722), under whom Fielding's father fought at Blenheim. For his victorious campaign against the French (1702–11), Marlborough was awarded with an estate and the publicly funded construction of Blenheim Palace. Fielding very much admired him.

9. *railed at the beautiful Creatures, in as gross Language as Juvenal himself formerly reviled them in.* An allusion to the Latin poet Juvenal's vicious attack on the female sex his *Sixth Satire.* In his youth Fielding had adapted a part of this satire, 'Modernised in Burlesque Verse' (published in his *Miscellanies*), when, as Battestin says, 'he, like Mr Wilson, was smarting from an injury done him by a young lady'.

10. *Coquette achevée.* An accomplished flirt.

11. *Whisk.* The card game whist.

12. *Eclaircissement.* A clearing up of what is obscure, an explanation; the term was common in the eighteenth century.

13. *Citizen.* 'A townsman; a man of trade; not a gentleman' (Johnson).

14. *Sp——wing.* i.e., spewing.

15. *These Gentlemen were engaged in a Search after Truth.* London coffee-houses were important meeting places for Freethinkers; in portraying the Rule of Right Men, Fielding possibly has in mind the club which included the leading Deists Anthony Collins (1676–1729) and John Toland, who used to meet in the Grecian Coffee-house in 1712. He is rounding up and satirizing several Freethinking tenets, extracted from their contexts in order to emphasize the incoherence of their beliefs and the dangers they posed to orthodox religion and morality. In rejecting Revealed Religion, the Deists rejected the sticks and carrots of divine punishment and reward, and thus the traditional sanctions for moral behaviour and social order. Deism seemed particularly dangerous to Fielding because a modified version, Natural Religion, was finding some acceptance in the orthodox Church of England.

16. *Prejudices of Education . . . Guide of Human Reason*. Key terms of the day. Freethinkers aimed to submit all inherited beliefs to the test of reason and to reject everything not consistent with common sense.

17. *Rule of Right*. The club members employ the teaching of Shaftesbury in order to cast off orthodox morality, then employ the rather different teachings on right of Hobbes and Mandeville to justify their immoral behaviour. Although he saw the usefulness of religion, Shaftesbury (see preface, *n.* 7, above) argued that people are born with an innate moral sense and will be led to virtue because of its natural beauty: we should love '*Right*, for its own sake, and on the account of its own natural beauty and Worth' (*An Inquiry concerning Virtue, or Merit*, I, iii, 1, in *Characteristicks*, 5th ed. (1732), II, 42). He also argued that in our 'Obedience to the Rule of Right . . . *the Excellence of the Object*, not the *Reward* or *Punishment*, shou'd be our Motive . . .' (*The Moralists*, II, iii, in *Characteristicks*, II, 273). Hobbes argued that there is a 'naturall Right of every man to everything' (*Leviathan*, I, xiv).

18. *without remembring to take leave of his Bail*. 'Apparently another member who has put up some financial surety that his friend will continue to attend regularly and pay his share of the club's expenses' (Goldberg).

19. *there was nothing absolutely good . . . of the Agent*. cf. Hobbes: 'For these words of Good, Evill, and Contemptible, are ever used with relation to the person that useth them: There being nothing simply and absolutely so; nor any common rule of Good and Evill, to be taken from the Objects themselves . . .' (*Leviathan*, I, vi), and Bernard Mandeville: 'It is in Morality as it is in Nature, there is nothing so perfectly Good in Creatures that it cannot be hurtful to any one of the Society, nor anything so entirely Evil, but it may prove beneficial to some part or other of the Creation: So that things are only Good and Evil in reference to something else, and according to the Light and Position they are placed in' (*The Fable of the Bees*, ed. F. D. Kaye (1924), I, 367).

20. *Tickets of other Poets for their Benefits long before the Appearance of their Performances*. 'The playwright received profits of the third, sixth, and ninth performances, if the play ran that long; but he also had to guarantee to cover the theatre's expenses for the first of these. Hence authors often sold tickets to their first benefit night in advance of the production' (Goldberg).

21. *voluntary Subscriptions for their Encouragement*. Subscription publishing could make the author independent of the bookseller (publisher) and the market, because it was a system whereby subscribers paid in full or part in advance for a work. Matthew Prior's *Poems on Several Occasions* (1719), Nicholas Rowe's *Tragedy of Jane Shore* (1714) and Pope's *Iliad* (1715–20) and *Odyssey* (1725–6) famously made their authors a fortune by this means. Fielding also made a profit by publishing his *Miscellanies* by subscription, but, as Wilson relates, the system was open to abuse.

22. *Plato himself did not hold Poets in greater Abhorrence than these Men of Business do*. See Plato, *Republic*, 2, 3, 10.

23. *on Sundays only*. Because of the Act for the Better Observation of the Lord's Day (1677), one could not be arrested for debt on Sundays.

24. *a Lottery-Ticket*. State lotteries were held at intervals from 1694 to 1826. Fielding satirized the corrupt and exploitative system in his ballad-opera *The Lottery* (1726) and in *The Champion*, 3 January 1740.

25. *He arrested me . . . for thirty-five Pounds*. Fielding repeatedly condemned the inhumane (and inefficient) practice of imprisoning debtors (see, for example, *The Champion*, 16 and 19 February 1740; *The True Patriot*, 3 December 1745; *Tom Jones*, VII, iii). The situation persisted into the nineteenth century.

26. *to procure myself Bread*. 'Jailors were not obligated to feed prisoners. Although an imprisoned debtor was legally entitled to fourpence a day subsistence, he was at the mercy of his creditor, who could refuse to pay this sum without fear of prosecution' (Goldberg).

CHAPTER IV

1. *the late famous King Theodore*. 'Late' means here 'recently'. The German adventurer Theodore Etienne, Baron von Neuhof (1686–1756) was crowned King of Corsica in 1736 by nationalists seeking independence from Genoa, but was expelled by the Genoese and French two years later. He came to England where he was imprisoned for debt but was later supported by benefactors and championed by opponents of Walpole's supposedly restrained foreign policy.

2. *Parterres*. Level spaces in the garden, usually facing the best front of the house, laid out with ornamental flower beds.

3. *The poor Girl, who was about eleven Years old*. Goldberg suggests that Fielding is inconsistent here: this girl appears to be his eldest child, but earlier Wilson had said that his second child was born 'almost twenty Years' ago (his eldest child, a son, was 'lost').

4. *had killed all the Dogs, and taken away all the Guns in the Neighbourhood*. See II, iii, n. 3, above. The Squire is obviously exceeding his rights.

CHAPTER V

1. *King's Scholars*. Scholars from public schools endowed by royal foundation who then went to one of the Oxford or Cambridge colleges associated with the school. Scholars from Westminster School could gain scholarships to Christ Church, Oxford, or Trinity College, Cambridge; those from Eton to King's College, Cambridge; and those from Winchester to New College, Oxford; these schools also controlled the appointment of fellows at their associated colleges.

2. *gloriari non est meum.* Latin meaning 'It is not for me to boast.'

3. *Hinc illæ lachrymæ.* Latin for 'Hence those tears'; first used literally by Terence, *Andria*, I, 125, it became proverbial and was quoted, in, for example, Horace, *Epistles*, 1, 14, 41.

4. *If Knowledge of the World . . . in Ignorance.* In Joseph Addison, *Cato* (1713), II, v, Juba says to Syphax: 'If knowledge of the world makes man perfidious,/ May Juba ever live in ignorance!'

5. *confer.* Conform.

6. *Chiron's.* In Greek legend, Chiron was the wisest of the centaurs. He was instructed by Apollo and Artemis, and tutored heroes such as Achilles and Jason and Asclepius, the god of medicine.

7. *Nemo mortalium omnibus horib sapit.* Pliny asks, 'What of the proverb that none among mortals is wise all the time?' (*Natural History*, 7, 40, 131.)

8. *Alexander the Great at the Head of his Army.* An allusion to the confrontation between Alexander the Great and the philosopher Diogenes the Cynic, recounted in many classical sources, including Cicero, *Tusculan Disputations*, 5, 32, 92, and Plutarch, *Life of Alexander*, 14, 1–3. In Fielding's retelling of the story in 'Of True Greatness' and *A Journey from this World to the Next* (both published in his *Miscellanies*), the philosopher's scorn of earthly riches seems as vain as the conqueror's pomp.

CHAPTER VI

1. *Moral Reflections . . . Parson Adams's miraculous Escape.* In this and the next chapter, Fielding takes hints from *Don Quixote*, II, xxx–xlvii (especially II, xxxii), relating an unsuccessful attempt to disenchant the knight by humiliating him. Again, Fielding departs significantly from his model.

2. *Ammyconni, Paul Varnish, Hannibal Scratchi, or Hogarthi.* Garbled references to Italian master painters Jacopo Amigoni (1675–1752), Paolo Veronese (1528–1609) and Annibale Carraci (1560–1609), and to Fielding's friend William Hogarth.

3. *but I defy the wisest Man . . . into Ridicule.* cf. Shaftesbury, *Sensus Communis: An Essay on the Freedom of Wit and Humour*, IV, i: 'One may defy the World to turn real *Bravery* or *Generosity* into Ridicule' (in *Characteristicks*, I, 129).

4. *Some Gentlemen of our Cloth . . . Book of Verses.* See Pope's *Epistle to Bathhurst* (1733), 250–90, where he praises the benevolence of John Kyrle (1634?–1724), the 'Man of Ross'. In his *Epilogue to the Satires* (1738), dialogue I, 135–6, Pope praises Ralph Allen in a line later used by Fielding in his dedication to *Tom Jones*.

5. *Henley himself, or as great an Orator (if any such be) had been in his Rostrum or Tub before him.* John 'Orator' Henley (1692–1756), notorious preacher, lecturer and hack writer, was in the pay of Walpole. He left the Church of England to set up on his own; from his ornate 'tub' (as the pulpits of Dissenters were satirically called), he preached primitive Christianity, and claimed to restore ancient eloquence. (This is a claim alluded to in '*Rostrum*', which was the term used for the speaker's platform in the ancient Roman forum.) Both Pope (in his *Dunciad* (1728), II, 2, 338; III, 195) and Fielding mocked Henley as a self-promoting and self-serving buffoon (see *The Author's Farce*; *The Champion*, 13 December 1739, 4 February 1740; *The Jacobite's Journal*, 16 January 1748). Henley called Fielding 'your Tragedy-Trimmer, your Farce-bundler . . . in short, your Flayer of dead Wits for live conceits, your Rat-Catcher of Poetic Images . . .' (*The Hyp-Doctor*, 15–22 June 1731).

6. *Fanny was wonderfully pleased . . . to threaten it.* Hunted hares are also associated with women in *Tom Jones*, XI, x, and *Shamela*, letter XII.

7. *Exuviæ.* 'Anything cast or taken off, such as skins or shells of animals, hence spoils' (*OED*).

8. *Hector or Turnus.* Both were heroes who fled before attack; for Turnus, see *Aeneid*, 12; for Hector, see *Iliad*, 22; cf. II, ix, *n.* 2, above.

9. *Hunter of Men.* An allusion to the biblical tyrant Nimrod (see Genesis 10.9).

10. *Mallet.* David Mallet (1705–65), Scottish poet, playwright and Opposition writer. Fielding alludes to his *Life of Francis Bacon* (1740), which was published by Andrew Millar, Fielding's bookseller.

11. *Thou who hadst no Hand . . . Life of Cicero.* A reference to *The History of the Life of Marcus Tullius Cicero* (1741) by Conyers Middleton (1638–1750). Fielding had already mocked the obsequious dedication to his political enemy Hervey in his dedication to *Shamela*. He was also angered by Middleton's preface, which dismissed *Observations of the Life of Cicero* (1731), by his friend and patron George Lyttelton.

12. *forced Colley Cibber to write English.* Another allusion to the Poet Laureate's badly written autobiography *An Apology for the Life of Mr Colley Cibber . . .* (1740); see I, i, *n.* 5, above.

13. *his Cudgel.* Descriptions of weapons and armour were common in the epic. This description specifically parodies Homer's famous setpiece descriptions of the genealogy of Agamemnon's sceptre (*Iliad*, 2, 100–9), and the shield of Achilles (*Iliad*, 18, 478–607). Both had already been feminized in Pope's mock-heroic *The Rape of the Lock* (1714), II, 117–22, V, 87–96. Fielding restores something of the heroic to the country boy's cudgel by insisting that it is *not* engraved with scenes of fashionable town life, and by having it immediately employed in violent action.

14. *a mighty strong Man of Kent.* William Joy (d. 1734), who performed feats of strength under the professional name 'Sampson, the strong man of Kent'.

15. *one of Mr Deard's best Workmen.* A reference to William Deard, or Deards (d. 17 June 1761), a fashionable London jeweller, toymaker and pawnbroker. Fielding filed a suit against him in November 1739, in a dispute that was probably financial, and frequently referred to him facetiously. His Homeric prototype is Hephaestus, Greek god of fire, who fashioned Achilles' shield.

16. *the Park.* The Mall in St James's Park was a fashionable promenade in this period.

17. *a certain long English Baronet.* Sir Thomas Robinson (1700?–77), commissioner of the Excise, appointed governor of Barbados in 1741. He was renowned for being both tall and long-winded, and for hosting lavish entertainments.

18. *As the first Night . . . Catcalls.* This refers to the noisy and premeditated damning of *The Modish Couple*, for which Fielding had written an epilogue, on its first night, 10 January 1732. The audience seems to have discovered that Captain Charles Bodens, Gentleman Usher (and pimp) to the King, was not its real author, but was probably covering for Lord Hervey and the Prince of Wales. The 'Cricks in Embroidery' were courtiers.

19. *Mr Cock.* Christopher Cock (d. 1748), auctioneer, who presided over fashionable auction rooms in the Grand Piazza, Covent Garden. Satirized in *The Historical Register* (1737) as 'Christopher Hen', a part played by a woman.

20. *swift of Foot.* Achilles is called this throughout the *Iliad*.

21. *no Babler, no Over-runner.* A 'babler' is a hound who barks indiscriminately; an 'over-runner' runs past a hare when it doubles back on itself to evade pursuit.

22. *opened.* Gave cry.

23. *Mr John Temple.* The Hon. John Temple, Esq. (1680–1752/3?), an admirer of Fielding's plays, whose estate, Moor Park, Surrey, was about 50 miles from the scene.

24. *Diana.* The virgin goddess of the hunt (Artemis in Greek mythology). Fielding is burlesquing the classical commonplace of divine intervention in human affairs. For possible classical parallels, see Battestin's article in *Studies in Bibliography*, 36 (1983), 102, 107, *n.* 10.

25. *cutting the Ears of the Dogs.* i.e. to bleed them; a common treatment for humans.

CHAPTER VII

1. *Roasting.* 'Ridicule . . . in a severe or merciless fashion' (*OED*). Fielding condemned the practice in *The Champion*, 13 March 1740.

2. *rusty.* Reasty, rancid.

3. *the Serpent.* i.e. a firecracker of that shape. Cibber taunted Fielding by saying that there was a law against throwing firecrackers, so there should be a law (the Licensing Act), against his satirical squibs (*Apology*, 2nd ed., viii, 237).

4. *Taw.* Marbles.

5. *Scipio, Lælius.* Scipio Aemilianus (*c.*185–129 BC), called Scipio Africanus Minor, was patron to many writers including his friend Gaius Lælius (b. *c.*186 BC). Although an important political figure, he reputedly resorted to childish pastimes, such as collecting shells, when on country holidays with Laelius. See Cicero, *De Oratore*, 2, 6, and *Tom Jones*, VII, i.

6. *Indeed, to confess the Truth . . . over Head and Ears in the Water.* According to

Goldberg, 'The same prank was played on the French philosopher Montesquieu a dozen years earlier by John, Duke of Montague (1688?–1749), an incorrigible practical joker.' Fielding expressed his disapproval of such jokes in 'An Essay on Conversation', *Miscellanies*, I.

CHAPTER VIII

1. *Commons.* Share of food.
2. *those who understand our Laws, will not wonder he was not over-ready to own it.* Because Roman Catholics were thought to be a danger to Church and State, and fears were particularly aroused by real or imagined Popish plots and Jacobite rebellions, a series of laws imposed severe restrictions and heavy taxation on Catholic clergy and laity. For example, priests returning from abroad, as presumably this one is, could be charged with treason (a statute, 2 William, 3, substituted a life sentence for the death penalty imposed by 27 Elizabeth, 2). Although not always enforced, there were restrictions on travel, residence, education, property ownership, the right to hold public office and to vote, as well as on worship. These were enforced by the threat of imprisonment and fines.
3. *Cable Rope . . . Camel.* A variant reading of Matthew 19.24.
4. *Rabbit.* 'Confound' (Partridge, citing Fielding).

CHAPTER IX

1. *Hanger.* A kind of short sword.
2. *a certain huge Stone Pot of the Chamber with one Hand, which six Beaus could not have lifted with both.* This fight is modelled on stock epic patterns and employs common tropes as well as specific allusions; cf. *Iliad*, 5, 302–4: Diomedes 'grasped in his hand a stone – a mighty deed – one that not two men could bear, such as mortals now are'; and *Aeneid*, 12, 896–902: Turnus casts a stone that 'scarce twice six chosen men could uplift upon their shoulders, men of such frames as earth now begets'.
3. *with a lumpish Noise, and his Halfpence rattled in his Pocket.* A parody of a recurring formula in the *Iliad*, where the dead frequently fall 'with a thud', while their armour clangs upon them (see, for example, *Iliad*, 12, 396; 13, 181).
4. *where, in some Men of Pleasure, the natural and artificial Noses are conjoined.* Another mock-heroic allusion, uniting a parody of Homer's manner (e.g., 'he smote Aeneas on the hip, where the thigh turns in the hip-joint' (*Iliad*, 5, 305–6)) with an allusion to the destruction of the nose by venereal disease.
5. *Don Quixotte would certainly have taken him for an inchanted Moor.* See *Don Quixote*, I, iii.

CHAPTER X

1. *some excellent piece of Satire or Humour called a Dance.* Entr'acte dances were common in all theatres after the Restoration, but Fielding excluded them from the Little Theatre in Haymarket when he was manager. Battestin suggests that Fielding might be referring here specifically to the elaborate entertainments of John Rich, see I, vii, *n.* 3, above.

2. *Booth . . . Otway.* Barton Booth (1681–1733), famous tragic actor. Thomas Otway (1652–85), poet and dramatist most famous for *The Orphan* (1680) and *Venice Preserved* (1682); he was said to be 'next to Shakespeare' (Goldsmith, *The Bee*, 24 November 1759).

3. *Bettertons and Sandfords.* Thomas Betterton (1635?–1710), the greatest actor of the Restoration stage. The crooked-featured Samuel Sandford (fl. 1661–1700) was famous for his portrayal of villains.

4. *Fenton's Mariamne, Frowd's Philotas, or Mallet's Eurydice. Mariamne*, performed 1722–3, earned its author, Elijah Fenton (1683–1730), nearly £1,000. Mallet's *Eurydice*, performed 1731, was also very popular, but mocked by Fielding in his *Tragedy of Tragedies* (1731). *Philotas*, a tragedy by Philip Frowde (d. 1738), performed 1731, was less successful.

5. *your Dillo or Lillo.* The poet's sneering jibe is Fielding's oblique defence of his friend George Lillo (1693–1739), a jeweller turned poet (hence the reference to commercial districts). He was much admired by Fielding for his 'domestic' tragedies, *The London Merchant* (1731) and *The Fatal Curiosity*, staged at the Little Theatre in 1736, with a prologue by Fielding, who also wrote a fine obituary for him in *The Champion*, 26 February 1740.

6. *Quin . . . Delane . . . Cibber . . . Macklin . . . Mrs Clive.* Famous actors, most of whom were admired by Fielding, all of whom but Delane acted in Fielding's plays. James Quin (1693–1766); Dennis Delane (d. 1750); Theophilus Cibber (1703–58), disreputable son of Colley Cibber (see I, i, *n.* 5, above); Charles Macklin (1697?–1797), actor and playwright; Catherine 'Kitty' Clive, née Raftor (1711–85), popular and respected comic actress.

7. *No more . . . sleep till Morn.* Quoted, with a few changes, from the bombastic tragedy *Theodosius: or The Force of Love* (1680), II, i, by Nathaniel Lee (1653?–92).

8. *Who'd be that foolish, sordid thing, call'd Man?* From Otway's *The Orphan: or, The Unhappy Marriage* (1680), I, i, where it reads, 'Who'd be that sordid foolish thing call'd Man . . . ?'

CHAPTER XI

1. *Containing the Exhortations of Parson Adams to his Friend in Affliction.* cf. Fielding's essay, *Of the Remedy of Affliction for the Loss of Our Friends* (1743).

2. *Seneca.* See II, xvi, *n.* 2, above. Seneca's works on this topic include *De consolatione ad Marciam, Ad Polybium* and *Epistulae morales ad Lucium* (*Letters*, 63, 98 and 99).

3. *Consolation, which tho' it was not Cicero's.* The *Consolatio Ciceronis* (first pub. Venice, 1583), supposed to have been written by Cicero on the death of his daughter Tullia, was thought to be spurious, but was admired by Fielding, who read it in times of affliction. It was a favourite of Walter Shandy too, see *Tristram Shandy*, V, iii; VIII, xix.

4. *Yes, I will bear . . . dear to me.* cf. *Macbeth*, IV, iii, 221–5: Macduff's speech on hearing the news of the slaughter of his family.

5. *Cato . . . Conscious Lovers.* Joseph Addison, *Cato* (1713), quoted by Adams in III, v, above; Richard Steele, *The Conscious Lovers* (1722). Both plays were admired for their moral sentiments.

CHAPTER XII

1. *advertised.* Informed.

2. *a Bond and Judgment.* A deed binding a person, his heirs and executors to pay a certain sum of money, which assigns his chattels as security for the debt.

3. *come to the Parish.* i.e., seek poor relief from the parish; see II, xiv, *n.* 12, above.

4. *Put.* 'A rustic; a dolt' (Partridge).

5. *which, to use the Language of a late Apologist . . . next Chapter.* Indicating a change of subject, Cibber announces: 'I shall therefore make use of those several Vehicles, to carry you thro' the rest of the Journey, at your Leisure' (*Apology*, 2nd ed., iv, 100).

CHAPTER XIII

1. *'Sir,' said Adams, 'my Definition . . . the Distressed'.* See Fielding's discussion of charity in *The Champion*, 5 April 1740.

2. *Gymnosophists.* 'The Greek name ("naked philosophers") for an ancient Hindu sect who regarded food and clothing as impediments to pure thought. Adams might have read of them in the *Geographica* of Strabo (*c.*64 BC–AD 19). Pounce substitutes the name of the righteous king of Judah (1 Kings 22.2–50; Chronicles 17–20)' (Goldberg).

3. *I had loved Money more and Land less.* cf. I, x, above. Pounce is based on the money-lending land steward Peter Walter (MP for Bridport, 1715–27), who acquired numerous properties during his career and was supposed to have purchased Fielding's own estate. On his death in 1746, he was said to be worth £300,000. See *The Champion*, 31 May 1740, and Pope, *Epistle to Bathurst* (1733), I, 125.

BOOK IV

CHAPTER I

1. *The Arrival of Lady Booby . . . Booby-Hall.* cf. the account of 'ominous Accidents that crossed Don Quixote as he entered his Village', in *Don Quixote*, II, lxxiii.

2. *Offalls.* Refuse, remnants.

3. *Character.* Character reference.

CHAPTER II

1. *the greatest Beauty in the Parish.* Pamela records that when the neighbouring gentry come to call, they are curious to see her, joking: 'Well, Mr B—, we understand, you have a servant-maid, who is the greatest Beauty in the County'. Mr B— claims that she is not as beautiful as all that (*Pamela*, 2nd ed., I, xxiii, 58).

2. *any Person who serves a Year, gains a Settlement in the Parish where he serves.* To restrict the number of people entitled to parish relief, several statutes established qualifications for settlement. The poor had 40 days to establish residence in a parish, or could claim settlement if they rented property worth £10 p.a., or if they paid taxes, performed a public office, were bound apprentices, or were unmarried servants hired for a year (see 13 & 14 Charles II; 3 & 4 William & Mary, chapter 11; 8 & 9 William III, chapter 30). A popular legal handbook, *The Clergyman's Vade-Mecum*, 6th ed. (1731), complains that some 'peevish and pragmatical' people try to forbid the banns of the poor to prevent their families becoming a burden on the parish; the author stoutly declares: 'Poverty is no more an Impediment to Marriage than Riches, and the Kingdom can no more subsist without Poor, than without Rich' (203).

3. *for indeed I have never been able to pay for a Licence.* According to Battestin, 'Adams's poverty has rendered his status in the Church technically illegal. Before he could legally officiate, a curate had to obtain a licence to preach and be admitted to his cure by the bishop of the diocese.' A licence might cost between 18 shillings and £3; many curates were unwilling to pay so much when their tenure was uncertain.

CHAPTER III

1. *Dowdy . . . Drab. Dowdy*: 'An awkward, ill-dressed inelegant woman' (Johnson); *Drab*: 'A whore; a strumpet' (Johnson).

2. *When a Man is married, he . . . is not removable.* Goldberg notes that Scout's opinion is supported by Jacob's *New Law Dictionary* (1729), but that research shows that married couples were frequently the subject of removal actions.

3. *Bridewell.* Bridewell Hospital in London, where the 'idle poor', vagrants and whores were condemned to menial labour. The name became generic for any house of correction. In 'A Proposal for Making an Effectual Provision for the Poor' (1753), Fielding argued for the reform of this system which he believed was likely to corrupt the morals of the inmates.

4. *in defiance of an Act of Parliament, to act as Lawyers in the Country.* 'An Act for the Better Regulation of Attorneys and Solicitors' (1729) imposed a £5 fine on those who practised law without having served a five-year apprenticeship with an attorney and being duly sworn in. Scout was technically exempt because the regulation was not extended to the Quarter Sessions until 1749.

CHAPTER V

1. *verbatim & literatim.* 'Word for word and letter for letter.'

2. *Jesu! said the Squire . . . both hanged.* According to the statute 43 Elizabeth I, chapter 7, anyone convicted of having cut any fruit trees, robbed any orchard or broken any hedges, pales or other fences, should pay the damages, or be committed to the constable to be whipped (see Wood, *Institute*, III, iii, 442).

CHAPTER VI

1. *puisny.* Puny.

2. *But the dear Man who is gone . . . how much I loved him.* Lady Booby perverts the advice typically offered in conduct literature; John Gregory, for example, argues that it is improper for a woman to show love even after marriage, 'that reserve and delicacy which always left the lover something further to wish, and often made him even doubtful of your sensibility and attachment may and ought ever to remain' (*A Father's Legacy to his Daughters* (1774), 51).

3. *almost six Weeks (it wants but a Day) ago.* Another inconsistency on Fielding's part, or possibly a sign of Lady Booby's exaggeration: it is three weeks minus a day since her husband's death.

4. *Common Garden.* A colloquialism for Covent Garden, then notorious for its brothels.

5. *Ifaukins!* In faith (truthfully).

CHAPTER VII

1. *their second Climacteric.* According to ancient belief, great changes, or climaxes, in a person's life and body were supposed to occur at intervals of the symbolic numbers seven and nine years. The second climacteric would therefore occur in the fourteenth year.

2. *a Commission in the Army.* 'An army regiment was like a corporation in which the officers owned shares according to their rank. In the time of Queen Anne, about thirty years earlier, a commission at the lowest rank of an ensign could be purchased for two hundred to five hundred pounds, depending on the regiment' (Goldberg).

CHAPTER VIII

1. *Speculation.* Perception.

2. *The Text will be . . . Matthew the 5th . . . foreign to my Purpose.* Adams omits the context which makes it clear that Jesus is preaching against adulterous rather than marital love: 'Ye have heard that it was said by them of old time, Thou shalt not commit adultery: but I say unto you, That whosoever looketh on a woman to lust after her hath committed adultery with her already in his heart' (Matthew 5.27–8).

3. *Had Abraham so loved his Son Isaac, as to refuse the Sacrifice required.* See Genesis 22.1–18.

4. *Cure.* Spiritual care.

5. *Quæ Genus.* Quite an advanced lesson for a boy of Adams's son's age, these are the opening words of the section on genders of irregular nouns in part 2 of *Lily's Grammar,* the *Brevissima Institutio*: '*Quae genus aut flexum variant . . .*' ('Those which change their gender or declension . . .').

6. *Jacky.* Another inconsistency: the boy is called Dick elsewhere. Jacky is the name of the boy in 'The History of two Friends', which Dick reads out in IV, x.

CHAPTER IX

1. *Non mea renidet in Domo Lacunar.* cf. Horace, *Odes*, 'The Vanity of Riches', 2, 18, 1–2: 'Not ivory or gilded panel gleams in my home'. The next sentiment might also be relevant: 'But I have loyalty and a kindly vein of genius, and me, though poor, the rich man courts' (2, 18, 9–10). See also II, iv, *n.* 9, above.

2. *Mr Didapper, or Beau Didapper . . . Now, to give him . . . Tho' he was born . . . so very large a Share.* A satirical portrait of the effeminate John, Lord Hervey, Baron Ickworth (1696–1743). Didapper's conduct, career and physical appearance all resemble those of this prominent politician and supporter of Walpole. '*Didapper*' suggests 'Dapper' – a name applied to Hervey by his enemies, and 'didapper' – a small diving water bird. Furthermore, the passage in quotation marks ('Tho' he was born . . . so very large a Share') travesties the sycophantic dedication to Conyers Middleton's *Life of Cicero* (1740), already parodied in the dedication to *Shamela* addressed to 'Miss Fanny'. (See Martin C. Battestin, 'Lord Hervey's Role in *Joseph Andrews*', *Philological Quarterly*, 42 (1963), 231–3.)

3. *And to finish his Character . . . any Imperfection in another.* An allusion to the dispute between Pope and Hervey. In *Verses Address'd to the Imitator of the First Satire of the Second Book of Horace* (1733), Hervey and Lady Mary Wortley Montagu (both of whom fell in love with the dashing Italian virtuoso Francesco Algarotti) had ridiculed Pope's poetry and made a personal attack on his physical deformities. Pope replied in a privately circulated manuscript, *A Letter to a Noble Lord* (1733), satirizing Hervey under the name of 'Fannius', an enemy of Horace. Fielding here combines two passages from the *Letter*, and alludes to Pope's most famous attack on Hervey, *An Epistle to Dr Arbuthnot* (1735), in which Pope dubs him 'Sporus' and 'that Thing of silk' (305). (See also 305–33: the whole magnificently disgusting description ought to be read.)

4. *Lest this should . . . polite Conversation.* cf. Jonathan Swift, *Genteel and Ingenious Conversation* (1738); in Swift's satire on the inanities and incivilities which passed for wit in polite society, Miss Notable tells Mr Neverout, 'don't ask questions with a dirty Face' (*Dialogue* II).

5. *Propria quæ Maribus.* This is the opening of the lesson from *Lily's Grammar* quoted by Adams in II, xi.

CHAPTER X

1. *Conviction.* Proof.
2. *Complacence.* Desire to please.
3. *scruple.* Doubt.

CHAPTER XI

1. *Settlements.* He offers her money to become his kept mistress.
2. *Complexion.* Temperament.
3. *Assurance.* Presumption.
4. *many Texts of Scripture.* See, for example, Ephesians 5.22–3; 1 Peter 3.1; and Colossians 3.18.
5. *Œconomicks.* 'Household management; the term retained its limited meaning and Latin spelling until the nineteenth century' (Goldberg).

CHAPTER XII

1. *for since the Decay . . . number of Recruits*. A hot concern in Opposition journals (e.g., *The Champion*, 15 and 31 October 1741), the cloth manufactury in Fielding's native West Country had been in recession since the 1720s, but wholesale army recruitment did not begin until 1739.

2. *Paméla or Paméla*. Pamela, a name taken from Sir Philip Sydney's *Arcadia* (1590), was indeed a strange name for a country wench. Derived from the Greek for 'all sweetness', it could be pronounced with a long 'e', as Pope scanned it in his 'Epistle to Miss Blount, with the Works of Voiture' (1712), 49. Claiming in a letter that 'Mr Pope has taught half the women in England to pronounce it wrong', Aaron Hill boasted that his verses 'for the unknown Author of the beautiful new Piece call'd *Pamela*' (which capped the adulatory introduction to the novel) had given Pamela a short 'e' as Richardson intended.

CHAPTER XIV

1. *Night-Adventures*. cf. the night adventures which occur in the inn mistaken for a castle in *Don Quixote*, I, iii; I, ii.

2. *an excellent Mimick*. Hervey was a noted mimic.

3. *Double-clout*. A kerchief or cloth worn on the head.

4. *the naked condition of Adams*. He is undressed, but wearing a nightshirt.

5. *Hylas*. The favourite of Hercules who, when he went to fetch water, was drowned by water nymphs enamoured of his beauty.

6. *hagged out*. Fagged out, exhausted.

7. *Statue of Surprize*. See I, viii, *n.* 5, above.

8. *He is an Infidel . . . Witchcraft . . . days of Saul*. Saul drove witches out of Israel, but then persuaded the witch of Endor to summon the spirit of the dead prophet Samuel (I Samuel 28.7–25).

CHAPTER XV

1. *Œdipus himself whilst his Fate was revealing*. At the climax of Sophocles' tragedy *Oedipus Rex*, Oedipus has to wait for the arrival of the old herdsman who will reveal to him his true parentage; he then discovers that he has murdered his father and married his mother.

2. *removed me, by Justices Warrants*. The law decreed that, as her husband was a soldier, Mrs Andrews could not claim settlement; thus, she could be removed by a warrant signed by two Justices of the Peace to the parish where she was last legally settled, where she was entitled to relief under the Poor Law (see II, xiv, *n*. 12, and IV, ii, *n*. 2, above).

3. *chopping*. 'Big and vigorous' strapping' (*OED*).

4. *Hic est quem quæris, inventus est, &c*. 'Here is the one whom you seek; he is found.' Battestin suggests that Fielding might be alluding to the words spoken by the angel to the women when they went to seek Jesus in the tomb (Matthew 28.5–6; cf. Mark 16.5–6, Luke 24.4–6, and John 20.15), and to the exclamation of the father on the return of the prodigal son (Luke 15.24). Goldberg thinks it is an allusion to the common device of recognition which resolved the action of many Roman comedies and Greek romances by revealing the hero's true identity.

CHAPTER XVI

1. *determined*. Concluded.

2. *Night-Gown . . . Shift . . . Thread Stockings*. *Night-gown*: an evening dress. *Shift*: a smock or chemise. *Thread-Stockings*: stockings possibly made from flaxen thread as opposed to silk or cotton.

3. *nor will be prevailed on . . . Appearance in High-Life*. A final hit at Richardson: in May 1741 a spurious continuation of *Pamela*, *Pamela's Conduct in High-Life*, by the hack writer John Kelly, was published by a group of booksellers, including Fielding's partner in *The Champion*, Richard Chandler. The furious Richardson denounced the continuation in the press and announced his own sequel, only to encourage more pretenders. Kelly published a second volume of *Pamela's Conduct in High-Life*, and another spurious work, *Pamela in High Life: Or, Virtue Rewarded*, appeared in September 1741 before Richardson could bring out his own sequel in December of that year. Although Joseph Andrews refuses to appear in high-life, Parson Adams enjoyed an after-life. He appeared 'in a political Light' as a correspondent in *The True Patriot*, 17 December 1745, 28 January 1746, and *The Jacobite's Journal*, 9 July 1748; he complained about people who pretend to have read Greek authors in the introduction to *A Journey from this World to the Next* (1743); and he replaced Thwackum in Allworthy's household at the end of *Tom Jones* (XVIII, xiii).